Books by Herman Wouk

Novels

AURORA DAWN

THE CITY BOY

THE CAINE MUTINY

MARJORIE MORNINGSTAR

YOUNGBLOOD HAWKE

DON'T STOP THE CARNIVAL

THE WINDS OF WAR

WAR AND REMEMBRANCE

Plays

THE TRAITOR

THE CAINE MUTINY COURT-MARTIAL

NATURE'S WAY

Nonfiction

THIS IS MY GOD

WAR
AND
REMEMBRANCE

WAR AND

a novel by

Little, Brown and Company

REMEMBRANCE

Herman Wouk

VOLUME ONE

BOSTON TORONTO

A limited edition of this book has been
privately printed.

ACKNOWLEDGMENTS

The author is grateful to the following publishers for permission to reprint ex-cerpts from selected material as noted below.

Chappell Music Company for "Hut-Sut Song" by Leo V. Killion, Ted McMichael and Jack Owens. Copyright © 1941 by Schumann Music Co. Copyright renewed, assigned to Unichappell Music, Inc. (Belinda Music, publisher). Inter-national copyright secured. All rights reserved. Used by permission.

Edward B. Marks Music Corporation and Chappell Music Company for "Lili Marlene" by Norbert Schultze. All rights for the United States © Copyright: Edward B. Marks Music Corporation. Used by permission. All rights for Canada and the Philippines Copyright © Chappell Music Co., Inc. International copyright secured. All rights reserved. Used by permission.

Southern Music Publishing Company, Inc. for "Der Fuehrer's Face" by Oliver Wallace. Copyright © 1942 by Southern Music Publishing Company, Inc. Copy-right renewed. Used by permission.

United Artists Music Publishing Group, Inc. and West's Ltd. for "Three O'Clock In the Morning" by Dorothy Terriss and Julian Robledo. Copyright © 1921, 1922. Renewed 1949, 1950 West's Ltd. All rights for North America administered by Leo Feist, Inc. All rights reserved. Used by permission.

Published simultaneously in Canada
by Little, Brown & Company (Canada) Limited

PRINTED IN THE UNITED STATES OF AMERICA

WRITE THIS FOR A REMEMBRANCE IN A BOOK . . . THAT THE LORD HAS A WAR WITH AMALEK FROM GENERATION TO GENERATION.

Exodus 17

Foreword

W AR AND REMEMBRANCE is a historical romance. The subject is
World War II, the viewpoint American.

A prologue, *The Winds of War,* published in 1971, set the historical
frame for this work by picturing the events leading up to Pearl Harbor.
This is a novel of America at war, from Pearl Harbor to Hiroshima.

It is the main tale I had to tell. While I naturally hope that some
readers, even in this rushed age, will find the time for both novels, *War
and Remembrance* is a story in itself, and can be read without the
prologue.

The theme of both novels is single. The last words of Victor Henry's
commentary on the Battle of Leyte Gulf give it plainly enough:

"Either war is finished, or we are."

I have put this theme in the colors and motion of the fiction art,
so that "he who runs may read," and remember what happened in the
worst world catastrophe. As to the history in both tales, I trust that
knowing readers will find it has been presented responsibly and with
care.

These two linked novels tend to one conclusion: that war is an old
habit of thought, an old frame of mind, an old political technique, that
must now pass as human sacrifice and human slavery have passed. I
have faith that the human spirit will prove equal to the long heavy task
of ending war. Against the pessimistic mood of our time, I think that
the human spirit—for all its dark side that I here portray—is in essence
heroic. The adventures narrated in this romance aim to show that essence in action.

The beginning of the end of War lies in Remembrance.

Washington
23 March 1978
Purim, 5738

Herman Wouk

PART ONE

"Where is Natalie?"

1

A LIBERTY boat full of sleepy hung-over sailors came clanging alongside the U.S.S. *Northampton,* and a stocky captain in dress whites jumped out to the accommodation ladder. The heavy cruiser, its gray hull and long guns dusted pink by the rising sun, swung to a buoy in Pearl Harbor on the incoming tide. As the boat thrummed off toward the destroyer nests in West Loch, the captain trotted up the steep ladder and saluted the colors and the quarterdeck.

"I request permission to come aboard."

"Permission granted, sir."

"My name is Victor Henry."

The OOD's eyes rounded. In his starched whites with lacquered gold buttons and his white gloves, with the ritual long glass tucked under an arm, this fresh-faced ensign was stiff enough, but he stiffened more. "Oh! Yes, *sir.* I'll notify Captain Hickman, sir—messenger!"

"Don't disturb him yet. He isn't expecting me. I'll just mosey around topside for a bit."

"Sir, I know he's awake."

"Very well."

Henry walked forward on a forecastle already astir with working parties in dungarees, who were dodging the hose-down by barefoot deckhands. The iron deck underfoot felt good. The pungent harbor breeze smelled good. This was Pug Henry's world, the clean square world of big warships, powerful machinery, brisk young sailors, heavy guns, and the sea. After long exile, he was home. But his pleasure dimmed at the tragic sight off the starboard bow. Bulging out of the black oil coating the harbor waters, the streaked red underside of the capsized *Utah* proclaimed the shame of the whole Pacific Fleet in one obscene symbol. Out of view in the shambles of Battleship Row, the ship he had come to Hawaii to command, the U.S.S. *California,* sat on the mud under water to its guns, still wisping smoke ten days after the catastrophe.

The *Northampton* was no *California;* a treaty cruiser almost as long, six hundred feet, but with half the beam, a quarter the tonnage, smaller main battery, and light hull far too vulnerable to torpedoes. Yet after his protracted shore duty it looked decidedly big to Captain Henry. Standing by the flapping blue jack and the anchor chain, glancing back at the turrets and the tripod mast, with bridge upon bridge jutting up into the sunlight, he had a qualm of self-doubt. This ship was many times as massive as a destroyer, his last command. Battleship command had been a dream; getting the *California* had never seemed quite real, and after all, it had been snatched from him by disaster. He had served in heavy cruisers, but command was something else.

The roly-poly gangway messenger, who looked about thirteen, trotted up and saluted. Altogether the crew appeared peculiarly young. Pug had at first glance taken for junior lieutenants a couple of young men sporting the gilt collar leaves of lieutenant commanders. Surely they had not served the grinding fifteen years that two and a half stripes had cost him! Fast advancement was a sugar-coating of wartime.

"Captain Henry, sir, Captain Hickman presents his compliments, sir. He's taking a shower, is all. He says there's mail for you in his quarters, forwarded from the *California*'s shore office. He invites you for breakfast, sir, and please to follow me."

"What's your name and rating?"

"Tilton, sir! Boatswain's mate third, sir!" Crisp eager responses to the incoming captain.

"How old are you, Tilton?"

"Twenty, sir."

Ravages of age; everybody else starting to seem too damned young.

The captain's quarters enjoyed the monarchical touch of a Filipino steward: snowy white coat, round olive face, dark eyes, thick black hair. "I'm Alemon, sir." The smiling astute glance and dignified head bob, as he handed Captain Henry the letters, showed pride of place more than subservience. "Captain Hickman will be right out. Coffee, sir? Orange juice?"

The spacious outer cabin, the steward, the handsome blue leather furnishings, the kingly desk, elated Pug Henry. Capital ship command would soon be his, and these perquisites tickled his vanity. He couldn't help it. A long, long climb! Many new burdens and no more money, he told himself, glancing at the batch of official envelopes. Among them was a letter from Rhoda. The sight of his wife's handwriting, once such a joy, punctured his moment of pride, as the overturned *Utah* had gloomed his pleasure at walking a deck again. In a wave of desolate sickness, he ripped open the pink envelope and read the letter, sipping coffee served on a silver tray with a Navy-monogrammed silver creamer.

December 7th

Pug darling—

I just this minute sent off my cable to you, taking back that *idiotic* letter. The radio's still jabbering the horrible news about Pearl Harbor. Never in my *life* have I been more at sixes and sevens. Those horrible little yellow monkeys! I know we'll blow them off the face of the earth, but meanwhile I have one son in a submarine, and another in a dive-bomber, and you're God knows where at this point. I just pray the *California* wasn't hit. And to cap it all I wrote you that perfectly *ghastly, unforgivable* letter six short days ago! I would give the world to get that letter back unread. Why did I ever write it? My head was off in some silly cloudland.

I am *not* demanding a divorce anymore, not if you really still want me after my scatterbrained conduct. Whatever you do, don't blame or hate Palmer Kirby. He's a very decent sort, as I think you know.

Pug, I've been so damned lonesome, and—I don't know, maybe I'm going through the change or something—but I've been having the *wildest* shifts of moods for months, up and down and up and down again. I've been very unstable. I really think I'm not quite well. Now I feel like a criminal awaiting sentence, and I don't expect to get much sleep until your next letter arrives.

One thing is true, I love you and I've never stopped loving you. That's something to go on, isn't it? I'm *utterly* confused. I just can't write any more until I hear from you.

Except—Natalie's mother telephoned me not half an hour ago, all frantic. Strange that we've never met or spoken before! She hasn't heard from her daughter in weeks. The last word was that Natalie and the baby were flying back from Rome on the 15th. Now what? The schedules must be all disrupted, and suppose we go to war with Germany and Italy? Byron must be wild with worry. I have never held it against him, I mean, marrying a Jewish girl, but the dangers, the complications, are all so magnified! Let's pray she gets out, one way or another.

Mrs. Jastrow sounds perfectly pleasant, no foreign accent or anything, except that she's so *obviously* a New Yorker! If you get news of Natalie, do send the poor woman a telegram, it'll be a kindness.

Oh, Pug, we've plunged into the war, after all! Our whole world is coming apart. You're a rock. I'm not. Try to forgive me, and maybe we can still pick up the pieces.

All my love
Rho

Not a reassuring letter, he thought, if wholly Rhoda-like. The passage about his daughter-in-law deepened Pug's sickness of heart. He had been burying awareness of her plight from his mind, laden with his own calamities and, as he thought, helpless to do anything about her. He was in a world crash, and in a private crash. He could only take things day by day as they came.

"Well! Is Alemon treating you right? Welcome aboard!" A tall officer with thick straight blond hair, a froglike pouch under his chin, and a belly strained into two bulges by his belt burst from the inner cabin, buttoning a beautifully ironed khaki shirt. They shook hands. "Ready for some chow?"

Alemon's breakfast, served on white linen with gleaming cutlery, was better than anything Victor Henry had eaten in months: half a fresh pineapple, hot rolls, steaming coffee, and a rich egg dish with ham, spinach, and melted cheese. Pug said, by way of breaking the ice, that he had short-circuited protocol and come aboard this way because he had heard the *Northampton* might be leaving soon with a carrier task force to relieve Wake Island. If Hickman wanted the change of command before the ship left, he was at his service.

"Christ, yes. I'm mighty glad you've showed up. I hate to go ashore with a war starting, but I've been putting off minor surgery and I'm overdue for relief." Hickman's big genial face settled into lines of misery. "And to be frank, Henry, I have wife trouble back home. It just happened in October. Some deskbound Army son of a bitch in Washington—" the thick shoulders sagged in misery. "Oh, hell. After twenty-nine years, and her a grandmother three times over! But Ruth is still gorgeous, you know? I swear, Ruth has got the figure of a chorus girl. And left to herself half the time—well, that's been the problem right along. You know how that is."

So often, Pug thought, he had heard such plaints before; the commonest of Navy misfortunes, yet not till it had struck him had he remotely imagined the searing pain of it. How could Hickman, or any man, discuss it so freely? He himself could not force words about it from his throat; not to a minister, not to a psychiatrist, not to God in prayer, let alone to a stranger. He was grateful when Hickman turned prominent eyes at him, ruefully grinned, and said, "Well, the hell with that. I understand you've had duty in Berlin and in Moscow, eh? Damned unusual."

"I went to Moscow with the first Lend-Lease mission. That was a short special assignment. I did serve in Berlin as naval attaché."

"Must have been fascinating, what with all hell breaking loose over there."

"I'll take the *Northampton*."

At Victor Henry's harsh tone of disenchantment with his years ashore, Hickman cannily winked. "Well, if I do say so, Henry, she's a good ship with a smart crew. Except this big fleet expansion's bleeding us white. We're running a goddamn training ship here these days." Hickman pulled the ringing telephone from its bracket on the bulkhead. "Christ, Halsey's barge is coming alongside." Gulping coffee, he rose, put on his gold-crusted cap, and snatched a black tie.

Pug was astonished. The *Northampton* was the flagship of Rear Admiral Spruance, who commanded Halsey's screening vessels. It was Spruance's place to call on Halsey, not the other way around. Straightening the tie and cap, Hickman said, "Make yourself at home. Finish your breakfast. We can get started on the relief this morning. My chief yeoman's got the logs and other records all lined up, and luckily we just did a Title B inventory. The registered pubs are up-to-date and the transfer report is ready. You can sight the books anytime."

"Does Halsey come aboard often?"

"First time ever." His eyes popping, Hickman handed Pug a clipboard of messages. "Something's afoot, all right. You might want to look over these dispatches. There's a long intercept from Wake."

Through the porthole Pug could hear Halsey piped aboard. As he glanced through the flimsy sheets, his pain over Rhoda faded. The mere look and feel of fleet communications, the charge of war electricity in the carbon-blurred dispatches, stirred life in him. Hickman soon came back. "It was the Old Man, all right. He looks madder than hell about something. Let's go to the ship's office."

Impeccable inventories, account books, and engineering records were spread for Victor Henry's inspection by young yeomen in spotless whites, under the glaring eye of a grizzled chief. The two captains were deep in the records when the flag lieutenant telephoned. The presence of Captain Victor Henry, he said, was desired in Admiral Spruance's quarters. Hickman looked nonplussed, relaying this to his visitor. "Shall I take you there, Henry?"

"I know the way."

"Any idea what it's about?"

"Not the foggiest."

Hickman scratched his head. "Do you know Spruance?"

"Slightly, from the War College."

"Think you can relieve me before we sortie? We're on seventy-two hours' notice."

"I intend to."

"Splendid." Hickman clasped his hand. "We've got to talk some about the ship's stability. There are problems."

"Hello, Pug," Halsey said.

It was the old tough wily look from under thick eyebrows; but the brows were gray, the eyes sunken. This was not Billy Halsey, the feisty skipper of the destroyer *Chauncey*. This was Vice Admiral William F. Halsey, ComAirBatForPac, with three silver stars on his collar pin. Halsey's stomach sagged, his once-thick brown hair was a gray straggle, his face was flecked and creased with age. But the square-set jaw, the thin wide crafty smile, the curving way he stuck out his hand, the hard grip, were the same. "How's that pretty wife of yours?"

"Thank you, Admiral. Rhoda's fine."

Halsey turned to Raymond Spruance, who stood beside him, hands on hips, studying a Pacific chart on the desk. Spruance was a little younger, but far less marked by time, possibly because of his austere habits. His color was fresh, his skin clear, his plentiful hair only touched with gray; he seemed not to have changed at all since Pug's tour under him at the War College. It was a Halsey byword that he wouldn't trust a man who didn't drink or smoke. Spruance did neither, but they were old fast friends. In Halsey's destroyer division, during Pug's first duty at sea, Spruance had been a junior skipper.

"You know, Ray, this rascal had the sassiest bride of any ensign in the old division." As Halsey chain-lit a cigarette, his hand slightly trembled. "Ever meet her?"

Spruance shook his head, the large eyes serious and remote. "Captain Henry, you worked on the Wake Island battle problem at the College, didn't you?"

"I did, sir."

"Come to think of it, Ray, why were you running a Wake problem in thirty-six?" said Halsey. "Wake was nothing but scrub and gooney birds then."

Spruance looked to Victor Henry, who spoke up, "Admiral, the purpose was to test tactical doctrine in a problem involving Orange-dominated waters, very long distances, and enemy land-based air."

"Sound familiar?" Spruance said to Halsey.

"Oh, hell, what does a game-board exercise away back then prove?"

"Same distances. Same ship and aircraft performance characteristics."

"Same doctrines, too—like *seek out enemy and destroy him.*" Halsey's jaw jutted. Pug knew that look well. "Have you heard the joke that's going around in Australia? They're saying that pretty soon the two yellow races may really come to blows in the Pacific—the Japanese and the Americans."

"Not a bad quip." Spruance gestured with dividers at the chart. "But it's over two thousand miles to Wake, Bill. Let's even say we sortie tomorrow, which isn't very feasible, but—"

"Let me interrupt you right there. If we have to, we will!"

"Even so, look at what happens."

The two admirals bent over the chart. The operation to relieve Wake Island, Pug quickly gathered, was on. The aircraft carriers *Lexington* and *Saratoga* with their support ships were already steaming westward, one to knock out the land-based air in the Marshalls south of Wake, the other to deliver reinforcements to the Marines, and attack any Japanese sea forces it encountered. But Halsey's *Enterprise* was being ordered to a station less than halfway to Wake, where it could cover the Hawaiian Islands. He wanted to go all the way. He was arguing that the Jap fleet would not dare another sneak attack on Hawaii, with the Army Air Corps on combat alert; that carriers operating together vastly increased their punch; and that if the Japs did try an end run for Hawaii, he could double back and intercept them in time.

The 1936 game-board exercise, Pug realized, had been prophetic. In the game, the Marines had been beleaguered on Wake after a sneak Japanese attack on Manila. The Pacific Fleet had sailed to relieve them and bring the Jap main body to action. The mission had failed. "Orange" air had clobbered "Blue" into turning back. "Blue" carrier attacks had not knocked out the enemy's island airfields, the umpires had ruled, due to bad weather, pilot inexperience, and unexpected Jap strength in AA and aircraft.

Spruance ticked off distances, times, and hazards until Halsey exploded, "Jesus Christ and General Jackson, Ray, I know all that. I want some arguments to throw at Cincpac so I can shake myself loose!"

Dropping the dividers on the chart, Spruance shrugged. "I suspect the whole operation may be cancelled."

"Cancelled, hell! Why? Those Marines are holding out splendidly!"

His sympathies all with Halsey, Pug Henry put in that while flying from Manila to Hawaii on the Pan Am Clipper, he had been under bombardment at Wake Island.

"Hey? What's that? You were there?" Halsey turned angrily glinting eyes on him. "What did you see? How are their chances?"

Pug described the Marine defenses, and said he thought they could resist for weeks. He mentioned the letter he had brought from the Marine commandant to Cincpac, and quoted the colonel's parting words in the coral dugout: *"We'll probably end up eating fish and rice behind barbed wire anyway, but at least we can make the bastards work to take the place."*

"You hear *that*, Ray?" Halsey struck the desk with a bony grayhaired fist. "And you don't think we're honor bound to reinforce and support them? Why, the papers back home are full of nothing but the heroes on Wake. *'Send us more Japs!'* I've never heard anything more inspiring."

"I rather doubt that message ever came from Wake. Newspaper stuff," said Spruance. "Henry, were you stationed in Manila?"

"I was coming via Manila, Admiral, from the Soviet Union. I was naval adviser on the Lend-Lease mission."

"What? Rooshia?" Halsey gave Victor Henry a jocular prod with two fingers. "Say, that's right! I've heard about you, Pug. Hobnobbing with the President and I don't know who all! Why, old Moose Benton told me you went for a joyride over Berlin in a Limey bomber. Hey? Did you really do that?"

"Admiral, I was an observer. Mostly I observed how frightened I could get."

Halsey rubbed his chin, looking roguish. "You're aboard to relieve Sam Hickman, aren't you?"

"Yes, Admiral."

"Like to come with me and handle operations instead?"

Victor Henry sparred. "I've got my orders, Admiral."

"They can be modified."

Pug knew this man well enough from the destroyer days. Lieutenant Commander Halsey had given him his first "outstanding" fitness report for duty at sea. Once Bill Halsey went charging into a fleet action—he was bound to do that sooner or later, he had always been hot for fame and a fight—his operations officer might decide the course of a big battle, for Halsey leaned heavily on subordinates. It was a temptation of a sort; much more so than the Cincpac staff assignment Pug had dodged.

But Victor Henry was tired of being a flunky to mighty men, tired of anonymous responsibility for major problems. The *Northampton* meant a return to the old straight career ladder: sea duty, shore interludes, more sea duty; and at last battle-line command, and the bright hope of flag rank. The *Northampton* was that all-important last rung of major sea command. He would be firing eight-inch guns in battle. He was a gunnery man to the bone.

Yet rejecting Vice Admiral Halsey to his face was an unhealthy undertaking. Pug was hesitating, wondering how to handle this, when Raymond Spruance, leaning over the chart with the dividers, remarked, "Bill, isn't that a three-striper slot?"

Halsey turned on him. "It damned well shouldn't be. Not the way operations are expanding! I can get that changed mighty fast."

With Spruance's casual words, Pug Henry was off the hook. He did not even have to speak. Halsey gave Pug a calculating glance and picked up his cap. "Well, I'm going back to Cincpac, Ray, and I mean to win this argument. Stand by to get under way tomorrow. Good seeing you, Pug. You've kept very well." Out swept the gnarled hand. "Still play tennis?"

"Every chance I get, Admiral."

"And read your Bible every morning, and Shakespeare at night?"

"Well, sort of. At least I still try."

"You clean-living types depress me."

"Well, I smoke and drink like anything now."

"Honor bright?" Halsey grinned. "That's progress."

Spruance said, "I'm going ashore, Bill."

"Well, come along. How about you, Pug? Like a ride to the beach?"

"Yes, thank you, Admiral, if I may."

At the quarterdeck, he gave the OOD a message for Hickman, then descended the ladder to the sumptuous black barge, and sat apart from the admirals. The boat cruised like a ferry through the malodorous oil and flotsam that since the Jap attack was fouling the harbor. On the fleet landing stood a gray Navy Chevrolet with three-star flags fluttering on the front fenders. A stiff Marine in dress uniform opened the door. "Well, gentlemen," said Halsey, "can I give anybody a lift?"

Spruance shook his head.

"Thank you, Admiral," Victor Henry said. "I'm going up to my son's house."

"Where does your son live?" Admiral Spruance asked as the Chevrolet drove off.

"Up in the hills over Pearl City, sir."

"Shall we walk it?"

"It's five miles, Admiral."

"Are you pressed for time?"

"Well, no, sir."

Spruance strode off through the clangorous Navy Yard. After a week of heavy drinking to blot out night thoughts of Rhoda, Pug had trouble keeping up with him. They began climbing an asphalt road through green hills. Though Spruance's khaki shirt blackened with sweat his pace did not slow. He did not speak, but it was not for lack of wind. Pug was embarrassed by his own puffing compared to the even deep breaths of the older man. Rounding a turn of the uphill road, they looked out on a broad panorama of the base: docks, cranes, nests of destroyers and of submarines—and the terrible smashed half-sunk battleships, burned-out aircraft, and blackened skeletal hangars.

Spruance spoke. "Good view."

"Too good, Admiral." The admiral's face turned. The big sober eyes flashed agreement. "I planned to spend the day aboard the *Northampton,* sir," Pug panted, now that they were talking, "but when Admiral Halsey thinks of getting under way tomorrow, I figure I better fetch my gear."

"Well, I doubt the urgency exists." Spruance patted a folded white handkerchief on his wet brow.

Wake Island's remote exposed location and the Navy's present weakness, he said, all but precluded a fight. Admiral Kimmel, no doubt wanting to recover face after December 7th, had ordered the rescue just before the President had fired him. But the Fleet was awaiting a new Cincpac, and its temporary commander, Vice Admiral Pye, was having second thoughts. Abandoning the relief mission would cause great controversy, and there were good arguments on both sides, but Spruance suspected that these Marines, like the phantoms in the War College exercise, were fated to spend the war in prison camps.

Talking in a calm War College vein, marching at a pace that made Victor Henry's heart gallop, Spruance said that December 7th had changed the Pacific balance of forces. The United States had been half-disarmed. The odds were now ten or eleven carriers to three, ten combat-ready battleships to none, and nobody knew where those heavy enemy forces were. The Japanese had shown prime combat and logistical ability. They had unveiled ships, planes, and fighting men as good as any on earth. The Philippines, Southeast Asia, and the East Indies might be theirs for the taking, stretched thin as the British were. Right now the Navy could do little but hit-and-run raids to gain battle skill and keep the Japanese off balance. But it had to hold a line from Hawaii to Australia at all costs, through the arc of islands outside Japanese aircraft range. New carriers and battleships would in time join the Fleet. Jumping off from Hawaii and Australia, they would start battering back Japan from the east and the south. But that was a year or more away. Meantime Australia had to be held, for it was a white man's continent. Its overrunning by nonwhites might trigger a world revolution that could sweep away civilization. With this arresting remark Raymond Spruance fell silent.

They trudged uphill through tall sweet-smelling green walls of sugarcane under an ever-hotter sun, amid peaceful bird song.

"Pessimistic picture, Admiral," Victor Henry ventured.

"Not necessarily. I don't think Japan can cut the mustard. Weak industrial base, not enough supplies for a long struggle. She'll have a hot run for a while, but we'll win the war if the spirit at home holds up. We've got a strong President, so it ought to. But our country's in a two-front war, and the German front is the decisive one, so we're second in line out here. And we've started with a big defeat. Therefore the realities are against any early heroics in the Pacific, such as an all-out battle to relieve Wake."

Set back from the road amid lawns and gardens, its verandas roomy and sprawling, Warren's home looked more suited to an admiral than to a naval aviator. Spruance said when they halted, pouring sweat, "Your son lives here?"

"His father-in-law bought it for them. She's an only child. He's Senator Lacouture of Florida. Actually, it's not that large inside."

Patting his red face with a handkerchief, Spruance said, "Senator Lacouture! I see. Rather changed his mind about the war, hasn't he?"

"Admiral, a lot of good people honestly thought we ought to stay out of it."

Lacouture had been a leading and noisy isolationist until the eighth of December.

"To be sure."

Spruance declined to come in and rest. He asked for a glass of water, and drank it in the doorway. Handing back the glass, he said, "So, you'll be bringing your gear aboard today?"

"Yes, sir. I'd better expedite the change of command," Pug said, "all things considered."

Amusement brightened Spruance's grave eyes. "Oh, yes. Always execute orders promptly." Neither of them had to mention Halsey's notion of recruiting Pug for his staff. "Join me for dinner, then. I'd like to hear about your flight over Berlin."

"I'll be honored, Admiral."

Janice crouched in a broad brown dug-up patch of the back lawn, wearing a damp lilac halter, soiled gray shorts, and sandals. Her wheat-colored hair was tumbled, and her long bare legs and arms were burned brown. Because of the special controls being imposed on Japanese truck farmers, fresh vegetables were already becoming scarce. She had started a victory garden and seemed the merrier for it.

She straightened up, laughing, wiping her brow with an arm. "My stars, look at you! Been gardening or something?"

"Admiral Spruance walked me up from the Navy Yard."

"Oh, *him!* I hear that all the junior officers hide when he comes on deck. Commanding the *Northampton* will put you in shape, if it doesn't kill you. Warren telephoned. He's coming home for lunch."

"Good. He can run me down to the fleet landing with my gear."

"You're going already?" Her smile faded. "We'll miss you."

"Dad?" Warren's voice sounded some time later through the bed-room door. Pug opened it, pushing aside two half-packed footlockers. Uniforms and books were piled on the bed. "Hi. I stopped by the *California* shore office. They're sending your mail to the *Northampton,* but these just came in."

The sight of British stamps jolted Pug. Alistair Tudsbury's office ad-dress was on the envelope. First he opened the cable, and without a word passed it to Warren.

WHERE IS NATALIE URGE REPEAT URGE YOU INQUIRE STATE DEPART-MENT CABLE ME DEVILFISH SUB BASE MARIVELES   BYRON

Warren wrinkled his sunburned forehead over the cable. In his flying suit, the everlasting cigarette dangling from his compressed mouth, he looked weary and grim. "Who do you know at State, Dad?"

"Well, a few people."

"Why don't you try phoning? Briny's pretty cut off out there in Manila."

"I will. I should have done it sooner."

Warren shook his head. "She may be in one hell of a fix." He gestured at the letter from London. "Alistair Tudsbury. Is that the British broadcaster?"

"That's him. Your mother and I met him on the boat to Germany."

"Great gift of gab. Lunch in half an hour, Dad."

Pug opened the letter after Warren went out. On arriving in Pearl Harbor, he had sadly mailed off a short dry letter to Pamela Tudsbury, finally breaking with her. She could not have received it and answered; the letters had crossed. In fact, he saw, hers was dated a month ago.

November 17th, 1941

My love:

I hope this will somehow reach you. There's news. The BBC has asked my father to make a sort of Phileas Fogg broadcasting tour clear around this tortured planet, touching the main military bases: Alexandria, Ceylon, Singapore, Australia, Pearl Harbor, the Panama Canal, and so on. Theme: the sun never sets on the Union Jack, and there's another possible foe besides Hitler—to wit, Japan—and the English-speaking peoples (including the reluctant Americans) must stand to their guns. Talky has stipulated that I go along again. More and more nowadays when he's fatigued or under the weather—his eyes are getting very bad—daughter writes up the broadcasts and even the articles. By now the product, though ersatz, is usable.

When he broached the thing to me, I heard only two words—*Pearl Harbor!* If the whole proposal doesn't blow up, and if we can maintain our dicey plane-and-boat schedule, we should reach Hawaii in a month or so. Where you will be with your blessed *California,* I don't know, but I'll find you.

Well, there you have it! I know you were supposed to write to me before I broke silence. Sorry I violated your rule, but for all I know your letter or cable will come next week and I'll be gone. Perhaps there's a screed for me already in the mail from Vladivostok, or Tokyo, or Manila. If so, I hope it was a love letter, not a prudent dismissal, which was what I feared and expected. Whatever it was, Pug, I never got it.

Dearest, you can love your wife and also love me. Do I shock you? Well, the fact is you already do. You know you do. You've even told me so. You have only to act realistically about it. To be blunt, it's just as possible for your wife to love you, and also love another man. Maybe that shocks you even more. But this sort of thing happens all the time, my sweet, I swear it does, especially in wartime, to perfectly good and decent people. You and Mrs. Henry have somehow spent a quarter of a century shut off in a very special church-and-Navy shell. Oh, dear! I haven't time to type this over, or I'd cut this last stupid paragraph. I know it's hopeless to argue.

I hate to stop writing to you now that I'm doing it at last. It's like the breaking of a dam. But I must stop. With any luck you won't hear from me again, you'll see me.

The weather in London is unspeakable, and so is the war news. It really looks as though we got out of Moscow none too soon; it actually may fall, as it did to Napoleon! What a prospect! But for me, to be quite honest, the only news that counts—and it's glorious—is that suddenly there's a chance to see you again. I had a horrible feeling in Moscow, for all your kindness and sweetness, that I was looking my last on you. Now (crossed fingers) here I come!

Love,
Pam

He could see the young face, hear the young warm elegantly accented voice pouring out these hurried words. The wistful, hopeless little romance with Tudsbury's daughter which had briefly flared in Moscow was best snuffed out. Pug knew that. He had tried. Moreover, until now he thought he had succeeded. The residue of the strange frail wartime relationship—a little more than a flirtation, pathetically less than an affair—had been a better understanding of what had happened to Rhoda, and a long start on forgiving her. He only wanted his wife back. He had already written her that in strong terms. There was no conceivable future with this young woman, twenty-nine or thirty, drifting in her celebrated father's wake.

Best snuffed out; yet his mind raced through calculations of where they might be now. Could they have made it to Singapore before December 7th? Tudsbury was a hard-driving traveller, a human bulldozer. If he could hitch rides on warships or bombers, he would keep going. Supposing by a freak the Tudsburys did show up in Honolulu? What a rich irony Pam's unwitting defense of Rhoda was! Pug tore up the letter.

Eating lunch on the back porch, Warren and Janice looked at each other as Pug came out humming in his blue service uniform.

"We're mighty formal," said Janice.

"Crease the uniform less if I walk it aboard."

"Mighty cheerful," remarked Warren.

"Prospect of sea pay." Pug dropped in a chair at the iron-and-glass table. He consumed a large plateful of the very savory stew, asking for more onions and potatoes; more food than they had seen him put away at midday since his arrival in Pearl Harbor.

"Mighty good appetite," observed Warren, watching his father eat. He and Janice knew nothing of Rhoda's divorce letter; they had ascribed Pug's boozing and his depression, which now seemed to be lifting, to his loss of the *California*.

"Admiral Spruance hustled me five miles uphill."

"Dad, Jan has an idea about Natalie."

"Yes, why don't you just call or cable my father?" Pug shot a sharp glance at his daughter-in-law. "He'll get some quick action from the State Department, if anyone can."

"Hm! What time is it in Washington? Is he there now?"

"There's five hours' difference. He's probably just leaving his Senate office. Try him at home a little later."

"That's a good notion, Janice."

When Warren helped Pug carry out the footlockers, Janice was bathing the baby. Little Victor was gurgling and splashing at her; she was a flushed, happy, sexy young wife, unabashed at the show of her breasts through the soaked halter. Recollection flashed upon Pug of Rhoda bathing Warren in just this way, in their bungalow on the San Diego base. A quarter of a century and more, gone like a breath! And an infant the image of this one had metamorphosed into the tall hard-faced young man in the flying suit, smiling down at his own baby son. Pug shook off an awed sad sense of passing time, made a joke about having drunk all of Janice's liquor, and kissed her wet smooth cheek.

"Come back whenever you're in port, Dad. Your room will be ready, and the bar will be stocked."

He held up a flat palm. "I'm back on the wagon while I've got a sea command."

Warren drove the pool jeep downhill with one hand. Cigarette bobbing in his mouth, he said after a silence, "Is the *Enterprise* going all the way to Wake Island, Dad?"

"What makes you think so?"

"You're in a big hurry to take over the screen flagship."

"And you're spoiling for a fight, are you?"

"I didn't say that." Warren looked sidelong at him through cigarette smoke. "I have my doubts about barrelling off with our last flattop. I don't trust the Army Air Corps all that much to protect this base, and my wife and kid. Well? Not talking?"

"I just don't know, Warren."

"It's all over the *Enterprise* that Halsey's screaming bloody murder up at Cincpac so we can get to go."

"Could be. How are your new pilots checking out?"

"Dad, they're green. *Green.* They haven't put in the hours. The squadron needs them, so they'll break their necks on the barriers, or drown, or learn. While we're in port, I'll drill the ass off them."

"You're an instructor now? That happened fast."

"My CO gave me the detail. I didn't argue. He's recommended me for instructor duty in the States, too, but I'm yelling plenty about *that*. This is no time to leave the Pacific."

Warren dropped his father at the telephone exchange, saying he would take the footlockers to the fleet landing. Their parting was almost as casual as if they expected to dine together, but they shook hands, which they seldom did, and stared for a moment in each other's eyes, smiling.

The small smoky telephone exchange was crowded with waiting sailors and officers. The chief operator, a buxom lady of forty or so with a heavy Southern accent, brightened when Pug mentioned Lacouture. "Now *thah*'s a great man! If he'd been President, we wouldn't be in this mess, would we, Captain? Ah'll do mah best to put you through."

Within a half hour Senator Lacouture was on the line, in his Georgetown home. Astounded to hear from Pug, quickly grasping the situation, he put a few terse questions. "Right. Right. Okay. Got it. I remember her from the wedding party. Maiden name again? Right. Jastrow, like that famous uncle of hers. Natalie Jastrow Henry. Dark girl, very pretty, quick tongue. Being Jewish may create problems. Still, Italy isn't bad in that regard, and travelling with a famous writer ought to be a help. Why, even I've heard of Aaron Jastrow!" Lacouture hoarsely chuckled. "She's probably all right, but it's best to be sure. How do I get back to you?"

"Just call Captain Dudley Brown at BuPers, Senator. He'll put the word on a Navy circuit. Make Byron an addressee on the *Devilfish*."

"Got that. And you're commanding the *California*, right?"

"The *Northampton*, CA–26, Senator."

A pause. "What happened to the *California*?"

Pug paused too. "I'm commanding the *Northampton*."

The senator, low and grave: "Pug, can we handle them out there?"

"It'll be a long pull."

"Say, I may resign from the Senate and go into uniform. What do you think? The Army's getting gouged on lumber and paper. I can save the war effort several million a year. They've offered me colonel, but I'm holding out for brigadier general."

"I certainly hope you get it."

"Well, give my love to the kids. You'll hear from me about the Jewish girl."

After twenty-four hours, Victor Henry felt as though he had been aboard the *Northampton* a week. He had visited the ship's spaces from the bilges to the gun directors, met the officers, watched the crew at work, inspected the engine rooms, fire rooms, magazines, and turrets, and talked at length with the executive officer, Jim Grigg; a laconic bullet-headed commander from Idaho, with the dark-ringed eyes, weary pallor, and faint air of desperation appropriate to a perfectionist exec. Pug saw no reason not to relieve Hickman straight off. Grigg was running the ship. Any fool could take it over; his incompetence would be shielded. Pug didn't consider himself a fool, only rusty and nervous.

He relieved the next day, in a ceremony pared of peacetime pomp and flourish. The officers and crew, their white sunlit uniforms flapping in a warm breeze, lined up in facing ranks aft of the number three turret. Standing apart with Hickman and Grigg, Victor Henry read at a microphone his orders to assume command. As his eyes lifted from the fluttering dispatch, he could see beyond the ranks of the crew the oil-streaked crimson bottom of the *Utah.*

Turning to Hickman, he saluted. "I relieve you, sir."

"Very well, sir."

That was all. Victor Henry was captain. "Commander Grigg, all ship's standing orders remain in force. Dismiss the crew from quarters."

"Aye aye, sir." Grigg saluted like a marine sergeant, wheeled, and gave the order. The ranks broke. Pug saw his predecessor piped over the side. Hickman was acting as though it were his birthday. A new letter from his wife, hinting that all might not be lost, had made him impatient as a boy to get back to her. He ran down the ladder to the gig without a backward glance.

All afternoon Pug read dispatches and ship's documents piled on his desk by Commander Grigg. Alemon served him in lone majesty a dinner of turtle soup, filet mignon, salad, and ice cream. A marine messenger brought him a handwritten note as he was drinking coffee in an armchair. The envelope and the sheet inside were stamped with two blue stars. The handwriting was upright, clear, and plain:

Dec. 19, 1941

Captain Henry,
    Glad you've taken over. We sortie tomorrow. You'll have the operation order by midnight. The new Cincpac will be Nimitz. The relief of Wake is looking more dubious. Good luck and good hunting—

                                        R. A. Spruance

Next morning, in calm sunny weather, the cruiser got under way. The deck force unmoored with veteran ease. On the swing of the tide the bow was pointed down-channel. With assumed calm that seemed to deceive the bridge personnel, Victor Henry said, "All ahead one third." The quartermaster rang up the order on the engine room telegraph. The deck vibrated—an inexpressibly heartwarming sensation for Pug—and the *Northampton* moved out to war under its new captain. He had not yet heard from Senator Lacouture about Natalie Jastrow Henry.

2

SHE was embarked in a very different vessel, a rusty, patch-painted, roach-ridden Turkish coastal tramp called the *Redeemer,* under-going repairs alongside a pier in Naples harbor; supposedly bound for Turkey, actually for Palestine. In the stormy week since she had come aboard, the old tub had yet to move. It listed by the stone wharf, straining at its lines with the rise and fall of the tide, wallowing when waves rolled in past the mole.

On the narrow afterdeck, under a flapping crimson flag with badly soiled yellow star and crescent, Natalie sat with her baby. For once the sky had cleared, and she had brought him out into the afternoon sun-shine. Bearded men and shawled women gathered around, admiring. There were some thin, sad-eyed children aboard the *Redeemer,* but Louis was the only babe in arms. Perched on her lap, he looked about with lively blue eyes that blinked in the chilly wind.

"Why, it's the Adoration," said Aaron Jastrow, his breath smoking. "The Adoration, to the life. And Louis makes an enchanting Christ child."

Natalie muttered, "I'm one hell of a miscast Madonna."

"Miscast? Hardly, my dear." Wrapped in his dark blue travelling cloak, gray hat pulled low on his head, Jastrow calmly stroked his neat beard. "Typecast, I'd say, for face, figure, and racial origin."

Elsewhere on the slanting deck, Jews crowded the walkways, swarm-ing out of the fetid holds to stroll in the sun. They squeezed past life-boats, crates, barrels, and deck structures, or they gathered on hatches, talking in a babel of tongues, with Yiddish predominating. Only Jas-trow and Natalie sat blanketed in deck chairs. The Palestinian organizer of the voyage, Avram Rabinovitz, had dug the chairs out of the bilges, mildewy and rat-chewed but serviceable. The baby worshippers thinned away, leaving a respectful patch of vacant rusty iron plate around the Americans, though the strollers kept glancing at them. Since arriving aboard, Jastrow, known as *der groiser Amerikaner shriftshteller,* "the great American author," had scarcely spoken to anyone, which had only magnified his stature.

Natalie waved a hand at the blue double hump of mountain, far across the bay. "Will you look at Vesuvius! So sharp and clear, for the first time!"

"A fine day for visiting Pompeii," Jastrow said.

"Pompeii!" Natalie pointed at the fat policeman in a green greatcoat patrolling the wharf. "We'd be scooped up as we stepped off the gangplank."

"I'm acutely aware of that."

"Anyway, Pompeii's so depressing! Don't you think so? A thousand roofless haunted houses. A city of sudden mass death. Ugh! I can do without Pompeii, obscene frescoes and all."

Herbert Rose came shouldering along the deck, a head taller than most of the crowd, his California sports jacket bright as a neon sign in the shabby mass. Natalie and Jastrow had been seeing little of him, though it was he who had arranged their flight from Rome and their coming aboard the *Redeemer*. He was berthing below with the refugees. The smart-aleck film distributor, who had booked most American movies in Italy until the declaration of war, was uncovering a Zionist streak, declining to share the organizer's cabin because—so he said—he was now just one more Jew on the run. Also, he wanted to practice speaking Hebrew.

"Natalie, Avram Rabinovitz wants to talk to you."

"Just Natalie?" asked Jastrow.

"Just Natalie."

She tucked Louis into his basket under the thick brown blanket. Rabinovitz had obtained the basket in Naples, together with other baby supplies, and a few things for Natalie and her uncle, who, with Rose, had fled Rome in the clothes in which they stood. The Palestinian had also brought aboard the tinned milk on which Louis was living. In Rome, even at the United States embassy, canned milk had long since run out. To her amazed inquiry, "Where on earth did you get it?" Rabinovitz had winked and changed the subject.

"Aaron, will you watch him? If he cries, shove the pacifier in his face."

"Is it about our departure?" Jastrow asked Rose as she left.

Dropping into the vacant deck chair, Rose put up his lean long legs. "He'll tell her what it's about." He was smooth-shaven, bald, lean, with a cartoonlike Semitic nose. His air and manner were wholly American, assured, easy, unselfconsciously on top of the world. "Solid comfort," he said, snuggling in the chair. "You Yankee-Doodles know how to live."

"Any second thoughts at this point, Herb?"

"About what?"

"About sailing in this wretched scow."

"I don't think it's a wretched scow."

"It's not the *Queen Mary*."

"The *Queen Mary* isn't running Jews to Palestine. Tough! It could run twenty thousand at a crack, and clear a million bucks on every run."

"Why have we been idle for a week?"

"It took two days to install the armature. Then came this three-day gale. We'll leave, don't worry."

A cold gust flapped the blanket off Louis. Rose tucked it back in.

"Herb, didn't we simply panic in Rome, the three of us? That mob around the American embassy was just a lot of loafers, I'm sure, hoping for a little excitement after the declaration of war."

"Look, the police were arresting people who tried to go in, right and left. We both saw that. God knows what happened to them. And at that, they probably weren't Jews."

"I'll bet," said Jastrow, "that if their passports were in order, Jews or not, they're now quartered in some pleasant hotel, awaiting exchange for Italians caught in the States."

Rose snapped, "I wouldn't go back to Rome if I could. I'm happy."

Jastrow said in perfect Hebrew, "And how are you progressing with your new language?"

"Jesus Christ!" Rose stared at him. "You could teach it, couldn't you?"

"There's no substitute," Jastrow smiled, stroking his beard and resuming his Bostonian English, "for a Polish yeshiva education."

"Why the devil did you ever drop it? I wasn't even bar mitzvahed. I can't forgive my parents."

"Ah, the greener grass," said Jastrow. "I couldn't wait to escape from the yeshiva. It was like a jail."

Natalie meantime made her way to Rabinovitz's cabin under the bridge. She had not visited it before. He offered her his chair at a desk piled with papers, dirty clothes, and oily tools, and sat on an unmade bunk, hunching against the bulkhead adorned with sepia nudes torn from magazines. The single electric bulb was so dim, and the tobacco smoke so thick, that Natalie could just make these out. At her embarrassed grin, Rabinovitz shrugged. He wore bulky grease-streaked cover-alls, and his round face was mud-gray with fatigue.

"It's the chief engineer's art collection. I took his room. Mrs. Henry, I need three hundred American dollars. Can you and your uncle help out?" Taken aback, she said nothing. He went on, "Herb Rose offered the whole amount, but he's already shelled out too much. We wouldn't have gotten this far if not for him. I'm hoping you and your uncle will give a hundred each. That would be fairer. Old men tend to be pikers, so I thought I'd put it to you." Rabinovitz's English was clear but heavily accented, and his slang was dated, as though it came from reading old novels.

"What's the money for?"

"Fetchi-metchi." He slid a thick thumb back and forth over two fingers, and wearily smiled. "Bribery. The harbor master won't clear us to depart. I don't know why. He started out friendly, but he changed."

"You think you can bribe him?"

"Oh, not him. Our captain. You've seen him, that drunken bearded old scalawag in the blue jacket. If we leave illegally, he forfeits his ship's papers. The harbor master's office is holding them. I'm sure he's done it often, he's a smuggler by trade. But it's an extra."

"Won't that be very dangerous?"

"I don't think so. If the coast guard stops us, we'll say we're test-running our repaired engine, and head back. We'll be no worse off than we are."

"If we're stopped, will he return the money?"

"Good question, and the answer is that he gets paid when we pass the three-mile limit."

All week long, with too much time to think, Natalie had been imagining calamitous reasons for the failure to depart, and wondering whether she had done the right thing in fleeing from Rome. The prospect of a trip across the Mediterranean in this hulk was growing uglier by the day. Still, she had clung to the thought that it would at least get her baby away from the Germans. But to start by breaking the Fascist law, and trying to outrun the coast guard's gunboats!

Rabinovitz said in a hard though not hostile tone as she sat silent, "Well, never mind. I'll get it all from Rose."

"No, I'll chip in," Natalie said. "Aaron will, too, I'm sure. I just don't like it."

"Neither do I, Mrs. Henry, but we can't sit here. We have to try something."

On a hatch cover near Dr. Jastrow, who was writing in a notebook, two young men were arguing over an open battered Talmud volume. Rose was gone. Jastrow paused in his work to listen to their dispute about a point in *Gittin,* the treatise on divorce. In the Polish yeshiva, Jastrow had earned many a kiss from his teachers for unravelling problems in *Gittin.* The sensation of those damp hairy accolades came to mind, and he smiled. The two arguers saw this and shyly smiled back. One touched his ragged cap, and said in Yiddish, *"Der groiser shriftsh- teller* understands the little black points?"

Jastrow benignly nodded.

The other young man—gaunt, yellow-faced, with a straggling little beard and bright sunken eyes, a pure yeshiva type—spoke up excitedly. "Would you join us, and perhaps teach us?"

"As a boy, I did once study the Talmud," Jastrow said in cool precise Polish, "but that was long, long ago, I fear. I'm rather busy."

Subdued, the pair resumed their study. Soon, to Jastrow's relief, they moved away. It might have been amusing, he thought as he resumed writing, to join the lads and astound them with memory feats. After fifty years, he remembered the very passage in dispute. The retentiveness of a boy's mind! But a long voyage lay ahead. Keeping one's distance in these crowded conditions, especially amid these tribally intimate Jews, was the only way.

Jastrow was starting a new book, to pass the time and make some use of his disagreeable predicament. In a deliberate echo of his big success, *A Jew's Jesus,* he was calling it *A Jew's Journey.* But what he had in mind was not a travel diary. As Marcus Aurelius had written classic meditations on the battlefield by candlelight, so Jastrow proposed to coin his wartime flight into luminous thoughts on faith, war, the human condition, and his own life. He guessed the idea would charm his publisher; and that if he brought it off, it might even be another book club selection. In any case, at his age, it would be a salutary reckoning of the soul. On this notion, characteristically combining the thoughtful, the imaginative, and the catchpenny, Aaron Jastrow was well into the first notebook borrowed from Rabinovitz. He knew the book could never be a success like *A Jew's Jesus,* which had hit the book club jackpot and the best-seller lists, with its novel portrayal of Christ in his homely reality as a Talmud prodigy and itinerant Palestinian preacher; but it would be something to do.

After the yeshiva boys had moved off, the little scene struck him as worth writing down. He detailed the subtle point in *Gittin* which, so long ago, he had disputed in much the same terms with his clever young cousin, Berel Jastrow, in the noisy study hall of the Oswiecim yeshiva. He described that distant scene. He made gentle fun of his own gradual change into a cool Westernized agnostic. If Berel were still alive, he wrote, and if he had been invited into this dispute over page 27A of *Gittin,* he would have picked up the thread with zest, and argued rings around the yeshiva lads. Berel had remained true to the old orthodoxy. Who could now say which of them had chosen more wisely?

But what has become of Berel? Does he yet live? In my last glimpse of him, through the eyes of my venturesome and well-travelled niece, he stands amid the smoky wreckage of the Warsaw Jewish quarter in 1939 under German bombardment—erect, busy, aged but sturdy as a peasant, with the full gray beard of the orthodox, a paterfamilias, a community leader, a prosperous merchant; and beneath that conventional surface a steely survivor, an Ahasuerus of Christian legend, the indestructible Wandering Jew. Seven or eight years younger than I am, Berel served four years on the battlefronts in the First World War. He was a soldier; he was a prisoner; he escaped; he fought on several fronts, in three different armies. In all that time, through all those perils (so he once wrote me, and so I believe) not only did he emerge unharmed; not a particle of forbidden food ever passed his lips. A man who could care so much about our old God and our ancient Law puts to shame, in point of gallantry, his assimilated cousin who writes about Jesus. And yet the voice of enlightened humanism, speaking with all respect, might well ask whether living in a dream, however comforting and powerful—

"Damn it, Aaron! How long has he been uncovered like this?" Crouched over the basket, Natalie was angrily pulling the flapping blanket back over Louis, who began to cry.

"Oh, has it come undone?" Jastrow said with a start. "Sorry. He's been quiet as a mouse."

"Well, it's time to feed him." She picked up the basket, giving him an exasperated glare. "If he's not too frozen to eat, that is."

"What did Rabinovitz want?"

She bluntly told him.

"Really, Natalie! That much money! An illegal departure! That's terribly upsetting. We must be careful with our money, you know. It's our only salvation."

"We've got to get out of here. That's our salvation."

"But perhaps Rabinovitz is just squeezing the rich Americans a bit—now Natalie, don't scowl so! I only mean—"

"Look, if you don't trust him, go ashore and give yourself up. I'll split the three hundred with Rose."

"Good heavens, why do you snap at me so? I'll do it."

Heavy vibration woke her. Sitting up, clutching over her nightgown the sweater in which she slept, she looked through the open porthole. Cold foggy fishy-smelling air came drifting in. The pier was sliding backward in the misty night. She could hear the slosh of the propellers. Aaron snored in the upper bunk. On the deck beside her, the baby rustled and wheezed in his basket.

She snuggled down again beneath the coarse blankets, for it was very cold. Under way! A departure was always exhilarating; this risky clandestine slip from the trap of Nazi Europe, doubly so. Her mind sleepily groped ahead to Palestine, to getting word to Byron, to making her way home. The geography of the Middle East was blurry to her. Could she perhaps find passage at Suez to Australia, and from there go on to Hawaii? To wait out the war in Palestine was impossible. At best it was a disease-ridden barren country. The Germans in North Africa were a menace. So were the Arabs.

At each change in engine sound she grew more wakeful. The rolling and pitching were bad right here in the harbor; what would they be like on the open sea? The extra oil tanks welded on the main deck clearly made the vessel very unstable. How long to reach the three-mile limit? Dawn was making a violet circle at the porthole. The captain would have to go slow in this fog, and daylight would increase the chance of being caught. What a business, what a predicament! So Natalie lay tense and worrying, braced against the unsteady bunk through a long, long half hour, while the porthole brightened to whitish-gray.

WHUMP!

On the instant she was out of her bunk, bare feet on the icy iron deck, pulling on a coarse bathrobe. Natalie had heard a lot of gunfire in Warsaw. She knew that noise. Cold wet wind through the porthole tumbled her hair. The fog had lifted a little off the rough sea, and she saw far ahead a gray ship with a white number on its bow. From this bow came a smoky yellow flash.

WHUMP!

The engines pounded, the deck shivered and tilted, the vessel swerved. She hastily dressed, shuddering in the raw air. So small was the room that she barked elbows and knees on the cold-water basin, the bunk, and the doorknob. Aaron slept on. She would not wake him yet, she thought. He would only dither.

At the porthole an enormous white 22 appeared, blocking off the black waves and the gray sky. The gun slowly moved forward into view —not very big, painted gray, manned by boyish sailors in black short raincoats. Both vessels were slowing. The gunners were looking at the *Redeemer* and laughing. She could imagine why: the motley paint job, patches of red primer, of white coat, of old unscraped rust; the extra fuel tanks, spread along the deck like bad teeth in an old man's jaw. Outside harsh voices bawled back and forth in Italian.

The deck trembled. The coast guard vessel fell away. Through the porthole Natalie saw the green crags of Capri and Ischia; then, swinging into view dead ahead, the hills of Naples, lined with white houses in wan sunlight. Through all this Aaron Jastrow slept. Turning back! She fell on the bunk, face down in the pillow. The trip she had been dreading now seemed a passage to lost bliss. The hunted feeling rose in her breast again.

"My goodness, what a commotion!" Aaron poked his frowsy head out of the bunk. Sunshine was streaming through the porthole, and the crewmen were cheerily shouting and cursing outside. The *Redeemer* was tying up to the same wharf, with the same potbellied policeman in green patrolling it. "Why, it's broad daylight. You're all dressed. What's happening? Are we leaving?"

"We've left and returned. The coast guard stopped us."

Jastrow looked grave. "Oh dear. Two hundred dollars!"

Rabinovitz came to their door, freshly shaved, in a stained dark suit, a gray shirt, a red tie. His face was set in hard angry lines, and he was holding out some American money. "I can only refund half, sorry. He wouldn't leave the pier unless I advanced half. I had to gamble."

"You may need the rest," Natalie said. "Keep it."

"If I need it, I'll ask again."

Jastrow spoke from the upper bunk. "We've never discussed paying for our passage, you know, and—"

Rabinovitz slapped the money into Natalie's hand. "Excuse me. I'm going to bust in on that damned harbor master. We're a neutral vessel. We just put in here for emergency repairs. Holding us up like this is a damned outrage!"

They were having their noonday tea when Rabinovitz reappeared at their cabin door. "I was short-tempered this morning. Sorry."

"Come in," Natalie said amiably. "Tea?"

"Thanks. Yes. What's the matter with your baby?" Louis was whimpering in his basket.

"He caught a chill. Is there any news?"

Rabinovitz squatted with his back to the door, holding the glass in two hands and sipping. "Dr. Jastrow, when we left Rome so suddenly, you seemed very upset about the manuscript you had to leave behind."

"I'm still upset. Four years of my life!"

"What was the title of your book?"

"*The Arch of Constantine.* Why?"

"In Rome, did you know anybody at the German embassy?"

"The German embassy? Obviously not."

"You're sure?"

"I had nothing to do with the German embassy."

"You've never heard of a guy named Werner Beck?"

"Werner Beck?" Jastrow repeated, half to himself. "Why, yes, I did know a Werner Beck, years ago. What about him?"

"There's a Dr. Werner Beck at the gangway. He's one of the two Germans I saw in your hotel suite in Rome, when Rose and I went looking for you. He just drove up in a Mercedes. He says he's from the German embassy in Rome, and he's an old friend of yours. And he says he's brought your manuscript of *The Arch of Constantine.*"

In sober silence, broken only by the baby's snorts and snuffles, Natalie and her uncle looked at each other. "Describe him," said Jastrow.

"Middle height. Sort of fat. Pale, a lot of blond hair, a high voice. Pleasant manners."

"Glasses?"

"Thick rimless glasses."

"It's probably Werner Beck, though he wasn't fat then."

Natalie had to clear her throat to talk. "Who is he, Aaron?"

"Why, Werner was a student in my last graduate seminar at Yale. One of the good German students, a demon for work. He had language difficulties, and I helped him over some hurdles. I haven't seen or heard from him since then."

"He says he took the manuscript from your suite," said Rabinovitz. "He was there, that I can assure you. He was the polite one. The other one was damned ugly."

"How did he track me here?" Jastrow seemed dazed. "This is very ominous, isn't it?"

"Well, I can't say. If we deny you're here, the OVRA will come on board to search. They do anything the Gestapo wants."

Shakily Natalie put in, "What about the Turkish flag?"

"Up to a point, the Turkish flag is fine."

Jastrow took a decisive tone. "There's really no alternative, is there? Shall I go to the gangway?"

"I'll bring him to you."

It was some comfort to Natalie that the Palestinian was showing so little alarm. To her this was a devastating, hideous development. She was frightened to the core for her baby. Rabinovitz left. Jastrow said meditatively, "Werner Beck! Dear me. Hitler wasn't even in power when I knew Werner."

"Was he for Hitler?"

"Oh, no. A conservative, gentle, studious sort. Rather religious, if memory serves. From a good family. He was aiming for the Foreign Office, I remember that."

The baby sneezed. Natalie busied herself trying to clean out his clogged tiny nose. She was too shocked to think clearly.

"Professor Jastrow, here's Dr. Werner Beck." Rabinovitz stepped into the cabin. A man in a gray overcoat and gray hat bowed in the doorway, lifting the hat and bringing together his heels. Under his left arm he carried a very thick yellow envelope wrapped in string.

"You do remember me, Professor Jastrow?" His voice was prim and high. He smiled in an awkward, almost apologetic way, half-shutting his eyes. "It's been twelve and a half years."

"Yes, Werner." Jastrow proffered a gingerly handshake. "You've put on weight, that's all."

"Yes, far too much. Well, here is *The Arch of Constantine.*"

Jastrow set the package on the bunk beside the restless baby, undid the string with shaking fingers, and riffled through the mass of onion-skin sheets. "Natalie, it's all here!" His eyes glistened at the man in the doorway. "What can I say, Werner, but thank you? *Thank you!*"

"It wasn't easy, Professor. But I knew what it would mean to you." Dr. Beck turned to Rabinovitz. "It was my Gestapo confrere, you see, who got it away from the OVRA. I don't think I could have. I regret you and he had words, but you returned him some very short answers, you know." Rabinovitz shrugged, his expression blank. Beck looked back to Jastrow, who was fondling his papers. "I took the liberty of reading the work, Professor. What an advance over *A Jew's Jesus!* You demonstrate a very special grasp of early Byzantium, and of the eastern church. You bring that whole lost world to life. The book will seal your popular fame, and this time the academics will praise your scholarship as well. It's your finest achievement."

"Why, how kind of you, Werner." Jastrow assumed his simpering way with admirers. "And as for you, your English has amazingly improved. Remember the trouble at your orals?"

"Indeed I do. You saved my career."

"Oh, hardly so."

"I've since served seven years in Washington. My boys—I have four— are bilingual in English and German. Now I'm first secretary in Rome. And it's all thanks to you."

"Four boys. Well, fancy that."

Natalie found it hard to believe that this small talk was going on. It was like dialogue in a dream. There the man stood in the cabin doorway, an official of Nazi Germany, a stoutish harmless-looking person, with glasses that gave him a bookish look. His hands holding the hat were folded before him in a peaceful, almost priestly way. Talking about his boys, praising Aaron's work, he made a benign appearance; if anything—especially with the alto voice and proper manners—a bit soft and academic. The baby coughed, and Werner Beck looked at him. "Is your child well, Mrs. Henry?"

Harshly she burst out, "How do you know my name? How did you know that we were at the Excelsior? And how did you find out we'd come here?"

She could see that Aaron was pained by her manner. Rabinovitz's face remained wooden. Dr. Beck replied in a patient tone, "The Gestapo keeps a current list, of course, of foreign nationals at Rome hotels. And the OVRA reported to the Gestapo that you had boarded this vessel."

"Then you're in the Gestapo?"

"No, Mrs. Henry. As I said, I'm a Foreign Ministry officer. Now, would you and your uncle care to lunch with me at the Grand Hotel? They say it has the best dining room in Naples."

Lips parted in silent stupefaction, Natalie looked to Jastrow, who said, "Surely you're not serious, Werner."

"Why not? You might enjoy some good food and wine. You'll be starting tomorrow on a long hard voyage."

"Tomorrow? That's more than I know," Rabinovitz spoke up, "and I've just come from the harbor master."

"Well, that is my information."

Natalie almost barked, "As soon as we set foot ashore we'll be arrested and interned. You know that. So do we."

"I have police passes for both of you." She shook her head violently at Jastrow. Dr. Beck quietly went on, "Suppose I withdraw so you can talk it over? If you're hesitant, let's just chat at the gangway before I leave. But it's quite safe for you to come ashore with me, and there really is much to discuss."

Jastrow struck in severely. "What were you doing in my hotel room, Werner?"

"Professor, when Mussolini declared war, I thought I'd better offer you my help. I brought the Gestapo man to handle the Italian police."

"Why didn't you call on me long before that?"

With a sudden hangdog look at Natalie, Beck answered, "Shall I be candid? So as not to inflict an odious presence on you." He lifted his hat, bowed, and left.

Jastrow glanced doubtfully from the Palestinian to his niece.

"Aaron, I'm not getting separated from Louis. Not for one minute!" Natalie turned strident. "I'm not even going out there to the gangway!"

"What do you think?" Jastrow said to Rabinovitz, who turned up his hands. "Well, d'you suppose it's all an elaborate scheme to collar me? Now that he's found me, can't he just get the OVRA to drag me off your ship, if that's what he's after?"

"This way he'd avoid a fuss."

"How much of a fuss?"

Rabinovitz bitterly grinned. "Not much of a fuss."

Jastrow pulled at his beard, eyes on his glowering niece. Then he reached for his hat and cloak. "Well, Natalie, I've been a confounded dunderhead right along. I may as well follow my nature. I shall go ashore with Werner Beck."

"Oh, by all means!" The baby was wailing now, and Natalie was beside herself. "Enjoy your lunch! Maybe his Gestapo pals will join you, to make things jollier."

Rabinovitz helped Jastrow with his cloak. "Find out all you can about our departure."

"I shall. If I don't return," said Jastrow to Natalie, as she rocked the screaming infant in her arms, "you'll simply be rid of a millstone, won't you?"

Two hours passed. Hard rain cleared the deck of strollers. Natalie waited alone at the gangway under an umbrella, watching the dripping policeman pace the wharf. A small black Mercedes at last appeared through the rain. Dr. Beck got out to open the door for Dr. Jastrow, waved to her, and drove off. Mounting the gangplank, Jastrow spread his arms under the blue cloak. "Well, my dear! I have returned, you see."

"Thank God for that."

"Yes. Now let's have a talk with Rabinovitz."

"Sure you don't want your nap first?"

"I'm not sleepy."

The Palestinian, in his greasy coveralls, opened the cabin door to their knock. The little room smelled strongly of sweat, grease, and cigarette ashes. Jastrow blinked at the pinups of naked women. "Please sit down," Rabinovitz said. "I'll have to get rid of those pretty ladies. I don't notice them, but everybody else does. So. I'm very glad you're back. You have guts. Was it an interesting lunch?"

"Rather." Jastrow sat stiffly in the desk chair, Natalie on a stool beside him. "To begin with, your Turkish captain betrayed you. He told the coast guard that you would try a clandestine departure. That's why you were caught. So Werner says."

Rabinovitz nodded, his face sour. "I thought as much. We can't charter another vessel, so I have to forget it—for the time being."

"The Turk also reported our arrival aboard last week. The harbor master decided to notify the OVRA in Rome, and clear up this matter of fugitive Americans, before letting you go. Hence the week's delay."

"Well. So it all fits together." Rabinovitz was clenching and unclenching clasped fingers in his lap. "What about our leaving tomorrow?"

"Yes, he says you will. Now, about that." Jastrow's tone sharpened. "Was this vessel formerly called the *Izmir?*"

"It's the *Izmir.*"

"Were you recently checked for seaworthiness?"

"A port inspector came to verify our certificate, yes."

"Werner says he appended a page of comment. You're overcrowded and overloaded. The added tanks topside have dangerously decreased your stability. In a panic, if the passengers all rush to one side, this vessel may actually capsize. Is that correct?"

"They're a disciplined group," Rabinovitz said very tiredly. "They won't panic."

"Your food, water, and sanitary facilities are acutely substandard," Jastrow went on. "Of course, Natalie and I have already observed that. Medical facilities are poor. The engine is thirty-five years old. Its log shows several recent breakdowns. You're certified only for coastal waters, not for the open sea."

Rabinovitz's tone turned acid. "Did you mention that we Jews have to accept such risks so as to escape German persecution?"

"Almost in those words. He didn't like it. But he said that if Palestine had been under a German mandate, most of Europe's Jews would have been sent there long since in seaworthy vessels. Your use of a floating death trap like this is due to Allied, not German, policy. England's closed Palestine off so as to win over the Arabs—a silly gesture, since they're heart and soul for Hitler. America has shut its gates. So your organization, which he knows all about, must try to smuggle refugees into Palestine, in derelicts like the *Izmir*."

"Yes, the Nazis are ardent Zionists," said Rabinovitz. "We know that."

Jastrow took an envelope from an inside breast pocket. "Now, here are the Italian police regulations for American internees. They're being sent to Siena to await exchange. As it happens, my home is in Siena. My staff is still living there."

Rabinovitz glanced through the mimeographed sheets, his eyes sad and dull.

"Those regulations could be faked," Natalie exclaimed.

"They're real." Rabinovitz handed the sheets to her. "So, does that settle it? Are you two getting off and going to Siena?"

"I told Werner," Jastrow replied, "that it's up to Natalie. If she sails with you, I'll sail. If she elects to return to Siena, I'll do that."

"I see. Very nice." With a brief shift of his eyes to Natalie, who sat pale and still, Rabinovitz asked, "What did Dr. Beck say to that?"

"Well, as a mother, he says, she'll no doubt decide wisely. The risks of the voyage for her infant are pointless and intolerable. She's not a stateless refugee. That's what he wanted to tell her."

"You haven't seen this man in twelve years, Aaron." Natalie's voice almost broke in mid-sentence. Her hands were crumpling the mimeographed sheets. "He's trying to keep you here. Why?"

"Well, why indeed? Do you suppose he wants to murder me?" Jastrow said, with tremulous facetiousness. "Why should he? I gave him straight A's in my seminar."

Rabinovitz said, "He doesn't want to murder you."

"No. I believe he wants to help his old teacher."

"God in heaven," Natalie all but shouted, "will you ever show a trace of common sense? This man is a high-placed Nazi. What makes you willing to accept a word he says?"

"He's not a Nazi." Jastrow spoke with calm pedantry. "He's a professional diplomat. He regards the Party as a pack of gross ill-educated opportunists. He does admire Hitler for unifying Germany, but he has grave misgivings about the way the war is going. The Jewish policy appalls him. Werner once studied for the ministry. I don't think there's an anti-Semitic bone in his body. Unlike some American consuls we've been dealing with."

There was a double knock at the door. The rough-looking man who was Rabinovitz's assistant looked in to hand him an envelope sealed with red wax. Rabinovitz read the letter and stood up, peeling the coveralls off a clean white shirt and dark trousers. "Well, all right. We'll talk some more later."

"What is it?" Natalie blurted.

"We're cleared to leave. I'm to pick up the ship's papers at once from the harbor master."

3

BEREL JASTROW, in a tattered Soviet army greatcoat, shuffles up to his ankles in snow along a road in southwest Poland. The long column of Russian prisoners is winding through flat white fields of the area historians call Upper Silesia. Green-clad SS men guard the column, clubs or machine guns in hand. Leading and trailing the column, two large clanking army vehicles full of more SS men ride. This labor draft, culled from the sturdiest prisoners in the Lamsdorf Stalag, has been walking the whole way. Death has shrunken it en route by about a third. The daily meal at 10 A.M. has been a slice of blackish woody stuff resembling bread, lukewarm soup made of nettles, spoiled potatoes, rotten roots, and the like. Even this ration has often failed, and the men have been turned loose in the fields to forage like goats under the SS guns. For twelve to fourteen hours each day, they have had to foot it at the pace of the stout healthy guards, who march and ride in two-hour shifts.

Berel Jastrow's oaken constitution is nearing collapse. All around him, men have been dropping in their tracks right along; often silently, sometimes with a groan or a cry. When kicking or clubbing does not rouse a man who falls, he gets a bullet through the head. This is a routine precaution, for partisans might otherwise revive and recruit him. Calmly but punctiliously the Germans blow each skull to pieces, leaving a red mass on the snow by the neck of the huddled Russian greatcoat.

The column is walking now from Cracow to Katowice; fresh signposts in heavy German lettering call it KATTOWITZ. Berel Jastrow numbly surmises that the trek may soon be ending, for Katowice is a center of industry and mining. He is too low in vital energy, too shrunken by cold, hunger, and crushing weariness, to wonder at the chance that brings him to familiar scenes. All his waning attention is focussed on keeping his eyes on the man ahead, his legs moving, and his knees stiff, for he fears if he relaxes the joints they will buckle, and he will go down and get his head blown off.

In forty years the old road has not changed much. Berel can predict each turn. He knows when the next peasant home or wooden church will loom through the fine dry blowing snow. Is the draft going to the Katowice coal mines? Not a bad fate! Mines are warmer in winter than the open air. Miners have to be well-fed to produce.

For all the suffering on this march, Berel is grateful to God that he is in the labor column and out of the Stalag. Nothing in his experience of the last war, nothing in the Warsaw ghetto, equals what he has seen at Lamsdorf. The Stalag is not really a prison camp, for there are no barracks, no buildings, no roll calls, no administration; no means of order, except fear of the manned machine guns on the watchtowers, and of the blazing searchlights at night. The installation is just a barbed-wire enclosure open to the sky, stretching farther than the eye can see, penning in two hundred thousand starving men. On the eastern front the Geneva Convention does not exist. The Soviet Union never signed it.

The Germans are not prepared, anyway, to support such a vast bag of captives. The supply of food and water is scanty. The rule of life at Lamsdorf is self-preservation, in filth, stench, snarling dogfights over edible scraps, and untended sickness. Dead bodies lie about in the muck and the snow. Daily the dead are cremated in heaps, fueled by wood and waste oil, outside the barbed wire. The pyres flame far into the night. The camp stinks as though a huge meat-packing plant were nearby, where animals are rendered and the hair or bristles scorched off their hides.

Prisoners captured in the Germans' November drive on Moscow make up this labor draft. Those who are dying in Lamsdorf were caught in the summer campaign. Reduced by now to walking skeletons, they collapse randomly, all over the place, day and night. Of the varied Lamsdorf horrors, one still scars Jastrow's soul. He himself has glimpsed, in the night gloom beyond the searchlights, the small packs of prisoners, insane with hunger, who rove the frozen wastes of the camp, eating the soft inner parts of new-fallen corpses. He has seen the mutilated corpses by day. The watchtower guards shoot the cannibals, when they spot them. Prisoners who catch them kick or beat them to death. But the instinct to live outlasts human nature in these creatures, and cancels fear. The cannibals are crazy somnambulists, idiot mouths seeking to be filled, with enough cunning left in their blasted brains to feed at night, skulking in shadow like coyotes. Whatever lies ahead in Katowice, Berel Jastrow knows that nothing can be worse than Lamsdorf.

Yet it seems the column is not going to Katowice. The ranks ahead are making a left turn. That will take the draft south to Oswiecim, Berel knows; but what is there for such a large labor force to do in Oswiecim? The place of his boyhood yeshiva is a town of small manufactures, isolated in the marshy land where the Sola meets the Vistula. Mainly, it is a railroad junction. No heavy labor there. At the turn in the road, he sees a new Gothic-lettered arrow, nailed above the faded Oswiecim signpost. The Germans are using the old name, which Berel remembers from his youth when Oswiecim was Austrian. Not only is it harsher, as German names tend to be; AUSCHWITZ hardly even sounds like Oswiecim.

4

Rabinovitz returned in a rusty van loaded with supplies, followed by two tank trucks carrying fresh water and diesel fuel. This touched off a frenzy of work through the twilight and into the night. Shouting, laughing, singing Jews passed the stores hand to hand up the gangway, across the deck, and down the hatches: sacks of flour and potatoes, net bags of wormy cabbages and other stunted, gnarled vegetables, bundles of dried fish, and boxes of tinned food. The ragged Turkish crewmen brought aboard the fuel and water hoses to throb and thump and groan; they fastened down hatches, tinkered at the anchor windlass, coiled ropes, blasphemed, hammered, and bustled about. The old vessel itself, as though infected with the excitement of imminent departure, creaked, rolled, and strained at its mooring lines. Frigid gusts were driving swells in past the mole, but despite the wind, happily babbling passengers thronged the unsteady deck watching the preparations. When they went below to eat, the wind was working up to a near-gale under a glittering half-moon.

In a purple crepe dress, her face touched with rouge and lipstick, Natalie stood hesitating on the wobbly deck outside Rabinovitz's cabin door. Close-wrapped around her shoulders was Aaron's gray shawl. She sighed, and knocked.

"Well, hello there, Mrs. Henry."

On the grimy bulkheads in place of the pinups were pallid yellow rectangles. Otherwise the rank disorder was as before: unmade bunk, piled papers, swirling tobacco smoke, workman's smells from clothes dangling on hooks. He said as he closed the door, "Isn't that Sarah Elowsky's dress?"

"I bought it from her." Natalie steadied herself against the doorway. "That everlasting brown wool dress of mine I've come to loathe, truly loathe."

"Sarah would wear that when we talked to the authorities at Nice. She has a way with Frenchmen."

"I hardly know her. I know so little about all you people!"

"How's your baby?"

"Cranky. He keeps pawing at his right ear, and he's feverish."

"You've had him to the infirmary?"

"Yes. They gave me pills for him."

"Well? And are you coming with us?"

"I'm trying to make up my mind."

"That shouldn't be hard." He offered her his desk chair, and squatted on the iron deck. "Decide what's best for yourself, and do it."

"Why did you ever bring us aboard, anyway? You only created trouble for yourself."

"Impulse, Mrs. Henry." He drew hard on a cigarette. "When we sailed from Nice we had no plan to stop here. The generator burned out. I had to get an armature and some more money in Rome. I contacted Herb Rose. He told me your uncle was there. I'm an admirer of his. So—"

"Are your passengers all from Nice?"

"No. None of them. They're Zionist pioneers, refugees now, mostly Polish and Hungarian. They'd have left from Constanta on the Black Sea—that's the usual route—but their Rumanian fixer ran off with their money. They got shunted around by the Jewish agencies for months, and ended up in Italian-occupied France. It's not a bad place for Jews, but they wanted to go on to Palestine, no matter what. That's what I do, get Jews to Palestine. So, that's the story."

"Are you going straight to Palestine, or via Turkey? I've heard both rumors."

"I'm not sure. I'll receive radio signals at sea about that."

"If it's via Turkey, you'll have to take your people through the Syrian mountains illegally, won't you? Hostile Arab country?"

"I've done that before. If we can go straight home, of course we will."

"Are your engines going to break down at sea?"

"No. I'm a marine engineer. The ship is old, but it's French. The French build good ships."

"What about the overcrowding? Those stacks of bunks down below—those long open latrine troughs! Suppose another three-day storm comes along? Won't you have an outbreak of disease?"

"Mrs. Henry, these people are trained for rough conditions."

"Hasn't it occurred to you"—she twisted the shawl in her hands—"that you may not sail? That the clearance could just be a trick to lure my uncle quietly away? It's quite a coincidence that you got your papers right after Werner Beck showed up." Rabinovitz made a skeptical face. She went on quickly. "Now I've thought of something. If we do leave the *Redeemer*—I'm not saying we will—but if we do, Aaron could insist on going straight to the Turkish consulate. There we'd wait for a signal from you, relayed through the coast guard, that you're past the three-mile limit. If no signal comes, we'd claim Turkish sanctuary, and—what are you smiling at?"

"There's no Turkish consulate here."

"You said there was."

"He's an honorary consul, an Italian banker. A converted Jew, as it happens, and he's been a help. The nearest consulate is in Bari, on the Adriatic."

"Oh, hell."

"Anyway, a consulate doesn't give territorial sanctuary, like an embassy." His smile broadened. "But you've been thinking hard, haven't you?"

"Oh, I even had the signal."

"Really? What was it?"

"Well—" with a certain embarrassment she brought it out—" '*Next year in Jerusalem.*' Just the last line of the Passover seder."

"I know what it is." His smile faded to a stern businesslike look. "Listen, Mrs. Henry, the Italians have no use for a lot of hungry stateless Jews. We'll go. You ought to come, too."

"Oh, I should? And why?" The swaying of the smoky little room, with the bumping against the wharf, was making Natalie queazy.

"Let's say because your baby's Jewish, and should go to the Jewish homeland."

"He's only half-Jewish."

"Yes? Ask the Germans."

"Look, don't you understand that I feel no emotion about Palestine? None! I'm an American, completely irreligious, married to a Christian naval officer."

"Tell me about your husband."

The question took her aback. She awkwardly replied, "I haven't seen him for ages. He's on a submarine somewhere in the Pacific."

He took out a worn wallet and showed her a snap of a big-bosomed dark girl with heavy hair. "That was my wife. She was killed in a bus that the Arabs blew up."

"That's frightful."

"It happened eight years ago."

"And you want me to take my baby there?"

"Jews live in danger everywhere."

"Not in America."

"You're strangers there, too. In Palestine you're home."

Natalie took from her purse a small colored photograph of Byron in uniform. "Here's my husband."

Byron came alive in her memory as Rabinovitz knotted his brows over the picture. "He looks young. When did you get married?"

For months she had been shutting her marriage from her thoughts—that hazy tangle of imbecile decisions, leading to delirious labor pains alone in a foreign hospital, surrounded by strange faces and half-understood medical babble in Italian. For all the delicious love flooding her at seeing the tiny wrinkled red baby, she had felt then that her life was wrecked. More or less, she still did. But as she sketched the story to the Palestinian, Byron Henry's charm and dash, his ingenuity, his boyish appeal, all came back to her; also the terrific sweetness, however harebrained the thing had been, of the fleeting honeymoon in Lisbon. She thought—though she did not say this to Rabinovitz—that a crippled lifetime might be fair pay for such joy. Besides, she had Louis.

Rabinovitz chain-lit a cigarette as he listened. "You never met any Jewish young men like him?"

"No. The ones I went out with were all determined to be doctors, lawyers, writers, accountants, or college professors."

"Bourgeois types."

"Yes."

"Bring your son to Palestine. He'll grow up a man of action like his father."

"What about the hazards?" Natalie feared she might be getting seasick, here beside the wharf. The motion was really nauseating. She got out of the chair and leaned against the bulkhead. "I hope this ship makes it across the Mediterranean, but then what? End up in a British prison camp? Or take an infant through Arab mountains, to be shot at or captured and butchered?"

"Mrs. Henry, it's risky to take him to Siena."

"I don't know about that. My uncle talked by telephone to our chargé d'affaires in Rome, during his lunch with Beck. The chargé advised Aaron to go to Siena. He called this trip an unnecessary hazard for us."

"Your chargé d'affaires told him to trust a Hitler bureaucrat?"

"He said that he knows Beck well. He's not a Nazi. Our own Foreign

Service respects him. Beck has offered to drive us back to Rome tomorrow, straight to the embassy. I don't know what to believe, and frankly— *Oh!*" The deck of the small cabin sharply pitched and bumped. Natalie staggered, he jumped up to steady her, and she fell against him, crushing her breasts on his chest. He caught her upper arms in a hard grip, and held her gently away.

"Steady."

"Sorry."

"Okay."

He let her go. She forced a smile, her arms and breasts tingling.

"The wind keeps backing around. The weather reports aren't good. Still, we sail at first light."

"That may solve my problem. Maybe Beck won't come that early."

"He will. You'd better decide. It's a tough one for you, at that. I can see it is."

Aaron Jastrow in a blue bathrobe, his thin gray hair blown about, knocked and opened the door. "Sorry to interrupt. The baby's acting strange, Natalie." Her face distorted with alarm. "Now don't be frightened. Just come and see."

Rabinovitz seized her arm and they went out together. In their scurry down the moonlit windswept deck, Natalie's hair blew wildly. Louis lay in his basket on the bunk, his eyes shut, thrashing clenched fists this way and that.

"Louis!" She bent over him, putting both hands on the writhing little body. "Baby! Baby! Wake up—oh, he won't open his eyes! What is it? He's wriggling so!"

Rabinovitz took the child up in a blanket. "It's a convulsion from the fever. Don't worry, infants come out of convulsions." Louis's head was jerking above the blanket, eyes still shut. "Let's get him to the infirmary."

Natalie ran after him, down into the fetid gloom of the lower decks, into the miasma of latrines, of crowded unwashed bodies and clothes, of stale overbreathed air. Rabinovitz pushed past the queue jamming the passageway outside the infirmary. In the narrow white-painted cabin he thrust the baby on the doctor, a haggard graybeard in a soiled white coat. With a harassed air the doctor unwrapped Louis, looked at the jerking body, and agreed that it was a convulsion. He had no medicine to give. He reassured Natalie in a hoarse weak voice, speaking a Germanic Yiddish, "It's that inflamed right ear, you know. It's a febrile episode, I'm sure, nothing involving the brain. You can expect he'll come out of it soon with no harm done." He did not look as cheerful as his words.

"What about a warm bath?" Rabinovitz said.

"Yes, that could help. But there's no hot water on this boat, only cold showers."

Picking up Louis, Rabinovitz said to Natalie, "Come."

They hurried down the passageway to the ship's galley. Even when the galley was cleaned up and shut for the night, as now, it was malodorous and greasy. One piece of equipment, however, a tremendous vat, shone in the flickering electric light. Soup was the mainstay of the refugees' diet. Rabinovitz had somewhere procured this restaurant boiler and installed it. Briskly he opened a faucet and a valve. Water poured into the vat, and from a nozzle at the bottom live steam bubbled up.

"Feel that," he said after a few seconds. "Too hot?"

She dipped in a hand. "No."

Stripping the writhing infant, she pushed back her purple sleeves and immersed the little body in the tepid water to the chin. "Get some on his head, too." She obeyed. The stiff arch of Louis's back soon loosened. Rabinovitz let in more cool water. The spasms weakened, her son went limp in her hands, and she glanced at Rabinovitz with nervous hope.

"When my baby brother went into a convulsion," he said, "that's what my mother always did."

The blue eyes opened, the baby's gaze focussed on Natalie, and he gave her a tired little smile that wrung her heart. She said to Rabinovitz, "God bless you."

"Take him back up and keep him warm," Rabinovitz said. "My brother used to sleep for hours afterward. Let me know if you have more trouble. There's a clinic on shore we can go to, if we must."

Later he came and looked into her cabin, which was lit by two candles. His face and hands were black with grease. Aaron was asleep in the upper bunk. Natalie sat by the baby, in a bathrobe, her hair pinned up, one hand resting on the blanketed basket.

"How's he doing?"

"He's in a deep sleep, but even so, he keeps rubbing his ear."

Rabinovitz produced a small flat bottle, and filled a small glass. "Drink this," he said to Natalie. "Slivovitz, if you know what that is."

"I've drunk slivovitz. Lots of it." She drained the glass. "Thank you. What's the matter with the electricity?"

"The dumb generator again. I'm trying to fix it. You have enough candles?"

"Yes. Can you sail if it isn't working?"

"It will be working, and we will sail. More slivovitz?"

"No. That was fine."

"See you later."

When the lamps flickered on about 2 A.M., Natalie began to pack a cardboard suitcase she had bought from a passenger. That took only a few minutes, and she resumed her vigil. It was a long bad night, a sterile churning of regrets and afterthoughts stretching back to her girlhood, interspersed with nightmarish dozes. The baby slept restlessly, turning and turning. She kept feeling his forehead, and to her it seemed cool; yet when the porthole began to pale he broke out in a flooding sweat. She had to change him into dry swaddlings.

Herb Rose met her on the breezy deck as she carried the suitcase to the gangway. The dawn was breaking, a clear pleasant day. The deck was full of jubilant passengers. On one hatch cover some were singing around a concertina player, their arms thrown over each other's shoulders. The Turkish crewmen were bawling back and forth from the wharf to the deck, and there was much noisy slinging around of tackle.

"Good God," Rose said. "You're not really doing it, Natalie? You're not putting yourself in the hands of that German?"

"My baby's sick as hell."

"Listen, honey, babies' fevers are scary, but it's amazing how they can recover. Just a few days at sea and you'll be safe, once for all. Safe, and free!"

"You may be at sea for weeks. You may have to cross mountains."

"We'll get there. Your baby will be fine. Look at the weather, it's a good omen."

What he said about the weather was true. The harbor had calmed down, the breeze was almost balmy, and Vesuvius seemed inked on the apple-green horizon. Happiness diffused all over the crowded deck like a flower fragrance. But when Natalie had changed Louis he had been trembling, pawing at his ear again, and whimpering. Her memories of the convulsion, the infirmary, the ghastly night, the pestilential air below decks, were overpowering. She set the suitcase down at the gangway. "I don't suppose anybody will steal this. Still, please keep an eye on it, for a minute."

"Natalie, you're doing the wrong thing."

Soon she returned, bearing the bundled-up baby in his basket, with Jastrow pacing behind her in cloak and hat. Beck's Mercedes, with its large diplomatic medallion on the radiator—crimson shield, white circle, heavy black swastika—drove up the wharf and stopped. Rabinovitz stood beside Rose at the gangway now, his hands, face, and coveralls black-smeared. He was wiping his hands on a rag.

The jocund chorus of passenger noise on deck cut off with the arrival of the Mercedes. Unmoving, the passengers stared at the car and at the Americans. The raucous cursing of the crewmen, the slosh of water, the cries of sea birds, were the only sounds. Rabinovitz picked up the suitcase, and took the basket from Natalie. "Okay, let me help you."

"You're very kind."

As she set foot on the gangplank, Herb Rose darted at her and clutched her arm. "*Natalie!* For God's sake, let your uncle get off if he insists. He's had his life. Not you and your kid."

Jostling the American aside, Rabinovitz grated at him, "Don't be a goddamned fool."

Sporty in a tweed overcoat and corduroy cap, Dr. Werner Beck hopped out of the Mercedes, opened the front and back doors, and bowed and smiled. The scene was swimming around Natalie. Jastrow got in at the front door as Beck loaded the two suitcases in the trunk. Carefully, Avram Rabinovitz bestowed the basket in the back seat. "Well, good-bye, Dr. Jastrow," he said. "Good-bye, Mrs. Henry."

Beck got into the driver's seat.

She choked to Rabinovitz, "Am I doing the right thing?"

"It's done." He touched a rough hand to her cheek. "Next year in Jerusalem."

Tears sprang to her eyes. She kissed his bristly, greasy face, and stumbled into the car. He shut the door on her. "Let's go!" he called in Italian at the crewmen. "Get the plank in!"

The Mercedes drove down the wharf, with Jastrow and Beck blithely chatting. Natalie bent over the baby's basket, dry suppressed sobs convulsing her throat. As the car headed north out of Naples on a deserted macadam highway, the sun rose in a white blaze. Its slanted afternoon rays were lighting the Via Veneto when Werner Beck halted his car at the American embassy, and helped Natalie alight. Louis had a high fever.

The Red Cross was handling mail for the internees. Before Natalie left for Siena, she wrote Byron what had happened, summing it up so:

Now that I'm back in civilization—if you call Mussolini's Italy that—I can see that I did the prudent thing. We're safe and comfortable, an American doctor's been treating Louis, and he's on the mend. That boat was a horror. God knows what will become of those people. Still, I wish I didn't feel so lousy about it. I'll not rest easy until I learn what happened to the *Redeemer*.

5

EXCEPT for the haunting uncertainty about his wife and baby, Byron Henry was enjoying the new war with Japan. It had freed him for a while from the *Devilfish* and its exacting captain, for salvage duty in the ruins of the Cavite naval base. Under the bombed-out rubble and broken burned timbers lay great mounds of precious supplies in charred boxes or crates—electronic gear, clothing, food, machinery, mines, ammunition, the thousand things needed to keep a fleet going; above all, spare parts now desired above diamonds. With a sizable work gang, Byron was digging out the stuff day by day, and trucking it westward to Bataan.

His feat of retrieving torpedoes under fire during the Cavite raid had brought him this assignment direct from Admiral Hart's headquarters. He had *carte blanche* in the burned ruins, so long as he produced the goods at the peninsula enclosing the bay to the west, where American forces were digging into the mountains for a possible long siege. This freedom of action enchanted Byron. His contempt for paperwork and regulations, which had gotten him into such hot water aboard the *Devilfish,* was a prime scavenger virtue. To get things moving he signed any paper, told any lie. He commandeered idle men and vehicles as though he were the admiral himself. For overcoming resistance and settling arguments, he used fire-blackened cases of beer and cartons of cigarettes—which worked like gold coin—from a vast cache he had come upon in the ruins. His drivers and loaders got plenty of these, too, and he made sure they were well fed. If he had to, he brought them into officers' messes, brassily pleading emergency.

Once during an air raid he marched his seventeen men into the grill of the Manila Hotel. The dirty, sweaty crew ate a sumptuous lunch on white napery to string music, while on the waterfront bombs exploded. He paid the enormous check with a Navy voucher full of fine print, adding a five-dollar tip from his own pocket; and he walked out fast, leaving the head waiter staring dubiously at the flimsy blue paper. Thus Byron got his raggle-taggle pickup gang of sailors, longshoremen, marines, and truck drivers—Filipino, American, Chinese, he didn't care—to drudge cheerily from dawn to nightfall. They stuck to him because he kept them on the move, rewarded them as a trainer throws fish to his seals, and turned a blind eye to their own pilferings in the rubble.

The stinking smashed-up Cavite base reminded him of battered Warsaw, where he had been caught with Natalie by Hitler's invasion. But this was a different war: sporadic bombings from the azure tropic sky setting ships ablaze and raising pretty bursts of flame among the waterfront palm trees; nothing like the storm of German bombs and shells that had wrecked the Polish capital. Nor was there yet the fear of an enemy closing in. Cavite had been a hot show, a thorough rubbing-out of a military target, but the base was just a smudge on the untouched hundred-mile coast of Manila Bay. The city itself kept its peacetime look: shimmering heat, glaring sunshine, heavy automobile traffic and crawling oxcarts, a few white men and hordes of Filipinos strolling the sidewalks. Sirens, fires, sandbags, tiny Japanese bombers glinting over green palm-feathered hills far above the thudding black AA puffs, made a war of it—a war slightly movie-ish in feel.

Byron knew things would get rougher. Pessimistic rumors abounded: as, that the entire Pacific Fleet had been sunk at Pearl Harbor, carriers and all, but that the guilty President was suppressing the catastrophic news. Or, that MacArthur's announcements of "small-scale" enemy landings on Luzon were lies; that the Japs were already ashore in force, thundering toward Manila with thousands of tanks. And so forth. Most people believed what General MacArthur told them: that the Jap landings in the north were light feints, well-contained, and that massive help was on the way. There were also optimistic rumors of a huge relief convoy, already en route from San Francisco with a Marine division and three mechanized Army divisions, plus two aircraft carriers crammed with fighters and bombers.

Byron wasn't much concerned either way. A submarine could leave Luzon at a half hour's notice. As for his father and brother at Pearl Harbor, Victor Henry seemed indestructible to Byron, and he doubted the *Enterprise* had been sunk. That would have come out. He would have been quite happy, had he only been sure that Natalie and the baby were homeward bound. The work was a godsend. It kept him too busy by day and too worn out by night to worry overmuch.

This pleasant time abruptly ended. Stopping his truck convoy in downtown Manila to report on his progress, he met Branch Hoban coming out of the Marsman building with a thick envelope in hand, blinking in the sunshine.

"Well, well, Briny Henry himself, loose as a goose!" The captain of the *Devilfish* caught at his arm. "This simplifies matters."

Hoban's handsome face had a hard set to it; the jaw was thrust far forward; the neat Clark Gable mustache seemed to bristle. He squinted at the four heavily laden trucks, and at Byron's work gang, all bare-chested or in dirty undershirts, drinking warm beer from cans. "Heading for Mariveles, were you?"

"Yes, sir, after making my report."

"I'll ride along. You're securing from this duty."

"Sir, Commander Percifield expects me, and—"

"I know all about Commander Percifield. Go ahead in. I'll wait."

Percifield told Byron that the admiral wanted to see him, and added, "You've done a 4.0 job, Ensign Henry. We'll miss you. Turn over your men and vehicles to Captain Tully at Mariveles."

Byron was led by a yeoman into the presence of the Commander-in-Chief of the Asiatic Fleet, a dried-up small old man in whites at an oversize desk, facing out on a spectacular panorama of the blue palm-lined bay.

"You're Pug Henry's boy, aren't you? Warren's brother?" Hart twanged with no other greeting. His round face, weathered in red-brown streaks and patches, wore a harried embittered look. His neck was all sunburned cords and strings. He held himself straight and stiff in the swivel chair.

"Yes, Admiral."

"I thought as much. When I was Academy Superintendent, Warren was a battalion commander. A real comer, Warren. And your father's an outstanding gent. Have a look at this." He tossed Byron a dispatch.

FROM: THE CHIEF OF PERSONNEL
TO: CAPTAIN VICTOR (NONE) HENRY
DETACHED CO CALIFORNIA (BB–44) X RELIEVE CO
NORTHAMPTON (CA–26)

So the *California* was out of action, and his father had a cruiser instead! This was news. But why was Thomas Hart, who bore naval responsibility for the whole Asian theatre, taking notice of an ensign?

"Thank you, Admiral."

"Not a bad consolation prize, the *Northampton*," Hart said in brusque gravelly tones. "The *California*'s sitting on the mud in Pearl, with a hell of a big torpedo hole in her hull. That's confidential. Now then. You seem to be an original, hey, Ensign?" The admiral picked up two papers clipped together. "Seems you've been put up for a letter of commendation, for pulling a quantity of torpedoes out of Cavite under fire. As a submariner, I deeply appreciate that exploit. We're very low on fish. And you've since been recovering other valuable stores, I understand, including mines. Well done! On the other hand, young fellow—" he turned over a sheet, and his face soured, "you've gone and applied for transfer to Atlantic duty!" Leaning back, Hart clasped his hands under his chin and glared. "I wanted a look at the Henry boy who would put in such a request at a time like this."

"Sir, my wife—"

Hart's hostile look softened, and his tone too. "Yes, I'm told that your wife is Jewish, and that she may be caught in Italy with a baby. That's a very bad business and I sympathize, but what can you do about it?"

"Sir, I'll be ten thousand miles closer, if by chance there is something to do."

"But we need submarine officers here. I'm combing them from the tender and the beach. For all you know, your wife's back home by now. Isn't that the real truth?"

"It's not likely, but even so, I've never seen my son, Admiral."

Hart stared at Byron and shook his head in a tired way. "Dismissed."

It was a long glum run to Bataan with Branch Hoban on the driver's seat beside Byron, in an Army truck groaning with crated mines. At the Mariveles Navy headquarters he said good-bye to his work gang. They responded with offhand waves and grunts as they began unloading. He doubted that they would stay together long.

"Now then," Hoban jovially remarked, as the dinghy puttered out past the green rocky island of Corregidor into the breezy bay, "the next question is, where's the *Devilfish?*" He stared around at empty waters stretching everywhere. Manila lay beyond the horizon thirty miles off. Smoke from an air raid marked its location. Not a ship was in sight; not a tug, not a garbage lighter. Fear of the bombers had cleared the bay. "The squadron's lying doggo on the bottom out around here, Byron. We'll just wait." For about an hour periscopes briefly rose from the waves, looked about, and vanished, while the dinghy lay to, tossing. Finally one scope popped up, turned, fixed a stare at the dinghy like the wet head of a sea serpent, and made for it. The dark hull broke the surface, streaming white water; and soon Byron was back aboard the cramped *Devilfish*, which, much as he disliked it, felt and smelled like home.

The executive officer staggered him by saying that his relief had reported aboard. At his hoot of disbelief Lieutenant Aster insisted, "He's here, I tell you. It's Ensign Quayne. You know him, that long drink of water off the poor old *Sealion*. They're reassigning her officers. You were up for a letter of commendation, my boy, but the admiral instead is transferring you to the Atlantic."

Byron said with false nonchalance, "Then when can I leave, Lady?"

"Hold your horses. Quayne's had only four months at sea. He has to qualify first. Wardroom meeting, incidentally, in a couple of minutes."

Ensign Quayne, a pale nail-biter, fresh off a submarine sunk at Cavite, was the one new face at the small green-covered table. Captain Hoban showed up clean-shaven. He looked not only younger, Byron thought, but less obnoxious; the dashing peacetime hotshot and lady's man giving way to an officer meaning business.

"If any of you are wondering about the soup strainer," Hoban grinned, unfolding the old scuffed H.O. chart of the northern Pacific on the table, "it's a war casualty. Not much chance of keeping it properly trimmed at sea, so—the word from headquarters, gentlemen, is to stand by for war patrol number one. Button up all maintenance work in three days, or scrub it. We top off, take on provisions and torpedoes, and go. The intelligence is that a mess of big transports have already left the Jap home islands, escorted by battleships, carriers, cruisers, and Christ knows what else, for an invasion of Luzon in force. Destination, probably Lingayen Gulf. Looks like Christmas on patrol for the *Devilfish* and most of the squadron. Our orders are simple. Targets, in order of priority: first, loaded troop transports. Second, major combat vessels. Third, any combat vessels. Fourth, any Jap ship."

A thrill rippled down Byron's spine. Around the table he saw tightened lips, widened eyes, sobered expressions; on Carter Aster's long face, a peculiar fleeting grin.

The captain tapped the blue and yellow chart. "Okay. First, to review the basics. We're eighteen hundred miles from Tokyo here. Five hundred from the Formosa bomber base that's been slugging at us. *Seven thousand miles from San Francisco, lads*. More than four thousand miles from Pearl Harbor.

"As you know, Guam and Wake look to be goners. They'll probably be operational Jap air bases in a week." Hoban's finger jumped from point to point on the worn creased chart. "So our line is cut. We're in

he Japs' back yard, surrounded and trapped. That's how it is. How we
ot into this mess, you can ask the politicians some time. Meantime
elp can reach the Philippines only by sea, by the long route via Sa-
1oa and Australia outside Jap air range. Ten thousand miles, *each
/ay.*" His meaningful look went round the table.

"Incidentally, that story about the big convoy from San Francisco is
orse manure to bolster civilian morale. Forget it. We'll patrol in waters
otally controlled by the enemy. The rest of the Asiatic Fleet will be
eading south to Java. They can't take the bomber raids. Only the sub-
1arines will stay. Our mission is to harass the landing of the main Japa-
ese expeditionary force—where, it goes without saying, destroyers will
e thick as fleas on a dog's back." Another glance around; a tough, ex-
ilarated smile. "Questions?"

Sitting in an easy slouch, Aster held up a hand. "What was that
ourth priority, sir? Any Jap ship?"

"Affirmative."

"Unarmed merchantmen and tankers, too?"

"I said any Jap ship."

"We follow Geneva Convention procedures, of course—warning,
earch, putting the crew into boats, et cetera?"

Hoban slid coarse gray mimeographed sheets from a manila enve-
ope. "Okay, here's orders on *that* point." He flipped pages. His voice
ecame monotonous and declamatory. "Here we are. 'On December 8,
his force received the following fleet order from the Commander-in-
Chief, Pacific Fleet: EXECUTE UNRESTRICTED REPEAT UNRESTRICTED
UBMARINE WARFARE AGAINST JAPAN.'" Hoban paused to give his
officers a meaningful look. "*Devilfish* will govern itself accordingly.'"

"Captain," Byron said, "didn't we declare war on the Germans in
917 for doing just that?"

"Glad you brought it up. Negative. The Germans sank neutral ships.
Ve'll attack only enemy ships. 'Unrestricted' here means warship or
1erchant vessel, no difference."

"Sir, what about Article Twenty-two?" Ensign Quayne said, holding
1p a bony finger with a chewed nail.

Sans mustache, Hoban's smile looked boyish. "Right. You just memorized the articles for the qualification course. Repeat it."

In a dull flat voice, Quayne self-consciously recited:

*"Except in the case of persistent refusal to stop on being duly sum-
1oned, a submarine may not sink or render incapable of navigation a
1erchant vessel, without having first placed passengers, crew, and*

ship's papers in a place of safety. For this purpose, the ship's boats are not regarded as a place of safety, unless the safety of the passengers and crew is assured, in the existing sea and weather conditions, by the proximity of land, or the presence of another vessel which is in a position to take them on board."

"Outstanding," said Hoban. "Unlearn it." Quayne looked like a startled fowl. "Gentlemen, the Japs attacked Pearl Harbor without warning in the middle of peace talks. We didn't throw away the rule book of civilized war. They did. This isn't the war we trained for, but it's sure as hell the war we've got. And it's just as well. By the time we'd go through that rigmarole, our target would shoot off an SOS and Jap planes would be swarming on us."

"Captain, let me understand you." Aster touched a match to a thick gray cigar. "Does this mean if we see them, we sink them?"

"We see them, Lady, we *identify* them, and we sink them." A jocularly ferocious grin lit his face. "When in doubt, of course, we give them the benefit of the doubt. We shoot. Any further questions? Then that's all, gentlemen."

As the officers left the wardroom the captain said, "Briny?"

"Yes, sir?"

Byron turned. Hoban was extending a hand and smiling. The wordless gesture, the youthful smile, seemed to wipe out six months of hostile tension. This was leadership, Byron thought. He grasped the captain's hand. Hoban said, "Glad you'll have at least one war patrol with us."

"I'm looking forward to it, Captain."

He had been up since dawn, working hard; and he worked late into the night in the torpedo rooms with his chiefs and crewmen, getting ready for a combat patrol. Falling asleep was seldom a problem for Byron Henry, but this night his thoughts kept drifting to his wife and son. In the cabin he now shared with Quayne were all his mementos: her picture taped on the bulkhead, her letters worn and wrinkled with rereading, the scarf he had filched from her in Lisbon, a single cracking snapshot of the infant. Lying wide-awake in the dark, he found himself reliving the best moments of the helter-skelter romance—their first meeting, their adventures in Poland, her declaration of love in the pink boudoir of Jastrow's villa, the rendezvous in Miami, the wild lovemaking of the three-day honeymoon in Lisbon, and their dockside farewell in a foggy dawn. He could call up these scenes in detail, her own words and his, her littlest gestures, the look in her eyes; but the memories were dulling, like old phonograph records played too often. He tried to picture where she was now, and what his baby might look like. He gave way to fantasies of a passionate reunion. Like a jewel in his possession was the knowledge that his relief was aboard; that this first war patrol would be his last voyage on the *Devilfish;* that if he survived it, he would be going to the Atlantic.

6

THE day Pamela Tudsbury wrote her letter to Captain Henry—three weeks before the Pearl Harbor attack—a chill November fog had been darkening London for a week, seeping through windows and keyholes and past closed doors, penetrating every cranny. Doorknobs and banisters were sticky to the touch. Indoors or out one breathed fog; there was no escaping the damp. Bronchitis had her feverish, shivering, and coughing up phlegm as she sorted out her things for tropic travel.

The six o'clock news droning out of her bedside radio chilled like the fog. The threat of the Japanese to enter the war was becoming acute. Rejecting Roosevelt's latest peace formula, they were massing troops and ships on the French Indo-China coast, a clear menace to Malaya and Singapore. Radio Moscow was denying that Rostov, the key to the Caucasus and its great oil fields, had fallen to the Germans, but every Nazi victory claim these days was lamely conceded by the Soviets within a week; by now they had confirmed that Leningrad was cut off and under siege, and that the Wehrmacht was surging toward Moscow. Moreover, a German submarine had in fact—as Radio Berlin had been claiming for days—sunk the carrier *Ark Royal* off Gibraltar. The announcer read out this budget of disaster with that BBC calm which was becoming so threadbare. She packed cheerfully, all the same, because she might see Victor Henry on the other side of the world. As for the news, she was numb to it. For months there had been only bad news.

The telephone rang. She turned off the radio to answer it.

"Pamela? It's Philip Rule."

A voice from the past; a deep, self-assured, unwelcome voice. Arresting an impulse to hang up, she said, "Yes?"

"That's a dim 'yes,' Pam. How are you?"

"I have a filthy cold."

"You do sound it. Sorry. What are you doing?"

"At the moment? Packing."

"Oh? For that round-the-world thing Talky's announced?"

"Yes."

"Is Singapore on the itinerary?"

"Yes. Why?"

"I'm going there myself next week for the *Express*. Getting a ride direct in a Blenheim bomber."

Pamela allowed a silence to lengthen.

"Pam, Leslie Slote's in town from Moscow. He's asking after you. I thought you might join us for dinner. He's told me quite a bit about your friend, Captain Henry."

"Oh? Is there any news about him?"

"Well, Pam, I don't know how up-to-date you are on Captain Henry."

"What's Leslie doing here?"

"He's on his way to the U.S. legation in Bern. That's his new post."

"Strange. He'd only been in Moscow a few months."

"He got into trouble there."

"Of what sort?"

"Something about the Jews, I gather. It's a sore point. Don't bring it up with him."

"Where are you dining?"

"At the Savoy."

"I can't get to the Savoy in this blackout and fog."

"I'll come for you, darling. Seven o'clock?"

At the attempted airy intimacy Pamela said, "How's your wife?"

"God knows. Last I heard, she was working in a factory outside Moscow. Seven o'clock, then?"

Pamela hesitated. She was resolved to steer clear of Philip Rule, but she did want to find out what Slote knew about Pug Henry's movements. Leslie Slote was an arid ambitious Foreign Service man, who had jilted Natalie Jastrow back in the old Paris days, after the four of them had had merry times together for about a year. He and Phil had seemed equally heartless then. She felt a bit more kindly to Slote now, because he regretted what he had done. It seemed extremely odd that he had had anything to do with Jewish matters; for he had dropped Natalie mainly to avoid the career problem of a Jewish wife.

"Are you there, Pamela?"

"Oh, all right. Seven o'clock."

At first glance the crowded Savoy Grill appeared to be riding out the war well. But tarnished sconces, dusty draperies, tablecloths washed threadbare, elderly waiters moving slowly in black uniforms gone green at the cuffs and elbows, showed the pinch. The diners too, the most prosperous of Londoners, had a peaked and shabby look. Slote took a spoonful of gummy Scotch broth, for which he had waited twenty-five minutes. With a grimace, he dropped the spoon. "The Savoy's gone downhill."

"What hasn't?" Pamela fingered the pearl choker around her thin throat. Slote guessed she must have a fever: red spots in her cheeks, glittering eyes, intermittent cough, gray cardigan buttoned up tight.

"Singapore hasn't," said Philip Rule. "Today I interviewed a general back on medical leave. They've got the place bristling with big guns and aircraft, and they're quite ready for the Japanese. Their peckers are up, the stengahs are flowing free at the clubs, and even the old Raffles Hotel is very jammed and gay. So he said. He found London shockingly run down."

Pamela said, coughing, "Like the inhabitants."

Rule pulled at his thick red mustache, grinning. "You, darling? You've seldom looked more desirable."

Long ago this crooked grin had affected her like alcohol. Rule's squarish face was fatter, his once-heavy hair was going, but his intent blue eyes still stirred her. She had thought herself cured of him. Not quite!

Their Paris affair had never run smooth. She had made trouble about his waitresses and whores, low tastes which he had seen no reason to alter for her sake. She had turned seriously nasty over a handsome Yale boy, an Antinous out of Bridgeport, with whom he had gone off for three blissful weeks in Majorca. At public school Rule had acquired a taste for this sort of thing, though by and large he preferred women. On his return she had forced a wild scene, and he had knocked her flat on her face; whereupon, half-insane with humiliated fury, she had drunk a bottle of iodine, and he had driven her at three in the morning, writhing and retching, to a hospital. The episode had finished them. Rule had gone on with his life as though nothing had happened, and from his viewpoint very little had.

Like Slote he had been studying Russian in Paris; this was how they had come to room together. Once settled in the Soviet Union as a corre-spondent, he had met a Bolshoi ensemble girl, so beautiful that he had married her—so he had written Pamela—simply in order to have her, be-cause she was extremely prim and would hear of nothing else. The cere-mony in a communist "wedding palace" he had described as comical bosh: a fat stern lady in a tailored suit, briefly lecturing them on communist marriage, while Valentina's parents, relatives, and Bolshoi chums stood about smirking, and the bride, all blushes, clung with one arm to her handsome British catch, and with the other to a bunch of wilting yellow roses. So it was that Rule had a Russian wife. When he was out of Russia he paid no attention to the circumstance.

Avoiding his intimate stare, Pamela spoke hoarsely. "You believe all that about Singapore?"

"Why not? Our monopoly capitalists built themselves the hell of a strong air force and defense system right here in Blighty under our noses, through several pacifist ministries. Surprised our own people, as well as Jerry! The Empire pivots on Singapore, Pam. If we want to go on oppressing and sweating half a billion Asiatics, and stealing the wealth of Australia and New Zealand from the silly aborigines, Singapore has to be impregnable. So no doubt it is."

"Oh, the Empire's finished, no matter what," said Slote.

"Don't be too sure, Les. Winnie's raised another alliance after all, to keep it gasping along. The Russians will beat the Germans for us. Sooner or later your sleepy countrymen will come in and thrash the Japanese. The whole monopoly capital system with its colonies is rotten, and has to go, but not just yet. The white exploiter is a tenacious world master. It will take a global revolution to get rid of him. At a guess that's half a century off."

"What on earth makes you think the Russians will beat the Germans?" Pamela put in. "Didn't you hear the evening news?"

Again the lopsided grin, the old lazy shift of the big body in the chair, the broad gesture with two hairy hands. "Darling, you don't know the Soviet Union."

"I do," Slote said. "I was in Moscow until last Thursday. I've never seen such a collapse of nerve. Everybody who could get wheels or a horse skedaddled."

"They're only human. They'll recover." Rule's voice dropped to a mellifluous rumble. "Isn't it disconcerting, dear boy, to have the main body of Hitler's army coming at you, fifty miles away?"

"I've been through it twice. It's hell. But I'm a damned coward. I expected more of the Russians."

Pamela and Rule laughed. Pamela liked Slote the better for his honesty, though nothing could make him seem attractive. The skinny pale ex-Rhodes Scholar with his rimless glasses, well-gnawed tobacco pipe, and nervous ways had always struck her as a physical neuter. He had made passes at her in Moscow, which she had yawned off. She had never comprehended Natalie Jastrow's old passion for him.

A shiver racked her. "Leslie, how long did Captain Henry stay on in Moscow?" To put this question she had come to the Savoy, ill as she was.

"Well, let's see. You and Talky went on the sixteenth, didn't you? At the height of the scare?"

"Yes."

"He stayed another week, trying to nail down train tickets beyond Kuibyshev. I thought it would be impossible in that panic but finally he did, and he headed eastward, across Siberia, Hawaii bound."

"Then he'll have gotten there by now."

"Should think so."

"Wonderful."

Rule said to Pamela, in the pleasantest way, "Were you lovers?"

Her tone was just as pleasant. "None of your bloody business."

"Leslie says," Rule persisted with a blink at the rebuff, "that la Jastrow has gone and married this same chap's son, a submarine officer much younger than she is. He also confides, in great secrecy, that his own heart still bleeds over Natalie. Why ever did she do such a grotesque thing? Did the lad get her pregnant?"

Pamela shrugged. "Ask Leslie."

"They were isolated in a villa outside Siena," Slote said gloomily. "I told you that. Month after month, before he joined the Navy. He was working for Aaron Jastrow as a researcher. I think they were the only two Americans under sixty left in Tuscany. No doubt nature took its course. I spent a whole night in Washington arguing with her about this mismatch. She was irrational. Turned to stone."

"You mean she was in love with him," Pamela said, "and out of love with you."

"Actually, I do mean that," Slote replied with a sudden sad grin that charmed Pamela. "She used to be damned sensible, but she's gone harebrained. Married this youth, stayed on in Italy with Jastrow, and she's still there, last I heard, with an infant on her hands."

Rule chuckled in his chest. "You shouldn't have spent that night in Washington arguing."

"Anything else would have gotten me a black eye."

"Well, if it's any consolation," Pamela said, "Captain Henry also tried to break it up and couldn't. It's a very passionate business."

"That's the man I'd like to meet," Rule said. "Captain Henry."

"Nothing easier. Get yourself an assignment to interview the commanding officer of the U.S.S. *California* in Hawaii," Pamela snapped.

"What do you like about him, Pam?"

"He's decent to the bone."

"I see. The charm of novelty."

The meal went by. Their desserts stood uneaten, gelatinous pud-
ings of tasteless pink goo. The waiter had been paid. Slote wished that
.ule would leave. He meant to have another try at Pamela, fever or no;
e had not had a woman in months, and unlike Rule he did not enjoy
hores. Rule called himself a man of pleasure; Slote thought him rather
n animal. He himself had mistreated Natalie, but never in the harsh
·ays that had driven Pamela to try suicide. Slote had muffed with
amela in Moscow, he believed, because of Captain Henry. Henry was
ır away now. Pam was likable and pretty; also easygoing and free-
pirited, or so Slote hoped.

"Well! Les is just in from Stockholm today, Pam," Rule said. Obvi-
usly he nursed similar notions. "Probably we shouldn't keep him up.
.et me drive you to your flat."

"As a matter of fact, I hear music," Pam said. "I'd like to dance."

"Dearest, since when? You haven't danced a step since I've known
ou."

"My American friends have been working on me. Pity you don't
ance. What about it, Leslie?"

"I'd be delighted."

Rule stood up, grinning in defeat. "My best to Talky, then. I'm off to
ingapore Monday. See you there, no doubt."

Pamela stared at his departing back, the spots crimson on her gray
heeks.

Slote said, "Are you sure you want to dance?"

"What? Of course not. I feel horrible. I just wanted to get rid of that
od."

"Come up to my room and have a drink." The invitation was plain,
·ut not leering.

A quick smile—knowing, amused, faintly giddy—illumined her face,
ovely even in its sickliness. She put a clammy hand to his cheek. "Bless
ıy soul, Leslie, you're still harboring indecent thoughts about me,
.ren't you? How sweet of you. Sorry, I'm in hopeless shape. I'm burn-
ıg with fever, and anyway, no."

Slote said, "Okay," with a resigned shrug.

"You really should have married Natalie in Paris, dear. She was so insistent!"

"Oh, Pamela, go screw yourself."

She burst out laughing, took his hand and placed it on her damp hot forehead. "Feel that? Honestly, I'd better find a cab and get on home, don't you think? Good luck in Switzerland. Thanks for the news about Captain Henry."

She wrote the ebullient letter when she got back to her flat.

In a flying boat circling over Singapore, Alistair Tudsbury pulled off his tie, threw open the white linen jacket strained over his paunch, and fanned his wet jowls with a straw hat. "This will be worse than Ceylon, Pam. We're dropping into a bloody inferno."

"Peaceful little inferno," said Pamela, looking down through the tilting window. "Where are the vast fortress walls, the masses of cannon, the swarms of Spitfires and Hurricanes?"

"Nothing shows, naturally. But that small green scorpion down there packs the hell of a sting. I say, there's the *Prince of Wales!* Can't miss those turrets."

Seen from the air Singapore was a broken-off tip of the craggy Malayan mountains; a green triangle in the wrinkled open sea, hanging to the mainland by a thread of causeway. Two gray warts blotched its jungle beauty: to the southeast a modern city sprinkled with red roofs, and up north, near the causeway, an expanse of sheds, cranes, barracks, streets, houses, and broad green playing fields: the Singapore naval base. The base looked oddly quiet. In its docks and wide anchorage not one vessel lay. On the other side of the island, warships and merchant vessels clustered by the city's waterfront.

"Hello there!"

In the immigration shed, Philip Rule pushed through the crowd and plunged past the wooden rail. He wore army shorts and shirt, his face and arms were burned red-brown, and he held a purple orchid in a swollen bandaged hand. "Barely in time. You're both invited to Admiral Phillips's reception aboard the *Prince of Wales.*"

"Admiral's reception!" Tudsbury limped up and shook hands. "Smashing."

Rule handed Pamela the orchid. "Welcome to the bastion of Empire, love. These things grow by the roadside here. Come, I'll whisk you through the formalities."

"What's wrong with your hand, Phil?"

"Oh, out on jungle maneuvers with the Argyll and Sutherland High-landers, I got bitten by a centipede. Nasty brute, a foot long. I hardly knew whether to step on him or shoot him! Charms of the tropics." Rule spoke cheerily over his shoulder, leading them to a small office. Here a perspiring red-faced little man in a brass-buttoned coat stamped the passports.

"Well, well! Mr. Alistair Tudsbury! What an honor. Correspondents are fairly pouring in now, but you're the most famous one yet."

"Why, thank you."

"Let me say, sir, that we've had these Jap scares before. They always blow over. The vultures are gathering in vain, so to speak. No offense, sir. Have a pleasant stay, sir."

Rule collected their luggage, piled it in his car, and raced them to town, where he drove slowly through narrow stifling hot streets, thronged with Asiatics of all ages and skin shades: some in native dress, some dressed Western style, some rich-looking and fat, some bony and naked but for rags. Sweet, spicy, and disgusting smells drifted turn by turn into the car windows. Brightly colored shop signs in strange alphabets lined the streets.

When the car emerged on a boulevard, the scene metamorphosed: broad avenues, green palm-lined parks, signs in English, tall buildings; glimpses of a waterfront, and gusts of refreshing sea breeze; dark-faced, white-gloved Bobbies directing traffic; a British seaport city, burning in un-British heat, its pavements crowded with colored faces. At the big ramshackle Raffles Hotel Rule dropped their bags. A navy launch took them from a steel and concrete pier, roofed with high arches, out to a gaudily camouflaged battleship moored to a buoy. Helped by Rule, clutching her flimsy skirt, Pamela climbed the accommodation ladder. Behind her Tudsbury painfully grunted.

"Oho!" she said as she set foot on deck. "The British! I wondered where they were."

"Everybody's here that matters," said Rule.

Under a brown awning the laughing, chattering guests were standing around drinking cocktails, or waiting in a reception line that stretched to the sunlit forecastle. The men wore white linen suits or bright-hued blazers, the women, flowery print dresses fluttering in the breeze. All the faces were white, unless the owner of the face carried a tray. Four long guns painted in garish patches like snakeskin projected beyond the awning.

"Mr. Tudsbury?" said a young officer at the gangway. "The admiral's compliments, sir. Please follow me."

They went to the head of the line. The admiral, a surprisingly small man with crusted gold shoulder marks on his white uniform, held out a small scrubbed hand. "Frightfully pleased. Very keen on your broadcasts."

He presented them to several stiff old men lined up beside him. Their sharply tailored tropical uniforms showed knobby gray-haired knees and elbows; their military titles were majestic, the highest brass in Singapore. The roar of airplanes interrupted the pleasantries; wave upon wave coming in low from seaward, scarcely clearing the *Prince of Wales*'s masts, then zooming over the waterfront. Distant guns boomed. Beyond the city, clouds of white smoke puffed up against the blue sky. Tudsbury shouted to the admiral, "Would those be our famous coastal guns?"

"Just so. Heaviest calibre in the world. Jolly good marksmanship, my target-towing ships report. Approaching Singapore in anger from the sea *not* advisable!"

"I'd like to visit those guns."

"It will be arranged."

All this was a series of yells through the racket of the air show. Tudsbury gestured upward. "And these planes?"

A tall grayhead in RAF uniform, standing next to the admiral, flashed pride from filmy wrinkled eyes. "Vildebeest and Blenheim bombers leading the pack. The fighters are American Buffaloes. Can't touch our Spitfires, but dashed good, better than what the Japs have got."

"How do you know that, sir?"

"Oh, Jap planes have fallen in China, you know." The gray eyebrows arched in cunning. "We have the book on them. Second-rate, rather."

Rule and Pamela stood at the rail amid a crowd of beaming British, watching the planes. He picked drinks off a tray passed by a Chinese boy. "God, Pam, your father does have a way with the brass. That's Air Chief Marshal Brooke-Popham talking to him. Boss of the whole theatre, Commander-in-Chief, Far East. They're chatting like old school chums."

"Well, everyone wants a good press."

"Yes, and they know he's got the popular touch, don't they? All acid and disenchanted in tone, yet in the end it comes out straight Rudyard Kipling, every time. For God and for Empire, eh, Pam?"

"Anything wrong with that?"

"Why, it's pure gold. False as hell to the future, but why should he care, since he believes it?"

The planes were dwindling in the distance. Pamela sipped her drink, peering fore and aft along the gigantic deck. "You know, Phil, Captain Henry visited this ship when it brought Churchill to Newfoundland. Now we walk its deck off Malaya, and he's commanding a monster like this in Hawaii. Unreal."

"Rather on your mind still, your Yankee captain?"

"That's why I'm here. Pearl Harbor's my destination. Talky knows that."

Rule grimaced and pulled at his mustache. "Look, I'm staying at the home of Jeff McMahon, the head of the Malayan Broadcasting System. Let's all go to dinner at Raffles tonight, shall we? Jeff wants to meet your father and put him on the air. Talky will like Elsa. She's the most beautiful woman in Singapore."

"Then her husband's a fool to have you in the house."

"Why, darling, I don't abuse a man's hospitality." Pamela's response was an arched eyebrow and a contemptuously wrinkled mouth. "You'll come to dinner, then?"

"I don't mind. I can't speak for Talky."

Later the fat old correspondent, in the highest spirits, readily agreed to dine with Singapore's most beautiful woman. "Of course, dear boy. Smashing. I say, the air chief marshal's a brick. I'm to visit the most secret military installations here. Not one door closed. And I'm to write what I bloody well please."

Elsa McMahon wore clinging ivory silk jersey, the only modish dress Pamela had yet seen in the colony. Her heavy glossy black hair might have been done in Paris. Four children milled and clattered about the rambling house, pursued by scolding servants; but the woman had a willowy figure, a cameo face, and the clear smooth skin of a girl, tanned to a rosy amber by tennis. She showed Pamela her house, her books, a whole wall of phonograph records, and before the sunset failed, her tennis court and the garden: a big disorderly expanse of lawn, high palms, flowering bushes and trees—gardenias, hibiscus, jasmine, and jacaranda —in air almost chokingly perfumed. Her easy English had a Scandinavian lilt, for her father had been a Norwegian sea captain. Her husband kept eyeing her as though they had been married a month.

They were killing time over drinks, waiting for Tudsbury to get away from an interview with the governor, when he rang up. The governor had just asked him to dine at the Tanglin Club. He was at the club now. Would Pamela and her friends forgive him, and join them, at the governor's invitation, for a drink?

Rule said testily, as Pam still held the phone, "Pamela, that's damned rude of him. Our dinner was all set. Tell him and that pompous-ass governor they can both go to hell."

"Nonsense, he can't turn down the governor," said Jeff McMahon amiably. "The Tanglin Club's on our way. Let's go."

It was a short drive from the McMahon house. Pulling to a stop at the club entrance, the director of the Malayan Broadcasting System turned to Pamela. "Here you are. Elsa and I will buzz on to the Raffles bar. Don't hurry for dinner. The music goes on till midnight."

"Nonsense. Park the car and come on in. The governor invited all of us."

"I resigned from the Tanglin, Pam, when I married Elsa."

"I beg your pardon?"

Elsa McMahon in the front seat turned her head. The dark eyes were solemn, the lovely mouth taut with irony. "My mother was Burmese, dear. See you at the Raffles."

The Tanglin was spacious, sprawling, and stuffy. Full-length court portraits of the king and queen dominated the foyer; London magazines and newspapers were scattered about; and under the slow-turning fans, the everlasting white-coated colored boys hustled with drinks. A bibulous and strident noise filled the club, for the evening was well along. Tudsbury sat at the bar amid the same people Pamela had seen aboard the *Prince of Wales*. The men were getting quite drunk. The women's evening dresses were as dowdy as their daytime getups. The governor was a placid, unbelievably dull person. Pamela and Rule downed one drink and left.

"Well, the McMahons didn't miss much!" she said, as they came out into a moonlit night heavy with flower scent. British clear through, Pamela believed in the happy breed's superiority, though she never spoke of it. She knew such clubs had such rules; all the same, the exclusion of Elsa McMahon had enraged her.

"Come along, you're surely not just discovering the hard facts of imperialism." Rule beckoned to a waiting taxicab. "How do you suppose twenty thousand whites, most of them frail ninnies, manage to rule four and a half million Malayans? Not by hobnobbing with them."

"She's as much a native as I am."

"One can't allow exceptions, love. The dikes of imperial snobbery hold back a raging sea of color. One pinhole, and they crumble. That's doctrine. Elsa's a wog." He put on a nasal aristocratic voice. "Dashed pity, and all that—so in you go, and let's join our wog lady friend."

In the open palm-lined courtyard of the Raffles, a five-piece band of old white men played listless out-of-date jazz. It was very hot and damp here. The McMahons sat at a table, watching three gray-haired couples sweatily shuffling on the floor. Their greeting to Pamela and Rule was untainted by rancor. They gossiped about the governor with tolerant amusement as they ate.

He was a harmless sort, they said, the son of a vicar. The heat, the bureaucracy, the confusion and complications of his job, had reduced him in seven years to a blob of benign jelly. Nothing could shake, change, or ruffle him. The Malay States were an administrative madhouse, with eleven separate local governments—including some touchy sultans—to deal with. Somehow half of the tin and a third of the rubber that the democracies used came out of this mess. There was money to be made, and it was made. Dollars had been steadily flooding into the British war chest. The people who did the work—two million Moslem Malays, two million Buddhist Chinese, about half a million Indians—all disliked each other, and united in loathing the white handful who ran things, headed by this serene white invertebrate living in Government House, on a high hill inside a big park, far from the congestion and smells of native Singapore. He had had seven years of continuous commendation from London, for keeping the wheels turning. He had done absolutely nothing except let it happen. In the British Colonial Service, said Jeff McMahon, that approached genius.

"Perspectives differ," Rule observed. "I heard a three-hour tirade today against him. The Associated Press man, Tim Boyle, says he's a tough bully with a censorship mania. Tim wrote a piece about the night life here. The censor killed it dead. Tim demanded a meeting with this governor, who bawled him out like a coolie. The governor's first words were, 'I read that story. If you were an Asiatic, I'd put you behind bars.'"

"Ah, that's different," said Elsa. "The British Colonial Office has a long memory. America started as a colony. Once a native, always a native."

The McMahons ate little. After the coffee they got up and danced sinuously to the thin music. Rule held out his hand. "Pamela?"

"Don't be an ass. I break out in a sweat here, with every move I make. Anyway, you know you can't dance. Neither can I."

"You asked Slote to dance with you in London."

"Oh, I was cutting you."

"Sweetie, you can't still be angry with me." The red mustache spread in an unoffended grin. "It all happened in another age."

"Granted, Phil. You're a yellowing diploma on the wall. Just hang there."

"Crushed again! Well, I like your indignation over Elsa. But she's a popular woman, and the Tanglin Club is a bore she can do without. What about the Chinese and Indians you saw uptown, swarming like rats in a garbage dump? That's Singapore's real color problem."

Pamela was slow to answer. She had no political, social, or religious certainties. Life was a colorful painful pageant to her, in which right and wrong were wobbly yardsticks. Values and morals varied with time and place. Sweeping righteous views, like Victor Henry's Christian morality and Rule's militant socialism, tended to cause much hell and to cramp what little happiness there was to be had. So she thought.

"I'm a duffer on those matters, Phil. You know that. Hasn't Asia always been more or less like this—a few rajahs and sultans eating off gold plate, building temples and Taj Mahals, while the masses multiply in cow dung and mud?"

"We came to change all that, love. So says Kipling. And Alistair Tudsbury."

"Haven't we made things better?"

"In a way. Railroads, civil service, a modern language. But Pam, there's just been the hell of a flap here at the Tanglin Club. They barred from their swimming pool the Indian officers—the *officers,* I repeat—of the Fifth Indian Regiment! Educated military men, stationed here to lead soldiers to fight and die for the Tanglin Club! The decision stuck, too. It undid fifty years of Kipling."

The McMahons left early to get back to their children; polite as they were about it, Talky's defection had made the evening pointless. Philip Rule walked with Pamela through the hotel lobby. "Tuck your mosquito netting in firmly, darling," he said at the stairway. "Check every edge. A few of those creatures can drain you like Dracula."

Pamela looked around at the Chinese boys in white coats, crisscrossing through the broad lobby with trays. "The boozing, the boozing! Does it ever stop?"

"I was told, the first day I came," said Rule, "and I've since heard it forty times in the white man's clubs—that Singapore is a place of 'drinks, Chinks, and stinks.'" He kissed her cheek. "Good-night. I shall now hang myself back on the wall."

The first bombs fell on Singapore at four in the morning. Pamela was half-awake, sweating under the mosquito net, when she heard thrumming overhead. Vaguely she thought it was a night fighter exercise. At the first distant thumps she sat up, swept aside the netting, and ran into the sitting room. Tudsbury lumbered out of his room blindly blinking, clutching pajamas over his hairy belly. "That's bombing, Pam!"

"I know it is."

"Well, the yellow bastards! They're really trying it on, are they? By Christ, they'll regret this!"

Airplane roars came and went overhead. Bombs were bursting closer and louder. Pulling off his pajama top, Tudsbury stumbled back into his room. Pamela called from the french windows, "Talky, we haven't even blacked out!" The streets were brilliantly lit. Clouds overhead reflected the glow. She saw no searchlights or tracer bullets, heard no sirens or ack-ack. It was nothing like a London raid. The one difference from other warm odorous Singapore nights, in fact, was that invisible planes overhead were dropping bombs, which the city was serenely ignoring.

His muffled answer came, "Well, nobody was expecting this. There are no land-based Jap bombers with the range to hit Singapore. Brooke-Popham told me that himself."

"Then what on earth is going on?"

"Carrier raid, maybe. Of course, the *Prince of Wales* will intercept and sink any flattop around, if the RAF doesn't get them first. One can't reckon on suicidal madness in the enemy."

Soon he hurried out of his room, untidily dressed. The bombing had moved farther off, but planes still drummed in the sky. She was at the desk, half-nude in her brief nightgown, dully leafing a typescript, hair falling around her face. "This broadcast is obsolete now, Talky."

"Why? My military summary stands. That's the meat of it. It's twice as timely now! I need a new opening about this onslaught, and a re-sounding wind-up. Have a go at those, won't you? I'll redictate your draft when I return."

"Where the devil do you think you're going, during an air raid?"

"Army Public Relations. I rang Major Fisher. He's holding a press conference right now, and—what's the matter?"

Her head was sinking on the desk in her naked arms. "Oh, it just depresses me so! The whole thing, starting up again out here."

"Courage, girl. These aren't Germans. The planes up there are made of bamboo shoots and rice paper. We'll smash these bastards. Ye gods, look at the lights, will you? This town's really ablaze like a Christmas tree. *Somebody* will catch hell for being asleep on watch! I'm off. You'll draft that new stuff?"

"Yes, yes. Go along," she muttered into her arms.

Pamela was thinking that Clipper flights would certainly stop at once; that the sea lanes to Hawaii would become infested with Japanese submarines; that in fact she was cut off from Victor Henry for years or for good. To have come so far in vain! Would she even be able to get out of Singapore?

Dawn was breaking, and a faint cool breeze through the open french windows was freshening the room with garden scents, when her father burst in, trumpeting like a mad elephant, "Pam! Pam, have you heard?" Still in her nightgown, she looked up blearily from the typewriter. "Have I heard what?"

"Why, you silly frippet, we've WON THE WAR!" Tudsbury's eyes were bulging from his head, and his hands were shaking. "Those yellow sods have gone and attacked *Pearl Harbor!*"

"What!"

"You heard me. Huge carrier raid! All kinds of enormous damage. The Yanks are in it, Pam! In it up to their necks this time! What else matters? We've won the damned war, I tell you! I must have a drink on it or I'll die."

He splashed whiskey into a tumbler, gulped it, and coughed. "Whew. We've *won it*. Won it! What a close-run thing. We've really won this damned war. I'll have to rewrite that piece from page one, but by God, what a glorious moment to live in! These are the days of the giants, Pam. Their footsteps are shaking the earth—"

"What ships were hit?"

"Oh, the Yanks aren't talking, naturally. But the damage is immense. That much comes straight from the wire services in Honolulu. *We* weren't caught short *here,* thank the Christ! They tried to come ashore at Khota Baru airfield, but we shoved them back into the sea. They did gain a beachhead in Thailand. We'll be marching up there this morning to knock them all on the head. Two crack divisions are on the border, ready to jump off. The Japs have really run their heads into a noose this time, and—*now* what's wrong?"

The back of her hand to her eyes, Pamela was striding to her bedroom. "Nothing, nothing, nothing!" She gestured at the desk. "There's your damned draft."

Tudsbury's broadcast brought telephone calls and cables of congratulations from London, Sydney, and New York. He spoke of vast secret stockpiles and fortifications that he had seen with his own eyes; of heavy reinforcements on the way, as he knew from the highest military sources; of the striking calm of Europeans and Asiatics alike under the bombing. His draft script had cited the street lamps burning during the raid, as a humorous instance of Singapore's sangfroid. Hesitantly, apologetically, the censor had asked him to cut this. He had amiably agreed.

Reeling off the statistics of America's giant industrial resources, Tudsbury closed with this peroration: "*Wars are not fought by cold statistics, true, but by warm-blooded suffering men. Yet statistics foreshadow outcomes. This war, though it must yet cause grisly tragedy to mankind, will be won. We know that now.*

"*For the grim closing struggle, I can report, Fortress Singapore is ready. Fortress Singapore does not expect a tea party. But it is well prepared for its uninvited guests. Of one thing, let the outside world rest assured. The Japanese will not enjoy—if they ever get close enough to taste it—the bitter brew that awaits them at Fortress Singapore.*"

When he walked into the bar of the Tanglin Club after the broadcast, the people there rose to a man and clapped, bringing tears trickling on his fat face.

The bombers did not come again to Singapore. There was little word of fighting up-country, either. For Pamela it was a queerly evocative tropical replay of the "phony war" in 1939: the same lift of excitement, the same odd unreality, the same "back to business-as-usual." The blackout was regarded as awkward novel fun, though the shortage of dark cloth gave the club ladies a cause for anxious twittering as they sat rolling bandages in sultry flowery gardens. Air raid wardens in tin hats self-importantly stalked the streets. However, there were no air raid shelters.

This lack bothered Tudsbury. He quizzed the governor. "Watery subsoil, dear fellow," said the governor. Tudsbury pointed out that at the naval base he had seen giant concrete bunkers deep in the earth endlessly stacked with cannon shells, food, and fuel. What about the watery subsoil? The governor smiled at his sharpness. Yes, those caverns had been sunk in the swampy ground at great cost, for the security of the Empire. But in the city such a drastic measure, quite aside from the expense, would alarm the Asiatic populace. Adequate instructions existed for taking shelter in cellars and stone buildings. If required, an elaborate evacuation plan was ready. Tudsbury reluctantly accepted all this. He was the lion of the Tanglin Club, Singapore's reassuring radio voice to the world.

But he had trouble filling his broadcast time. In the first army communiqués the Jap invasion vessels were reported retiring, leaving a few troops behind on surrounded beachheads, and these stranded invaders were being wiped out according to plan. Since then the information had been getting sparser. The place names had been sliding strangely southward. One day the communiqué in its entirety read, *"Nothing new to report."* A theory began circulating at the white men's clubs. Like the Russians fighting Hitler, the military command was cleverly trading space for time, wearing the Japs out in the equatorial jungle, which was as hard on troops as the Russian winter.

Then there was the "monsoon" theory. Army experts had long held that after October, Singapore could rest easy for half a year, since the enemy could not land during the northeast monsoon. But the Japs had in fact landed. The experts now were explaining that any rash military plan could be tried, but the Japanese invasion, fatally weakened by losses in monsoon surf, was bound to peter out in the jungle. Though Tudsbury broadcast these theories, the absence of hard news gnawed at him. The way he had been welcomed, and the impact of his first broadcast, had pushed upon him the role of optimist, but he felt he was getting out on a limb.

Then came the sinking of the *Prince of Wales* and the *Repulse*. Here was hard news! Disaster at the outset, with a strong odor of blundering; sickening, yet familiar in British war-making. Two correspondents returned alive from the *Repulse,* shaken and ill, with historic scoops. Tudsbury had to compete. He burst in on his high military friends, demanded the truth, and got it. The brave little admiral had steamed north, intending to surprise the invasion force, smash it up fast, and escape from the Jap land-based bombers. He had had no air cover. The nearest British carrier was in India. The local RAF command had lacked the planes or had missed the signals; that part was vague. Japanese torpedo planes and dive bombers had roared in and sunk both capital ships. The admiral had drowned. The Empire lay open now to a Japanese navy that included ten battleships and six major aircraft carriers, with only a much-weakened American navy at its back to worry about.

Tudsbury rushed to the Raffles and dictated this hot story to Pamela, centering it on one theme: air power. His broadcast was half an editorial. England had just bought with blood the knowledge that warships could not stand up against land-based air. He pleaded: turn the lesson against the enemy! The Royal Air Force was the world's greatest air arm. Quick massive air reinforcements of Malaya could cut off and doom the Jap invaders. Here was an opportunity worth any sacrifice on other fronts; a turnabout that would redeem the disaster and preserve the Empire.

He sent the draft to the censor's office by runner. Three hours before broadcast time, the censor telephoned him; the broadcast was fine, except that he could not say the ships had lacked air cover. Not accustomed to such interference, Alistair Tudsbury sped to the censor's office in a taxi, sweating and muttering. The censor, a frail blond man with a pursed little smile, shook with terror at Tudsbury's roars, staring at him with round moist little eyes. His military adviser was a navy captain, plump, white-haired, pink-skinned, clad in faultless tropic whites, who gave no reason for his ruling except a reiterated, "Frightfully sorry, old chap, but we can't have it."

After long arguing Tudsbury thrust quivering grape-colored jowls right in his face, bellowing, "All right, before I go directly to Air Chief Marshal Brooke-Popham, WHY can't you have it?"

"It's vital military information. We must deny it to the enemy."

"The *enemy?* Why, who do you suppose *sank* those ships? My broadcast can bring Singapore such a cloud of fighter planes that nothing like that will happen again!"

"Yes, sir, that part is splendidly written, I grant you."

"But unless I *say* there was no air cover, the story is pointless! Can't you see that? Incomprehensible! Idiotic!"

"Frightfully sorry, sir, but we can't have it."

Tudsbury catapulted out to the nearest telephone. The air chief marshal was unavailable. The governor was out inspecting defenses. The time before his broadcast shrank. Arriving at the broadcasting studios in a rage, he proposed to Jeff McMahon that he go on the air, read his uncut script, and take the consequences.

"Good Lord, we're at war, Tudsbury!" McMahon protested. "Do you want us all to go to prison? We'll have to switch you off."

The fat old correspondent was running out of indignation and energy. "I broadcast for four years from Berlin, McMahon," he grated. "Goebbels himself never dared to tamper with my scripts like this. Not once! The British administration of Singapore does dare. How is that?"

"My dear fellow, the Germans only talk about being the master race," Elsa McMahon's husband said drily. "You're on in ten minutes."

7

I N a heavy sea, in the early darkness of the morning watch, the U.S.S. *Devilfish* pounded along the west coast of Luzon toward Lingayen Gulf. Byron stood wedged by the gyroscope repeater on the tiny bridge in sticky foul weather clothes, and with every plunge of the forecastle, warm black spray struck his face. The lookouts were silent shadows. They wouldn't doze tonight, Byron thought. Except for this sense of heading toward trouble, and for running darkened, Byron's first OOD watch under way in wartime was like any other night watch: uneventful peering into the gloom on a windy wet rolling bridge, through long empty hours.

About the trouble ahead, he knew more than the crewmen. This was less a patrol than a suicide mission; Aster had showed him on the Lingayen Gulf chart the shallow depth figures, and the reefs that nearly blocked the mouth of the gulf. The clear entrance to the east would be crawling with Jap antisubmarine vessels. If an American sub did by some fluke slip past them to torpedo a troop transport, thereby alerting the whole invasion force—well, as Aster put it, from then on life aboard might be disagreeable and short.

Byron accepted all this. Yet Prien's penetration of Scapa Flow to sink the *Royal Oak* had been as dangerous a venture. The U-boat captain had brought it off, and come home safe to a hero's welcome and a medal from Hitler's hands. Advancing through the dark in a lone submarine, toward a huge enemy force that commanded the air and sea, filled Byron with high-strung zest; possibly a stupid feeling, he knew, but a real one. The exec obviously felt the same way. Carter Aster was smoking a long brown Havana tonight. That meant his spirits were high; otherwise he consumed vile gray Philippine ropes. As for Captain Hoban, he was almost fizzing with combat verve.

Byron's resentment of his commanding officer was gone. The captain had ridden him hard, but that contest of wills now seemed his own fault; his persistence in sloth had been childish. Branch Hoban was a superb ship-handler. He had proved it again, threading out through the tricky new mine fields laid in Manila Bay to block Jap I-boats. He was a skilled submarine engineer, ready and quick to get his hands dirty on a diesel engine, or to sting them with battery acid. His failings were only those of any Academy eager beaver; anxiety to make a record, tough punctiliousness about paperwork, a tendency to grease four-stripers and admirals. So what? He had won E's in engineering and tor-pedo shooting. Those were the things that mattered in combat. Heading toward the enemy, Hoban was a reassuring boss man.

When the east showed a faint graying, the captain came up on the bridge for a look at the lowering sky. "Lady wants to submerge at 0600. Why the devil should we, with this visibility? We're a long way from Lingayen. I'm not crawling there at three knots, and let the *Sal-mon* and the *Porpoise* beat me to the attack. Put on four extra look-outs. Conduct continuous quadrant searches of the sky, and go to full speed."

"Aye aye, sir."

The day brightened. The *Devilfish* nauseatingly corkscrewed and jarred through gray wind-streaked swells at twenty knots. Hoban drank mug after mug of coffee, and smoked cigarette after cigarette in a cupped hand, ignoring the spray that drenched him. Coming off watch, Byron found Aster bent over the navigator's chart in the conning tower, gloomily chewing a dead cigar. To Byron's "Good morning," he barely grunted a response.

"What's the matter, Lady?"

With a side glance at the helmsman, Aster growled, "How do we know the Jap planes don't have radar? They're full of surprises, those yellow monkeys. And what about Jap subs? In daylight we're a sitting tin duck. I want to get to Lingayen fast, too. But I want to *get* there."

Over Aster's shoulder, Byron glanced at the chart. The peninsula projected northwestward of Luzon's land mass like the thumb of a yel-low mitten; the U-shaped blue space between thumb and hand was Lin-gayen Gulf. The course line showed the submarine halfway up the thumb. Beyond the tip, the projected course was a turn east along the reefs and shoals, then a turn south, back down the whole length of the thumb to the assumed landing beach, the point nearest Manila.

"Say, Lady, did you ever hear of Gunther Prien?"

"Sure. The kraut that sank the *Royal Oak* at Scapa Flow. What about him?"

"He gave a lecture in Berlin. I was there." Byron ran a finger along the line of reefs. "He penetrated Scapa Flow through stuff like this. Found a hole and slipped through on the surface."

Aster turned his long-jawed face to Byron, forehead knotted, mouth corners curled in his strange cold smile. "Why, Briny Henry, you getting eager to polish medals? *You?*"

"Well, we'd get there faster if we cut through the reefs, wouldn't we? And we'd duck the destroyers up at the entrance."

Aster's satiric look faded. He reached for the coastal pilot book.

A-OOGHA! A-OOGHA! A-OOGHA!

"Dive, dive, dive." Branch Hoban's voice, urgent but calm, boomed through the boat. The deck pitched forward. Lookouts dropped trampling through the dripping hatch, followed by the OOD, the captain, and last the quartermaster, slamming the hatch and dogging it shut. Byron heard the old hiss and sigh, as though the boat were a live monster taking a deep breath, and felt in his ears the sudden airtightness, before the chief below called, *"Pressure in the boat!"* The *Devilfish* slowed, plowing sluggishly downward with loud gurglings and sloshings.

Hoban wiped his streaming face. "Whitey Pringle spotted a low-flying plane. Or maybe it was a seagull. Pringle has good eyes. *I* didn't argue. The sun's starting to break through, anyhow, Lady. Level off at three hundred."

"Aye aye, sir," Aster said.

Byron slithered down to the control room, and walked forward on the downslanted deck. The Christmas tree of small lights on the port bulkhead, flashing the condition of every opening in the hull, showed solid green. The planesmen at their big wheels had calm eyes fixed on the depth gauges; no trace of combat anxiety here.

"Blow negative to the mark!"

The routine procedure scarcely registered on Byron. In the forward torpedo room he found Chief Hansen and his crewmen affixing warheads to two torpedoes newly loaded aboard. Byron's eyes smarted; he had had no sleep since the departure from Manila, but he wanted to confirm torpedo readiness for himself. Hansen reported all six bow tubes loaded; all fish checked out in working order; the new secret exploders ready for insertion in the warheads. Racked along the bulkheads were yellow dummy warheads, which in peacetime had been filled with water for practice shots; compressed air would empty them, and the torpedoes would float for recovery. Unpainted iron warheads full of TNT now tipped the torpedoes; impossible to detonate without exploders, yet Byron had seen the crew handle these gray warheads with gingerly respect for the havoc and murder in them.

As Byron drank coffee with the torpedomen, crouched on a bunk slung over a torpedo, Lieutenant Aster appeared. "By the Christ, Briny, he's going to try it."

"Try what?"

"Why, that notion of yours. He's been studying the chart and the sailing directions. We're going to surface and look for a break in the reefs. He wants to talk to you about that U-boat skipper's lecture."

In a sparkling noonday, the black snout of the submarine broke the surface. Byron stepped unsteadily out into brilliant hot sunshine on the pitching slippery forecastle, still aslosh with foaming seawater. Lookouts and leadsmen in bulky life jackets stumbled and slipped after him. He could not help a swift glance up at the cloudless blue sky. After the stale air below, the fresh wind was delicious as always, and the pleasure was sharper today because of the danger. Dead ahead, where the dark ocean merged into green shallows, foaming breakers roared against tiny palm islands and jagged brown rocks. White gulls came cawing and screeching over the submarine.

"All ahead one-third! Heave your leads!" Hoban's shout from the bridge was muffled by the heavy wash on the hull and the grinding sound of the breakers. Coral heads were showing, far down in the deep —pink spires, rounded gray domes. The *Devilfish* was heading for a notch between two rocky little islands.

"Mark! Four fathoms, starboard!"

Byron perceived yellow coral sand slanting up, full of immense waving sea fans. Blown dry of ballast, the *Devilfish* was drawing about thirteen feet.

"Mark! Three fathoms, port!"

Eighteen feet. Five clear feet under the keel. With each swell the boat was rising and falling, staggering Byron's party and drenching them with spray. The smaller island was drifting so close that he could count the coconuts on the trees. On the bridge, at the bullnose, and on the fantail, lookouts were combing the sky with binoculars. But in this sunlit waste of air, water, palms, and rocks, the only sign of man was the grotesque black vessel risen from the deep.

"All engines stop!"

From the bridge, Aster yelled through cupped hands, "Fathometer's showing fifteen feet, Briny! What do you see?"

Slipping about, wet to the skin, Byron flailed both arms forward. "Okay! Keep coming!" he bawled, for the water shaded toward blue again beyond the notch. On either side of the submarine, ugly breakers were smashing and creaming on pitted brown rocks. The propellers thrashed; a heavy swell lifted and dropped the vessel. With a crunching *clang, clang!* the *Devilfish* shuddered and jolted forward. Byron caught a fragrant whiff of palm fronds as the islands slid by, near enough to hit with a thrown hat.

"Four fathoms, port!"

"Four fathoms, starboard!"

Coral heads drifted below the hull like anchored mines, deeper and deeper. The bow was heading into blue water now. Over the crash and slosh of the breakers came the captain's exultant bellow. "Secure leadsmen and lookouts! Prepare to dive!"

Byron stood in his cabin naked amid sodden clothes piled on the deck, drying himself with a rough grimy towel. Grinning from ear to ear, Aster looked in, green eyes brilliant as emeralds. "How about this? Well done."

"You found the hole," Byron said.

"Lucked into it. That chart is goddamn vague. Glad the patrol plane pilots were having their noon sukiyaki, or whatever."

"What happened there? Did we ground?"

"Starboard screw struck a coral head. The shaft's not sprung. The captain's pleased as hell, Briny. Get some rest."

Yawning and yawning, Byron slipped into the mildewy hot bunk. The *Devilfish* had sneaked itself into a tight predicament, he thought, with no easy way out. However, that was the captain's problem. He turned off his mind like a light—Byron could do that, and it contributed much to his health, though it had often infuriated his father and his naval superiors—and fell asleep.

A shake and a husky whisper woke him. He smelled the tobacco-chewer's breath of Derringer, the chief of the boat. "Battle stations, Mr. Henry."

"Huh? What?" Byron slid aside the curtain, and confronted the jowly smelly face in the dim light from the passageway. "*Battle* stations?"

"Screw noises."

"Oh ho."

Now through the thin hull Byron heard the underwater commotion, and a high faint shuddery *ping*—a very familiar sound from exercises at sea and from the attack teacher. This echo-ranging was different: shriller, more vibrating, with a peculiar timbre.

The enemy.

They were runing silent, he realized. The ventilators were off. The air was stifling. Chief Derringer's heavy face was tightly lined with worry and excitement. Byron impulsively put out his hand. The chief grasped it with a horny paw, and left. Byron's watch showed he had been asleep for an hour.

At general quarters he was the diving officer. Hurrying to his battle station, he was reassured by the cool working demeanor of every man in the control room—the bow and stern planesmen at their big wheels watching the depth gauges, Derringer and his plotting team huddled around the dead reckoning tracer, Whitey Pringle on the trim manifold, just as in peacetime exercises off Pearl Harbor. They had been through this a thousand times. Here was the payoff, Byron thought, of Hoban's stiff monotonous drill schedule. Aster, smoking a long rich Havana, stood with the chief of the boat, watching the plot take form. The echo-ranging was getting louder; so was the confused noise of propellers. Ensign Quayne was at the diving officer's post. Of all the men in the control room, only he had the wide-open eyes and shaky lips of fear. Quayne wasn't yet part of the team; he had just survived a sinking; he was not long out of sub school. With these forgiving thoughts, Byron relieved him.

"Lady, when did all this break?"

"We picked up these clowns on sonar at about nine thousand yards. All of a sudden. We must have come out from under a thermal layer."

"Sounds like a mess of them," Byron said.

"Sounds like the whole goddamn landing force. This stuff is spread across a hundred degrees. We can't sort it out yet." Aster lightly mounted the ladder to the conning tower, gripping Byron's shoulder as he passed.

Byron strained to hear the low conversation of Aster and the captain in the tower. A command down the voice tube, Hoban's confident voice, quiet and tense: "Briny, come up to seventy feet. No higher, hear? *Seventy feet.*"

"Seventy feet. Aye aye, sir."

The planesmen turned their wheels. The *Devilfish* tilted up. The gauges reeled off the ascent. The outside noises grew louder still: pings and propeller thrums, now plainly ahead.

"Seventy feet, Captain."

"Very well. Now, Briny, listen carefully. I'm going to raise number two periscope all the way." The captain's voice was firm and subdued. "Then I want you to come up exactly a foot, and level off—another foot, and level off—just the way we did it in that last run on the *Litchfield*. Nice and easy, you know?"

"Aye aye, sir."

The narrow shaft of the attack scope slid softly upward behind Byron, and stopped.

"Coming to sixty-*nine* feet, sir."

"Very well."

A level-off. A pause. "Coming to sixty-*eight* feet, sir."

The planesmen were the best on the boat, an ill-sorted pair: Spiller, the freckled Texan who said "fuck" at every third word, and Marino, the solemn Italian from Chicago, never without the crucifix around his neck, never uttering so much as a "damn"; but they worked like twins, inching the submarine upward.

"Okay! Hold it! That does it!" Hoban's voice went high, loud, almost frantic. "Wow! *Jesus Christ! Mark!* Target angle on the bow forty starboard. Down scope!"

A silence. A crackling in the loudspeaker.

P-i-i-i-ing . . . P-i-i-i-i-ng . . .

The captain's voice through the quiet submarine, controlled but with a fighting thrill in it: "Now all hands, listen to me. I've got three large transports in column, screened by two destroyers, one point on the port bow. The Rising Sun is flapping plain as day on all of them. It's brightly sunny up there. This is it! I'm coming to normal approach course. Prepare the bow tubes."

Hot pins and needles ran along Byron's shoulders and arms. He could hear Aster and the captain arguing about the range. The periscope bobbed up behind him, and straightway down again. There was rapid talk in the conning tower about masthead heights, and the captain harried the quartermaster for recognition manuals. The echo-ranging grew sharper and stronger, the propeller noises louder. Byron had done enough work on the torpedo data computer to picture the trigonometry in his head. On the dead reckoning tracer, the problem showed clearly: the *Devilfish* as a moving spot of light, the enemy course and its own course as two converging pencil lines. But the target's line was jagged. The transports were zigzagging. They were still beyond torpedo range, according to Aster; or, in the captain's judgment, barely within range. The two men were equally adept at guessing distance by masthead heights. On a submarine there was no more precise range-finder. The transports were on a zig away, and they moved faster than the crawling sub.

Utter silence fell in the conning tower. Silence throughout the boat. All the noise now was outside, a cacophony of machinery sounds and the plangent searching probes of the Japanese sonar.

Piiiing! Piiiing! P-i-i-i-ing! Pi-i-i-i-ing!

"Up scope. *Okay, here they come! They've turned back!* Mark! Range forty-five hundred. Mark! Bearing zero two zero. Mark! Target angle on the bow seventy starboard. Down scope!"

A pause. The captain's voice, hushed and urgent on the PA system: *"Now all hands, I intend to shoot. Open outside doors on bow tubes."*

His natural voice, in the conning tower: "Damn! An absolute setup, Lady, but an outside range. We're not going to close them much with that angle on the bow. What stinking luck!"

"Captain, why don't we hold our fire and track them? It's a fantastic chance. That zigzag plan will slow their advance. Maybe we can pull ahead and close the range."

"No, no, no. *Now's* our chance, Lady. They're making fifteen knots on a radical plan. If they zig away again we may lose the bastards. I've got a setup and a solution, and I'm going to shoot."

"Aye aye, sir."

"Outside doors are open, sir!"

"Very well. Slow setting!"

Concentrating on holding depth, Byron could scarcely grasp that at last this was the real thing; not the launch of a yellow-headed dummy, but a TNT warhead attack on ships filled with Japanese soldiers. Except for the different sonar sound and the choking tension, it was so much like an attack school drill, or an exercise at sea! It was going very fast now, along old familiar lines. Hoban had even used this slow setting for the hit on the *Litchfield* that had clinched the E.

"Up scope! Mark! Bearing zero two five. Range four thousand. Down scope!"

The aiming was harder on a slow setting, the chance for missing greater, detection of torpedo wakes by the enemy more likely. In this decision to make his first wartime shot on slow setting, Hoban was accepting marginal conditions. Fifteen years as a naval officer, ten years as a brilliant peacetime submariner, lay in back of that decision. . . . Byron's heart thudded, his mouth was dry as dust . . .

"Fire one! . . . Fire two! . . . Fire three! . . . Fire four!"

With the usual jolts and rushing water noises, the torpedoes left the *Devilfish*.

"Up scope. Oh, wow. Four wakes! Four beautiful wakes, running hot, straight, and normal. Down scope!"

Heart-stopping expectant silence again, all through the *Devilfish*. Byron watched the second hand of the control room clock. It was easy to calculate the time to target, at slow setting, on the last called range.

"Up scope!"

A long, long silence. Time passed for all four torpedoes to hit. Byron stiffened with alarm. No impacts; and the periscope had been up for ten seconds, and was staying up! Maximum safe exposure was six seconds.

"Down scope. Four misses, Lady. Goddamn." The captain sounded sick. "At least two wakes had to go under the lead transport. I *saw* them heading there. I don't know what went wrong. Now they've spotted the wakes, and turned away. The near destroyer's coming at us, with a hell of a bone in its teeth. Let's go to ten knots." He called through the tube, "Byron! Take her down to two hundred fifty feet."

On the loudspeaker his voice turned dull and cranky. "Now all hands, rig for depth charge on the double."

Two hundred fifty feet? Lingayen Gulf was nowhere deeper than a hundred seventy feet. The captain's impossible order shocked and baffled Byron. He was grateful for Aster's lively interposition. "You mean a hundred fifty, Captain. That's about down to the mud here."

"Right. Thanks, Lady—a hundred fifty, Byron."

With a silent jar of acceleration, the submarine tilted and dove. Aster spoke again. "What course, Captain?"

It was almost a silly question, but Hoban was giving no order for the all-important evasive turn. Overhead on the surface of the sea, four slick white bubbly torpedo wakes certainly led straight to the *Devilfish*. The destroyer must be charging up those visible tracks at forty knots. The pitch of the echo-ranging was rising to a scream, and the probes were coming thick and fast on short scale: *ping, ping, ping, ping!*

"Course? Oh, yes, yes, left full rudder! Come to—oh, make it two seven oh."

"Left to two seven oh, sir," called the helmsman.

The diving vessel tilted sideways. The oncoming Japanese ship sounded much like the *Litchfield* in practice runs, but noisier and angrier, though that very likely was Byron's imagination; like a train approaching on loose old tracks, *ker-da-trum, ker-da-trum, KER-DA-TRUM!*

Throughout the *Devilfish,* shouts, slams, clangs of maximum watertight rigging.

The destroyer came closer, passed right overhead—*ker-da-TRAMM-TRAMM-TRAMM-TRAMM*—and moved away.

The pitch of the sonar dropped. White faces in the control room turned to each other.

Byron heard one clear *click,* as though a ball bearing had bounced off the submarine's hull. Another quiet second, and the depth charge exploded.

8

CHRISTMAS carols filtered scratchily over the loud drunken talk and the clack-clack of iron wheels. Palmer Kirby disliked club cars, and Christmas carols depressed him, but he needed to drink. This express train howling toward Washington through the snowy night carried no gloomier passenger.

Rhoda Henry would be waiting at Union Station. He was hungrily glad of that, yet ashamed of his yearnings. She was the wife of another man, a battleship captain out fighting the Japanese. After stumbling into this affair, he had tried to right himself by proposing marriage to her. She had considered it, but backed off. Resuming the sex relationship after that had been ignominious; so he now thought, in his low mood. Dr. Kirby had no religious or moral scruples; he was a dour decent atheist, a widower of old-fashioned habits. This constrained and messy adultery was a damned poor substitute for having a wife. He had to limit his attentions to avoid scandal, yet his sense of honor tied him down like a husband. In his travels he now was ignoring attractive secretaries and receptionists, whose eyes sometimes glinted at this tall ugly bony-faced man with thick grizzled hair. He had been telephoning Rhoda regularly. Pug's cable from Pearl Harbor that she had read him, AM FINE HAVE JUST BEGUN TO FIGHT, had both gladdened and humiliated Kirby. He liked and admired the man he was cuckolding. It was a wretched business.

The root of Dr. Kirby's dark mood, however, was the war. He had been touring a land legally a belligerent, yet paralyzed by frivolity, indecision, lack of leadership—and above all, by Christmas, Christmas, Christmas! This whoop-dee-do of buying, selling, decorating, gorging, and guzzling, to the endless crooning of Bing Crosby's inescapable gooey voice, this annual solstice jamboree faking honor to the Christ child, this annual midwinter madness was possessing the country as though Hitler did not exist, as though Pearl Harbor were untouched, as though Wake Island were not falling. The Lucky Strike ads showed jolly red-cheeked old Santa Claus wearing a tin soldier hat, cutely tilted. In one sickening image, that was the national attitude.

Kirby had found some sense of war on the West Coast: hysterical air raid alarms, brief panics, spotty blackouts, confused and contradictory orders from the Army and from Civil Defense, rumors of submarines shelling San Francisco, fear of the Japanese mixed with inexplicable cocksureness that America would win the war. Eastward even this shallow awareness dimmed. By Chicago the war had faded to a topic for talk over drinks, or a new angle for making money. The thought of defeat entered few people's minds. Who could beat America? As for the Armageddon swirling before Moscow, the terrific counterstrokes of the Red Army against the Wehrmacht hordes—to most Americans Santa Claus in a tin hat was considerably more real.

Perhaps in the muddled turmoil of Franklin Roosevelt's management agencies, production boards, and emergency committees, now multiplying in Washington like amoebas, something was being accomplished. Perhaps in army camps, naval bases, shipyards, and airplane factories, a capacity for war was growing. Kirby didn't know. He knew he was returning in despair from a tour of the country's resources for producing actino-uranium. He had seen a national industrial plant so disorganized and swamped by war orders that even if the scientists solved the theory of nuclear explosives, the factories could never produce the weapons. Everywhere the wail was not enough copper, not enough steel, lack of labor, lack of parts, lack of machine tools, skyrocketing prices, ignorant government officials, favoritism, corruption, and confusion. He had travelled with good credentials from Washington, but men with such credentials were swarming over the land. He had been unable to reveal what he was after. If he could have—and he had tried some hints—it would not have helped. To the harassed factory managers, atom bombs belonged in science fiction tales with spaceships and time machines. Warning articles had long since appeared in scientific journals, and even in *Time* and *Life*. But people could not grasp that this futuristic horror was upon them.

Yet it was.

Uranium had been disintegrating harmlessly through aeons. Human awareness of radioactivity was not fifty years old. For about forty years it had seemed a minor freak of nature. Then in 1932, the year before Franklin Roosevelt and Adolf Hitler had simultaneously come to power, an Englishman had discovered the neutron, the uncharged particle in atoms, and after only seven years of further unsettling discoveries in Italy, France, Germany, and America—seven years, a micro-second of historical time—the Germans had shown that neutron bombardment could split uranium atoms and release vast primordial energies.

In 1939, Kirby had attended a physicists' convention where chilling news had started as a whisper and swelled to an uproar. Columbia University scientists, following up on the German experiments, had proved that a splitting uranium atom emitted, on the average, more than one neutron. This answered the key theoretical question: was a chain reaction in uranium possible? Ominous answer: *yes*. A new golden age of available power was thus opening. There was, however, another, and very horrible, aspect. An isotope discovered only four years earlier, called U-235 or actino-uranium, could conceivably fire off in a self-sustaining explosion of incalculable magnitude. But could any country produce enough pure U-235 to make bombs for use in this war? Or would some blessed fact of nature crop up, in dealing with large lumps instead of tiny laboratory quantities, that would render the whole doomsday project a harmless failure, a physical impossibility? Nobody on earth yet knew these things for sure.

So the race was on to isolate enough of the fearsome isotope to try to make bombs. On all the evidence of Palmer Kirby's senses, and of the information available to him, Adolf Hitler's scientists were going to win this race hands down. They had a formidable lead. British science and industry were already too strained for an all-out atomic bomb effort. Unless the United States could overtake the Germans, the superb Nazi war plants were likely to furnish the lunatic Führer with enough U-235 bombs to wipe out the world's capitals one by one, until all governments grovelled to him.

Such was Palmer Kirby's view of the actino-uranium picture. If the future really held that shape, what other military plans or operations mattered? What human relationships mattered?

In a black cloth coat with a silver fox collar, a tilted little gray hat, and gray gloves, Rhoda Henry was pacing back and forth at the train gate well before its arrival time. She was taking a chance on being seen meeting him; but he had been away almost a month, and this reunion was bound to be pivotal. Kirby did not yet know that she had written Pug to ask for a divorce, that the Pearl Harbor attack had intervened, and that she was now vaguely craw-fishing. All these disclosures now lay before her.

The letter to Pug had been a desperate thing. Several bad developments had made Rhoda spring like a frightened cat. For one thing, his letter from Moscow about the *California* had arrived; and though that was fine news, she had feared that next he might ask her to come to Hawaii. Palmer Kirby, a much less inhibited man than Pug, had wakened late-blooming lusts in her. She dreaded giving him up. She loved Washington, and detested life on Navy bases overseas. Kirby was right here in Washington, doing his hush-hush work, whatever it was. She had never asked; his presence was what mattered.

But at the time Pug's letter came, her relationship with Kirby had been getting shaky. His work had taken him off on long trips. The anniversary of his wife's death had dejected him. He had once again begun muttering about feeling guilty, and about breaking off. Thoroughly scared by a long lugubrious talk over dinner in a restaurant, she had gone with him one evening to his apartment, instead of bringing him to her house. By rotten luck they had run straight into Madge and Jerry Knudsen in the lobby. Madge had a big mouth, and the Navy wives' grapevine was the fastest communication network in the world. A nasty story might well be winging to Pug in Hawaii!

Pushed into this corner, in a spell of three straight days of sleet and rain, alone in the twelve-room Foxhall Road house, with Kirby off on another trip, and not telephoning her, Rhoda had sprung. Now that the children were grown, she had decided, only five or eight tolerable years were left to her before she shrivelled into an old dry crone. Life with Pug had run down. Kirby was a vigorous lover, a self-made wealthy man. He was mad about her, as Pug had not seemed for many years. Perhaps the collapse of the marriage was her own fault and she was not a very good person (some of this had crept into what she wrote to her husband), but it was now or never. Divorces among four-stripers were common, after all, as Navy families grew up and apart, and the long separations took their toll. Come to that, she knew a tangy tale or two about Madge Knudsen!

So off the letter had gone. Hard upon it, by the most appalling mischance, the Japanese had attacked, and blown all Rhoda's little calculations to smithereens. Rhoda's reactions to the bombing of Pearl Harbor had been not admirable, perhaps, but human. After the shock, her first thought had been that the start of a war spelled a quick sharp rise in the prospects of naval officers. Commanding a battleship in the Pacific, Pug Henry was poised now for a brilliant recovery to—who could say? Certainly to flag rank; perhaps to Chief of Naval Operations! In asking for the divorce just now, had she blundered like the Wall Street man who held an oil stock for twenty years, and then sold out a week before the corporation struck a new field?

With this practical concern went genuine regret at having hit her husband at a bad time. She still loved him, somewhat as she loved her grown children. He was part of her life. So she had fired off the repentant cable, and the short agitated letter which he read aboard the *Northampton*, withdrawing her divorce request. His reply to the request had filled her with remorse, pride, and relief; remorse at the pain traced in each sentence, pride and relief that Pug could still want her.

So Pug knew the worst, and she still had him. But what about Kirby? One look at him, hurrying up the train platform with those long legs, coatless and hatless in the billowing vapor, told Rhoda that she still had this man too. Her risky spring was turning out well. You never knew! She stood there waiting, gray-gloved hands outstretched, eyes wide and shining. They did not kiss; they never did in public.

"Palmer, no coat? It's ARCTIC outside."

"I put on long johns in Chicago."

She darted him a mischievous intimate glance. "Long johns! Shades of President McKinley, dear."

Side by side they left the thronged terminal, clamorous with train announcements and with Bing Crosby blare. Dr. Kirby peered through whirling snow as they walked out into the lamplit night. "Well, well! The Capitol dome's dark. There must be a war on."

"Oh, there's all kinds of a war on. The shortages are starting already. And the prices!" She hugged his arm, her motions elastic and happy. "I'm one of these awful unpatriotic hoarders, dear. Do you LOATHE me? I bought two dozen pairs of silk stockings yesterday. Paid double what they cost three weeks ago. Cleaned out two stores of my size! Silk's all going into parachutes, they say, and soon we'll be lucky to get even nylon stockings. Ugh! Nylon! It bags around the ankles, and it's so CLAMMY."

"Heard again from Pug?"

"Nary another word."

"Rhoda, on the West Coast they're saying we lost all the battleships at Pearl Harbor, the *California* included."

"I've heard that, too. Pug's letter sort of did sound like it. Real low. But if it's true, he'll get some other big job. It's inevitable now."

Kirby slung his suitcase into Rhoda's car in the dark parking area. Once inside the car they kissed, whispering endearments, his hands straying under her coat. But not for long. Rhoda sat up, switched on the lights, and started the motor. "Oh, say, Madeline's here, dear."

"Madeline? Really? Since when?"

"She fell in on me this afternoon."

"Staying long?"

"Who knows? She's muttering about becoming a Navy nurse's aide."

"What about her broadcasting job?"

"I guess she's quitting—oh, BLAST you, you IMBECILE!" A red Buick pulled out from the curb ahead of her, forcing her to brake, skid, and wrestle with the wheel. "I swear, the MORONS who have the money to buy cars nowadays! It's SO AGGRAVATING."

This kind of irascible snap was normal for Rhoda. Her husband would not even have noticed. But it was new to Palmer Kirby, and it grated on him. "Well, in wartime prosperity does seep down, Rhoda. That's one of the few good things that happens."

"Possibly. All I know is, Washington's becoming UNLIVABLE." Her tone stayed shrill and hard. "Just BOILING with dirty pushy strangers."

Kirby let it pass, weighing the news of Madeline's presence in the house. Would Rhoda consent to come to his apartment? She didn't like doing that, she knew too many people in the building. So the reunion looked to be a fiasco, at least for tonight. His inamorata had a family, and he had to put up with it.

In point of fact, Rhoda was counting on Madeline's surprise visit to help her through a difficult evening. Madeline's presence luckily postponed certain tactical and moral questions; such as, whether she should sleep with Palmer, after having written to Pug that she wanted to preserve their marriage. In a quandary Rhoda's rule was "If possible, do nothing." With her daughter in the house, doing nothing would be simple. Her casual announcement of Madeline's presence had masked great tension about how Kirby would take the news, and this lay under her little outburst at the Buick. Her natural crabbiness had hitherto been unthinkable with Kirby; in irritated moments she had bitten her tongue, choked down her bile, and kept her face smiling and her voice honeyed. It amused and relieved her to note that he reacted like Pug; after one admonishing remark, he did not speak again. He too was manageable.

They were driving past the darkened White House, on the side where the Christmas tree stood on the lawn, amid crowds of gawkers. "I suppose you know that Churchill's in there," she said gaily, sensing that the silence was getting long. "Churchill himself. What a time we're living in, love!"

"What a time, indeed," he replied with deep moroseness.

Like most pretty girls, Madeline Henry had a doormat suitor. She had briefly fallen in love with Midshipman Simon Anderson at her first Academy dance because his white uniform fitted so well and he could rhumba so smoothly. He too had fallen in love, mooning and carrying on about the beautiful Henry girl, and sending her atrocious poems; and upon graduation he had fecklessly proposed to her. She was barely seventeen. Enchanted with this very early bloody scalp on her belt, Madeline of course had turned him down.

Scalped or not, Simon Anderson was a dogged customer. Five years later he still pursued Madeline Henry. He was with her tonight. On her telephoning him from New York that afternoon, he had made himself free for her. A prize-winning physics student at the Academy, Lieutenant Anderson was now working at the Bureau of Ordnance, on a secret radical advance in antiaircraft fuses. But to Madeline Sime remained the doormat: good for filling an evening on short notice, and for pumping up her ego when it lost pressure. Anderson accepted this status, tolerated her treading on him, and bided his time.

Rhoda and Dr. Kirby found them drinking by a log fire in the spacious living room of the Foxhall Road house. Rhoda went off to the kitchen. Kirby accepted a highball and stretched his legs, chilled despite the long johns, before the blaze. He was struck by Madeline's almost blatant allure. Her red wool dress was cut low, her crossed silk-clad legs showed to the knee, and she had a roguish buoyant sparkle to her. "Oh, Dr. Kirby. The very man I want to talk to."

"Delighted. What about?"

Madeline did not dream, of course, that there was anything between her mother and Kirby but elderly friendship. Rhoda's church activities and her prim manners and speech had in no way changed. Kirby seemed a nice old gentleman, with a hint in his eye of relish for women, which decades ago might have been beguiling.

"Well, we've been having the maddest conversation! My head's spinning. Sime says that it's become possible to make radioactive bombs that may blow up the world."

Anderson spoke crisply. "I said conceivable."

Kirby gave Anderson a cautious glance. This blond middle-sized lieutenant looked like any other junior naval officer: young, clean-cut, commonplace. "Are you a physicist, Lieutenant?"

"That was my major, sir. I did postgrad work at Cal Tech. I'm a regular officer of the line."

"Where are you stationed?"

Erect on his chair, Anderson rapped out his words like answers to an oral examination. "BuOrd Proving Ground, sir."

"I have an E.E. from Cal Tech. How would you go about making this frightful bomb?"

"Well, sir—" he glanced at Madeline—"it requires a new technology. You of course know that. All I said was that Germany might be well along toward it. Their technology is outstanding. They made the first discoveries, and they have high military motivation."

"Why, I'd be *petrified*," Madeline exclaimed, "if I could believe any of that. Imagine! Hitler drops one of those things on the north pole, just to show his power, and it melts half the polar cap and lights up the night sky, clear to the equator. Then what happens?"

"Good question," Kirby replied mournfully. "I wouldn't know. How long will you be in Washington, Madeline?"

"I may just stay here."

Kirby saw surprised gladness on Anderson's face. "Oh? You're giving up your radio work?" As he said this, Rhoda came in wearing a frilly apron over her gray silk dress.

"I'm not sure. It's getting hard to take—same idiotic cheerfulness, same grubby commercials, war or no war. Just phony patriotic stuff. Why, we had a songwriter on the show last night, singing his brand-new war ditty, 'I'm Going to Find a Fellow Who's Yellow, and Beat Him Red, White, and Blue.' What a creep!"

Anderson's sober face cracked in a boyish laugh. "You're kidding, Mad."

Her mother asked, "Now what is this, dear? Have you quit your job or not?"

"I'm trying to decide. As for Hugh Cleveland, that egomaniac I work for, what do you suppose *he's* contributing to the war effort, Mom? Why, he's bought his wife a sable coat, that's what. And he's taken her off to Palm Springs. Just left the show on my hands, with a dumb comedian named Lester O'Shea to interview the amateurs. Christ, what a coat, Mama! Huge collar and cuffs, solid sables down to mid-calf. I mean it's *vulgar* to own and wear such a coat in wartime. I plain got disgusted and came home. I need a vacation myself."

Madeline had told Rhoda with great indignation of Mrs. Cleveland's unjust suspicions about her and Cleveland. The mother now had a clue

to Madeline's conduct. "Madeline, dear, was that quite responsible?"
"Why not? Didn't *he* just up and leave?" She jumped to her feet.
"Come on, Sime, feed me."

"Won't you two eat here, dear? There's plenty."

Madeline's ironic glance at Kirby made him feel his years, it declared
so plainly her lack of interest in the idea.

"We're just snatching a bite, Mom, before the movie. Thanks."

Rhoda treated her lover, in the matter of creature comforts, as she
had her husband. She served him excellent lamb and rice, and a good
wine. She had a hot mince pie for him, and the heavy Italian coffee he
preferred. They brought the coffee into the living room by the fire.
Kirby lolled his great legs on the sofa, mildly smiling at her in warm
well-being over the coffee cup.

This was the moment, Rhoda thought, and she walked out on the
tightrope. "Palmer, I have something to tell you. I wrote Pug about a
month ago, asking for a divorce."

His smile faded. His heavy brows knotted. He put down his coffee
and sat straighter. Rhoda was not surprised, though this was a letdown;
he might have showed gladness. In good balance, she ran lightly along
the rope. "Now, darling, listen, you're free as air. Just remember that!
I'm not sure I ever want to marry again. I'm in a terrible turmoil. You
see, I thought he might ask me to come and set up house in Honolulu. I
simply couldn't face leaving you. So I did it, and now it's done."

"What reason did you give him, Rhoda?"

"I simply said that we'd been seeing each other, and that I'd fallen so
hopelessly in love that it was wrong not to tell him."

Slowly, heavily, he shook his head. "Gruesome timing."

"I agree. I'm not clairvoyant, my darling. I couldn't know that the
Japs were about to bomb Pearl Harbor."

"Has he answered yet?"

"Yes. A lovely, heartbreaking letter."

"Let me see it."

She went to her bedroom to get it.

Kirby clasped his hands between his knees, staring at the fire. He at
once thought of repeating his proposal. In the circumstances, it seemed
mandatory. But marrying Rhoda Henry now wore a different aspect
than it had in his hotel room fantasies. He was on the spot. This development struck Kirby as a maneuver. He was a hard-grained man, he
knew maneuvering, and on principle resisted being outmaneuvered.

The war rose again in his mind. How much better was he, after all, than the Christmas celebrants he despised? Stuffed with lamb, rice, mince pie, and wine, hoping to sleep with another man's wife, and perhaps to steal her for good while the man fought the war; could self-indulgent pettiness sink any lower? Right now his place was back in the apartment, writing a report for the meeting tomorrow with Vannevar Bush . . .

In the bedroom, meantime, Rhoda read over her husband's letter, as it were with the engineer's eyes. For an instant, she saw herself as shallow, tawdry, and unworthy of either man. She weighed making some excuse to withhold it from Kirby. But she had observed in his eyes all evening that he desired her. That was the main thing. Let the rest go as it would. She brought him the letter where he sat hunched, poking the fire. He read it, studied the scuffed snapshot of Natalie and Louis, then without a word handed the envelope to her. He rested his head on the back of the sofa, rubbing his eyes.

"What's the matter, dear?"

"Oh, nothing. I've still got a report to write tonight."

"It is awkward, isn't it—I mean, Madeline being here and all?"

With a grimace and a shrug of one shoulder Palmer Kirby said, "It really doesn't matter."

So chilly were those words, all of Rhoda's recently gained security was blasted away. "Palmer," she said in a charged voice, "take me to your apartment."

This startled life into his drooping eyes. "What? Is that what you want?"

"What do you think, you fool?" They looked at each other. Rhoda's expression smouldered and a little half-smile curved her thin pretty lips. "Don't you?"

She returned to the house around one. The living room was dark and Madeline was not in her bedroom. Having already bathed in Kirby's apartment, Rhoda changed into a housecoat and went downstairs. She felt a bit silly about all this rapid-fire dressing and undressing. Otherwise she felt very good indeed—an afterglow in her body, a new peace in her mind. Kirby had proposed, as expected, after the lovemaking. She had firmly put him off. She could not consider, she had told him, a proposal made under pressure. Brilliant response! He had wonderfully cheered up, his dutiful manner vanishing in a great grin and a strong hug.

"Well, meantime, Rhoda, will we—well, go on seeing each other?"

"Dear, if 'seeing' is what you choose to call this, why yes, by all means. I loved being seen by you tonight. Very penetrating vision." Rhoda enjoyed such wheezy ribaldry with Kirby; a taste that somehow, with Victor Henry, she seldom indulged. Her remark brought Kirby's sudden vulgar smile, showing teeth and gums. Then when she left, some time later, his unreflecting remark, "When will I see you again?" made them both whoop with laughter.

She threw logs on the red embers, mixed herself a drink, and reread Pug's letter. With Kirby's proposal in hand, it affected her differently. She was a grandmother twice over, and here she was loved and wanted by two fine men! Not since her adolescent days, when the phone had jangled with dance invitations, and she had turned down two boys in the gamble that a preferred third one would call, had she felt quite this pleasure in her own power to attract.

With such thoughts running through her mind, she jumped when the telephone rang. It was the long-distance operator, calling from Palm Springs for Madeline Henry.

"She's not here. I'm her mother."

Rhoda heard Cleveland's unmistakable voice: "Operator! Operator! I'll talk to this party . . . Hello, Mrs. Henry? Sorry to disturb you." The celebrated rich rumble charmed and soothed the ear. "Is Maddy really in Washington?"

"Yes, but she's out for the evening."

"Look, how serious is she about becoming a nurse's aide? I mean, I'm all for patriotism, Mrs. Henry, but that's a ridiculous notion. Any nigger girl can become a nurse's aide."

"Frankly, Mr. Cleveland, I admire her. There's a war on."

"I realize that." Cleveland heavily sighed. "But the morale effect of *The Happy Hour* is a great war service, I assure you. You should see the letters from admirals and generals framed in my office!" The voice grew warmer and more intimate. "Rhoda—if I may call you that—with two sons and a hubby in the armed forces, aren't you making enough of a sacrifice? Suppose they send her overseas? You'd be alone all through the war."

"Madeline didn't like your going off on a vacation at this time, Mr. Cleveland. She feels you're indifferent to the war. And she said something about sables."

"Oh, Jesus! What did she say about the sables?"

"Sables for your wife, I believe."

With a low groan, Cleveland said, "Christ, if it isn't one thing it's another. She manages the show backstage, Rhoda. I can step out for a week, but she can't. We have to train a replacement for her. Please tell her to call me when she gets in."

"I'll probably be asleep. I can leave her a message."

"Thanks. Write it in lipstick on her mirror." That made Rhoda laugh. "I'm not kidding. I must talk to her tonight."

Rhoda was finishing her drink by the fire when she heard Madeline in the hallway saying good-bye to Sime Anderson. The daughter marched in perkily. "Hi, Mom. Nightcap? Think I'll join you."

"Dear, Hugh Cleveland called."

The daughter halted, frowning. "When?"

"Not long ago. His number in Palm Springs is on the telephone table."

Tossing her nose in the air like a little girl, Madeline sat down by the waning fire, and picked up the snapshot beside her father's letter. "Wow, Briny's baby, hey? Poor Natalie! She looks fat as a cow here. Mom, can't you find out what's happened to them?"

"Her mother wrote to the State Department. I haven't heard from her since."

"That's a weird marriage anyway. Most marriages seem to be. Take Claire Cleveland. She hasn't grown with Hugh, and that makes her insanely jealous. Did Dad write anything about that stupid letter I sent him?"

"Only in passing."

"What did he say?"

Rhoda looked through the three sheets. "Here we are. It's short. 'I don't know what went wrong with Madeline. I'm kind of sick about that, and don't propose to dwell on it. If the fellow wants to marry her, that may clean the mess up as much as anything can. If not, he'll be hearing from me.'"

"Oh, dear. Poor, poor Dad!" Madeline struck a little fist on the sofa. "She'd no more have divorced Hugh! I should never have written. I just panicked, because I was so astounded at her accusations."

"Write him again, dear. Tell him that it was all nonsense."

"I intend to." With a huge yawn, Madeline stood up. "Sime is sort of sweet, you know? So crushed, so obliging! If I asked him to cut off his own head, he'd fetch an axe and do it. Boring, actually."

"Do go and call Mr. Cleveland, Madeline."

The daughter went out. Later Hugh Cleveland called again. The phone rang and rang until Rhoda answered. She went to her daughter's room and shouted at her through the bath door, over the sound of gushing water, to take the call.

"What the Christ does he want?" Madeline yelled. "I can't be bothered. Tell him I'm covered with soap."

Cleveland said he would wait until Madeline dried herself.

"Oh, Jesus! Tell him I like to soak myself for half an hour before I go to bed. This is outrageous, pestering me at half past two in the morning!"

"Madeline, I'll NOT go on with this idiotic bellowing through a door. Dry yourself and come out."

"I *WON'T*. And if he doesn't like it, tell him I quit, and to kindly go and hang himself."

"Hello? Mr. Cleveland? Better wait until morning. She's truly in a very bad mood."

"He'll call *you* in the morning," she carolled, her teasing sing-song conveying Madeline's victory.

"I couldn't care less," Madeline sang back.

Rhoda tossed in the darkness for almost an hour, then got up, fetched a writing pad and pen, and sat up in bed.

Dearest Pug—

I could write forty pages, expressing how I feel about you, and our life together, and the wonderful letter you've written me, but I'll keep this short. Of one thing I'm sure. You're mighty busy now!

First of all, Madeline. It's a long story, but the nub of it is she was frightened by an utterly false accusation and an utterly scurrilous threat. I'm sure she's innocent of any wrong-doing. She's come to stay with me for Christmas, so I don't feel totally alone, and I must say she's turned into quite the spiffy New York gal. Believe it or not, Sime Anderson still dances attendance! He took her out tonight. She's in excellent control of her situation, and you can put that problem out of your mind.

If you can do it, please put me out of your mind, too, for the next few months, except as the little old lady back home. You have a war to fight. What I said in my last letter still goes, but there's this *horrible* time lag in our correspondence, and we just can't thrash anything out this way. I've been around a long time, and I'm not going to do anything drastic. When you get back, I'll be right here in Foxhall Road, waiting like a good Navy wife in my best bib and tucker, with a full martini jug.

I cried when I read your offer to forget my letter and go on as before. That's like you. It's almost too generous to accept, and we both ought to take time to think about it. It may well be that I'm "not a schoolgirl," and that I've actually been going through a sort of middle-aged "hot flash." I'm doing my best to "sort myself out," right down to the bottom. That you would be willing to forgive me is almost inconceivable—to anyone who doesn't know you as I do. Believe me, I have never respected and loved you more or been more proud than when I read your letter.

There's no news yet about Natalie and her baby, is there? None here. Please send any news of Byron. Love to Warren, Janice, and little Vic—

And of course, and forever to you—

Rho

Having written this, and meant every word of it, Rhoda turned out the light and slept the sleep of the just.

9

POUNDING at the door.

The floor of the old Raffles Hotel bedroom shook as Pamela went running out, fumbling a negligee around her. "Who is it?"

"Phil Rule."

She opened the door and got a shock.

She had last seen him on the morning after the Japanese attack, all nervy and dashing in jungle war rig, about to fly a rented private plane to the front. Rule was a sport flyer, and in pursuing a combat story he could be foolhardy. He had first fascinated Pamela during the Spanish Civil War with tales of his wild plane flights; his romantic yarns salted with Marxist rhetoric had put her in mind of Malraux. Now he was sodden wet, his hair hung in strings, his unshaven face was gaunt and hollow-eyed, and his bandaged hand was horribly swollen. Beside him, just as drenched, a short hard-faced army officer with iron-gray hair slapped a dripping swagger stick on a palm.

"My God, Phil! Come in."

"This is Major Denton Shairpe."

Tudsbury limped out of his bedroom in droopy yellow silk pajamas. "Bless me, Philip, you're drowned," he yawned.

"There's a cloudburst outside. Can you give us some brandy? Penang has fallen. We've just come from there."

"Good Christ, *Penang?* No."

"Gone, I tell you. Gone."

"Are they *that* far south? Why, that island's a fortress!"

"It was. All Malaya's falling. It's an utter rout, and your broadcasts are criminal lies. Why in Christ's name are you sucking up to the mendacious incompetent bastards who've botched this show and probably lost the Empire—not that it was worth saving?"

"I've told the truth, Phil." Tudsbury's face flushed as he handed the two men glasses of brandy. "Such as I could find out."

"Bollocks. It's been a lot of *Rule Britannia* gooseberry jam. Malaya's gone, gone!"

"I say, jolly good brandy!" The major's voice was astonishingly high and sweet, almost like a girl's. "Don't mind Phil, he's got the wind up. He's never been through a retreat like this. Malaya isn't gone. We can still defeat these little bastards."

"Denton was on General Dobbie's staff," Rule said hoarsely to Tudsbury. "I don't agree with him, but listen to him! He'll give you something to broadcast."

Pamela went into her room for a bathrobe because Philip Rule kept staring at the thin silk over her breasts and thighs.

"Do you have a map of Malaya about?" Shairpe piped, as Tudsbury refilled his glass.

"Right here." Tudsbury went and lit a hanging lamp over a wicker table in mid-room.

Using his swagger stick as a pointer on the map, Shairpe explained that this campaign had all been foreseen. He had himself helped to plan General Dobbie's staff exercises. Years ago they had predicted where the Japs would probably land for an invasion, and how they would advance. Dobbie had even staged a mock invasion during the monsoon, to prove its feasibility. But nobody in the present Malaya Command seemed aware of the Dobbie studies. Indian and British troops in the north, caught off guard in a wild night storm, had retreated pell-mell from the Japanese beachhead. The Japs had come on fast. Fixed fallback positions around Jitra, built and stocked to hold out for a month, had fallen in hours. Since then the army had been stumbling backward without a plan.

Moreover, the troops were weakly dispersed over the peninsula— Shairpe flicked the stick here and there—to protect airfields foolishly sited by the RAF without consulting the army. Their defense could not be coordinated, and several fields had already fallen. So the Japs had taken control of the air. Furthermore, they had tanks. There was not one British tank in Malaya. The War Office in London had decided that tanks would be useless in jungle warfare. Unfortunately, Shairpe said in dry high nasal tones, the Japanese had not been informed of this piece of wisdom. Though their tanks were poor stuff, they were punching along unopposed, panicking the Asiatic troops. Antitank obstacles were piled in Singapore, but nobody was putting them in place.

With all this the defenders still had the edge, Shairpe insisted. Three Jap divisions had landed. The British could muster five, with plenty of air and ground reinforcements on the way. The Japs were well trained for jungle war—lightly dressed, able to live on fruits and roots, equipped with thousands of bicycles for fast movement down captured roads—but Japan was attacking all over the Pacific; and most likely this landing force had to live and fight on whatever supplies it had brought or could seize. If the defenders would scorch the earth, and force the invaders with delaying actions to use up their food, fuel, and bullets on the long march south, the attrition in time would halt them. They could then be destroyed.

Shairpe showed on the map where strong fall-back defenses ought to exist. General Dobbie's report had called for building these in peacetime. It hadn't been done—a major folly—but there was still time. The material lay ready in warehouses. A labor pool of two million Chinese and Malayans, who all hated and dreaded the Japs, was available. They could do the work in a week or ten days. Two very strong lines were needed, close in: one in Johore on the other side of the strait, the other along the north shore of Singapore Island itself, with underwater obstacles, petroleum pipes, searchlights, pillboxes, barbed wire, machine gun nests—

"But that's been done," Tudsbury interrupted him. "The north shore's already impregnable."

"You're wrong," Shairpe replied, his oddly girlish voice roughened by brandy. "There's nothing on the north shore of this island but marsh."

After a pop-eyed pause, Alistair Tudsbury said, "I saw massive fortifications there myself."

"You saw the outer walls of the base. They're to keep out busybodies. The base is not a defensible strong point."

"Are you telling me that the BBC has been lied to, by the highest officials in Singapore?"

"Oh, my dear fellow, the BBC's a propaganda channel. One uses you. That's all I'm here for. I hope you can somehow get the Malaya Command cracking." Shairpe thinly smiled and slapped the stick on his palm. "Phil says you've a heart of oak, and all that sort of thing. The Empire's teetering in the balance, Tudsbury. That's not journalism. That's a military fact."

Tudsbury stared at this calm, wet, powerfully convincing officer. "All right. Can you come back about nine this morning?" He was limping about the room in agitation. "I'll say up all night to draft this story. Then I want you to vet it."

"Really? Nine o'clock? Jolly good! Keen to help."

"But you've got to shield Denton," Rule put in, "even if they twist your balls in red-hot clamps."

Shairpe left. Rule asked if he might stay and doze in an armchair. He meant to go to a hospital at first light.

"Look, get off those wet clothes. Hang them up and have a bath," Tudsbury said. "Then use the extra bed in my room."

"Thanks awfully. I do stink all over. At Jitra we went wading through bogs. I had to pick forty leeches off myself. Filthy little horrors!"

"What's happened to your hand?" Pamela said. "It looks awful."

"Oh, an imbecile army medico lanced it at Jitra." Rule gave the hand a miserable, worried glance. "I hope I don't lose it. I may have a touch of blood poisoning, Pam. I'm shaking from head to foot."

Pamela smiled. With all his daredeviling, Rule had always been a hypochondriac. Tudsbury asked, "Where's your plane, Phil?"

"The Malacca airfield. We caught an army lorry from there. They wouldn't refuel me. Denton and I flew there from Penang. We had to beat people off the plane at Penang, Talky, and I mean white people. Army officers, in fact!"

Pamela drew a bath and laid out fresh towels, but then she found him asleep in his clothes. She took off his boots and outer uniform, which had a foul swampy odor, and tucked the mosquito netting about him. As she rolled him about, he muttered in his sleep.

Memories assailed her. Up till now, here in Singapore, he had been the ex-lover: older, sleekly flirtatious, repellent. But this big worn-out dishevelled blond man, lying asleep in his dank underwear with everything showing, seemed much more the Phil Rule of Paris days. Russian wife and all, at least he was not ordinary! In Paris he had always been—in his jagged and tormenting fashion—fun.

"What the devil, Pamela?" Tudsbury called. "Get at the typewriter and let's go."

Stumping here and there, waving his arms, he dictated a broadcast called "Conversation with a Defeatist." At the Golf Club, he recounted, he had talked with a crusty old retired army colonel, full of alarmist opinions. Denton Shairpe's views came out as this old carper's words. Defeatism tended to conjure up such nightmares, Tudsbury pointed out, and the story showed a human side of the Singapore defenders. He himself was sure that the fixed defense lines existed, that the fighting retreat was going wholly according to plan, and that the north shore of Singapore Island was a bristling death trap. This episode merely proved that free speech still prevailed in Fortress Singapore, that democracy in Malaya remained self-confident.

When he finished, Pamela opened the blackout curtain. The sky was gray. Rain was still coming down hard.

"Adroit, what?" her father asked, when she failed to comment. "Tells the story, yet they can't fault me."

She said, rubbing her eyes, "You'll never get away with it."

"We'll see. I'm going to catch an hour's sleep."

Major Shairpe, much spruced up and wearing a pith helmet, arrived on the dot of nine. Making a few small rapid corrections on the script in pencil, he piped, "I say, you've got the hell of a retentive memory, Tudsbury."

"Long practice."

"Well, it's a smasher. Most ingenious. Congratulations! Hope it has some effect. I shall be listening for it up-country. Jolly glad Phil got me to come."

Pamela dropped the script at the censor's office and went shopping. Buyers were crowding in and out of the stores, mostly run by Chinese, and still crammed with peacetime goods at far cheaper prices than in London—silk lingerie, jewelry, gourmet food and wines, kid gloves, elegant shoes and purses. But in nearly every store there now hung a copy of the same sign, newly printed in vaguely Oriental red lettering: *Cash Only Please—No More Charge Accounts or Chits.*

"Is that you, Pam?" Tudsbury called as she dropped her bundles on the map table.

"Yes. Any news?"

"Rather. I've been summoned to Government House." He emerged from his room freshly shaved and ruddy, in a white linen suit and a rakishly tilted hat, with a pugnacious gleam in his eye. "Berlin all over again!"

"Did Phil ever wake up?"

"Long since. He left a note in your bedroom. Cheerio!"

Rule had written in childish block letters: *"Excuse left hand printing luv. Appreciate thoughtfulness mosquito netting. Sorry you had to put on bathrobe due my sudden attack of memory and desire. My hand's killing me. A toi, Malraux."*

She threw the note into a wastebasket, and fell fast asleep on a couch. The telephone woke her. An hour had passed.

"Hello, Pam?" Tudsbury sounded excited and gay. "Throw together a bag for me. I'll be travelling for about a week."

"Travelling? Where to?"

"Can't talk now."

"Shall I also pack?"

"No."

He soon arrived, his suit dark-patched with sweat at the armpits. "Where's the bag?"

"On your bed, all ready."

"Let me have a stiff gin and bitters. The fat's in the fire, Pamela. My destination's Australia."

"Australia!"

"I am in very, very hot water, my dear." He threw off his jacket, opened his tie, and fell into an armchair with a creak. "It's *worse* than Berlin. By God, that script raked raw nerves! The governor and Brooke-Popham were fairly jigging with rage. I got the unruly native treatment, Pam. These two lords of creation actually tried to bully me. Bloody fools, they're the ones who are in trouble. But they're determined to throttle anybody who wants to shake them out of their dream world. It was an hour of revelation, Pam, bitter and ominous revelation. What I saw was dry rot, pervasive and terrible, at the very top. Ah, thank you." He gulped the drink.

"What am I to do? Follow you?"

"No. Brooke-Popham's about to be relieved. Find out what you can. Keep notes. I'll hurry back and cover this battle, but that script must go on the air."

"Talky, there's censorship in Australia."

"Nothing like this. It can't be. The unreality, the unreality! The self-contradiction! Do you know, they first said they had the fixed defense lines. Then no, they admitted they hadn't, because the labor wasn't available! As for Shairpe's native labor pool idea, they called it ignorant poppycock. Malaya's mission is to earn dollars. Every native taken from the gum trees or the tin mines hurts the war effort—this, mind you, with mines and plantations falling day by day to the Japs! Also, the government can't compete with the pay scale of the planters and mine companies. To commandeer the labor at government rates would take three months of correspondence with the War Office. That's how their minds are working, Pamela, with Penang gone and the Japs roaring south."

"Singapore will fall," Pam said, wildly wondering how she could get out of this place.

"Not if Shairpe's view prevails. I've lent myself to this government's suicidal sham. Now I must make amends. Thank God Phil brought Shairpe here—hullo, here we go!" He sprang at the ringing telephone. "Yes? Yes?—Ah, beautiful! Superb. Thank you—Pam, they did it! They bumped a poor American merchant off the flying boat. I'm on my way."

"You'll be in Australia for Christmas, then. And I'll be here."

"Pam, what's to be done? It's the war. This should be a historic broadcast. The BBC can sack me afterward. I don't really care. Once the deed's done, and the dust settles, I'll come back, or you'll fly to Australia." Tudsbury babbled all this as he combed his hair, straightened his tie, and ran to get his bag. "Sorry to bolt like this. It's only for a few days."

"But will the Japanese come in those few days? That's what I'm wondering."

"Do you think I'd abandon you to face that? They're three hundred miles away, and advancing only a few miles a day."

"Well, good. Given the choice, I'd rather not be raped by platoons of slavering Orientals."

"See here, do you feel I'm treating you badly?"

"Oh, Talky, on your way! Merry Christmas."

"That's my girl. Cheerio."

Major Shairpe had told the plain truth. Fortress Singapore was a phantom. What the Tudsburys had seen from the arriving aircraft was the simple fact. It wasn't there.

When an empire dies, it dies like a cloudy day, without a visible moment of sunset. The demise is not announced on the radio, nor does one read of it in the morning paper. The British Empire had fatally depleted itself in the great if laggard repulse of Hitler, and the British people had long since willed the end of the Empire, by electing pacifist leaders to gut the military budgets. Still when the end was upon them, it was hard to face. Illusion is an anodyne, bred by the gap between wish and reality. Such an illusion was Fortress Singapore.

It was not a bluff. Nothing is clearer from Churchill's memoirs than that he himself believed that there was a fortress at Singapore. Of all the people on the spot—army officers, naval officers, colonial administrators, all the way up the grand chain of command—there was not one man to tell the Prime Minister that Fortress Singapore did not exist. And the British belief in the "bastion of Empire" was infectious, at least for Europeans. Hermann Göring warned a visiting Japanese general, months before Japan struck, that Fortress Singapore would hold out for a year and a half. This same general later captured Singapore in seventy days.

Nor was the illusion generated out of thin air. Singapore did command the main eastern trade routes, at the water passage between the Indian Ocean and the South China Sea. In the lean pacifist years, many millions in military funds had been poured into it, for the Japanese threat had been anticipated. Early in the century the English had themselves built Japan's modern navy, with great profit to British shipyards. The quaint feudal Japanese had caught on fast, defeating Czarist Russia's navy to the warm applause of the British press. But when the smoke of the First World War cleared away, the shift in world forces made it conceivable that those same quaint Nipponese might one day try to vex the Empire. Accordingly, the gigantic naval base at Singapore, capable of servicing the whole Royal Navy, had been constructed. The plan was that if ever trouble from Japan threatened, the main fleet would steam to Singapore, to end the trouble by awe or by force. That the Germans might make trouble at the same time, requiring the main fleet to stay at home, seems to have been overlooked.

So Singapore was stocked with food, fuel, and ammunition for a siege of seventy days. That was the time the fleet would need to muster up and get there. Great fixed cannon pointed seaward, to hold off any attempted assault by the Japanese fleet before help came. All this did give the feeling of a fortress.

Yet the sea did not entirely moat Singapore. An attack could come by land from the north, down the wild Malayan peninsula and across the narrow Johore Strait. But the planners judged that four hundred miles of jungle made a stouter barrier than fortress walls. Moreover, actual walls on the island's north side, they felt, would suggest a fear that the Japanese might come from the north one day, and that the British army might not be able to stop them. The British ruled in Asia by an aura of invincibility. With the main fleet seventy days away, what pressing need was there for such a mortifying precaution? The walls were not built. Instead, to make assurance doubly sure, Singapore Island's stockpile was doubled to last one hundred forty days.

Thus the "Fortress Singapore" image arose. The years of planning, the outpouring of treasure, the rivers of ink in newspapers and journals, the resounding political and military debates, fostered an all but universal fantasy, reaching to Britain's highest leaders, and all over the Western world, that a fortress was there. The lifeblood of the British working class went into a naval base twenty miles square, with the largest docks in the world, with cranes, repair shops, every conceivable spare part and machine, elaborate housing and recreation facilities; and with enough ammunition, food, and oil to supply the whole fleet for many months, squirrelled away in the giant concrete caverns sunk in the swamps. In its way it was as striking an engineering feat as the Maginot Line.

But to the last, to the moment when the last retreating Scots brigade crossed the causeway in February with bagpipes playing, and demolition charges blew a hole in the one link to the mainland swarming with oncoming Japanese soldiers, the north side of Singapore remained without defenses: defenses that Churchill always assumed were there, as—in his own words—he assumed that "a battleship could not be launched without a bottom."

In the event, the fleet never came. It was too busy fighting the Germans in the Atlantic, in the Mediterranean, and in home waters. The vast facilities stood empty until, with the Japanese army a mile away, the British did their best to blow up or burn the base. But it fell in usable condition, a staggering military haul. Churchill's insistence on trying a ragged remnant of the seventy-day plan, by dispatching the *Prince of Wales* and the *Repulse,* only doomed them.

Airfields had also been laid out in Malaya and heavily stocked up—except with planes. The RAF never came in force. It had lost too many planes saving England from the Luftwaffe, and had shipped hundreds more to the Soviet Union; though of those a large number never flew, sunk in the sea by German torpedoes. The few aircraft on hand in Malaya were shot from the sky fast. The Japanese planes "made of bamboo shoots and rice paper" turned out to be Zeroes, the most advanced fighter aircraft then on the planet. The Japanese seized the splendid airstrips, which they called "Churchill aerodromes"; and from these richly supplied fields their planes helped batter Singapore into surrender.

So the confused Singapore record now reads. Congress investigated Pearl Harbor, but Parliament did not investigate Singapore. Churchill shouldered the blame, stooped an inch or two lower, and went on with the fight.

The confusion still extends to the very name. What was "Singapore"?

Singapore was the city; Singapore was the island; Singapore was the naval base; Singapore was "the bastion of Empire." But at bottom "Singapore" was a narcotic myth, which dulled the pain while the gripping hand of white Europe on Asia was amputated.

The unused strategy of General Dobbie—so it turned out after the war—had been absolutely sound, for the invaders did arrive at Singapore at their last gasp, greatly outnumbered by the defenders, their fuel and bullets almost spent. In one final assault, they daringly burned up and shot off everything they had left. The Singapore command caved in, and the colored Malayans had new masters with colored skins.

Alistair Tudsbury made his broadcast from Australia. Pamela heard him in the McMahons' guest cottage, where Philip Rule, arm in a sling, was bedridden. The hand had been lanced again, and he had to rest for a week. The McMahons and their dinner guests down at the main house had shown little interest in listening to her father. After a copious *pahit* and a big meal with several wines, they were singing carols around a piano. Through the darkness, over the drumming of the rain and the bass croaking of bullfrogs from nearby mangroves, their voices dimly floated to the cottage, where Pamela sat under a large slowly turning fan that stirred her hair and fluttered her thin long skirt. Perhaps half as bright as a candle, the radio dial diffused a faint orange glow in the room. Through the open window came sprays of rain and wisps of frangipani scent.

The reception was good, the script almost intact. The fictitious colonel no longer asserted that the island's north shore was undefended; it needed "some dashed double-quick stiffening." The charge that the RAF had put down airfields without regard for their defensibility was gone; and Tudsbury's closing disclaimer was more strongly phrased.

"Was it worth it, Phil?" Pamela asked, turning down the sound but leaving the dial to glow.

He drew on a cigarette, his face shadowed with deep lines of bitter irony. He was looking better. Rule was very strong, and a few days of rest pulled him out of most distempers. "A wee bit too clever. The dotty old crank came off quite lifelike. It won't be taken seriously, not by anybody who counts."

"How else could Talky have done it?"

"I don't know. I'm amazed it got by, even so."

"Phil, will Singapore fall?"

Rule harshly laughed. "Darling, I fear so. But blaming the governor, or Brooke-Popham, or Duff Cooper, or even Churchill is pointless. There's just a general collapse. Nothing's working. The system's just rotten-ripe to fall apart. Up-country there's simply no leadership. The men want to fight. They *try* to fight, even the Indian troops do. But again and again come these pusillanimous orders from Singapore—fall back, pull out, retreat. I've seen the men crying over their orders. These Tanglin Club overlords down here have bad consciences, Pam. They're played-out funks. They fear the Japs, and they fear our own Asiatics. When you think about it, this domination of Asia by white Europeans has always been damned silly. It was bound to be temporary. Why grieve at its passing?"

"How do I get out of Singapore?"

"Oh, you'll get out. The Japs are still far off. There are vessels waiting to evacuate the white women and children. That's what they did at Penang, you know. They got out the Europeans—soldiers and all—and left the Asiatics with their women and children to face the Japs. Do you know that? And then Duff Cooper went on the air and announced that *all the inhabitants of Penang had been rescued!* He really meant it, Pamela. To Duff Cooper, the Asiatics were part of the animal life of Penang. It's causing an uproar now—what happened, and what he said. I don't think the Asiatics care anymore who's top dog here. Maybe we're gentler than the Japanese, but at least they're colored. The Asian endures brutality better than contempt."

"You don't believe in the American rescue expedition everyone's talking about?"

"Wishful fantasy. The Americans have no fleet. It was all sunk at Pearl Harbor."

"Nobody knows what happened at Pearl Harbor."

"Denton Shairpe does. They lost all eight of their battleships. The Americans are finished for two years in the Pacific, if not forever. A rescue expedition for Singapore is as likely to come from Switzerland, but—what the hell's the matter with you?" Pamela Tudsbury was burying her face in an arm on the back of the chair. "Pamela! What is it?" She did not answer. "Oh, Christ, you're thinking of your Yank! Sorry, old girl. When Denton first told me, I thought of him myself. Pam, I know nothing about the casualties. There's every chance your man's all right. They were sunk inside a harbor, in shallow water."

Still she said nothing and did not move. Outside, the rain, the bull-frogs, and a distant chorus—

> *God rest ye merry, gentlemen,*
> *Let nothing you dismay—*

Suddenly a wild gibbering and giggling just outside the window, as by a frightened lunatic, made Pamela sit up with a shriek. "Oh! My God! What's *that?*"

"Easy now. That's our apricot monkey. He comes and goes in the trees. Sounds dreadful, but he's harmless."

"God Almighty, I hate Singapore! I would have hated it in peace-time." Pamela stumbled to her feet, wiping her moist brow. "Let the Japanese have it, and good riddance! I'm going back to the house. Are you all right? Do you want anything?"

"I'll be lonely, but that's no reason for you to miss the fun. Run along."

"Fun! I just don't want to be rude to my hosts. They'll be thinking I've gotten into bed with a sick man."

"Well, why don't you, Pam?" She stared at him. "Truly, wouldn't it be charming? Christmas Eve and all that? Remember Christmas Eve in Montmartre? When Slote and Natalie had that monumental fight at dawn, and we went sneaking off to Les Halles for onion soup?" The mustache twisted in a slow beguiling well-remembered smile, shadowy in the orange radio glow. He held out his good arm. "Come, Tuds-bury."

"You're a swine, Philip, an unchanging swine"—Pam's voice trembled—"and everything else I called you in our little Bastille Day chat."

"Darling, I was born in a rotting system, and so perhaps I'm a rotter, if the word has any meaning. Let's not have that old quarrel again, but aren't you the inconsistent one? When everything's breaking up, there's nothing but pleasure. You believe that yourself. I take my pleasures lightly, you insist on drama. That won't change, I grant you. I do love you."

"And your wife? I'm just curious. In Paris you had no wife, at least."

"Sweetie, I don't know if she's alive. If she is, I hope she's screwing the brains out of some nice deserving Russian fighting man on leave. Though I doubt it, she's a worse prig than most Englishwomen are nowadays."

Pamela plunged out the door.

"You'll need the umbrella," he called after her.

She returned, snatched the umbrella, and darted outside. She had not gone ten steps in the blackness, when, almost at her ear, the monkey set up its blood-freezing cry. With a little scream Pamela sprinted forward and ran into a tree. The bark scratched her face. The branches swept the umbrella from her hand and showered her. She caught it up and stood paralyzed, soaking wet. Almost straight ahead she could hear the singing—

> *There'll always be an England,*
> *While there's a country lane—*

but the night was pitch-black. She had come by starlight, in an interval between showers. She had no clear idea of how to proceed. The path twisted steeply through the banks of oleanders and bougainvillea.

It was a bad moment for Pamela. Her father's broadcast had sunk her spirits. The familiar voice, coming from so far away, had intensified her nervous sense of being alone and unprotected. In recent days, threatening Japanese broadcasts in broken English had scared her. The guttural alien voices had sounded so close, so horrible! She had almost felt calloused hands with tough nails ripping at her underwear and forcing her thighs apart. More than most threatened females she knew how weak Singapore was.

And now Rule had Shairpe's word that Victor Henry's ship had been sunk! Even if Henry had survived, he would be reassigned. Even if she got out of Singapore, she would probably never see him again. And if she should, by some bizarre chance, then what? Did he not have a wife? She had set out on a wild goose chase around the world, and here she was, wet and lost in the hot black night, under an umbrella in the garden of strangers in a downpour, on Christmas Eve, perhaps her last.

> *There'll always be an England,*
> *And England shall be free—*

She did not want to join these drunken Singapore British in their songs. This cheap ditty unbearably brought back the first days of the war, the brilliant summer of the Battle of Britain, and the best moment of her life, when Commander Henry had come back from the flight over Berlin and she had flung herself into his arms. All that glory was crumbled now. She liked the McMahons, but their friends were dullards from the club crowd and the army. Two young staff lieutenants had been paying court to her, from the *pahit* drinking onward; both crashing bores but handsome animals, especially a long-faced blond lieutenant with a languid Leslie Howard air. They would be after her again, as soon as she returned to the house—if she could find her way without falling on her face in muck. Obviously they both were intent on sleeping with her; if not tonight, another night.

How wrong were they? What did it matter? What was her spell of continence, vaguely for Victor Henry's sake, but a stupid out-of-character joke, after all the damned screwing she had done in her life?

Behind her, the open window of the guest cottage was a faint orange oblong in the dark. To someone who did not know it was really there, it would have seemed an optical illusion. In the all-encompassing blackness and rain, it was the only hint of light, the only way to go.

10

BYRON had never heard a depth charge detonate under water; nor had anybody else on the *Devilfish*.

A hideous ear-splitting *BONG* shuddered through the whole vessel, like the blow of a sledgehammer on a giant bell. The control room tumbled in nauseating earthquake motions; glass smashed, loose objects flew, and the lights blinked scarily, all in the roaring reverberation of a thunderclap. While the planesmen managed to cling to their control wheels, the plotting party went staggering, Chief Derringer falling to his hands and knees, the others toppling against bulkheads. Byron felt such sharp stabbing pains in his ankles that he feared they were broken. An instrument box sprang off the overhead and dangled on an electric cable, emitting blue sparks and the stinking smoke of burning rubber. Confused yells echoed through the vessel.

BONG!

This second metallic thunderbolt blacked out the lights and flung the deck bow-upward. In the darkness the blue sparks kept flaring, terrified groans and shouts arose over the thunderous roaring outside the hull, and a heavy body with flailing arms fetched up against Byron, crushing his back agonizingly against the ladder to the conning tower.

This time it truly felt like the end, with the submarine on a horrible upslant, sounds of breakage all around, Derringer weighing him down like a warm corpse—he could smell the tobacco breath—and the Japanese sonar baying loud, fast, and triumphant on short scale: *peeng-peeng-peeng-peeng!* Another explosion made the tortured hull scream and ring. A squirt of cold water struck Byron's face.

Except for the lancing death in its torpedoes, the *Devilfish* was very weak and very slow. Even on the surface it could go only half as fast as the destroyer overhead. Underwater its sprint was eleven knots, its usual crawl three knots. The destroyer could run circles around it, probing for it with sonar; and the tumbling depth charges did not even have to hit. Water transmits an explosion in a shock wave. A miss thirty feet off could finish the *Devilfish*. It was just a tube of nine long narrow cylinders joined together, a habitable section of sewer pipe. Its pressure hull was less than an inch thick.

It had only one military advantage to balance its feeble sluggishness—surprise; and it had blown its surprise. Now it was a creeping scorpion in a flashlight beam. Its only resort was to dive; the deeper it dove, the less the chance of being found and pinned by sound echoes. But in Lingayen that refuge was denied. The test depth of a fleet submarine, then a guarded secret, was four hundred twenty feet, and the safety margin was close to a hundred percent. *In extremis* the submarine captain could as a rule burrow down as far as six hundred feet, with some hope that his poor tube might survive the leaks springing at the fittings. Deeper, the heavy black fist of the sea would crumple the steel hull like tinfoil. Hoban would gladly have risked the *Devilfish* beyond test depth now; but the end of the line for him in most of Lingayen was shallow muck at about a hundred feet.

There were other hazards. A surface ship had a natural balance, but a submerged submarine was a waterlogged object. Trapped air bubbles in its tanks held it suspended, a wobbly thing hard to control. Water and fuel oil, pumped here and there through pipe mazes, made the long tube tilt one way or another, and the submarine unfolded planes much like an aircraft's to steady it. But the vessel had to keep moving or the planes would not work.

Stopped for long, a submarine like the *Devilfish* was done for. It would slowly sink below its test depth—or in this case, into the muck—or it would pop to the surface to face the destroyer's five-inch guns. And it could not keep moving underwater for more than a few hours, at any speed. For underwater there is no air for a combustion engine to consume. As it had only so much bottled air for its crew to breathe in a dive, so it had only so much stored power to use. Then it had to stop, lie on the bottom, or come up for air to burn fuel and get itself going again.

On the surface, the submarine wound itself up for moving underwater. The diesels not only drove the boat but also charged two huge banks of batteries with energy to their chemical brim. Submerged, the *Devilfish* would draw on these batteries. The faster it moved underwater, the quicker the batteries would go flat. At three or four knots it could stay down for about twenty-four hours. Doing radical escape maneuvers at ten knots, it would be finished in an hour or so. In extreme hazard, the captain could try to outwait his pursuer, lying on the bottom while the crew used up its air. That was the final limit: forty-eight to seventy-two hours of lying doggo, and a submarine had to choose between asphyxiation below and destroyer guns above.

The lights flickered yellowly on. Byron wiped the salt water off his face—from some fitting strained by the explosion but holding, thank God! The chief pushed himself off Byron, his mouth forming apologetic words the ensign was too deafened to hear. However, as through cotton wool he did hear Aster directly overhead bawling, "Captain, he's got our depth cranked in. We're getting creamed. Why don't we go to fifty feet and give him a knuckle?"

The captain's voice blared in the tube, "Briny, come up to fifty feet! *Fifty feet!* Acknowledge!"

"Fifty feet! Aye aye, sir!"

The planesmen steadied the vessel to climb. Their response was calm and expert, though both of them looked over their shoulders at Byron with round eyes in livid faces. As it climbed through the depth charge turbulence, the *Devilfish* made a sharp turn to create the "knuckle," more turbulence to baffle the echo-ranging. The sailors clung to anything handy. Locking an elbow on the ladder, Byron noted on the depth gauges that the power plant must still be working, for at this angle and rate of climb they were making ten knots. Four more explosions shook the deck; hideous sounds, but farther off. This time nothing broke in the control room, though the sailors swayed and staggered, and particles of loose debris rattled in Byron's face.

"Levelling off at fifty feet, Captain!"

"Very well. Everything okay down there?"

"Seems to be, sir." Derringer was yanking at the broken sparking cable. The other sailors, shakily cursing, were picking instruments and rubbish off the deck.

Several more charges rumbled and grumbled below, each one duller and farther away. Then Byron's heart jumped, as the pings of the Jap destroyer shifted to long scale: *p-i-i-i-ng! pi-i-i-ng!* In the Pearl Harbor drills that had been the moment of triumph, the hunter's mournful wailing confession that he had lost the scent, and was forced back to routine search; and the down Doppler—the lowered pitch of the sound—betrayed that the destroyer had turned away from the *Devilfish*.

A joy as intense as his previous fear, a wave of warm physical delight, swept over Byron. They had shaken loose, and he rode in a blooded submarine! The *Devilfish* had survived a depth charging! It had taken hard punishment, and it had eluded its pursuer. All the submarine action narratives he had ever read paled once for all into gray words. All the peacetime drills seemed child's play. Nobody could describe a depth charging, you had to live through it. By comparison, the bombings he had experienced in Warsaw and Cavite had been mild scares. This was the real thing, the cold skull-grin of the Angel of Death, frightful enough to test any man at war. Such thoughts shot through Byron Henry's mind with the joyous relief, when he heard the destroyer pinging again on long scale with down Doppler.

Things became quieter. The plotting team gathered again around the dead reckoning tracer. Aster and Captain Hoban descended from the conning tower to watch the picture form. The plot soon coalesced into two course lines; the destroyer heading toward the beachhead at Lingayen, the *Devilfish* moving the opposite way.

Aster said, grinning with relief, "I guess he figures we'd still try for the landing area."

"I don't know what he's figuring, but this is just great!" Hoban turned to Byron. "All right. Tour the compartments, Briny, and let me have a survey of the damage."

"Aye aye, sir."

"And talk to the crew. See how they're doing. We got some crazy screaming about water in the after torpedo room. Maybe a valve came unseated for a minute, or something."

The captain spoke in collected tones, and seemed in every way himself, yet something about him was changed. Was it the vanished mustache? No, not that. It was the look of his eyes, Byron thought; they seemed bigger and brighter, yet dark-ringed as though with fatigue. Hoban's brown eyes now dominated his face, alert, concerned, and shiny. The boss man had tasted his full responsibility. That would sober anybody. As Byron left the control room, Lady Aster, moistening the end of a Havana, gave him a contorted wink.

Every compartment had some minor breakage or malfunction to report—dangling bunks, shattered lamp bulbs, overturned tables, jammed water lines—but under the pounding the *Devilfish* had proved remarkably resilient; that was the sum of what Byron saw. Nothing essential to operations was down. The crew was another matter. Their condition ranged from pallid shock to profane defiance, but the note all through the submarine was dispirited; not so much because of the depth charging, though there was much obscene comment on its terrors—and in one compartment a strong smell of befouled trousers—but because the torpedoes had missed. They had taken the beating for nothing. It was a sour outcome after all the E's in drills. This crew was used to success. Some sailors ventured mutters to Byron about the captain's hasty shot on slow setting.

When Byron brought back his report to the wardroom, Aster and Hoban had their heads bent over a sketch for the battle account. The captain was diagramming his attack in orange ink for the enemy track, blue for the *Devilfish,* and red for the torpedoes. Hoban's diagrams were always textbook models. "I *saw* those wakes, goddamn it, Lady," he said wistfully, inking ruled lines. "Those new magnetic exploders are defective. I'm going to say so, by God, in the war diary and in the action report both. I don't care if I hang for it. I know our range was long, but we had an excellent solution. The wakes went directly under the first and third ships. Those ships should have had their backs broken. The torpedoes never exploded."

"Better check in with plot before you take the watch," Aster said casually to Byron. "We're heading for the entrance."

"The entrance?"

The captain's dark-ringed eyes gleamed at the puzzled note. "Of course. The whole landing area is on submarine alert now, Briny. We can't accomplish anything there. Up at the entrance we might find some fat pickings."

"Yes, Captain."

Over Hoban's head, as he bent over the diagram, Aster grotesquely winked again. The implication was clear and jarring to Byron. The mission of the *Devilfish,* the only way it could now justify twenty years of maintenance and training, was to oppose the Japanese landing at the beachhead, no matter what the risk. They were being paid for extra-hazardous duty! Byron had assumed that, once out of the attack area, Hoban would unquestionably circle and make for the troop transports. This was the submarine's moment, the reason it had been built and manned. Giving prudent arguments, Branch Hoban was abandoning the mission with an intact submarine, still loaded with twenty torpedoes.

They had evaded but not shaken off the destroyer. Its long-scale pings still shivered sadly and faintly in the *Devilfish*'s sonar receiver.

On Derringer's plot the Japanese search plan soon became clear: a pattern of widening squares, much as in American antisubmarine doctrine. Off Pearl Harbor, in the peacetime exercises, a submarine that had gotten clear of its pursuer would send a sonar signal, and the destroyer would speed over for another attack run; the search phase being a tedious boring process that wasted time and fuel. But now the process was far from boring; it was the real thing, ugly, tense, and perilous. The searcher above intended to find and sink the *Devilfish*. His chances still were good.

For though the scorpion was out of the flashlight beam now, and crawling away in the dark, there was no satisfactory place to hide. Hoban had heavily depleted his batteries. The pursuer, fresh from Japan with full oil bunkers, could steam at eight or ten times Hoban's normal underwater speed. In another few hours the *Devilfish* would have a "flat can"—no battery juice left. Much now depended on brute luck. Hoban was making a beeline away from the point where the destroyer had lost him. That was doctrine, though Byron (and obviously Aster, too) thought he should not be heading for the entrance. The destroyer captain, having completed two tight squares, was heading out on a wider sweep. If he happened to choose the right turns, he might pick up the unseen crawler again. But the night sea was a gloomy tossing blank, the choices were infinite, and failure was discouraging. Also, he might be called off to other duty. These were the hopeful factors in the problem; except that "problem" was a peacetime word, somewhat too bland for the dogged pursuit by this anonymous menace.

Standing watch in the conning tower, Byron heard the captain and the exec discuss tactics. The time of sunset had passed, and Aster wanted to surface. Running on the diesels, they could race out of the destroyer's search pattern at flank speed, and charge up the can for more underwater action; perhaps for an attack on this very pursuer. Hoban roundly vetoed the idea. "Goddamn it, Lady, surface? How can we gamble on unknowns? What's the weather like up there? Suppose it's a calm crystal-clear night? We might be up-moon from him—ever think of that? A black tin duck in the moonlight! Even the periscope could show up in binoculars. How reliable are our sonar ranges? Plus or minus a mile, we figure, but with five-inch guns waiting for us up there, maybe we'd better make that *two* miles, hey? All right. Plot has him at what now—seven thousand?"

"Seventy-five hundred and opening, sir, with strong down Doppler."

"All right. Even so! At three or four thousand yards a lookout can pick us up with binoculars. It's all poppycock that Japs can't see in the dark. If that destroyer spots us surfaced with a flat can, we've had the course. Now if *we* could open the range to twelve or fourteen thousand, surfacing might make some sense. In fact, that's the thing to try for. Byron! Go to seven knots."

"Seven knots, sir?"

"Are you deaf? Seven knots."

"Seven knots. Aye aye, sir."

The decision baffled Byron. Aster's face went dead blank. At seven knots the *Devilfish* had little more than an hour of underwater propulsion left. Captain Hoban, in an attempt to be cautious, seemed to be invading the last margin of safety.

Plot reported the Japanese destroyer making a turn; and after a short interval, another turn. Sonar announced, "Up Doppler." The destroyer was now closing the *Devilfish*. The power-consuming time dragged on, while in the conning tower Aster and the captain speculated on the pursuer's last action. Had the Jap picked up a stray sonar echo? Had he by bad luck gotten an echo from a school of fish, in the submarine's direction? Should they change course? Hoban elected to bear on toward the entrance. The sonar range gradually dropped to seven thousand yards; twenty minutes later, to six thousand—three miles. If the night was dark or rainy, Byron thought, they still might surface and flee at twenty-one knots. Why didn't the skipper at least chance a periscope glimpse of the weather? As the range dropped to four thousand, the option to surface was dimming. Sonar pings now began reverberating faintly through the hull itself. Byron's remaining hope was that the destroyer would pass without picking up an echo; but this faded too, when he heard Derringer announce below, in a sepulchral voice, that the destroyer was turning to a collision course.

Aster came scrambling up the ladder, eyes narrowed, dead gray cigar clenched in his teeth. "Battle stations, Briny."

"What now?"

"Well, he's found us, all right. The captain's going to the bottom."

"Will that work?"

"Depends."

"On what?"

"For one thing, on how good his sonar is. Maybe he can't screen out bottom return."

Byron remembered this tactic from submarine school exercises off New London. Echo-ranging on a vessel on the bottom was inexact; the random return diffused the readings. Hurrying down the ladder to his post as diving officer, he saw Captain Hoban staring at the plot, where the destroyer's pencilled course was curving in, dot by dot, toward the white moving point of the *Devilfish*.

"Flood negative! Retract sonar head!" Hoban plunged for the ladder, shouting up through the hatch. "Lady, give me a fathometer reading and pass the word for all hands to stand by to ground! Hard right rudder!"

The submarine mushed downward, slowing and turning. Byron levelled off, well above fathometer depth. Shortly there came a jolt, another jolt, and the *Devilfish* settled, rocking and grinding, on the mud; according to the depth gauges, at the exact figure of the fathometer reading—eighty-seven feet.

Silence, dead waiting silence, in the *Devilfish;* outside, loud long-scale pings, and the mutter of propellers. On the dead reckoning tracer, the destroyer track moved closer and closer to the halted point of light. The propeller noise intensified. Derringer was getting no sonar ranges now, the attacker was too close; he was projecting the destroyer's track by using his ears and his judgment. As Byron's breath all but failed him, the pencil line passed the point of light, and slowly moved away. A sharp fall of pitch of the long-scale pings to down Doppler confirmed Derringer's guesswork plot. All the men in the control room heard it—the young sailors, the young officer, the old chief—and all looked around at each other with wan hope.

How totally a submariner depended on the captain, Byron thought, how crucial was confidence in him! Though he had once hated Hoban, he had never until now doubted his skill; he had in fact resented his crushing superiority. Now the rat of panic was gnawing at Byron's spirit. Was he in shaky or amateurish hands, after all, a hundred feet down in the sea in a long vulnerable metal tube, waiting for a ship on the surface to dynamite him to a vile death by drowning? Black seawater under terrible pressure gripped the thin hull; one opened seam, one blown valve, and his life would be choked out by flooding salt water. He would never again see Natalie, nor even once lay eyes on the baby he had fathered. He would rot on the floor of Lingayen Gulf, and fish would swim in and out of his bones.

This awareness of being in peril under water, which submariners suppress but never for a moment wholly forget, was clamping a cold hold on Byron Henry. Not forty-eight hours ago, just before reporting to the Marsman building, he had been jolting down a Manila boulevard in hot sunshine, perched in the back of a truck on a crated mine, jocularly drinking beer with his working party. And now—

Derringer said huskily, "Mr. Henry, I think he's turning back."

The pinging outside shifted to short scale.

Now fear stabbed Byron's very bowels. This time the submarine was caught; caught dead on the bottom and almost out of power, and he was caught in it, and all this was no dream, dreamlike though the horror seemed. Death under the sea was now coming at him, screaming through the short-scale pings in malevolent rising glee, *"Found you! Found you! Found you!"*

The faces in the control room took on one expression—stark terror. Chief Derringer was not looking at the plot, but staring vacantly upward, his heavy mouth wide open, his big fat face a Greek mask of fright; the man had five children and two grandchildren. The propellers came drumming and thrashing directly overhead once again—*KER-DA-TRAMM! TRAMM! TRAMM!* Morelli at the bow planes clutched his crucifix, crossed himself, and muttered a prayer.

Click, click, click, like little pebbles or balls bouncing on the hull; it was the arming of the depth charges at their preset depth, though Byron did not know that this caused the noise. He too was praying; nothing complicated, just, "God, let me live. God, let me live."

11

THE block leader's yells and curses rouse the Russian prisoners at
4:30 A.M. from their uneasy dozing. It is the only sleep they can
get, jammed three in a bunk in the cold and stench of the quarantine
camp blockhouses, on straw pallets crawling with vermin. Getting down
from his upper bunk for roll call, Berel Jastrow murmurs the obligatory
Hear O Israel morning devotion. He should wash first, but that can't
be done, water is a hundred yards away and forbidden at this hour. He
adds the Talmud's brisk summary prayer for times of danger, and con-
cludes, *"Yehi ratzon sheekhye*—Let me live." Next will come an hour
or more of standing at attention in ranks, in the icy wind and darkness
of the Polish midwinter, clad in a thin prison suit of striped ticking.

"Let me live" is a practical heartfelt plea. What with the heavy beatings at any provocation or none, and the physical drills that go on till
the weakest drop, and the starvation, and the long roll calls of nearly
naked men, in subzero frost, and the hard work—digging drainage
ditches, hauling lumber, dragging rocks, demolishing peasant houses in
the evacuated villages, and carrying the materials, sometimes several kilometers, to the new blockhouse sites—and what with the guards
shooting on the spot men who falter or fall, or finishing them off with
the butt-ends of their rifles, the roster of Russians in the quarantine
camp at Oswiecim is rapidly shrinking.

The Soviet prisoners of war are in fact proving a major disappointment to the Commandant.

Draft after draft they arrive sick, emaciated, all but prostrate with
exhaustion, in half the promised numbers, the rest having died on the
way. With this deteriorated rubbish as a labor force he is supposed to
execute not one but several urgent construction projects: to double the
size of the base camp, located in the tobacco monopoly buildings and
the old Polish army barracks; to lay out and man the ambitious experimental farms and fisheries that Reichsführer SS Himmler plans as the

real showpieces of the Auschwitz establishment; to erect a whole new camp of unprecedented magnitude out at Birchwoods, three kilometers to the west, accommodating *one hundred thousand prisoners of war* for labor in armament factories; and to commence surveying and preparing the factory sites! No German concentration camp until now has held much more than ten thousand prisoners. It is a breathtaking job, an assignment to be proud of, a great chance for advancement. The Commandant realizes that well.

But he is not being given the tools. The whole thing would be impossible, if he did not have a solid base of Polish and Czech political prisoners who can still put in a good day's work, and a steady supply of fresh ones. Only the strongest Russians, maybe ten percent of each draft, are of any use in the labor gangs. Given any feeding at all, these can still revive and do a job. Hardy fellows! But right there is the big problem: confusion from the top down about the true mission of the Auschwitz Interest Area, these forty square kilometers of marshy farmland allotted to the Commandant's rule. Conscious of the responsibility entrusted to a mere SS major, he is eager to do a job. For a year and a half he has put heart and soul into Oswiecim. It was just a dismal swamp with a straggle of buildings and a few scattered villages when he came here in 1940 to start the camp up. Now it is looking like something! But what is really wanted of him? Maximum production for war, or maximum elimination of the nation's enemies? He is still not clear.

The Commandant considers himself a soldier. He will do either job. He cannot do both at the same time! Yet contradictory orders come down in a steady stream. Take the very matter of these Russian POWs! In retaliation for the inhuman treatment of German prisoners in the Soviet Union, they are to be used "without pity." For those with any trace of political responsibility, execution at once; for the rest, swift working to death, at slave labor on rations below what dogs need to survive.

. . . *Very fine, Reichsführer Himmler; but how about the hundreds and hundreds of barracks, just by the way, that you've ordered me to build out in Birchwoods (Brzezinka, in the uncivilized Polish spelling; adapted into smooth German as Birkenau). Oh yes, the barracks; and oh yes, the experimental farms; and oh yes, the factories! Well, well, let Sturmbannführer Hoess worry about all that. Hoess is a chap who delivers. He complains, sends long pessimistic reports, declares assignments are impossible. But in the end Hoess carries out orders. There's a chap you can rely on . . .*

The Commandant values this reputation of his. Even in these heartbreaking conditions he means to maintain it, or kill himself trying. Like the next fellow, he wants to rise in the service, do well by his family, and all that. But Reichsführer SS Himmler is taking advantage of his outstanding conscientiousness, and this sinks him in depression. It just is not fair.

In a cloudy noonday, shielded from the knifelike wind by a heavy greatcoat, the Commandant waits in the snow outside the crematorium for the arrival of the three hundred Russians. Combed out of several drafts as political officers or ratings, they have been sentenced to death by the military circuit court from Kattowitz. The Commandant has no quarrel with the sentence. The life-and-death struggle with Bolshevism is what this war is about. If European culture is to be saved, no mercy can be shown to the barbaric eastern foe. It is just too bad that some of the condemned appear so ablebodied.

At least their deaths will not be a total waste. They will yield important information. Major Hoess accepts no optimistic reports of subordinates. He learned the hard way, as Rapportführer in Sachsenhausen, to see things for himself. The tendency in a concentration camp chain of command is to lie, to cover up, to pretend that things are more efficient than they are. Reports on a previous gassing with the camp's strongest insecticide of some condemned Russians in the cellar of Block 11, while the Commandant was off reporting to Reichsführer SS Himmler in Berlin, have been contradictory. One subordinate, whose idea it was, claims they all died almost at once. Others say that it took forever for the Russians to croak; that they rushed one door of the cellar and almost broke it down, even as they were being gassed. What a hell of a mess, if they had actually forced their way out and released a cloud of that smelly poisonous blue stuff all over the main camp!

Just the usual thing, inattention to detail. The door wasn't reinforced enough, and the supposed airtight sealing of the cellar was done with clay; what stupidity! This experiment in the morgue room of the crematorium is being run under the Commandant's personal supervision. Airtightness has been tested with chlorine under pressure; satisfactory, just a faint sort of swimming-pool odor near the door, which has since had its rubber gaskets doubled up. The crematorium is off in the grassy area beyond the camp, not smack in the middle of the main buildings like Block 11. Just a little common sense!

The Russians approach—drawn, ghastly, with white-rimmed sunken eyes, in their ragged uniforms marked *SU* in huge black letters. They are flanked by guards with tommy guns. Their faces show awareness that they are going to their deaths. Yet their formation is good. Their wooden clogs squeak in the snow with a ghostly echo of military precision. Strange people! He has seen them in their work area, fighting like wolves over a dump of garbage from the SS kitchen, grasping each other by the throats for a rotten potato, snarling and cursing; he has seen them wandering like sleepwalkers, skin and bones, dead on their feet, impervious to the blows and threats of guards, crumpling and falling bloody to the ground without complaining. But put them in a formation, give them an order, a sense that they are in a group; and feeble and terrorized though they are, these Russians come to life and work and march like men.

The prisoners disappear single file into the gray flat-roofed building. Guards wait on the roof with canisters, by pipe apertures recently pierced. Three hundred men can be packed into the wide low cement room. That detail has been tested. The aperture flaps seal tight; that too has been tested. The Commandant walks up and down in the snow, swinging his arms to keep warm, three aides at his heels, all in well-fitted green uniforms. He is a martinet about uniforms. Sloppy appearance in guards is the beginning of a breakdown in camp morale. He saw that in his early service at Dachau . . .

Activity on the roof!

In due course he enters the building with his aides. The gas-masked SS men on duty inside give the Commandant a momentary remembrance of his service in the last war. Accepting and donning a mask, he observes that the process in the mortuary is not a silent one. That is for sure. Muffled yells, screams, shouts sound through the door, although this noise did not carry outside. He glances at his wristwatch. Seven minutes since activity on the roof began. He steps up to the thick glass peephole in the door.

The harsh mortuary lights are blazing, but this damned glass will have to be replaced; poor quality, it makes everything yellow and wavering, distorts details. Most of the prisoners are already down, piled all over each other, some not moving, others rolling or writhing. Perhaps fifty or so are still on their feet, stumbling and jumping about. Several right here at the door are pounding and clawing, with open yelling mouths in crazy faces. An ugly sight! But even as he watches, they are one by one dropping away like flies in a spray of pyrethrum. The Commandant has seen many and many a flogging, hanging, and shooting, having been himself eight years an unjustly sentenced political prisoner under Weimar, and eight more years a concentration camp officer. One learns to take this sort of thing; one gets hard. Yet he feels rather sick to see this process. It is something different. Still, what can one do? One is carrying out orders.

The stuff works, no doubt of that. With decent airtightness it really seems to do the job. For an instant the Commandant lifts his mask. No odor out here in the corridor, none whatever. That is important; no danger to personnel. Perhaps masks can be dispensed with in time.

It is getting quiet in there now. The mass of bodies is quiescent but for a hump here and there still heaving and flopping. No reason to linger. He leaves, handing his mask to the guard at the door. Outside he fills his lungs with the cold air of snowy Auschwitz, sweet and delicious after the nasty, rubbery, chemical smell of air filtered through a mask.

He closely questions the lieutenant in charge of ventilating the chamber. Until it is safe, he wants no show-off personnel going in there, even with masks. The ventilation is poor, the lieutenant admits. Big portable fans will be used. They should do the job in an hour. The Commandant issues a flat order: for three hours after ventilation begins, nobody inside the mortuary! Safety factor of two hundred percent; that's how to run a hazardous operation.

His personal aide drives him in his staff car to the Residence, where his wife and children await him for Christmas dinner. The Commandant is in no mood for festivity. He has kept a hard calm face all through this business. It is up to him to set the example! But he is human, though nobody in the Interest Area especially thinks so. That is how it must be, with the orders that he has to carry out. He takes a hot shower, scrubbing himself vigorously, and puts on a fresh uniform though the other is fresh, too, and carries no smell. He cannot relax on the base, he is always in uniform when he is not asleep; and there is something unseemly in eating Christmas dinner in the same uniform he wore before.

As he showers and dresses, trying to be cold and businesslike in his thoughts, he has to be pleased with the results. Reichsführer Himmler already told him back in July—honoring him with a long private interview in his inner office—about the big Jewish project. It is something so secret that he half-suppresses it, even in his thoughts. The orders come direct from the Führer, so there can be no argument. Several other camps will take some of the load, but Auschwitz is to be a main disposal center.

Hoping all the while that it may be an exaggerated scheme—a lot of Himmler's ideas are mostly talk—the Commandant has nevertheless been compelled to look into the problem. Visits to camps where such actions on a small scale are already under way have convinced him that no existing means will serve to do what Himmler forecasts. The asphyxiation by carbon monoxide at Treblinka is a drawn-out, messy affair, very wasteful of fuel and of time, and not one hundred percent effective. Shooting on the projected scale is also out of the question. The psychological effect on the execution squads would be unendurable, setting aside the serious ammunition problem.

No, the poison gas in rooms of large capacity has always been an idea worth trying; but which gas? Today's experiment shows that Zyklon B, the powerful insecticide they have been using right along at the camp to fumigate the barracks, may be the surprisingly simple solution. Seeing is believing. In a confined airtight space, with a plentiful dose of the blue-green crystals, those three hundred fellows didn't last long! Much larger rooms, carefully built, with a humane and orderly procedure to pack large numbers in at a time, will give satisfactory results. The problem of disposing of the bodies remains. That tough one is just being dumped in his lap, as usual. No bright suggestions from above; leave it to Hoess. But the present small crematorium can barely handle the prisoners who die a natural death and the various offenders who are shot or hanged.

Well, time for Christmas dinner. The Commandant joins his family. But it is not a gay occasion, though the handsomely furnished Residence is full of fine decorations, and a nice tree twinkles its ornaments in the foyer. His wife keeps filling his wineglass with Moselle, an apprehensive look on her face. The kids are all dressed up and shiny-faced, but they too have scared expressions. The Commandant would like to create a warm home atmosphere, but his burdens are too heavy. He can't be the good German husband and father he'd like to be. He is morose. His brief conversation has a growling note. He can't help it. The roast goose is excellent, the brisk services of the Polish girls can't be faulted, but the Commandant has had a rotten day, Christmas or no Christmas, and that's that.

He does feel sorry for the kids. When he goes off with the brandy bottle, to smoke a cigar and drink by himself, he ponders again about sending them back to Germany to school. His wife objects. Life is lonely enough on the base as it is, she keeps saying. Of course, she knows nothing about what goes on across the road, beyond the barbed wire. She can't understand that the atmosphere of Oswiecim is just not the best for growing kids. He will have to look into it again. The private tutoring they are getting from young educated SS officers is no way for German children to grow up. They need friends their own age, merry games, athletics, a normal life.

As the Commandant methodically empties the brandy bottle, worrying despite the welcome numbing of alcohol about his kids and about a dozen pressing camp problems, and getting unpleasant intermittent mental pictures of the heaving flopping pile of Russians seen through the yellow peephole, dusk is falling over the long rows of blockhouses in the quarantine camp. The Russian POWs are marching in from their day's work at the Birkenau site. Some stagger under the weight of limp bodies in striped ticking. All the corpses must be brought back from the work site for the evening roll call, since the count of living and dead has to match the number of men who left in the morning, to establish that nobody has escaped Auschwitz except by dying. The prisoners' band is thumping out a march, for the workers always leave and return to merry, brassy music.

Berel Jastrow bows beneath a very light corpse. The head swings like a stone on a rope. It is a man unknown to him who, just before work stopped, fell and died before his eyes in the lumberyard. He lays the body down in the row of corpses on the parade ground, and hurries to his place in ranks. When roll call ends it is dark. Returning to his block, Berel finds it less crowded than before. Some of the gassed men came from this house.

"Yuri Gorachov!" the block captain yells. That is the false name Berel used to join the Red Army in Moscow. He stiffens, pulling off his striped cap and dropping his arms rigidly to his sides. The block captain, a Ukrainian kapo and a very ugly customer, approaches him in the gloom, holding a piece of paper.

"Get your belongings!"

Carrying his ragged little sack, Jastrow marches after him out on the snow, and far down the line of floodlit buildings. Berel is too weary, starved, and numbed by cold and constant terror to be overconcerned about what may well be his imminent death. Let come what God wills.

They enter a block near the gate. The light is brighter in this block. The crowded prisoners look cleaner and better fed. Nor are they Russians, for Berel sees nowhere the big black *SU* that is painted on his own back.

The Ukrainian hands over the gray paper to a big man in a kapo armband, with a tremendous red beard and tiny wrinkled blue eyes; he gestures at Berel, mutters in garbled German, and goes. Taking the prisoner roughly by an elbow, the red-bearded man hustles him down the wooden tiers of bunks to the far end of the block. There, Jastrow sees Sammy Mutterperl, leaning his back on a tier, talking to another prisoner.

This is as stunning and gladsome a surprise as a reprieve from execution.

For, recognizing Mutterperl in the lumberyard that afternoon, just before picking up the light corpse, Berel took his life in his hands to whisper to him. Talking between prisoners is punishable with instant death by clubbing, whipping, or shooting. But Mutterperl was obviously a privileged prisoner—not a kapo, but some sort of foreman—for he was shouting orders at a squad of big Poles stacking lumber. There was no mistaking Mutterperl, an Oswiecim building contractor, formerly a fellow yeshiva student; a very pious, very burly man with a mashed nose from an accident on a construction job. So Berel risked brushing past him and whispering his name and his block number. Mutterperl, fat and powerful-looking as ever in the striped prison garb, his matted hair and whiskers still almost all brown, made no sign of recognition or even of hearing him.

The red-bearded kapo gestures to Berel that he will sleep in the topmost bunk of the tier Mutterperl leans against; and off he goes. Not looking at Jastrow, Mutterperl drops into his Polish chatter with the other prisoner a brief, *"Sholem aleichem, Reb Berel."*

It is Jastrow's first hint that God may let him live.

12

THIS time the *Devilfish* caught a barrage. The thunderous clangs, the jolting shocks, the sharp pain in the ears, the blackout, the agonizing bouncing and grinding of the darkened submarine on the sea floor, the sounds of breakage, the panicky yells, the unseen things hitting Byron's face—one of them felt jagged and cut his cheek—all seemed weirdly natural, all part of one simple experience, one sudden catastrophe, his death in the *Devilfish*. Even the previous depth charging had been nothing to this black bombinating ringing bedlam, this chaos of life bursting apart.

"I'm taking her up. Blow tanks! Surface! Surface!" He could barely hear the captain's strained bellow in the voice tube, but before he could issue orders to the planesmen, there came another hoarse howl. *"Belay that, Byron. I'm taking her up to fifty feet! Blow negative! Maximum up angle! All ahead full!"*

The lights came on, showing the planesmen clinging for dear life to their control wheels. The other sailors clutched stanchions, valve heads, anything that would keep them from breaking their limbs or their skulls in this tossing quaking space with its hundreds of iron projections. The depth charges boomed and crashed in a hell without letup. Books, cups, measuring instruments, were clattering and flying about; cork fragments rained in the air. Nevertheless, the planesmen obeyed orders, frantically twisting their wheels, and the submarine with a grind and a bound went forward, wallowing, shuddering, bucking in the roiled water. It was proving a tough vessel. Whatever the havoc so far, the hull was holding, there was some charge left in the can, and the engines were turning; but the control room had a wrecked look, two of the sailors were bleeding—Byron too put his hand to a wet spot on his cheek, and brought it away red—and Chief Derringer was horribly gagging and vomiting behind the dead reckoning tracer. Death still seemed very close at hand.

However, the submarine had gained a shade of advantage from the attack. Even in the deep ocean, the heavy explosions would have created a screen of turbulence opaque to sonar, and therefore a new chance to sneak away. With the *Devilfish* on the bottom, the rain of depth charges had raised a broad cloud of mud. Through this cloud it moved off, momentarily hidden from the enemy's sonar. Astern the depth charges blasted and rumbled. Obviously the destroyer captain, his charges set by fathometer, was plastering the area to bring up debris as proof of his victory.

But Byron's awareness of this tactical situation was nil. Somehow they were under way again; that was all he knew. As he stanched the cut on his face with a handkerchief, Carter Aster's voice on the loud-speaker startled him. *"Now pharmacist's mate to the conning tower on the double."* The quartermaster came trampling down from conn to tell Byron in a low voice that the captain had been thrown off his feet by one of the explosions, fallen in the darkness, and struck his head. When the lights came on Aster had found him on the deck, eyes closed, bleeding from his forehead. So far he had not revived. The exec didn't want to alarm the crew; he had sent the quartermaster to let Byron know why he would be giving the voice tube orders for a while.

Aster did not alter Hoban's tactics. The *Devilfish* ran on, just above the bottom, squandering its last reserve voltage at ten knots while the pharmacist's mate worked on the captain. The depth charging astern ceased. The pinging continued on short scale with up Doppler. So the destroyer was once more on the move and closing the range. In search, or in direct pursuit? No telling.

And now sonar reported propeller sounds of two other vessels, approaching at high speed from the direction of the entrance. Derringer began plotting them on the tracer at a range of five miles. "There're two more goddamn destroyers, Mr. Henry," the chief said, rolling his eyes at Byron. "Speed thirty knots." He repeated the news by telephone to the conning tower.

Aster's voice in the speaking tube, choked and tense: "Periscope depth, Briny!"

"Aye aye, sir. Periscope depth."

The planesmen turned their wheels. The polished oily shaft of the attack periscope slid noiselessly upward behind Byron. The submarine climbed.

"Sir, levelling at sixty-one—"

An exultant yell cut Byron off. "Why, it's raining! Pouring! It's a goddamn squall, black as a black cow's inside!" Aster shifted to the loudspeaker. "Surface, surface, surface! *STAND BY TO MAKE TWENTY-ONE KNOTS!*"

Seldom had Byron Henry heard more welcome words, or more welcome sounds than the roar and swash of the blowing tanks. Swiftly the *Devilfish* rose. He could feel the motion of the sea, the steep pitching, the levelling off, and he knew that the submarine was breaking into the rainy night. His ears recorded the change of pressure. Sweet damp air poured in through the vent. The diesels coughed and roared into life. The *Devilfish* smashed forward, once more a surface vessel breathing and burning the open air!

Rude cheers, happy blasphemies, roistering obscenities rang through the long vessel in every compartment. Temporarily, anyway, praying time was over.

They were still at battle stations. Red-stained handkerchief to his face, Byron mounted the ladder on his way to his post on the bridge. Aster, at the chart desk, said, "Stand by, Briny." The pharmacist's mate was bent over the captain, who sat with his back to the torpedo data computer, eyes open, complexion bluish, head bandaged, khaki shirt splashed with blood. Hoban gave Byron a sickly smile. "Well, I see you caught it, too." His voice was hoarse and weak.

"It's just a cut, sir."

"You were luckier than me."

Aster said, "Captain, do you want to try walking?"

"In a minute. You're heading south, you say? Why south?" It was a tired, petulant query. "The entrance is the other way."

"That's it, sir. He's tracked us, he knows where we were heading. A line between the two contact points shows him. With two more tin cans coming for us, I figure we better do a wide end run. Ten miles south, ten miles east, and then up the east coast to the entrance."

"Very well. Help me up." Aster and the pharmacist's mate lifted him by his elbows. On his feet, Hoban weaved and grasped a stanchion. "Whew! Dizzy. That's not a bad plan, Lady. But keep the men at battle stations. I'd better take a half hour or so in my bunk."

"Aye aye, sir."

Aided by the pharmacist's mate, the captain tottered to the ladder, and the bloody bandaged head sank through the hatch. Aster took up rulers and divider. "Briny, better have Doc Hviesten fix you up."

"I'm all right, Lady. I'll just go to my station." Byron wanted to climb outside, see the waves, breathe fresh air.

Aster gave him a hard penetrating look. "Do as you're told. And put on foul weather gear."

"Aye aye, sir."

When he did get to the bridge, he found blackness, spray, wind, rough swells. These were beautiful to him. The fire control officer had the deck; a blond lieutenant from Virginia, Wilson Turkell II, nick-named Foof in some forgotten Annapolis episode. But only the captain and Aster called him Foof. He was an accomplished officer with two marked habits: total silence except on ship's business, and a way of drinking himself insensible on the beach. Turkell said nothing when Byron arrived, and nothing thereafter.

The bridge was the captain's battle station. Half an hour passed and he did not come. Aster shouted an order through the open hatch to turn east. From the dark form of Turkell, surprising Byron almost like speech from a tree, issued five words: "This is a bad business."

"What? Why, Wilson?"

But the tree had spoken its wooden piece. Except for orders Turkell said nothing more.

Half an hour passed in rainy, pitching, tossing silence, and the dark. Sonar lost the three destroyers. The *Devilfish* turned again to run along the coast. The loudspeaker grated, "Now secure from battle stations. Meeting of officers in the wardroom."

The captain was not at the meeting. In his place sat Aster, looking grim, smoking a gray cigar. When all the officers were seated, he pulled the green curtain. "Okay, I'll make this short," he said in low troubled tones. "I've been with the captain for the past hour. His concussion seems serious. Doc Hviesten says his pulse is elevated, so's his blood pressure, and his vision is impaired. He may have a fractured skull. The *Devilfish* has to return to base."

Aster paused, looking around at the officers' set faces. Nobody said a word or made a gesture. He took a long puff at his rank cigar. "Now I guess you all feel as badly about this as I do. We came here to do a job. But there's no alternative. We can't break radio silence. If we could, ComSubRon 26 would just order us in. Captain Hoban isn't up to con-ducting attacks, and he can't delegate command. The safety of the boat and crew becomes paramount. The thing to do is get the hell out of here. Let's hope the *Salmon,* the *Porpoise,* and those other guys get some scores down at the landing beach."

"How do we get out, Lady?" Turkell asked in an offhand way. "And when?"

"On the surface, Foof, straight through the entrance at twenty-one knots"—Aster glanced at his watch—"approximately forty minutes from now."

Turkell's reaction was a marked downcurving of his mouth and a single nod. "Any comments?" Aster inquired, after a silence. "We're all in this together."

The engineering officer lifted a hand, an awkward formality among *Devilfish* officers. He was a peppery little lieutenant j.g. from Philadelphia named Samtow, a humorless fanatic about machinery maintenance, but otherwise rather a joker. "The captain's conscious? He's aware of what's going on?"

"Of course. He's ill and dizzy. He doesn't feel up to conducting attacks, and there's no point in wasting torpedoes."

"Does he know we'll transit the entrance on the surface?"

"Yes."

Turkell's lips barely moved. "That's his desire?"

"Well, Foof, we tossed it back and forth." Aster slouched, puffing on his cigar, shedding some of his forced dignity. "It's a tough one. Destroyers and sub chasers will be thick up there as whores on Market Street. We know that. These monkeys may even have mined the entrance. For all we know they have radar, too, though our intelligence says no." Aster swept both his arms wide, and shrugged. "On the other hand we've got zero visibility topside, haven't we? With the diesels we can run through and get away in a quarter of an hour. This hole is twelve miles wide, and that's one hell of a big expanse to bottle up solid with patrol vessels on a rainy night. But if we pull the plug it'll take us four times as long to transit the hot zone, with all those tin cans pinging for us. I grant you, two hundred feet of water overhead is a nice margin of safety. The captain finally said I'd have the conn, and to do it my way. So I say again, any comments?"

The officers looked at each other.

"That's the way to go," Turkell said.

Aster let several wordless seconds go by. He nodded. "Okay then. One more thing. Captain Hoban told me to express his regret at aborting the patrol. He says the boat, the crew, and the officers all performed admirably. If not for malfunctioning torpedoes we'd be heading home with a couple of major sinkings chalked up. We've learned that the *Devilfish* can catch a lot of hell and still go on fighting. The patrol hasn't been a dead loss, and he says well done." Aster spoke all this in a dry monotone. In his natural tone he added, "And that's that. Back to battle stations. I just secured for a while to give the crew a chance to grab a sandwich and a piss."

"You mean," said Samtow, "there's somebody left in this boat who hasn't pissed in his pants?"

The meeting broke up in coarse relieving laughter. The escape through the entrance was an anticlimax. Aster, Byron, and Turkell stood on the bridge in rubber clothes, peering into driving black rain. The sonar operator, stammering with excitement, reported more and more screw noises and pinging; far ahead at first, then getting closer, then sounding all around the *Devilfish*. Apparently in the sonar receiver terrifying pandemonium was echoing, through 360 degrees, but on the bridge all was wet, dark and peaceful. They went cruising straight through the heavy Japanese patrol line and saw no sign of it as they plunged and wallowed uneventfully through the night out of the gulf and into the open ocean.

"Just goes to show you, Briny," Aster remarked while the sonar operator was chattering alarm after alarm, "that ignorance is bliss. Here we are absolutely ringed by these yellow rascals, and it's like a pleasure cruise. Let's just hope we don't ram one."

He kept the submarine at General Quarters until the pinging had faded from the sonar, far astern; then he stationed the watch. "Briny, when you're relieved, see me in my cabin."

"Aye aye, sir."

He was lying on his bunk in jockey shorts, smoking a cigar, when Byron came. "Hi. Draw the curtain and sit down." Aster raised himself on an elbow. "How do you like submarine duty?"

Byron took a moment to answer, then spoke the truth. "It's for me."

Aster's green eyes flashed, and his mouth corners curved in his highly individual, cold, almost mirthless smile. "Now listen carefully." Aster leaned toward him—their heads were only a foot or so apart—and spoke almost in a whisper, *"There's nothing wrong with Captain Hoban except that he's scared absolutely shitless."*

"What? No concussion?"

"Nah! He confessed to Doc Hviesten. Doc told me. Then the three of us had it out. He did fall, but he wasn't knocked cold, he simulated it. It isn't malingering or cowardice, he just can't hack it, Briny. He got the message when the first depth charge went off. You know, I guessed it, watching him. It was pitiful. He crumpled up in a ball like a girl caught naked. I guess he's doing the right thing, because he sure as hell can't conduct an attack. He's broken. He's in terror. Doc had to put him to sleep with a strong sedative. As soon as we reach Manila, he's going to transfer out of submarines."

This was staggering news to Byron. "Oh, he'll think better of that. His whole career—"

"No, he won't. He's through. He told me that, Briny."

"Ten years in submarines, Lady—"

"Look, he was in the wrong business. There was just no way he could find out. I'll never blame any man who decides he can't hack this, and I feel sorry for him. Actually he did well in his condition. He kept his self-control, and he maneuvered properly under fire."

"Who else knows about him?"

"Well, Foof was right there. You can't deceive Foof. But he's no blabbermouth. Doc Hviesten won't talk, he's very ethical. I think the sailors were too scared to notice. I'm backing Hoban's story. When he's transferred the truth will get out. Meantime we have to run this submarine. We're returning to base with our tail between our legs, and that's poison for the crew. So if we make a fat contact on the way back, I'm going to ask Hoban's permission to shoot. We've still got twenty torpedoes left. If we do run an attack, Foof will be my kibitzer, he'll punch the Is-Was, and you'll man the TDC. Got that? You're the best diving officer I've ever seen, except maybe me, but Quayne will have to do that."

"Jesus Christ."

"What's your problem?"

"I can't run that TDC."

"You did all right in the attack trainer. Better than Samtow. There's nobody else."

"Dive, dive, dive." Through the mists of sleep Byron heard the loudspeaker and the clamorous flooding of the ballast tanks. On the instant he was out of his bunk naked. Sitting at the tiny desk writing a report, his roommate, Samtow, yawned. "Easy. It's almost dawn, so Lady's pulling the plug."

"Dawn? It is? How could I sleep five hours?"

"It's a talent."

"What's happening?"

"We're about fifty miles out of Manila."

"What about the captain?"

Samtow shrugged. "Haven't seen hair nor hide of him."

Byron dressed, drank coffee, and went to check on the torpedo rooms, bow and stern. The submarine stank. Listless cleanup and repair went on here and there, but the mood of defeat was as pervasive as the odor of malfunctions and decay. Most of the sailors were taciturn, but their feeling was plain—stunned humiliation that the red-hot *Devilfish* crew should be skulking home empty-handed from their first patrol, mauled by Japs, barely saving their skins.

Then the sonar operator reported the faint beating of a propeller. The plotting party came on duty. The count of propeller turns per minute gave the vessel's approximate speed. Its very slow movement relative to the submarine showed it some forty miles away. The distance was astonishing, but depending on sea conditions, the equipment could sometimes pick up screw noises at great ranges. Several times the contact faded out and returned, still on the same closing course at the same speed.

A rumor flashed through the compartments that Lieutenant Aster was going after it; and, as by a blast of compressed air, the sickly atmosphere in the vessel blew away. The torpedomen came to life, feverishly checking their weapons. The engineering gang fell earnestly to work on jammed valves, malfunctioning pumps, and broken fuel and water lines. The crew began an intensive cleanup. A cheerful fragrance of frying chicken soon obliterated the stench of leaking drains and filthy men. About midday curiosity overcame Byron. Pulling the curtain behind him, he stepped into Aster's cabin, where the exec, quite naked, sat correcting typed logs. "What's the dope, Lady?"

"About what?"

"Will we attack this target?"

"Oh, you require a special briefing, do you?"

"Sorry if I'm off base."

"Well, since you ask, I have the captain's permission to close him and take a look." Aster was distant and uncordial.

The propeller sounds slowly grew stronger, hour by hour. Derringer's plot showed that with this submerged approach, the *Devilfish* would not sight the ship much before evening, but a daylight run on the surface in these waters was far too risky.

Byron had the afternoon watch. At five o'clock Aster appeared in the conning tower in clean khakis, freshly shaved, smoking a long Havana, and humming the "Washington Post March," his habit when in the highest spirits. "Well, now, gentlemen, just let's see if this rascal is in view yet, hey? Plot says he ought to be. Up periscope!—Well, well, well! By the Christ, there's our friend. Bearing. Mark! Two one zero. Range. Mark! Fourteen thousand yards. Down scope!"

He shouted in the tube, "Chief, right on the money! He's there over the hill, hull down." Happy laughter resounded from the control room. Aster turned to Byron, his face glowing. "Briny, let's go to General Quarters."

At the alarm the usual racket ensued: loud scurrying and shouting, clanging of watertight doors, barked reports by telephone talkers. Turkell arrived and slung around his neck the Is-Was, a convoluted plastic instrument that gave bearings for a torpedo shot if the TDC failed. Byron nervously took his place at the computer. He had worked the black-faced instrument and its constantly turning dials in sub school and the simulator on shore, but had never before manned one at sea. The device put together the three moving elements of the attack problem—torpedo, submarine, victim—boiling down all the evolving data to one crucial number: the final bearing on which to launch the torpedo. The information coming in was of varying reliability. Course and speed of the *Devilfish* were precise; but the data on the target ship consisted of sonar readings and periscope glimpses, inexact and fleeting. The officer on the TDC had to guess which readings were fluky, which more or less accurate, in feeding new numbers into the machine. Wilson Turkell had rare insight for this. The responsibility weighed on Byron but excited him, too.

On the plot and on the computer, submarine and target continued to draw together. Aster paced and smoked, waiting for the time of sunset to put up the periscope again. "I'm not scaring off our plump little friend up there," he observed to Turkell. His usually pale face was bright pink, and his lithe nervous pacing and finger-snapping were working up tension in the attack party which Byron could see on the sailors' faces.

"All right," Aster said at last, crouching at the periscope well, "up scope!" He caught the handles and snapped them in place. Rising with the scope as stylishly as Hoban had done, he was looking through the eyepiece as it went up. "Range. Mark! Six thousand. Bearing. Mark! Two two four." The periscope had scarcely stopped when he ordered it down again. "Okay. Angle on the bow, twenty port. It's a medium-sized tanker, Foof. About five thousand tons."

"Jap silhouette?"

"Hell, tanker silhouette! What other nationality is chugging around in the South China Sea?"

"That's what we don't know, Lady," said a melancholy voice.

Like a ghost's, the bristly face of Branch Hoban rose through the hatchway. He climbed into the conning tower, his eyes haunted and sickly bright, his head bloodily bandaged, his lean frame stooped in his old tiger-pattern bathrobe, which dragged on the deck. "Maybe some fool Dutchman hasn't got the word. Maybe it's one of our own ships out to rendezvous with a fleet unit. We just don't know."

"Sir, it sure as hell doesn't look American."

"Lady, we've got to *know*."

"Okay. Identification manual, Jap merchants, tankers," Aster snapped at the quartermaster. Again he raised the periscope to call range, bearings, and angle on the bow. "Come on, come on, Baudin. Where's the manual?"

"Here, sir!" Hurriedly the sailor spread the open book on the navigator's desk. "Tanker silhouettes."

"I see them." Aster stared at the book, seized a red pencil, heavily ringed a silhouette, and showed it to Hoban. "That's the type, forty-five hundred tons. You can't mistake the broken line of that bridge house. It even looks like a goddamn pagoda. Take a look, sir. He's like a cardboard cutout in the sunset."

"Up scope," said Hoban. His movements were slow and slack. He called no data as he peered through the eyepiece. "All right, down scope. . . . Well, it's a setup, Lady. My vision's very fuzzy. You've identified him, so go ahead."

"Attack, Captain?"

"Yes, if you want to, go ahead and shoot him."

"Byron! Normal approach course?"

"Normal approach course one six zero, sir," Byron rapped out.

"Helmsman, come to one six zero."

"Coming to one six zero, sir!"

"Make ten knots!"

Aster took the loudspeaker microphone. "All hands. The *Devilfish* is commencing an attack on a tanker."

Hoban said rapidly and hoarsely, "One piece of advice. Those new magnetic exploders are lousy. I fought this fight in BuOrd years ago. I know. They cost me two hits yesterday. Set your torpedoes to strike the hull, otherwise you'll miss the way I did."

"We have orders to shoot ten feet under the keel, sir."

"True, but I hear the Japs are building flat-bottom tankers, Lady." Hoban winked. In his sad chalk-white face the effect was peculiarly clownish. "Don't you know about that? Drafts of six inches and less."

With a keen glance at the captain, Lieutenant Aster ordered a shallow setting for the torpedoes.

From the start, this second attack was so like the drills in the Cavite attack trainer that Byron's sense of reality became numbed. Aster had conducted dozens of mock torpedo runs, with Turkell as kibitzer, and Byron on the computer. This situation seemed exactly like a school problem, complete with a rapid fire of reports, orders, questions, and course changes to keep the TDC officer frantically at work. The conning tower in the trainer on the beach had looked the same, even smelled the same—mainly of sailors' sweating bodies, Aster's cigar, and the acrid odor of the electric equipment. Byron became utterly absorbed. He wanted to do well at this game and to earn praise. He knew that they were underwater and that a real target ship was generating the data, but that was a foggy awareness compared to his sharp hot focus on the numbers, the trigonometry, the turning dials, and the oncoming moment for his solution—that all-important final bearing, which would fix the gyro angle of the torpedo.

The whole thing seemed to race. Aster approached even closer than he had in the school drills. The computer showed the target at nine hundred yards before he said in brisk tight tones, *"Final bearing and shoot.* Up scope. Mark! Bearing one nine eight. Down scope!"

"Bearings on," Byron called. "Gyro angle one seven port!"

"Shoot!"

"Fire one!" The torpedoman pressed the firing key. "Fire two!"

The jolts of the launch shook Byron into realizing that two TNT-loaded weapons were now lancing through the water to destroy a ship and its unsuspecting crew, guided by his mathematics of death. The tanker had not once changed course or speed. This was unrestricted warfare, all right, he thought: a shotgun to the head of a pigeon. If only the torpedoes worked this time! The seconds ticked away—

BRAMM!

BRAMM!

Another surprise! Exploding torpedoes at nine hundred yards knocked the *Devilfish* about almost like depth charges. The deck jerked, the hull rumbled, the attack party staggered. Yells echoed through the submarine, and Lady Aster shouted, "Oh, WOW! Oh Jesus! Oh my *God,* what a sight! Captain, Captain!"

Hoban hurried to the periscope, his robe flapping around his bare shanks, and bent to the eyepiece. "Oh, beautiful! By Christ, Lady, it's a

successful patrol! This does it! It just takes one! Oh, that's just beautiful! Magnificent!"

Byron snatched the ship's camera from a drawer, and as the captain
stepped away, he fitted it to the eyepiece. Slapping his back, Aster
chortled, "Goddamn, Briny, well done! Just get a couple of shots, then
take a look, baby, take a look. He'll burn for a good while. It's the sight
of a lifetime! Foof! You look next. Let *everybody* take a look. Everybody in the attack party!"

As Byron stooped to the eyepiece, a spectacular night scene leaped
into view, framed in the black circle of the scope. Against a starry sky a
flame shaped like a candle flare hundreds of feet high was rising from a
black tanker shape half-enveloped in a red ball of darker fire. Pouring
from the top of the candle flame, billows of black smoke blotted out
many stars. The sea was a bath of gold. Lady Aster slapped his bent
back. "How about that? A perfect solution, you young sack rat. Perfect! Two out of two! Well done! Have you ever seen anything more
beautiful in your life?"

Byron was trying to grasp that all this was true, that this was a kill,
that the depth charging was avenged, that Japs were dying horribly in
that gorgeous holocaust, but a sense of reality still eluded him. His honest sensations were above all heart-pounding triumph at the good shot,
admiration of the wild thrilling fire spectacle, and a trace of theatrical
sadness, as at the end of a drama or a bullfight. He searched his spirit—
all in these few seconds at the periscope—for compassion for the frying
Japanese sailors, and could find none. They were abstractions, enemies,
stepped-on ants.

"I never have seen anything half as beautiful," said Byron Henry,
yielding the scope to Turkell. "I swear to God I never have, sir."

"You bet you haven't!" Aster threw long arms around the ensign and
squeezed him like a gorilla. "Merry Christmas! Now you've got a story
to tell Natalie!"

13

LESLIE SLOTE tended to see Natalie Henry in any lithe tall girl with heavy dark hair pulled back in soft waves. When he spied one at an eggnog party in Bern, the usual slight shock ran along his nerves. False alarm, of course. Natalie was capable of showing up almost any place, but he knew where she was.

This pseudo-Natalie was chatting with the host of the Christmas party, the British chargé d'affaires, under a bright painting of King George VI in a much-bemedalled uniform. Slote maneuvered in the noisy polyglot crowd for a better look at the oval face, the big slanted dark eyes set far apart, the high cheekbones with slight hollows underneath, even the too-orange lipstick—remarkable resemblance! She was certainly Jewish. Her figure was slighter and therefore more seductive than Natalie's, which to Slote's taste had always been a bit large-boned. He kept watching the girl as she moved through the smoky reception room. She began to return his glances. He followed her into a panelled library, where she halted, sipping a tall drink, by a globe on a bronze stand.

"Hello."

"Hello." The intense eyes turned up to him were clear and innocent, like the eyes of a clever teenager, though she looked to be in her twenties.

"I'm Leslie Slote, first secretary at the American legation."

"Yes, I know."

"Oh, have we met?"

"I asked someone about you, because you kept staring at me." She spoke in a mild sweet voice with a British accent, faintly Germanic in intonation.

"My apologies. You look amazingly like a girl I'm in love with. She's happily married, so it's rather idiotic of me, but anyway, that's why I stared."

"Really? Now I already know too much about you, while you don't even know my name. It's Selma Ascher." She held out a thin hand with a grip less firm, more girlish than Natalie's. She wore no rings. "My friend said you were transferred from Moscow for being too partial toward Jews."

This irritated Slote. The story was all over Bern. Who in the legation was spreading it? "I wish I could claim such martyrdom. My transfer was routine. I'm glad to find myself where food is good, lights go on at night, and guns don't go off."

She shook a schoolteacherish finger at him. "Don't! Don't be ashamed of it. Can't you realize how that distinguishes you in your Foreign Service?" She turned the creaky globe with a pale hand. "A big world, isn't it? And yet there is not one place left on it for Jews to go. Always before, down all the centuries, there's been at least one open gate. Now all are barred."

Slote had not thought to run into such heavy weather. Could this girl, with her smartly tailored suit, her assured manner, her laughing demeanor with other men, be a refugee? He had long since become callous to the woes of the driven unfortunates who haunted the legation. There was no other way to keep one's sanity.

"Are you in difficulties?"

"I myself? No. My family left Germany when I was a child. We're Swiss citizens. People thought Hitler was a joke then, but Papa was not amused." She tossed her head, and her tone changed. "Well! Tell me about the girl I resemble. But first, please, get me more soda water with lemon peel."

At the bar he paused to throw down a hooker of gin. When he returned, Selma Ascher stood at the globe, arms crossed, one hip and leg thrust to a side, outlining a delicious thigh under the slim blue skirt; an old Natalie pose. "Well, about this girl," he said, "she's the niece of Aaron Jastrow, the author—if that means anything to you."

"Oh? *A Jew's Jesus,* and *A Jew Named Paul?* Of course. I didn't much care for the books. They're brightly written, but rather shallow and atheistical. So she's Jewish! How did you meet, and where is she now?"

She avidly took in his story about Natalie. Selma Ascher could focus her pellucid brown eyes like a light beam. Slote's eyes kept going to the strong pulse beating in her white throat above a lacy blue blouse. High nervous energy here.

"But what a strange business! Why didn't she abandon this leech of an uncle, famous or not?"

"She was gradually sucked in. When it was too late she frantically tried to get herself and the baby out. The Pearl Harbor attack trapped her."

"And where is this young Gentile naval officer now, the father of her baby?"

"On a submarine in the Pacific."

"Most peculiar! I feel sorry for her, but her judgment must be very bad. How do you know she's in Siena?"

"I'm working on the exchange of interned nationals. That's where Italy's housing our journalists. She's on the list with Dr. Jastrow."

"Does she know you're trying to effect her release?"

"I hope so. The Swiss legation in Rome transmits our messages, and I've written to her."

"Will you get her out?"

"I don't know why not. Her uncle's published magazine articles, and she's been his researcher. A lot of Italian journalists are caught in my country. It'll take time, but there shouldn't be too much trouble."

"Perfectly fascinating." Selma Ascher offered her hand. "You must write her about the girl you met in Bern who resembled her."

"Let me take you home."

"I have my car, thank you."

"But I'd very much like to see you again."

"Oh, no, no." Her eyes rounded in ironical amusement. "I'd only depress you, reminding you of your lost love."

With a swing of hips as pleasant as waltz music, she left the library.

"Then you think the Soviet Union will hold out?" said Dr. Ascher, a plump man with heavy gray hair and a big hooked nose. He sat at the head of the table, his deathly tired face sagging on his chest.

Slote was disconcerted by the bald question, much as he had been by the unlooked-for dinner bid, and by the wealth of the Ascher home. They were dining off heavy gold-trimmed china. On the panelled walls two Monets glowed in pencil-beams of light from ceiling apertures. Selma smiled across the table at Slote. "Papa, you'll never get such a flat commitment from a diplomat."

She sat between a red-faced priest in clerical garb, who was eating and drinking with lusty appetite, and a tall stringy old Englishman with an ugly wart on his nose, who accepted only vegetables and left them almost untasted. There were ten at the table, all strangers to Slote but Selma. The father and Selma's brother, a prematurely bald little man, wore black skullcaps. In all his travels, Leslie Slote had never before dined with Jews who wore caps at table.

Selma's mother touched Slote's hand. On her slim fingers red and blue fire danced in two large diamonds. "But you're fresh from Moscow. Do tell us your impressions."

"Well, things were at their worst when I left in November. They've somewhat improved since."

Slote slipped smoothly into his monologue on the winter counterattack: generals' photographs in *Pravda* over victory headlines, sheepish officials streaming back to Moscow from Kuibyshev, improved food supply, fading air raids, columns of unshaven gaunt Germans marching down Gorki Boulevard in the snow under Red Army tommy guns, wiping snotty noses on their ragged sleeves. " 'Winter Fritz,' the Russians call these fellows," Slote said, and his hearers laughed and looked happy. "But here it is mid-January. The Germans gave some ground, but Hitler still holds western Russia. The counterattack looks to be petering out. One can't be too optimistic. Except that the Russian people do impress me with their stamina, patriotism, and sheer numbers."

Dr. Ascher wearily nodded. "Yes, yes. But without ninety percent of her heavy industry, how can the Soviet Union go on with the war?"

"They moved factories behind the Urals all during their 1941 defeats. It was a superhuman job."

"Mr. Slote, Hitler's factories didn't have to be moved. They're the best in the world, and they have steadily been grinding out mountains of arms. He'll start a big new offensive as soon as the mud dries from the spring thaw. Can those transplanted factories give the Russians enough arms?"

"They're also getting Lend-Lease supplies."

"Not enough," snapped the old Englishman. "Not for them, and not for Britain."

"What I fear," said Ascher sadly, "is that if he takes the Caucasus in 1942, and Leningrad and Moscow are still cut off, one can't exclude a separate peace."

"Precisely what Lenin did in 1917," said the Englishman. "Communists will sell out their allies at the drop of a hat. They're total realists."

Selma's mother said, "That would be the end for the Russian Jews."

The priest, his small eyes darting at Slote, paused in his vigorous attack on half a duck. "What's the condition of those Jews in Russia now?"

"Behind the German lines? Probably fearful. Elsewhere, tolerable.

The regime shunts them about like cattle, but that's how Russia more or less handles everyone."

"Are the stories coming out of Russia and Poland true?" said Dr. Ascher. Slote did not answer. "I mean about the big massacres."

Hard stares at him, from all around the table.

"Such things are difficult to prove." He spoke hesitantly. "It's wartime. The world press is shut out of those areas. Even the German press is. Massacre victims can't talk, and of course the murderers wouldn't."

"Drunkards talk, and Germans drink," Selma said.

Mrs. Ascher touched his hand again. The strands of gray in her hair, the pretty bone structure of her wrinkled face, the long-sleeved black dress buttoned to the throat, all gave this woman of sixty or so a stately charm. "Why did you say conditions behind the German lines are fearful?"

"I saw some documentary evidence before I left Moscow."

"What kind of documentary evidence?" The question came sharp and fast from the priest.

Less and less comfortable, Slote evaded. "Pretty much the sort of thing one hears about."

The Englishman cleared his throat, rapped the table with a knuckle, and spoke in a rheumy voice. "Bern is such a gossipy small town, d'you know, Mr. Slote? One's told you were sent from Moscow to Switzerland by your State Department for being too concerned about the Jews."

"There's no truth in it. My country's State Department itself is very concerned about the Jews."

"One's told, in fact," persisted the Englishman, "that you disclosed your documentary evidence to American newspapermen, and so incurred the displeasure of your superiors."

Slote could not handle this probe smoothly. "Gossip is seldom worth discussing," was all he said.

In the long silence that fell, a maid put small prayer books by each diner's place. Dr. Ascher and his son solemnly intoned a grace in Hebrew, while Slote, feeling awkward, turned pages of German translation. When the men and women went to different sitting rooms for coffee, Selma cut Leslie Slote off in a hallway, putting both her arms on his. Her black velvet bodice half-revealed pretty breasts smaller than Natalie's. Glancing around and seeing nobody else, she leaned to him, and gave him a little cool kiss on the mouth.

"What's that for?"

"You are so skinny. We must feed you up." She rushed away.

An entire floor of the house was Dr. Ascher's library: a long dark room with floor-to-ceiling rows of volumes, most of them leather-bound. The smell was heavy, bookish, musty. On the wall behind a broad cluttered desk hung signed pictures of politicians and opera stars. A wooden stand nearby displayed a war map of the world full of colored pins.

"You've been listening to Radio Berlin again, Jacob!" At the map, the Englishman rapped shaky fingers on the Malay peninsula. "The Jap has been stopped much farther north than this."

Ascher said to Slote, "You see, I am fool enough to bring the war into my spiritual retreat."

"You've a better picture here than we do at the legation. We tend to forget the Pacific entirely."

"But, Herr Slote, it's the key, isn't it? If Singapore should fall, that starts a slide"—he raked spread fingers down across India to Australia—"which may not end short of world chaos." He swept the fingers up to the German front in Russia, a wavy north-south row of red pins from the Arctic Ocean to the Black Sea. "Look at what Hitler holds! The Soviet Union is a cripple without arms or legs."

"Singapore won't fall," said the Englishman.

"And a sovereign nation can grow new limbs," Slote said. "It's a rude tough form of life, like a crab."

Ascher's whey-pale face wanly lit up at the comparison. "Ah, but Germany is so strong. If only she could be struck from behind!" The fingers jumped to the Atlantic coast. "But now the slide in East Asia will drag America and England in the other direction." Ascher heavily sighed, and dropped on the brown leather sofa beside Slote.

"That jolly well mustn't happen!" The Englishman, perching himself in a high-backed chair, began to needle Leslie Slote about the U-boat sinkings off the Atlantic shore. Couldn't Slote's countrymen exert enough self-discipline, even in wartime, to black out their coastal cities? Radio Berlin was openly boasting that the glow set up for the U-boats their easiest hunting of the war. The BBC had just confirmed appalling German figures for December sinkings off the American coast. At this rate the Allies were lost.

Furthermore—the old man was almost jumping from his chair, in worked-up indignation—why were the Japanese advancing so rapidly on Luzon? The British army was stretched all over the earth, and it had been at war for over two years; small wonder Singapore was threatened. But American forces in the Philippines had had two precious extra years of peace to prepare, and the United States wasn't fighting any-where else in the world. Why weren't the invaders being thrown into the sea? If America could not pull even *that* much weight in this war, well, then England would save civilization alone, and then confront the Russian bear afterward. But it would be a damned long haul. America had the resources, but it wanted the will to fight.

The tirade did not much anger Slote, for the manner and the cracking voice were senile. A peaceful nation needed time, he calmly re-turned, to get into the war mood. England under Chamberlain had showed that. But he had a question or two also. How did it help the British war effort to shut out of Palestine the Jewish refugees fleeing Hitler? How could a supposedly civilized democracy force women and children to keep sailing hopelessly around the Mediterranean in danger-ous old hulks?

"There are reasons—reasons of regional policy, reasons of state—" the Englishman's eyes watered, and he dashed a hand across them. "Empire brings responsibilities and dilemmas, you know—one's some-times between the devil and the deep—excuse me." He got up and bolted from the room. In a moment his unpainted and unattractive daughter appeared and said, "We must be leaving." With a reproachful look at Slote, she turned on her heel and went out.

"I'm sorry," Slote said to Ascher.

"When Treville was on duty here in the legation," Ascher said firmly, "he was our good friend. He's unwell, he loves his country, and he's old."

So the party broke up. Slote and the priest went out together into a freezing windy starlit night. Putting up his collar, Slote said he would walk to his flat. The priest proposed to accompany him for the exercise. Slote thought the fat small cleric might hold him back, but it was he who had to hurry, as they strode under bare-limbed trees and past dry fountains. In the quiet night Slote could hear the priest's hard even breathing. Vapor jetted from the broad nose as from a little steam en-gine. They did not exchange a word, walking about a mile.

"Well, here we are," Slote said, halting outside his apartment house. "Thanks for the company."

The priest looked straight in his face. "Would further documentary evidence about what is happening to the Jews interest you?" This was said abruptly in crisp German.

"What? Ah—certainly my government, as I said at dinner, is con-cerned to alleviate the sufferings of the Jews."

The priest's hand waved toward a gloomy little children's park across the street, where swings and seesaws stood amid empty benches. They crossed the street and walked once around the park in silence.

"Frightful. Frightful. Frightful." The words burst from the priest in a tone so different, so grief-stricken and intense, that Slote halted, shaken. The priest looked up at him, his face distorted in the light of a distant street lamp. "Herr Slote, I am Bavarian by birth. I watched this pile of filth, Adolf Hitler, make speeches on street corners to twenty people in Munich in 1923. I saw him make insolent speeches at his trial in 1924 after the putsch. At the 1936 *Parteitag,* I saw him speak to a million people. He has always been the same pile of filth. He has never changed. He hasn't to this day. The same hand on the hip, the same shaking fist, the same vulgar voice, and dirty language, and stupid primitive ideas. And yet he is Master of Germany. He is the evil genius of my people. He is a scourge sent by God."

Suddenly the priest resumed walking. Slote had to run a few steps to get beside him. "You must understand Germany, Herr Slote." The tone was calmer. "It is another world. We are a politically inexperienced people, we know only to follow orders from above. That is a product of our history, a protracted feudalism. We have been wavering for a century and a half between our dreamy socialist optimists, and our romantic materialistic pessimists. Between sweet visions of utopia, and brutal power theories. Basically, today, we are still caught between the liberal epicureanism of the western democracies, and the radical atheism of the eastern Bolsheviki." The priest stretched his arms wide, as the abstract phrases rolled in a practiced way from his tongue. "And between them, a hideous gap, what a vacuum, what a void! Both these modernist humanisms propose to ignore God. We Germans know in our hearts that both these theses are equally oversimple and false. There we are right. There we are not deceived. We have been groping to put love and faith and, yes, Christ back into modern life. But we are naïve, and we have been humbugged. An Antichrist has beguiled us, and with his brutish pseudoreligious nationalism he is leading us on the path to hell. Our capacity for religious fervor and for unthinking energetic obedience is unfortunately bottomless. Hitler and National Socialism are a ghastly perversion of an honest German thirst for faith, for hope, for a sound modern metaphysics. We are drinking salt water to quench our thirst. If he is not stopped, the end will be an immeasurable cataclysm."

Deeply stirred, as much by the ever-tightening grip of the priest's heavy hand as by this passionate outburst, Slote said, "I believe all that, and it is well said."

The bullet head nodded. The priest said with a simper, in a ridiculous change to a casual tone, "Do you like the cinema? I'm very partial to the films myself. It's a frivolous misuse of time, I confess."

"Yes, I go to films."

"How nice. Perhaps we could go together, some day."

Foreign Service officers were approached from time to time with offers of intelligence, and movie houses were a commonplace rendezvous. It had never before happened to Slote. Nonplussed, he sparred, "What is your name again? I'm very sorry, I should have caught it, but I didn't."

"I am Father Martin. Shall we count on taking in a film together, one of these days? Let me give you a call."

After a considerable pause, Slote nodded.

What went into that small gesture? Often thereafter Leslie Slote wondered, because it shaped the rest of his days. The sense of representing America, and the feeling that America was at bottom—whatever the surface cross-currents and prejudices—compassionate; his own haunting belief that he had been a short-sighted ass in rejecting a splendid Jewish girl; an itch to conquer his own timidity, which was beginning to disgust him; an awareness that his revelation of the Minsk documents to the Associated Press, however it had harmed his career, remained a source of perverse pride; finally, as much as anything else, curiosity; these things impelled him into a new life.

Three weeks went by. This strange talk in the night faded from Slote's mind. Then out of the blue Father Martin called. "Mr. Slote, do you like Bing Crosby? I find him so amusing. The latest Bing Crosby film is playing at the Bijou cinema, you know."

The priest was waiting with tickets already bought. For the seven o'clock showing the house was less than full. Father Martin took an aisle seat and Slote slipped in beside him. For a half hour or so they watched Bing Crosby, dressed as a collegian, caper and swap jokes with pretty girls in very short skirts. Without a word the priest left his seat to move farther down front. Shortly a thin man in glasses came and sat down, juggling a hat, an umbrella, and a thick envelope. The hat dropped to the floor. *"Bitte,"* he said, laying the envelope on Slote's lap as he groped under the seat. On the other side of Slote, a pimply girl, watching Bing Crosby open-mouthed, observed none of this. The man retrieved the hat and settled down. Slote kept the envelope. When the picture ended he tucked it under his arm and left, his heart beating fast. In the twilight outside, nobody in the departing audience gave Slote a glance.

He strolled back to his flat, resisting the impulse to hurry, in fact to run. Behind locked doors and drawn shades, he pulled out of the envelope a sheaf of photostat pages, white on black; a copy of an official German document, stained on some pages with a brown slop that blurred the words. An acrid chemical smell rose from the dark sheets as he riffled them.

A rubber stamping on the top page stood out clearly, white on black —*Geheime Reichssache* (*National Secret*). The title of the document was

CONFERENCE PROTOCOL
Meeting of Under Secretaries of State
Held in Gross-Wannsee, 20 January 1942

The first pages listed fifteen high government officials with orotund titles. Reinhard Heydrich, the deputy chief of the SS, had chaired their meeting in the Berlin suburb of Wannsee. Slote was just starting to sight-translate the text when his telephone rang.

"Hello. It's Selma Ascher. Will you take me to dinner?"

"Selma! God, yes!" She burst into rich laughter at his enthusiasm. "When? Where?"

Before dressing, he skimmed the document. The main topic was a transfer by railroad of large numbers of European Jews to the conquered eastern territories, for forced labor on highways. This was neither novel nor very shocking. Russian and French war prisoners were being used as slave labor. The Germans were pressing even Italians into their factories. They were harsh overlords, and harshest to the Jews, hence the road-building project. Slote wondered why the priest had been at such pains to get the material to him. He tucked the envelope under his mattress for a close reading later.

Selma picked him up in her gray Fiat two-seater. Half-hidden by a white fox collar, her face was solemn as she greeted him, her eyes bright and shy. She drove to a tiny restaurant in a side street.

"Since meeting you I've done two bad things for the first time in my life." Selma clasped and unclasped her small hands on the checked tablecloth. "One of them is to ask a man to take me to dinner."

"That's not so bad, and I'm happy you did. What's the other thing?"

"Far worse." She suddenly, heartily laughed, touched her hand on his, and jerkily withdrew it.

"Selma, your hand's cold."

"No wonder. I'm awfully nervous."

"But why?"

"Well—to get one thing out of the way, it wasn't my idea to ask you to dinner last month. Papa took me by surprise. You seem not to mind a forward girl—from what you've said about your friend in Siena—but that's the last thing I am. I did tell my parents I'd met you. They'd heard about you. Papa's headed the Jewish Council here for years. It's been an education for me," Selma exclaimed, talking rapidly after her first halting sentences, "a real education in cynicism, to see our friendships here in Bern dwindle down with every German victory. Papa has supported the hospital, the opera, the repertory theatre, everything! We used to be a popular family. Now—well—"

"Selma, who was the priest I met at your house?"

"Father Martin? A good German. Oh, they exist. There are many, but unfortunately not enough to make a difference. Father Martin has helped Papa get many South American visas."

"He offered me secret information on German mistreatment of the Jews."

"He *did?*"

"Would his information be reliable?"

"I can't really judge anything about a priest, even a friendly one. I'm sorry." She made an agitated negative gesture with both hands, as though waving the topic away. "Things are in such a turmoil at home! I had to get out tonight. Papa's moving his business to America. He's just exhausted, and Mother doesn't want him to die of grief and worry. It's a very complicated deal, it involves trading off factories in Turkey and Brazil, and I don't know what else, and—I'm talking my head off."

"I'm glad you're confiding in me. I never repeat anything."

"Does Natalie talk so much?"

"Much more. She's quite opinionated, and very argumentative."

"I think we're not really much alike."

"I'm rapidly forgetting the resemblance."

"Truly? Poor me. That's the only reason you were interested in me."

"Not once you spoke half a dozen words."

Selma Ascher colored and turned away her head, then faced him, bridling. "The other reason, the real one, that my father is moving is that I'm going to marry an American, a lawyer in Baltimore, quite orthodox."

"Are you—well, are you yourself actually religious? Or do you conform to your parents' wishes?"

"I have a fine Hebrew education. I even know some Talmud, which girls aren't supposed to learn. I've always been a serious student. It makes my father happy. He and I are studying Isaiah together right now, and it's really glorious. But as to God"—again she made the nervous negative gesture—"I grow more skeptical all the time. Where is He nowadays? How can He allow the things that are happening? I may yet become a lost soul."

"Then what about marrying that devout young man?"

"Oh, I couldn't possibly marry any other kind." She chuckled at his puzzled frown. "You don't understand that? Well, you don't have to."

It was now perfectly evident to Slote that there was nothing doing with this girl. They talked aimlessly until the food came. He began to look for her unattractive points, an old trick of his when trying to back off. All girls had flaws. Selma's long drippy earrings were badly chosen. Her sense of style was deficient: prudishness and femininity were awkwardly at odds in the high-necked dress, which concealed her throat but made provocative mounds of her small breasts. Her eyebrows were heavy and unplucked. What had seemed at first remarkable freshness and innocence apparently was nothing but overprotected narrowness. He was dining with—of all things—a pious virgin! He began to feel taken in. What was the point of this dinner?

"Do you like to dance?" Selma was picking idly at her steamed fish.

"So-so," said Slote with faint ungraciousness. "And you?"

"I dance abominably. I've done it so little. I would like to dance tonight."

"By all means." It was a way, if no very satisfying one, of taking the pious virgin in his arms.

"You're angry at me."

"Not in the least."

"Can't you guess the other bad thing that I've done for the first time in my life?"

"I'm afraid not."

"All right. Then I'll tell you. It was kissing a Gentile. I've not kissed many Jews, either."

They went to a casino where two bands spelled each other. She kept stepping on his feet, turning the wrong way, holding herself a foot away from him, seeming at once confused, distraught, and delighted. Holding this slim clodhopping girl in his arms at whatever distance, and with whatever punishment to his toes, brought back wistful memories of high school proms. She kept watching a large wall clock, and precisely at a quarter past eleven, she said, "We must go now. That was very nice."

She let him out of the Fiat at his flat without a handshake and roared off. He plodded upstairs, knowing that Selma Ascher's image, and the remembered sensations of embracing her body and smelling her hair, would keep him awake for hours. Mixing himself a dark whiskey and water, he dropped in an armchair. His eye fell on the bed. With a sigh he got up and went for the Wannsee Protocol, thinking that translating official German prose might make him sleepy. Settling down with a yellow pad, a pencil, and the black sheets, he began to read and write.

After an hour or so, he let the sheet he was reading fall to the floor. "Jesus . . . Christ!" he exclaimed, more wide awake than ever, staring with horror-stricken eyes at his own dead-white face in a mirror on the wall. "Jesus . . . CHRIST!"

*   *   *

World
Holocaust

by General Armin von Roon
(adapted from his *Land, Sea, and Air Operations of World War II*)

English Translation by
VICTOR HENRY

14

Translator's Foreword

(with a note on "The Wannsee Protocol")

Time usually hangs heavy on the hands of a retired naval officer, but in recent years I have been well occupied translating General Armin von Roon's *World Empire Lost* and its sequel, *World Holocaust*.

These strategic summaries are extracted from Roon's massive two-volume operational analysis of World War II, written in prison while serving a sentence for war crimes. Without the battle analyses that documented these summaries, Roon's judgments may seem sweeping. But his whole work is for military specialists, and they can read German. Other people must get Roon's views in this short form, first compiled by a German publisher as a two-part popular history of the war.

Though much colored by Roon's nationalism, the strategic overview in these two volumes should interest readers who want a clear and readable account of the whole war as it looked "from the other side of the hill." Roon's penetrating analyses of the sea battles in the Pacific, a theatre so remote from his own field, show German military professionalism at its soundest. Where I have felt compelled to dissent from Roon's views, my comments are plainly set off in italics.

I have prefaced this book with an essay Roon wrote for a military journal shortly before his death, entitled "The Wannsee Protocol." I believe this essay should be required reading for first-year students in all military academies.

Since the publication of *World Empire Lost* I have received a number of letters, some from old friends and comrades-in-arms (including a Soviet general), wondering at my willingness to spread the views of a convicted German war criminal. I hold no brief for the Germans. They started the worst war in mankind's history and came too close to winning it, and under the cloak of wartime secrecy they committed unheard-of crimes. I believe we must study the German state of mind that generated their huge (and militarily remarkable) assault, and their persisting fealty to an insane tyrant. Without the Armin von Roons who followed him and fought for him to the last, Adolf Hitler would have lived and died an impotent fanatical loudmouth, instead of becoming the most powerful monster of history, who all but brought down the civilized world. That is why I have translated Armin von Roon; and why I think "The Wannsee Protocol" should be required reading for military men.

Victor Henry

Oakton, Virginia
12 September 1970

Note to the Third Edition

Readers continue to write and argue with me as though I shared Armin von Roon's views; whereas I translated his books just because his views appall me.

As a professional military analyst, Roon is often sound, sometimes brilliant. His facts are seldom wrong. Where they are, I have said so in my notes. But his interpretations of the facts tend to be twisted by the German nationalism that led to Hitler; and if I had noted all my disagreements, the books would have been twice as long. In these pages, therefore, one peers into an able but distorted mind. Readers who find themselves agreeing with Armin von Roon had better take a good hard look at themselves and their ideas; readers who disagree with him are probably in my camp.

Victor Henry

Oakton, Virginia
17 October 1973

The Wannsee Protocol

BY GENERAL ARMIN VON ROON

Military writers tend to shun the topic of this paper, but the Jewish question affected the conduct of the Second World War and its outcome. The question cannot be forever ignored. Nor need one fear a frank probing of the problem, for the honor of the German soldier emerges intact.

Long before the war, the National Socialist policy on Jewry had created a military perplexity. Eleven million dispersed inhabitants of Europe had been designated as our nation's blood enemies. In Germany the Nuremberg decrees had expelled them from civic, business, and professional life. The Third Reich, once it began its armed drive to normalize Europe, therefore had to reckon at the outset with this closely knit community branching all over the continent, with powerful connections and substantial resources overseas. The army could not dig back into the origins of the problem. It had to deal with the security situation as it existed.

The Jews had to be classed as a potential underground, formidable in numbers, cleverness, and means. The worst enemy is always the desperate one who has nothing to lose. Partisans of other nationalities could change their allegiance and side with us. This option was not open to Jews. The army had no choice but to cooperate with the regime's special Jewish measures.

The nature of the measures was not a responsibility of the army. Various federal police agencies shared in this task: RSHA, Gestapo, SD, regular SS, and so on, a multiple façade for the various Nazi bigwigs contending for power. These all added up to a single iron instrument of Adolf Hitler's will, for from Adolf Hitler alone proceeded the policy regarding the Jews. The essence of this policy was the elimination of the Jewish race in Europe. It should be noted that this policy failed. Despite the regime's grip on the continent for almost four years, approximately half of the European Jews survived. Bureaucratic botching, thoroughly unmilitary, characterized the execution of the policy from start to finish.

Indeed, of Hitler's actual aim, the German army, from the lowest foot soldier to the highest general in Supreme Headquarters, had no knowledge

*whatever until the war ended and the so-called death camps were uncov-
ered by the victorious armies.*

The surviving documentation of this secret policy is naturally tenuous.
The policy was carried out with circumspection. Crucial orders were given
verbally, "under four eyes." So thin is the paper record, in fact, that some
authorities soberly contend that the so-called extermination never took place.
In this view, all the Jews except a few hundred thousand really escaped to
the Soviet Union, to the West, or to Palestine; the so-called death camps
were concentration camps of undesirables, where conditions were under-
standably harsh; and the crematoriums were routine hygienic installations
for the disposal of those who died in confinement.

Unhappily the written record, slender though it is, suggests the contrary.
For instance, the camp rosters that have survived show few entries of death
by execution; but several thousand prisoners often died on the same day
of "heart failure." Obviously such mass simultaneous heart failures had to
be induced. To distinguish these demises from executions is to split legalistic
hairs.

There are, moreover, SS documents which discuss the merits of Zyklon B
gas for euthanasia purposes versus shooting and carbon monoxide asphyxiation, etc., etc., also detailed correspondence between German industrial
firms and SS officials on the design and building of very large-scale crematoriums, etc., etc. All these undeniably authentic papers suggest a plan to
produce and dispose of great numbers of human corpses on a systematic
basis. Thus, one is forced to grant that the elimination process took place.

Of these surviving German documents, none is more instructive than the
Protocol of the Wannsee Conference of January 20, 1942.

The Wannsee Protocol

The Protocol came to light because of the sudden collapse of our fronts.
Many tons of our nation's most secret papers, which by standard security
practice should have been burned, fell intact into American, British, or Russian hands. Among these papers was the Wannsee Protocol.

Had Moscow suddenly fallen to our Army Group Center in December
1941, documents equally compromising would have come into our hands.
Stalin was fully as ruthless a personage as Hitler. He ordered many vast
secret slaughters of his own Russian people, which his minions obediently
carried out. The figure has been put as high as sixty million! But no official
records have been exposed to horrify the world. Consequently, nobody
brands the Russian people as a nation of murderers.

Or supposing that we had taken London, in the swift cross-Channel attack which I vainly advocated in June 1940? What shameful Whitehall records might we not have uncovered of hideous episodes in India, in Egypt, in Malaya, in South Africa, in fact wherever British imperialism carried the Union Jack, and British arms brutally suppressed native populations which resisted being bled dry for Anglo-Saxon enrichment? But these things remain shrouded secrets.

Only Germany suffered the ignominy of having her records unveiled. Only Germany was stripped naked. Even the defeated Japanese were allowed to keep their emperor and their government structure, which ensured suppression of their papers on the sack of Nanking and the Bataan Death March.

"Wannsee Protocols" exist in the secret papers of every nation. Human nature is everywhere alike. Let America uncover its files about its extermination of the Red Indian, its robbery of Texas from Mexico, its oppression of the Nisei after Pearl Harbor. Then let us see how the facts compare with the disclosures in the Wannsee Protocol.

The Wannsee Conference

The Protocol, a fifteen-page mimeographed secret document, was found by American investigators digging through the vast captured files of our Foreign Ministry. A notation shows that thirty copies originally existed. Only number 16, the Foreign Ministry's copy, survived. On such a slender thread hung world history's insight into Hitler's Jewish policy. The secret was almost kept!

The document describes a conference held at the International Police Building in the Gross-Wannsee section of Berlin on January 20, 1942, shortly after America entered the war. The chairman was Heydrich, a shady cashiered naval officer, who in the topsy-turvy Nazi era became chief of the Security Police and head of the Reich Security Main Office.* This Heydrich person was number two man under the unsavory Himmler in the SS. Already early in 1942 the SS had gained control over our federal security and police departments. So when Heydrich called this conference, undersecretaries of state came scurrying. They met for about an hour and a half with seven SS men, one of whom, Lieutenant Colonel Adolf Eichmann, kept the minutes. These minutes, edited by Heydrich, constitute the Wannsee Protocol.

The eight high officials came from the Ministry of Justice, the Ministry

---

* In German this is *Reichs-sicherheits-haupt-amt*, run together as one word; acronym RSHA.—V.H.

for the Interior, the Foreign Ministry, the Ministry for the Occupied Eastern Territories, the Government General in Poland, the Reich Chancellery, and the Plenipotentiary for the Four-year Plan——in fact, from every major government department except the armed forces. *No evidence exists that any member of the armed forces ever knew the conference took place.*

This is the crucial fact that emerges from the Wannsee Protocol. The honor of the German nation was entrusted to our armed forces, and the armed forces were innocent. It was a joint meeting of the secret police and the federal bureaucracy. The Eichmann-Heydrich document proves this.

—————

TRANSLATOR'S NOTE: *General von Roon does not usually resort to such fudging of the facts in his writings. He is not being a military historian here, however, but a special pleader. In fact, though no Wehrmacht representative attended the Wannsee Conference, the documentation of the German army's involvement in the Jewish policy is all too real and depressing.——V.H.*

—————

Heydrich seems to have called the conference to impress his superiors. Six months earlier, on July 31, 1941, when our invasion of the Soviet Union was rolling, Reichsmarschall Hermann Göring had ordered him in a top-secret letter to organize a disposition of the Jewish problem; to bring in other government departments as needed; and to submit to Göring, "as soon as possible," a draft showing what action had been taken, and what the further plans were. Despite the usual SS practice of not putting such things on paper, the Wannsee Protocol evidently came into existence to impress Göring with Heydrich's diligence.

Göring's letter used the words, "a final solution to the Jewish question." Since the exposure of the Protocol, this expression, "The Final Solution,"* has come to take on unpleasant overtones in anti-German literature. Heydrich often used a more precise term, "the territorial solution." This term will be used here.

The Territorial Solution

Three alternative solutions to the Jewish question had emerged in policy analyses over the years: the *emigration* solution, the *expulsion* solution, and the *territorial* solution.

At first the Nazis believed that once they took power, most of the Jews

* German: *Endlösung.*——V.H.

would emigrate. But the German Jews, as it turned out, were reluctant to abandon their homes and businesses, and the graves of their ancestors, even after Hitler's Nuremberg laws made them pariahs. They hoped that the Nazi regime would prove a passing storm. Elsewhere in Europe few Jews seemed to believe that war would come, or that if it did, Germany would win. As a result, far more Jews remained in Germany than left. Outside our borders, Jewish emigration was insignificant.

But even for the few who wanted to leave, the emigration solution hit a snag. If Hebrews were no longer welcome in Germany, it developed that they were not much more welcome anywhere else. Year by year after Hitler took power, western Europe stiffened its restrictions against admitting Jews. The sparsely settled vast lands of the New World, led by the "haven of oppressed mankind," the U.S.A., clanged iron doors shut in the Jews' faces. This was a black chapter in the tale of man's inhumanity to man.

When it became clear to the Hitler regime that the Jews would not emigrate and would find it hard at all events to get in elsewhere, the *expulsion* solution came forward: i.e., forcibly removing them. The awkward question remained: where to?

Of all the expulsion ideas, the one most prominent in the surviving documents is the *Madagascar Plan*. The forcible resettling of Europe's Jews on this French island off South Africa received some study. But in view of the gross difficulties—lack of shipping to transport eleven million people, enemy control of the seas, stupendous cost, offense to Vichy France whose collaboration we were seeking, and nonviability of this wild tropical island for Europeans—it is hard to say how serious this project was. When the navy indicated to Hitler that the British might one day land in Madagascar to protect their Indian Ocean sea lanes, all talk of settling the Jews there ended. The Führer declared that the British would only "let the bacillus loose again on the world."

Thus it developed that the problem would have to be solved on European soil: hence, *territorial solution*. At Wannsee, Heydrich lifted the veil of secrecy, so that the federal bureaucrats would understand plainly, once for all, what the nature of their job was.

The Program

This draconic program should certainly have had no place in the twentieth century. Alas! Cologne, Dresden, Katyn, and Hiroshima showed that this kind of moral failure in wartime was certainly not confined to Germany. The territorial solution of the Jewish question was a harebrained scheme dreamed up by irresponsible and inept Berlin desk officials. Administratively, it was from start to finish a mess. Like most projects dreamed up in the comfortable suites of a government building, it had about it a specious neatness and clarity, but in the field it broke down. All too many Jews did perish in the process, but on the whole it was a monumental fiasco.

The key to the territorial solution lay in our vast 1941 conquests. *The occupied eastern areas were at last the long-sought place where the Jews could be sent.* For here no government had to be consulted, and no local population had to be mollified. It was a thinly settled half-continent under German guns.

Heydrich outlined a most plausible and simple plan. The Jews of Europe would be "cleaned up from west to east," temporarily collected in transit ghettos, and then shipped to the Occupied Territories in huge labor columns, separated by sexes. There they would build roads, of which this backward region stood in great need for military purposes. In the course of this action "a great part of the Jews would undoubtedly be eliminated by natural causes," that is, by poor conditions and debilitating labor. As for the few who survived the ordeal, Heydrich said bluntly that they would have to be "treated accordingly," since as the tough product of natural selection they would otherwise constitute a spore for the rebirth of the Jewish people. Such was the unrelenting ideology of the government of the time.

The unanimous reaction of the cabinet officials was extreme enthusiasm, and a variety of suggestions for improving or speeding up the plan. The conference ended on a note of cordial agreement, and an excellent and convivial luncheon followed in the usual high bureaucratic style.

But the scheme collapsed almost at the outset. The labor columns were never organized. The roads were never built. From 1943 on in our forced-march retreats from Russia, the army felt keenly the impact of this failure. True, the Jews were collected all over Europe and shipped eastward, to transit ghettos of Poland. But there they stayed—a colossal prison population, an immense drain on German resources, and a festering rear-area threat both to health and to security.

No subsequent SS protocol has survived to explain why Heydrich's plan was abandoned. The territorial solution was modified in a haphazard way to become the construction of big factories near the ever-swelling transit ghettos, and the use of Jewish forced labor on the spot. The hoped-for natural diminution was sought through reduced nutrition, drastic work schedules, etc., etc. But the uprooting and resettling of a population of eleven million people proved an almost unimaginable administrative task, quite beyond the Berlin bunglers in charge of the program, with the result that half the

Jews, as has been stated, escaped elimination. No more than five and a half, or by the highest estimate six, million were caught by the scheme.

The Mercy Deaths

We still do not know exactly when or how the switch to euthanasia (mercy death) in gas chambers occurred. This difficult aspect has been widely distorted and misunderstood.

Heydrich's plan turned out to be a vast folly, projected by soft-living bureaucrats not experienced, as soldiers are, in large-scale suffering, privation, and death. The resources of the human spirit and body are remarkable. Prisoners of war endure wretched conditions for years. They learn to eat or drink almost anything. The demands of their depleted bodies shrink almost to zero, in the natural urge to live on. All these phenomena occurred in the transit ghettos. The slow rate of attrition became worrisome. Plagues broke out, and plague germs do not distinguish between captors and prisoners. The weakened Jews therefore became a standing menace to the local populations and to our armed forces.

These developments apparently brought forward the thought: since these people were in any case condemned to death, would not a quick, unexpected, painless end free them from long woes? And would it not simultaneously relieve our forces of a clogging problem, the proportions of which had not been realized in time?

Here, in these essentially humane considerations, lay the reason for the gas chambers. Rescuing the Jews was out of the question. Adolf Hitler had decreed their end, and his will was law. One could only carry it out in the most decent, practical, and civilized fashion. Much has been made of the undeniable fact that a million children were thus gassed to death, and it is an unfortunate episode to recall. Yet starvation would have been a slower, more painful demise for the children, and their parents would have endured the misery of watching them waste away.

As for the spoliation of the arriving Jews, and even of the dead bodies of these unfortunates, such practices cannot be extenuated. The SS amassed several billion marks' worth of gold, jewelry, and goods in this fashion, but whether the German war effort benefitted remains doubtful, for the Himmler-Heydrich agency was a high-handed and corrupt one. The story of soap manufacture from the bodies was, of course, a baseless British fabrication from the First World War.

Military Effects: (1) Manpower

This was not a rear-area matter of no military weight. The territorial solution materially damaged our armed effort.

The worst damage was in *manpower*. Large numbers of healthy German men were diverted from combat roles to the herding of Jews. Round-up squads, camp guards, etc., were recruited from local populations, but even so enough Germans for several divisions may have been fussing with Jews in bureaus and in camps, instead of fighting.

The manpower shortage was also chronic in our factories. The prisoners of war and the forced laborers from occupied lands gave halfhearted service at best, and they persisted in sabotage no matter how many were shot. But the Jews constituted a vast pool of clever workmen and artisans, or professional men and women quick to learn any skilled labor. They were so used, in fact, until the inexorable round-up squads came to ship them off. They committed very little sabotage. Rather, they displayed a desperate anxiety to preserve their own lives and those of their loved ones by turning in superlative work. We thus lost the labor of several million workers of high reliability, motivation, and productivity.

Finally, it was fashionable under National Socialism to sneer at the fighting capacity of the Jews. Indeed, under SS handling they appeared a docile and vulnerable lot. But that this was a condition capable of startling reversal has been shown by postwar events in Palestine. How well we could have used on the eastern front one or two million fighters of the calibre of the present-day Jewish armies! At the time the idea would have seemed a joke. Today, when it is too late, we can only wonder.

Military Effects: (2) Supplies and Services

The railroading burden was oppressive and continuous. No matter how tightly the trains were packed——and that this was carried to excess is common knowledge——the tying up of rolling stock remained a grave problem. There never were sufficient trains and locomotives for the fighting fronts. Combat divisions sat shivering at rear depots while trains devoted to shuttling the Jews rolled eastward jam-packed and went back empty, cut off from use for any other purpose. This noncombat usage had a secret overriding priority such as in America was given only to making the atomic bomb.

Military Effects: (3) Morale

While the ultimate intent of the policy remained secret, many German army formations did see the process in action. That is a matter of record. Regrettably, some units were also coopted to assist not only in transporting or guarding the Jews, but in the liquidation process.

Local army commanders sometimes supplied and transported the mobile execution squads, since they were on government business. These SS squads,

called *Einsatzgruppen* (Special Action Units), had entered Russia close behind our advancing armies. They had orders to shoot political commissars
without trial, in order to nip partisan activity in the bud; this was the well-
known "Commissar Order" of March 1941. They also were instructed to
liquidate forthwith, as a prime menace to German security, all the Jews they
could round up. Local populations gladly volunteered to join the *Einsatzgruppen* against their Jews, with episodes of frightfulness resulting, especially in Lithuania, Rumania, and Hungary. By the more orderly German
squads themselves, hundreds of thousands of Jews were systematically shot
within areas of army cognizance.

German soldiers could not always avert their eyes from these happenings.
Isolated instances occurred of misguided local army commanders allowing
or even ordering their units to take part. Thus authentic photographs exist
of men in Wehrmacht uniform, shooting Jewish women holding babes in
their arms. Such occurrences unquestionably spread in our ranks a certain
demoralization, and a questioning of our aims in fighting the war. When
this happens in an army, its fighting spirit has been injured. Like so many
aspects of the territorial solution, one cannot state this morale damage in
our army in percentage points, or other meaningful figures. It was, however,
a real factor on the eastern front. Like defeatism, self-doubt is an invisible
but heavy weight on a war effort.

A soldier is trained to the job of killing. It is his life against the enemy's;
that is soldiering at its cleanest. Soldiers sometimes have to do sadder,
dirtier jobs. They must shoot spies and partisans who are standing blind-
folded and helpless. On orders, they must sometimes hang boys, girls, and
women, who make good partisan fighters. But that does not mean that the
soldier—especially a German soldier, trained to decency and honor, as
much as to hardness in the field—can always stomach such work. What the
Nazis did, in this regard, to our German youth is hard to forget or to excuse.

The Nature of the Enemy

We come therefore to the heart of the whole matter: was the solution,
with all these drawbacks, nevertheless an imperative wartime security measure? Were the Jews the ultimate security menace to the Reich that Hitler postu-
lated? Within this question lies another question—"*Which Reich?*"

Ever since the French Revolution two irreconcilable Reich concepts had
emerged in our philosophy and in our politics:

(a)   The *liberal* concept: a peaceful Reich universalist in culture, with free-
      dom for the Jews, the establishment of bourgeois democracy in imi-

tation of France and England, and a subordinate military position for Germany.

(b) The *nationalist* concept: the Reich as a rising world force, the natural successor to the British Empire; a German culture purged of foreign strains; armed forces on the Bonapartist basis of "the nation in arms"; a hard mystical loyalty to king, to soil, and to old Christian virtues.

Cutting across both ideas came *socialism,* with its sentimental and poisonous farrago of world brotherhood, egalitarianism, and the abolition of private property. But nationalism was the truly German essence. Whenever the nationalist Reich prevailed——in 1866, in 1870–71, in 1914, in 1917—— we were strong and victorious. Whenever the liberal and socialist elements surfaced, Germany suffered.

It was Adolf Hitler's political genius to weld the mistique of the nationalist Reich to the rabble-rousing appeal of socialism. *National Socialism* resulted, an explosive mass movement. The modified socialism of Hitler was unobjectionable to the army. It amounted to spartan economic controls, and basic employment, health, and welfare measures for all the people except the Jews.

But the Jews were the backbone of German liberalism. Liberalism had given them the rights and privileges of citizens. Liberalism had turned them loose to use their energy and cleverness in finance, the professions, and the arts. These people who had been kept apart were now to be seen everywhere——prosperous, exotic, holding high places, and indiscreetly displaying their new-won gains. To the Jews, liberalism was their salvation. Therefore, to a dedicated nationalist like Adolf Hitler, the Jews appeared as ultimate enemies.

Tragically, it all depended on the point of view.

The Actual Power of the Jews

Yet all attempts to justify the territorial solution finally fall before one practical historical truth. The Jews proved unable to save themselves, or to influence anybody else to save them; and self-preservation is the test of a nation's true power.

The Jews beyond Hitler's reach looked on helplessly while their European blood brothers were going to an obscure but grim fate. Where then was their political stranglehold on the West, that Hitler took as an article of faith? Where was their boundless wealth, when they could not induce or bribe a single country——not even one small South American republic——to open its doors? In 1944, where was their all-penetrating influence, when the secret began to leak out, and they in vain implored the Anglo-Americans to bomb Auschwitz?

These things speak for themselves. Hitler exaggerated the threat of the Jews, and badly led astray the well-meaning German people. The Jews would have served us well. Their weight in manpower, skill, and international influence, added on our side instead of subtracted from it, would have been most welcome. Perhaps the war might even have ended differently!

For if the Jews outside Europe lacked the power to command deliverance, they did have a strong voice. Their outcries lent credence to Roosevelt's and Churchill's unfair portrayal of our folk as Huns and savages, even while we were fighting the battle of Christendom against the Red hordes. And so arose the two policies fatal to our cause—"Germany First," and "unconditional surrender"—which ranged the two powerful plutocracies irrevocably on the side of Eurasian Bolshevism.

Had the Nazi regime handled the millions of Jews under our rule with wisdom, none of this need have happened. This is the tragic military paradox of the territorial solution. The Jews were not strong enemies; but they might have been strong friends. Seen in this light, the Nazi policy toward the Jews must be called a costly military blunder. But the armed forces were not consulted and cannot be blamed. This is the inescapable conclusion from the prime surviving document of the matter, the Wannsee Protocol.

TRANSLATOR'S NOTE: *When I first submitted this article in translation to the U.S. Naval Institute* Proceedings, *the editor, Vice Admiral Turnbull C. "Buck" Fuller, USN, returned it with a large red-ink scrawl, "Just what is the purpose of offering to the* Proceedings *this obtuse, cold-blooded, sickening drivel?" He was an old salt and a good friend. I wrote under his words, "To show ourselves what we might be capable of," and sent the piece back. Six months later the article appeared in the* Proceedings. *I met Buck Fuller on many occasions thereafter. He never once referred to Armin von Roon's essay. He still has not.—V.H.*

*   *   *

15

1. Commencing at sunrise, Task Group 8.1 (this vessel with *Salt Lake City* and *Dunlap*) will bombard Wotje atoll in the northern Marshall Islands.

    a. Air strikes from *Enterprise* will neutralize enemy air strength and shore batteries before bombardment commences.

    b. Charts of these enemy waters being old and unreliable, and hazards from coral reefs abounding, condition Zed will be set at 0000 hours.

2. *Northampton* is proud to be flagship of bombardment group North, under Vice Admiral Halsey's Task Force 8, as the Pacific Fleet at last hits back at the treacherous Nips throughout the Marshall and Gilbert island groups.

3. "This is It." All hands govern themselves accordingly.

JAMES C. GRIGG
EXECUTIVE OFFICER

"Commence firing!"

The *Northampton*'s three turrets thundered out white smoke and pale fire. The deck jerked and shuddered. Though plugged with cotton, Victor Henry's ears rang. The flash, the roar, the smell of gunpowder from this first salvo at the enemy that had wrecked Pearl Harbor and the *California,* filled him with exultation. Astern, at the same moment, the *Salt Lake City*'s main battery blasted and flamed, and the two clusters of eight-inch projectiles, plain to see with binoculars, arched off toward the vessels anchored in the lagoon.

Off the port quarter, the rim of the sun was blazing up over a sharp horizon. The two cruisers and the destroyer *Dunlap,* flying huge battle flags, were steaming in column at full speed, broadside to the smoking green lump on the sea that was Wotje Island. The *Enterprise* planes, mere specks in the sky (Warren's no doubt among them), were heading back to the carrier, barely visible to the north. They had struck the island at dawn, on schedule.

Pug was still seething over the messy catapulting of his own four spotter planes. One craft had just missed going into the sea. Another had been twenty minutes loading on the catapult, for the crane had jammed. Damned bad start! Admiral Spruance, standing beside him on the bridge in the brightening dawn, had said not a word, but disappointment at the performance had radiated from him. He was clearly disappointed too at the lack of targets in Wotje. There were no warships, only a scattering of merchantmen. Halsey's first hit-and-run raid against the Japs would not amount to much if the pickings were no better at the other atolls.

But even this minor gunnery action began badly. The enemy ships weighed anchor, made smoke, and dodged and twisted in the lagoon, hard to see and harder to hit. Not one visibly sank or even flamed under continuous heavy gunfire. The spotter planes reported splashes as hits, then corrected themselves. A nervy little minesweeper sortied from the lagoon, shooting its popguns and zigzagging. The destroyer *Dunlap* engaged it at point-blank range, with five-inch salvos that kept churning up futile splashes in the sea. Lookouts on all three ships next began sighting periscopes, in a hysterical wave of reports. Neither Pug Henry nor the admiral could see the periscopes, but Spruance had little choice. He ordered an emergency turn. The attack fell apart. The three warships milled about on the quiet sunny sea off the smoking island, preoccupied with dodging reported torpedo tracks and avoiding collisions. At last Pug Henry resolved to ignore periscopes and torpedo wakes he couldn't see. Heading into Wotje on a firing course, he blasted away at the elusive merchant vessels, lavishing the costly shells to give his crew at least the experience of failure, the exposure to the thumping shore batteries, the practice of rushing shells from magazine to gun breech, the smell and the sound and the fear of combat; and to force into the open the humiliating realities of a warship system still clogged with peacetime fat.

Rear Admiral Spruance, issuing order after order on the TBS, finally regained a semblance of control. The *Dunlap* sank the minesweeper. The three ships formed up, moved in close to shore, and set ablaze most of the island's rickety buildings. But the shore batteries found the range, and colored splashes began howling up around the attackers. When Spruance saw the *Salt Lake City* straddled twice, he called a cease-fire. Ordering Captain Henry to lead Task Group 8.1 back to the *Enterprise* screen, the admiral left the bridge frozen-faced. The action had lasted an hour and a half.

"Meeting of all officers not on watch in the wardroom," Pug said to Jim Grigg.

"Aye aye, sir," said the exec, his countenance under the new blue-painted helmet as fallen as Spruance's.

A subdued crowd of young men in khaki got to their feet as the captain came into the long narrow room. He kept them standing for his short talk. They had just taken part in a nuisance raid, he said. They had failed to be much of a nuisance. A long war lay ahead. The *Northampton* would commence improving its combat readiness. Dismissed.

All day, all evening, past midnight, department heads were summoned to the captain's quarters, where, speaking without notes, he ticked off weak points and ordered remedial action. The *Northampton*'s poor showing had not greatly surprised Pug Henry. In his first month or so as captain, sizing up his ship, he had kept his eyes and ears open and his mouth more or less shut. There were too many raw recruits and draftees aboard; the experienced personnel, enlisted and officers alike, were a sparse lot. Ship routine went well, spit-and-polish was adequate, but everything was slack, grooved, comfortable, and faintly civilian. Still, the men looked good to Pug, and he had been waiting for just such a crisis to show his hand.

He startled all the officers from the exec down with his hard manner and precise criticisms, for they had been taking him as a quiet sort, out of touch after all his years on the beach. The conferences went on for fourteen straight hours. Alemon kept brewing and serving fresh coffee, pot after pot, and made hamburgers for dinner, which Grigg and the captain ate as they conferred. When Grigg, having taken hundreds of notes in his "urgent" notebook and drunk a dozen cups of coffee to stay alert, looked ready to faint, Pug quit. "Prepare a dispatch to ComCru-Pac," he said, "requesting a tug with target upon our return to base."

"We can't break radio silence, sir," said Grigg nervously. "Not for that."

"I know. Send a scout plane with it."

Halsey's task force, a long column of gray warships streaming battle flags, entered Pearl Harbor to a wild welcome: sirens, whistles, bells, cheers, and rainbows of flags decking every ship in port. For journalists and radio commentators the raid had been a mighty shot in the arm. They were hailing Admiral Halsey's gigantic attack on the Marshalls and Gilberts as the resurgence of American power in the Pacific, the turn of the tide, the proof of the resilience of free governments, and so on and so forth. Coded intercepts of battle reports had told Victor Henry a different story. Air attacks at Kwajalein had destroyed some planes and probably sunk a few small ships. The coordinated air strikes by the *Yorktown* in the Gilberts had produced small results. Surface bombardments had nowhere been effective.

The captain summoned his officers to the wardroom as soon as the *Northampton* moored. They had all been out on deck enjoying the tumultuous victory greeting, and they looked fresh and happy. "Let's understand one thing," he said. "The purpose of all the hoopla out there is to boost civilian morale. Hirohito isn't losing any sleep over what this raid did. As for what the *Northampton* did, the less said the better. We sortie at dawn for gunnery runs."

He had some trouble obtaining the target vessel. ComCruPac summoned him by messenger mail to explain his failure to schedule liberty for his crew after their arduous combat cruise. He went ashore and brusquely confronted the chief of staff, an old classmate. The *Northampton* had to be jolted into war, he said. Wives, girl friends, bars, beds, would all be there when the cruiser returned from forty-eight hours of hard drills. He got a promise of a target.

Returning aboard, he found on his desk a pile of personal mail: two letters from Rhoda, a thick one from Madeline, one from his father, who at eighty-one seldom wrote, one from his brother, a soft-drink dealer in Seattle, also one from Senator Lacouture, which he tore open as he settled in the armchair of his inner cabin. The news that Natalie was interned with a group of journalists in Siena upset him, though the attached State Department letter was reassuring about her prospects of getting home. It was better than not knowing where she was; at least, he hoped Byron would take the news that way. Rhoda's letter written at Christmas was long, conciliatory, submissive—"When you get back, I'll be right here in Foxhall Road, waiting like a good Navy wife in my best bib and tucker, with a full martini jug. . . . I have never respected and loved you more . . ." The other, a short note, merely gossiped, as though nothing had ever gone wrong, about a big snowfall on New Year's Eve, and the dinner at the Army and Navy Club.

The thickness of Madeline's letter proved deceptive. It was a single typed yellow sheet, triple-spaced, with a folded page from a theatrical trade paper. Madeline bubbled that she hated publicity and couldn't imagine how this silly story had gotten into print, but here it was.

. . . Love to Byron and Warren, if you see them. Tell them I'll write them both long letters very soon. To you, too. This one doesn't count.

Hugh is screaming at me to start the script conference. Just wanted you to know that your wandering girl is fine and happy, and not exactly unknown anymore.

Love,
Madeline

P.S.—Look, about that last dopey letter of mine, just pretend you never got it. Mrs. Cleveland is a very sick woman. It's a good thing she didn't go ahead with all those threats, especially about naming *me*. I guess she's not that crazy. I could have sued her to kingdom come.

M.

In the *Variety* page, a marked paragraph was all about Madeline Henry, Hugh Cleveland's assistant. "Maddy" came from a great Navy family. Her father commanded an aircraft carrier, one brother led a squadron of fighter planes, and the other was skipper of a submarine. A publicity agent had used the Henry background, obviously, to puff Cleveland; he was mentioned four times. Aside from the inaccuracies and the wisenheimer slang, the whole thing revolted Pug. His pretty, clever daughter, once his darling, had sunk into a world of crass fools, and was turning into one herself. He could do nothing about it; best to close his mind to that misfortune.

On a tan envelope addressed with green ink in an unfamiliar hand, the postmark was Washington, the posting date blurred. The single sheet was undated and unsigned.

Dear Pug,

This is from a true and well-meaning friend, who has known you and Rhoda for years. I realize what war can do to marriage, but I can't stand to see it happening to a "model couple" such as you two dear people have always been.

Write Rhoda and ask her about that *very* tall man (his name begins with K) that she plays tennis with at the St. Albans court. That isn't all she "plays." She has been seen with him in the wrong places and at the wrong times—*if* you know what I mean, and I *think* you do. Everybody in Washington who knows you two is talking about it. Rhoda stands in awe of you, as we all do, and a word from you probably can still make her "straighten up and fly right." Better do it before it's too late. That's a "word to the wise" from a well-wisher.

The letter had come by surface mail. It could be months old, dating back to the time before Rhoda's request for a divorce. Still, it brought back the full pain of the first disclosure, with the bitter new knowledge that his misfortune was on people's tongues.

While the other crews of Halsey's task force celebrated victory on the beach, the *Northampton* went back out to sea. The word was going around the decks that this bastard meant business. After the first mutterings subsided, there was little real dissatisfaction. The crew had tasted the disgrace of bad shooting. They had passed through showers of warm salt water from close misses of enemy salvos. They had seen the *Salt Lake City* straddled, and they had heard that five men in a twin-forty mount had been hit and blown to bloody smears. They were ready to learn how to fight. From the first collision drill, which started with sirens and alarm gongs while they were still in the channel, the sailors responded to the whip. Catapulting and recovering the float planes, a chronic sore of the Hickman days and the prime disgrace at Wotje, smoothed down in a day to a controlled chore. The time for setting condition Zed was halved. Surprise fire drills, air attack drills, abandon ship drills, broke out at all hours. It was hell, but by 2300, when Pug's drastic drill schedule at last ended, the crew was exhilarated as well as exhausted.

Not Pug. The anonymous letter had sapped him. He sat in his cabin well past midnight, leafing through three weeks' accumulation of news magazines. They showed a country still grinning at itself from giggly advertisements, still failing in any way—war production, war training, combat operations—to show awareness that defeat was not only possible, but coming on. The whole country was like the *Northampton* at Wotje. Meantime, the U-boats had wolfishly lunged against American shipping. The figures passed all belief; *over a million tons sunk in one month!* Rommel was sweeping across North Africa, smashing up the British armies. With the Americans falling back on Bataan, and the British retreating to Fortress Singapore, Pug could see little hope anywhere, except in the Russian counterattacks. These, too, seemed mere holding actions, while the tough gigantic Wehrmacht regrouped for the summer knockout.

In his War Plans service, Victor Henry had come to know well the inventory of armed force and natural resources of the planet. The changing picture seemed to him frightening. Java, Sumatra, and Borneo, which looked sure to fall, were immense prizes, greater in area and in warmaking potential than Japan itself. The Japanese advance into Burma threatened the United States, because it shook the British hold on the murmuring hundreds of millions of Indians. The loss of India could close the Persian Gulf, the best Lend-Lease route to the Soviet Union, and the great fountain of petroleum, the propellant of this whole world disaster. All the land masses, all the oceans, were strategically interlocked in this war. Everywhere except on the Russian front the situation was growing catastrophic; and nothing was worse in the whole flaming panorama than the continuing softness, complacency, and ignorance of the American people.

The secret mail he had read during the day reinforced his gloom. The landing craft program was stalled. Production was far behind the schedule he had himself drawn up in the War Plans section. Like a tidal wave a thousand miles off, a crisis was rolling toward President Roosevelt: a shortage that would one day halt major landing operations, or lead to shoestring assaults and bloody defeats. Pug felt he could avert that. He knew the problem to its core. He had grappled with the chief people in design and manufacture. He knew how to get raw material priorities. The Navy decision makers listened to him. Even Ernest King did, on the matter of landing craft. Many four-stripers could command a heavy cruiser. Nobody else had his grip on this key aspect of the war.

The fact he was coming to face was that he had plunged for forgetfulness into a past which he had outgrown. Big ship command was a challenge and an honor, but it was less than the best he could do in the war. Wotje had in any case deepened his doubts about heavy cruisers. The submarine panic had reflected the fear of the *Salt Lake City* skipper—fear he had himself felt—of the vulnerability of these beautiful, heavily armed, thin-skinned monsters. All operations plans now starred the carriers. The battleships were finished; and what was the *Northampton* but a kind of flimsy battleship that one torpedo or bomb could finish off? Wotje had rubbed his nose, too, in the mistake of his career, his choice of big guns over naval air. His son Warren, in a gnatlike dive-bomber, with one enlisted gunner, had perhaps caused more damage at Kwajalein than he had at Wotje, with his ten-thousand-ton cruiser and its crew of twelve hundred officers and men.

Worry about Warren, too, plagued him. Not till his visit to ComCruPac, when he had telephoned Warren's home and heard his son's cheery casual "Hello!" had his heart leaped with relief. Warren crashing, Warren burning, were anxious pictures that rose in his bad nights, and this was one of them. At two in the morning he went and woke the ship's doctor, a paunchy old regular, and asked him for a sleeping pill. The doctor sleepily proposed a good dose of medicinal brandy: it would promote the skipper's slumber better than a pill, he said, and might be a hell of a lot more fun. Victor Henry, standing in the doctor's cabin in an old bathrobe, barked, "Never suggest that again, Doc. Not to me. Not to any other officer or man on this ship. Not for sleeplessness."

The doctor stammered. "Well, ah, Captain, sometimes in the case of excessive nerve fatigue et cetera—you know, Captain Hickman, he—"

"Insomnia and nerves at sea in wartime are not emergencies. They're common nuisances. You prescribe brandy for them, and I'll end up with a wardroom of closet drunks. If they can't have the stuff, I can't. Understood?"

"Ah—understood, Captain."

Next day the concentration was on shooting. ComCruPac sent out a minesweeper with a sled and a plane towing a red sleeve-target. Everything about the cruiser's gunnery—rate of fire, ammunition handling, communications, fire control, score of hits—improved. So did Pug's mood. Recruits or draftees, these sailors were quick learners. When the *Northampton* moored in Pearl Harbor at sunset, the exec announced that, except for a skeleton watch, there would be liberty for all hands. Usually only half the crew went ashore at once. A cheer went up that sealed the status of Captain Henry; he was no longer the new skipper, he was the Old Man.

The flag lieutenant brought Pug a handwritten note:

Captain—Will you be dining ashore with your family? Otherwise, please join me. Armed Forces will rebroadcast your friend Tudsbury from Singapore at eight.

R. A. Spruance

Since the admiral had walked off the bridge at Wotje, Victor Henry had not once seen him. Through several days of fine weather, he had failed to appear topside. Pug showered and was dressing for dinner when the mail orderly came in. There was only one personal letter, another tan envelope addressed in green, this time sent airmail, its postmark clear, January 25; one month after Rhoda's contrite Christmas letter.

Dear Pug,

You may hate me, "sight unseen," because the truth often hurts. But the whole thing is now getting too *blatant* for words, and unless you do something "p.d.q." you can kiss your marriage good-bye. They go to the theatre together now, and to restaurants and I don't know "what all." *Everybody* who has ever known you two is talking about it, and I mean *talking*. Write to any "old pal" who is stationed in Washington. Tell him you're getting letters from this "awful person" (me) and ask him on his honor what he knows about Rhoda. "Nuff sed!"

With this black acid eating at his heart, Pug Henry went to dine with the admiral.

He found Spruance neat and erect as ever, but morose and dull of eye. Silence stretched through the meal, but it did not embarrass either of them, for they had come to know each other. Addiction to exercise was their bond. Spruance would stride the main deck for an hour or more in fair weather, and in port he would walk daily five or ten miles. Pug went along when he could, and their walks passed for the most part in such long silences. When Spruance now and then asked him to his quarters for a meal, they sometimes talked about their sons in submarines, and about themselves. The admiral, like Pug, harbored rueful second thoughts about having stayed in surface ships. Halsey's foresight in learning to fly at fifty Spruance considered masterful. He was not happy with a cruiser division, and foresaw a war career pass in obscure drudgery. Pug thought that the Wotje fiasco must be weighing on him as a blight on that career.

Over a dessert of canned peaches, Spruance surprised Pug by telling him to prepare for an award ceremony at morning quarters. He, Spruance, would receive the Navy Commendation Medal from Nimitz's own hands for his distinguished leadership in the Wotje bombardment. Bitter humor glimmered in the admiral's eyes as he said this. "The Navy needs heroes right now. To get decorated, it's enough to have been shot at. All I did at Wotje was lose control of a small task group. Turn on the radio, it's time for your friend. My compliments, incidentally, on what you're doing with the *Northampton*. It's needed."

Tudsbury sounded shaken and grave. Japanese heavy artillery was shelling downtown Singapore across the Johore Strait, the correspondent reported, killing hundreds of civilians each day. The enemy army was in plain sight on the far shore, making large-scale preparations to cross the water barrier. The military authorities now conceded (here Tudsbury's voice sharpened) that Singapore's one hope lay in letting the democratic world know exactly how desperate the situation was, since if help were ever to come, it had to come now.

Spruance and Pug Henry exchanged quizzical looks near the end, when Tudsbury said, *"My American friends will forgive me if I quote one of the many gallows-humor jokes circulating here. It goes so: 'Do you know where the American Navy is? Well, it can't operate because it's still under contract to Metro-Goldwyn-Mayer.'*

"Still, whether relief comes or not, I still believe that the Europeans and the Asians of Singapore, rallying shoulder to shoulder, can them-

selves, even at this late hour, turn the tide and destroy the badly worn-down invaders. I will gamble my overstuffed old hide on this belief, but not the person of my daughter, Pamela, a clever and lovely young woman who assists me in my work. So off she goes tomorrow with the other women and children who are being evacuated. She told me a story not two hours ago that I want her to share with you. Here, then, is Pamela."

With a strong effort of the will, Pug kept his face calm and his attitude relaxed.

"My story is a short one." The remembered husky sweet voice cut into him with a sensation of joy verging on agony. *"For the past two weeks, I have been working at a troop hospital as a volunteer. Today a badly wounded man left his bed, took me aside, and gave me a thing called a Mills bomb. It's a sort of grenade. 'Ma'am, you've been very nice to us. If you think a Jap is about to rape you, ma'am,' he said, in a charming Aussie accent, his face calm and serious, 'just pull the pin and you'll know nothing more.'*

"I have only one thing to add. I leave under protest. Good-night."

"Good-night," came the other voice, *"from Alistair Tudsbury in Singapore."*

"There are interesting parallels, Henry," said Spruance, reaching over and snapping off the radio, "between the battle problems in Malaya and Luzon. White garrisons plus mixed native troops defend water-girt land masses with Asian populations. An Asian invader advances on a north-south axis. The defenders execute a fighting fall-back toward a heavily armed island citadel in the extreme south. We seem to be doing a bit better with the problem than the British. After the war, it'll be instructive to compare the campaigns in detail."

"Yes, sir," said Pug, for once having not the vaguest idea of what an admiral was talking about.

16

LESLIE SLOTE gave the Wannsee photostats to the minister of the American legation in Bern, describing the material as "explosively urgent."

William Tuttle was a retired California railroad millionaire, a West Point graduate. The loss of an eye to German shrapnel in the First World War had cut off his Army career. Instead, he had gotten rich. This tall paunchy Republican grayhead naturally hated the New Deal and had strongly opposed a third term for that socialistic son of a bitch in the White House. With the fall of France in June 1940, however, and the nomination by the Republicans in July of a political amateur named Wendell Willkie, Tuttle had decided that the socialistic son of a bitch had better stay in the White House. He had headed the California branch of "Republicans for Roosevelt," earning the disgust of his friends and family before the election, and the sugarplum of a diplomatic post afterward. Slote liked this maverick legation head. If the railroad man was short on diplomatic experience he was long on horse sense, and he could make tough decisions without dithering.

Slote did not hear from Tuttle for three days, then the minister telephoned him in mid-morning. "Oh, say, Les, come on up and let's chin a bit."

It was a modest office for the representative of the United States of America in Switzerland: bookshelves stacked with unread-looking official volumes, dark old furniture, and three windows facing out on bare trees in mist, through which on clear days one could see the Alps. The minister puzzled Slote with aimless war talk, leaning back in his swivel chair with thick fingers folded over his belly. The successful escape from Brest of the *Scharnhorst* and the *Gneisenau,* he said, was a worse sign of British decay than the crumbling of Malaya. "Ye gods and little fishes, Les! Malaya's on the other side of the earth. But if the Royal Navy and Air Force between them couldn't stop two damaged German battleships from slipping away up the English Channel, right

inder their guns, then something's rotten—their intelligence, their combat readiness, or both."

Slote caught a whiff of rum-flavored tobacco, and the third secretary,
August Van Winaker, walked in with the portfolio in which Slote had
put the Wannsee papers. This appalled Slote. Van Winaker was the
legation's stickiest man on Jewish matters; whether because of a con-
sular background—he had shifted over not long ago to the Foreign Service track—or a bone-deep genteel anti-Semitism, Slote could not tell. He
knew that Jastrow had had trouble with this same fellow in Florence.
Slote thought Van Winaker a pompous nuisance, absurdly preoccupied
with his genealogy.

"Les, Augie's had some intelligence background," said Tuttle. "Mind
if he sits in?"

"Not at all, sir."

Van Winaker smiled and sat down, crossing short plump legs and
laying the portfolio on the desk.

"Okay, then," said the minister, "what's your evaluation of this material, Les? And what action do you recommend?"

"I believe it's an authentic document of grave import. The legation
should shoot off an urgent summary cable to the Secretary of State, and
send him the document by special air courier."

The minister looked toward Van Winaker, whose smile indulgently
broadened. "Augie thinks differently."

"Indeed I do. A kindly description would be 'a compassionately mo-
tivated fraud.'"

Slote forced a grin. "Let's hear your reasons, Augie."

Van Winaker puffed blue rum-smelling smoke through his smile.
Okay. Let's start at the point of contact. You meet a pretty girl at a
party, Leslie. Some time later her father, one Dr. Jacob Ascher, unexpectedly invites you to dinner. You're a new arrival, not too familiar
with Bern, with a reputation for compassion to Jews. Whereupon—"

"Now, stop right there—"

"Just let me finish, laddie." Van Winaker rolled his eyes at the
minister, and ran a hand through his close-cropped blond hair.
"Whereupon a priest at that dinner party offers to slip you documentary evidence on the Jewish situation. Interesting! Jacob Ascher happens to be president of the Jewish Council of Bern, a rich man who
hounds all the legations for refugee visas. Still, he's an honest sort, so
let's say some wily fabricator put one over on him and your priest, possibly with this so-called document, perhaps mulcting Ascher of a goodly

sum in the process. Of course, he'd jump at it, it's a fine propaganda tool for him."

"Augie, that's just theorizing. If the Germans are committing mass murder under cover of war—and I think they are—President Roosevelt can turn world opinion against them with this document."

"Oh, come on, laddie. The Nazi mistreatment of Jews was wrung dry years ago. People are numb to it. As for mass crime, the document is sheer fantasy."

"Why?"

"Why? Well, for pity's sake, cabinet-level government men meeting and discussing such a gruesome scheme so calmly—and putting it into writing! Not a word of such business would ever appear on paper. Oh, the stilted language, the labored jocularity, the coffee-hour tone! The whole thing is amateur romancing, Leslie, very badly done." Languidly Van Winaker picked up the portfolio and slid out the black sheets, releasing the nasty chemical odor. "And just look at this mess! The Germans have the best copying equipment in the world, and white on black, incidentally, is *not* the way they reproduce documents. They print from a negative film, and it comes out black on white. I mean, I respect your compassion, but—"

"Never mind my compassion," snapped Slote. "I'm well aware who Dr. Ascher is. Now as to the text, I say it's real. It's turgid, boring, like most German official documents we've both waded through. Everybody at the meeting is a droning pedant. Everybody's fawning German-fashion on the chairman, Heydrich. It's all Teutonic government prose to the life. Moreover, as to the reduction of an inhuman plan to writing"—Slote turned to Tuttle—"sir, nothing is more German than that. I took my degree in German political history. Look, Augie, read Treitschke. Read Lueger. Read Lagarde. Christ, read *Mein Kampf!* Hitler's just a self-educated street agitator, but even he uses thick political jargon, and a grandiose pseudophilosophical moral frame, to justify the most bloodthirsty proposals. I don't want to make a classroom lecture of this, but—"

"I've read *Mein Kampf*," said Tuttle.

Slote struck the desk with a fist. "Well, sir, I say a person from the submerged Germany, the liberal Germany, copied this document. I say he was risking torture, death, and the exposure of his anti-Nazi group. I say he sneaked a portable apparatus into a top-secret file room, his heart in his throat, and did a hurried job. Printing this copy was as risky as taking the pictures. You probably can't even buy black-on-white photocopy paper in Germany today without signing a receipt that can hang you."

"You're a warm advocate, laddie." Van Winaker was smiling again. "But notice that the thing is dated January twentieth. A top-secret report written, approved, mimeographed, filed, surreptitiously copied, and secretly delivered to Bern, all in less than three weeks? No, Les, I sympathize with your compassion, but—"

"Jesus *Christ*, Augie," Slote exploded, "stop using that goddamned word! Of course they'd rush it to the outside world! It describes a crime almost beyond human imagination!"

"Why, I admire compassion, Les," Van Winaker returned softly. "Just let me tell you a little story. A document came to me in Florence, in much the same cloak-and-dagger way, about top-secret Italian war plans. In language and physical appearance, unlike this crude botch, it was flawless. I guessed it was a fraud, all the same. I *said* so. Our embassy in Rome swallowed it, however, and gave it to the British. Well, they analyzed it and laughed it off. It was hogwash, intended to misdirect their entire North Africa strategy. So there you are. These things are an art, and that"—he waved limp fingers at the photostats—"is the work of a low-grade bungler."

"Okay, Augie," Bill Tuttle said. "Many thanks."

With a friendly, even apologetic smile at Slote, and a wave of the pipe, the third secretary got up and left.

Swivelling his chair in a half-turn, Tuttle laced his fingers behind his head. "Sorry, Les, I'm with Augie. That stuff is the pipe dream of an ignoramus, making up a horror story and doing a bum job."

This was a real shock to Slote, though he had anticipated Van Winaker's reaction. "May I ask why you say that?"

Tuttle was lighting a cigar. He rolled it with relish in his mouth, and waved it at the portfolio. "The railroading part. I've been handling intelligence on European railroads since I got here. General Marshall asked me to do that. I've known George forever. I send him periodic summaries. The rolling stock in all of German-held Europe couldn't do it. You're talking here about transporting millions upon millions of civilians, Leslie, with a deteriorating rail system that's already in a bind. Hitler's having trouble just moving his troops, his supplies, and his foreign laborers around. Depots are piling up with vital things like food, fuel, tanks, and shells. Whole divisions are sitting on their duffs on sidings because the trains can't get them to the front, and the British are bombing the hell out of their locomotive factories and railroad yards.

It's not going to get better but worse. Okay? Now how does such a broken-down system go shunting eleven million people all over the continent for some crazy massacre scheme?" Tuttle shook his head. "It's stupid nonsense. The faker who did that document didn't know anything about railroading. He should have done a little research."

Slote was chewing on his cold pipe during the minister's tirade, slumped in the armchair, a picture of pale discouragement. "Sir, at the risk of seeming compassionate, may I respond?"

"Go ahead," grinned Tuttle.

"It's just that the job isn't that big. It's a sweep of a dragnet through western Europe, sort of fanwise"—Slote made a half-circle in the air with spread fingers—"Scandinavia, Holland, Belgium, France, then Italy and the Balkans, all spilling into Poland and conquered Russia. Out of reach of the Red Cross and the press. Away from liberal populations. Backward areas, where communication is bad or nonexistent, and anti-Semitism is rife. But, sir, *most of the Jews are there already, in Poland and occupied Russia.* That's the whole point. They don't have to be moved far, if at all. Bringing the Jews from the west shouldn't overtax the rails. There's no fighting in the west."

The minister puffed at his cigar, cocking his good eye at Slote. "How would you go about authenticating this document?"

"What would you consider authentication, sir?"

"That's the problem. I don't believe the damned thing, not one bit. I say the railroading problem's insurmountable. Now, I'm not telling you to forget this thing. Bring in some authentication, if you can, and meantime give the document maximum security storage."

"I will, sir."

"Maximum security storage isn't, for instance, the hands of an Associated Press reporter."

His face hot and tingling, Slote replied, "Nobody will see it unless you release it."

"Okay, then."

Returning to his office with the portfolio, Slote felt drained, defeated, stupid, with no notion of what to do next. He drudged through the lunch hour on official papers, haunted by a sense of defeat which made his lips tremble. About three o'clock a secretary looked in. "Will you see Dr. Jean Hesse?"

"Absolutely."

The Swiss diplomat entered briskly, a decent, sad little man Slote had known since Warsaw, with a red tuft of chin beard. They sometimes played chess, and Hesse gloomed over the board in Spenglerian tones about the collapse of European man. "Well, I have been to Siena, and I have seen Mrs. Natalie Henry," said Hesse, rasping open his briefcase. "A handsome woman. Jewish, isn't she?"

"Yes, she's Jewish."

"Mmmmm!" The sidewise look and a pull at the beard expressed concurrence with a naughty erotic taste. "I gave her your letter. Here's an answer."

"Thank you, Jean. How are the other journalists doing?"

"Desperately bored. Drunk all day. In that respect I could envy them. I'm going to report now to your minister. They'll probably come out in March or April, the way the negotiation is going."

Slote locked his door, ripped open the letter, and read the yellow sheets at the window.

Dear old Slote:

Well, what a marvelous surprise! Your nice Dr. Hesse is having a cup of tea out in the lemon house with Aaron while I hammer this off.

First of all, I'm fine and so is Louis. It's crazy, how comfortable we are here. But I feel sick to the heart whenever I think of the *Izmir*. We almost sailed on that boat, Leslie! A German diplomat who knew Aaron got us off and drove us to Rome. I still don't know what his motives were, but he rescued us from terrible danger, possibly from death. The BBC didn't make much of the story, but apparently the *Izmir* just vanished after the Turks forced it to leave Istanbul. What in God's name became of it? Do you know? The news here is so scanty! I still have nightmares about it. What a world! I saved my baby, and I suppose I should be thankful, but I keep thinking about those people.

We found the house in good shape. Took off the dust covers, put sheets on the beds, lit the fire and there we were! Maria and Tomaso are going on with their work in exactly the old way. The weather is chilly, but lovely once the morning mists lift. Only the internees down at the Excelsior Hotel remind us of the war. They come up here for lunch, one or two at a time. The police are nice about that. Correspondents, wives, a singer, a couple of clergymen—an odd lot, bored to death, mostly staying ossified on Tuscan wine, and full of cranky little complaints, but perfectly okay.

Oh Lord, I can't *begin* to tell you how glad I am to have your letter! When Dr. Hesse left the room just now, I cried. It's been so goddamned lonesome here! And you're in Bern—so close, and working on our release! I still haven't caught my breath.

Well, one thing at a time. I'd better jump to what's most on my mind.

Slote, Aaron is playing with the notion of staying on here, war or no war.

Between the archbishop and the chief of police, both old friends of his, he's being treated like royalty in exile. It's eerily like peacetime, for us. Last Sunday he was even allowed to go and have lunch with Bernard Berenson in his mansion outside Florence—you know, that old American art critic. Well, Berenson told Aaron that he has no intention of leaving. He's too old to move, Italy is his home, etc., etc., and he'll stay and take what comes. Berenson's a Jew too—of sorts, like Aaron. Aaron came back with this bee in his bonnet. If Berenson can do it, why can't he? As for me, I'm free to go home, of course.

GRRRR!

Bernard Berenson, I have pointed out, has important, powerful connections. He has authenticated paintings for billionaires, lords, national museums, kings. He may well be under Mussolini's protection. None of this applies to Aaron in the least. He grudgingly admits that. But he says he too is old. His home too is Italy. His rheumatism is worse (that is true). A long rail trip and an Atlantic crossing could knot him all up, maybe disable him. He's started what he considers his most important book, "the last panel," about Martin Luther and the Reformation. The book does begin well, and I must say it's kept us both occupied.

But what he apparently can't picture is his plight once the rest of us leave. His isolation will be frightful. If he becomes ill, he'll be in the hands of hostile strangers. *He's in enemy country!* That's the brute fact he won't face. He says Mussolini's declaration of war on America was a comedy to keep the Germans quiet. He has an answer for everything.

He squirrels and gloats over one sweaty little ace in the hole, Leslie. During some futile little romance in his early twenties, Aaron was once converted to Catholicism. Did you know that? He dropped it fast but he's never de-converted, if there is such a thing. A friend of his in the Vatican obtained copies of the American documents and gave them to him. Aaron now regards these scruffy photographs as his shield and buckler. It's a curse that he ever obtained them!

You see, he's read up on the Nuremberg laws. I'm not sure of the details, but it seems that a conversion before 1933, when Hitler came to power, makes a material difference for German Jews, or maybe it's for half-Jews. Anyhow, Aaron says he can handle the Italians; and as for the Germans, why, between his precious conversion documents and his position as an American journalist, he refuses to worry. In short, he has only a few years to live, the one thing he cares about is his work, and he works best here.

I beg you to get word to Aaron to drop this notion. Possibly he'll listen to you. I have no effect on him any more. He's apologetic toward me, and in every way tries to mollify me. He's made me the heir of all his property and copyrights. Aaron's a prudent man, and quite wealthy. But I remain furious at him, and terribly concerned.

I really don't know why I should be so upset about Aaron. It's his life. I came to work for him simply to be nearer you, in those simple lost days when my only worry was a messed-up romance. (God, how young I was!) I hardly knew him then. Now my destiny's bound up with his. My father's gone. My mother's a million miles away in body and spirit, playing canasta and going to Hadassah meetings in Miami Beach while the world explodes. Next to Louis, my uncle seems almost the only family I have. Byron himself is a disembodied idea, an aureate memory, compared with Aaron. I know even you much better than I do my baby's father.

Omigosh, I hear the voices of Aaron and your Swiss friend, and I have to end this—

Old Slote, my dear, you can't imagine how GOOD it makes me feel, just knowing you're close by. You were a fool not to marry me in Paris, when I proposed. How I loved you! Oh, if one only understood sooner that things happen *once* and then roll away into the past, leaving one marked and changed forever, and—well, this hasty maundering is to no avail. Think of something to do about Aaron, my dear, please!

I'm a lot thinner again in the enclosed, and at least I'm smiling. Isn't Louis cute?

Love,
N

Slote sat at his desk and stared at the snapshot, comparing Selma Ascher in his mind to this young woman in a plain housedress, holding a pretty baby on her arm. How Selma faded! Something was wrong with him, he thought. When one lost a girl, it ought to be like having a tooth out; brief sharp pain, then a rapid healing of the hole. Every man went through it. But Natalie Jastrow, utterly gone, preoccupied him yet like a teasing mistress. The very look of the letter gave him a poignant bittersweet sensation; ah, the passionate outpourings he had received on just such yellow sheets, in this Remington typeface with the crooked *y!* Gone, all gone, that fiery love, that once-in-a-lifetime golden chance!

Though it might be a couple of weeks before a letter could even start back to her through the diplomatic channel, he stopped work and wrote a three-page reply. Pouring out words to Natalie Henry was in itself a real if frustrating pleasure. Then he wrote a short letter to Jastrow, cautioning him against the plan to remain in Italy. He tore up a draft referring to "new documents" about the danger to Jews that he had come upon. He did not want to scare Natalie uselessly. The minister's reproof about security before authentication troubled him, too.

But what would be authentication?

17

STEPPING from an ice-cold shower in a shivery glow, Natalie towelled herself fast and hard at the tall antique mirror framed in pink-and-gilt curlicued wood; turning here and there, feeling thankful for the flat belly she saw. Louis's passage into the world had left, after all, only a few fading purple stretch marks. Even her breasts were not too bad, not too bad. Meager wartime rations helped! She might be twenty.

Her nakedness struck memory sparks of the Lisbon honeymoon. Sometimes she could hardly remember how Byron looked, except in the few old snapshots she still had. At this moment she could picture his mouth curling in the old beguiling grin, feel the thick red-brown hair in her fingers, feel the touch of his hard hands. What a dry death-in-life this was, what a waste of love, of young years! She bent one knee in the female pose common to the Venus de Milo and Rabinovitz's girlie pictures. This fleeting thought of Rabinovitz sobered her. "Vain old bag," she said aloud, wondering how to dress for the unusual dinner guest. The telephone rang. She pulled the damp towel around her and answered it.

"Hello, Mrs. Henry. Dr. Beck here. I've finished my meeting at the bank, so I can still get to Florence for the seven o'clock train to Rome. May I take a cup of tea first with you and Professor Jastrow?"

"Tea? But we're expecting you for dinner."

"You're very kind, but dinner guests in wartime are a trouble. Now tea—"

"Dr. Beck, we've got veal."

"Veal! Amazing."

"The archbishop sent it over for Aaron's birthday. We saved it for you. Do come."

"I'm flattered. And hungry! Ha ha! The morning train's faster, anyway. Veal! I accept."

The black and white cathedral in slant sunset light, rising out of Siena's old walls and ascending red roofs, made a fine view through the all windows of Jastrow's sitting room. But Italy was full of fine views and virtually empty of Scotch whiskey. The bottle of Haig and Haig which Natalie brought in with glasses, soda, and ice really impressed Dr. Beck. Jastrow explained that Bernard Berenson had given him the whiskey "out of sheer gratitude at hearing another American voice." She also briefly fetched in the baby. Dr. Beck cooed at Louis, his glasses misting, his face glowing. "Ach, how I miss my kiddies," he said.

The Scotch put Jastrow in his vein of jocose persiflage. The philosopher George Santayana had also lunched with him and Berenson, and Jastrow satirized the foibles of both men at table, such as Santayana's drinking a whole bottle of wine, and Berenson's hogging the conversation and admiring the play of his own shapely little hands. He was waspishly amusing about all this. Dr. Beck roared with laughter, and Natalie yielded up a few giggles.

She found herself warming a bit to the visitor. She never could truly like or trust him, but his admiration of her baby pleased her, and they owed him their present safety. His square face topped with thick lank blond hair was not unhandsome, and he even had a clumsy humor of his own. She asked him when he had last eaten veal. "I'm not sure, Mrs. Henry," he said. "I was served veal two weeks ago in Rome, but I think that particular calf had been well broken to the saddle."

The dinner was a decided success. Happy to be cooking veal again, the housekeeper had made superb scallopini in Marsala. The archbishop had also sent champagne for Aaron's birthday, and they quaffed both bottles. Natalie drank more than she wanted to, mainly so that Aaron would not get her share of the wine. In his isolation, and perhaps in a suppressed state of nerves, he was becoming a toper, and when he had had too much his mood could turn unstable, and his tongue could loosen. At the end of the meal, as they ate raspberry tarts and ice cream, an exquisite aroma drifted in.

"My dear professor, *coffee?*" said Beck.

Jastrow smiled, dancing his fingertips together. "The Swiss chargé l'affaires brings Berenson little gifts. My generous friend shared half a pound with me."

"One begins to understand," said Beck, "why Berenson has decided not to leave."

"Ah, creature comforts aren't everything, Werner. There are shortages at I Tatti. The place is in shocking disrepair. B.B. has spells of depression about it. But he says it's his only home now. As he puts it, he'll 'ride out the storm at anchor.'" With an arch and not exactly sober smile he added, "B.B. thinks it will all end well, meaning that your side will lose. Of course, he's an expert on Italian paintings, not warfare."

"Dr. Freud might call that wishful thinking," Beck replied, pursing his lips. "In view of what's happening in Singapore, and Burma, and the Atlantic, and North Africa. However, whichever side wins, such a prominent person needn't worry."

"A prominent Jew?" It was a measure of Natalie's unbending that she could say this without edginess.

"Mrs. Henry, victory softens harsh wartime policies." Beck's tone was calm. "That's my profound personal hope."

The housekeeper proudly bore in the coffee service. They watched the steaming brew fill the cups, as though a magician were pouring it from an empty pot.

"Ah," Beck exclaimed over his first sip. "Worth the trip to Siena."

"Of course Santayana has no problem, he's neither Jew nor American," Jastrow mused aloud, sipping his coffee. "He's a strange personality, Werner, a true exotic. A fixture at Harvard for twenty years, writing and speaking exquisite English, yet he has retained Spanish nationality. He explained why, but I couldn't follow. Either he or I had had too much wine. He's Gentile to the bone, a bit of a Spanish grandee, and not too fond of the Hebrews himself. One could hear that in his subtle digs at Berenson's opulent surroundings. Santayana holes up in a little cell in a Roman convent, writing his memoirs. He says that a scholar living in one small room near a major library is as close to happiness as a man can come on earth."

"A true philosopher," said Beck.

"Well, I could live like that, too." Jastrow waved a hand around at the walls. "When I bought this place with the book-club money for *A Jew's Jesus,* I was fifty-four. It was my fling. I can leave with a cheerful shrug and never look back."

"You too are a philosopher," said Beck.

"Then again I can always get my niece angry"—Jastrow's glance at her was sly and tipsy—"by suggesting that she and the baby go home while, like Berenson, I ride it out at anchor."

"I'm enjoying my coffee," said Natalie sharply.

"And why should you do that?" said Beck.

"Because a philosopher is above worrying about concentration camps," said Natalie. Jastrow shot her a vexed look. "Is that discourteous? I have trouble making Aaron face realities. Somebody must."

"Perhaps not all Germans, either, are enthusiastic about concentration camps." Beck's voice was kindly and sad. His fat cheeks reddened.

"And what about the stories coming out of eastern Europe, Dr. Beck? Stories that your soldiers have been massacring the Jews?"

Jastrow stood up, raising his voice. "We'll have brandy and more coffee in the sitting room."

That they were unendurably on each other's nerves was all too evident. "I take it, Mrs. Henry," Beck said, settling into a corner of a sofa in the other room, carefully lighting a cigar, and making his voice easy and conciliatory, "that your question was not merely provocative. I have standard replies to standard provocations. I can also give you an honest opinion about your uncle's safety, if he should elect to stay on."

"Can you?" She sat tensed on the edge of the sofa, facing Beck. Jastrow stood at a window, brandy glass in hand, glowering at her. "How much do you really know about what's happening to Jews?"

"In Italy? Nothing is happening."

"And elsewhere?"

"The Foreign Service does not operate in the Occupied Territories, Mrs. Henry. The army governs the combat areas. Drastic measures are imperative there, and life is hard for both occupiers and the occupied."

"Worse for the Jews, no doubt," said Natalie.

"I don't deny it. Anti-Semitism is rife all through eastern Europe, Mrs. Henry. I'm not proud of our own excesses, but the Jews had to be rounded up for their own safety! Of that I assure you. They would otherwise have been plundered and murdered en masse in places like Lithuania, Poland, and the Ukraine. The local hooligans were amazed, when German forces arrived, that they didn't want them to join in straightway to rob and kill the Jews. They expected an 'open season,' as one might say."

Jastrow cut in. "What excesses by your own forces?"

"Professor, our police units are not always the highest types," Beck replied, looking unhappy. "Scarcely the representatives of an advanced culture. There has been rough handling. The Jews have passed a bad winter. There were outbreaks of disease. True, in the snow outside Moscow and Leningrad our soldiers have also suffered terribly. War is a vile business." He faced Natalie and his voice rose. "But when you ask me, Mrs. Henry, whether the German army is massacring Jews, I respond that this is a lie. My brother is an army officer. He has spent much time in Rumania and in Poland. He assures me that the army has not only refrained from atrocities, but has at times interfered to protect the Jews from the local population. That is God's truth, as I know it."

Aaron Jastrow said, "I was born and grew up in eastern Europe. I believe you."

"Don't let me gloss things over. Our regime will have much to answer for." Werner Beck spread his pudgy hands, puffed at his cigar, and drank brandy. "Even in victory decent Germans are not going to forget, I promise you. This is excellent brandy, Professor. Your friend Berenson again?"

"No." With a pleased look, Jastrow passed his glass under his nose. "I'm rather a fancier of French brandy. I had enough foresight to lay in several cases of this stuff back in 1938."

"Yes, my brother told me some fantastic things. Strangely enough, one can visit these wretched ghettos. Imagine that! The elegant Polish ladies and our officers sometimes enjoy a night of slumming among the Jews. There are even grotesque little nightclubs. Helmut went several times. He wanted to see conditions for himself. He tried to do something about improving supplies. He's in the quartermaster corps, and he had some success in Lodz. But the whole thing remains bad. Very bad."

"Has your brother visited concentration camps?" Natalie inquired very politely.

"Let's change the subject," said Jastrow.

"Mrs. Henry, those are secret political prisons." Beck gave a miserable shrug.

"But that's where the worst things are happening." The studied patience of his manner was impressing Natalie, for all her rising irritation. She regretted having started this topic, but why had Aaron brought up his fatuous maddening notion of remaining in Italy?

"Mrs. Henry, dictatorships use terror to keep order. That is classic politics. What forced the German people to submit to a dictatorship is a long, complex question, but the outside world—including America—is not guiltless. I have never so much as seen the outside walls of a concentration camp. Have you ever visited an American prison?"

"That's not a reasonable comparison."

"I'm comparing only your ignorance and mine about penal institutions. I'm sure that American prisons are very bad. I imagine our concentration camps are worse. But—" he passed a hand across his forehead and cleared his throat. "We began with the question of your uncle's safety, if he should stay in Italy."

"Never mind!" Jastrow knit his brow fiercely at his niece. "We asked Werner here to give him a good dinner, Natalie. It's not his problem. Bernard Berenson is a very shrewd and worldly man, yet he too—"

"*Damn* Berenson!" Natalie exploded, and she thrust a demanding finger at Beck. "Supposing Germany occupies Italy? Is that so impossible? Or supposing Mussolini decides to ship all Jews to the Polish ghettos? Or just supposing some Fascist bigwig up and decides that he'd like to live in this villa? I mean it's so incredible, so childish, to even *think* of taking such risks—"

"It would be I, only I, taking those risks," Aaron Jastrow burst out, slamming down his glass so that the brandy flew, "and frankly I'm getting sick of this. Werner is our guest. You and your baby are alive because he rescued you. Anyway, I never said I wouldn't leave." Jastrow jerkily, noisily threw open a casement window. Cool air streamed in, and a patch of blue moonlight fell on the Oriental rug. He stood with his back to the window, and picked up his glass in a badly shaking hand. "One crucial difference between you and me, Natalie, is that you're hardly Jewish. You know nothing about our culture and our history, and you're not interested. You married a Christian without turning a hair. I'm a Jew to the core. I'm a *Polish* Jew!" He said this with a proud glare. "A Talmud scholar! I could resume the study tomorrow if I chose. All my writings turn on my identity. My nerve ends are antennae for anti-Semitism, and I detected it in George Santayana before we'd been in the same room five minutes. *You* needn't warn *me* about the hazards of being Jewish!" He turned to Dr. Beck, "You haven't an anti-Semitic bone in you. You serve a detestable regime, and whether you should be doing that is another and a very large question—one you and I should discuss another time—but—"

"Professor, this was for me, and still remains, a radical ethical dilemma."

"I should think so. What your government has done to the Jews is unforgivable. But alas, how far back it all goes! There are anti-Jewish rules in Aquinas's *Summa* that make your Nuremberg laws look mild. The Church has yet to repudiate them! We're the eternal strangers, the outsiders in Christian Europe, and in times of breakdown we feel the impact first and hardest. It happened to us during the Crusades, it happened in the plague years, it has happened during most wars and revolutions. The United States is the modern liberal oasis, full of natural wealth and protected by the oceans. We're able and we're hard workers, so we've done well there. But Natalie, if you think we're any less strangers there than in Germany, *you're* the childish one, not I! If the war should take a bad turn, a defeated America will be uglier than Nazi Germany. Louis will be no safer there than here, and perhaps less so, because the Italians at least love children and are not very violent. These are simple truths you can't grasp because your Jewish blood runs so thin."

"Nonsense! Plain nonsense!" Natalie shot back. "Nazi Germany is a freakish monster of history. Not Christian, not Western, not even European. To equate it with America, even in defeat, is just drunken babble. As for my Jewish blood—"

"Why? What's so freakish about Hitler? Why are the Germans more wrong, in trying for world mastery, than the British were two centuries ago when they succeeded? Or than we Americans are, for making our own bid now? What do you suppose this war is about, anyway? Democracy? Freedom? Fiddlesticks! It's about who rules next, who fixes the currencies, who dominates the markets, who gets the raw materials and exploits the vast cheap labor of the primitive continents!" Jastrow was wound up now, and his wine-loosened tongue flew; not at all blurrily, but with the clipped edged classroom accents of an enraged professor. "Mind you, I think we'll win. I'm glad of that, because I'm a liberal humanist. Radical nationalism like Hitler's or Stalin's tends to crush free thought, art, and discourse. But I'm honestly not sure at this late hour of my life, Natalie, whether human nature is happier under tyranny, with its fixed codes, its terrorized quiet, its simple duties, or amid the dilemmas and disorders of freedom. Byzantium lasted a thousand years. It's doubtful whether America will last two hundred. I've lived more than ten years in a Fascist country, and I've been more at peace than I ever was in the money-chasing hurly-burly back home. I really fear an American 1918, Natalie. I fear a sudden falling apart of those unloving elements held together by the common pursuit of money. I foresee horrors in defeat, amid abandoned skyscrapers and grass-grown highways, that will eclipse the Civil War! A blood bath with region against region, race against race, every man's hand against his brother, and all hands against the Jews."

Werner Beck made a gesture and wink at Natalie as though to say, *Don't stir up the old fellow any more.* He took a soothing, almost unctuous tone. "Professor, you surprise me with your penetrating insight about America. Frankly, when I was in Washington I was shocked.

Some of the best-connected persons whispered in my ear total approval of the Führer's position on the Jews, never supposing that I might not agree."

"Ah, upper-crust anti-Semitism is epidemic, Werner. Elites always detest gifted and nimble outsiders. Who made the British policy to turn back the refugee ships, but old-school-tie anti-Semites? The upper-crust anti-Semites who run our State Department have closed all the Americas to refugees. Why am I still here? Only because of obscure sabotage of my papers."

Natalie said, striving for a calm note, "You were dilatory, Aaron."

"Granted, my dear. Granted." He sank into an armchair. *"Mea culpa, mea culpa, mea maxima culpa.* But it's done. The question is, what next? I quite understand that those bored newspaper soaks down at the Excelsior Hotel can't wait to get out of Siena, and I know that you want to take Louis home. But I believe there may be a negotiated peace this year, and I for one would welcome it."

"Welcome it!" Natalie's face and Beck's showed almost the same degree of astonishment. "Welcome peace with Hitler?"

"My dear, the best chance for mankind's survival is simply for the war to stop. The sooner the better. The fabric of civilization has been shaken loose already by the industrial and scientific revolutions, the collapse of religion, and two mechanized world wars. It can't stand much more of a pounding. In a bitter way I almost welcome the fall of Singapore—"

"It hasn't fallen—"

"Oh, that's a question of days," put in Beck. "Or for all we know, hours. The British are finished in Asia."

"Let's face it," said Jastrow, "the Japanese belong there and the Europeans don't. The Russian front is at a stalemate. The Atlantic front is at another stalemate. A negotiated peace would be the best thing for the world, for America, and certainly for the Jews. It's much more desirable than a vengeful five-year crusade to destroy the have-nots. I suppose if we marshal all our industrial power we'll crush them, but to what purpose? They've shown their mettle. The hegemony can be shared. The British and the French learned to do that after centuries of bloodletting. It will have to be shared in any case with the Russians. The longer the war goes on, the worse things will get for Jews behind the Nazi lines, my dear, and if we do crush Germany, the end of it will merely be a Soviet Europe. Is that so desirable? Why shouldn't we hope instead that the bloody madness will stop? And if it does stop, how silly

I'll look to have uprooted my whole life for nothing! Nevertheless, you won't go without me, so I'll leave. I've never said otherwise. But I'm not a soft-headed old fool to consider remaining, and I'll not have you take that tone with me again, Natalie."

She did not answer him.

"Mrs. Henry, I find your uncle's vision of the war lucid and inspiring," said Werner Beck excitedly. "He gives all this stupid carnage a theme, a direction, and a hope."

"He does? Peace with Hitler? Who can believe a word Hitler says, or have faith in a paper he signs?"

"That is not an insoluble problem," Beck quietly returned.

"Exactly. There are other Germans. There are even other Nazis," said Jastrow. "The skin of the tyrant is not steel plate. So history teaches."

"Professor, I have not had such a conversation, except with my brother, in ages." The eyes of Werner Beck strangely flashed at Jastrow, and his voice quavered. "I will pretend I never had this conversation. Yet I will tell you, my old and trusted teacher, that my brother and I have more than once discussed into the dawn the ethics of tyrannicide."

"My baby gets fed now." Natalie stood up, and Werner Beck jumped to his feet.

"Let me thank you for the best dinner I have had in months, Mrs. Henry."

"Well, we probably owe you our lives. I'm not unaware of that. So if I—" Without looking at her uncle, she broke off and hurried from the room. Jastrow stood at the open casement, his thin hair blowing, his face heavily shadowed by the moonlight.

"Professor, your discussion of the war stunned me," said Dr. Beck. "You spoke with the grasp of a Thucydides."

"Ah, Werner, it was just an angry rush of words. Poor Natalie. Even an animal mother fears for her baby. She's not very good company these days."

"I would urge you, Dr. Jastrow, when you get home, to write a short book developing those thoughts. A book like *The Last Palio,* your exquisite little elegy over the Europe of the Versailles Treaty."

"Oh, did you read that?" Jastrow sounded flattered. "A minor *jeu d'esprit.*"

"But your vision of the war! That a man like yourself, a humanist, a Jew, can speak with such understanding of the Japanese problem, and of the German revolution! Can even suggest that 'sharing the hegemony,' in your brilliant phrase, might be preferable to a grim five-year mutual bloodletting! It's breathtaking. It restores one's faith in the possible brotherhood of mankind. What a profound tribute to the Jewish spirit!"

"You're too kind, but I shall write nothing about this accursed war. I shall get on with Martin Luther. Well! Shall we have a nightcap?"

"*Bitte*. Let me telephone for my car."

Beck made his call, while Jastrow poured two snifters fuller than usual. They drank standing at the open window, chatting about the view and about the quiet charm of Siena. "I understand your reluctance to leave," Beck said. "What you have here is a private little paradise."

"Well, I've been happy here." Jastrow's mood was much improved. "And brandy has helped me snare many an elusive theme and thought."

"Professor, would you consider coming to Rome and talking to press correspondents of neutral countries? *Only* of neutral countries. None of Goebbels's propagandists or Gayda's hacks."

"To what purpose?"

"Your views on the war would command attention. They are original, magnanimous, and wise. Their impact would be great. I can tell you"—the diplomat's voice sank low—"that better elements in Germany would be encouraged."

Jastrow stroked his beard, his face wrinkling into sharp smiling lines. "Hardly. I'm a very minor writer."

"Not so. You have news value. Only Berenson and Santayana, besides yourself, have lived so long in the Italian dictatorship. I urge you to think about this."

"Out of the question. On my return home, I should be pilloried." A car came rolling into the driveway, the same bank limousine that had brought the diplomat. "Ah, then you must go?" said Jastrow. "Pity. I did want you to see my library."

Beck leaned out of the window and spoke a few crisp words to the driver. Jastrow led him upstairs to the library, where they made a circuit of the room, brandy glasses in hand. "Bless my soul," said Beck, "don't you have as good a private collection on Christianity as one will find anywhere?"

"Oh, no! This is a pathetic scratch of the surface. And yet—" Jastrow's eyes moved along the shelves, and the look on his face was deeply sad. "You know, Werner, I've had no family life. No children. If my love has an object, it's this collection of books. Santayana's right, of course, an institutional library is best. Yet there's something personal and—this will sound mawkish—alive for me in this room. These books speak to me. The authors are all my friends and colleagues, though some of them crumbled to dust fifteen centuries ago. I shall leave the villa with no regret, but it will hurt to leave these books behind, knowing that it may be the end of them."

"Dr. Jastrow, could I not have them crated up for you, after you go, and sent to Switzerland or Sweden? All wars end. Then you could retrieve them."

The mournful aged eyes shone with delight. *"Could* you do that, my dear fellow? Would it work?"

"I will find out details on my return to Rome, and telephone you about it."

"Why, I'll never forget you! And I'm already so much in your debt."

"Please! You pulled me through my doctorate. That shaped my whole career. And now I bid you good-night. I thank you for a grand evening. Dr. Jastrow, I shall be pressing you yet again to share your prophetic insights with a suffering world. Fair warning."

"I am not a prophet, nor the son of a prophet, Werner," said Jastrow archly. "Pleasant journey."

18

LESLIE SLOTE came trudging back to the legation after a too-heavy Swiss lunch with too much Swiss wine, all ingested to comfort himself in his mood of profound futility. Head down to the wind-driven rain, collar turned up, he almost butted Augie Van Winaker, coming out of the legation building. "Steady there, laddie."

"Hi."

"No offense, I hope, about that meeting yesterday."

"No offense."

"Good. You'd have looked very silly—or worse—if the matter had gone further."

In his office Slote threw his wet coat and hat down, seized the telephone, and called Selma Ascher. A heavy weary voice came on. "Ja? Who is that?"

"Ah—it's Leslie Slote, Dr. Ascher."

"So." Pause. "You wish to speak to my daughter? My daughter is not here."

"It's not important. Thank you."

"My daughter will return at six. Shall she telephone you?"

"If she has a moment."

He went to work, and ground through his paper pile at half his usual speed. The telephone rang at the stroke of six. "Hello? This is Selma Ascher speaking."

"Are you free to talk, Selma?"

"Certainly. What is it I can do for you?"

The stiff cool tone was warning enough. "Well, I'd rather like to call the English girl I met at your house."

"You mean Nancy Britten? They live at 19 Tellenstrasse in the Pension Gafen. Would you like Nancy's number?"

"Please. Sorry to trouble you."

"No trouble. One moment—here we are. Nancy's number is 68215."

"I'm much obliged."

"Good-bye then, Mr. Slote."

He was stuffing his briefcase despondently when the phone rang again. Her voice was breathless and gay. "Yes, Leslie? I'm in a pay telephone down at the corner garage."

"Selma, that priest I met at your house—"

"Father Martin? What about him?"

"I have to talk to him. Your father mustn't know, and I can't telephone his parish house."

"Oh. I see. Is that it?" The girlish tone turned brisk. "I'll have to call you back."

"I'm about to go to my flat. The number—"

"No, stay where you are."

She called again half an hour later. "The corner of Feldstrasse and the Boulevard. You know where that is?"

"Of course."

"Wait there. I'll pick you up."

He had scarcely arrived at the busy boulevard corner when the gray Fiat roadster came zipping up and the door flew open. "Nancy Britten, indeed!" Selma exclaimed with an agitated smile. "Hop in."

"Well, I had to say something." He slammed the door shut. The smell of the leather seats and of her perfume brought back strongly the mood of their one clumsy night out. "Wasn't your father standing beside you?"

"Indeed he was." She shifted gears and went off in a jackrabbit start. "I hardly know Father Martin, but I drove over and saw him. He gave me some strange instructions. I can take you only partway. He said you mustn't involve me again. I've never been in such a situation before. It's like a film." Slote laughed. She added, "No, truly. Is there any danger?"

"No."

"Has this to do with his information about the Jews?"

"Never mind."

"My father found out about our evening together."

"How?"

"He asked me. I can't lie to him. I'm disobeying him by seeing you again."

"What is his objection to me?"

"Oh, Leslie, don't talk rot."

"I'm serious. His attitude puzzles me."

"Don't you find me attractive?" The question shot out at him as she whisked the car into a dark side street.

"Terrifically."

"I find you attractive. I'm engaged to be married. We're a religious family. What puzzles you about my father's attitude?" In these crackling commonsense sentences, Slote could hear Natalie Jastrow, as in old days, pinning him to the wall.

Selma braked the car on a hill lined with town houses, near a street-lamp where two bundled-up children played hopscotch in the pool of light. "Here I leave you. You walk to the top of the hill and turn left. Go along the park until you come to a stone parish house, with a wooden garden door in the stone wall. Knock at that door when nobody else is in sight."

"Selma, won't we see each other again?"

"No."

Round soft eyes glistened under a red shawl. Shawled in much the same way against winter, Natalie had often looked like this—aroused, melancholy, tense from the effort at control. Once again he felt the throb of recognition and regret. She took his hand and pressed it hard in her cold fingers. "Be very careful. Good-bye."

"Ja?" A woman's voice responded to his knock at the heavy wooden garden door.

"Herr Slote."

The door creaked open. A short shapeless person led him toward a bay window glowing orange in the darkness, where he could see the priest at a candlelit table. As Slote came inside, Father Martin rose and waved to a dinner setting beside him. "Welcome! Join me." He lifted the lid of a tureen. "These are tripes *à la mode de Caen.*"

"What a pity," said Slote, glancing down at the steamy pungent-smelling brown mass. He had eaten tripe once in his life, and classed it, like octopus, as a rubbery abomination to be avoided. "I've eaten."

"Well, then," said Father Martin as they sat down, pouring red wine from a clay jug. "Try this."

"Thank you. —I say! It's superb."

"Ah?" The priest looked happy. "It is from my brother's family vine-yard near Würzburg."

Father Martin did not speak again while he methodically and plac-idly devoured a loaf of bread, chunk by chunk, with the tripes, sopping up brown juice from his plate. Each time he broke the bread, his ges-tures and his shiny red face showed pleasure at the feel and smell of the loaf. He kept refilling his glass and Slote's. The thick-lipped moon face remained almost stupidly serene. The roly-poly housekeeper, a middle-aged woman with a bristling mustache, in a full black skirt down to the floor, brought in a yellow cheese and another bread loaf.

"You will take a bite of cheese," said the priest. "Surely you will."

"I guess so, thanks." By now Slote was ravenous. The cheese, the fresh bread, the wine, were all delicious.

Father Martin happily sighed and wiped his mouth after demolishing most of the cheese. "Now let us have a little air."

A wind was springing up outside, making the tall old trees in the garden creak their leafless boughs. "What is it you want?" The voice turned businesslike and anxious. "I can say nothing within walls, even my own."

"It's about the document I received in the theatre. Have you read it?"

"No."

"I have to establish its authenticity."

"I was told the authenticity was self-evident."

Silence, and the crunching of their steps on the gravel walk.

"Does Jacob Ascher know about it?"

"No."

"Did he arrange our meeting at his house?"

"He did not."

"May I tell you how things stand at my end?"

"Bitte."

Slote recounted his interview with the minister and Van Winaker, and he described the contents of the Protocol. The priest uttered peculiar gasps and grunts. Up and down the garden they paced as the wind gusted heavily and the trees whipped.

"Frightful. Frightful! But as to the authenticity, Herr Slote, are you not butting a stone wall, *the will not to believe?*" He spoke the words slowly, sternly, bitterly, grasping Slote's elbow and thrusting a stubby finger toward his face. "The will not to believe! It's nothing new to me. I meet it on deathbeds. I hear it in the confessional. I hear it from deceived husbands, from parents whose sons are missing in action, from trapped bankrupts. The will not to believe. It is simple human nature. When the mind cannot grasp or face up to a horrible fact it turns away, as though refusing credence will conjure away the reality. That is what you're encountering."

"Father Martin, our minister is an able and tough-minded man. He'll face up to hard facts, if I can provide them."

"What hard facts? What would your minister accept as authentication, Herr Slote? How can one argue with the will not to believe? Supposing I persuaded a certain man in the German legation to meet him face to face? Do you appreciate the risk? The Gestapo net spreads all through Bern. It might mean the man's death. And what would be gained? Your minister suspects he has seen fake papers. Well? Won't he simply suspect he has talked to the faker?"

"I could identify a man from the German legation. You'd better tell your man that all the risk so far has been in vain. Tell him Americans say about the document, 'Incredible contents. Dubious origins.' "

The priest let go of his arm, opened the garden door, and peered out. "Good-night. Straight on beyond the park, outside the Café William Tell, you will find a taxi stand."

"You won't help me any further?"

"Herr Slote, I have asked my Provincial to transfer me from Bern." The priest's voice was shaking badly. "You must not approach me anymore. You Americans really don't comprehend Europe. And in the name of God do not bring in the Aschers again."

August Van Winaker poked his head into Slote's office a few days later. "Hi. I've just been having a long hot session with a friend of yours. He'd like to say hello."

"Certainly. Who is it?"

"Dr. Jacob Ascher."

In a black homburg, and a black suit that hung loose on his bowed shoulders, Dr. Ascher looked like an invalid forced from his bed by an emergency. But his handshake was surprisingly strong.

"Well, I'll leave you two lovebirds together," Van Winaker said with a jolly wink. "I'm sure you have lots to talk about."

"I have only come for a moment," Ascher said, "and I beg you to join us."

Wagging a finger at him Van Winaker replied in sing-song, "Ah-ah. Two's company, thre-e-e's a crow-w-wd, ta-ta," and he danced out, gaily winking.

Dr. Ascher sat down heavily in the chair Slote offered him. "Thank you. We are going to America earlier than planned. In fact, next Thursday. This has involved the hurried execution of some complicated international contracts. That is why I was seeing Mr. Van Winaker."

"Has Augie been helpful?"

"Oh, yes." The look from under Dr. Ascher's heavy gray eyebrows was veiled. "Most helpful. Well!" Ascher looked hard at Slote, with eyes sunk in terrible dark hollows. "I seldom ask a personal favor of any man. Yet I've come to ask such a favor of you, sir, though I hardly know you."

"Please!" Slote returned.

"We leave only eight days from now. If my daughter Selma should happen to telephone you during this time, I ask you not to see her." Slote quailed before the stern face of the old Jew. "Is that a very difficult request?"

"I happen to be hard pressed with work, Dr. Ascher. I couldn't see her anyway."

Painfully, Dr. Ascher rose, holding out his hand.

"I wish you happiness in the United States," Slote said.

Ascher shook his head. "It has taken me sixteen years to feel at home in Bern. Now I'm going to Baltimore, a place I don't know at all, and I'm seventy-three. Still, Selma comes first. She is a brilliant and good girl, though all girls are difficult at times. Since my son is an old bachelor, her future is the only future I have. Good-bye, sir."

Slote went back to work. He had the Vichy France assignment in the legation. A treaty was in the works for continuing three-way trade, despite the war, between Switzerland, the United States, and occupied France. For their own practical reasons, the Germans were allowing this. But it was tricky business, and a mountain of paper had accumulated. Slote was pushing through a draft for a meeting that afternoon when his telephone rang.

"Mr. Leslie Slote?" The aged high voice was very British. "Treville Britten here. We met at the home of the Aschers."

"Of course. How are you?"

"Splendid. We had some interesting talk that evening, didn't we? Ah, Winston Churchill will broadcast tonight, you know, and ah, my daughter Nancy and I thought if you cared to join us for dinner—it's frugal vegetarian fare, but Nancy does it rather well. We might listen to Churchill together. Discuss the new developments."

"I'd be charmed," said Slote, thinking that few invitations could be less attractive, "except that I must work straight through the night, pretty near."

The hemming and hawing ceased. "Mr. Slote, I'm not going to take no for an answer."

Slote caught a professional hardening of the elderly voice that was a signal. This was a British Foreign Service man, after all. "How nice of you to insist."

"Pension Gafen, 19 Tellenstrasse, apartment 3A. About seven."

Perhaps there were two gray Fiat roadsters like Selma Ascher's in Bern, Slote thought that evening, seeing the car parked in front of the pension, a dismal-looking house in a dilapidated part of Bern. Question: did his promise to Selma's father bind him not to go up to the flat and see? Doing rapid mental casuistry, he mounted the stairs two at a time. Selma had not telephoned him. He wasn't sure that she was in the Britten apartment. He had accepted the dinner invitation in good faith. In short, the worried old Jewish father be damned! For all Slote intended to do, Selma Ascher would leave Bern *virgo intacta*.

There she was in a dowdy blue frock, little more than a housedress, with her hair carelessly pinned up. She had a tired unhappy air, and her greeting was anything but flirtatious; offhand, rather, and faintly resentful. She and the English girl worked in the kitchen while, in a small musty study crammed with old books and magazines, Britten poured very stiff whiskeys. "How fortunate that alcohol is a vegetable product, what? If it were distilled from animal corpses, all my principles would have to give way. Hee hee." Slote felt Britten had made this joke and giggled this way a thousand times.

The old man was eager to talk about Singapore. Once the Japanese had landed in Malaya, he explained, the obvious strategy had been to lure them all the way south with a fighting retreat, to within range of Singapore's terrible guns. The news meantime had been depressing, but now the turnabout was surely at hand. Winnie obviously had something exciting to impart tonight about Singapore. *"The will not to believe,"* thought Slote; what an egregious example was here! Even the BBC was broadly hinting that Singapore was falling. Yet Britten's crack-voiced optimism was utterly unfeigned.

It was a strained, impoverished meal. The four people crowded the small table. The peculiar mock-meat puddings and stews that the daughter served were insipid stuff. Selma ate little, scarcely looking up, her face sullen and withdrawn. They were starting on a dessert of very tart stewed rhubarb when Churchill's cadences began to roll out of the shortwave radio. For a long time in his sombre talk he did not mention Singapore. Britten conveyed to Slote, with reassuring winks and gestures, that all this was quite in line with his prediction. The great disclosure was coming.

Churchill paused, and took an audible breath.

And now, I have heavy news. Singapore has fallen. That mighty bastion of Empire, which held out so long against insuperable odds, has honorably surrendered to spare its civilian population from further useless slaughter . . .

The old man's wrinkled face wilted into a pained smile, getting redder and redder, his watery eyes taking on a queer gleam. They listened in silence to the very end of the speech:

. . . and so let us go on, into the storm, and through the storm.

Shakily Britten reached over and turned off the radio. "Well! Bit mistaken on that one, wasn't I?"

"Oh, the Empire's gone," said his daughter with vinegary satisfaction. "High time we all faced that, Father. Especially Winnie. What an obsolete romantic!"

"Just so. Night falls. A new world order cometh." Britten's voice fell into the rhythms of Churchill, a reedy grotesque echo. "The Hun will join hands with the Mongol. The Slav, the born helot, will serve new masters. Christianity and humanism are dead creeds. The thousand-year night of technological barbarism descends. Well, we English fought the good fight. I have lived my life. You young people have my sympathy."

He was so obviously distraught that Slote and Selma left almost at once. On the staircase she said, "Is it really that bad, the fall of Singapore?"

"Well, to him it's the end of the world. It may spell the end of the British Empire. The war will go on."

On the street she seized his hand, twining the fingers in hers. "Come into my car."

She drove to a busy boulevard and parked at the curb with the motor running. "Father Martin gave me a message for you. Here are his exact words. *'It is arranged. Wait for a visitor in your flat at six o'clock Sunday evening.'*"

Immensely surprised, Slote said, "I thought he didn't want you involved."

"He was at the house last night. Papa told him we'd be gone by next Thursday. I suppose he decided that I'm a safe messenger, since I'll be gone so soon."

"I'm sorry you had to disobey your father."

"Did you mind Nancy's horrible food?"

"It was worth it."

She stared at him and turned off the motor. "I suppose you had an affair with this Natalie girl?"

"Of course I did. I told you that."

"Not in so many words. You were very diplomatic. Do you imagine you could possibly have had an affair with me?"

"I wouldn't have dreamed of it."

"Why not? I thought I was like her. How am I different? Not sexually exciting?"

"This is a stupid conversation, Selma. Thanks for the message."

"I can't forgive my father for going to you. It's so humiliating!"

"He shouldn't have told you."

"I got it out of him. We had some bitter words. Well, you're quite right, this *is* a stupid conversation. Good-bye." She started the motor, and held out her hand.

"Ye gods, Selma, your circulation must be bad. Your hands are always icy."

"Nobody but you has ever mentioned that. Well—what do the English say? 'In for a penny, in for a pound.'" She leaned to him and kissed him hard on the mouth. The sweetness of it shook Slote deeply. Her voice dropped to a whisper. "There! Since you find me so exciting, remember me a little. I'll remember you always."

"And I you."

She shook her head. "No, you won't. You've had so many adventures! You'll have so many more! I've had my one, my very little one. I hope that you get your Natalie back. She'd be happier with you than with that Navy fellow"—Selma's expression turned darkly mischievous—"as long as she insists on having a Gentile husband."

Slote opened the car door.

"Leslie, I don't know what your business with Father Martin is," Selma exclaimed, "but take care! I have never seen a more frightened person."

Nobody came to Slote's flat on Sunday evening. The front page of the Zurich *Tageblatt,* lying on his desk Monday morning, had a spread of Japanese photographs about the Singapore victory, furnished by the German news service: the surrender ceremony, the hordes of British troops sitting on the earth in a prison compound, the celebration in Tokyo. The story about Father Martin was so short that Slote almost missed it, but there it was at the bottom of the page. The truck driver, who claimed that his brakes had failed, was being held for questioning. The priest was dead, crushed.

19

A Jew's Journey
(excerpt from Aaron Jastrow's manuscript)

APRIL 23, 1942.

American bombers have raided Tokyo!

My pulse races as it once did when, an immigrant in love with everything American, infected with baseball fever, I saw Babe Ruth hit a home run. For me America is the Babe Ruth of the nations. I unashamedly confess it. And the Babe has come out of his slump and "hit one over the fence"!

Strange, how Allied airplane bombs infallibly fall on churches, schools, and hospitals; what a triumph of military imprecision! If Berlin radio speaks the truth—and why should Germans lie, pray?—the RAF has by now flattened nearly all institutions of worship, learning, and healing in Germany, while unerringly missing all other targets. Now we are told that Tokyo was unscathed in the raid except for a great number of schools, hospitals, and temples demolished by the barbarous Americans. Most extraordinary.

My niece calls this "Doolittle raid" (an intrepid Army Air Corps colonel of that name led the attack) just a stunt, a token bombing. It will make no difference to the war; so she *says*. What she *did*, when the news came through on the BBC, was to entrust her baby to the cook, rush down to the Excelsior Hotel where our fellow journalists are housed, and there get joyously drunk with them. They are drunk nearly all the time, but I have not seen Natalie inebriated in years. I must say that when her chief local admirer, a banal-minded Associated Press reporter, brought her back, she was full of amusing raillery, though scarcely able to walk straight.

Her mood was so gay, in fact, that I was tempted to disclose then and there the grave secret I have been harboring for two weeks, not even entrusting it to these pages. But I refrained. She has suffered enough on my account. Time enough to reveal this bombshell when the fuse has burned down to the danger point. This it may never do.

The departure date of the American internees in Siena has been fixed for the first week in May. We are to proceed to Naples or Lisbon, embark in a Swedish luxury liner, and sail for home. On the first of April (I remember noting that it was April Fool's Day!) my old friend, the Siena chief of police, paid me a visit. With many a Tuscan sigh and shrug and circumlocution, he hinted that for us there might be a hitch. He would not elaborate.

Detailed word came within a few days, in a letter from our embassy in Rome. The nub of the matter is this: the Nazis claim that three Italian journalists, interned in Rio de Janeiro and awaiting trial as German agents in disguise, are in fact *bona fide* journalists, barbarously detained by the Brazilian authorities at Allied instigation. In retaliation, since the Germans can lay their hands on few Brazilians, they have asked the Italians to detain three Americans so as to force our State Department to persuade Brazil to set these men free. It is just crude Teutonism, of course, a game to recover clumsy spies who got themselves caught. Unhappily, the three hostages, if it comes to that, may be myself, my niece, and her baby, since our "journalist" credentials are marginal, to say the least. The international dickering has, in fact, already begun, and we are among those marked for possible detention. So the embassy has disclosed.

But that it will happen is unlikely. Brazil will probably bow to the intercession of our State Department. Then again, our friend and rescuer, Dr. Werner Beck, is moving heaven and earth to get us released, or at the very least, to designate three other Americans from the list for the retaliation, if it comes to that. Probably I should not let him do this, but I have learned already to turn feral in wartime. *Sauve qui peut* is the cry.

I have concealed this news from Natalie. Her dread of the Germans and what they may do to her baby borders on the psychotic. As for me, I am not alarmed. I would just as lief work on here to the last, and—when the worst befalls and however it befalls—have my ashes scattered in the garden. For one way or another, my time of ash is not far off. I cannot say how I know this. My health is fair. Nevertheless I do know it. It neither frightens nor saddens me. It strengthens my resolve to wring all the work I can out of the passing days, and finish my *Luther*.

For Natalie's sake, however, I must do all I can to ensure that we will go. Upon completing my morning's work, I shall go and have a word with the archbishop. He is not without influence in the Italian Foreign Ministry. The time has come to pull every string, and turn over every stone.

20

THE red beard scratched and tickled Janice Henry's cheek. She hugged Byron a shade tighter than family affection called for, thinking that he had been out on that submarine a pretty long time. Too, though incest was as far from her thoughts as parricide, she did feel—she always had—a mild fugitive attraction to Warren's younger brother. She didn't mind the rum reek on his breath, nor the grease streaks on his rumpled khakis, for she knew that he had come straight from the victory celebration of the *Devilfish*. A double frangipani lei, heavily and sweetly odorous, dangled around his sunburned throat.

"Well!" She touched the beard. "Are you going to keep that?"

"Why not?" He took off the lei and hung it around her neck.

Flustered, sniffing at the flowers, she said, "I feel so dumb about your phone call. You and he do sound alike, you know."

Janice had begun blurting a sexy wife-to-husband greeting on hearing his voice. "Look, it's Byron," he had interrupted, and after an embarrassed pause they had both roared with laughter.

Byron shyly grinned. "Expecting Warren, were you?"

"Well, the scuttlebutt is that Halsey's due back with the carriers."

"Minus the *Lex,* I hear."

"Minus the *Lex.*" She shook her head sadly. "Sunk in the Coral Sea. That's definite."

"Where's my nephew?"

"In the nursery. Bathed, fed, sleepy, smelling like a rose."

"More than you can say for me, I guess." Byron did, in fact, smell rather gamy. "We just piled off the boat and started celebrating—hi, Vic. Holy cow, Janice," Byron called from the nursery, "he's gigantic."

"Don't rouse him. He'll give us no peace."

Byron strolled into the kitchen after a while and dropped on a chair. "Marvelous kid," he said, with a faraway look. He sounded doleful.

Janice crouched at the stove in an apron, a shirt, and shorts, the pink lei hanging loose. She pushed heavy yellow hair away from her face.

"Sorry I'm such a mess. Seems I never dress up any more. Warren's so seldom home."

"I'd call Washington," Byron said, "but it's midnight there. I'll call in the morning. Natalie and my kid are interned in Italy, I suppose you know that."

"Briny, they're out."

"What! They *are?*" Byron sprang joyfully to his feet. "Jan! How do you know?"

"I talked to my father in Washington—oh, three, four days ago. He's been keeping after the State Department about it."

"But, was he positive?"

"Yes, there's this Swedish liner en route from Lisbon with the interned Americans. She's aboard with her baby."

"Fantastic!" He seized Janice and hugged and kissed her. "Maybe I'll telephone him."

"He's left there. He's a brigadier general, assigned to MacArthur's staff in Australia. You can talk to him when he passes through here, probably Saturday."

"Oh, Lord, how I've waited for this news!"

"I'll bet. Some reunion coming up, eh?" Her grin was sly as he released her. "How much time did you two have on your honeymoon, three days?"

"Less. Dunno about the reunion, though." He dropped in the chair again. "Aster wants me to stick with the *Devilfish.* Most of our squadron's been pulled back off patrol. That's damned unusual. There's a smell around the sub base. Something brewing."

She gave him a worried glance. "Yes? At Cincpac, too."

"Aster heard that the Japs are going to try to take the Hawaiian Islands. Biggest battle of the war coming up. No time for me to leave, that's his argument."

"Don't you have orders to SubLant?"

"He has to detach me. I could stay aboard for the battle, if there's one imminent. Maybe I ought to, I don't know."

"So Aster's got command now?"

"Yes, it's Captain Aster, no more Lady."

"I don't like him."

"Why not?"

"Oh, God's gift to women, isn't he? And he grins like the phantom of the opera."

That made Byron laugh. "Phantom of the opera! Not bad."

He helped her carry food and wine out to a table of wrought iron and glass on the lanai. She lit candles, though the sunset still glowed beyond the trees. They drank California burgundy with the meat loaf she had hastily prepared. Byron emptied glass after glass as he talked about Aster's first patrol. They had sunk two ships before the summons back to base, and Byron thought Carter Aster was going to be one of the great skippers of the war. His eyes began to gleam. "Say, Jan, can you keep a secret?"

"Indeed I can."

"We sank a hospital ship."

"My *God*, Byron!" She stared and gasped. "Why, that's an atrocity, it's—"

"Just let me *tell* this, will you? It was the goddamnedest experience of my life. I spotted the ship myself when I had the deck, about midnight. Unescorted, floodlights on a white hull, brilliant running lights, huge red cross painted on her side. This was in the Makassar Strait off Java. Aster came topside, took one look, and ordered a dive and an approach. Well, I figured it was a practice run. But when he said, *'Open the outer doors,'* I cracked. 'Captain,' I said, 'is this an attack?' He ignored me, just kept boring in. I was on the computer. At about fifteen hundred yards I had a perfect solution, but I felt guilty as hell, and the exec was just scratching his head and keeping his mouth shut. 'Captain,' I said, 'this target is a hospital ship. If there's a general court martial I'll have to say so.' 'Yes, you do that, Briny. I'm going to shoot him now,' he says, cool as a popsicle, chewing on his cigar. 'Stand by! Up periscope. Final bearing and shoot!' And off went four fish."

"Byron, he's a maniac!"

"Janice, will you listen? That baby blew up in a fireball you could see for a hundred miles! It was a disguised ammunition ship. Nothing else could have blown like that. We surfaced and watched it burn. It kept whizzing and popping and spraying fire. It took forever to sink. The fireworks just went on and on. And once it did go down, why, the sea was full of strange dark floating shapes. We hove to till dawn, and they turned out to be huge balls of crude rubber, ten or fifteen feet across. Those things were bobbing all the way to the horizon. That ship was transporting rubber from Java, honey, with a big load of ammo. Probably captured Dutch stuff."

"How could he know that? He might have drowned two thousand wounded men."

"He guessed right. Don't ever repeat that story, Jan."

"Horrors, no."

The doorbell rang. She left the table and soon reappeared. "Speak of the devil." Carter Aster followed her in dress whites, clean-shaven, slim and straight, cap under his arm.

"Briny, the base pool ran out of jeeps. Will you give me a lift down the hill about ten? The cabs won't come up at curfew time."

"Where will you be?"

"I'll turn up here again." Aster directed his strange grin—curled corners on a hard mouth—at Janice. "If that's okay with you."

Janice said to Byron, "Won't you be sleeping over?"

"I hadn't thought about it. A hot bath, a real bed? Thanks, I sure will."

"We're on twenty-four hours' notice, Byron," Aster said.

"I'll be back at 0800, Captain."

"Made up your mind yet about staying aboard?"

"Let you know in the morning."

Janice could guess why Byron was saying nothing about Natalie. The news would only intensify Aster's pressure on him to remain with the *Devilfish.*

"The latest poop is that they're coming in force to invade Alaska," Aster said to Janice. "Heard anything like that at Cincpac?"

She shook her head, unsmiling. He grinned at her and left.

"Which lucky lady is he visiting up here?" Janice asked.

Byron's answer was an evasive shrug.

"Now that's mean, Briny. I'll suspect every wife on the hill."

"Can't help your evil mind, Jan."

As they chatted into the evening about the family and the war, moving inside and drawing the blackout curtains, Byron's manner began to strike Janice as odd. He was wandering in his talk, and giving her awkward, sombre glances. Too much wine? Sexual stirrings? In her brother-in-law that seemed inconceivable. Still, he was a young sailor back from the sea. When he went off for a bath she decided to stay dressed, to keep the lights turned up, and to put away the liquor.

"God, that was marvelous." He emerged in Warren's pajamas and robe, towelling his head. "I haven't had a bath since Albany."

"*Albany?*"

"Albany, Australia." He flopped loose-limbed on the rattan couch. "Lovely tiny town, as far away as you can go on God's green earth. Wonderful people. Our tender was berthed there. Got any bourbon, Jan?" His manner was quite matter-of-fact.

Janice felt ashamed of her imaginings. She brought two drinks. Stretching out on the couch, he took a swig, and morosely shook his head. "God, to think of seeing Natalie again! And the baby. Incredible."

"You don't sound all that happy."

"There was a girl in Albany. Maybe I'm feeling guilty."

"Wow." She made a small drama of falling in an armchair.

"I met her in church. She sang in the choir, a small choir, everything's small in Albany. Just three other singers and this girl. She played the organ, too. It's a tiny little toy seaport, Albany—just three streets and a church and a town hall. Clean, charming, lots of lawns, flowerbeds, old nice houses, old oaks, totally British and nineteenth-century. It's another world."

"Who is she?"

"Her name's Ursula Cotton. Her father owns the little town bank. Very sweet, very proper. Her guy is a tank corps officer in North Africa. Our sub had two overhauls, two months apart. Both times we were inseparable, every minute I could get ashore."

"And—?"

Byron made a despairing gesture with both hands. "*And?* And we sailed, and here I am."

"Byron, I'm not clear on one point. Did anything happen?"

"Did anything happen?" He angrily frowned. "You mean did I get into her pants?"

"Well, you put it rather horridly."

"Christ! You, too? Carter Aster, every time I'd come back to the sub, he'd say, '*Well, did you get into her pants?*' I finally said if he'd come ashore, and forget about being captain, I'd straighten him out about Ursula once and for all. That ended that."

"Dear, it makes a difference—"

"Look, I said her guy was fighting in North Africa. What do you take me for? That was a torment, but still it was beautiful. It made life endurable. I'll never write her. It's no use. But by God, I'll never forget Ursula."

Janice got out of her chair, and placed both hands on his shoulders. Leaning over him so that her scented yellow hair cascaded on him, she kissed his lips. With a businesslike rub of a thumb on his mouth she said, "Natalie's lucky. Brothers can sure be different. What Warren has put *me* through!"

"Well, you married a hell-raiser, you knew that."

"I did, indeed."

Byron yawned and shook his head. "Strangely, I only got crazier about Natalie all that time. I kept thinking of her. Ursula was lovely, but compared to Natalie! Natalie's a powerhouse. There's nobody in the world like her."

"Well, I envy Natalie. I envy Little Miss Ursula, too. Natalie would forgive you and her both. That's my guess." A bitter wrinkling smile. "Even if you had gotten into her pants, as Lady Aster would say. It's war, you know. Good-night, Byron. Vic gets me up at five."

Next morning she was feeding the baby in the kitchen when she heard the dying cough of a jeep. In came Warren in fresh khakis. She had not seen him in almost a month. He was strikingly bigger and heavier than Byron, and very tanned and bright-eyed. "Janice, what's another jeep doing out here? Got some guy in a closet, with thirty seconds to live?"

As he swept her into a crushing hug, she put a finger on his mouth. "Byron's asleep in the guest room."

"What, Briny's back? Great!"

Janice stammered, her mouth against his, "Darling, Vic's in his high chair—"

Warren strode to the kitchen. The baby turned an egg-smeared face and large solemn eyes on him, then smiled from ear to ear. Warren kissed him. "He smells good. Grows half a foot every time I go out. Come along, feller."

"Where are you taking him?"

The aviator wiped his son's face, carried him to a crib in the nursery, and handed him his teddy bear.

"Darling, listen," Janice protested in low tones, following him, "Byron will come stumbling out any second, looking for eggs and coffee—"

He circled her waist in a powerful arm, took her into the bedroom, and quietly locked the door.

Prone and naked, half-stuporous, she heard the scratch of a match, opened her eyes, and gave her husband a sad, heavy, mischievous look. He was sitting up in the bed. "Honestly," she said, in an unexpected baritone voice that made them both laugh. The sun fell in golden bars on Warren's bronzed chest, and the smoke from his cigarette made blue coils in the sunlight.

"Well, you're a sailor's wife."

"Jesus. Not one of Magellan's sailors."

"Jan, I hear Byron stirring about."

"Oh dear. Well, the coffee's on. I guess he'll find it."

He said a shade gruffly, "I love you." She reared up on an elbow to look at him. He dragged on the cigarette, and blew out a gray cloud. "Quite an exercise, this last one. In futility, that is. A two-carrier task force, roaring thirty-five hundred miles to the Coral Sea and back, and missing the battle by three days. If we'd got there in time we'd have smashed the Japs, instead of losing the *Lex*. The *Yorktown's* kaput, too. Seven thousand miles for nothing. Halsey's lucky he doesn't have to pay his oil bill."

Janice said, "What's this thing cooking up now? Do you know?"

"Oh, you hear scuttlebutt. Something big, that's for sure. We sortie again in two days."

"Two days!"

"Yep. Working parties replenishing ship around the clock." Yawning, he put a brown arm around her. "Action will be a novelty. All we did on those seven thousand miles was patrol, baby. Patrol, patrol! Two hundred miles out, two hundred miles back, grinding along over clouds, water, hours on end, days on end. I never saw anything except whales. There was lots of leisure to think. I figured out that time's getting precious, and that I should stop screwing around and hurting you. I've done too much of it. I'm sorry. No more. Okay? Guess I'll shower up and talk to Briny. How does he look?"

"Why, why, sort of haggard and scrawny." Stunned with delight at his contrition, Janice tried to sound just as casual. "Thick red beard, like Dad told us." She touched his face. "I wonder how you'd look in a beard."

"Negative! It comes in half-gray. Balls to that. Well, Dad will sure be glad to see Briny, beard and all. The *Northampton* was following us in."

"Byron says the *Devilfish* got two Jap ships."

"Hey, won't that give Dad a charge!"

On the sunny wing of the *Northampton's* bridge, maneuvering to buoys in a strong ebb tide, Pug Henry could see Spruance pacing the main deck far below. The barge lay to, waiting to take them to the *Enterprise,* where the admiral would pay his respects to Halsey. Then they would walk the five miles to Warren's house. That was their routine. As the drenched sailors down on the pitching buoys wrestled with the shackles of the massive anchor chains, Pug and Commander Grigg were talking about urgent yard repairs that they might get done before going back to sea. The magazines were still loaded from the vain Coral Sea dash, but food and fuel were low. Forty-eight hours for turnabout, after seven thousand miles of high-speed steaming! All hell must be about to break loose in the Pacific; but what it was all about, Pug Henry had no idea.

The *Enterprise* was usually bleak and quiet in port; an abandoned nest, the birds having flown off before dawn from a hundred miles out. But this time the utter lack of life was eerie: no pipings at the approach of Spruance's barge, no loudspeaker calls for sideboys and ceremonies; the gangway deserted, not even the OOD in sight. In the cavernous hangar deck there was a cold, ghost-ship feeling. The flag secretary came toward them on the run, his tread thumping and echoing down the empty steel cavern. Unceremoniously he took Raymond Spruance aside by the elbow, turning a pale unshaven face over his shoulder. "Excuse me, Captain Henry. Had coffee with your son at 0300, incidentally, before he took off."

Pug nodded, showing none of the relief he felt. Off the New Hebrides he had seen a Dauntless dive-bomber cartwheel from the *Enterprise* into the sea; probably not Warren, on the odds, but until this moment he had wondered and worried.

"Okay, Henry. Let's go," said Spruance, after a muttered colloquy. The barge rocked and clanged its way to the sub base. Spruance volunteered nothing, Pug asked no questions. The admiral's face looked almost wooden in its calm. He broke his silence as they stepped ashore. "Henry, I have a little business at Cincpac. I suppose you want to join your family right away?" Plainly, from his tone, he hated to give up the walk.

"I'm at your pleasure, Admiral."

"Come with me. It shouldn't take too long."

In a hard chair outside Nimitz's gold-starred doors, twisting his cap round and round, Pug waited, noting the extraordinary bustle all around him: typewriter clatter, telephones ringing, hurrying foot traffic this way and that of yeomen, Waves, and junior officers. The Cincpac building was as stirred up as the *Enterprise* was dead. Momentous business was in the air, and no mistake. Pug hoped that it was not another Doolittle-type raid. He was a conservative military thinker, and he had been skeptical of that Doolittle show since the task force had first sailed.

With an irrepressible spine tingle he had read over the *Northamp-*

ton's loudspeakers Halsey's message. *"This force is bound for Tokyo."* But how could two carriers, he had thought at once, venture within range of the land-based Japanese air force? Through the crew's cheers and rebel yells, he had skeptically shaken his head at Spruance. Next day, when the *Hornet* had joined up, its deckload of Army B-25 bombers had of course solved the mystery. Watching the oncoming carrier, Spruance had remarked, "Well, Captain?"

"My hat's off to those Army fliers, Admiral."

"Mine too. They've been training for months. They'll have to go on to China, you realize. That deck can't take them back aboard."

"I know. Brave souls."

"Is this good war-making, Captain?"

"Sir, my inferior understanding prevents my grasping the unquestionable soundness of the mission."

For the first time since Pug had met him, Raymond Spruance had laughed heartily. They had not discussed the raid again until a few days ago. At dinner in Spruance's quarters, Spruance had been bemoaning the way they had missed the Coral Sea battle, the first in history in which the opposed warships had never sighted each other; an all-air duel at ranges of seventy-five miles or more. "That's something new in sea warfare, Henry. A lot of War College thinking goes overboard. Possibly you were right about that Tokyo raid. Maybe we should have been down south all that time, instead of roaring back and forth over the Pacific to make headlines. Still, we don't know to what extent Doolittle upset the Japanese war plans."

Spruance remained in Cincpac's sanctum for about half an hour. He emerged with a strange look on his face. "We're on our way, Henry." When they were out of the Navy Yard, and plugging uphill through weedy dusty sugarcane fields on a tarred road, he abruptly remarked, "Well, I'm leaving the *Northampton*."

"Oh? I'm genuinely sorry, sir."

"I am, too, since I'll be going on the beach. I'm to become Admiral Nimitz's chief of staff."

"Why, that's splendid. Congratulations, Admiral."

"Thanks," Spruance said coldly, "but I don't recall your leaping at staff duty when offered."

That closed the topic. They trudged around a bend. The base came in sight, sprawled out far below, beyond flowering trees and terraced green truck gardens; the wharves, drydocks and anchorages crowded with warships, the channels full of small craft moving about; on the wrecked battleships, workmen swarming over the temporary repair structures, and—the most striking sight—along the capsized hull of the *Oklahoma,* the long row of righting cables stretched to winches on Ford Island.

"Henry, you've read the *Yorktown*'s damage report dispatches. How long would you say repairs will take?"

"Three to five months, sir."

"Captain Harry Warendorf is your classmate, isn't he? The Captain of the Yard?"

"Yes, I know Harry well."

"Can he put her back to sea in seventy-two hours? Because he's going to have to. Admiral Nimitz has ordered it."

"Harry will do it, if any man can," Pug answered, astounded. "It's bound to be a patch job."

"Yes, but three carriers instead of two is a fifty percent increase in striking power. Which we'll soon need."

Over steak and eggs on the back porch, Byron was telling Warren about the torpedoes he had salvaged from Cavite. The brothers, both barefoot, both in shorts and beach-boy shirts, had been talking at a great rate for an hour.

"Twenty-six torpedoes!" Warren exclaimed. "No wonder you got your transfer to the Atlantic."

Byron was enjoying, in fact revelling in, this conversation. Eternal months ago in peacetime, Warren had warned him to kowtow to Branch Hoban if he wanted his dolphins. Now Warren knew of Hoban's cave-in, and dolphins were pinned to the sweaty khaki shirt hanging in the guest room. "Warren, Aster's pressuring me to stay aboard the *Devilfish.*"

"Do you have a choice?"

"I've got my orders, but it could be managed."

"Rinkydink administration in submarines."

"Sort of."

Warren had no ready advice to give. His self-confidence was solid and deep; he had overwhelmed Byron from boyhood; yet he had always sensed an original streak in Briny that he lacked. Attracting and marrying a brilliant Jewess, the niece of a famous writer, was a deed outside his range; and given the opportunities of wartime, Byron was fast closing the gap as a naval officer.

"Well, let me tell you a story, Byron. Halsey brought the Doolittle fliers to their takeoff point. I suppose you know that."

"That's the word at the sub base."

"It's true. When those Army bombers took off from the *Hornet,* I stood out on our own flight deck and watched them form up and head west for Tokyo. Tears ran down my face, Byron. I bawled."

"I believe you."

"Okay. It was a hell of a brave deed, yet what did it amount to? A token bombing to pep up the home front. There's only one service really hurting the enemy in the Pacific right now, and that's the submarines. There won't be another moment like this in your lifetime. If you go to SubLant you'll boot it. You asked my opinion, and I'm giving it to you. You know Natalie's okay now, and—"

Janice poked her head out of the kitchen. "Your dad and Admiral Spruance are rounding the Smiths' terrace, men, going full steam."

Byron glanced down at his shirt and shorts, and rubbed his beard. "Spruance?"

Warren yawned, scratching a dirty bare foot. "He just drinks a glass of water and goes back down the hill."

The bell rang. Janice went to answer. The brothers jumped to their feet, as the white-clad admiral, his face streaming sweat, walked out on the porch, followed by their father.

"Byron!" Pug grasped his son's hand and they embraced. "Well, here's my submariner, Admiral. I haven't seen him since Thanksgiving."

"My submariner's out in the *Tambor.*" Spruance patted his crimson face with a square-folded handkerchief. "How's the hunting been, Lieutenant?"

"Two confirmed sinkings, Admiral. Eleven thousand tons."

Victor Henry's eyes brightened. Spruance smiled. "Indeed? You're ahead of the *Tambor.* What about the Mark Fourteen torpedo?"

"It stinks, Admiral. It's a disgrace. My skipper got his three kills with contact exploders. Against orders, but they worked."

At the impudent freedom of the response, Pug's pleasure subsided. "Briny, when torpedoes miss it's always a temptation to blame the exploders."

"Sorry, Dad. I know you were involved with that magnetic device." In peacetime, Victor Henry had received a letter of commendation for his work on it. "It's gone sour in production, that's all I can tell you. Even with contact exploders, the Mark Fourteen keeps failing. All of

SubPac's skippers are up in arms, but BuOrd won't listen. It's sickening, I tell you, to sail five thousand miles to make a torpedo attack, and then have the fish hit the target with a dull thud."

Spruance relieved Pug by commenting, "My son says much the same thing. Admiral Nimitz has taken the matter up with BuOrd." He accepted a glass of iced tea from Janice, and turned to Warren. "Incidentally, what's the range of the Dauntless, again, Lieutenant?"

"We tend to think in hours, Admiral. Three and a half hours airborne, more or less."

The admiral's expression was abstracted. "Your book range is seven hundred fifty miles."

Warren tartly smiled. "Sir, just forming up burns a lot of gasoline. Then over the target the fuel disappears like there's a hole in the tank. Most of us wouldn't get back from a target at two hundred miles."

"And the fighters and torpedo bombers?" Spruance asked as he sipped the tea. "Same speed and range?"

"Approximately, sir." Warren concealed any puzzlement at the questions, answering briskly. "But the TBD is a lot slower."

"Well!" Spruance emptied his glass and stood up. "Most refreshing, Janice. I'll be going down the hill now."

The others were all on their feet. "Admiral, one of the boys can drive you back," Pug said.

"Why?"

"If you have pressing business, sir."

"Not necessary." As he went out, Spruance beckoned to Pug to follow him. Closing the front door he paused, squinting at Victor Henry in the noon sun. He looked much sterner when he put on the big white cap. "Those boys of yours are different in character, but they're both cut from the same cloth."

"Byron should curb his tongue."

"Submariners are individualists, as I well know. It's good they're both in port. Spend all the time with them you can."

"There's much to do on my ship, Admiral."

Spruance's face took on a sudden hard cast. "Henry, this is for your information only. The Japanese are heading east in great force. They're already at sea. Their objective is to seize Midway Island. A Japanese base a thousand miles from Hawaii is unacceptable, so Admiral Nimitz is sending everything we've got up there. We're about to fight the biggest battle of the war."

Pug groped for a response to these stunning words that would not sound defeatist, alarmed, swaggering, or plain stupid. The *Hornet,* the *Enterprise,* with possibly the patched leaky *Yorktown* and their meager train, against that Japanese armada! At least eight carriers, perhaps ten battleships, only God could know how many cruisers, destroyers, submarines! As a fleet problem, it was too lopsided for any peacetime umpire to propose. His hoarse words came unbidden, "Now I know why you don't want to go on the beach."

"I won't just yet." The calm eyes glowed in a way Victor Henry never forgot. "Admiral Halsey has gone to the Cincpac hospital. Unlucky outbreak of a skin disease. He can't fight this battle. He has recommended to Admiral Nimitz that I assume command of Task Force Sixteen, so I'll transfer my gear to Halsey's flag quarters this afternoon. My new assignment starts after the battle."

This was just as stunning as the first disclosure. Spruance, a nonaviator, taking the *Enterprise* and the *Hornet* into battle! Trying to maintain a level tone, Pug asked, "The intelligence is all that certain, then?"

"We think so. If all goes well, we may achieve surprise. Incidentally, I intend to invite you to the battle conference." He held out his hand. "So as I say, spend some time with your boys while you can."

Returning to the back porch, Pug Henry paused in the shadows of the doorway. His sons were talking on the lawn now, folding chairs pulled close, each clasping a beer can. *Cut from the same cloth!* They looked it. What could they be discussing so earnestly? He was in no hurry to interrupt them. He leaned in the doorway, taking in the picture he might not see again for a long time, trying to digest Spruance's savage news. He was ready himself to sail against those odds in the thin-skinned *Northampton.* He had been paid through thirty years to prepare for such an encounter. But Warren and Byron, in their twenties, were just starting to taste life. Yet on the *Northampton* he would be the safest of the three.

In these two young men in gaudy shirts and tan shorts—one lean and red-bearded, the other big and solid, with gray-sprinkled hair—he could still see ghostly shadows of the boys they had been. Byron had smiled just such a smile at five. Warren's emphatic push of both hands outward had been his main gesture as an Academy debater. Pug remembered Warren's great moment, his graduation from the Academy, a battalion commander with a prize in modern history; and poor Byron's sad Columbia commencement, when he had almost failed to graduate because of an overdue term paper. He remembered the rainy March day in 1939 when he had received his orders to Germany, and Warren had come in all sweaty from tennis to say he had applied for flight training, and Byron's first letter from Siena about Natalie Jastrow had arrived. He would break into their talk soon, Pug thought, to ask about her. Not yet. He just wanted to look at them a little longer.

About Warren, Pug thought, he could have done nothing. Warren had always wanted the Navy. By becoming an aviator, he had outdone the father he was emulating. The aviators who survived would become the Navy's next wave of admirals. That was already clear. As for Byron, Pug knew he had forced him into submarines and parted him from his Jewish wife. This was a sunken rock always to be steered around when they were together. Byron would have been called up anyway, and he might even have chosen submarines. But Pug could not clear himself of muddying Byron's life, and—proud as he was of the *Devilfish*'s sinkings—of pushing him into hazard.

A poignant sense engulfed him of the one-way flow of time, of the offhand decisions, the slight impulsive mistakes, that could swell and become a man's fate. There they sat, the little boys he had stiffly disciplined and silently loved, transformed into naval officers and combat veterans. It seemed the work of a master illusionist who could just as easily, if he chose, reverse the trick and change the red-bearded submariner and the broad-chested aviator back into quarrelling lads on a Manila lawn. But Pug knew those lads were gone. He himself had changed into a grim old dog, and they too would keep changing in one direction. Byron would at last come to the adult form and personality that still eluded him. Warren—

The strange thing was that Victor Henry could not picture Warren changing any further. Warren as he sat there in the sun, holding that beer can, the cigarette slanting from his thin mouth, his body developed, full, and powerful, his face carved in lines of self-confidence and resolution, his blue eyes glinting with suppressed humor, was Warren as he would always be. So the father could not help thinking, and as the thought took root, a stinging cold shiver traversed his body. He shouted, stepping out of the doorway, "Say, is there any beer left, or have you two problem drinkers soaked it all up?"

Byron jumped to his feet and brought his father a tall frosty glass of beer.

"Dad, Natalie's coming home on a Swedish boat! That's what Janice's father has heard, anyway. How about that?"

"Why, that's glorious news, Briny."

"Yes, I'm still trying to call the State Department to confirm it. But

Warren thinks I shouldn't transfer, because SubPac's where all the glory is."

"I never mentioned glory," said Warren. "Did I say glory? I don't give a shit about glory—pardon me, Dad—I said the subs are carrying the fight in this ocean, and you've got the chance of a lifetime to take a hand in history."

"What else is glory?" said his father.

Byron said, "What do you think, Dad?"

Here was the sunken rock again, thought Pug. He answered at once, "Take your transfer and go. This Pacific war will be a long one. You'll get back here in time to make all the history you can handle. You've never seen your son and—now, why the wise grin?"

"You surprise me, that's all."

The telephone was ringing and ringing in the house.

"By God," Pug said, "that's something to celebrate, Natalie coming home! When were we last together like this, anyway? Wasn't it at Warren's wedding? Seems to me an anniversary party is overdue here also."

"Right," Warren said. "I remembered the date, but I was flying patrols off Samoa."

The ringing stopped.

"Well, I'm for having a champagne dinner at the Moana Hotel tomorrow night," Pug said. "How about it?"

"Hey! Janice would love that, Dad, getting off this hill, maybe dancing—"

"I'm in," said Byron, getting up and making for the kitchen door. "I buy the wine. Maybe that's my call to Washington."

Janice came running out on the lanai, flushed and wide-eyed. "Dad, it's for you and guess who? Alistair Tudsbury. He's calling from the Moana."

PART TWO

Midway

21

The Road to Midway

(from World Holocaust by Armin von Roon)

TRANSLATOR'S NOTE: *The German edition opens with an analysis of the Soviet counterattacks in the winter of 1941–1942. For American readers a better starting point is Roon's fine prologue to the Battle of Midway, which also touches on the Russian picture. The different theatres of war affected each other more than is generally appreciated, and Roon is well aware of the linkages.—V.H.*

The Japanese Surge

After Pearl Harbor we had to face the United States of America as a full and angry belligerent. We gained a brave but poor comrade-in-arms, a far-off Asiatic island folk with less land surface and natural wealth than just one American state, California; and a fresh enemy in the field wielding the greatest war-making potential on earth. The odds had mounted against us. Yet in our General Staff we could still see in the situation elements of an upset victory.

For the bedrock of war is geography, and geographically our posture remained awesome. With one boot on the Atlantic shore and the other on the snows outside Moscow, the Führer bestrode Europe more completely than Napoleon at his far reach, or Charles V of Spain, or the Antonine emperors. From the Arctic to the Mediterranean, every nation was either our ally, or a friendly neutral, or a conquered subject. Under our submarine onslaught, American Lend-Lease help and Britain's colonial resources were going to the sea bottom. Each month fewer Allied ships were left afloat, for all the feverish work in their shipyards. Churchill himself has confessed in his memoirs, *"The one thing that really frightened me during the war was the U-boat campaign."*

As for the Soviet Union, its winter counterattack had achieved local gains at bloody costs; but as it petered out, our battle-hardened troops still gripped the rich bulk of Russia west of the Volga. As a nation we had burned our bridges, and had turned with one will to fighting the war. Despite England's air bombings, our war production was still mounting.

And now Japan was debouching on the world battleground with blazing victories!

Adolf Hitler at once embraced these doughty little Asians as comrades. The mystical bunkum of Nordic supremacy was for Nazi fanatics. We Wehrmacht officers despised it, and we observed with relief that Hitler did too. If a people twelve thousand miles away could help us gain world empire, their skins might be yellow, black, or green for all the Führer cared. The Japanese were not disturbed by Nazi theories, because by their Shinto faith they themselves were the "master race." Unlike our General Staff, the Japanese high command seems to have allowed this rubbish to affect their judgment.

Military judgment should never stray far from the basic factors of time, space, and force. The key to an Axis upset victory was *time*. As to space, we had the advantage of operating on strong interior lines in Europe, while our foes were scattered around our rim; but our one effective ally lay on the other side of the globe. The cold arithmetic of force, in the long run, added up much to our disfavor. Yet the Americans at the moment were weak, and their impact in the field was at least a year away. Because of their thirst for revenge on Japan, we could expect a fall in their Lend-Lease aid to the hard-pressed British and Russians. In short, we still had an edge in time in which to snatch a victory, or compel a tolerable peace.

The Spherical Battlefield

In December 1941, with the industrial civilization all around the northern hemisphere leaping into flame, one grand theme loomed through the smoke. *The battleground had become the surface of a sphere.* This posed unprecedented strategic choices. England and Russia had to exert all their strength just to contain Germany, but Japan, the United States, and the Third Reich now had to decide: "Which way to strike?"

Ever since 1918, as is well known, the American armed forces had been planning for simultaneous war against Germany and Japan. Their notorious Rainbow Five doctrine, drawn up years before Adolf Hitler ever marched, provided a ready answer to the question: eastward, or "Germany first," on the Clausewitz rule, *strike for the heart.* Franklin Roosevelt had the willpower and the sense, in the face of the storm in his country against Japan, to hold to this sound military precept. Under his bluff jolly exterior of a Christian humanitarian, President Roosevelt was a devious and frigid conqueror, much more fitted for war on the surface of a sphere than the impulsive, romantic, European-minded Führer.

Japan's problem was more complex. To the north lay rich Siberia, half-denuded of troops for the defense of Moscow; to the west, China, on its knees but still mushily resisting; to the southwest, the treasures of Indo-China, the Indies, and vast India; to the south, New Guinea and white Australia; to the southeast, the valuable island chains athwart the supply line from Australia to the United States. To the east America glowered, distant and enfeebled, yet thrusting into Japan's *Lebensraum* its thorny imperialist outposts of Hawaii and Midway.

Japan's oil stocks were burning down like a candle. Six months earlier, Franklin Roosevelt had embargoed Japan's fuel supply, and this cruel bullying had compelled her to go to war. She lacked steel; she lacked food; she lacked most of the necessities for a long war. A reckoning for her spree of early victories had to come. With her limited strength, in her limited time, Japan had to strike one decisive blow. But—"Which way?"

For the moment Siberia was out. Before attacking the imperialist plutocracies, Japan had prudently signed a neutrality treaty with the Soviet Union. Hitler had fatuously failed to demand, as a quid pro quo for his declaration of war on the United States, that Japan denounce the treaty and come in against Russia. Thus Japan's rear was safe, and we could not combine with her against the Bolsheviks.

Truly Germany's position was bizarre! All the members of a world-girdling alliance were attacking us, while Japan, our strongest ally, stayed at peace with Russia, our strongest foe! Already the German people were paying dearly for the *Führerprinzip*, which placed total reliance on Hitler's politics. Italy had a sizable navy and air force and numerous troops; but with her cardboard dictator and unwarlike people, she was a drain on our fuel and steel, and her long open Mediterranean coastline was our worst weak spot.

These factors all pointed one way. Against the English, all three Axis powers could still combine. Even Italy would be of some use in the Mediterranean and in North Africa. Obviously we had one best course: speedily to unite in smashing the faltering British Empire, while going on the defensive against stronger foes—in our case Russia, in Japan's case America. This could be done, *and this could be done in time.* Like nothing else, the fall of England would signal a turn in world history, multiplying the impact of Japan's triumphs in the Far East.

The Mediterranean Strategy

The way to destroy the British Empire was by closing the Mediterranean and cutting its lifeline to India and Australia.

Admiral Raeder had first suggested the plan in 1940. It called for the seizure of Gibraltar, a landing in Tunis, and a drive across Libya and Egypt to the Suez Canal and the Middle East, where we could count on an open-arms welcome from the Arabs and the Persians. A glance at a map shows the glitter of the concept. Spain, France, and Turkey, the three major soft spots in our hegemony, would drop into our camp. With French North Africa in hand, the Greater German Empire would become a hard pyramid, based in the south on Sahara sands from Dakar through Egypt, Palestine, and Syria to the Persian Gulf; its apex in Norway under the midnight sun; its western slope the Atlantic Ocean and its fortified coasts; its eastern slope (in 1940) the border with the Soviet Union.

Our weak southern ally, Italy, would be safely locked within an Axis lake. The island of Malta, Britain's flinty little bastion in mid-Mediterranean, would starve and fall. The riches of Africa would flow in ships to German Europe. We would gain the oil of the Persian Gulf, and the raw materials of Asia. From the bulge of Dakar we would dominate opulent South America. It was the beckoning of the golden age, the dawn of the German world imperium itself.

As early as 1940, and again for a while in 1941, Hitler had shown serious interest in this farseeing plan. The Arabs of the region loathed their French and British masters, and the Arab Freedom Movement welcomed our propaganda and agents. Hitler had actually explored with Franco the Gibraltar question. But the cautious Spaniard had equivocated, and the Führer's heart had been in the coming assault against Russia, so Barbarossa had temporarily eclipsed the Mediterranean strategy.

But now the hour of this historic idea had surely come. A strong German presence had arisen in Greece, Crete, and Yugoslavia. Rommel was on the march in Africa. The Soviet menace had been rolled back almost one thousand miles, far out of bombing range of the Fatherland. The naval forces of England were stretched paper-thin, and the sinking of the *Prince of Wales* and the *Repulse* had created a seapower vacuum in the Indian Ocean. Australia and New Zealand wanted their troops back from North Africa to defend Singapore and their own homelands. We were, in fact, witnessing the crack-up of the British world system before our eyes.

When the foe is staggering, that is the time to knock him out. At that moment, we had the world's strongest navy allied with the world's strongest army. If Japan would assault the British Empire westward via the Indian Ocean, while we attacked eastward overland along the Mediterranean littoral, would not this antiquated imperium be crushed like a rotten hazel nut in a steel nutcracker?

The Kuroshima Strategy

There emerged in Japanese naval circles at this time a wonderfully conceived secret war plan, the Kuroshima strategy. It showed professional insight and daring worthy of a Manstein. The swift fall of the British plutocracy, and a different end to the Second World War, were real possibilities under this plan.

Captain Kameto Kuroshima was the senior fleet operations officer of the Japanese fleet; an eccentric intellectual of unmilitary habits but flashy strategic genius. It was he who had designed the masterly Pearl Harbor attack. Ever since, the Japanese navy had been studying long-range follow-up plans; thrusts to the east, to the south, to the west. The navy's fighting spirit was high, and Captain Kuroshima's concept of "westward operations" was the counterpart of our Mediterranean strategy. His ideas still stir the soul:

Operations should be timed to synchronize with German offensives in the Near and Middle East.

The objectives would be

 a. destruction of the British fleet

 b. capture of strategic points and elimination of enemy bases

 c. establishment of contact between the Japanese and European Axis forces.

Kuroshima's superior, Rear Admiral Ugaki, put aside his own breathtaking plan for seizing the Hawaiian Islands, and set his entire staff to studying Kuroshima's scheme. At that time a Japanese-German military agreement was actually being negotiated in Berlin. Unhappily, it turned out to be a shallow document. The scant two pages made no provision for joint staff studies or combined strategy. The globe was parted into two "operational zones" by a line through western India. Orotund generalities followed: west of the line Germany and Italy would destroy the enemy, east of the line Japan would do likewise, etc., etc. Empty pleasantries about exchanging information, cooperating in supply, and conducting the "trade war" closed the footling instrument. Discouraged by this diplomatic bungling, the Japanese navy planners gave up "westward operations" as a lost cause.

Alas!

Hitler Berserk

Ironically, Hitler just then had been re-examining Raeder's Mediterranean strategy.

An isolationist American newspaper, the *Chicago Tribune*, had got hold of the top-secret Rainbow Five war program, and had printed the full text under big black anti-Roosevelt headlines.* This strange act of treason was of course a fine intelligence break for us. The document was unmistakably genuine; Hitler referred to it in declaring war on America. It called for a gigantic invasion of Europe in 1943 by a newly recruited United States Army of millions, with the British Isles as the main invasion base, and large British supporting forces. Admiral Raeder pounced on this information. Clearly a knockout of England would foil the whole scheme and stun the United States.

Even while Hitler was mulling this over, the Japanese smashed Pearl Harbor. Euphoric days ensued. Hitler heard the navy, the army,** and the Luftwaffe argue in favor of Raeder's plan. He fully grasped the main idea—to crush the weakest foe in speedy joint Axis attacks—and at last he indicated tentative approval, and went off to the easten front. Our staff speedily worked up Führer Directive Number 39, switching to the defensive in Russia, with the necessary withdrawals and preparations of rear positions; and we forwarded it to him at his headquarters.

Thereupon all the devils came storming out of Hell!

Hitler summoned General von Brauchitsch, the army commander-in-chief, and his chief of staff, General Halder, to a midnight meeting. He screeched insults, called Führer Directive Number 39 "drivelling nonsense," and declared that there would be no withdrawals on the eastern front; that every German soldier would dig in where he stood, there to fight or die. He summarily relieved Brauchitsch and took personal command of the army—a corporal, relieving a field marshal! The new strategy, of course, went glimmering, for the heart of it was the release of forty or fifty divisions from the east to clean up the Mediterranean. No doubt this was why our January agreement with Japan came out so thin and trivial.

What had happened to Hitler's thinking?

* Roon is in error. The *Tribune* printed excerpts from the top-secret "Victory Program," a resources analysis.—V.H.

** Army advocacy was less than unanimous. My memorandum in support of Raeder survives in my files. Generals on the Russian front tended to scorn the Mediterranean strategy as a "fantasy." It was no more a "fantasy," as it turned out, than the notion of beating the Soviet Union.—A.v.R.

Returning to his gloomy snowbound field headquarters, he had had to face some nasty facts. Against staff advice he had driven for Moscow into December. Weather and supply difficulties had halted our cold exhausted troops in exposed positions. Russian counterattacks had begun, and local penetrations were occurring. Most unsettling, for a dictator used to nothing but victories!

Hitler was haunted by the spectre of Napoleon. We all knew that; copies of Caulaincourt's *Memoirs* were actually forbidden at staff headquarters, like pornography in a boys' dormitory. Our shaken Führer undoubtedly pictured the front disintegrating, the Wehrmacht routed, the Germans harried out of the land by the Cossacks. This was mere nightmare. Our broad solid front from Leningrad to the Black Sea was nothing like Napoleon's narrow, horse-mounted penetration to Moscow on thin supply lines. But the false analogy obsessed Hitler, so he issued his draconic "Hold or Die" order, and took personal command to see that it was obeyed.

Granting that every supreme commander is entitled to his *nuit blanche* fears, there was no need to send to the Japanese such a dispiriting scrap of paper. Had Hitler dispatched even a small military mission to Tokyo— perhaps Admiral Raeder with General Warlimont or myself—it might have sufficed to tip the scales for the Kuroshima strategy. Or if Hitler, after Pearl Harbor, had invited some high Japanese commanders to Berlin to consider joint planning, we might have closed the Mediterranean and forced England to her knees even while the Russian front remained static in the snow, and we tooled up for our summer Caucasus thrust. *But no Japanese liaison officer was ever admitted to Supreme Headquarters.*

"Hold or Die"

Some historians and military analysts still hail the "Hold or Die" order on the eastern front as Hitler's great achievement, a deed of sheer will that "saved" the Wehrmacht. But the truth is that with this order, the Austrian adventurer's star began to wane. The political chief needs detachment in the midst of a war, to keep the big picture in view. Once Hitler took on supreme field command, in which he was merely a headstrong dabbler, he was lost.

The "Hold or Die" order was in point of fact a hysterical military blunder. Defiant toughness in adversity is a sound doctrine; however, elasticity of defense is another. Far outnumbered in Russia, we excelled the Slav hordes in leadership, fighting ability, and maneuvering skill. Hitler's order froze maneuver, paralyzed leadership, and discouraged fighting spirit by commanding meaningless death. Our image of invincibility evaporated. A new

German soldier appeared in Russian propaganda: "Winter Fritz," a pathetic helmeted scarecrow with icicles on his pinched nose, "holding and dying" in an untenable post.

And thus Raeder's plan, the last coherent idea for German victory, faded. One can turn one's imagination free for extravagant pictures of what might have been: Japanese battleships and aircraft carriers sailing into the Mediterranean under the Rising Sun flag, through a Suez Canal flying the swastika! The political effect would have shaken the earth. And it was feasible. Our defensive lines in Russia, properly shortened and reinforced under Directive Number 39, would have held toughly and bathed the Russian earth in Bolshevik blood. Japan could easily have shielded her Pacific perimeter against the weak Americans in the spring of 1942, with small holding forces.

But dismiss all this as wistful romance. It remains a sober fact, attested by the Churchill memoirs, that Japan could have taken Madagascar at will, and cut the supply line up the East Africa coast to Egypt. There would then have been no Battle of El Alamein. The starved British African army would have fallen to Rommel in June after his brilliant *coup de main* at Tobruk. Churchill would then probably have fallen too; and the war would have taken a major favorable turn for us.

Instead, the Mediterranean strategy dwindled into a phantom "Great Plan," the global stroke with which Hitler would wind up the war after beating Russia. He liked to talk about it at dinner, and that was what it remained: table talk.

The Forgotten Victory

The great Japanese navy dawdled and dawdled. Not until the end of March was Admiral Nagumo, the conqueror of Pearl Harbor, given a real task. Until then he roamed the blue ocean wastes in minor carrier strikes, "cracking eggshells with a sledgehammer," as the commentator Fuchida says. Japan's fast battleships swung to anchor at their base near Hiroshima as the sands of time trickled away. In March Nagumo finally sailed westward to hit British surface and air forces in the Indian Ocean. The purpose was to support the Japanese army's advance into Burma.

Here at last was a trial run of the Kuroshima strategy, and a huge victory resulted. Nagumo's dive-bombers sank an aircraft carrier, two heavy cruisers, and a destroyer. He demolished two bases in Ceylon, and much merchant shipping. His Zeroes wrought such havoc among the defending Swordfish, Hurricanes, and Spitfires that Winston Churchill in his memoirs confesses the Royal Air Force was never so outfought over Europe. The surviving British battleships fled to British East Africa. British seapower, after two centuries of hegemony, vanished from the Indian Ocean. De facto, it became a Japanese lake. Western historians pass over this stupendous event, except for Churchill, who candidly records his own real shock and fear at the time.

Thus the Kuroshima concept was vindicated. Madagascar, the African coast, the Suez Canal, the Persian Gulf, the Mediterranean itself, lay open to the advance of the Japanese fleet. But by now it was too late. Nagumo was recalled for other operations. The Axis edge in time had run out unused.

The Doolittle Raid

A brave if harebrained Yankee propaganda action at this time, the notorious Doolittle terror raid against Tokyo, stung Imperial Headquarters into making at last the long-deferred decision, "Which way?" In near-panic, they chose the worst possible course.

Underestimating the Americans is a mistake their enemies often make. They seem frivolous and easygoing; in fact they are highly mechanically minded, and capable of considerable ferocity once aroused. The Yanks were too weak in the Pacific just then for anything but light carrier raids. However, they concocted this savage little stunt, the launching of a few Army Air Force bombers against Tokyo from the decks of a carrier. Since Japanese patrols covered only carrier plane ranges, this achieved total surprise. It had no military effect beyond random murder of civilians, a practice the Americans kept up through Dresden and Hiroshima. The aim was to inspirit the home folks and to jolt the foe.

Technically it was no easy feat. But the Americans modified the bombers and altered carrier routine in their usual clever fashion. A group of volunteer pilots under the able army flier Doolittle made the sneak attack. Out of a clear sky, bombs exploded over Tokyo. America rejoiced, the world was astounded, and Japan was jarred to its foundations. After only four months of war the sacred emperor had been exposed to Yankee bombs!

Yamamoto, the daring supreme admiral who had made the Pearl Harbor decision, now determined that this must not happen again; that the impudent Americans must be taught a lesson, and pushed forever out of carrier range. The answer to "which way" thus came, clear and fatal: *"Eastward!"* Eastward, where there was nothing material to be gained; but eastward, where the American fleet might be forced to come out and be annihilated. And Japan would seize an enemy outpost, from which she could ward off all future Doolittle outrages. So Nagumo was recalled and the die was cast. *Eastward!*

In this way, with such misguided leadership, we and the Japanese turned our backs on each other, sparing the British Empire. We each rode off in the wrong direction on the spherical battlefield. The Wehrmacht set forth on the long march to Stalingrad, and the Japanese navy sailed for Midway.

———————

TRANSLATOR'S NOTE: *This analysis is a study topic at the Naval War College. I have lectured on it. As an army officer, Roon tends to minimize the logistical problems of sea supply lines spanning the whole Indian Ocean, and the flanking threat by sea and air from India. Still, the best course for the Axis in the spring of 1942 may well have been to hold against us and Russia, and hit the British hard from both sides. Losses to U-boats were reaching a peak. A Japanese drive toward Suez, combined with Rommel's advances in North Africa, might have had grim consequences for the Churchill government. If Churchill had fallen, it could have been a long step to a separate peace.*

But Roon throughout ignores the fact that combined operations are not congenial to totalitarian governments. Typically they are founded by extremists and fanatics, who come to power through conspiracy and crime. Once power is seized and the conspiracy becomes a government, these traits persist. As thieves tend to fall out, so totalitarians make poor allies.—V.H.

*   *   *

22

Brigadier General Lacouture had been misinformed about Natalie's whereabouts.

A black cloudburst was drenching Siena at midday. In a bad mood, Jastrow was writing at his study desk by lamplight, beside a streaming window. Rainy weather made his shoulders ache; it stiffened his old fingers; and the words always flowed better when he worked out in the sunshine. Natalie's quiet tap signalled, *"Minor matter; if you're busy, ignore."*

"Yes? Come in."

The passage he was writing demanded a long further look at Martin Luther's views on celibacy. Feeling the weariness of his years and the endlessness of his task, Jastrow welcomed the break. In the shadows cast by the lamplight, her bony face looked pale and sad. She was still not over the blow of their detainment, he thought.

"Aaron, have you ever met Mosé Sacerdote?"

"That Jew who owns the cinema, and half of the real estate on the Banchi di Sopra?" Pettishly he pulled off his glasses. "I may have. I know who he is."

"He's on the telephone. He says you've met at the archbishop's palace."

"What does he want?" Jastrow waved the glasses in annoyance. "If he's the man I remember, he is a walleyed and very glum old gent."

"He'd like you to autograph his copy of *A Jew's Jesus*."

"What? After I've been here eleven years, he asks that?"

"Shall I say you're busy?"

With a slow calculating little grin, Jastrow breathed on his glasses and polished them. " 'Sacerdote,' you know, means *Cohen* in Italian. 'Priest.' We'd best find out what Mr. Moses Cohen actually wants. Let him come after my nap."

The storm had passed, the sun shone, and raindrops sparkled on the terrace flowers when an ancient car wheezed up to the gate. Natalie picked her way around puddles to greet the pudgy elderly man in black.

Jastrow, drinking tea in a lounge chair, waved Sacerdote to a bench beside him.

"Well, well. The Italian edition, *Il Gesù d'un Ebreo*," Jastrow said, as the old man handed him a plain blue-bound volume, one of two he carried. Donning glasses, Jastrow turned the pages of cheap coarse paper. "I no longer have a copy myself. Isn't this rather a collector's item? The printing was only a thousand or so, back in 1934."

"Oh, yes. Very scarce. Very precious.— Ah, thank you, no milk and no sugar." Natalie was pouring tea at a small portable table. Sacerdote spoke Italian with a pure Tuscan accent, mellifluous and clear. "A prize possession, Dr. Jastrow. A fine book. Your discussion of the Last Supper, for instance, carries such impact for our young people! They see *Last Suppers* on church walls, and they attend Passover seders—not always willingly—but they don't connect the two until you do it for them. Your proof that the Romans executed Jesus as a political radical, and that the Jewish common people really loved him, is most important. If only that were better understood! Our mutual friend the archbishop once mentioned that very passage to me."

Jastrow inclined his head, smiling. He loved praise, however trivial, and these days got little of it. "And the other book?"

Sacerdote extended to Jastrow a scuffed little volume. "Another scarce item. I have been spending much time on it lately."

"Why, I didn't know anything like this existed." He held it out for Natalie to see. "*La Lingua Ebraica Contemporanea.* Imagine!"

"The Zionist organization in Milan brought it out long ago. A small group, but well funded." Sacerdote dropped his voice. "Our family may go to Palestine."

Natalie stopped slicing cake and cleared her throat. "How on earth will you get there?"

"My son-in-law is arranging that. I believe you know him. Doctor Bernardo Castelnuovo, he treats your baby."

"Of course. He's *your* son-in-law?"

With a weary gold-toothed smile at the surprised note, Sacerdote nodded.

"He's Jewish, then?"

"Nowadays one doesn't flaunt it, Mrs. Henry."

"Well, I'm amazed. I had no idea."

Jastrow handed back the primer, unscrewed the cap of his pen, and started to write on the flyleaf of *Il Gesù d'un Ebreo*. "Don't you feel secure here? You're contemplating a very risky journey. We know that from experience."

"You refer to your time aboard the boat *Izmir?* My son-in-law and I partly financed the sailing of the *Izmir.*" Natalie and Jastrow exchanged astonished glances. "This evening is the Sabbath, Dr. Jastrow. Won't you and your niece come and dine with us? Bernardo will be there. How long since you've had a real Sabbath meal?"

"About forty years. You're very kind, but I imagine our cook has already started dinner, so—"

Natalie spoke up curtly. "I'd like to go."

Aaron said, "And Louis?"

"Oh, you must bring the infant!" Sacerdote said. "My granddaughter Miriam will adore him."

Jastrow completed his scrawl on the flyleaf. "Well, then, we will come. Thank you."

Sacerdote clasped the book. "Now we have a family treasure."

Natalie ran a hand over her hair, pulled straight back in a bun. "What happened to the *Izmir?* What happened to Avram Rabinovitz, do you know? Is he alive?"

"Bernardo will tell you everything."

The Sacerdotes and the Castelnuovos lived in the modern part of Siena outside the ancient walls, atop an ugly stucco apartment house which Mosé Sacerdote owned, and which he called a "palazzo." The lift was not working, and they had to climb five flights of musty stairs. Manipulating several keys and locks, he let them into a roomy apartment, full of appetizing dinner fragrances, highly polished heavy furniture, whole walls of books, and elegant silver and china in massive breakfronts.

Dr. Castelnuovo met them in a hallway. Natalie had never thought much of him; a small-town doctor, but the best Siena could offer, and his gallant office manners had rather charmed her. His heavy black hair, liquid brown eyes, and dark long face gave him the wholly Tuscan look one saw in old Siena paintings. It had never crossed Natalie's mind that this man might be a Jew.

In the dining room the doctor presented them to his wife and mother-in-law, who also looked quite Italian: both stout, both dressed in black silk, with heavy-lidded eyes, large chins, and similar sweet unworldly smiles. The mother was gray and unpainted; the daughter had brown hair and wore a touch of lipstick. In sunset light that reddened the tall windows, they were preparing to light Sabbath candles on a lavishly set table. As they donned black lace caps, a sallow little girl in brown velvet ran lightly into the room. Halting by her mother's skirt, she smiled at the baby on Natalie's arm. The candles flared up in four ornate silver candlesticks. The two women covered their eyes and murmured blessings. The girl dropped in a chair, holding out her arms and piping in lucid Italian, "I love him. Let me have him."

Natalie put the infant in Miriam's lap. The thin pale arms closed around the baby in a comically competent way. Louis looked her over and nestled against her, hanging on her neck.

Sacerdote spoke hesitantly. "Would you be interested, Dr. Jastrow, to come to the synagogue with us?"

"Ah, yes. The archbishop did tell me, years ago, that a synagogue did exist, somewhere down near the Piazza del Campo." Jastrow sounded surprised and amused. "It is architectually interesting?"

"It's just an old synagogue," Castelnuovo said irritably. "We're not very religious. Father is the president. It's never easy to assemble ten men, so I go. One sometimes hears news there."

"Will you forgive me if I don't go?" Jastrow said, smiling. "It would so startle the Almighty, it might ruin His Sabbath. I shall enjoy looking at your library instead."

While Natalie and the doctor's wife fed the children in the kitchen, Anna Castelnuovo chattered away woman-to-woman. She wasn't a believer at all, she cheerily confessed, but kept up the rituals to please her parents. Her husband's Zionism left her just as cold. Her passion was reading novels, especially by Americans. Having an American author in the house, even though he wasn't a novelist, greatly thrilled her. At Natalie's tale of her marriage to a submarine officer, the doctor's wife was enchanted. "Why, it's like a novel," she said. "A novel by Ernest Hemingway. Romantic." They fell to laughing as Miriam took over the feeding of Louis, both children being ridiculously solemn about it. Then they put the girl and the baby in Miriam's toy-crammed room. "She'll take better care of him than any governess," said Anna. "I hear Father and Bernardo. Come to dinner."

Sacerdote and Dr. Castelnuovo looked gloomy on their return. The older man put on a worn white skullcap to make a blessing over wine, then removed it. Natalie gathered from murmurs among the family that somebody was late. "Well, we will eat," Sacerdote said. "Let us sit down." One place was vacant.

The food was neither Italian nor in the kosher style Natalie half-expected. There was a spicy fish dish, a fruit soup, a chicken dish, saffron-flavored rice, and eggplants cooked with meat. Conversation lagged. Halfway through the meal a son named Arnoldo came in; lean, short, twenty or so, his grimy sweater, long tousled hair, and open shirt in jarring contrast to the family's formality. He ate silently and voraciously. Once he arrived the halting talk died. Sacerdote donned his skullcap to lead a little Hebrew song in which the others joined, but not Arnoldo.

Natalie began to regret that she had pushed Aaron to accept this dinner. He was getting through it by emptying his wineglass as fast as the doctor's wife filled it. Uncomfortable looks kept passing among the family, and a vague dread seemed to compound the gloom. Natalie was dying to ask the doctor about Rabinovitz and the *Izmir,* but his face wore a forbidding aspect that stopped her.

Jewish ceremonies depressed Natalie anyway, and the Sabbath candles still burning on the table were a special sore point. Watching Miriam tonight, she had felt an old deep forgotten ache. Standing beside her mother in the same way twenty years ago, she had asked why mama was lighting candles in the daytime. The reply, that making fire was forbidden after sunset on the Sabbath, had seemed perfectly reasonable, since life to a little girl was full of arbitrary prohibitions. But then after the heavy Friday night dinner, her father had struck a flaring wooden match to his long cigar. She had said in all innocence, "Papa, that's not allowed after sunset." A glance of embarrassment and amusement had passed between her parents. She did not remember what her father had replied as he went on smoking; but the glance she could never forget, for in an instant it had destroyed the Jewish religion for her. Her rowdiness at Sunday school had dated from that night, and soon, though her father was a temple officer, the parents had been unable to make her attend.

Straightening his stained sweater, Arnoldo got up while the others were still eating. In rapid Italian, with a winning white-toothed smile, he said to Jastrow, "Sorry I must leave. I read your book, sir. Quite a book."

His mother said sadly, "On a Sabbath when we have visitors, Arnoldo, can't you stay awhile?"

The smiling face turned sullen. A girl's name whipped out of him in a hostile hiss, "*Francesca* is waiting for me. Ciao."

He left behind a heavy silence. Dr. Castelnuovo broke it by turning to Jastrow and Natalie. "Well! Now I have a good report for you. The boat *Izmir* reached Palestine, and the British didn't catch the passengers as they went ashore."

"Ah, my God!" Natalie exclaimed, in a surge of glad relief. "You're sure?"

"I'm in touch with Avram Rabinovitz. There were bad moments, but on the whole it was a success."

Jastrow put a small damp hand on Natalie's. "Great news!"

"That trip cost us a lot of money." Sacerdote was beaming. "It's satisfying when the results are good. That doesn't always happen."

Natalie said to the doctor, "But the papers and radio said the ship disappeared. I had nightmares that it was the *Struma* all over again."

Castelnuovo bitterly grimaced. "Yes, you do hear about the disasters. The world press is not unsympathetic to Jews, once they're destroyed. It's best to keep the successes quiet."

"And Rabinovitz? What about him?"

"He made his way back to Marseilles. That's his base. He's there now."

"What's your connection with him? May I know?"

Castelnuovo shrugged. "Why not? My father-in-law used to rent his films from that man Herbert Rose who went on the boat. When Rabinovitz ran short of money in Naples—what with delays, and repairs— Rose suggested that we might help him. Avram came up here by train. We gave him a lot of money."

"But one must be careful about such things," Sacerdote put in unhappily. "So incredibly careful! Our position here is delicate, *very* delicate."

The doctor said, "Well, that's it. Since then he and I have stayed in touch. He's a good man to know."

Castelnuovo talked of the growing danger to Italian Jews. Jews had no future anywhere in Europe, he said. He had decided that long ago, while going to medical school in Siena. That tough uphill fight had made him a Zionist. All of Europe was poisoned by nationalist hatred for the Jews; the Dreyfus case in ultraliberal France had been the warning sign, long ago. Under Mussolini's anti-Semitic laws, he himself could practice medicine only because the Siena health authorities had declared him essential. His father-in-law was retaining control of his property through tenuous legal fictions, which put him at the mercy of Christian associates. That very evening in the synagogue they had heard that the Fascist regime was preparing concentration camps for Italian Jews, such as already existed for Jewish aliens. The roundup squads would strike on Yom Kippur, four months hence, when the Jews could be caught in their synagogues. Once collected, they would be handed over to the Germans for shipping eastward, where terrible massacres were taking place.

Sacerdote broke in to insist the report was panicky nonsense. The man who had brought it was a rumormonger with no high connections. The stories of secret massacres were all foolishness. The archbishop himself had assured Sacerdote that the Vatican's intelligence net was the best in Europe; and that if the stories had any truth to them, the Pope would have long since denounced Nazi Germany and excommunicated Hitler.

"I've given fortunes to the archbishop's projects." Sacerdote turned moist and worried dark eyes to Jastrow. "I'm the chairman of the orphanage, his pride and joy. He would not lead me astray. You know him. Don't you agree?"

"His Excellency is an Italian gentleman, and a good soul." Jastrow again emptied his glass. He was very red in the face, but he spoke clearly. "I do agree. Even with a madman as their leader—for it has become my settled view that Hitler is unbalanced—the advanced culture of the Germans, their passion for order, and their legal scrupulosity preclude the truth of these rumors. The Nazis are indeed brutal open anti-Semites, and on such a base of fact, erecting gruesome fantasies becomes all too simple."

"Dr. Jastrow," said Castelnuovo, "what about Lidice? The work of an advanced culture?"

"This fellow Heydrich was a leader of the SS. Reprisal is commonplace in war," Jastrow answered, in a tone of cool academic riposte. "Don't ask me to defend the calculated military frightfulness of the Boche. He doesn't want it defended. He proclaims it. He has proclaimed with great fanfare the annihilation of that poor Czech village."

Castelnuovo came out with a burst of dry quick Italian. The archbishop didn't know all the Pope knew. The Pope had his reasons to keep silent, mainly the protection of the Church's property and influence in German-held lands; also, the old Christian dogma that the Jews must suffer down through history, to prove they had guessed wrong on Christ, and must one day acknowledge him. Miriam could not live much longer within reach of German claws; he and his wife had decided that. He was already communicating with Rabinovitz about ways and means of getting out.

Here again the old man struck in. The decision to leave would be a terrible one for himself and his wife. Siena was their home. Italian was their language. What was worse, Arnoldo was determined to remain; he was in love with a Sienese girl. The family would be torn apart, and the property gathered in a lifetime would be lost.

Louis and Miriam were laughing in a distant room. "Why, it's incredible that that child's still awake," Natalie said. "He's having the time of his life, but I must get him home and to bed."

"Mrs. Henry, why didn't you leave with the other Americans?" The doctor spoke with abrupt sharpness. "Rabinovitz is very puzzled and concerned. He has asked about you repeatedly."

She looked at her uncle, feeling color come into her cheeks. "We've been temporarily detained."

"But why?"

Jastrow answered, "Again, reprisal. Three German agents in Brazil, posing as Italian journalists, were arrested, and so—"

"German agents in Brazil?" Castelnuovo interrupted, wrinkling his forehead. "What has that got to do with you? You're Americans."

His wife said, "That makes no sense."

"None whatever," declared Jastrow. "Our State Department is pressing the Italian government through Bern to send us to Switzerland at once. And they're working on the release of those agents in Brazil, in case this pressure fails. I am not concerned."

"I am," said Natalie.

Jastrow said lightly, "My niece finds it hard to accept that our government has one or two other things on its mind besides our release. As, for instance, that it seems to be losing the war on all fronts, at the moment. But we have other protection. Protection of an unusual nature." He gave Natalie a teasing inebriated smile. "What do you say, my dear? Shall we confide in our pleasant new friends?"

"As you please, Aaron." Natalie pushed back her chair. His patronizing of these well-to-do but miserable people was annoying her. "The children are strangely quiet, suddenly. I'll have a look at Louis."

She found him asleep on Miriam's bed in his favorite slumber pose: face down, knees drawn up, rump in the air, arms sprawled. He looked very uncomfortable. Often she had straightened him out, only to watch him return to the pose, still fast asleep, as though he were a rubber baby rebounding to his manufactured shape. Miriam sat beside him, hands folded in her lap, ankles crossed, swinging both feet.

"How long has he been sleeping, dear?"

"Just a few minutes. Shall I cover him?"

"No, I'll take him home soon."

"If only he could stay!"

"Well, come to our house tomorrow and play with him."

"Oh, may I?" The little girl softly clapped her hands. "Will you please tell my mama that?"

"Of course. You should have a baby brother. I hope you will, one day."

"I did. He died," said the girl in a calm way that chilled Natalie.

She returned to the dinner table. Aaron was describing Werner Beck's intervention to quash the summons from the secret police, at the time when alien Jews had been interned. "We've been living in tranquillity ever since," Jastrow said. "Werner couldn't be more thoughtful and protective. He even brings us mail from home, illegally transmitted. Imagine! A high-placed German Foreign Service officer, keeping two Jews from being interned by the Fascists, because I once helped an earnest young history student with his doctoral thesis. Bread cast upon the waters!"

The old lady spoke up. "Then why doesn't he help you, Dr. Jastrow, with all this nonsense about Brazil?"

"He has, he has. He's been burning up the wires to Berlin. He assures us that this outrage will be corrected, that our release via Switzerland is only a matter of time."

"Do you believe that?" Castelnuovo addressed Natalie.

She gnawed her lower lip. "Well, we know that a diplomatic fuss is going on, and that he's taking an interest. I have a friend in the American legation at Bern who's written me as much."

"My guess would be," said the doctor, "that this Dr. Beck is preventing you from leaving Italy."

"How preposterous!" exclaimed Jastrow.

But Castelnuovo's words stirred a horrible dark sickness in Natalie. "Why? What would there be in it for him?"

"You ask the right question. It's to his advantage to have the famous Dr. Jastrow trapped in Italy and dependent on him. In what way, you will find out."

"You are quite a cynic," Jastrow said, beginning to bristle.

"About my Jewish identity, at this time, and in this place, I believe only the worst possibilities. It's not cynicism, it's common sense. Now I have a message for both of you from Avram Rabinovitz," the doctor said to Natalie. "He says, 'Get out, while you can.' "

"But how?" she almost shrilled at Castelnuovo. "Don't you think I want to get out?"

Jastrow looked at his watch, and said stiffly to the Sacerdotes, "You've taken us into the bosom of your family. I warmly thank you. We must go. Good-night."

23

P UG HENRY stood in the reception line with his sons, Janice, and
Carter Aster at a big lawn party on the grounds of the governor's
mansion. Amid the palms, the flamboyant tropical shrubbery, the very
noisy swanky crowd, the guest of honor visibly stood out. Alistair Tudsbury's ordeal in an open boat on the high seas had not slimmed him; or
if it had, he had managed to eat himself back into shape with a net
gain. He wore a yellow silk suit with a bright yellow tie; a yellow lei
ringed his neck, and he leaned on a yellow malacca cane; and in the
yellow sunshine of a late Hawaiian afternoon, he was altogether a
rather blindingly buttery sight. A black patch covered his left eye.

When Pug came up, Tudsbury pulled him into a bear hug. "Awrr-
hawrr! *Pug Henry,* by God! Late of Berlin, London, and Moscow! By
God, Pug, how are you!"

Stepping forward to embrace Pug, he disclosed his daughter, standing
there in a gray sheath dress. Until that moment Pug wasn't sure she was
at the party, though the papers said she had arrived with Tudsbury. The
correspondent, out of coyness or mischief, had not mentioned her over
the telephone. Engulfed in the hug, losing sight of her in a perfumed
crush of yellow flowers, Victor Henry thought how small she was, and
how white those bare slender arms were; had she had no sun in all her
months in the tropics? She wore her light brown hair as before, un-
fashionably piled up on her head.

"Well, Yank," boomed Tudsbury hotly and moistly in his ear,
"you're in it with us now, aren't you? Up to your necks! In to the
death!" He released Pug. "Awr-hawrr-hawr! And none too soon, none
too soon, by God. Well! You do remember Pam, don't you? Or had you
quite forgotten her?"

"Hello there." The voice was low, the clasp of her hand dry and
brief. Her pale face was almost as calm, distant, and unrecognizing as it
had been in their first meeting on the *Bremen.* But the illusion that she
was tiny had been created by the eclipsing mass of her father. Pamela's

green-gray eyes were almost level with his, and her bosom under the thin gray dress was fuller than he remembered.

Tudsbury said, "Governor, this is Captain Victor Henry of the *Northampton.* The confidant, as I've told you, of presidents and prime ministers." The florid introduction was wasted on the governor, a wrinkled weary-looking man in seersucker, who gave Pug an empty smile suited to a mere cruiser captain. Tudsbury bellowed over the party noise, "What say, Pug, *three* stalwart sons, eh? I thought I remembered two. And hello, here's the senator's pretty daughter."

When Pug introduced Lieutenant Commander Aster the governor's bored eyes came alive. "Ah, the captain of the *Devilfish?* Really! Well, now, I've heard of *you.* Giving the Japs back some of their own, aren't you, skipper? Well done!"

"Thank you, Governor." A modest bob of the head.

Tudsbury's good eye flashed alertly. "Submarine hero, eh? Let's have a chat later."

Aster answered with a frigid grin.

Under a palm tree far down the garden, Spruance was standing beside Admiral Nimitz, who had his hands folded before him. Spruance's were on the back of his hips, as though he did not know where else to put his hands. Both admirals wore pained squints. Spruance beckoned to Pug. He approached Cincpac with some trepidation, for he had never met Nimitz.

"Sir, this is Captain Henry."

"Well! We'll be seeing you at the planning conference tonight, Captain."

Dolphins were pinned over Nimitz's breast pocket and its bright layers of campaign ribbons. White close-clipped hair, ruddy skin, composed blue eyes, a square jaw, a flat waistline; here was a healthy hardy old submariner with a gentle look, yet a sufficient air of supreme command. Nimitz inclined his head toward the receiving line. "You're a friend of this newspaperman, I'm told."

"We became acquainted, Admiral, when I was serving in Europe."

"I was advised to show my face here because the Army was turning out in force." Nimitz's gesture took in the khaki uniforms clustering around General Richardson, the military governor, and his hand swept out at the jocund mob of Hawaiian high society filling the lawn. "Is the man worth all this?"

"He has a world audience, sir."

"Public Information also wants me to talk to him tomorrow." The blue eyes probed. The statement was a question. The weight of the coming battle was already on Nimitz, Pug reflected. The request made him think of the little puff for Madeline in *Variety*.

"Admiral, if you have the time for any correspondent, he's a fine one."

Nimitz made a wry face. "Time is a problem. But they keep telling me we've got to keep up public morale back home."

"A good way to do that, Admiral, is with a victory."

Nimitz dismissed him with a flash of the eyes and a nod. A few minutes later, Pug saw the admirals thread through the crowd and slip out of the garden. Tudsbury now bulked yellow and huge at the tent bar beside General Richardson, in a ring of brightly dressed eagerly crowding women.

Pug stood alone, not drinking. To avoid being jostled by the throng of guests he backed up to the palm tree, and unconsciously put his knuckles to his hips as Spruance had, looking around with much the same pained squint. Pamela Tudsbury, drinking with Janice, his sons, and Aster, was telling a story; an anecdote of Singapore, Pug guessed, from the close attention of the others. He was glad to see Byron enjoying himself, for he had seemed sunk in gloom this afternoon, after a second unsatisfactory talk in two days with some evasive nobody in the State Department, who would not confirm or deny that Natalie was on her way home. As for Pamela, hungry though Pug was to talk to her, he would not intrude on that young group. Half a year had gone by since their parting in Moscow. A few more minutes didn't matter. How youthful she looked, after all! Her age was thirty-one, so she was older than his boys. But not by much; not by much.

Heavy on Pug's mind was awareness of the Japanese fleet plowing the high seas toward Midway. A ludicrous trifle by comparison, but weighing just as much on his spirit, was Pamela Tudsbury's distant greeting to him. He had not expected an affectionate outburst, but even in a receiving line a woman could signal feeling with a mouth twitch, a hand pressure, a glance. Nothing! At first glance Pam had looked less attractive than he had expected; a bit ordinary, even drab, and rather run-down. But now, a few yards away, animated in talk with young people, she was recovering the iridescent aura she had worn in memory and in fantasy; and he felt the same frustration that had ached in him at sea when daydreaming about her, though there she stood, solid and alive.

This whole twittery festive gathering, to his dour view, seemed a game of dressed-up children. There came vividly to his mind the Waterloo eve scene, recounted in poems, novels, and movies, of the grand ball in Brussels; beautiful women, handsome officers, music, wine, the Duke of Wellington himself dancing; and then the distant mutter of the French artillery, and the dissolution of the gaiety in panic, scurry, tears, farewells, and hasty arming. This noisy fancy crush in the garden of Washington Place might lack the rich glitter of Napoleonic times, but the oncoming battle muttered in Victor Henry's imagination like Waterloo. Its consequences, he thought, could be more cataclysmic for the side that lost.

"What, what, Pug Henry?" Alistair Tudsbury left the bar and came limping toward him. "Standing aside and alone, with the worries of the world on your manly phiz?"

"Hi there. Enjoying your party?"

"Oh, one sometimes can't say no." Tudsbury made a grotesque grimace. "Bloody waste of an afternoon. Is that anniversary dinner still laid on for tonight?"

"It's laid on."

"Smashing."

"What about your eye, Talky?"

"Trifling irritation. Having it checked in your naval hospital tomorrow after I interview Nimitz."

"Sure you'll see him?"

"Why, Pug, the man came to this silly do, didn't he? These chaps are never too busy for me. They're always panting to get their ducks in a row for the public and for history. Why, Air Marshal Dowding talked to me at the height of Göring's September seventh raid! If I'd been at Waterloo, Napoleon would have talked to me on horseback while fleeing the field, I assure you. No matter how badly his piles were hurting him! Ah, hawr, hawr!"

Pug gestured at the jolly crowd all around them. "I've been thinking about Napoleon. About that ball in Brussels before the battle."

"Ah yes. 'There was a sound of revelry by night—' But at the moment, at least, one doesn't hear the thunder of approaching cannon." The eye blinked and stared. "Or does one?"

"Not that I know of."

"Now come on, Pug!" A crafty tough look hardened the fat face. "Something's brewing on this island. Something damned tremendous. Tell me what you know."

"Can't help you."

"You do have the most damnably worried look."

A blonde girl came simpering up to Tudsbury in a cloud of white or-gandy, with an autograph book and a pen projecting in little pink hands from the cloud. "Would you, Mr. Tudsbury?" she tinkled. Snorting, he scrawled his signature. The cloud wafted away in giggles.

"I'll tell you what this reminds *me* of," growled Tudsbury. *"Pahits* and dances I attended in Singapore, while those little yellow devils were marching or bicycling down the peninsula. With all those smashed be-hemoths out there in your harbor, and a whole American army in the Philippines captured by the yellow men, who are also swarming over Southeast Asia and the Indies, sweeping up the wherewithal to wage war for a century; with Singapore gone, with the Empire shattered, with Australia naked as a bride for her deflowering, with the Japanese fleet four or five times as strong as anything you've got left in the Pacific— with all that, one would expect in Hawaii, shall we say a concerned air, a hint of urgency, a trace of resolve such as we showed in Old Blighty during the blitz? But the tropics unfit the white man for modern war." Tudsbury flipped the lei with a fat paw. "The natives seem so simple to handle, one gets a false sense of invincibility. There's no such delusion in Australia. They are hellishly alarmed. They know that the Doolittle raid was a fine brave Yank stunt, but not a mosquito bite on Japan's war capacity. Every third person at this party has asked me about the Doolittle raid, popping buttons with pride. Why, man, the RAF's send-ing hundreds of bombers over Germany several times a month—in one night we sent a thousand bombers over Cologne—and we haven't dented the enemy's will yet. Perhaps my nerves are shot, but what I see about me here is more or less a Singapore with Yank accents and pineapples."

"Sounds like your next broadcast, Talky."

"It is, more or less. These people need waking up. I didn't like scuttling out of a falling British bastion under the artillery fire of Asians. Nor will they. I liked getting torpedoed by them even less. And I would gladly have skipped a week in a whaleboat on the open water, under an equatorial sun."

"If you get to talk to Nimitz you'll be reassured."

Pamela strolled by on Carter Aster's arm, both talking at a great rate. "How do you think my Pam looks?"

"Sort of tired."

"She's had a rotten time. We became separated when they sent off a drove of women in an old Greek tub bound for Java. Pam came down with dysentery on board, had to be hospitalized in Java, and then by God the Japs started landing there. So it was march aboard ship again when she could scarcely walk. Pam's resilient, and she's snapping back. I say, is that submarine hero coming to your dinner?"

"He hasn't been asked."

"Would you ask him, old cock? I do so want a word with him. Well, I must drivel a bit more with General Richardson. Awful stick, isn't he?"

As Tudsbury stumped off, Pug mulishly decided that he wouldn't invite Aster. He didn't like the *Devilfish* captain. Under his fawning politeness a hard ego jutted, with a hint of condescension to an older man commanding a treaty cruiser. The Navy tended to pound touchiness out of a man, and Pug Henry was used to letting the other fellow have his plaudits. But the snub from the governor of Hawaii in Pamela's presence, in favor of the younger officer, had nettled him.

Byron came weaving up, grasping a tall planter's punch. "Hi, old Dad! Get you a drink?" His eyes were sparkling and red, his grin foolish. "Great party, hey? What'll you drink, Dad?"

With a glance from the glass to his son's face, Pug said, "What's left?"

Byron laughed. "Dad, you can't put me down, not this afternoon. I'm feeling too damn good. I haven't felt so good in a year. Say, Dad, let's ask Lady Aster to the dinner, okay? He's peculiar, but in submarines you have to be somewhat goofy. He's a great skipper."

Through a gap in the crowd, Victor Henry could see Pamela and Aster at the bar, still in merry converse. All right, Pug thought. Suppose this able officer, back from a brilliant war patrol, likes Pam and she likes him? What's objectionable in that? What claim have I on her, and how would I propose to execute a claim if I had one?

"Sure, ask him, by all means. If you find yourself a nice girl, ask her."

"I've got one."

"Fine! And on second thought, bring me a rum collins with some hair on its chest."

"*Now* you're talking." Byron gave his father a one-armed hug, and startled Victor Henry to his bones by muttering indistinctly, "I love you," or "God love you." The father wasn't sure which.

Off Byron lurched toward the long bar under the striped tent, where Janice was talking to an Army general with thick white hair. Pug saw her wave excitedly to Byron. Beside her Pamela and Aster were laughing into each other's eyes. Victor Henry smiled at his own ridiculous pain; then he realized that the white-haired Army man was Senator

Lacouture. He strode to the bar. "Hello there, General! Welcome, and congratulations."

"Why thanks, Pug." The brigadier general's uniform was bandbox new, the brass buttons too bright. The senator's plethoric face radiated good humor. "Yes, I'm still getting used to it! Why, General Richardson's driver met me at the airport, and zoom!—whisked me straight to this party. I think I'm going to like the Army, ha ha!"

Byron said to his father in a flat frigid sober voice, "She's not on that boat."

"What!"

"They detained her and Jastrow. She's still in Siena. All the other Americans are coming home but not her."

"Yes, but don't worry, young man," said Lacouture cheerily. "Somebody at State slipped up, not to notify you by cable. Sorry I had the wrong information. It's a temporary snag, so State assured me, a matter of weeks at most, some problem involving Italian journalists in Brazil."

"Senator, two very beautiful ladies here are absolutely dying to meet you," General Richardson called.

Lacouture hurried away.

"One rum collins with hair on its chest," said Byron calmly, his face ashen. "Coming up, Dad."

"Byron—"

Byron's back was to him, pushing through the brown Army crowd at the bar.

The main dining room of the Moana Hotel was a kaleidoscopic whirl of brass-buttoned uniforms and colored frocks, crowded to the walls and tumultuous with talk and brassy jazz. Young officers, mostly from the SubPac rest center in the nearby Royal Hawaiian Hotel, were spinning excited girls around and around in the Lindy Hop. The band's singer, in a strapless red dress that exposed billowy bosoms, was wriggling, jiggling, and howling *"and the boogie-woogie washerwoman washes away"* to an audience packed at tables around the dance floor; at which tables military uniforms predominated, and pretty laughing girls, bejewelled, bepainted, and dressed in splendid half-nude evening finery. Elderly civilians at a few tables, by their look wealthy and retired, were gazing wistfully at all this amorous wartime dazzlement, lit by a sinking sun through open windows. Though it was still day, the restaurant fizzed like a ballroom at midnight because the revelry, off to an early start, had to end at ten. The ten o'clock curfew had teeth.

Pug had reserved a large table by the dance floor. Carter Aster sat there alone. As Pug came into the room with the Tudsburys, the submariner jumped to his feet.

"Where's Byron?" Pug asked.

"Sir, I thought he must be with you. I couldn't find hide nor hair of him at the party." Aster pulled out a chair for Pamela with a gallant flourish. "I even went looking inside the governor's mansion. I figured he must have caught a ride with you."

"He didn't."

Dancing past them, Warren called, "Where's Briny, Dad?"

Pug turned up his hands.

"*And the boogie-woogie washerwoman washes away . . .*" Warren was blocked from sight by jostling dancers. Aster and Pamela fell at once into animated chatter. Pug thought that at this rate he might never get to talk to her. The Cincpac conference was scheduled for ten. The fleet was sailing for Midway in the morning. In the car Tudsbury had held forth without cease on Singapore, the Russian front, Rommel, the Japanese advance toward India, and such cheerful matters. Meantime Pamela had sat in the back seat mum as a fish. Now, putting his mouth almost to Pug's ear, Tudsbury began badgering him again for inside dope on what was brewing. "The Boogie-Woogie Washerwoman" gave way to total gibberish bawled by the gelatinously shaking singer. "*Hut-Sut rawlson on the riller-ah and a braw-la, braw-la soo-it*" were the approximate noises Pug heard. With this *Götterdämmerung* babble at one ear, with Tudsbury's pesky questions yelled into the other, with Aster and Pamela getting up to dance, with worry about Byron's disappearance plaguing him, with an ever-growing sense of the Japanese fleet's approach, Pug Henry was not having much fun.

Byron came in view, carrying a large brown envelope and leading a girl. "Hi, Dad. Hi, Mr. Tudsbury. This is Ursula Thigpen. Remember Ursula, Mr. Tudsbury? You gave her your autograph. Don't you think Ursula's a pretty name?"

Ursula plumped down in the chair beside the correspondent before he could reply. "Now, that's *Thigpen,* Mr. Alistair Tudsbury." She tapped his arm with a stiff little pink finger, spelling, "*T-h-i-g-p-e-n!* Thigpen! Not 'Pigpen,' see? Just in case you do broadcast about me. Hee hee!"

"Well, well, Briny, so you surfaced," said Aster, returning with Pamela. "Where the hell did you get off to?"

Warren and Janice came back to the table. "Like dancing in a subway rush," Warren said.

"*Hut-Sut rawlson on the riller-ah . . .*" Ursula inquired whether either Janice or Pamela cared to press their shoelaces. Byron had been driving her all over the island, she said. He had even brought her aboard the *Devilfish*, but there was no little girls' room on submarines. "My back teeth are floating," she elaborated.

Janice took her off, wondering why Byron had this imbecile in tow. While fixing her makeup in the powder room Ursula spilled a condom from her vanity case and unblinkingly put it back, tittering that in Hawaii you never knew when it was going to rain, did you? "Although frankly, your brother-in-law doesn't seem exactly the type," she said. "He's cute, but strange."

"What were you doing in the submarine?"

"Oh, he went to fetch a big wooden box. It's out in the jeep. Getting it up those ladders was a problem, but nothing like *my* problem, honey. Why, those awful submarine sailors! They could see everything. And they sure looked! I'll bet they've got eyestrain, the lot of them." Ursula chortled about this all the way back to the table, where a waiter was serving drinks.

Out on the floor Byron was now doing a Lindy Hop with Pamela, who, keeping him at arm's length, was observing his elegant antics with a half-dismayed, half-amused look.

Warren said to Janice, "Briny's flying to San Francisco tonight. He's brought his footlocker. At nine thirty we take him to the NATS terminal, he says, and pour him on board the plane."

Janice said to Aster, "But have you detached him?"

"There are his orders." Aster made a limp resigned gesture at the envelope on the table. "I've just signed them."

"What about air priorities?"

"He got himself an air priority. Byron does these things."

"Byron has two gaits," remarked his father, "a snail's crawl, and the speed of light in a vacuum." He was watching Byron dance, doing the best jitterbugging in sight, shaping the faddish angular prances and wild twirls of the Lindy Hop into fluid motions charming to watch. Pamela Tudsbury's sedate careful stepping-about, with her outstretched hand barely touching his, made a ludicrous contrast.

"Ursie Thigpen!" A fat perspiring lieutenant whose dolphins were green with sea tarnish wrapped a thick arm around her waist. "Good old Ursie! How about a dance, Urs? Will you excuse her, folks?" And away they gyrated.

Holding out a hand to Janice, Warren jumped up. "Well, let's go, anniversary girl. Tonight's your night."

"These damned Lindys!" bubbled Janice. "Don't they play anything for old married folks?"

"It's hopeless," Pamela said to Pug, dropping into a seat beside him, patting at her forehead with a wisp of gray handkerchief. She smiled up at Byron. "You were a darling to put up with me."

"I'm sorry you quit." Byron went back to his place, drank off a tall rum collins like a glass of water, and signalled at the waiter for another.

Aster and Tudsbury were in a low earnest colloquy quite drowned out by the music. Here was Pug's chance to talk to Pamela. How to start? She was looking away from him toward the dance floor. He had thought so much about her that here at his side, in the flesh, she had an unreal quality that disconcerted him; a minor actress, as it were, not quite filling the stupendous Pamela role of his yearnings and visions. Her face seen this close was strained and older; her cheeks were darkly hollow, her lipstick was carelessly applied, and on her upper lip there was a trace of moist down. He touched her bare white forearm.

"I'm sorry to hear you've been ill, Pam."

She faced him. Her tone was as low as his. "I do look it, don't I?"

"I didn't mean that. You look grand." Bad beginning! He lurched awkwardly on. "You didn't by chance get a letter I sent you from here, months ago?"

"A letter? No. I've never had a letter from you."

"I received one from you."

"Oh, did that missive actually reach you? Written in another epoch, wasn't it?"

"I was very glad to get it."

"How's your wife?"

"She asked me for a divorce."

Pamela stiffened, clenched her hands, and thrust her bare pale arms forward on the table, hectic eyes flaring at him. "How could she? You couldn't have given her any cause."

"Claimed she'd fallen in love with someone else."

"How ghastly for you."

"Well, she's since expressed regret about it, in a fashion. It's all up in the air."

Looking straight at Byron, whose eyes were on them, she murmured, "Do your sons know?"

"They haven't a notion."

"I'm terribly sorry to hear this. And you lost your battleship, too."

Victor Henry wanted to reply, *Now that you're here it's okay,* but her cool casual manner forbade it.

"How long will you and your father stay in Honolulu?"

"I'm not sure."

Janice and Warren glided by, a straight-backed pair in the crowd of flailing prancing couples. "Didn't you propose, on the *Bremen,* to match me up with a son of yours?"

"Oh, you recall that?"

"Warren, no doubt?"

"Yes. But meantime, Janice hogtied him."

Pamela's mouth wrinkled, and she shook her head. "Never. Byron, possibly. Though when you first told me about him and Natalie Jastrow, I confess I was surprised. I thought wow, Natalie, my contemporary, and a son of yours—a *son*—"

"I still think that."

She contemplated Byron, slumped low in his chair over a second rum collins, his dark red hair falling in his eyes. "Oh, I understand her now. Devastating charm. Quiet, effortless, lethal. As for Warren, he's fine, but formidable. Are Natalie and her baby in real danger?"

"I suppose they'll get out all right."

"Why's Byron going to the Atlantic? What can he do for them?"

"Don't ask me."

Waiters arrived with champagne bottles and shrimp cocktails. Ursula, holding down her skirt close by in an animated twirl, left her partner with a twiddle of her fingers. "Ooh, champagne, yum, yum! Bye-bye, Bootsie!" Byron ordered the champagne opened at once.

"Well, founder of the feast," he said to Pug, "how's for the first toast?"

"Okay. Raise your glasses. Janice, many happy returns. Of the day, and of your man. Warren, good hunting."

Next Byron held up his glass. It happened that the music just then stopped. "Mom," he said. The sharp clear word caught Victor Henry unaware.

Warren raised his glass. "And Madeline."

Janice said, "Natalie and her baby, and their safe return."

Byron gave her a dark glance, raised his glass to her, and drank.

Over the shrimp cocktails Pug lost Pamela to Aster. The submariner made some joke he didn't hear, Pamela threw her head back in hearty laughter, and soon they got up to dance again. So did the others. He was left at the table with Tudsbury, who leaned over and jogged his elbow. "I say, Pug, how well do you know this submarine man? Does he enjoy leading one up the garden path?"

"Pamela can take care of herself."

"Pamela? What the devil has she got to do with it? He's just told me the most astounding story about his last patrol."

"To what effect?"

Tudsbury shook his head. "Come up to our suite after dinner, won't you? Some things can't be bawled over music."

Thinking of the Cincpac conference, Pug said, "I will, if there's time."

More champagne arrived with the roast chicken. Pug wondered by what legerdemain Byron had lined up these scarce bottles of California wine. A frenetic spirit was animating and jamming the dance floor as nine o'clock approached. The waiter had trouble getting through to their table with the cake. In the white icing, a blurry blue aircraft trailed red skywriting: *Janice and Warren.*

"Lovely," said Janice.

"Wrong war," said Warren. "Biplane."

The waiter poured out the last of the wine as Warren cut the cake. Tudsbury seized his glass. "Well, in concluding this splendid feast," he grandiloquently boomed, getting to his feet, "I propose our host, and his two sons. Gentlemen, your disguise of simple Yank sailors is convincing, but the Homeric marble shows through. You are three figures from the Iliad. I drink to your health, and to your victory."

"Jehosephat, that's some toast," said Pug.

"Three figures from what?" Ursula said to Byron.

"Three figures from *The Idiot,*" he said. "It's a Russian novel."

Pamela burst into a shriek of laughter and spilled her champagne.

The room darkened for the floor show. A master of ceremonies trying to sound like Bob Hope told jokes about rationing, Hitler, Tojo, and the curfew. Two Hawaiian men played guitars and sang. Then half a dozen hula-hula girls came undulating barefoot into the pink spotlight, their grass skirts audibly swishing. They danced and sang, then broke their chorus line to move out along the cleared floor, inviting diners to dance with them. One by one men jumped up to face the girls and hula, some kicking off their shoes. Mostly they clowned. The most beautiful girl, who looked more Eurasian than Hawaiian, came weaving her hips toward the Henry table. Seeing the decorated cake at Warren's place, she turned a brilliant smile at him, and extended beckoning hands.

"Go ahead, darling," said Janice. "Show them how it's done."

With a serious expression Warren got to his feet and faced the grass-skirted girl. He did not take off his shoes. Moving with grace, maintaining the dignity of his gold-winged white uniform, he danced a cold correct hula-hula, bringing to Pug's mind the naval officer in *Madame Butterfly,* the imperturbable and lordly young white man toying with an Asian beauty.

"I didn't know men did this dance," said Pamela to Pug.

"It seems he does."

The fixed entertainer's grin on the hula-hula girl's face changed to a sweet smile of pleasure. She looked full into Warren's eyes, and impulsively hung her lei around his neck. Her dancing became sexier. Guests at other tables watched and whispered. Glancing around the table, Victor Henry saw that Janice, Pamela, and Ursula had admiring eyes fixed on Warren, while Aster and Tudsbury were gazing with appetite at the dancing girl. Byron was not looking at her. His face frozen in a drunken expression, he was staring at his brother, and tears were trickling down his cheeks.

24

PREDICTABLY, Tudsbury occupied the presidential suite, with the predictable huge living room full of overstuffed modernist sofas and armchairs, but with an unpredictable wallpaper of large red stallions charging around the room. The best feature of the suite, Tudsbury told Pug, was shrouded by the blackout curtains: a wide balcony facing the sea and Diamond Head. "Smashing view in the moonlight," he said, entering the suite with Pug as Pamela went off to her room down the hall. "What'll it be, Victor? Brandy? Or a warm whiskey and soda? There's a fridge, but it doesn't work. Shades of Singapore."

Since taking command of the *Northampton,* until this evening, Pug had drunk nothing. He asked for brandy. The first taste brought back a glimmer of his time of acute pain over Rhoda's divorce letter. Tudsbury flopped in an armchair, gulping dark whiskey and water. "Charming dinner, Victor, truly. Frightfully keen on your sons. One seldom runs into such a sense of family nowadays. Well, what cheer, old cock? What's the real news? Come on! There's a great sea battle making up, isn't there?"

"What was Aster's shocking story?"

"You really don't know? Why, my dear fellow, the second vessel the *Devilfish* sank was a hospital ship."

Sitting up straight, Pug jabbed a forefinger at Tudsbury's face. "He never told you that."

"But he did, dear boy."

"You misunderstood him."

"Softly, softly. It turned out to be a disguised ammunition ship. He's got photographs to prove it. Before it sank it popped off for half an hour like a pyrotechnics factory. And it was carrying tons of crude rubber. He retrieved samples."

"Was Aster very drunk?"

"No. Possibly Pam made him feel expansive. She rather took to him, I thought."

"Forget you ever heard that story."

"Why? Camouflaging an ammunition ship with the red cross is a filthy trick. Typical Jap insensitivity to civilized rules of war. They're barbarians, Pug." A fat fist waved in the air. "Lieutenant Commander Aster is one white fighting man who can be as ruthless as they are, an ingratiating young Yank with a killer's heart. Superb copy."

"Do you want him to go on killing?"

"Of course."

"Then blot the thing from your mind. Alcoholic babble. What are your plans, Talky? Where do you go from here?"

"San Francisco. Washington. And so home to Old Blighty, and thence to the desert army in North Africa." He leaned forward, his good eye popping, his paunch straining at the yellow silk, and dropped his voice to a hissing whisper. "See here, Pug Henry, *what's up?* I ask you man to man, *what's up?* Damn it all, I'm a friend of yours and a friend of your country."

A pleasant brandy fog wisped in Pug's brain. The battle was coming on, he thought, Tudsbury did happen to be here, and it would be a disservice to the Allies if he left. Ingrained total secrecy in this case could be modified. "Okay. You forget that hospital ship and I'll tell you something." He extended his hand. "Done?"

"But you're offering a pig in a poke."

"Yes."

"Well, for once, I'll trust a Yank." Tudsbury clasped hands. "Done! Now talk."

"Don't leave Honolulu."

"No? Good-o! Why not? Go on, *go on,* tell me all about it, dear fellow. I'm panting." Tudsbury was indeed breathing heavily, somewhat like a leaky bellows, with considerable wheeze.

"That's it."

"What's it?"

Henry reiterated, with the level droning emphasis of words issuing from a warship's bullhorn, *"Don't . . . leave . . . Honolulu."*

"That's *all?* But you're a damnable swindler!" Tudsbury's face contorted in a huge scowl. "I *know* I shouldn't leave. Your Cincpac building is boiling like an anthill, I saw that! What in hell have you given me?"

"Confirmation," Pug said.

Tudsbury's one-eyed indignant glare slowly faded into a crafty capitulating leer. "All right, dear boy. But it's *you* who's been diddled, you know, not me. I gave my word of honor to Aster not to use his story, before he'd tell me a word of it. No Allied correspondent could touch that tale. Heh heh. You're an easy mark." He leaned over and patted Henry's arm. "Tremendous battle cooking up, eh? Trafalgar of the Pacific, what? On their way already, the yellow beggars? Going to try to invade Hawaii?"

Pamela came in. Droplets of water clung to her hair at the forehead and temples. She looked very pale, almost ill. Pug stood up, and her father waved his glass.

"Ah, here's my charmer, my right hand. Nobody will ever know, Victor, how much I owe this girl. I've dragged her through fire and water in these past six months. She's never faltered or complained. Pour yourself a drink, Pam, and give me another stiff whiskey and soda."

"Talky, go to bed."

"I beg your pardon?"

"You've had a very long day. Go to bed."

"But Pam, I want to talk to Victor."

"So do I."

Tudsbury peered at his daughter's chill nervous face, and reluctantly pushed himself up out of his armchair. "You're being hard on me, Pamela, very hard," he whined.

"I must help him dress his eye," she said briskly to Pug. "I shan't be long. Take a look at our view."

Victor Henry slipped through the swaying blackout curtains. The night was starry, and the low moon cast a golden path on the calm sea. Eight or nine days from full; the Japs' battle plan called for full-moon nights, obviously. A deceitfully peaceful prospect here: the quiet plash and hiss of the phosphorescent surf, flower scents from the gardens below, the moonlit cone of Diamond Head beyond the blacked-out Royal Hawaiian Hotel. Under this same moon, lower in the sky thousands of miles to the west, the Japanese armada was even now plowing toward Midway, swells breaking and foaming on hundreds of iron bows —pagoda-masted battleships, crudely built carriers with flight decks propped by naked iron girders, tubby transports crowded with landing troops, and the vessels of the train swarming like waterbugs from horizon to horizon.

"I wondered where you'd got to." A touch on his shoulder. Pamela's voice, cool and low.

"Hi." He turned toward her dark shape. "That was quick. Is his eye bad?"

"Your Navy doctors call it an ulcer. They say it'll heal." A pause. "Your wife's demand for a divorce is shattering news."

"Well, it was blurred at the time by other things, Pamela, such as losing the *California*. And seeing Pearl Harbor from the air, a smoking junkyard."

"Something like my last glimpse of Singapore."

"I heard you broadcast from there. About the Mills bomb."

"Oh, did you?" Another awkward pause. Arms folded, she was staring out to sea.

"Last time we stood on a balcony like this the view was different," he ventured.

"I should say. The Thames docks on fire, searchlights on a black sky, sirens, AA popping, German planes falling—" She turned her face to him. "And then you went off to ride a bomber over Berlin."

"And that made you furious."

"Indeed it did. Look, I've lost my taste for tropic nights. The Southern Cross now signifies for me—and probably always will—nothing but godawful sickness and fear. Let's go in." She led him through the french window and rustling blackout curtains. A streak of yellow light shone under the bedroom door.

A muffled call: "I say, Pam, is that you?"

"Yes, Talky. Why aren't you asleep?"

"Going over my notes. Where's Victor?"

"He's just leaving now."

"Oh, is he? Well, good-night there, Victor."

"Night, Talky," Pug called.

"Pamela, will you bring your pad and take just a little dictation?"

"No, I won't. Turn out the light. You're exhausted."

"Well, since you're so eager to go to bed, all right." The streak of yellow disappeared. "Pleasant dreams, Pam," Tudsbury called in a teasing tone.

"He's a small boy," Pamela muttered. "We'll go to my room."

The corridor smelled very hotel-like. The lights glared. As she took a key from a little gray purse, the elevator door slid open, and with a heart-thump Henry saw his son Warren step out. The discomfort lasted only a second or two. It wasn't Warren, but a tall young man in a white uniform with gold wings, who gave Pamela an admiring glance as he passed.

She unlocked her door and in they went. The room was small and dingy, as Pug expected it to be on the hotel's landward side: the gray paint faded and peeling, the red curtains in need of a dusting, the double brass bed hiding a threadbare carpet.

"I suspect it's a chambermaid's quarters," Pamela said. "I couldn't argue. The hotel was jammed and they did give him the royal suite. I wasn't expecting to entertain, anyway." She tossed aside key and purse, and held out her arms. "But I guess I am, at that."

Pug seized her.

"Oh, God Almighty, high time," Pamela gasped. She kissed him hard, sending sweet fire shooting all through him. Pug's awareness of other things—battle conference, oncoming enemy, sons, wife—was blotted out by a sensation forgotten since his honeymoon: the unique and fiercely exalting thrill of a woman in his arms signalling with mouth and body her love and her first surrender.

The worn lonely wounded man returned her kisses, crushing her close. Their rush of endearment, an incoherent blaze of kisses and broken words, at last slowed. They caught their breaths. There was the squalid little room again, and the big bed.

"This is one hell of a surprise," he muttered against her questing mouth.

"Surprise?" She leaned back in his arms, her eyes dancing with a joyous light. "How? Why? Didn't I declare myself very crudely in Moscow?"

"I thought tonight it was all off, from your manner."

"Dearest, your sons were *right there*."

"I thought you liked young Aster."

"Oh? He was handy." She put caressing fingers to his face. "My problem was to keep my eyes off you. Now then. What's all this about a conference tonight?"

"I have to leave in half an hour."

"Half an hour! My God! Can we spend all day tomorrow together?"

"Pam, the fleet sails in the morning."

"NO! Damn! Oh, damn, damn!" She pulled free, and made an agitated gesture at a small seedy armchair. "What a disaster! Sit down. Damn! In the morning! There's *never* time, is there? Never! I should have hunted you up directly we got here." She sat on the bed, and struck the brass frame with a clenched white fist. "I *thought* of it, but I wasn't sure how you felt. It's been half a year, you know, and I'd never heard from you. What was in the letter you sent me?"

Pug said miserably, "I was giving you up."

"Had you heard from your wife when you wrote it?"

"No."

"She's reprieved me. Oh, how *could* the misguided woman do it? Do you know who the man is?"

"You met him at our house. That tall engineer, Fred Kirby. He's not a bad fellow."

"He made no impression on me. Half an hour! Oh, blast! Oh, hell!"

She swung up her legs and hugged them, leaning her back against the frame. The girlish pose troubled Pug. Madeline sat so, sometimes. Pam looked piercingly sweet and desirable, but young, young, hunched there with white slender arms clutching her folded legs and thighs outlined in gray silk.

"Now listen, darling," she said, talking fast. "Before I left London, I checked on ways and means of staying on in Honolulu. The chief of our military liaison here, a Commodore Alexander Pike, rather likes me. Also I've brought a high-powered letter from Lord Burne-Wilke. Milord's a dear boring man who'll do anything for me. In short, my love, I've got an offer of a job here. Just today I put down a month's rent to hold a sublease on a small flat. You see—" She was ticking off all this like an executive secretary, but at his headshake she stopped and grinned. "Have I been a trifle forward, *mon vieux?* My plan was to offer myself to you on a silver platter, all set, no problem. I couldn't foresee that we'd have so little time tonight. Or that your wife would go dotty on you. Exactly how does that stand, Pug?"

He repeated passages from Rhoda's divorce letter that were branded into his brain; and he spoke of the breezy tone of her writing since then, and of the anonymous notes.

"Oh, ignore that filth!" A disgusted headshake. "It's only what Rhoda writes that counts."

"She's stringing me along, Pam. That's my strong hunch. Maybe she feels it's her duty, because I'm out here fighting the war. Or maybe it's because the other fellow isn't nailed down yet. There's a phony note in her letters."

"You can't be sure. She's self-conscious, Pug. She's put herself in a false position. Can't you see that? Don't be too quick to judge her." Pamela glanced at her wristwatch. "Hell, time's burning down like a fuse. You're off to sea, and Talky will want to leave for the States. What a mess Rhoda's made! It's my golden opportunity, of course, but would it complicate your poor life if I stayed on?"

"Talky isn't going to leave. I've advised him to stay."

"You have?" She waited. He said nothing more. "Well. Interesting! Still, I'd better let old Alex Pike know about that job."

This lovely creature was no dream girl, Pug thought. She was almost as tough and pushy as her father. She sat there within reach, real as a rock, pale and anxious-looking, demanding a decision. Matters were blazing forward between them, after the long slow empty months.

"So the ball's in my court, then," he said.

Anger flashed across her face. "There's no ball and no court. This is no game." She sat up straight, her legs on the floor. "I'm here. If you want me, I'll stay. If you don't, I'll go. Is that explicit enough? I want to be where you are. *I love you.* To me you're life. You're distressed about Rhoda, and I can't blame you. Well, make your regulations and I'll obey them. But there's no place for me to go from here, Victor, unless you send me away. Do you understand, or don't you?"

How many men would give all they had to hear such words from such a woman? It was his God-granted chance to rebuild a ruined life. He got to his feet and pulled her up into an embrace. All but overwhelmed by the power of the moment and the joy of her body seeking his, he could only choke out, "I'm too damned old for you."

"I have to tell you something," she said, clinging to him hard, bowing her face on his white jacket. The words came muffled and fast. "In Singapore I went back to Phil Rule. He was there. I don't know why. It was the end of the world. He's the same old swine. Still, I went back to him. It happened once. I didn't plan it. I'm still sick about it." She raised her face. It looked as pale and ill as it had earlier.

Pug said, quelling agonized anger and hurt, "You didn't owe me anything. Now, you asked about regulations. Here's regulation number one. Never make me late for a Navy conference."

"Oh, Lord, that bloody conference! Is it time?" Her voice shook. "Be off with you, then. No, wait. Here." She darted at her purse, pulled out a white card and put it in his hand. "Here's where you'll find me when you get back. It's an apartment hotel."

" 'Dillingham Court,' " he read. "That still exists?"

"Yes. Seedy, but convenient and—why that peculiar smile?"

"Rhoda and I stayed there once. Before we had the kids."

She looked him straight in the eyes. "When will you return? Do you know?"

His face turned grave. "I'm telling this to you alone. We're heading out to fight a hell of a big battle, Pam. The odds are against us. I'm going now to Admiral Nimitz's headquarters."

Her face stiff with tension, her eyes huge and brilliant, she took his head in her hands and lingeringly kissed his lips. "I love you, Pug. I'll never change. When you come back, *and you will*, I'll be here."

She opened the door for him.

Thin brown smoke wisped from the *Northampton*'s stacks as it rode to a chain hove short. Through the smoke, the morning sun dappled a deck alive with sailors hurrying here and there under the long guns and the float planes on catapults, securing the heavy cruiser for sea. In his cabin, Victor Henry was downing a breakfast of fresh pineapple, oatmeal, ham and eggs, and hashed brown potatoes, as his amazed steward poured cup after cup of steaming coffee for him.

"Appetite fine this morning, Cap'n."

"Food's fine," said Pug.

The sunlight that fell through the porthole in a brilliant oval on the starchy white cloth seemed to be streaming into his spirit. He had slept only two or three hours, yet he felt wonderful; a half-year of funk was blasted away, like fog by a fresh sea wind. Before springing from his bunk for exercise and a cold shower, he had lain in the dark thinking it all over: an amicable settlement with poor fouled-up Rhoda, a second marriage, perhaps a second family—why not, *why not?* He knew men his age who lived in bliss with glowing young wives (none like Pamela Tudsbury!), even with fresh crops of babies around them. Fantasy was finished; fact was sweeter.

His concern about the battle was dissolving into nervy relish, now that his spirits were up, and he knew what would probably happen—that is, if Cincpac's cryptanalysts were right. Even with this intelligence break, the battle estimate went massively against the Pacific Fleet's chances of survival. Yet in the peculiar configuration of the Japanese attack plan there was some hope. Their power would be spread out from the Aleutians to the Marianas. In at least the first phase, carriers against carriers, the odds might be endurable, though the damaged *Yorktown* and the unblooded *Hornet* were weak sisters compared to the battle-hardened Japanese flattops. Anyway, he was heading for a fight, and he was a fighting man; and Pamela's love made him feel ready to take on any odds.

A ringing telephone broke into Pug's reverie.

"Sir, this is the OOD. Your son's come aboard."

"Send him along."

Warren appeared in the doorway in workaday khakis, with gold wings pinned on a faded shirt. "Hi, Dad. If you're too busy for me, say so."

"Come in. Have something to eat."

"No thanks." Warren held up a hand, dropping into an armchair. "Janice just gave me the royal send-off. Steak and eggs for breakfast." He looked around at the sunny cabin. "Hm! I've never yet seen you in your glory. Nice quarters."

"Well, you've been invited often enough."

"I know. My fault."

"Byron get away all right?"

"Oh, he's in San Francisco by now. With a historic hangover, no doubt."

Pug glanced at the steward, who bobbed his head and vanished. Warren lit a cigarette, saying quietly, "It's Midway, isn't it, Dad? And the whole damn Jap fleet?"

"Where'd you hear that?"

"Guy on Halsey's staff."

"Sorry to hear Halsey's staff is a sieve."

"What about this Admiral Spruance? You've been steaming around with him for months."

"What about him?"

"Well, to begin with, he's a battleship man, isn't he? The word is that he's an electrical engineer, a War College type. Not even qualified in aviation like Halsey. They say he's Halsey's buddy, and that's how he got the job. The staff's worried."

"Cincpac's choice of task force commander isn't your business or the staff's."

Warren's tone hardened like an echo. "Dad, the boss man of this show has to understand aviators. Halsey's flight qualification was just one of those things, but at least he went and did it. Actually he doesn't think like an aviator. When we struck the Marshalls he wanted to launch unescorted bombers beyond flight range, and at that his staff navigation was off. Half of us would have fallen in the drink getting back to Point Option. We staged a pilots' sit-down, damn near, and got the orders changed." His father shook his head in stern disapproval. Warren threw up both hands. "Well, that's what happened. You can't shoot off dive-bombers like sixteen-inch shells. They have to turn around and come back. It's a big difference, but admirals have no end of trouble remembering that."

"Spruance will remember it."

"Well, I'm glad you say that. If he'll just close the range and give us a chance, we'll do a job for him." Warren blew out a thick smoke ring. "Two carriers against the whole Jap navy. Should be interesting."

"Three carriers." Somewhat piqued, Pug added, "Also some nine cruisers, Warren."

"Three? The *Sara?* She's in California, isn't she?"

"The *Yorktown.*"

"Dad, the *Yorktown* had her insides blown out. It's a six months' repair job."

"The Yard has promised to put her in combat shape in seventy-two hours."

Warren whistled. "I'll believe that when I see it. Incidentally, did you hear the morning news—that battle around Kharkov?"

"No."

"Biggest tank fight of all time. Both sides say that. Did you ever get to Kharkov?"

"The Germans held Kharkov when I was in Moscow. It's been taken and retaken since. I've lost track."

Warren nodded. "And Rommel's fighting still another tank battle in Africa. Where do the Germans get all these tanks? The RAF's supposed to be levelling their factories."

It struck Pug that this gossip had an empty, wandering note not like Warren. "See here, it's 0814. I'm getting underway at 0900. Shall I send you to Ford Island in my gig?"

"In a minute." Warren crushed his cigarette, audibly blowing out gray smoke. "Look, I was going to give Byron this, but he's gone." Warren pulled out a white envelope from a back pocket. "It's just some financial dope. Janice is a smart cookie, as you know, but arithmetic throws her into catalepsy." Victor Henry silently accepted the envelope and dropped it in a drawer. "Dad, coming back from a strike, I'll make a pass over the *Northampton* and waggle my wings. If I don't that won't mean anything. I may be in formation or low on gas, or something. But I'll try to do it."

"I understand perfectly. That'll be fine, Warren, but I won't count on it."

Warren's glance, avoiding his father's, rested on a desk photograph of Rhoda beside very young pictures of himself, Byron, and Madeline. "I missed Mom and Madeline last night."

"There'll be family reunions yet, Warren. And you'll do the hula again for us."

"The hula! *Ha!* It'll be some other dance by that time."

As they walked up to the passageway, Victor Henry could not resist asking, "What did you think of the Tudsburys?"

"He's sort of a blowhard. I liked the daughter."

"Oh, you did? Why?"

"Well, the way she devotes herself to her father. Also, though she's quiet, she strikes me as sexy as hell."

The comment gave Victor Henry a long-forgotten kind of male satisfaction, the pleasure of a midshipman hearing his girl praised.

In the sunlight on the main deck Warren squinted, put on dark glasses, and looked fore and aft along the busy six-hundred-foot deck. "It's a magnificent ship, Dad."

"It's not an aircraft carrier."

"Attention on deck!" The OOD rapped out the order. Hurrying sailors froze. As Victor Henry and his son shook hands at the gangway, Warren looked into the father's eyes and smiled. Never before had he smiled in quite this way at his parent: a remote reassuring smile, almost like a pat on the back, as though to say, *"I'm not your little boy any more, though you don't quite believe it. I'm a dive-bomber pilot, and I'll do all right."*

Harry Hopkins's phrase leaped into Pug Henry's mind: *the changing of the guard.*

"Good hunting, Warren." The son tightened his grip, then turned and saluted the OOD. "Request permission to leave the ship."

"Permission granted, sir."

In his loose-limbed jaunty way Warren went down the ladder. "Carry on," Pug said, freeing the rigid sailors. He stood at the gangway, watching the gig pull away and head for Ford Island with his tall son standing arms akimbo in the stern sheets, steady despite the choppy waves.

The destroyers of the task force screen were steaming down channel for the sortie, signal flags flying. The long gray shape of a destroyer, passing close aboard, hid Warren from view. Pug felt self-conscious about lingering on the quarterdeck, just for another glimpse of his son. He went up to his bridge to take the *Northampton* out to sea.

25

WERNER BECK was having problems.

A letter had landed on his desk from Subsection IV B-4 of the Reich Security Main Office, requesting a report on the possibilities of deporting Italian Jews to the east. For such ticklish matters, Beck handled liaison with Mussolini's comatose bureaucracy. It was he, for instance, who was getting drafts of Italian workers shipped to German factories. Beck knew how to handle Rome officials, those smiling eels whose life specialty was paralyzing positive action with charm, paperwork, and words. An electric shock of fear from the OVRA would cause the smiling eel to cease smiling and wriggling every time, straighten into a man, and get the desired job done.

However, Beck was no miracle worker; and this Jewish project he considered hopeless. No Italians, right up to Mussolini himself, were likely to cooperate in sending off the Jews to a shrouded fate. Even fanatical Fascists smirked at the anti-Semitic laws. Most Italians liked the Jews, or at least felt sorry for them. So Beck adopted the appropriate obfuscating tactics: he wrote official queries to the right bureaus, got official evasions in reply, made official appointments for useless secret talks, and wrote official minutes of these. He sent an official negative summary to the Reich Security Main Office, with a file of all the negative responses, and trusted that that would end the matter.

Back came another letter from the SS lieutenant colonel who headed Subsection IV B-4, saying that he would himself visit Rome. For a lieutenant colonel, the man wrote in peremptory style. SS rank was nothing like a genuine Wehrmacht commission. An offspring of Hitler's strong-arm squads, now a swollen private army of Nazi faithfuls, the SS was, in Beck's view, really just a phony "elite" of government police terrorists—even if reserve status in the SS had become a token of Nazi fealty, and Beck therefore was himself a reserve Sturmbannführer. But this Lieutenant Colonel Eichmann seemed to swing some weight, for the ambassador next received a terse tough top-secret letter from Heydrich—an SS general of frightening reputation second only to Himmler—saying in effect, "Do whatever Colonel Eichmann wants." Shaken, the ambassador demanded from Beck a detailed written rundown on Lieutenant Colonel Eichmann's Subsection IV B-4. This compelled Beck to review the whole dreary and opaque tangle of security agencies, which puzzled the oldest heads in the Foreign Service.

It was all a mess of political empire-building. Division IV of Main Security was the old Gestapo, forged by Göring out of the Prussian political police into a secret service arm. Himmler and Heydrich of the SS had co-opted the Gestapo into Main Security, a bureaucratic octopus sprawling through Berlin's official buildings, combining the intelligence and police functions of both the government and the Nazi party. In no state structure had the Nazis made a worse hash of things. The RSHA was a sinister and ill-defined catchall outfit, but it was obviously just what the party wanted: a secret total police power operating outside federal law, answerable only to Hitler.

Section B of the Gestapo was devoted to "sects." The fourth "sect" was the Jews. Subsection IV B-4 of the RSHA thus was the Gestapo desk for Jewish affairs. So this Lieutenant Colonel Eichmann governed the destiny of all the Jews in German-held Europe, for they were classed as a security matter. His peremptory style became more understandable; he held sway over eight to ten million souls, a larger domain than Sweden. Beck developed a somewhat anxious curiosity about him.

Eichmann arrived in Rome by car, shortly after the assassination of Heydrich. Despite the gasoline shortage, he had driven all the way from Berlin. One of his first remarks, in a meeting in the ambassador's grandly furnished reception suite, was that he never flew in airplanes; they were too unreliable. At this meeting there was only chitchat over coffee among the three men. Despite his ominous and splashy black-and-silver SS uniform, Lieutenant Colonel Eichmann looked and acted quite pleasant; scarcely military, rather with the brisk intelligent crispness of a high-level accountant. But he lacked class. He sipped coffee with a vulgar noise. The ambassador was an erect, ruddy, elderly gentleman of great affairs and polished deportment, descended from a field marshal; yet it was the old ambassador who deferred to this businesslike bureaucrat in his thirties, rather than the other way around. Assuring Eichmann that the embassy was at his disposal, begging him to convey his cordial regrets to Reichsführer SS Himmler over the sad death of General Heydrich, the ambassador fobbed the lieutenant colonel off on Werner Beck.

In Beck's office Eichmann turned peremptory again. About the negative responses of the Rome officials he was coarsely scornful. Italians were not to be taken seriously, he said; mere strutters and posers, with no conception of the Jewish problem. Security police and the Foreign Ministry would solve this Jew business in Italy despite the government. For in the Führer's view, said Eichmann, making frequent pedantic gestures with a stiff forefinger, the Jewish problem had no boundaries. Could a European epidemic of bubonic plague, for instance, be stamped out if the germs were allowed to multiply unchecked beyond invisible lines on the ground called "boundaries?" The Führer's unshakable will was to cleanse the continent of the Jews. Hence Herr Dr. Beck, as political secretary in Rome, would have to do better than file mere negative reports.

"But Italy is not an occupied country," Beck mildly rejoined. "It's a sovereign nation, I need hardly point out, a full military ally. And these Jews are still Italian nationals."

A trace of pleased approval widened Eichmann's broad thin mouth. Herr Dr. Beck was a realist, after all! Yes, in occupied capitals it was simpler. Main Security could put men in the German embassies to take over the Jewish question. But in Rome this would prick tender Italian feelings of national honor. So the delicacy of the task made the challenge all the more bracing.

He, Eichmann, had come to give Beck the guidelines. He had been dealing with this Jew business in all its aspects since well before the war. No government outside the Reich wholly understood the Führer's farseeing policy, said Eichmann, plying his forefinger like a schoolteacher. They were all more or less confused by Christian or liberalist notions. They were ready enough to revive the anti-Jewish laws that had once been in all European law codes; to kick their Jews out of the government, the professions, and the good neighborhoods, and to tax them into beggary. On more radical measures the politicians tended to drag their heels.

Beck should bear in mind, Eichmann went on, warming to his topic, smoking cigarette after cigarette, one crucial point: *it was imperative to get Italy to hand over some Jews, however few, and on whatever basis, to Germany at once.* Once the line was crossed, the principle established, the ice broken, resistance to the German policy would gradually crumble. That was his repeated experience. For despite the toughest taxes, Jews could cleverly hang on to their property with one dodge or another; but when they were physically removed, *kaputt!* The wealth remained behind for confiscation. Once a government could be induced to hand over some Jews and sample the surprising revenue that resulted, its attitude usually changed to warm enthusiasm. This had happened in country after country. The timid politicians simply had to learn for themselves how easy it was, how little their population really objected, how willingly the Jews complied, how blandly the rest of the world looked on, and above all, how much profit there was in the Führer's wise policy.

For example, Eichmann said, he was just now working up a deal with Bulgaria. That was a bad setup, a wobbly satellite ready to jump either way. Now that the Wehrmacht's summer offensive was rolling, the Bulgarian czar was softening up. The triumphs of Rommel and the big advances in the Crimea had really got him talking business at last. The key to hauling in all the Bulgarian Jews was a handful of them now living in Germany. A swap was in the making. Bulgaria would get control of all German Jews who had fled there, and Germany would take charge of the Bulgarian Jews on Reich soil. The Bulgars were getting the better of it, profit-wise, *but they were officially acquiescing in the radical German policy; they were abandoning Bulgarian citizens who were Jews to the Germans.* That was the main point won. Italy was not too unlike Bulgaria, a bunch of treacherous politicians running a weak country. Hence Dr. Beck might try the same approach.

It was all a question, Eichmann went on, of the existing status of various Jews. Italian-born Jews now in Italy would be the toughest ones to nab. Alien Jews would be easier, but they still had sanctuary of a sort. The way to start was with *Italian Jews who were in Germany.* There were exactly one hundred eighteen of these delightful people, Eichmann said. He would send Dr. Beck dossiers showing each Italian Jew's place of origin, present place of German residence, age, health, important connections, and net worth statement. Dr. Beck should then propose the Bulgarian formula to the Fascist bigwigs. And Dr. Beck could use a fine humanitarian argument. If the German policy toward Jews was indeed so harsh—though of course he should deny that—this deal would only help the Jews, wouldn't it? A lot more would get out of German control than would pass under it, since there were many hundreds of German Jews in Italy. Eichmann added, with the sly grin of a close bargainer, that Beck needn't worry about the German Jews in Italy thus traded off; one way or another, they would be picked up in the end.

To sum up, Eichmann said, the opening wedge was what counted. Hadn't Herr Dr. Beck ever laid a virgin? That was the whole idea: gentle persuasion to start with, lots of soothing words and disarming talk, and then, at the proper moment—sock it home! After the first time, no problems! This Italian Jew situation called for a persuasive diplomat. The Labor Ministry had warmly recommended Herr Dr. Beck, and positive results were confidently expected by Reichsführer Himmler.

The clearer Eichmann's drift became, the less Werner Beck liked it. He had heard enough knowing hints about the Jewish camps in the east. Anti-Semites abounded in the Foreign Service, creatures of Ribbentrop. One of the worst was an undersecretary incongruously named Martin Luther, head of a high-security section called *Deutschland,* which was somehow involved in Jewish affairs. Beck had talked to this gross drunkard at a Berlin party. Very much in his cups, Luther had volunteered, with a gloating smile and a wink behind his hand, that the Jews were finally "getting it in the ass" in the eastern camps, just as the Führer had predicted. Among the better class of Germans, the subject was smothered in silence. Werner Beck had never asked anybody for details, and had tried to shut his mind to this whole unfortunate business. His army brother had lately dropped the entire subject.

Now this round-shouldered obscure functionary, with the long lean face, foxy nose, high balding forehead, and brisk manner, in a black uniform that heightened his paper-shuffler's pallor, was suggesting that he plunge himself up to his neck in that morass. One thing Beck never forgot, as a seasoned diplomat with a doctorate in history: all wars ended, and postwar accountings could be onerous. He was not quite at ease about his role in drafting Italian workers. The hardship pleas which he had vetoed wholesale had often upset him. War was war, and orders were orders, but this business with the Jews was entirely out of bounds.

He spoke up decisively, to nip the thing in the bud. "Let me point out one fact. In setting up the labor drafts I've had to give explicit written guarantees of destinations, wages, and working conditions of the laborers."

"Of course, but those were Italians. These are Jews."

The tone nonplussed Beck, for Eichmann might as well have said, "These are horses."

"Rome officials still regard them as Italian citizens. I'll be asked exactly where these one hundred eighteen Jews will be resettled, what they'll do there, and in what circumstances. I'll have to put an official written reply from the Foreign Ministry in the record."

"Fine!" Eichmann shrugged and smiled, quite unperturbed. "Just write whatever you please. What will all this shit ever amount to?"

Beck winced, but he tried to be patient. He was used to Nazi commonness, and perforce had to put up with it. "That's not how the Foreign Service works, you see. We've been very factual in the labor matter. We've made good on our representations. That's how we've gotten such favorable results."

The two men stared at each other. A change came over Lieutenant Colonel Eichmann's face. All the lines slightly stiffened, and into his narrow eyes there came a strange vacant look. "If you like," he said in deep sarcastic tones from his hollow chest, "I'll be glad to tell you exactly where the Jews will go, and what the disposition will be, by the Führer's direct orders. Then you can decide just what story to write for the Italians." There was no focus in the man's eyes. Behind the glitter of his glasses two dark caverns seemed to open, and in those caverns Dr. Werner Beck saw horror, a vision of mountains of dead bodies. Not a word passed between them, but the moment of silence told the political secretary what happened to deported Jews. It was disheartening to have to face this. With chills rippling on his backbone, he seized at a straw. "The ambassador would have to know."

"Oh, I can see what you mean." The long livid face relaxed. Eichmann said in a humorous familiar tone, "He's just the sort of backward old fart to make trouble for us, isn't he? Well, the Foreign Minister himself will put him in the picture. That'll squelch him, I assure you, and he'll be quiet as a mouse. He won't say 'boo' to Ribbentrop." Eichmann emitted a pleased sigh, and waved the forefinger. "I'll tell you this, you can look for a very positive effect on your career once you pull this off. Old fellow, do you happen to have a spot of brandy in the office? I drove two hundred kilometers this morning, and I've had no breakfast."

Producing a bottle and two glasses, Werner Beck did some fast thinking while he poured. He must not even seem to assent; otherwise, when he failed to deliver, disaster could befall him. The Italians would not budge on the Jews; of that he was all but sure. They might round them up in camps, treat them roughly, and so forth; but handing them over for deportation—no. As they clinked glasses and drank, he said, "Well, I'll try. But the Italians will have the last word. I can't help that. Nobody can, unless we occupy Italy."

"So? You can't help it." Brusquely, as to a barman, Eichmann held out his empty glass. Beck refilled it. The lieutenant colonel drank again, and folded his hands in his lap. "I now request from you," he said, "an explanation of the Jastrow case."

"The Jastrow case?" Beck stammered.

"You've sequestered in Siena, Herr Dr. Beck, a stateless Jew named Aaron Jastrow, aged sixty-five, a prominent author from the U.S.A., with a niece and her infant. You have visited them. You have written to them. You have telephoned them. Yes?"

In handling Jastrow Beck had of course repeatedly used his Gestapo contacts. He realized that this must be Eichmann's source. He had been open and aboveboard, and there was nothing to fear. The lieutenant colonel had simply startled him with his abrupt change of front and uncanny recall of detail. Eichmann was now sitting up straight, wrinkling his whole face in suspicion, the embodiment of a malevolent secret police officer.

As nonchalantly as he could, Beck explained what he had in mind for Aaron Jastrow.

Shaking a cigarette from a pack and slipping it in his mouth, Eichmann said, "But Dr. Beck, this is all very puzzling. You mention the poet Ezra Pound, and his shortwave broadcasts for Rome Radio. That's fine stuff, very fine. The Propaganda Ministry records and uses the broadcasts. But the poet Ezra Pound is a rarity, a very sophisticated American anti-Semite. He gives it in the ass to the Jewish bankers and to Roosevelt more than our own shortwave does. How can you compare this Jastrow person to him? Jastrow's a full-blooded Jew."

"Ezra Pound's talks are no good for American audiences. Please take my word for that. I know the United States. He must be regarded there as a traitor or a lunatic. What I plan for Jastrow—"

"We know you studied in the United States. We also know that Jastrow was your teacher."

Feeling that he was getting nowhere—that his conception was beyond the SS mentality—Beck yet had to plow on. What he hoped for, he said, was a farseeing, forgiving, Olympian broadcast, or series of broadcasts, picturing the Germans and Japanese as deprived and misunderstood proud peoples, the Allies as fat cats clutching riches gained by armed force, and the whole war as a useless bloodletting that should be settled at once by a "sharing of the hegemony." This brilliant phrase was Jastrow's own. Coming from a prominent Jewish author it would have great impact in America to weaken the war effort and encourage a peace movement. Perhaps other high-level alien intellectuals like Santayana and Berenson would follow Jastrow's example.

Eichmann looked unconvinced. Santayana's name clearly meant nothing to him. At "Berenson" his eyes sharpened. "Berenson? There's a smart millionaire Jew. Berenson has a lot of protection. Well, all right. When will this Jastrow make his first broadcast?"

"That's not definite yet." Under Eichmann's hard surprised gaze he added, "It's a question of persuading him, which takes time."

The lieutenant colonel gently smiled. "Really? Why should it? Persuading a Jew is simple."

"To be effective, this has to be done of his own free will."

"But Jews will do anything that you want them to do, of their own free will. Still, I believe I understand you now. He is your old teacher, a fine man. You have a soft spot in your heart for him. You don't want to upset or frighten him. It isn't that you're coddling or protecting a Jew—" Eichmann happily smiled, and waved the schoolteacher's forefinger— "it isn't that, but rather that you think you'll catch more flies with honey than with vinegar. Hm?"

Dr. Beck began to feel cornered. The man had a streak of the actor, and his changing moods and manners were hard to deal with. Yet he was *just an SS lieutenant colonel,* Beck told himself, whatever his role with Jews. He, Beck, must not let himself be bullied into an untenable commitment. His reply was as light and confident as he could make it. "I'm sure that my approach is correct and will get the right results."

Eichmann nodded and briefly giggled. "Yes, yes, providing you get the results before the war is over. By the way, is your family here with you in Rome?"

"No, they're at home."

"And where is home?"

"Stuttgart."

"And how many kids do you have?"

"Four."

"Boys? Girls?"

"Three boys. One girl."

"Girls are so sweet. I have three boys. No luck on girls." Eichmann sighed and produced the forefinger. "I try once a week, no matter what, to get home to the kids. Even if it's only for an hour, once a week religiously I must see the kids. Even General Heydrich respected that, and he was a goddamn hard boss." Eichmann sighed again. "I suppose you're as fond of your kids as I am." Every time Eichmann said "kids" he managed to edge the word with freezing menace.

"I love my children," said Beck, trying to control his voice, "but I don't get to see them once a week, or even once a month."

Eichmann's face took on a drawn, faraway look. "Enough, Dr. Beck. Let's talk straight. Can Reichsführer Himmler expect a progress report fairly soon on those one hundred eighteen Jews? You'll have all their documents by courier tomorrow."

"I'll do my best."

With a wide friendly grin, Eichmann said, "I'm glad that I came here and we thrashed it out. This Jastrow business is not 'kosher.'" Eichmann repeated the Jewish word with rude amusement. "Not 'kosher,' Dr. Beck. When you walk in shit, it sticks to your shoes. So tell the old Yid to make his broadcast quick. Then let the OVRA put him and his niece away with the other Yids."

"But they have a guarantee of safe conduct back to America, as part of the journalist exchange."

"How can that be? All the American journalists have already left Italy. Anyway, he's no journalist, he writes books."

"I delayed their departure myself. It's a temporary thing, we tied it to a mess in Brazil which sooner or later is bound to clear up."

The lieutenant colonel's narrow face brightened into a jolly smile. "Well, but you did manage that delay! See? When you want to be, you're a live wire. So do a job now for the Führer."

Eichmann accepted another glass of brandy. As Werner Beck walked out with him to the entrance of the embassy, they exchanged banalities about the way the war was going. The colonel's walk was rather bowlegged in the varnished black boots; and as he creaked and clicked along on the marble floor, he was very much the preoccupied civil servant again. At the door he turned and saluted. "You have a big responsibility here, Dr. Beck, so good luck. Heil Hitler."

The greeting and the outstretched arm gesture were in almost total disuse around the embassy. Both came rustily to Beck. "Heil Hitler," he said.

The black figure clumped down the steps, frightening away into the flowering shrubbery two peacocks that had the run of the embassy grounds. Beck hurried to his office and called Siena.

By mere chance, Natalie's hand was resting on the telephone when it rang. She stood by Jastrow's desk, holding the baby on her arm. Mrs. Castelnuovo, with Miriam clinging to her skirt, was admiring the Madonna and child over the mantel; and the little girl kept looking from the painted baby to the live one, as though wondering why the wrong one had the halo. Dr. Beck came on the line, gay and high-spirited. "Good morning, Mrs. Henry! I hope you're theeling well. Is Dr. Jastrow fere?" Beck had this odd speech defect of mixing up his f's and th's in moments of excitement or tension. Natalie had noticed it first when a highway patrol car had stopped the Mercedes on the drive from Naples to Rome.

"I'll call him, Dr. Beck." She went out to the terrace, where Jastrow was writing in the sunshine.

"Werner? Of course. Does he sound cheerful?"

"Oh, merry as could be."

"Well! Maybe it's news of our release." Laboriously he got out of the lounge chair, and began hobbling toward the house. "Why, bless me, both my legs are numb! I'm tottering like Methuselah."

Natalie took Miriam and Anna to her bedchamber, where the pink satin hangings and bedspread were getting threadbare with age, and the painted cherubs on the ceiling, what with the decay of the plaster, looked somewhat leprous and perspiring. She laid Louis in his crib, but he promptly pulled himself to his feet with tiny fists clenched on the rail. The women sat chatting while Miriam played with him.

Natalie was growing very fond of Anna Castelnuovo. Mere snobbish self-isolation, she realized, had deprived her of this warm bright companion in all her long Italian exile. What a waste! Neither she nor Aaron had imagined that the few shadowy Sienese Jews might be worth bothering with. No doubt because Dr. Castelnuovo had sensed this, he had not told her he was Jewish.

Aaron looked in. "Natalie, he's coming by overnight train for lunch tomorrow. He has letters for us from America. Also—so he hinted—great news he can't discuss by phone." Jastrow's wrinkled face was animated by hope. "So talk to Maria about the lunch, my dear, and tell her I'd like some tea and a little compote on the terrace now."

When Louis fell asleep in his rump-to-ceiling pose, Natalie strolled with Anna Castelnuovo and her daughter to the bus stop. They sat in the rickety wooden shed talking on and on, until the ancient bus wound smokily into sight, far up among the green vineyards along the ridge. Anna said, "Well, I hope your news will be truly good. It's so curious that a German official should be your benefactor."

"Yes, it's decidedly curious." They exchanged looks of wry skepticism.

The bus went off, and she walked back to the villa feeling very much alone.

When Dr. Beck arrived next day, he at once gave two letters to Natalie, and one to Dr. Jastrow. They were waiting for him on the terrace. "Don't be polite, please. Go ahead and read your mail." Smiling benignly, he sat on a bench in the sun while they ripped at the envelopes.

"*The Arch of Constantine!* It arrived safely!" Jastrow burst out. "Werner, you must tell Father Spanelli and Ambassador Titman. Natalie, just listen to this, from Ned Duncan. '*We can never thank the Vatican enough. . . . The Arch of Constantine is your best book yet . . . a permanent contribution to popular understanding of both Judaism and Christianity—*' I declare, what a satisfying description! '. . . *Of classic stature . . . certain book club selection . . . brilliant panorama of decadent Rome . . . honored to publish such a fresh and seminal work . . .*' Well, well, well! Isn't that capital news, Natalie?"

"That is good news," said Dr. Beck, "but not all the good news."

Natalie looked up alertly from Slote's discouraging letter. The German and Italian red tape over the Brazil affair seemed endless, he wrote; it would all work out, but he could no longer guess when. She passed this letter to Beck, who after a glance handed it back with a shrug and a smile. He looked very pale and his eyes were bloodshot, but his manner was jocose. "Yes, yes, but all that is quite out of date. May we have lunch? Otherwise we've so much to discuss, we may forget to eat."

Natalie was skimming a piece of microfilmed V-mail from Byron, poorly printed and scarcely readable, which had fallen out of the three-page scrawl from her mother. Nothing really new in either letter; Byron was writing from Australia in a lonesome mood, and her mother was complaining about the coldest Miami Beach spring in years, and fretting about Natalie's detention. She jumped up. "Lunch is only a soufflé and a salad, Dr. Beck."

"Ah, I didn't expect your veal coup to be repeated."

"But at any rate," Jastrow said, "we'll share the last of Berenson's coffee."

After lunch Beck asked Natalie's permission to light a heavy black cigar. With his first puff he leaned back, sighed, and gestured toward the open window. "Well, Dr. Jastrow, won't you be sorry to leave this view behind?"

"*Are* we leaving it?"

"That's why I've come."

He talked for a long while. His pace and tone were leisurely, with frequent long cigar puffs, yet he began mixing up his f's and th's. The official Italian radio, he disclosed, wanted to put Dr. Jastrow on the air! The shortwave section was planning talks by famous enemy aliens, to project abroad an image of intellectual tolerance in Fascist Italy. Speakers would have *carte blanche*. The plan called for big names: Bernard Berenson, George Santayana, and of course Aaron Jastrow. The OVRA had just come through with a written commitment to Beck that Jastrow, his niece, and the baby would leave for Switzerland directly after the broadcast. So this development was proving a quick solution of the departure snarl. If Jastrow would simply come to Rome with Mrs. Henry and her infant, and record a leisurely two-hour interview—or four half-hour broadcasts, whichever he preferred—the Brazil business would be set aside. Beck would arrange in advance three exit visas, and tickets on the Rome-Zurich plane. They would not even have to return to Siena! And the sooner this happened, the better. Rome Radio was very hot on the idea.

Having said all this, Beck sat back, relaxed and smiling. "Well, Prothessor? How does it strike you?"

"Dear me, I confess I'm bewildered. Would they want me to discuss something in my field of work, like Constantine?"

"Oh, no, no. Absolutely out of the question! They want a philosophical view of the war, simply showing that all the right is not on one side. Remember what you said in this very room, Dr. Jastrow, on the occasion of our famous veal dinner? That would precisely fill the bill."

"Oh, but Werner, I'd had far too much wine that night. I couldn't rail against my own country like that on enemy shortwave. You can see that."

Pursing his lips around the cigar, Beck cocked his head. "Professor, you're creating difficulties, aren't you? You're a genius in the use of words, and in the subtle elaboration of ideas. You have a great original vision of this world catastrophe, a remarkable God's-eye view of the whole tragic panorama. That theme of 'sharing the hegemony' is perfect. Once you put your mind to it, the words would come easily. I'm sure you'd not only please Rome Radio, but impress your own countrymen as well. And to state matters bluntly, you'd get out of Italy at once."

Jastrow turned to his niece. "Well?"

"Well, you and Ezra Pound," said Natalie.

An unpleasant expression flashed across Beck's jowly face. "Comparisons are odious, Mrs. Henry."

"What about Berenson and Santayana?" Jastrow asked. "Have they agreed to this?"

Beck took a long puff at the cigar. "The Italian radio people consider you the key personality. Santayana is very old, and as you know he lives up in the clouds, with his theory of essences and all that philosophical mumbo-jumbo. He'll just mystify people. Still, a great name. Berenson, well, Berenson's whimsical and very independent. Rome Radio feels they'll get Berenson once you agree. He thinks very highly of you."

"Then neither of them knows about this yet," Natalie said.

Reluctantly Beck shook his head.

"No, no, no!" Jastrow suddenly rapped out. "I can't possibly become bracketed with Ezra Pound. His critical writings are undeniably brilliant. He has an original mind, though his verse is willfully obscure. The few times we've met I've found him an untidy, overbearing egotist, but that's neither here nor there. The thing is, I've heard his broadcasts, Werner. His attacks on the Jews are worse than anything even on your Berlin broadcasts, and his wild ravings about Roosevelt and the gold standard are simple treason. After the war he'll be hanged or shut up in an insane asylum. I can't imagine what's gotten into him, but I'd rather rot here in Siena than become another Ezra Pound."

With a curl of his lips, and a total confusion of f's and th's, Beck retorted, "But there's also the question of Mrs. Henry and her baby 'rotting here.' And there's the more serious question of how long you can stay on in Siena." He pulled out a gold pocket watch. "I've made a long trip to put this before you. I didn't expect a rejection out of hand. I thought I had earned your confidence."

Natalie interjected, "What's the question about our staying in Siena?"

Deliberately crushing out the cigar, grinding it on the ashtray, Beck replied, "Why, the OVRA pressure never lets up on me, Mrs. Henry. You realize that you belong in a concentration camp with the rest of the alien Jews. I was reminded of this very pointedly, when the broadcasting idea came up, and—"

"But I can't fathom this!" Jastrow expostulated, his flecked little hands shaking on the table before him. "We're *guaranteed* eventual passage to Switzerland! Aren't we? Even Leslie Slote's new letter affirms that. How can Rome Radio blackmail me into wrecking my reputation?

Just be firm, Werner. Tell them to put it out of their minds. I won't consider it."

Beck rolled his bloodshot eyes at Natalie. "That, I must tell you, is a grave statement, Professor."

"Nevertheless, that's my answer," cried Jastrow, his excitement mounting, "and it's final."

An auto horn sounded outside.

"Dr. Beck, are you expecting a taxi?" Natalie folded her napkin on the table. Her tone was low and calm. Her face seemed all bones and eyes.

"Yes."

"Let me walk out with you. No, Aaron, don't you come."

"Werner, if I seem obstinate, I'm sorry." Jastrow stood up and held out an unsteady hand to Dr. Beck. "Martin Luther once put it well. *'Ich kann nicht anders.'*"

Beck stiffly bowed, and went out after Natalie. On the terrace, she said, "He'll do it."

"He'll do what? The broadcasting?"

"Yes. He'll do it."

"Mrs. Henry, his resistance was very strong." Beck's eyes were hard, questing, anxious.

From behind the gate came the cracked wheeze of the horn again.

"I know him well. These explosive reactions pass. I set him off by mentioning Pound. I'm terribly sorry. When does Rome Radio want him?"

"That's not definite," Beck said eagerly, "but what I must imperatively have from him at once is a letter consenting to make the broadcasts. That will get the hounds off my back, and start the wheels turning —the wheels of your release, Mrs. Henry."

"You'll have the letter by the end of the week."

They were at the open gate, where a large old touring car was waiting. Beck said in harsh harried tones, "I'd raffer bring fee letter back to Rome now. Fat would take a vast load oth my mind. I'd even postpone my return."

"I can't press him when he's in this mood. I promise you the letter will come."

He stared at her, and with a decisive flourish held out his hand. "I must count on your good sense, then."

"You can count on my concern for my baby."

"The greatest pleasure for me," said Beck, pausing with his hand on the taxicab door, "will be to see you all off to Zurich. I'll be waiting anxiously for that letter."

She hurried back into the villa. Jastrow still sat at the dining table, wineglass in hand, staring out at the cathedral. With a hangdog look at her, he said in a voice that still trembled, "I just couldn't help it, Natalie. The proposal is outrageous. Werner can't think like an American."

"Indeed he can't. But you shouldn't have turned him down flat, Aaron. You'll have to equivocate and stall."

"Possibly. But I'll never make the broadcasts he's asking for. Never! He took my perverse half-serious tirade over the veal far too literally. There's a German for you! You had provoked me, I'd drunk a lot, and anyway I relish arguing on the wrong side. You know that. Of course I loathe the Axis dictatorships. I exiled myself to save money and live quietly. Clearly it was the mistake of my life. No matter how badly the State Department has mistreated me, I love the United States. I will not go on the air for the Axis, to disgrace my scholarship and mark myself a traitor." The old man lifted his bearded chin, and a stony look settled on his face. "They can kill me, but I won't do it."

Alarmed, and thrilled too, Natalie said, "Then we're in danger."

"That may be, and you had better consult Dr. Castelnuovo about his escape plans, after all."

"What!"

"Making a dash for it seems farfetched, but it may come to that, my dear." Pouring a glass of wine, Jastrow spoke with cheery vigor. "Rabinovitz is a very able man. This young doctor seems a resolute sort. It's best to be prepared. Chances are our release will come through meantime, but I can't say I like Werner Beck's new tune."

"Christ almighty, Aaron, this is a change."

Jastrow rested his head wearily on a hand. "I didn't bargain for adventuring in my old age, but the one important thing is to get you and Louis out safely, isn't it? I shall have this wine and take my nap. Please draft up a letter to Werner, dear, agreeing in principle, and apologizing for my outburst. Say I'm commencing now to lay out four broadcasts. Be terribly vague about a completion date, for I shall be weaving Penelope's cloth, you know. Then you had better go and talk to that young doctor. The OVRA may well be watching him, so it's best you make it look like an office visit. Take the baby."

Dumbly Natalie nodded. She went to the library to draft the letter, feeling—half with terror, half with relief—that the lead had in an eyeblink passed from her to her uncle, and that she and her baby were now in the dark rapids.

26

JUNE flowers are springing up all over Auschwitz. Even in the muddy heavily trodden camp sectors, in nooks between the blockhouses missed by the wooden clogs of the prisoners, the flowers peep out.

The Auschwitz Interest Area of the SS spreads over some forty square kilometers of greenery and woodland, at the confluence of the Sola and the Vistula, where the Vistula begins its long meander north to Warsaw and the Baltic Sea. Everywhere inside the high barbed-wire fences of this huge enclave, spaced with signs in German and Polish warning of instant death to trespassers, wildflowers make bright splashes, except where construction crews are churning the marshy grassland into brown muck and putting up blockhouses. Berel Jastrow is working in one of these crews.

The peasants who dwelled in the villages within the enclave are gone. A few of their evacuated thatched houses still stand. Most have been razed and their rubble used in camp blockhouses. Near the mucky holes where the houses once stood, fruit orchards in bloom perfume the warm June winds. The sweet odors die in the rows of prison blocks with their terrible latrine huts. But out in the fields where Berel is working, the orchards still sweetly scent the air. In the past six months Berel has been gaining back some of his old gnarled strength. As an assistant foreman to Sammy Mutterperl, with the armband of a *Vorarbeiter,* a leading worker, he eats and sleeps better than most Auschwitz inmates, though wretchedly enough.

Mutterperl wears the armband of an *Unterkapo.* But he is something more. The *Arbeitskommando,* work gang, of SS Sergeant Major Ernst Klinger, is actually a construction crew managed by Mutterperl; six hundred inmates of two blockhouses in Camp B-I. The job here is the rush construction of Camp B-II-d Birkenau, one of six subcamps of thirty-two blockhouses each. Completed, the whole sector will have one hundred fifty blockhouses in all, planned by the Central Building Board for erection north of the main roadway. With a twin sector, B-III, not yet begun, and B-I, already standing, Birkenau is projected by the Central Building Board as the largest detention center on earth. More than a hundred thousand working prisoners will be housed in Birkenau as slave labor for SS factories.

Sammy Mutterperl is doing in the Oswiecim prison camp what he did when he was a free man in Oswiecim town. He was a contractor there; in a peculiar way he is a contractor here. His client now is the Commandant of Auschwitz, and Sergeant Major Klinger is the Commandant's deputy on the spot. In theory Reichsführer SS Himmler is the high ultimate Client, but Himmler is an unseen god in Auschwitz. Even the SS men speak his name seldom, and with awe. The Commandant's chauffeured black Mercedes, however, is a familiar intimidating sight in the area, fluttering the double lightning-flash insignia flags of the SS. Berel glimpses it often. The Commandant believes in personal supervision from the top—"the eye of the master" is his word.

The Klinger gang has been turning out good work for many months, laboring in all weather, in haste, silence, and submissiveness. The crew routinely endures curses and beatings from SS men and the kapos. Prisoners who weaken, faint, and fall get beaten bloody by the kapos for malingering. If they really look done for, the kapos finish them off with shovels or sticks, and other workers drag back their bodies for evening roll call. Fresh prisoners, of which the supply is endless, replace them on the next shift.

As Auschwitz goes, Mutterperl considers Klinger's a good kommando to serve in. He has been in Auschwitz for a year and a half. In 1941 the Commandant, desperate at the crazy expansion orders from Berlin, combed the countryside for builders and mechanics and put them to work at once—Jew, Pole, Czech, Croat, Rumanian, it made little difference, Mutterperl among them—in conditions of housing, nourishment, and discipline that were by outside standards unspeakable, but in Auschwitz something like luxury.

Sammy has come to know Auschwitz well. In on the ground floor, so to speak, he is surviving handily. Because of the rush to start construction he was spared quarantine camp, those fearsome isolation weeks of maltreatment and hunger which reduce many prisoners to bony automata, blank to any thought but self-preservation. Klinger as SS overseer and Mutterperl as Jew foreman have worked together since they did the SS barracks job a year ago. Both are wily burly fellows in their late fifties, anxious to produce results: Klinger to please his superiors, Mutterperl to stay alive. For his own benefit, Klinger has gradually pushed the Jew into an informal protected status as a construction foreman. As such, Sammy can recruit prisoners for the kommando. That is how he has rescued Berel. Pulling in a Russian prisoner is nonregulation procedure, but Auschwitz regulations have no consistency or coherence. SS noncoms and officers constantly trade off favors and loot, and bend the rules to suit themselves. Nobody is a better hand at such maneuvering than Hauptscharführer Ernst Klinger.

Klinger is an old file of the camps, a stout blond Bavarian going gray. Like the Commandant, he is a veteran of Dachau and Sachsenhausen; in fact, the Commandant requisitioned him for Oswiecim. Once a policeman in Munich, turned Nazi when he lost his job in the depression, Klinger found in the SS a haven. Since toughness was a requirement, this once easygoing family man became tough. In the line of duty Klinger has flogged the skin off prisoners' backs, wiping the blood-dripping whip with a casual grin as the victim sagged raw and unconscious. He has lined up with execution squads and shot condemned men. His normal tone of communication with prisoners is a menacing bellow. With a blow of a club he can collapse a man like a scarecrow of sticks. Nevertheless, Sammy Mutterperl considers him "all right." Klinger does not, like so many SS men and kapos, get his kicks from inflicting fear, pain, and death on terrified living skeletons. Moreover, he is very corrupt, which is a big help. You can do business with Klinger.

Klinger considers the Jew "all right," too, for a Jew. When getting drunk with his SS buddies, he can even boast about "my smart clipcock Sammy." For in the Central Building Board office back at the base camp, where several hundred German architects, engineers, and draftsmen work in comfort on Auschwitz's never-ending expansion plans, the word is "Give it to Klinger," when a job requires quick, visible results. Klinger's efficiency ratings have shot up since he left Sachsenhausen. Promotion to Untersturmführer, second lieutenant, is in the wind; a big leap at his age, from the noncom ranks to a commission, with big dividends in prestige and pay. How pleased his wife and kids will be, if it really comes off! He knows that he owes all this to his Sammy. So strictly in self-interest, he watches out for the Jew.

Klinger now has a big rush job going: to throw up all thirty-two blockhouse frames of Birkenau Camp B-II-d in a hurry. Never mind the walls and roofs, is the word from the board—just frames, frames, frames, as far as the eye can see. A big shot is coming to inspect. Klinger's gang is at the outer edge of new Birkenau construction. Farther west a horde of shaven-headed prisoners in striped ticking, knee-deep in marshy grass, are clearing rocks, pulling stumps, and levelling the ground with spades and hoes for still more camps, but those are only on the drawing-board. B-II-d is under construction, and the more actual structures in sight, the better for the Commandant.

Every day in Auschwitz can bring surprises; and on this day at the Klinger work site comes a frightening surprise. Seven covered gray trucks pull up on the road. Klinger orders Berel's subsection of seventy men—SS guards, kapos, and all—into the trucks, to load up studs and rafters at the timber yard. This is a very strange business. Human time and muscle are in infinite supply at Auschwitz, zero cost items. Prisoners carry lumber to building sites, if necessary several miles. The Germans do not waste gasoline and tires on such errands. So what is going on? Fear distorts their faces as the prisoners enter the trucks; some drag their feet, and the cursing kapos club them aboard.

But the trucks do go to the timber yard. Under the yells and the blows of the kapos, the prisoners rush about to load up, then jam aboard again pell-mell, and rumble back to B-II-d. Berel guesses that the deadline is drawing close, and for once, fast action matters. Ordinarily, Auschwitz is a slow machine-free world, paced by the human body. Over-slaves beat under-slaves, government taskmasters beat them both, and it is all—so he has thought often—a throwback to Pharaoh's Egypt, as the Torah pictures it. Only in this Egypt, twentieth-century trucks grind by sometimes, and the taskmasters have twentieth-century machine guns; and death is not for Jewish male babies only.

When the trucks arrive, another surprise. The Commandant himself stands there with a couple of green-uniformed aides, frowning in the sunlight at the strange sight of slaves riding. His Mercedes is parked by the roadside. Klinger is shuffling and scraping before him. The kapos and the guards pile on abuse and blows in the unloading. The prisoners run frantically with lumber several hundred yards to the northernmost framing sites, then scamper back for more. An old frog-faced kapo who has long had it in for Berel, a former Viennese bank robber who wears the high-status green triangle patch of a professional criminal, suddenly and blindingly clubs Berel's skull. *"Who do you think you are, you lazy old pile of shit, just because you've got a shitty armband? Grab a plank and shake your ass!"* Berel staggers, almost goes down, but seizes a brace and runs with it, dizzily thinking that the kapo has picked his time well. With the Commandant looking on, there is no protection in Auschwitz. But the Commandant never stays long.

The Commandant for his part is in bad shape, though his square-hewn calm face shows no sign of it. Not since his own solitary confinement for a political murder in Brandenburg prison, under the Weimar regime, has he suffered such wrenching griping stomach pains. The agony is impervious to whiskey, sedatives, or any medicines he has tried. He simply must endure and go on.

He is busily muttering to an aide. After a while the aide takes Klinger aside. Fresh orders: work straight through the night, under floodlights! The Commandant is waiving the air defense rules. Halt work on framing. Switch to covering walls and putting on roofs. Put up wallboards only on the side facing the road, and only on every other blockhouse.

The Commandant gets in his Mercedes. Back to the Residence for lunch, he tells the chauffeur. Lunch! He will be lucky to hold anything on his stomach. All morning he has been driving over the route they will traverse tomorrow. He has been seeing every site for himself, anticipating questions, throwing questions at the SS overseers to get them on their toes. The dam site is the worst problem. Berlin hasn't come up with the labor, materials, and supervision. I. G. Farben has been swallowing up everything for its Buna Werke at the Monowice subcamp. One can't flog starving unskilled Poles and Jews into building a dam. Flog them to death, yes, but the Vistula will still flow merrily on its way! If Reichsführer SS Himmler really wants to dam the Vistula, then let him see how far behind the project really is, and come up with the wherewithal. Dr. Kammler, chief architect of Auschwitz, is an SS major general, not a lowly major like the Commandant. Berlin can issue these impossible orders, but Kammler's deputies in Auschwitz have to implement them. Himmler will listen to Kammler. The Commandant feels fairly safe about the dam.

His one worry about the whole inspection visit is the damned Jewish transport. Himmler wants to see an action from the beginning to the end. The Commandant has tried to anticipate all the things that can go wrong, and that have gone wrong in the early months: the troublemakers who scream and cause panics, the sanitary squad idiots who fail to drop in enough stuff, so the people don't die, and the like. By now the process has been smoothed out and usually goes off all right. But if things get gummed up, nobody will be blamed but himself!

Then there is the disposal problem. This mass-grave burial technique is not going to work much longer; not in Auschwitz. This is no small cleanup of Jews like Chelmno or Sobibor. Those pen-pushers in Berlin don't picture what a disposal problem thousands and thousands of bodies can be. They don't care. All they want is impressive figures to show the boss. But these tons—many, many tons—of organic material, piling up week by week in Auschwitz soil, are a hell of a headache and a health hazard. And it's only the beginning! Let the Reichsführer see for himself.

And those Berlin pantywaists are plenty jittery about the big boss's visit. They've been giving him glowing reports, sidetracking the Commandant's desperate pleas for personnel and material and his complaints about impossible schedules. Now they have to pray that the Commandant will protect their asses. They wouldn't dream of soiling their own shiny boots with Auschwitz mud; not them, those desk-bound *Standartenführer* and *Obersturmbannführer,* leading the soft life back home! And he is just a major, running an establishment bigger than any army camp, bigger probably than any military installation in the world, and still growing! Berlin keeps telling him to go easy on the complaints, emphasize the positive things. The hell with them.

The Commandant is writhing in pain as the Mercedes drives up before the prettily flowering front garden of the Residence, where his wife is working in a sunbonnet. He knows very well what is causing these cramps. His career hangs on the next seventy-two hours. He can be relieved in disgrace and expelled from the SS; he can be promoted on the spot to Obersturmbannführer—lieutenant colonel—a recognition scandalously overdue; those are the extremes, and in between are a lot of possibilities. A visit from Reichsführer SS Himmler doesn't happen every day.

His wife wants to show him how the roses are coming along, but he brusquely passes her by. His adjutant is standing in the bay window. She sees them talking inside. Her husband glances eagerly at a document the adjutant hands him. He looks happy, then suddenly he begins to glare. He lets out such a roar, throwing the document in the adjutant's face and waving both fists, that she hears him through the closed windows. He makes that old infuriated gesture: *Upstairs!* That means top-secret talk, in the den off the bedroom. She hurries inside to warn the cook not to dry out the roast.

The Commandant has in fact been pleased by his first glimpse of the fine paper and the good printing job. The schedule started off well:

REICHSFÜHRER VISIT
KONZENTRATIONSLAGER AUSCHWITZ

First Day

0800–0830.   *Aerodrome.* Arrival and reception. Motorcade to Base Camp.

0830–0845.	*Parade Ground.* Trooping of colors. Band serenade. Honor review of troops.
0845–0930.	*Officers' Mess.* Breakfast, with map demonstration of camp layout.
0930–1000.	*Architect's Office, Central Planning Board.* Reichsführer SS views models: Vistula dam, new drainage canal system, animal husbandry center, Birkenau Camp.
1000–1100.	*Motor Tour.* Monowice, Raisko, Budy. General view: I. G. Farben construction, dam site, agricultural areas, reclaimed lands, botanical laboratories, tree nurseries, stock breeding sector.
1100–1330.	SPECIAL.
1330–1500.	Lunch.

It was on seeing these last two items that the Commandant has thrown the schedule in his adjutant's face and ordered him upstairs.

Screaming so that the whole household hears him through closed doors, and his children quake in their rooms, and his wife and cook in the kitchen exchange scared looks, the Commandant demands an explanation. The trembling adjutant stammers that the railway directorate at Oppeln has scheduled the transport arrival before lunch, with instructions to expedite the return of the emptied train. If the Commandant will telephone Oppeln to see if the cars can be retained in the Auschwitz yards for a few more hours, then perhaps the Jews can just wait in the cars and get off after lunch.

The explosion that follows is the worst the Commandant's wife has ever heard. The Himmler visit, she thinks, is making nervous wrecks of everybody. How glad she will be when it is over! He has gotten dead drunk every night for a week, taken strong sedatives, and yet he has not slept. This job is too much. As for the children and herself, the sooner they get out, the better. The flood of new toys and picture books day by day for the young ones, the fine clothes for the big boy, the excellent servants, expert gardeners, the stacks of lovely expensive underwear and negligees for herself are all very well, but a decent home life would be better than any of that.

Upstairs the Commandant is roaring that the whole schedule will be printed again at once. The SPECIAL item will come *after* lunch as ordered. He, the Commandant, personally orders this. The train will re-

main in the freight yard as long as necessary! If the Oppeln railway directors have doubts, they can take a few months in the Auschwitz
quarantine camp to think it over. This is REICHSFÜHRER SS BUSINESS!
Understood? Nothing, *nothing* can interfere. What idiotic asshole could
think of showing a special operation to the Reichsführer *before* lunch?
What kind of appetite will he have to eat after that?

This is the gist of a ten-minute chewing-out that has the adjutant,
himself a hardened SS captain with a Sachsenhausen background,
whey-faced and shaking as a Jew before a quarantine camp flogging.
Never has the Commandant thrown a fit like this. He himself is trembling all over when he dismisses the adjutant, who hurries out and
barely makes it to the garden before throwing up everything in his
stomach, with blood streaks in the vomited mess.

The Commandant gulps half a tumbler of brandy. It calms him.
When he goes down to lunch the gnawing at his gut is gone. He eats
well, and is pleasanter to his wife and children than he has been in a
month. The rest of the schedule, after all, looks good. But God in
heaven, if he had not insisted on seeing that printed schedule! His old
rule never fails—*"the eye of the master!"*

The train has been waiting out of sight around the bend. Now its
mournful whistle blows at five minutes to three.

The Reichsführer SS and his high-brass aides stand with the Commandant on the long wooden platform, waiting. Happily, it is another
beautiful day. The leafy trees around the siding give pleasant shade
from the hot afternoon sun. They have all lunched heartily at the senior
officers' mess, and so far the whole inspection tour has been going
smoothly. Himmler has been very gracious about the stalled dam. He
has obviously been impressed by the camp's explosive growth. He has
shown real delight in the agricultural installations, always his pet
Auschwitz undertaking, farmer that he is. The impressive unfinished
I. G. Farben structure at Monowice has won his approval, too. The Commandant is on pins and needles. If this business goes off without a
hitch, positive results from the visit may well impend.

The smoke of the locomotive shows over the trees. The train pulls
into sight. It is a small transport, deliberately planned that way by the
Commandant; ten freight cars, about eight hundred people. The Kattowitz police have held them rounded up for several days. The bunker
can take just about eight hundred, tightly packed. Himmler's personal
letter to the Commandant was specific: *"a whole action, from the be-*

ginning to the end." Two shifts would have dragged the thing out and depressed the Reichsführer SS. It will be bad enough as it is!

The Commandant has watched the process many times—*"the eye of the master"*—but he has never gotten quite used to it. He is tough. He knows that the Reichsführer is tough. He knows about Himmler's visit to a Special Action Unit in Russia during the dispatch of a lot of Jews. Crude stuff, that, from what he has heard: making them dig their own mass grave, then mowing them down and burying them, clothes and all. The Auschwitz process is far more humane, practical, *German*. Still, in its own way it is sad. The Commandant knows how hard it is on his own officers. He is intensely curious to see how Heinrich Himmler will take it. After all, it is a damn sticky proceeding. What if Germany loses the war? The Commandant never voices such doubts, naturally. He squelches the faintest hint from his subordinates. Still, these thoughts do trouble him every now and then.

The train stops. The Jews begin to descend. SS guards along the edge of the siding stand back, avoiding any bullying or menacing appearance. These are Jews from a big town, and they look prosperous. They blink in the sunlight as they clumsily tumble out of the cattle cars, helping down the old people, the cripples, and the youngsters. They peer around anxiously, the women holding their children close. But they show no great alarm, and listen intently to Untersturmführer Hössler's smooth announcement about where they will be housed, what skills are most in demand, and so on and so forth. It is convincing stuff at that. Hössler and his sidekick Aumaier keep polishing and improving the spiel.

Next, the Jews line up for the selection without difficulty. Soon the few men picked for the labor camp march off on foot through the thick trees toward Birkenau. The rest climb quietly into the waiting trucks. The abandoned platform is piled high with their baggage; handsome goods, a lot of real leather there. It will be quite a haul when the cleanup squad sorts it out. The Jews really seem to believe everything Hössler has said, down to the detail that the luggage will all be delivered to their living quarters. Living quarters! There is something very human in their credulity. Nobody wants to believe he is about to die, especially on such a pretty June day, with the sun shining and birds chirping in the trees. Some of the Jews cast apprehensive looks at the clump of SS officers watching the process; but it does not seem to the Commandant that any of them recognize the great Reichsführer SS Himmler. Maybe they are too preoccupied.

The loaded trucks wait while the SS party drives ahead to the bunker site for a quick look around. The Commandant is proud of its innocuous appearance. DISINFECTION, reads the large wooden sign by the roadside. One sees only a large thatched peasant cottage like thousands in Polish villages, set in an apple orchard. On the cottage door, a neat arrow sign says, *This Way to Disinfection.* The undressing huts, new structures of raw wood a few meters away, are not in the least scary. The inspection party enters the hut labelled *Women and Children.* Benches line the walls under numbered hooks where the Jews will hang and fold their clothes. A sign on the wall reads in several languages:

> *Remember your hook number, to recover your*
> *belongings after the disinfection!*
> *Fold clothes neatly!*
> *Be tidy!*
> *No unnecessary talking!*

The hot sun makes for a strong smell of fresh lumber in the hut, which mingles with the sweet scent of the apple blossoms drifting through the open door. Himmler offers no comments. His short, characteristically sharp and jerky nod shows he has seen enough: on to the next thing!

The SS officers cross the orchard and enter the cottage. Here the very heavy wooden doors on the four big empty whitewashed rooms, and the back door with a large sign reading *This Way to Bathroom,* look somewhat odd. An SS man in a white coat stands in the corridor beside a table piled with towels and bars of soap. The odor here is of some powerful disinfectant. The room doors are hooked open. The Commandant unhooks one, and shows Himmler the heavy bars that will screw the doors airtight. Wordlessly, he indicates the wall apertures where the gas crystals will tumble in. The Reichsführer SS nods. He makes an inquiring gesture at the sign about the bathroom. "Leads outside," says the Commandant. "Disposal."

Short jerky nod.

The trucks rumble up. The inspection party leaves the bunker and gathers under some apple trees, at a discreet distance, to watch the operation.

In the leading truck, as usual, are about a dozen of the Sonderkommandos, the squad of Jewish prisoners required to take part in the process. This small subsquad consists of Sonderkommandos who know several languages. They jump from their truck and run to assist their fellow Jews out of the other trucks. They are dressed respectably in civilian clothing: in this warm weather, good shirts, trousers, and leather shoes. No striped suits for these Sonderkommandos, and no wooden clogs, of course, only the obligatory striped camp cap. They help down the women and kids, talking in Yiddish or Polish about the disinfection procedure, the camp accommodations, the working conditions. By now the transport Jews have only a few minutes to live, so no chances are taken. The SS guards line up in a double cordon from the trucks to the undressing hut, with dogs, guns, and clubs. The Jews have no choice but to march straight on to the hut, accompanied by the Sonderkommandos, who are describing the food, the mail service, and the visiting privileges. These fellows will go all the way into the bunker with them, maintaining the humane hoax to the very last second, as the Commandant explains to the silent Himmler. They will dart outside only when the SS guards actually march in to bolt the gas-tight doors.

In his explanation the Commandant does not give credit to Aumaier and Hössler, the two SS officers who have worked up this really clever arrangement of the Sonderkommandos. After all, not they, but he himself will get the blame if something goes wrong! But these officers did create the whole concept. They train the Sonderkommandos in groups. Periodically they gas them and train more. Sonderkommandos are recruited from the new arrivals in the quarantine camp; the weak, the easily terrified, the ratty ones who tend to collapse under the shock of Auschwitz conditions, are the ones to look for. Hössler and Aumaier select them, isolate them in a special blockhouse, and confront them with this assignment in no uncertain terms. They can do as they are told and live, or they can be shot at once. That is their choice. There are always enough Sonderkommandos, though many prefer the *Kugel,* the bullet in the neck, terrorized though they are. They get their request. But even afterward there are those who break down on the job; try to warn the new arrivals, or even to undress and commit suicide with them. The SS keeps a sharp eye out for these, and usually catches them. They get a punishment designed to discourage the others; they are burned alive. Sound practice.

As the Commandant watches these wretches urging women and children along to their doom, he wonders at them, as always. How can they be so absolutely dead to all natural feelings, particularly toward their co-religionists? Jews are a riddle, that's all. He steals a look at Heinrich Himmler, and gets a nasty shock. Himmler is looking glassily and fixedly at him. The Commandant realizes with a cold shudder that this may be the decisive moment of the whole inspection, the only real point of it. The Reichsführer has come to see with his own eyes—*"the eye of the master"*—whether the Commandant of Auschwitz has what it takes. If he flinches now, shows the slightest nervousness or compunction, it is his career, possibly his neck. How long can he be allowed to live, knowing what he knows, if he can't cut the mustard? He has seen SS men—high-placed ones, too—get a *Kugel.*

The Jews are hurrying now in a drove toward the undressing hut. He sees a sight that unexpectedly tries his taut nerves. A dog lunges and barks at a child, no more than four or five years old, a little girl in a short blue dress who looks a lot like his own youngest daughter: fair hair, blue eyes, round German face, nothing "Jewish" about her. The pretty little thing shrinks against her mother and screams. The mother catches her up in her arms and to distract her, she breaks off a small branch of apple blossoms and holds it to the little girl's nose. So they disappear into the hut among the crowding Jews. The Commandant has seen dozens of pathetic incidents here; but something about the look of that little girl, the mother's impulsive seizing of the flowering branch—the mother, too, didn't look Jewish. The propaganda caricatures are stuff and nonsense; these mortal enemies of the Reich look like any other Europeans, most of them. He has found that out long ago. The Commandant feels a pain in his gut; the cramps are starting up again. He puts on his stoniest face.

Now at least it will go fast.

The SS double cordon lines up again in a tight path from the hut to the cottage. The naked men come out first, as always a sorry crowd—tubby ones, scrawny ones, cripples, gray or bald ones—their sorry circumcised cocks shrunken up with fright, no doubt. He seldom sees a Jew with a really big cock here. Maybe the able-bodied ones are more virile. The fully dressed Sonderkommandos among them are still talking, trying to cheer them up. But now these Jews are too close to death not to show it on their faces. The Sonderkommandos, too, have sick expressions. The Commandant is tough, but he never likes to look at the faces of the Jews walking to the bunker, especially the men.

Somehow the women have more courage. Or maybe the shock to their modesty distracts them; that, and concern for their kids. They do not look so ghastly as they come out next and troop naked through the two rows of young German uniformed men. These SS men are under strict orders to keep silent and serious, but nevertheless they can't help smirking at some of the lovely ones. There are always pretty ones among them, and after all, there is nothing in the world more charming than a naked woman; and when she is carrying or leading a nude child, in a strange way it adds to her beauty.

This, for the Commandant, has always been the supreme moment of the process, in its beauty, sadness, and terror—the walk of the naked women with their children to the bunker. He wants to look at Himmler, but he is afraid to. He keeps his face rigid, yet he almost loses his composure when, among the last of the women coming out of the cottage, he sees the mother who broke the branch. She has a sweet figure, poor creature. Like so many of the others, she has uncovered her tits so as to hold the child in one arm and protect her cunt with the other. Invariably they will let the tits go, if they carry a baby, to cover their bushes; it is a strange fact of feminine nature. But what shakes the Commandant is the sight of the naked little girl. She is still holding the branch of apple blossoms.

The last woman's pink backside disappears into the cottage. The SS men dash in, and out come the Sonderkommandos, with the white-coated man who stood by the soap and towels. The inspection party can hear the loud slamming of the doors, and the screeching of the bolts that fasten them tight. The Red Cross ambulance, which has driven up during the undressing time, now disgorges the SS men from the sanitary squad in their gas masks, carrying the cans of cyanide crystals. After the naked women, not a very handsome sight! But it's nasty stuff they handle. The precautionary rules are strict. They do their job in a few moments, opening the cans and dumping them into the wall slots. They pile back into the ambulance, and off it goes.

The Commandant, keeping his voice absolutely steady, asks the Reichsführer SS if he would like to listen at the bunker door and look in. Himmler goes with the Commandant, listens and looks. A transport of Jews sounds different inside; mournful, resigned, almost prayerful wails and groans, not the animal screeches and bellows of Russian prisoners or Polacks. As Himmler puts his eye to the peephole, his face contorts: a grimace of disgust or a smile of amusement, the Commandant cannot be sure.

Himmler does a surprising thing. He asks an aide for a cigarette. Like the Führer, Himmler does not smoke, or is reputed not to. But now he lights up and puffs calmly, as the Commandant takes him around to the back of the bunker, while they wait for the gas to do its work. He shows Himmler the enormous and ever-expanding area of the mass graves, and explains the mounting problems. For hundreds of meters in every direction, there are vast mounds of earth here and there in the grassy field. A rail track runs through them, ending near a large hole with earth piled high beside it, where the special kommandos are still digging. The expression on Himmler's face sharpens. His lips disappear as he puffs the skin around them in his curious fashion; a sure signal that he is intensely interested.

For the first time since their arrival at the bunker, he speaks; in a low calm voice, not to the Commandant, but to an aide, a tall good-looking colonel, who pulls off his black glove and makes rapid notes on a pad.

The gate in the back fence swings open. From the open back door of the bunker comes a cart heaped high with naked bodies rolling toward the inspection party on the rails, hauled and pushed by different Sonderkommandos, the burial detail. As the cart passes the SS officers, there is a whiff of the disinfectant, rather like carbolic acid. The naked people look not much different than they did less than half an hour ago, except that they are absolutely still now, streaked with excrement, and all jumbled together, some with jaws hanging open and wide eyes fixed and staring—old men, little children, pretty women, in an inert heap. One can still admire the looks of the women and the charm of the kids.

These Jew kommandos couldn't be more businesslike about the whole thing. Where the rails end, they crank the cart up so that the bodies slide to the ground in a tangle. A few of them push the cart back toward the bunker. The rest, together with the diggers who come climbing out of the pit, haul the bodies to the edge of the hole by an arm or a leg—some of them use big meat hooks, which the Commandant finds personally distasteful—and toss the dead down out of sight. Reichsführer Himmler is interested. He walks to the rim of the pit, and observes the kommandos laying out the warm naked bodies in rows, and sprinkling white powder on them. This, the Commandant explains, is quicklime. Something must be done, because the water table of the whole area is being contaminated. The bacteria count even of the drinking water at the SS barracks has gone up to the danger level. In the long run, as he has repeatedly complained to Berlin, burial is no answer; certainly it won't be once the actions that Lieutenant Colonel Eichmann has projected, on a scale of hundreds of thousands of Jews every few weeks, start to materialize.

The whole system will break down, he insists, if drastic steps are not taken at once. Nothing is adequate. The cottage bunker is a makeshift. Another one is being readied nearby, but it too is only a stopgap. The crematoriums remain pretty models in the Central Building Board office, and Berlin has simply been ignoring the disposal problem. The

Commandant, in his honest preoccupation with this serious matter, pours out his heart to the Reichsführer SS, while the special kommandos continue to cart out bodies, throw them in the hole, and stack them in rows. So caught up is he in his pleas that when he sees the dead baby girl come tumbling out of the cart with the broken branch in her hand it does not bother him.

Sincerity pays off. He can see that he is making an impression. Himmler gives a sharp jerky nod; he puffs out his mouth so that his lips disappear, and he glances around at his aides.

"So?" says the Reichsführer. "And what is next?"

"The crematoriums will be built," he says next day to the Commandant, in a private meeting just before going to the aerodrome.

The meeting is almost over. The last serious request, for permission to use Jews in sterilization experiments, which the Commandant put with some trepidation, has been cheerfully granted. They are in an inner office at the Building Board. Only Schmauser, the SS general in charge of all of south Poland, and therefore of Auschwitz, is present.

"The construction of crematoriums will take priority even over I. G. Farben," Himmler states. "They will be completed before the end of the year. Schmauser will override all other projects in this province for labor and materials." Himmler waves his black swagger stick at the general, who hastily nods. "You will hear from me further about the disposal problem. You have told me all your difficulties, and given me an honest look at Auschwitz. I am satisfied that you are doing your best under very tough conditions. It is wartime, and we have to think in terms of war. Assign your best construction crews to the crematoriums. When they are completed, liquidate the crews. Understood?"

"Understood, Herr Reichsführer."

"I promote you to Obersturmbannführer. Congratulations. Now I am on my way."

Lieutenant Colonel! Spot promotion!

A week later, Ernst Klinger is promoted, too, to Untersturmführer. At the same time, he receives a different assignment for his construction crew. They have a new designation: *Arbeitskommando, Crematorium II.*

*   *   *

27

Midway

(from *World Holocaust* by Armin von Roon)

One of the decisive battles in the history of the world was fought at sea at this time on the other side of the globe, almost unnoticed in Germany, even in our Supreme Headquarters. The failure of our Japanese allies to furnish us the truth about Midway amounted to bad faith. However, Hitler hated gloomy news, and most likely would have ignored an honest report of it. The serious German reader must grasp what happened at Midway in June 1942 to understand the course of the entire war.

Strangely, the democracies themselves gave Midway small play at the time. In the United States the news of the battle was scanty and inaccurate. To this day few Americans grasp that at Midway their navy won a sea victory to stand in military chronicles with Salamis and Lepanto. For the third time in planetary history, Asia sailed forth to attack the West in force, with ultimate stakes of world dominion. At Salamis the Greeks turned back the Persians; at Lepanto the Venetian coalition halted Islam; and at Midway the Americans stopped, at least for our century, the rising tide of Asiatic color. Pacific battles thereafter were in the main futile Japanese attempts to recover the initiative lost at Midway.

Before Midway, for all the missed chances and miscalculations of Adolf Hitler and the Japanese leaders, the war still hung in the balance. Had the United States lost this passage at arms, the Hawaiian Islands might well have become untenable. With his West Coast suddenly naked to Japanese might, Roosevelt might have had to reverse his notorious "Germany first" policy. The whole war could have taken a different turn.

Why then is this decisive event so underestimated? The anomaly stems from the nature of the battle. Victory at Midway turned partly on the analysis

of Japanese coded radio traffic. The feat could not be revealed in wartime.*
The United States Navy's version of Midway was foggy and guarded, and it
came out several days late. A long time passed before the setback to Japanese war plans was fully assessed. So the realities of Midway were obscured.
The war rumbled on, and the battle faded from sight, as Mount Everest can
be obscured by a whirl of dust raised by a truck. But as time passes, this
turning point looms ever larger and clearer in the military history of mankind.

"Flattop" Warfare

The German reader accustomed to land warfare needs a brief sketch of
the tactical problem at sea. On the water of course there is no terrain. The
battleground is all one smooth level unbounded field. This simplifies combat
as the land soldier knows it, but adds weight to fundamental elements. The
aircraft carrier developed as a radical advance in *range of firepower.*

In ancient sea fighting, warships rammed each other, smashed each
other's banks of oars, cast arrows, stones, lumps of iron, or flaming stuff
across a few feet of open water. Sometimes they came alongside each other
with grappling hooks, and soldiers leaped across and fought on the decks.
Long after guns were installed in men-o'-war, hand-to-hand waterborne
fighting continued. John Paul Jones won the first big sea fight for America
by grappling and boarding the British man-o'-war *Serapis,* exactly as a
Roman sea captain would have done to a ship of Carthage.

But the great nineteenth-century revolutions in science and industry brought
forth the *battleship,* a giant steam-driven iron vessel, with rotating center-
line guns that could fire a one-ton shell almost ten miles to port or starboard.
All modern nations hastened to build or buy battleships. The front-running
race between our own shipyards and England's to build ever-bigger battleships was a prime cause of the First World War. Even before that, English
capitalists had obligingly built a fleet of these monsters for the Japanese,
who in 1905 used it to trounce czarist Russia at Tsushima Strait. Only one
other large battleship engagement ever took place. At the Battle of the
Skagerrak, in 1916, our High Seas Fleet outfought the British navy in a
classic action. Twenty-five years later, at Pearl Harbor, the type went into
final and futile eclipse.

The battleship was the dinosaur of sea warfare, misbegotten and short-
lived. Each one was a drain on a nation's resources like the equipment for
many army divisions. But it did bring long-range firepower into sea war. The

---

* In fact, a Chicago newspaper did dig out and print the story of the code-breaking. The
Japanese missed it, evidently. President Roosevelt wisely ignored this treason, instead of
prosecuting it in a blaze of publicity.—V.H.

trajectories of its big guns required a correction *for the curvature of the earth!* Thus the industrial age brought man face to face with the physical limits of his tiny planet.

After the First World War a few farseeing naval officers perceived that the airplane could far outrange the battleship's big guns. It could fly hundreds of miles, and the pilot could guide his bomb almost onto the target. Against the crusty advocacy of battleship admirals, they fought and won the argument for building "flattops," seagoing airdromes. Pearl Harbor settled the twenty-year dispute in an hour, and the Pacific conflict became an aircraft carrier war.

————

TRANSLATOR'S NOTE: *I was a battleship man all my life. Roon ignores the role of the battleship in maintaining the balance of power for a turbulent half-century, though nobody can disagree that it failed at Pearl Harbor. His casual claim of German victory in the Jutland stand-off (Battle of the Skagerrak) is ridiculous. The Imperial German High Seas Fleet never sailed to fight after Jutland. Much of it was scuttled at Scapa Flow. Eventually Hitler scrapped the rest, after the Bismarck was sunk and the other battleships immobilized at their moorings by RAF bombs.*——V.H.

————

Carrier Combat Tactics

All Pacific flattops, U.S. and Japanese, carried three kinds of airplanes.

The *fighter* plane was defensive. It escorted the attacking planes to the target, and protected them by knocking down fighters that tried to intercept them. It also protected its own fleet against enemy attackers, by hovering overhead in a combat air patrol.

There were two attacking types: the *dive-bomber* plane and the *torpedo* plane. The dive-bomber dropped its missile through the air. The torpedo plane aimed for the death blow below the waterline; its technique was riskier, its missile heavier. It had to fly for many minutes on a straight course low over the water, and slow down to drop its torpedo. During this approach, the torpedo plane pilot was suicidally vulnerable to AA fire or to a fighter plane attack. He therefore needed strong fighter protection.

Carrier battle doctrine was the same in both navies. The three types of aircraft were launched for a mission by squadrons. The fighters, dive-bombers, and torpedo planes would join up and wing together to the target. The fighters would engage the defending fighters, the dive-bombers would attack, and when the enemy was most distracted the vulnerable torpedo planes would slip in low for the kill. This was called *coordinated attack,* or *deferred departure.*

In this scheme there were variations: i.e., a fighter could carry a light bomb; and the Japanese from the start designed their torpedo plane, the Type-97 bomber, as a two-purpose machine. Instead of a torpedo, it could carry a very large fragmentation bomb, thus giving it a strong capability against land targets as well.

On this dual-purpose Japanese bomber, in the end, the whole battle turned.

Code Book C

Intelligence too was crucial. By analysis of encoded radio traffic and by fractional decipherment of the code, the Americans discerned the enemy battle plan. The Japanese should have foreseen and avoided this. In modern war all codes and ciphers must be frequently replaced. This was a standard rule in our Wehrmacht commands. One has to assume that the enemy is copying all the broadcast gibberish, and that what the mind of man can devise the mind of man can unravel. Japan's communication doctrine called for code replacement, but her navy's preparations for Midway were plagued by both overconfidence and hurry. The hurry resulted from the Doolittle raid.

Navy Code Book C had been in use by the Japanese since Pearl Harbor. Aided by pioneer use of IBM machines, American and British teams had worked on the texts for half a year. A Code Book D was supposed to go into use on April first. Had this been done the Japanese signals for the Midway attack would have been secure. But the replacement was postponed to May first and then to June first, in the post-Doolittle scramble. On June first the opaque curtain of Code Book D did at last fall, but by then only three days remained before the battle, and Japan's plan was largely known to the enemy.

The Damaged Carriers

The Japanese faults of overconfidence and hurry showed up after the Coral Sea battle, a carrier skirmish that took place when they tried to capture Port Moresby in New Guinea, to create an air threat to Australia. The expedition ran afoul of two American carriers. The Japanese had the better of the two-day melee, a comedy of blundering decisions and airborne blindman's buff in bad weather, during which the opposing vessels never sighted each other. The Japanese sank the big flattop *Lexington* and an oiler, and damaged the *Yorktown*. They lost a light carrier, and took bomb damage and aircraft attrition in the fleet carriers *Shokaku* and *Zuikaku*.

The flattops of both sides went limping home from the Coral Sea. Fourteen hundred Yankee workmen at Pearl Harbor, laboring around the clock, patched up the badly hit *Yorktown* in three days, and it fought at Midway. But the two damaged Japanese flattops were *dropped from the operation*. The high command refused a postponement to train and replace air crews, and ordered no urgent repair effort. To ensure a full moon for the landing, or for some such footling reason, the weight of two carriers was nonchalantly forgone.

Plan and Counterplan

Yamamoto's battle plan for Midway was the work of Captain Kuroshima, who had devised the great but aborted "westward" strategy. His judgment seems to have waned. The Midway scheme was grandiose in scope and dazzling in its intricacy, but it lacked two military virtues: *simplicity,* and *concentration of force*. It was a dual mission, always a hazardous business.

1. Capture Midway atoll.
2. Destroy the United States Pacific Fleet.

The plan started with a replay of Pearl Harbor, a surprise carrier strike at the atoll. Under Admiral Nagumo, four carriers—instead of the six originally called for—would approach from the northwest by stealth. They would wipe out the air defenses at a blow, and the landing force would then capture the atoll before Nimitz could interfere. It was assumed (quite soundly) that Nimitz would have to come out and fight, no matter how weak he was. Yamamoto himself planned to lie with his battleships several hundred miles astern of Nagumo, out of aircraft range, prepared to close and annihilate the Nimitz fleet elements that would survive Nagumo's air onslaught.

The plan included a feint at the Aleutian Islands off Alaska. There other carriers would blast American naval bases, and an invasion force would land. The feint might decoy Nimitz's meager forces far to the north, thus enabling Yamamoto to get between the Pacific Fleet and the Hawaiian Islands, a stupendous opportunity; if not, Japan would still seize and hold the Aleutians, thus tearing loose the northern anchor of the American line in the Pacific.

So, despite his overwhelming advantage in power, Yamamoto elected to base his operation on deception and surprise; but there was no surprise. Nimitz gambled that what his decoders told him was true, and that he might win against odds by surprising the surprisers. He thus cut the Gordian knot of military theory: should operations be based on what the enemy would *probably* do, or on the *worst* he could do? Chester von Nimitz even shrugged off the barbed nagging from Washington of Fleet Admiral King, who kept pointing out that the Japanese fleet might be heading for Hawaii. Had Nimitz proved wrong, his disgrace would have been greater than that of the Pearl Harbor commander-in-chief who was cashiered.

But Chester von Nimitz was made of good stuff. He was of pure German military descent, and he had bred true. His Texas family traced its line directly to one Ernst Freiherr von Nimitz, an eighteenth-century German major, with a crowned coat of arms. This ancestor in turn derived from von Nimitz military forebears going back to the Crusades. Recent generations of Nimitzes, lacking the means to keep up the aristocratic style of life, had dropped the "von," and of course in Texas it would have been a handicap.

Nimitz made one simple grand decision: to ambush Yamamoto. He determined to position his carriers well northeast of Midway, as Nagumo's carriers were steaming down from the northwest. In this deadly game played around a wide water-girt bulge of the earth, much hung on who saw whom first. Placing his heavy pieces so, concealing them by distance, Nimitz seized a big advantage.

For Midway's land planes could search an arc of seven hundred miles, while Yamamoto's carrier craft could at best patrol three hundred miles. Also, Nimitz could receive patrol reports in Hawaii by underwater cable from Midway, so that no increase of broadcast traffic from the atoll would warn Yamamoto that the Americans were alerted. From Hawaii, Nimitz could then broadcast the patrol reports in code to his carriers, while Yamamoto's forces plodded within range, oblivious and unseeing.

Such was Nimitz's ambush. Yamamoto's fleet steamed right into it.

Yet not all ambuscades succeed. Surprise is a great but fleeting advantage. Yamamoto's powerful and battle-toughened forces quickly rallied from Nimitz's surprise, and in its opening phase the Battle of Midway took shape as a smashing Japanese victory.

———

TRANSLATOR'S NOTE: *Fleet Admiral Nimitz was a quiet man of broad vision, with a good sense of humor. Shortly before he died he read in manuscript my translation of this chapter. At Roon's usage of "von Nimitz" he enjoyed a hearty laugh, but he remarked that the details of his genealogy were accurate.*

A Navy adage runs, "If it works you're a hero, if it doesn't you're a bum." Actually there was much guesswork in the Midway intelligence break. Clues had to be teased out of the Japanese by deceptive signals. Admiral Nimitz's decision to act on this inconclusive "dope" was daring. He did not know the Japanese plan. Rather, he had a fair indication of what might be going on. He proceeded on hunches that proved brilliantly right.

The Wehrmacht coding precautions were not all that adequate. At this writing I can say no more, but the fact is that German communications were deeply penetrated.—V.H.

* * *

28

THE air squadrons flew out from Oahu to join the departing carriers in clear calm weather. On its approach, the leading *Enterprise* torpedo plane went into a spin, crashed, and tumbled overboard with pieces flying. To Warren, circling high above in a new dive-bomber, it looked like a toy breaking up. The plane guard destroyer rushed to the wreckage, boiling smoke like a locomotive and streaking the sea white. The plane crew was rescued, as he learned on landing. Such accidents were not uncommon, yet this one struck him as a bad omen.

TASK FORCE SIXTEEN IS PROCEEDING TO INTERCEPT A JAP LANDING ATTEMPT AT MIDWAY

Flashing across the teletype screens shortly after the pilots landed aboard, the words generated cheery excitement in the ready rooms. But in a long, long, dull week of northward zigzagging at standard speed, the excitement faded into an uncomfortable mix of boredom and mounting tension. The *Enterprise* and the *Hornet,* ringed by cruisers and destroyers, slowly moved from sunny tropical seas to gray swells, gray skies, and cool winds. Under the umbrella of the Hawaiian air patrol, there was nothing for the fliers to do. The newcomers, three-year Academy men or reserve ensigns, gloried in their prima-donna freedom from ship routine: sleeping late, playing acey-deucey and cards, fogging the ready rooms with tobacco smoke, drinking gallons of coffee and lemonade, eating big meals and great mounds of ice cream, killing time between drills and lectures with chatter of sex, shore leave, airplane mishaps, and the like, perpetrating ham-handed practical jokes; and generally mimicking, in their green self-consciousness, the Hollywood picture of combat fliers.

Usually Warren enjoyed the ready-room camaraderie play, but not this time out. Too many of the squadron mates with whom he had started the war were dead, missing, or transferred. The high-spirited recruits, mostly unmarried, made him feel old and irritable. The protracted idleness ate at him. He was flight operations officer, third in command, and he tried to keep busy reviewing tactics manuals, devising navigation problems and blackboard combat drills, exercising violently on the flight deck, and haunting the hangar deck to check and recheck the squadron's aircraft.

Idleness breeds gossip. Idleness plus tension is a bad brew. As the slow days passed, the talk in the ready rooms drifted to the topic of Rear Admiral Spruance. Word was trickling down from flag country that Halsey's staff was not cottoning to him. Halsey had built up the former screen commander, his old friend, to them as a brilliant intellectual. The staff was finding him a damned queer fish: cool, quiet, inaccessible, the Old Man's absolute opposite. He was content at meals to sit almost mum. He depressed Halsey's loyal and ebullient subordinates, who had absorbed their style from the rollicking Old Man. Why had Halsey pushed forward this taciturn nonflyer to fight a carrier battle, when red-hot aviators like John Towers had been available? Out of friendship? At lunch on the first day out, so rumor ran, Spruance had opened up after a long boring silence by saying, "Gentlemen, I want you to know that I'm not worried about any of you. If you weren't any good, Bill Halsey wouldn't have you." He seemed unaware that he himself was under worried scrutiny.

His ways were altogether odd. He tramped the flight deck alone by the hour, but otherwise he seemed rather lazy. He went to bed early and slept long and well. During an alarm over a night surface contact he had not turned out, merely ordered an evasive maneuver and gone back to sleep. Each day he ate an unvarying breakfast of toast and canned peaches, and drank only one cup of morning coffee, which he made himself, with the fussiness of an old maid, from special beans he had brought aboard. When it rained or blew hard topside, he sat in the flag mess reading old books from the ship's library. Almost, he seemed to be along for the ride. Halsey's chief of staff, Captain Browning, was running the task force, and Spruance was just initialling Browning's orders.

All in all, the staff was counting on Spruance for very little. Browning would fight the battle, and if the patched-up *Yorktown* got to the scene in time, Frank Jack Fletcher would take charge, since he was senior to Spruance. Fletcher had not done so well in the Coral Sea, but at least he had been blooded in carrier combat. Thus went the idle talk in the ready room, which irked Warren and troubled him too.

Arriving on station, a spot in the trackless sea designated "Point Luck," Task Force Sixteen steamed back and forth through two more tedious days, waiting for the *Yorktown*. This was the place of ambush, some three hundred twenty-five miles from the atoll; beyond the range of enemy carrier planes, yet close enough for a quick attack once Midway aircraft espied the foe. Dolphins frisking among the slow-moving ships found no scraps to eat; the crews were forbidden to throw so much as a paper cup overboard.

At last, making full speed, with no outward mark of its Coral Sea battering, the *Yorktown* hove into view. Like the ship, its decimated air squadrons were a patch job of Coral Sea survivors and *Saratoga* aviators hastily thrown together; but another flattop, patched or not, was mighty welcome. With Fletcher now in tactical command, more fleet alarms began to break out. *Yorktown* warnings about enemy submarines or aircraft touched off the old frenzied routines time and again: sharp turns of all ships, flight decks crazily canting, crews scurrying to man and train guns, destroyers foaming and crisscrossing; then would come the bored wait, the standdown, the recovery of aircraft, and the resumed plan of the day. None of the alarms proved genuine. The two task forces milled around and around Point Luck: the *Yorktown* with its own screen of cruisers and destroyers called Task Force Seventeen, the *Hornet* and the *Enterprise* still designated Task Force Sixteen, under Spruance as subordinate to Fletcher.

Warren scheduled himself out on the first dawn search. When his new Dauntless bounded forward between lines of hooded yellow guide lights on the deck and roared off into the cold night toward the crowded stars and the Milky Way, his spirit lifted too. The new fliers had looked grave during the ready-room briefing when told of the absolute radio silence orders; the carrier would send out no homing signals and if they had to make emergency water landings, distress calls were forbidden. Thus the chilly reality of the approaching enemy was thrust on them. Not having patrolled in an SBD-3 before, Warren too was uneasy at these tough rules. But the new machine purred out two hundred miles; then, in a soft lilac dawn and a beautiful sunrise, its new electronic homing device returned him dead on Point Option. A pleasant sight, those two carrier islands nicking the horizon! He landed with a clean catch of the number three wire. A great airplane, sure enough: improved navigation gear, a sweet engine, self-sealing tanks, extra guns, thicker armor. Even his gunner, a gloomy Kentucky mountain boy named Cornett, who seldom spoke and seemed to be using a foreign language when he did, climbed smiling out of the rear seat.

"Not a bad crate at that," said Warren.

Cornett spat tobacco juice and said something like, "Rakn rat smat new dew."

"Warren! Warren! It's started. They're bombing Dutch Harbor."

"Jesus." Warren sat up on his bunk, rubbed his eyes, and seized his trousers. "What do you know! Alaska, hey? Screwed again."

His roommate's eyes shone. Peter Goff was an ensign new to the squadron, a youngster from upstate New York with a red beard like Byron's. He said eagerly, "Maybe we'll head north, cut off their line of retreat, and cream 'em."

"That's three days' steaming, fella." Warren jumped barefoot to the cold iron deck.

When they got to Scouting Six ready room the big reclining chairs were full. Silently the aviators stared at words crawling across the yellow teletype screen:

DIVERSION MOVE AT ALASKA EXPECTED MAIN THRUST WILL BE AT MID-WAY DUTCH HARBOR PREPARED AND WELL DEFENDED

The commander of Scouting Six, a tough stocky old hand named Earl Gallaher, hung the big Pacific chart over the blackboard to discuss time and distance problems of a possible dash against the Japs to the north. The younger fliers listened hungrily. This was getting down to business. But Warren noted a new fleet course being chalked up: *120 degrees,* southeast, away from the Aleutians, away from Midway, away from the wind. Just another routine turn to hug Point Luck; no action.

Within the hour words were sliding across the screen again:

PBY PATROL PLANE REPORTS QUOTE MANY HEAVY ENEMY SHIPS BEAR-ING 237 DISTANCE 685 FROM MIDWAY UNQUOTE

The word "Midway" triggered shouts and rebel yells in the Scouting Six ready room. Everybody started talking at once. The CO jumped to the chart and drew a heavy red crayon ring at the point of the sighting. "Okay, here we go. Range about one thousand miles. They'll be in striking range in sixteen, seventeen hours."

The fliers were still clustering at the chart, spanning distances with fingers and arguing, when the teletype came to chattering life:

FROM CINCPAC URGENT THAT IS NOT THE ENEMY STRIKING FORCE THAT IS THE LANDING FORCE THE STRIKING FORCE WILL HIT FROM THE NORTHWEST AT DAYLIGHT TOMORROW

"Son of a bitch!" said Pete Goff at Warren's elbow. "How do they *know* all that in Pearl Harbor?"

Night fell. Midnight drew on. Few Scouting Six pilots went to their bunks. They were reading, or writing letters, or going on with the ever-lasting talk about women and flying; but the buzz of words had a different sound, lower and more tense. Staff gossip kept drifting in. Spruance was receiving the dispatches not in flag plot, but on a couch in the flag mess where he sat reading a mildewy biography of George Washington, merely initialling the message board. Meanwhile, in a flag plot like an overturned beehive, Captain Browning was already making out the preliminary battle orders.

The teletype now and then clicked out a burst of words about Dutch Harbor, or about the oncoming Jap landing force; Army Air Corps bombers from the atoll claimed to be pounding it and sinking battle-ships, cruisers, and whatnot in high-level attacks. Nobody placed any stock in that. The dive-bomber pilots had a word for high-level bomb-ing at sea: it was like trying to drop a marble on a scared mouse. *"What about the flattops? Where are their carriers? Any dope about the goddamned carriers?"* All through the ready rooms that was the restless litany.

Warren went topside to check the weather again. Moon almost full; stars, light clouds, cold crosswind, the Big Dipper on the starboard quarter. Loud splashing far below of a high-speed run. Closing the enemy fast now! On the flight deck aft, moonlight glinted on the wings of jammed-together planes, and here and there the pencil-thin red flash-light beams of repair work barely showed. The enlisted plane captains squatted in small knots, where sailor talk went on and on: about the better torpedo planes coming to the fleet in August, about religion, about sports, about family, about Honolulu whorehouses; not much talk about the subject most on every man's mind, the battle coming with the dawn.

Wide awake, Warren strode the breezy steady deck. The sea all around danced with moonlight. Passing through the hangar deck below, he had noted with peculiar clarity the quantities of explosive materials all about—bombs, gassed-up planes, full ammo racks, oil drums, tor-pedo warheads. The *Enterprise* was an iron eggshell eight hundred feet long, full of dynamite and human beings. Of this, he was edgily aware as never before. Jap eggshells just like it were probably only a few hun-dred miles away and closing.

Who would surprise whom? Suppose an enemy submarine had spotted this force? Far from unlikely! In that case Jap aircraft might strike at sunup. And even if this force did get the jump on the Japs, would the assault come off? In fleet exercises, even with no enemy opposition, a coordinated attack of fighters, dive-bombers, and torpedo planes had never yet worked. Some leader had failed to get the word, someone's navigation had gone wrong, or bad weather had scattered the formations. Too many *Enterprise* fliers were green recruits like Pete Goff. The battered *Yorktown*'s aviators were a sandlot team, scraped together off the beach after the Coral Sea losses. What would such a ragtag force do against seasoned Jap airmen who had wrecked Pearl Harbor and driven the British navy out of the Indian Ocean?

Yet there would be no more rehearsals, no more drills. This was it. Unless a surprise attack came off with total success, swift skilled Jap reprisal would explode the *Enterprise* into a grandiose fireball. He would either burn up in it, or if he was airborne he would fall in the sea when his fuel ran out. These were not fifty-fifty prospects.

And yet, Warren accepted them as all in the day's work. He no more expected to die in the coming battle than does a passenger who buys an air ticket from New York to Los Angeles. He was a professional flying man. He had flown through a lot of enemy fire. He thought he knew enough about it to get through the day alive, with any luck. At the after end of the flight deck, aft of the last dark row of planes, with the wind whipping his trousers, he stood and watched the broad moonlit wake rushing away. There was no place he would rather be, he thought, and nothing he would rather do than fly against the Japs tomorrow.

He wanted a cigarette. Returning to the island to go below, he glanced up again at the sky and he halted, his face turned upward, recalling a scene he had not thought of for years. He was a boy of seven, walking at night under just such a sky, on a wharf piled with fresh snow, hand in hand with Dad, who was telling him about the big distances and sizes of the stars.

"Dad, who put the stars there? God?"

"Well, Warren, yes, we believe the Lord God did that."

"You mean Jesus Christ himself stuck the stars up in the sky?" The boy was trying to picture the kindly long-haired white-robed man hanging gigantic balls of fire in black space.

He could recall his father's silence, then the hesitant reply. "Well, Warren, you sort of get into rocks and shoals there. Jesus is our Lord. That's true enough. He's also the son of God, and God created the universe and everything in it. You'll understand more about all this when you're older."

Warren could date the start of his doubts from that talk. In one of their rare arguments about religion, many years later, his father had cited the night sky as his old proof that there must be a God.

"Dad, I don't want to offend you, but to me those stars look pretty randomly scattered. And think about their size and distance! How can anything on this earth matter? We're microbes on a grain of dust. Life is a stupid and insignificant accident, and when it's over we're just dead meat."

His father had never again discussed religion with him.

The stars were majestically rocking over the prickly radar masts. They had never seemed so beautiful to Warren Henry. But despite the vivid patterns of the constellations, they still looked randomly scattered.

He lay in the dark in his cabin, chain-smoking. Pete Goff softly snored in another bunk. The third roommate, the squadron exec, was writing in the ready room. Warren yearned for just a couple of hours' sleep. He thought he had better try reading, and switched on the bunk light. Usually his glance passed over the black-bound Bible as though Dad's gift weren't in the book rack. Just the thing to make him drowsy! He propped himself up, and on a fortune-telling impulse opened the book at random. His eyes fell on this verse in the second Book of Kings:

Thus saith the Lord, set thy house in order; for thou shalt die, and not live.

It gave him a turn. He had never quite stopped believing in God, though he thought He must be more like his father, for forbearance and a sense of humor, than the thundering blue-nosed God of the preachers. "Well, ask a silly question, hey?" he thought. "I better mind my own business and leave the rest to You."

He read the Creation chapters, then the stories of Noah and the Tower of Babel. He had not looked at these since Sunday school days. Surprisingly, they seemed not boring, but terse and perceptive. Adam's dodging of responsibility was something he saw every day in the squadron; Eve was a lovely troublemaker like too many he had tangled with; Cain was every envious hating son of a bitch in uniform; and the storm description in the deluge chapter was damned good, the real thing. He began to bog down in the patriarchs, and Jacob's troubles with Laban did the trick. He fell asleep clothed, his gold wings gleaming in the light he was too drowsy to turn off.

"Now General Quarters. General Quarters. Man your battle stations."

The dawn GQ call boomed over the windy flight deck. Stars still twinkled in the black sky, and in the graying east one cloud glowed pink. Pulling on helmets and life jackets, sailors poured out on the gloomy deck, some to the gun tubs, some to the aircraft, some rolling out fire-fighting equipment. Warren was in his plane, checking a balky canopy. Most of the aviators were still in the ready room; they had all long since breakfasted, and were just waiting. Warren, usually a sausage-and-eggs man, had taken toast and one cup of coffee to keep his insides quietly in order. In the dark morning hours the teletype had fallen silent. Of enemy carriers, still no word.

The canopy was moving freely, yet Warren lingered in the plane. The stars faded, the sky went from indigo to blue, the sea brightened. Starkly clear in Warren Henry's mind was a relative movement diagram of what was probably happening. The Jap carriers—if Pearl Harbor was right about a dawn strike—would now be about two hundred miles west of the *Enterprise*. In a God's-eye view, the two moving carrier forces and the motionless Midway atoll made an equilateral triangle on the sea, and the triangle shrank as both forces speeded toward the atoll. Some time this morning the distance between the forces would close to strike range, and that would be the flash point of the battle. Of course, the Japs might not be there at all. They might be down off Hawaii, in which case Admiral Nimitz had fallen for a historic sucker play.

The sun pushed a blazing yellow arc over the sharp horizon and mounted. Well, no Jap daybreak attack; one hazard passed! That was what Warren had really been waiting for. He went down to the ready room, and as he was walking in, the loudspeaker rasped, *"Pilots, man your planes."*

"Okay . . . This is it . . . Here we go . . ."

The fliers jumped from their chairs, boots thudding on the metal deck, faces taut and eager. This time by a common impulse they turned to each other and shook hands. Then, slapping shoulders and joking, about half of them had crowded through the door when in the passageway the loudspeaker bawled, *"Now belay that last word. Pilots return to their ready rooms."*

Angry and jumpy as racehorses pulled up short after a bad start, the aviators trudged back to their chairs, trading rude comments about "those idiots up there." A bad business, Warren thought, some nervous faltering on the command level.

What had happened "up there" was that Captain Miles Browning had given the order, and Rear Admiral Spruance had countermanded it.

Spruance had already discomfited Halsey's chief of staff well before dawn. Prior to the GQ alarm Browning and his operations officer had mounted to Halsey's flag shelter, a small steel eyrie high up above the flying bridge; and as Spruance had left no call, Browning had not disturbed him. A short shadowy form in the starlight outside the shelter had greeted them. "Good morning, gentlemen."

"Ah—Admiral?"

"Yes. Looks like we'll have good weather for it."

As day broke, Spruance leaned on the bulwark outside, watching the ship come to life. Captain Browning was nervily ready for battle, his head was full of contingency plans, but this early presence of the placid Spruance was unsettling. Halsey would be pacing now like a caged cat. The chief of staff, who was wearing a leather windbreaker like Halsey's, did all the pacing, smoking cigarette after cigarette with Halsey gestures, fuming at the lack of news, arguing with the operations officer about where the Jap carriers could be.

Abruptly he seized a microphone and issued the summons to the pilots that had greeted Warren in the ready room.

Spruance called in, "Why are we doing this, Captain?"

"If you'll look here, please, Admiral."

Spruance amiably came to the chart table.

"By now, sir, the Japs have certainly launched. It's broad day. They probably launched well before dawn. We know the range of their planes. They *must* be somewhere along this arc, give or take twenty miles." He swept a stiff forefinger in a slim circle near Midway. "They'll be sighted any minute. I want to be ready to hit them."

"How long does it take our pilots to man their planes?"

Browning glanced at the operations officer, who said with a touch of pride, "On this ship, Admiral, two minutes."

"Why not leave them in their ready rooms for now? They'll be in those cockpits a long time today."

Spruance walked out on the sunlit platform, and Browning testily broadcast the recall.

The flag shelter was a small area, cramped by the chart table and a couple of settees. A rack of confidential publications, a coffee maker, microphones, telephones, and radio speakers made up the equipment. One speaker, tuned to the frequency of the Midway patrol planes, was emitting a power hum and loud popping static. About half an hour after

sunrise this speaker burst out in gargling tones, *"Enemy carriers. Flight
58 reports."*

"Kay, that's IT!" Browning again snatched the microphone.
Spruance came inside. The three officers stared at the humming and
popping receiver. Browning exploded, pounding the chart table with
his fist, "Well? *Well,* you stupid son of a bitch? *What's the longitude
and latitude?"* He glanced in angry embarrassment at Spruance.
"Christ! I assumed the squirt would give us the location in his next
breath. What kind of imbeciles are flying those Catalinas?"

"Their combat air patrol may have attacked him," said Spruance.

"Admiral, we've *got* the yellow bastards sighted now. Let's get the
pilots to their planes."

"But if the enemy's out of range we'll have to close him, won't we?
Maybe for an hour or more."

With a miserable grimace, as Spruance went out in the sunshine,
Browning slammed the microphone into its bracket.

A dragging interval ensued; then the same voice, much clearer, broke
through the random popping: *"Many enemy planes bearing 320 distance 150. Flight 58 reports."*

Again, humming silence.

More violently, the chief of staff cursed the PBY pilot for giving no
position. He poured coffee, let it stand and cool; smoked, paced, studied the chart, paced some more, turned the pages of an old magazine
and hurled it into a corner, while his operations officer, a burly quiet
aviator, kept measuring with dividers and ruler on his chart. Spruance
lounged outside, elbows on the bulwark.

"Flight 92 reports." It was a younger, more excited voice barking out
of the speaker. *"Two carriers and battleships bearing 320 from Midway, distance 180, course 135, speed 25 Dog Love."*

"AH! God love *that* lad!" Browning plunged for the chart, where the
operations officer was hastily marking the position.

Spruance came inside, took a rolled-up maneuvering board graph he
had tucked in a wall rack, and spread it beside him on a settee. "What
was that position again? And what is our present position?"

Rapidly measuring, scrawling calculations, barking questions into the
intercom to flag plot several decks below, Browning soon rattled off the
latitudes and longitudes to Spruance.

"Is the message authenticated?" Spruance asked.

"Authenticated, authenticated? Well, is it?" Browning snapped. The
operations officer threw open a loose-leaf book while Spruance was

spanning distances on his small graph with thumb and forefinger. *"'The farmer in the dell,'"* the operations officer quoted, *"'any two alternate letters.'* The pilot gave us *Dog Love.* That works."

"It's authenticated, Admiral," Browning said over his shoulder.

"Launch the attack," said Spruance.

Startled, Browning jerked his head around from the chart to look at Spruance. "Sir, we've received no orders from Admiral Fletcher."

"We will. Let's go."

At the chart, the air operations officer lifted a worried face. "Admiral, I make the distance to the target one eighty. At that range our torpedo planes won't get back. I recommend we close at least to one fifty."

"You're quite right. I thought we were about there now." The admiral turned to Browning. "Let's put out a new fleet course, Captain Browning, closing them at full speed. Tell the *Hornet* we'll launch at a hundred and fifty miles."

A sailor in dungarees, life jacket, and helmet came thumping up the long ladder with a message board. Spruance initialled it and passed it to Browning. "Here are the orders from Fletcher."

URGENT. COM TF 17 TO COM TF 16. PROCEED SOUTHWEST AND ATTACK ENEMY CARRIERS WHEN DEFINITELY LOCATED. WILL FOLLOW AS SOON AS MY SEARCH PLANES RECOVERED.

Miles Browning was a fighting man, everybody acknowledged that, and he had been waiting most of his professional life to see such a dispatch. His ill humor vanished. A beguiling masculine grin lit his lean weathered face (he was a well-known ladykiller, too) and he squared his cap and saluted Raymond Spruance. "Well, Admiral, here we go."

Spruance returned the salute and went out in the sun.

In the ready rooms, when the carrier sighting printed out on the teletypes, the nervous irritation of the pilots cleared away. False alarm forgotten, they cheered, then fell to plotting and calculating. Guesses fired back and forth about probable time of launch. The range of the torpedo planes was of course the problem. Their chances of survival were reckoned poor at best, and the torpedo pilots deserved a decent chance to get back.

Visiting the ready room of Torpedo Squadron Six to kill the slow-grinding time, Warren found his friend Commander Lindsey in flying suit and life vest, his bandages gone, blood-caked scars on his hand and on his pale sunken face. This was the man whose plane had crashed on the first day out. "Ye gods, Gene, did Doc Holiwell shake you loose?"

Commander Lindsey said, unsmiling, "I've trained for this, Warren. I'm leading the squadron in."

The torpedo squadron room was unusually quiet. Some aviators were writing letters; some doodled on their flight charts; most of them smoked. Like the dive-bomber pilots they had stopped drinking coffee, to avoid bladder discomfort on the long flight. The effect here was one of taut waiting, as outside an operating room during surgery. At the blackboard a sailor wearing earphones was chalking new numbers beside RANGE TO TARGET: *153 miles.*

Lindsey said to Warren, glancing at his own plotting board, "That checks. We're closing fast. I figure we'll close to a hundred thirty miles. So we'll be launching about an hour from now. This is for keeps, and we've got to get the jump on the little bastards, so even if we strain a bit—"

"Pilots, man your planes."

Glancing at each other and at the pallid squadron commander, the pilots of Torpron Six got out of their chairs. Their movements were heavy, not eager, but they moved. So alike were the expressions of grave hard resolve on their faces, they might have been nineteen brothers. Warren threw an arm around Lindsey's shoulder. His old instructor slightly winced.

"Happy landings, Gene. Give 'em hell."

"Good hunting, Warren."

The fliers of Scouting Six were trampling by in the passageway, shouting high-strung banter. Warren fell in with them. As the squadron ran out on the gusty sunny flight deck, a sight met his eye that always thrilled him: the whole task force turning into the wind, the *Enterprise,* the *Hornet,* the far-flung ring of cruisers and destroyers, all moving in parallel; and old Dad's *Northampton* right up there, swinging from the port beam to a station almost dead ahead in dazzling sun glare. With farewell shouts and waves the pilots climbed into their planes. Cornett nodded at Warren from the rear seat, placidly chewing tobacco in long bony jaws, his red hair flying in the wind.

"Well, Cornett, here we go to get ourselves a Jap carrier. You ready?"

"Stew lot yew dang sartin cummin," Cornett approximately replied, then broke into clear English to add, "The canopy is freed up."

Thirty-five dive-bombers were spotted on the flight deck, their motors coughing, roaring, and spitting dense blue fumes. Warren's plane, among those farthest aft, carried a thousand-pound bomb; as flight operations officer he had made sure of that. The take-off run for some of the others was too short, and their load was a five-hundred-pound bomb, with two more hundred-pounders. Warren's launch was heavy and lumbering. The SBD-3 ran off the end of the deck, settled much too close to the water, then began a wobbling climb. The rush of warm sea air into the open cockpit was soul-satisfying. A professional calm settled on Warren as he wound up the wheels and flaps, checked his dancing dial needles, and climbed skyward in a string of soaring blue bombers. The *Hornet* dive-bombers too were single-filing into the air in steep ascent about a mile away. Far above some shreds of high cloud, the gleaming specks of the combat air patrol circled.

At two thousand feet, as the squadron levelled and circled, Warren's exaltation dimmed. He could see, on the shrunken *Enterprise* far below, that the launch was lagging. In their square deck wells the elevators sank and rose, tiny men and machines dragged aircraft about, but the time crawled past seven thirty, seven forty-five. Soon almost an hour of gasoline was gone, and still no fighter escorts or torpedo planes were airborne! And still the two carriers plowed southeast into the wind, away from the atoll and the enemy, slaves to the wind in launch or recovery, no less than sailing ships of old.

A signal light flashed on the *Enterprise,* beaming straight up. Letter by letter, Warren read the message, addressed to the new group leader, Commander McClusky: *Proceed on assigned mission.*

A second shocker, after the very long-range launch—suddenly, no coordinated attack! What was going on? No fighter protection, no torpedo planes for the knockout punch: the *Enterprise* dive-bombers ordered to go in alone against the Jap interceptors! Rear Admiral Spruance was jettisoning—or allowing Halsey's staff to jettison—the whole battle plan at the outset, with the drills of a year, the fleet exercises of many years, and the entire manual of carrier warfare.

Why?

A barometer in Warren's spirit registered a quick sharp rise in the danger of this mission, and in the chances of his dying. He could not be sure what "those idiots down there" had in mind. But he suspected that between the inexperienced Spruance and the overeager Browning—who was something of a joke among the veteran pilots—the thirty-six *Enterprise* dive-bombers were being squandered in a jittery shot from the hip.

Warren Henry knew too much military history for a young flier. To him all this strongly smelled of the Battle of Balaclava:

> *Theirs not to reason why,*
> *Theirs but to do and die—*

Resignedly, he made hand signals to his wing mates. From planes roaring along a few yards below and behind him, they grinned and waved. They were both new ensigns; one was Pete Goff, clutching a cold corncob pipe in his mouth. McClusky waggled his wings and swooped around to the southwest. Warren did not know McClusky except to say hello. He had been the squadron CO of the fighters, but there was no telling how he would perform as group leader. The other thirty-five planes gracefully veered to follow McClusky. Making his turn over the screen, Warren saw from his tilted cockpit the tiny *Northampton* straight below, cutting a long white wake ahead of the *Enterprise.* "Well, old Dad," he thought, "there you are, sitting way down there, and here I go."

On the bridge of the *Northampton,* Pug Henry stood among crowding officers and sailors in gray helmets and life jackets. He had been watching the *Enterprise* since dawn. As the departing bombers dwindled to dots, he stared after them through binoculars. Everybody who served on the cruiser's bridge knew the reason.

The wind was smartly flapping the signal flags. Below, noisy swells were breaking on the hull like surf. Pug raised his voice to the exec at his elbow, "Secure from GQ, Commander Grigg. Maintain condition Zed. AA crews stand easy at their guns. Float plane pilots stand by the catapults ready to go. Double the regular lookouts for aircraft and submarines. All hands be alert for air attack. Where men remain on battle stations, serve out coffee and sandwiches."

"Aye aye, sir."

In a different tone Pug went on, "Say, incidentally, those SBDs won't be breaking radio silence till they're over the target. We've got the right crystals for the aircraft frequency, haven't we?"

"Chief Connors says that we do, Captain."

"Okay. If you hear anything, call me."

"Aye aye, sir."

In the sea cabin, Victor Henry slung helmet and life jacket on the bunk. His eyes smarted. His legs were leaden. He had not slept all night. Why were those dive-bombers flying off unescorted to face a cloud of Jap interceptors? His own prize lookout, Traynor, a sharp-eyed Negro youngster from Chicago, had spotted a Japanese float plane slipping in and out of low clouds. Was that the reason? Pug did not know what orders had gone out to the squadrons of the *Yorktown* and the *Hornet;* he could only hope the whole battle picture made more sense than he could yet discern. The game was on, that was sure.

From the old triple photograph frame on the chart table, between Madeline and Byron, Warren looked out at him sternly in the Academy graduation picture: a skinny solemn ensign in a big white officer's cap. Well, thought Pug, a damned good lieutenant was flying off against the Japs, with fitness reports that were a string of "outstandings," and a solid combat record. His next job would be as a Stateside flight instructor, no doubt. The air cadet programs were clamoring for combat veterans. Then he would rotate back to an air group in the Pacific, to gain command experience and reap medals. His future was radiant, and this day was the needle's eye of his destiny. Hardening himself to endure the wait for a break in radio silence, Pug took up a detective novel, reclined on his bunk, and numbly tried to read.

Why, in fact, did Spruance send off the dive-bombers?

The battle decisions of a commander are not easily analyzed; not even by himself, not even in reminiscent tranquillity. Not all men of war are at ease with words. Events evaporate and are *gone,* especially the evanescent moments of a battle. The memoirs composed long afterward are as often misleading as illuminating. Some truly proud men say or write little. Raymond Spruance left few words about his Midway conduct.

He was acting in the battle under a Nimitz directive that is on the record: *"You will be governed by the principle of calculated risk, which you shall interpret to mean the avoidance of exposure of your force to attack by superior enemy forces without good prospect of inflicting, as a result of such exposure, greater damage on the enemy."* The Navy had a sour slang translation for this: "Sock 'em and rock 'em, but don't lose your shirt"; a standard admonition to a weak force going out against odds. Boiled down, it meant little but "Try to win with conservative tactics." Few military orders are harder to obey. And he had unwritten orders from Nimitz not to lose his carriers, even if it meant giving up Midway. "We will get it back later," Nimitz had said. "Save the fleet."

Some hard truths had been squeezing Spruance, under these hobbling instructions. He was a stranger to the ship, to Halsey's staff, and to air operations. He could not force a speedup of the appallingly slow launches on the *Enterprise* or the *Hornet* merely by throwing an admiral's tantrum. In this matter he was in fact helpless. The *Yorktown* had drifted aft below the horizon while recovering its search planes, so he couldn't consult Fletcher. A Jap float plane had been sighted, and the special intelligence officer who knew Japanese said that it had sent a position report. So the edge of surprise was melting away like butter on a hot skillet. Midway atoll was reported under attack by enemy aircraft. His dive-bombers were circling and circling overhead, burning up gasoline.

Given the distances in the combat triangle, and the known aircraft ranges and speeds, Spruance could hope that his dive-bombers, if they left now, might reach the enemy in his moment of weakness, when his planes were getting back from Midway low on bullets and gas. But there was one grim catch to that. The PBY had seen only two carriers. Nimitz's intelligence staff had predicted four or five. *Where were those missing flattops?* Were they coming at Task Force Sixteen from the north, the south—even in an end run from the east? Would they pounce when all his dive-bombers were off, attacking the first two?

An oppressive urgent choice confronted him: either hold back the bombers for a full coordinated attack, and hope meanwhile for news of the missing carriers; or hit out now, gambling that they would show up near the two in sight.

Spruance hit out. It was hardly a "calculated risk." It was the steepest and gravest of gambles with the future of his Navy and his country. Such decisions—only such once-in-a-lifetime personal decisions —test a commander. Within the hour his far more experienced and stronger opponent, Vice Admiral Chuichi Nagumo, would face much the same hard choice.

29

A Jew's Journey
(*from Aaron Jastrow's manuscript*)

JUNE 4, 1942, MIDNIGHT.
SIENA.

I have just listened to the BBC and to Radio Berlin, hoping for I know not what—a last-minute turnabout in the war news, possibly, to justify putting off a desperate decision. There was none. Under the propaganda cosmetics—the German paint whorish, the British ladylike—one discerns the same grim face of events: *Germany and Japan triumphant*.

In my meeting with the archbishop today I encountered a subtle change. His Excellency is something of a peasant, with a red jowly face, a solid build, and an earthy vocabulary. But he is cultured and tolerant. I like him and tend to trust him. This time he received me not in his cozy wood-panelled study, but in his cold grand outer office. He sat behind a splendid old desk. When I came in he did not stand up, but motioned me to a chair. I understood. I am no longer the well-known American author at whose villa he can now and then enjoy a good dinner, fine wine, and jocose pedantic talk. I am a suppliant. The wheel has turned, and the archbishop with it.

Still, he has looked into the matter. As to the Italian authorities, no immediate harm threatens us. Of this he assures me. He knows of no new program to round up Jews. Our status as enemy aliens under house arrest is of course most singular. He has been told we are marked for privileged treatment, and for release to Switzerland when various problems are cleared up. The question of concealing ourselves may therefore not arise.

Still, if it does, hiding out in the countryside would be a possibility, he agrees. But taking refuge in Siena's environs would be unwise. The story of *il famoso scrittore americano* trapped by the war is common Sienese gossip, and no hiding place around here would be secure.

He has cautiously raised the topic with the bishop of Volterra, an old walled town some fifty miles to the northwest, on the winding mountain road down to Pisa. Many years ago, I visited the Etruscan antiquities in Volterra. An alabaster bowl I bought there sits on my desk now, filled with roses. It is a town forgotten by time. The inhabitants are a darkly handsome dour lot. His Excellency jokes that they are probably Etruscan by blood and pagan at heart. Several people wanted by the Fascist regime are lying low in Volterra. Should the worst come to the worst, he can put us in touch with the Volterra bishop, who will be sympathetic. But he feels we should just keep calm and await our eventual. release. He stood up smiling to see me out, thus cutting the meeting quite short.

I am shaken by his having talked to the Volterra prelate. How do I know that he can be trusted? Under all the bland reassurance, the archbishop offers us no hiding place himself; and as for future emergencies, he holds out only a promise of sympathy from the bishop of Volterra, a man I don't know, who owes me nothing. This dusty outcome brings me to the alternative.

[*The following passage in* A Jew's Journey, *eight and a half handwritten pages in all, is in the original manuscript a series of strange marks. Such sections occur all through the notebooks after June 4. The key to the cipher is given in the clear English text below. The first line of the passage looks like this:*

ﾘ. ⟨⟨ ɾ ﾘﾉﾘ. ɾｌ ɾ ﾘｲﾌ.ﾉ ｢ﾌﾉ. ɛɿ ﾦﾉﾚ.ﾞ.ſﾌ ɛ. ﾘﾌﾌﾚ⟨ｨﾌ ﾌ .//]

I have avoided until now describing the alternative in these pages. Once it contains such things, my notebook becomes a ticking bomb. Bethinking me of Leonardo's mirror handwriting. I have decided to spell out perilous matters in English, but in the backward-running Yiddish alphabet, which will look to the uninitiated like hen scratchings: a temporary shield against prying eyes, or a sudden pounce by Italian police. A simple device, but the short-term security is good.

I scarcely dreamed, when I began *A Jew's Journey,* that I would be using spy tricks in writing it! My life's candle sputters and flares as it burns down, making melodramatic shadows leap about me. Yet I intend to record everything of consequence that happens from now on. By touching a match to tinder-dry faggots in my fireplace, I can in seconds reduce this book to ash.

To the alternative, then.

A Sienese doctor has revealed himself to us as a Jew and a secret Zionist. He plans to flee Italy with his family, hoping to reach Palestine; he is sure that all of Europe's Jews are doomed. Avram Rabinovitz, the tough Palestinian organizer of the *Izmir* voyage, has been in touch with this man, whose departure plans are now complete. Tomorrow he will send a confirming message to Rabinovitz. They are willing to include us in the flight arrangements. I must tell the doctor by morning whether we wish to come along.

The plan envisages an escape route via Piombino, Elba, Corsica, and Lisbon. The nub of it is a Turkish ship, once again; this time a freighter, which carries a cargo of Turkish tobacco from Istanbul to Lisbon every two months. This flavoring tobacco is important to the Allied war effort, so the vessel has British clearance. The ship's captain reaps a fortune by stopping at dead of night off Corsica and taking on Jewish stowaways for gold. In Lisbon we and our Zionist friends would part company. They would hope to go on to the Holy Land, one way or another, and we of course would simply walk into the American consulate.

The doctor does not blink at the hazards of this project. Italian and French underground groups are both involved. Rabinovitz deals with both. Sticky points abound from the start at the Siena bus station to the end at a Lisbon wharf. The whole thing could scarcely be less inviting.

Yet this is our last chance to struggle free; otherwise, in an ever-darkening war scene, we must helplessly wait. If I believed that release to Switzerland was genuinely in prospect, I would brave it out here. My rule, "When in doubt, *wait*," has served me well in life. But for a Jew in Europe, I begin to grasp, all rules are confounded. The compass needle spins in a violent magnetic storm. Even without those unthinkable broadcasts hanging over me, I would be tempted to flee. The archbishop pooh-poohs the stories of secret Nazi massacres of Jews; and anyway, he says, no Italian government will ever give Jews over into German hands, as the occupied countries are doing. So he thinks. He sits in an archdiocesan palace. My safety trembles on a thread.

If an Allied victory were in sight, if only as a glow from below the horizon, I would not budge. A month ago that was my resolve. Against the huge Allied array of raw materials, factories, and manpower, I couldn't see Germany and Japan ever winning. Rather, I was sure, Tocqueville's vision was coming to birth, of a world divided between America and Russia; these two great unions, aided by the doughty though sinking British imperium, would roar into central Europe, shatter the moonstruck Hitler tyranny, and set free not only the occupied countries, but the benighted bled-white Germans. Nor could Japan long survive the end of Hitler.

But what is now sinking in, after shock upon shock, is the example of Macedon. The forces of Alexander were small in number, compared to the hordes of Asia. But his phalanx smashed gigantic empires, and humbled the whole known world to his tiny state. Cortez, an adventurous butcher leading a handful of bravos, plundered and destroyed Montezuma's empire. Pizarro did the same to the great Inca civilization. Wars are won by will, by readiness to die, and by skill in killing, not by advantages, however lopsided, in numbers.

One hoped that the Russian winter, having halted the Germans outside Moscow, might have blunted the *furor Teutonicus* once for all. Alas, the monster was but leaning on his sword, catching his breath to spring again. The Italian papers show mind-boggling photos of the siege of Sevastopol. Nightmarishly huge guns are throwing shells tall as houses at the city. A perfect rain of artillery fire and aircraft is blanketing Sevastopol with smoke like a volcano in eruption. Following on the Russian defeat near Kharkov, the grinning mannikin Dr. Goebbels is announcing astronomic bags of prisoners. On the high seas, Hitler's U-boats are so close to cutting the American supply route to Europe that the Allied press itself trumpets alarm, admitting that the sinkings are in the millions of tons. In North Africa, the British once again flee before Rommel.

Meanwhile, Japan grows in military stature like a genie towering up out of a bottle. The list of Japanese conquests is Kiplingesque: Singapore, Burma, Java, and now they threaten India! The photographs of defeated and captured white men look like the end of civilization. Dejected British prisoners in Singapore squat on the ground as far as the camera can focus; and on palm-lined Philippine roads, columns of unshaven, ragged, bowed Americans march to captivity from Bataan under the guns of scowling yellow dwarfs.

The lesson was writ plain by Thucydides centuries before Christ was born. Democracy satisfies best the human thirst for freedom; yet, being undisciplined, turbulent, and luxury-seeking, it falls time and again to austere single-minded despotism.

I may be giving way to gloom, blinded by scanty information and a dismal ambience. The pinched nagging shabbiness of life in wartime Italy, with the poor food and drink, weakens one's body and mind. I have not tasted decent meat or wine since the American journalists left. The rationed vegetables are stunted or rotten. The clayey bread sticks in one's throat. Still, I believe I am thinking straight. An Allied victory in the near future seems to me too silly to be discussed. The tides of war do not reverse so easily. The opposite is the more likely quick result: collapse of the Soviet Union, expulsion of the British from Asia and of the Americans from the Pacific, and an Axis triumph on terms. Otherwise the prospect is for stalemate. If the war drags on long enough, a tortuous Allied victory may ensue as Axis-plundered metals, fuel, and food run out. But the fall of Hitler in 1945 or 1946 will not help Natalie, her baby, or me. We would probably not survive such a long wait; but more than that, a showdown with Werner Beck cannot be put off many months, let alone several years.

I do not fear apocalypse. The armies of Germany and Japan are not going to land in New England and California. The oceans are broad, and America remains populous and strong, only impotent to wield its strength in time. Once the despots have swallowed their conquests there will be a pause for digestion and a peace of sorts, perhaps for a decade or two. Should the United States adopt a Vichy-like regime, there may be no third war at all, only a long gradual sucking dry of America's riches by the tyrannies. I need to plan for five or at most ten more years of life. *Après moi, le déluge.* And I must deliver Natalie and Louis if I can.

The decision does seem to be in my hands. Natalie is all but paralyzed. The hoyden who dashed to her lover in Warsaw while war was breaking out, who met another lover in Lisbon in wartime and married him on the spot, has become a mother. It has changed her. She says she will follow my lead. If she is willing to make this rash journey with an infant, it can only be because Avram Rabinovitz is involved, the man who awed and attracted her aboard the *Izmir.* Her submariner husband is half a world away, if indeed he is alive at all. For a bizarre and shadowy adventurer like Rabinovitz she can have only fugitive feelings, but I am glad this shred of moral assurance exists for her.

We will start for Lisbon, then. God help us! I wish I were on better terms with Him. But alas, as with the bishop of Volterra, I don't know Him and He owes me nothing.

If the worst comes to the worst, Natalie will learn that I am not altogether a blundering wool-head. Like Hamlet, when the wind is southerly, I know a hawk from a handsaw. There are the diamonds.

30

V ICE ADMIRAL Nagumo's wartime photograph shows a stern bald old Japanese gentleman in a European-style admiral's uniform—thick gold epaulettes, diagonal sash, banks of medals—in which he looks choked and cramped. Nagumo far outclassed Raymond Spruance in rank and in achievement. He had not fought in the Coral Sea; that mess had been botched by lesser men. The victory record of his striking force from Pearl Harbor to the Indian Ocean was unstained. Of samurai descent, a destroyer and cruiser man of high repute, he was the veteran world master of carrier operations.

Steaming out of the melancholy rain and fog that had screened him for a week, Nagumo had launched his strike against Midway at dawn: half of each carrier's fighters, dive-bombers, and Type-97 torpedo planes; these last, dual-purpose machines having been loaded with fragmentation bombs for a land strike. Then he had ordered the remaining one hundred eight planes in the four flattops spotted on deck in readiness to attack any enemy warships that might show up; these Type-97s armed with their usual torpedoes, and the dive-bombers with armor-piercing bombs. But Nagumo and his staff did not expect to encounter the enemy; this was just a conservative precaution.

Just before the strike launch Nagumo in his own hand had drawn up an *Estimate of the Situation:*

1. *The enemy fleet will probably sortie to engage once the Midway landing operations are begun. . . .*
4. *The enemy is not yet aware of our plan, and he has not yet detected our task force.*
5. *There is no evidence of an enemy task force in our vicinity.*
6. *It is therefore possible for us to attack Midway, destroy land-based planes there, and support the landing operation. We can then turn around, meet an approaching enemy task force, and destroy it.*
7. *Possible counterattacks by enemy land-based air can surely be repulsed by our interceptors and antiaircraft fire.*

Radioed victory reports, familiar but exhilarating, began to pour in from the Midway strike aviators. The atoll had sent up a large fighter force, but the Zeroes were mowing them down, and the bombers, without a single loss, were laying waste to the two little islands of Midway. Hangars, power plant, barracks were aflame, guns were silenced, ammunition and fuel dumps were exploding skyward, and the whole garrison was a smoking shambles.

There was one disappointing note. The Yank aircraft had not been caught on the ground as at Pearl Harbor; they had taken the alarm and scrambled out of sight. The hangars and runways had been found empty. Of course, those planes would soon have to land and refuel, and that would be the time to destroy them. So the strike commander had radioed, *"There is need for a second strike."*

Here was the first snag of the day. The Midway airpower had to be smashed, or the landing would be a delayed and bloody one. But the planes now spotted on deck were armed to hit ships. The Type-97s would certainly have to change weapons; torpedoes were no good for a strike on land. Nor were the armor-piercing shells in the dive-bombers as suitable as incendiary and fragmentation bombs.

Nagumo and his staff were debating this pesky problem when air raid bugles sounded, black smoke poured from destroyers to signal *Planes sighted,* and roaring enemy aircraft swooped in low over the wave crests, unmistakable blue U.S. attackers with white-starred wings. Unescorted by fighters, the enemy craft fell like shot fowl under AA and Zero attack. A few launched torpedoes before they went down in flames, but these weapons porpoised, broached, or broke in pieces on striking the water. Not one hit or ran true. It was a miserable display of American ineptness, a brilliant clean sweep by Nagumo's combat air patrol. One plane crashed on the flight deck of the *Akagi* right before Nagumo's eyes, cartwheeling harmlessly over the side. The vice admiral and his staff saw the twin engines, the white star on the flaming blue fuselage, and inside the canopy the blood-soaked pilot, probably already dead. This plane was too big for carrier launching. It was a B-26 medium bomber, and it could only have come from Midway.

That settled it for Nagumo. He would have to make that second strike. As for any enemy fleet nearby, search planes had been aloft since dawn and had reported nothing. Farfetched precautions had to go by the board. The planes now on deck would hit Midway, and to speed matters, only the Type-97 torpedo planes would be rearmed. The two big flattops of his division, the *Akagi* and the *Kaga,* had that chore to rush through. The Type-97s of the smaller *Hiryu* and *Soryu* in Division Two were all off over Midway. Their decks held only fighters and dive-bombers, ready to go. So the orders went out to Nagumo's division. The elevators whined up and down. The big Type-97s were struck below to the hangar deck. Crack crews swarmed to switch the weapons.

A decided surprise came at half past seven. The heavy cruiser *Tone* relayed word from its search plane that ten ships, "apparently enemy," had been sighted about two hundred miles to the east, heading southeast, away from Nagumo and the atoll. The message said nothing about carriers. Surface ships two hundred miles distant could not rescue Midway now. Once the atoll's air force had been obliterated, these vessels could be picked off; but first things first. The rearming of the Type-97s with bombs for land attack went on apace.

Then Nagumo or a staff officer had alarming second thoughts. Enemy course southeast—that course was *into the wind*. Could that float plane pilot have seen carriers and idiotically failed to specify them?

To the carriers: *"Suspend rearming! Leave torpedoes in Type-97 bombers!"*

To the float plane: *"Ascertain ship types and maintain contact."*

So the chances of war froze the whole vast Japanese operation to the vagaries of one young pilot in one obsolescent cruiser scout plane. Half the Type-97s were already respotted on the flight decks with bombs. The rest were still below with their torpedoes. Now the air raid bugles blared once more, destroyers puffed black smoke balls, and dots in the sky grew to Douglas dive-bombers, approaching from the direction of Midway—again, with no fighter escort—at a peculiar shallow angle, contrary to the usual tactics of U.S. "hell-divers."

These planes were in fact being flown for the first time by raw Marine pilots, last-minute reinforcements for Midway, and their commander was trying to glide-bomb. A second massacre ensued; to the cheers of Japanese deckhands and gun crews, Zeroes picked off the blue planes one after another, and they burst into pretty rosettes of flame and arched smoking into the sea. Not a single bomb landed.

Perhaps this cold-blooded squandering of American pilots' lives in a second attack without fighter escort surprised Nagumo. It was not what one might expect of a soft decadent democracy. But then, the Zeroes had probably shot down all the fighters Midway had started with. The main point stood out: the skies this day were his. The Americans, though brave, were outmatched.

Now the far-off bumbler in the float plane answered up: *Enemy ships consist of five cruisers and five destroyers.* Well! No carriers; the rearming of Type-97s could proceed. But the air raid bugles sounded again, and this time a formation of gigantic land planes came drumming high, high overhead: B-17s by their silhouettes, the dreaded "Flying Fortresses." A harsh apparition; tiny Midway was peculiarly set for air combat! Yet what could the monsters actually do against moving ships with their high-level bombing? The test of this long peacetime debate was at hand as the huge bombers approached at twenty thousand feet.

They had no fighter escort. With their terrible gun-blisters they needed none. The Zeroes did not rise to challenge them. Ponderously, the four carriers scattered as heavy black bombs came showering down, plain to see, on the two smaller flattops, the *Soryu* and the *Hiryu*. Dark watery explosions engulfed them, again and again. The high-flying giants grumbled away in the sky, the splashes subsided; and out of the smoke into the sunlight, unscathed, the two carriers steamed!

With this historic defensive success, after slaughtering two low-level bomber waves, Nagumo was riding high. Obviously, however, Midway crawled with bombers. The second strike was imperative. He had been right to switch the Type-97s to bombs, and that process must now be speeded up.

Before he could act, four almost simultaneous jolts threw the old hero off balance again.

There was always much uproar around Nagumo during operations—clang of elevator warning bells, bark of flight deck loudspeakers, roar of engines warming up, chatter of radio receivers, shouts of flag bridge signalmen. Long habit enabled him to shut out this familiar racket, but the cataract of crises and tumult that burst on him now was something new. He had to make decision after decision—on some of which hung the future of his country, and indeed of the world order—in haste, in uncertainty, in a very hurricane of noise, alarm, confusion, upsets, and contradictory advice. A high commander lives for such moments, and he began to breast the storm with veteran calm.

First, still another wave of bombers came diving out of the clouds.

Second, as the bugles were shrilling and the remaining fighter planes on deck were scrambling to reinforce the combat air patrol, a stricken-faced officer brought Nagumo an addendum from the *Tone* pilot: *Enemy appears to be accompanied by a carrier bringing up the rear.*

Third, even as Nagumo was digesting this shocker, a different alarm signal flashed through the task force: *"Submarine!"*

Fourth, at precisely this juncture, his own first-strike airplanes began arriving back from Midway, winging in sight, low on fuel, some shot up and in distress, demanding to land on the cluttered carrier decks.

Nagumo found himself driven to the wall. A second strike on Midway? No, not *now;* not with an enemy aircraft carrier full of elite pilots within range! The order of his two missions was rudely reversed. No longer was he attacking the atoll; he himself was threatened with a crossfire of land-based bombers and carrier aircraft. Before anything else, he had to get that carrier.

The air raid proved to be only some old-type scout bombers buzzing a battleship of the screen and then running away from the Zeroes into the light clouds. Destroyers swarming over the supposed submarine found nothing. What to do now? The obvious course was to hit out at that carrier at once: turn into the wind, order the *Soryu* and the *Hiryu* to launch their planes all spotted and ready to go, and send off the Type-97s crowding his own decks. These now were armed with bombs, of course, not torpedoes—the ones with torpedoes were below—but bombs were better than nothing. That would clear the decks to recover the first strike, while getting right after the foe.

But it was such a weak gesture for the great Nagumo Force! A fraction of his power, without the punch of torpedoes, without fighter escort, for the fighters were mostly aloft and low on fuel. All morning Nagumo had been watching the slaughter of unescorted bombers. And what about that cardinal rule of war, the concentration of force?

Then again, he could keep calm, and call for cool heads and quick hands; clear *all* decks, including the *Soryu* and the *Hiryu,* by striking aircraft below; recover all planes from Midway, and all fighters of the combat air patrol; refuel and arm all aircraft, while closing the enemy at flank speed; and *then* hit him in the coordinated attack prescribed by doctrine, with his massed air might.

Of course, that would take time; perhaps as much as an hour. Delay in carrier warfare could be risky.

As Vice Admiral Nagumo weighed this momentous choice, surrounded on the flag bridge by the anxious faces of his staff—while all over the task force antiaircraft guns still rattled, and ships heeled and turned in a tangle of crisscrossing white wakes on the remarkably smooth blue sea, and the planes returning from Midway roared low, round and round the *Akagi,* and Zeroes drove off the last of the slow enemy bombers, and the thousand noises of a carrier in action rose all around him—at this fateful moment Nagumo got a message from his subordinate, the division commander of the *Soryu* and the *Hiryu*:

URGENT. CONSIDER IT ADVISABLE TO LAUNCH ATTACK FORCE IMMEDI-
ATELY.

The officer who had to hand Nagumo this paper probably did not dare look him in the face. In any navy in the world, such a message from a subordinate in the heat of battle would have been an insult; in the Imperial Japanese Fleet it was suicidal effrontery. This man Yama-guchi was considered the most brilliant officer in the navy after Yama-moto, whom he was destined to succeed. Surely he knew the gravity of his act. He apparently thought that the battle might hang on this mo-ment, and that sacrificing his career didn't matter.

Old men are not to be pushed that way. Nagumo immediately did the opposite: ordered all planes struck below—*including Yamaguchi's*—and directed the entire task force to recover aircraft. So the die was cast; it would be a full coordinated attack.

And now for the first time he broke radio silence to inform Admiral Yamamoto, idling three hundred miles away with the seven battleships and one carrier of the Main Body, that he was heading to destroy an enemy force of one carrier, five cruisers, and five destroyers. Until that moment, ten long days after leaving Hiroshima Bay, the commander-in-chief had been utterly in the dark about what was happening to his at-tack plan.

So once again the Type-97s rolled to the elevators; once again they sank to the hangar decks; once again switching commenced. Bombs had at first replaced torpedoes, now torpedoes were replacing bombs, and still these airplanes had never left the ships. Possibly some Japanese muttering about "the idiots up there" went with the loaders' heavy labor, under the lash of loudspeakers howling exhortations from the flag bridge. But if so, it must have been good-natured. These sailors had seen American dive-bombers flying to pieces, dropping into the sea, streak-ing down afire like meteors, in defeated wave upon wave. They had watched the harmless fall of giant bombs from cowardly B-17s flying too high for the Zeroes, and the impotent American torpedoes flounder-ing and breaking. Overhead they could hear the roar and the thud of the triumphant first strike returning from Midway. A more glorious vic-tory than Pearl Harbor was in the making! So these hard-working youngsters, stripped to the waist and pouring sweat, undoubtedly felt as they scattered seventeen-hundred-pound bombs in disorder on the deck and feverishly strapped in place the heavy torpedoes.

In less than an hour the four carrier crews recovered all aircraft, rearmed them, refueled them, and spotted them on the flight decks ready to go. No doubt pleased with this superb performance, and with his own sturdy decision not to go off half-cocked, Nagumo was speeding northeast to pull away from Midway's annoying bombers and to strike at the American carrier.

The sun had now been up for almost four and a half hours.

The unescorted *Enterprise* dive-bombers, reaching the point where the staff navigators had predicted that they would intercept the enemy, saw nothing but cloud-flecked ocean, fifty miles in every direction. Onward and westward they flew. Warren's fuel-gauge needle was wobbling below the halfway mark. If within twenty minutes they turned back, he calculated, they might make it to the *Enterprise,* since it was steadily closing the range. But to go back with loaded bomb racks! For years he had imagined a combat dive at an enemy flattop, and now the reality was so goddamn close! Did anybody in charge, from Rear Admiral Spruance down to Lieutenant Commander McClusky, know what the hell he was doing? This harum-scarum Charge of the Light Brigade through the clouds was hardly a match for the Japs' brute professionalism. Would he even see the *Enterprise* again, without first dropping in the drink?

It seemed such a pitiful, stupid trap—a great flight of dive-bombers howling down the sky in disciplined echelons, loaded to strike, but heading nowhere except for the water. The enemy already lay behind and to the northeast, Warren was sure of that. Browning's staff navigators must have assumed that the Japs would continue to close the atoll at full speed, but obviously they had slowed to evade bomber attacks from Midway, and perhaps to launch aircraft. Gagged by radio silence, how could he point this out to McClusky, whose plane led the serried blue bombers hundreds of yards up ahead and above; was it his place to do it, and would the group commander listen to him, anyway?

Impulsively he slid back his oil-streaked canopy. The thin frigid air swept cigarette smoke and stale machine smells from the heated cockpit. He was breathing hard as on a mountain top, but he did not want to use oxygen; the soppy mask was irksome, and he preferred to smoke. His fuel predicament did not worry him too much. On the return from the Marcus raid his damaged engine had quit, and he had ditched, hitting into a foaming swell with an impact like a crash on land; but he and his rear gunner, Cornett's predecessor, had gotten the raft out of the sinking bomber and had floated for six hours, eating chocolate and swapping stories, before a destroyer had picked them up. Ditching was a nasty but manageable maneuver.

But this futile wandering of the two dive-bomber squadrons angered him to his heart. Stoically, he hoped that the *Hornet* and *Yorktown* planes, and maybe Gene Lindsey's torpedo squadron, would find the son-of-a-bitching Japs and so some harm; or that McClusky would turn northeast, or else go back and gas up for another try, instead of deep-sixing thirty-three Dauntlesses.

At this point, Wade McClusky did turn northeast.

Warren could not know—happily for him—what a sorry farce the whole American attack was degenerating into.

In the Japanese strike on Midway, one hundred eight aircraft from four carriers—fighters, dive-bombers, Type-97s—had joined up and flown out as a single attack group, performed their mission like clock-work, and returned in a disciplined formation. But in this American strike each carrier had sent off its own planes at odd times. The slow torpedo squadrons had soon lost contact with the fighters and the dive-bombers. No American pilot knew what other squadrons than his own were doing, let alone where the Japanese were. Disorganization could go little further.

The *Hornet* dive-bombers and fighters, in abysmal futility, had already fallen out of the fight. At the vacant intercept point their group leader had turned south toward the atoll, away from Nagumo's force. This group had then broken apart, some flying on to Midway to refuel, others turning back to the *Hornet*. Most of the latter would splash with dead engines.

While the *Enterprise* squadrons under McClusky were blundering westward, the *Yorktown* had finally launched, well after nine o'clock—but it had sent off only half its planes. Rear Admiral Fletcher was saving the rest for some emergency. Nagumo's carriers meanwhile were plowing northward, his intact air force fueled and rearmed, preparing to launch at half past ten a total coordinated attack with a hundred two planes.

Only one eccentric element—as it were, one wild card—remained in this all but played-out game: the three slow American torpedo squadrons. These were operating out of sight of each other, in a random and quite unplanned way. No torpron had any idea where another torpron was. The commanders of these weak and outmoded machines, three tough mavericks named Waldron, Lindsey, and Massey, were doing their own navigation. It was they who found the Japanese.

"Fifteen torpedo planes, bearing 130!"

Nagumo and his staff were not caught by surprise, though the absence—again!—of fighter escort must have astounded them. The bearing showed the planes were coming from the carrier Nagumo was closing to destroy. Fifteen planes, one squadron; naturally the Yank carrier would try to strike first. But the vice admiral, with an advantage, as he believed, of four to one in ships and planes, was not worried. He had no idea that he was closing three carriers. The float plane pilot from the cruiser *Tone* had never reported the other two.

There was an ironic fatality about this search pilot. He had been launched half an hour late, and so had made his crucial sighting late. He had failed at first to recognize the flattop he saw; and thereafter he had not mentioned the other carriers. Having turned in this sorry performance, he vanished from history; like the asp that bit Cleopatra, small creature on whom the fortunes of an empire had briefly and sadly turned.

The fifteen aircraft sailing in against Nagumo were Torpedo Squadron Eight of the *Hornet*. Their leader, John Waldron, a fierce and ironminded aviator, led his men in on their required straight slow runs—with what feelings one cannot record, because he was among the first to die—through a thick antiaircraft curtain of smoke and shrapnel, and a swarming onslaught of Zeroes. One after another, as they tried to spread out for an attack on both bows of the carriers, Waldron's planes caught fire, flew apart, splashed in the sea. Only a few lasted long enough to drop their torpedoes. Those who did accomplished nothing, for none hit. In a few minutes it was over, another complete Japanese victory.

But even as the fifteenth plane burst into flames off the *Akagi's* bow and tumbled smoking into the blue water, a strident report from a screening vessel staggered everybody on the flag bridge: *"Fourteen torpedo planes approaching!"*

Fourteen MORE? The dead, risen from the sea as in some frightful old legend, to fight on for their country in their wrecked planes? The Japanese mind is poetic, and such a thought could have flashed on Nagumo, but the reality was plain and frightening enough. American carriers each had but one torpedo squadron; this meant that *at least one more carrier was coming at him.* The report of the accursed *Tone* float plane was therefore worthless. There might be four more carriers, or seven. Who could tell what devilry the ingenious Americans were up to? Japanese intelligence had flatly failed. As Nagumo had once sneaked up on Pearl Harbor, could the enemy not have sneaked several new carriers into the Pacific Ocean?

"Speed all preparations for immediate takeoff!"

The panicky order, abandoning coordinated attack, went out to the four carriers. The air raid bugles brayed, the thick black-puffing AA thumped out from the screen, the carriers broke formation to dodge the attackers, and the Zeroes, halting the slow climb to combat patrol altitude, dove at this new band of unescorted craft. These were Gene Lindsey's squadron from the *Enterprise.* The scarred, unwell commander had led them straight to the enemy while McClusky groped westward. Ten planes went down, Lindsey's among them. Four evaded the slaughterers, dropped their torpedoes, and headed back for their ship. If any torpedo hit, it did not detonate.

Yet another big victory! But all steaming order was now gone from the Carrier Striking Force. Evasive maneuvering had pulled the *Hiryu* almost out of sight to the north, and strung the *Akagi,* the *Kaga,* and the *Soryu* in a line from west to east. The screening vessels were scattered from horizon to horizon, streaming smoke and cutting across each other's long curved wakes. The sailors and officers were working away on the carrier flight decks with unabated zest. They had already cheered the flaming fall of dozens of bombers from Midway, and now two waves of Yank torpedo craft had been minced up by the Zeroes! The four flight decks were crammed with aircraft; none quite set for launch, but all fueled and bomb-loaded, and all in a vast tangle of fuel lines, bombs, and torpedoes, which the deck crews were cheerfully sweating to clear away, so that the airmen could zoom off to the kill.

Warren Henry had thought of the *Enterprise* as an eggshell eight hundred feet long, full of dynamite and human beings. Here were four such eggshells; more nearly, four grandiose floating fuel and ammunition dumps, uncovered to the touch of a match.

"Enemy torpedo planes, bearing 095!"

This third report came after a short quiet interval. The Zeroes were heading up to the station whence they could repulse dive-bombers from on high, or knock down more low-skimming torpedo planes, whichever would appear. The four carriers were turning into the wind to launch; but now they resumed twisting and dodging, while all eyes turned to the low-flying attackers, and to the combat patrol diving in a rush for more clay-pigeon shooting. Twelve torpedo planes were droning in from the *Yorktown.* These did have a few escort fighters weaving desperately above them, but it made little difference. Ten were knocked down; two survived after dropping torpedoes in vain. All three torpedo squadrons were now wiped out, and the Nagumo Carrier Striking Force was untouched. The time was twenty minutes past ten.

"Launch the attack!"

The order went out all through the force. The first fighter escort plane soared off the deck of the *Akagi*.

At that very moment the almost unrecognizable voice of a staff officer uttered a scream which perhaps rang on in Nagumo's ears until he died two years later on the island of Saipan, under attack by another Raymond Spruance task force:

"HELL-DIVERS!"

In two slanting lines stretching upward into the high clouds, unopposed by a single fighter, dark blue planes were dropping on the flagship and on the *Kaga*. The Zeroes were all at water level, where they had knocked down so many torpedo planes and were looking for more. A more distant scream came from a lookout pointing eastward: *"HELL-DIVERS!"* A second dotted line of dark blue aircraft was arrowing down toward the *Soryu*.

It was a perfect coordinated attack. It was timed almost to the second. It was a freak accident.

Wade McClusky had sighted a lone Japanese destroyer heading northeast. It must be returning from some mission, he had guessed; if so, it was scoring a long white arrow on the sea pointing toward Nagumo. He had made the simple astute decision to turn and follow the arrow.

Meantime, the torpedo attacks of Waldron, Lindsey, and Massey had followed hard upon each other by luck. McClusky had sighted the Striking Force at almost the next moment by luck. The *Yorktown's* dive-bombers, launched a whole hour later, had arrived at the same time by luck.

In a planned coordinated attack, the dive-bombers were supposed to distract the enemy fighters, so as to give the vulnerable torpedo planes their chance to come in. Instead, the torpedo planes had pulled down the Zeroes and cleared the air for the dive-bombers. What was not luck, but the soul of the United States of America in action, was this willingness of the torpedo plane squadrons to go in against hopeless odds. This was the extra ounce of martial weight that in a few decisive minutes tipped the balance of history.

So long as men choose to decide the turns of history with the slaughter of youths—and even in a better day, when this form of human sacrifice has been abolished like the ancient, superstitious, but no more horrible form—the memory of these three American torpedo plane squadrons should not die. The old sagas would halt the tale to list the names and birthplaces of men who fought so well. Let this romance follow the tradition. These were the young men of the three squadrons, their names recovered from an already fading record.

• • •

U.S.S. YORKTOWN

TORPEDO THREE

Pilots	*Radiomen-Gunners*
Lance E. Massey, Commanding Descanso, California	Leo E. Perry San Diego, California
Richard W. Suesens Waterloo, Iowa	Harold C. Lundy, Jr. Lincoln, Nebraska
Wesley F. Osmus Chicago, Illinois	Benjamin R. Dodson, Jr. Durham, North Carolina
David J. Roche Hibbing, Minnesota	Richard M. Hansen Lakefield, Minnesota
Patrick H. Hart Los Angeles, California	John R. Cole La Grange, Georgia
John W. Haas San Diego, California	Raymond J. Darce New Orleans, Louisiana
Oswald A. Powers Detroit, Michigan	Joseph E. Mandeville Manchester, New Hampshire
Leonard L. Smith Ontario, California	William A. Phillips Olympia, Washington
Curtis W. Howard Olympia, Washington	Charles L. Moore Amherst, Texas
Carl A. Osberg Manchester, New Hampshire	Troy C. Barkley Falkner, Mississippi
	Robert B. Brazier Salt Lake City, Utah

Survivors

Harry L. Corl Saginaw, Michigan	Lloyd F. Childers Oklahoma City, Oklahoma
Wilhelm G. Esders St. Joseph, Missouri	

U.S.S. ENTERPRISE

TORPEDO SIX

Pilots

Eugene E. Lindsey, Commanding
San Diego, California

Severin L. Rombach
Cleveland, Ohio

John T. Eversole
Pocatello, Idaho

Randolph M. Holder
Jackson, Mississippi

Arthur V. Ely
Pittsburgh, Pennsylvania

Flourenoy G. Hodges
Statesboro, Georgia

Paul J. Riley
Hot Springs, Arkansas

John W. Brock
Montgomery, Alabama

Lloyd Thomas
Chauncey, Ohio

Radiomen-Gunners

Charles T. Grenat
Honolulu, Hawaii

Wilburn F. Glenn
Austin, Texas

John U. Lane
Rockford, Illinois

Gregory J. Durawa
Milwaukee, Wisconsin

Arthur R. Lindgren
Montclair, New Jersey

John H. Bates
Valparaiso, Indiana

Edwin J. Mushinski
Tampa, Florida

John M. Blundell
Fort Wayne, Indiana

Harold F. Littlefield
Bennington, Vermont

Survivors

Albert W. Winchell
Webster City, Iowa

Robert E. Laub
Richland, Missouri

Edward Heck, Jr.
Carthage, Missouri

Irvin H. McPherson
Glen Ellyn, Illinois

Stephen B. Smith
Mason City, Iowa

Douglas M. Cossitt
Oakland, California

William C. Humphrey, Jr.
Milledgeville, Georgia

Doyle L. Ritchey
Ryan, Oklahoma

William D. Horton
Little Rock, Arkansas

Wilfred N. McCoy
San Diego, California

U.S.S. HORNET

TORPEDO EIGHT

Pilots	Radiomen-Gunners

John C. Waldron, Commanding
   Fort Pierre, South Dakota
	Horace F. Dobbs
	   San Diego, California

James C. Owens, Jr.
   Los Angeles, California
	Amelio Maffei
	   Santa Rosa, California

Raymond A. Moore
   Richmond, Virginia
	Tom H. Pettry
	   Ellison Ridge, West Virginia

Jefferson D. Woodson
   Beverly Hills, California
	Otway D. Creasy, Jr.
	   Vinton, Virginia

George M. Campbell
   San Diego, California
	Ronald J. Fisher
	   Denver, Colorado

William W. Abercrombie
   Merriam, Kansas
	Bernard P. Phelps
	   Lovington, Illinois

Ulvert M. Moore
   Bluefield, West Virginia
	William F. Sawhill
	   Mansfield, Ohio

William W. Creamer
   Riverside, California
	Francis S. Polston
	   Nashville, Missouri

John P. Gray
   Columbia, Missouri
	Max A. Calkins
	   Wymore, Nebraska

Harold J. Ellison
   Buffalo, New York
	George A. Field
	   Buffalo, New York

Henry R. Kenyon, Jr.
   Mount Vernon, New York
	Darwin L. Clark
	   Rodney, Iowa

William R. Evans, Jr.
   Indianapolis, Indiana
	Ross E. Bibb, Jr.
	   Warrior, Alabama

Grant W. Teats
   Sheridan, Oregon
	Hollis Martin
	   Bremerton, Washington

Robert B. Miles
   San Diego, California
	Ashwell L. Picou
	   Houma, Louisiana

	Robert K. Huntington South Pasadena, California

Survivor

George H. Gay, Jr.
   Houston, Texas

• • •

Warren Henry had, of course, not a glimmer of this tactical miracle.

Shut in his cockpit, isolated by radio silence, locked into the array of blue bombers roaring through the sky over a thickening cloud cover, all he knew was that McClusky at last had—for one blessed reason or another—turned northeast; that radio silence had been broken by one weak garbled aircraft transmission and another, suggesting that somebody must have found the Japs, the next by a ship's high-powered radio, squawking in the unmistakable high-strung tones of Miles Browning, *"Attack! I say again, ATTACK!"*

For the first time in over two hours, Warren then heard the baritone voice of McClusky, calm, clear, faintly sarcastic, the young professional cooling the excited old fud, *"Wilco, as soon as I find the bastards."* At once he felt a surge of warm confidence in McClusky. Within minutes the Japanese fleet burst into view, a stunning spread of ships from horizon to horizon, showing through breaks in the layer of clouds.

It looked just like the Pacific Fleet on a major battle exercise. That was Warren's first thought, and to dive-bomb them seemed like murder. McClusky droned orders to commence the descent to the attack point. The bomber group sank toward the dazzling white clouds, and broke through the upper layer for a panoramic view of the whole enemy force under wisps of low cloud.

The formation was in bad disorder. Long wakes curled and crisscrossed in the sea like a child's finger painting of white on blue, the screening ships raggedly headed this way and that; black AA puffballs floated all over the scene; and the pale yellow lights of gun muzzles winked everywhere. In his first glimpse Warren had seen only one carrier, but here were three almost in column, all heading into the wind, with black smoke and long, long white wakes streaming straight back; and far to the north was another big ship, possibly a fourth one, in a clump of escorts.

Tiny aircraft in a swarm were flitting and darting at wavetop height among the ships. Warren saw one trail smoke, another burst into flame; some kind of action was going on down there, but *where was the combat air patrol?* The sky was eerily vacant. McClusky was already issuing attack orders! One squadron to one carrier, Scouting Six for the rear flattop, Bombing Six for the second one; let that third one go for now. It was all happening fast, for there was McClusky starting to push over into his dive, and Warren's squadron leader was following him.

From here on this was familiar stuff, plain squadron attack drill, the

ABC of dive-bombing. The one difference—so he told himself in these last seconds, with his hand on the diving brake lever, when he was beginning to feel better than he had ever felt in his whole life—the one difference now was that the oblong thing which he had to hit fifteen thousand feet down there on the sea wasn't a target sled but a carrier! That made the shot a hell of a lot easier. The flight deck was a hundred times the size of a sled. He had more than once splintered the edge of a sled with a dummy bomb.

Yet again, *where was the combat air patrol?* That had been his worry right along, unescorted as they were. This thing so far was an unbelievable cinch. He kept glancing over his shoulders for Zeroes pouncing out of the clouds. There wasn't a sign of them. McClusky and the first few bombers, already on their steep way down far below, one staggered behind the other, weren't even catching any AA. Warren had often pictured and dreamed of attacks on carriers, but never of a walkover like this.

He said into the intercom in high spirits, "Well here we go, I guess, Cornett. All set?"

"Yes, Mr. Henry." Matter-of-fact drawl. "Say, where the heck are the Zeroes, Mr. Henry?"

"Search me. Are you complaining?"

"No sir, Mr. Henry! Just you drop that egg in there, sir."

"Going to try. We'll have the sun on our starboard side. That's where they're likely to show up."

"Okay, Mr. Henry. I've got my eye peeled. Good luck."

Warren pulled the lever of his diving flaps. The perforated metal V opened all along his wings. The airplane mushily slowed. The flattop went out of sight beside the fuselage, under the wing. The nose came up, the plane gave its almost living warning shudder; Warren pushed over, dizzily dropped the nose straight toward the water far, far below, and straightened out in a roller-coaster plunge.

And there, by God, was the carrier in his telescopic sight, right over the little wobbling ball. Now if the telescope only wouldn't fog up as they plunged into the warmer air! Visibility through the oily film of the canopy wouldn't be very good.

It was an excellent dive. The danger was always overshooting and standing on your head, when the dive was almost impossible to control, but he was dropping toward the flattop at a beautiful angle, maybe sixty-five, seventy degrees, from almost dead astern, a little to port, perfect. He wasn't sitting on his seat now but hanging facedown in his straps, the pure dive sensation. He always thought it was like jumping off a high dive board. There was the same headfirst feeling, the same queaziness in gut and balls that you never got over. It was a long way down, almost a whole minute, and he had excellent controls to straighten out slips or wobbles, but this dive was going fine. With a pedal jammed in hard to neutralize the SBD's usual yaw, they were skimming down sweetly, the throttled-back engine purring, the air whiffling noisily on the brakes—and that flight deck was sitting right there in his little lens, not fogging over at all, growing bigger and plainer, with the hardwood decking bright yellow in the sunlight, the big red ball conspicuous in the white oblong forward of the island, the planes crowded aft in a jumble, and minuscule Japs running around them like insects. As his altimeter reeled backward his ears popped and the plane warmed.

All at once he saw the great white splash of a near-miss jump up alongside the island; and then a huge fiery explosion ripped the white paint all around the meatball, with a blast of smoke. So there was one hit! He could see two bombers zooming away. His ears ached like hell. He swallowed, and they popped again. Right now that carrier was in trouble; one more good hit could really cream it. Warren was at five thousand feet. Doctrine called for the bomb drop at about three thousand feet, but he meant to bore down at least to twenty-five hundred. Joyously in control, watching his dials, watching the rapidly expanding deck almost straight below him, he was nerving himself for a split-second decision. He intended to slam the bomb in among those aircraft sitting there in his scope; but if this carrier took yet another hit first, then instead of plastering it again with a precious half-ton bomb, he might still veer over and try to hit the third carrier, far ahead.

But what a target, that mess of airplanes rushing up at him now in the telescopic sight, so clear that he could see white numbers on the fuselages, and the little Japs running and gesticulating as he plunged toward them! No other hits yet; *he'd go*. Now his heart was racing, his mouth was parched, and his ears seemed about to burst. He yanked the bomb release, felt the jolt of lightness as the missile flew clear, remembered to keep going to make sure he didn't throw the bomb, and he pulled up.

His body sagged to the seat, his head swam, his stomach seemed to plop against his backbone, the gray mist came and went; he kicked the plane's tail and glanced backward . . . Oh, *CHRIST!*

A sheet of white fire was climbing out of those airplanes, billowing black smoke; and even as he looked, the fire spread and exploded along the deck and arched into the air in beautiful colors, red, yellow, purple, pink, with varicolored smoke towering up into the sky. What a terrific change in a second or two! Debris was flying in every direction, pieces of airplanes, pieces of the deck, whole human bodies tumbling upward like tossed rag dolls; what a horrible unbelievable magnificent sight! The whole wild holocaust of fire and smoke went roaring skyward and streaming astern, for the stricken carrier was still rushing at full speed into the wind.

"Mr. Henry, there's a Zero at eight o'clock angels about one thousand." Cornett on the intercom. "He's making a run on us."

"Roger." Warren nosed over and dove for the water, violently jinking and yawing. The waves were breaking in long white crests, and he hurtled along through spume that spattered his canopy like hail, dodging erratically, grateful for the sturdy response of the SBD-3 to the crazy maneuvers. This was doctrine: hug the water, make the Jap miss, lure him to dive into the sea. The plane shook and his teeth jarred as Cornett's gun began a furious rattle. Warren saw bullets splashing a line in the water a few yards forward of his nose, and glancing up he caught sight of the Zero diving at him, squirting yellow flame and white smoke. The fighter that had knocked him down over Pearl Harbor had been a peacetime silver color; this was a dirty mottled greenish-brown, but those big red balls on the wings were just the same. The Zero pulled up smack at the waterline and disappeared into AA smoke; ye gods, those damned things were maneuverable.

Warren flew past a tragic sight, caught in a flash out of the corner of his eye—a blue wing with a white star, sticking out of the water; just the wing. It vanished, and a huge gray ship slid into view before his windshield with forty yellow lights blinking at him, surely a battleship or a heavy cruiser. Antiaircraft began bursting around him in sooty explosions that rocked and hammered the plane. In seconds the vessel stretched out dead ahead, blocking his way, a vast gray steel wall. Warren pulled up for dear life and the Dauntless soared over the forecastle, much lower than the crooked pagoda mast, barely clearing the forward turret of long gray guns.

So he was out of the screen now! If his luck would hold and he could outdistance the AA batteries that from behind were spattering shrapnel on the water all around him—

"Mr. Henry, that sumbitch is *back*. He been follerin' us all the way."

"Roger."

Warren tried to repeat his wild dodging, flying as close to the water as he dared, but the airplane was now acting sluggish. The red tracers from the Zero came raining down along his port side, kicking up white water spurts. He veered hard right and almost caught a wing in a wave top. The plane was not answering as before.

"*Yippee!* Mr. Henry, I think maybe I got the sumbitch." Cornett sounded like a kid at a high school ball game. "I swear he's headin' home to mama. Take a look, Mr. Henry, he's dead astern. He's smokin'."

The Dauntless turned and climbed. The attacker was shrinking away toward the enemy task force, trailing a smudge of smoke; and beyond it, beyond the ships of the screen, all three carriers were vomiting flame and black smoke upward into the blue sunny sky. Who had got the third carrier, he wondered? Had some other pilot done what he'd thought of doing? That third flattop was on fire, not a doubt in the world of it. Those three black smoke pillars were rising high over the task force like three black plumes on a hearse.

Now he looked at his watch, at the fuel gauge, and at the flight chart. It was 10:30, and he had winged over for the attack at 10:25; he had lived a lot of his life in five minutes! The fuel was too low to bear thinking about. He was sure the staff's Point Option position was wrong. Those stupid staff bastards had probably figured that Spruance would advance at full speed—same mistake as with the Japs—when chances were he had turned into the wind to recover the combat air patrol or returning aircraft. Warren headed for the 1000 position bearing, grimly noting that the craft's response was still sluggish.

"That was some hit, Mr. Henry. Gee, did that baby go up!"

"Say, Cornett, watch the tail assembly. I'm going to waggle the controls. Tell me if there's any damage to the surfaces."

"Yes, Mr. Henry. Oh, Judas Priest, you got no rudder, sir. Just a small ragged hunk."

"Well, okay." Warren quenched an upwelling of alarm. "We're heading home to mama ourselves."

"We gonna make it, Mr. Henry?"

"Dunno why not," Warren said with more cheer than he felt. "We may have to sling a couple of chocolate bars in the tank."

"Well, anyway, Mr. Henry," Cornett said with a most un-Cornett-like merry laugh, "whatever happens, it was worth it, just to get that hit, and watch them sumbitches burning back there."

"Concur."

Now the thought came to Warren as a gladsome surprise that radio silence was finished. He gambled the gasoline to climb to two thousand feet, and tuned in on the *Enterprise*'s Y-E homing signal. Loud and clear, from the 1000 position dead ahead, came the Morse-code letter he expected. He throttled back near stalling speed, and settled down near the tossing whitecapped swells. It would be a close thing, but there were always the rescue destroyers. In his exalted mood, a water landing held no terror for him. He could still see the flames billowing, the planes exploding, the bodies flying on that Jap carrier. He had done it; *done it,* and he was alive and heading back in glory.

Many miles astern, Vice Admiral Nagumo was being dragged off the flaming, listing *Akagi* by his staff officers. Picking his way among the broken corpses roasting with a kitchen stench on the red-hot deck plates, which still shuddered with explosions, he was fussily insisting that there was no real need yet to abandon ship. He had not authorized his subordinate Yamaguchi in the unhit *Hiryu* to take command, or even to launch at discretion. Climbing down a rope ladder to a cruiser's whale boat, the distraught old gentleman remained the commander-in-chief of the ruined Carrier Attack Force. But Yamaguchi was not waiting any longer for orders from Nagumo, who had probably just lost the war for Japan. On seeing the first bombs raise smoke and fire on the *Kaga,* he had commenced an immediate counterstrike.

*   *   *

31
Midway (Concluded)

(from *World Holocaust* by Armin von Roon)

Second Phase

The opening phase of the battle occupied most of the morning of June 4.
The middle phase lasted five minutes.
The end took four days.

The annals of military conflict, from their dim origins in Chinese and Egyptian accounts to the present era, show no equal to the world-historical second phase, the Five Minutes of Midway.

Between 10:25 A.M. and 10:30 A.M. of that fateful day, in that mere instant of combat time, three Japanese carriers, with their full complements of aircraft, were reduced to smoking flotsam. These giant victims embodied the national strength and treasure of Japan, the culmination of half a century of heroic effort to become a first-class military power. In those five explosive minutes, Japan's world status, laboriously built up from Tsushima Strait to Singapore, Manila, and Burma, was shattered; though she had yet to suffer three years of defeat and final atomic-blast horror before accepting this fact.

After Midway, as Admiral von Nimitz once put it, "We fought the Pacific war just as we had worked it out for twenty years in the War College" (a remark that sufficiently suggests the long-range aggressive intent of the Anglo-American plutocracies). The rest of that war is tangential to German readers' interests, but this brilliant classic of sea warfare must be studied.

Chance thrust an unknown junior flag officer into full command of the combined American task forces in mid-battle. Vice Admiral Halsey, a sort of seagoing General Patton full of dash and swagger, had fallen ill just before the fleet sortied, otherwise he would have led the fight. The replacement he suggested was his friend Raymond A. Spruance, a quiet man who commanded his screen. Rear Admiral Frank Jack Fletcher, commanding Task

Force Seventeen, was senior to Spruance. Nimitz intended that Fletcher run the battle. Luck dropped it into Spruance's hands, and Spruance proceeded to show himself one of the great admirals of world history. The United States of America has been a lucky nation, and this luck held remarkably on June 4, 1942. How long it will hold in the future, only the dark gods know who bestowed on this crass mercantile nation of mongrelized blood and cowboy culture a virgin continent with almost infinite natural resources.

Spruance made three historic decisions at Midway. This shy and reticent man, of no remarkable blood or background, unveiled an astounding capacity to think and act in the thick of battle. After Midway he won many victories in command of ever-vaster forces; yet in history, like Nelson of Trafalgar, he will remain Spruance of Midway.

The First Decision

Spruance's first great decision was to launch all the aircraft of the *Hornet* and the *Enterprise* at extreme range at seven o'clock in the morning, risking everything to get in the first surprise blow. The risk proved costly. Several of his squadrons could not even find the enemy. Almost half his planes ran out of gasoline and fell in the water, or returned with their bombs, or flew on to Midway atoll without fighting. Yet enough dive-bombers reached the Nagumo force to execute the blitz that left the *Akagi*, the *Kaga*, and the *Soryu* in flames. Nothing else mattered. Spruance won this world-historical gamble.

Here too he enjoyed American luck, for his wandering squadrons met up over the Japanese fleet for a combined attack by chance. The dive-bombers did all the damage. The torpedo planes were wiped out. By contrast, later that day, Japanese torpedo planes from the *Hiryu* drove home an attack and wrecked the *Yorktown*. Technically as well as numerically, the Americans were outclassed at Midway. This only highlights Spruance's leadership.

Rear Admiral Fletcher cautiously delayed his *Yorktown* launching for over an hour. He then sent out only half of his aircraft. When the torpedoed *Yorktown* had to be abandoned, Fletcher moved his flag to a screening cruiser, and passed command of all forces to Spruance. This was the only important act in the military career of Fletcher that this historian has been able to ascertain.

TRANSLATOR'S NOTE: *When Fletcher had to abandon the* Yorktown, *he signalled Spruance, "I will conform to your movements," thus generously yield-*

*ing up leadership of a great battle. That was more than Nagumo ever did.
Fletcher knew that Spruance had the staff, the communications, and the
carriers to continue the battle. He did the sensible thing.—V.H.*

Nagumo's Dither

In even sharper contrast to Spruance stands the performance of Nagumo.

Here was a carrier flag officer as experienced as Spruance was green, commanding the best carrier force afloat. Under the same pressures that beset Spruance, with a seasoned staff that swiftly executed his every wish, with vessels and air squadrons that operated with ballet precision, Nagumo fell apart, and threw away a battle that almost could not be lost.

Here was more American luck. The catapult of the cruiser *Tone* was defective, so the search plane assigned to the sector where the Americans happened to be hiding did not get off on time. The pilot sent vague reports. But popular accounts make too much of the famous "*Tone* float plane." Nothing is commoner in warfare than unreliable scout or sentry reports. As soon as Nagumo learned of the presence of American ships, he should have assumed that they were carriers, and urgently prepared to attack. Instead, he dithered. Under air harassment from Midway that did him no harm, he kept changing his mind about his next move, and switching the armament of his Type-97 planes. Spruance's dive-bombers resolved his dilemma by destroying him.

Nagumo himself escaped with his life from the *Akagi* by climbing down a rope from his bridge. Unlike Fletcher, he clung to command, though in Rear Admiral Yamaguchi aboard the *Hiryu* he had a fine subordinate in position to fight on. One wonders what Vice Admiral Nagumo's feelings must have been as he boated in the open sea while three carriers burned in the morning sunshine before his eyes, the funeral pyres of Japan's first-line carrier pilots and aircraft, a loss beyond replacing. His conduct afterward suggests he was in shock, for he ordered pell-mell retreat and reported to Yamamoto at one point that five American carriers were chasing him. Yamamoto relieved him in the middle of the night. Yamaguchi, who might have won the battle, elected to go down with the *Hiryu*.

Aside from the dither, Nagumo committed another unpardonable mistake. Just prior to the fatal five minutes, he allowed the whole combat air patrol to abandon altitude and swarm down on the torpedo planes. Where torpedo planes appeared, dive-bombers could not be far behind. Had half the fighters stayed aloft, the whole story of the battle and possibly of the

Second World War might have been different; but at the moment of maximum peril the upper sky was unguarded.

Spruance's Second Decision

The tragic dispatch of the disaster came to Fleet Admiral Yamamoto, three hundred miles away, after long tense hours of silence, during which he had every reason to suppose that Nagumo was enjoying his customary success. As though sensing trouble ahead, Yamamoto for days had been sick at his stomach. Now, learning the worst, the ailing old man rallied.

Very well, he seems to have decided, Japan had lost the first round. Aggressive American naval doctrine would undoubtedly draw Nagumo's conqueror westward in pursuit. Here then was a golden chance to counter-ambush and smash the thin Nimitz forces! He was on sound ground; many famous victories have followed on initial setbacks in the field. Yamamoto still had the enemy heavily outnumbered and outgunned in his Main Body. The four dispersed light carriers could be summoned. The *Hiryu* was intact. Urgent dispatches shot out to the scattered Imperial Fleet to close in around Yamamoto's battleships.

From then until nightfall of June 4, on the flag bridge of the great battleship *Yamato,* the mood seesawed with the flux of the news. The reply of the carriers in the Aleutians caused gloom. They could not join up for three days. The *Hiryu* reported that her pilots had dive-bombed an enemy carrier, and then that her torpedo planes had left a second carrier dead in the water. This caused great joy, but it was a mistake. The *Hiryu* had struck the *Yorktown* twice—once with dive-bombers, again and fatally with torpedo planes—but good American damage control had totally quenched the fires of the first attack. The glee died when at sunset the *Hiryu* reported that it too was hit and ablaze.

Still Yamamoto grimly bore eastward. His aim now was to force a night action. If only he could himself encounter the thin-skinned American carriers! His great guns could sink them like ferryboats, lay waste to the screening vessels, and turn defeat into victory; and he could then still take Midway. The whole hope now was that Americans in hot pursuit would spit themselves on the eighteen-inch guns of the *Yamato,* the tremendous firepower of the other battleships and cruisers, and the devastating "long-lance" torpedoes of the Japanese destroyer squadrons.

Had Vice Admiral William F. Halsey been in command of the United States ships that probably would have happened. In such situations Halsey's nature was to fling himself with impetuous bellicosity after his wounded foe.

But Raymond Spruance was in command. Spruance steamed toward the oncoming Yamamoto force just long enough to catch the *Hiryu* and destroy it. He then recovered his aircraft *and reversed course to the eastward away from the enemy.* After midnight he again reversed course, and at dawn he was back in position to protect Midway with air cover from a possible landing.

This maneuver was the key to the victory at Midway; the finest command decision in the Pacific war, and one of the finest in the history of sea combat. It was wisdom itself, simplicity itself, with world consequences at stake.

It was not so regarded at the time. Spruance was chided even during the battle by his superiors in Pearl Harbor and Washington for failing to pursue the beaten foe that night. His own staff—or rather, Halsey's staff, which did not like or understand their new nonaviator admiral—was disconcerted by his decision. Afterward, staff officers asserted that radar would have detected oncoming surface forces, and so the task force should never have lost contact with the enemy. This view persists in American military literature, and Raymond Spruance is still sometimes called an overcautious officer.

The criticism is erroneous. Having already won a crucial battle with far inferior forces, this brilliant commander would not stake his victory on a new electronic gadget. Instead, he put his fleet where without question it remained both secure and dangerous. Neither Spruance nor Nimitz knew where Yamamoto's battleships were. Rear Admiral Spruance escaped Yamamoto's terrible trap by acting on perfect military instinct. Not till many months later did American intelligence ferret out the facts about Yamamoto's moves, which confirmed Spruance's blind second decision as a historic masterstroke.

Spruance's Third Decision

Shortly after midnight Yamamoto sensed that he had been foiled, that the night action would not take place, and that daylight might find him well within range of Midway's airplanes. Anguished flag conferences ensued. For Yamamoto and his staff, huddling in the luxurious undamaged flag country of the mightiest battleship afloat, leading a battle line of stupendous firepower through the night, there must have been a sickening sense of frustration. The combined fleet was like a gorilla confronting a cobra; if only once it could lay its paws on its puny foe and tear it to ribbons! But the cobra had struck and vanished.

Yamamoto's operations officer, the same Captain Kuroshima, now put forward a gallant proposal. Let the Imperial Fleet steam straight on to the atoll, and with dawn's first light let it pulverize the air installations with gunfire and proceed with the landing! The atoll's planes had failed against Nagumo, after all, and a swarm of them had splashed. The ones that remained must be poor stuff. As for the American carriers, they had suffered huge plane losses, and two (as he thought) were out of action or sunk. The concentrated AA of the Main Force, with cruiser float planes and the aircraft of two light carriers, could surely handle the surviving American carrier strength.

But the plan was hooted at as suicidal folly. There was little impulse for daring left in the staff. Yamamoto straightway rejected Kuroshima's idea, and with all respect to this great warrior's memory, the present writer wonders why. Spruance was in fact substantially weakened by plane losses. The Midway air strength was a shoddy mishmash of ineffective army and marine units. However, there is an inexorable rhythm to battles. The time for dash had passed on the Japanese side.

Nevertheless Yamamoto was more than ready to fight on in his own way. The atoll could not now be seized, but the small Pacific Fleet had been drawn far out beyond its Pearl Harbor air umbrella, and that was a great chance. If only it could be brought to battle and smashed, history would still call the Midway operation a success.

Yamamoto projected two more traps for the foe. He would retreat westward. No doubt the enemy would pursue with harassing tactics. He hoped now to lure the foe within the seven-hundred-mile airpower circle of Wake Island, and there pounce on him with his great force——battleships, heavy cruisers, and destroyer divisions. This giant force had not yet fired a gun or seen an enemy aircraft. That it was in retreat from two battle-worn American carriers and their escorts was grotesque.

Simultaneously, he ordered the carriers in the Aleutians to attack again. The capture of Attu and Kiska was to proceed. The American fleet might then be ordered north, where it would run into four heavy cruisers, a light carrier, and the formidable carrier *Zuikaku,* at last repaired, replenished with fresh pilots and aircraft, and making for the Aleutians at top speed.

The two arms of the gorilla, as it were, would grasp at the cobra from the west and the north.

Spruance did pursue. Naval men say that "a stern chase is a long chase." The last phase dragged on for two days as Yamamoto fell back and the American fleet hunted him. Spruance's surviving dive-bombers did very poorly against targets smaller than aircraft carriers. The only other sinking during the long chase, in fact, was an already damaged heavy cruiser, which had collided with a sister ship in a submarine scare. Kuroshima may have been profoundly right in guessing that Spruance was no threat to the heavy

Main Force. But the staff on the *Enterprise* kept urging Spruance ever westward. The requirement to pursue and annihilate was for them holy writ.

Spruance's third major decision was to disregard this urging, and strong messages from Nimitz as well; to break off the pursuit, and end the battle. He would not enter the airpower circle of Wake Island. This seems a sort of clairvoyance. He is reported to have put it very simply to his staff: "We have done just about all the damage we are going to do. Let's get out of here." His vessels were low on fuel; his aviators were exhausted; an enemy of unknown but heavy strength eluded him beyond the horizon; the known menace of land-based air cancelled out the doctrine of pursuit. So Rear Admiral Raymond Spruance decided, and so he sealed the Midway victory.

At the last moment his work was almost undone, for Chester von Nimitz took the Aleutian bait, and ordered Spruance north! Fortunately, Nimitz later thought better of this, and cancelled the order. On June 11th, Task Force Sixteen returned to Pearl Harbor to learn that Army Air Corps bombers had won the Battle of Midway by sinking four carriers, several battleships, etc., etc. The story was in every newspaper. It was in the weekly magazines. All Hawaii believed it. For a time, all America believed it. Raymond Spruance never issued a contradictory public account. In footnotes to postwar reports and memoirs, the Army Air Corps acknowledged that it did no damage at Midway.

Once, much later in life, when complimented on his victory, Raymond Spruance responded, "There were a hundred Spruances in the Navy. They just happened to pick me for the job." In fact, there was only one Spruance and luck gave him, at a fateful hour, to America.

Strategically, the great Nimitz-Spruance victory accomplished three things:

1. American submarines could continue to depart with full fuel bunkers from Midway instead of Pearl Harbor, a round-trip difference of 2300 miles. This multiplied their killing power in the war. William F. Halsey later wrote that the submarine campaign was the first cause of Japan's defeat.
2. Japan's first-line carrier squadrons were drowned or shot down off Midway. The loss of this cadre of leaders and trainers could never be made up.
3. Japan passed overnight, in morale, from élan to desperation. Morally, from 10:30 A.M. June 4, 1942, onward, Japan was on the run, though this brave race gave a good account of itself to the last.

Yamamoto: Vale

The trounced Imperial Fleet skulked back into Hiroshima Bay. Yamamoto still did not know that he had been beaten not by Nimitz, nor even by the famous Halsey, but by an anonymous replacement, plucked from the ranks of American rear admirals.

The Americans sent but four rear admirals into the fight: Fletcher, Spruance, and the two screen commanders. By contrast, the Imperial Fleet sailed under the great Fleet Admiral Yamamoto himself, flanked by five vice admirals and thirteen rear admirals. In essence, Yamamoto took his headquarters to sea. Nimitz elected to keep his ashore, where it could use the radio, get information, and maintain broad perspective. Nimitz's course was the sounder.

Yamamoto, who had brought off the monumental air victory of Pearl Harbor, rode through Midway on a silenced giant, the world's biggest gunship. In retrospect, he seems not to have grasped the lesson of sea-air power which he himself taught the world. In his battle plan, the carriers were to clear away the land-based air menace; then he was to steam forward in massive grandeur with the Main Body, meet the Nimitz fleet head-on, and win the Pacific Battle of the Skagerrak. This delusory vision kept him out of action at Midway.

Radio Tokyo claimed a vast triumph, but the name of Midway was thereafter blotted from Japanese war reporting. The survivors were put into quarantine. So many records were suppressed or lost that the Japanese side of the battle will never be adequately documented. Yet Yamamoto did not fall. He was Japan's greatest military figure. He had been a naval attaché in the United States. He had represented Japan at the naval conferences of the 1920s, and had won equality for her with the white man's sea powers. He had been against the war with America, but given his sailing orders, he had done his best.

Yamamoto continued to lead his navy until April 1943, when Admiral von Nimitz, learning that Yamamoto was making an air tour of the South Pacific, ordered his plane ambushed and destroyed. So this great man perished. The final stain was on Nimitz. Between Achilles and Hector, there might have been more honor than this sneak murder.

At Midway, the colored man's dramatic military surge in the industrial age was thrown back; perhaps not for all time, since most of mankind is colored; but certainly for fifty or a hundred years. Midway was a solid recovery of the upper hand by the Caucasian after his collapse at Singapore.

Yet before the figure of Isoroku Yamamoto, the military analyst must pause. If Nagumo turned in the typical performance of the colored man under pressure—erratic, dilatory, dithering—Yamamoto rose to disaster with firmness, nobility, and ingenuity worthy of a Moltke or a Manstein. Europe and America should remember that Asia can produce such men.

Midway: The Final Lesson

The five-minute overturn that struck the Japanese nation at Midway compels a final reflection.

Industrial-scientific developments since that time have made possible Midway-style lightning holocausts of entire countries. The new Midway which now threatens is, as is well known, atomic surprise and counter-surprise with colossal rockets, between U.S. capitalism and Russian Bolshevism. These twin brutish materialisms of our age are spiritual hells, incapable of controlling the forces they wield. Today both carry the logic of the aircraft carrier much further. Their entire land masses and their whole populations are now flattop and crew; and both nations are vulnerable and destructive to an unheard-of degree.

The tale must proceed to its dark end. Perhaps our own prostrate, sundered, and mutilated Fatherland will out of its great agony in World War II produce a new philosopher—a Kant, a Hegel, a Nietzsche—to point a way out of mankind's dread cul-de-sac. The German genius has always been for such Faustian reaching beyond the given.

Otherwise the prospect is grave. The Americans and the Russians are blood-brothers in uncultured hardness, though the Americans sometimes seem comfort-mad and the Russians woolly-headed. It means little or nothing to them that in their duel of dimwitted giants most life on earth is menaced, and all human advancement since Roman times seems condemned. As things stand now, one or another of their small allies will one unexpected day prove the Serbia or Poland of the Third World War. It will be no war in the old sense, however. It will be a lightning Midway of the continents.

———

TRANSLATOR'S NOTE: *Roon's racial viewpoint is beneath comment. The shooting down of Fleet Admiral Yamamoto was ordered by the Secretary of the Navy, Frank Knox, a former newspaper publisher. Chester Nimitz was apprised of the plan, and endorsed it on the grounds that Yamamoto was irreplaceable, and in military value to Japan, equal perhaps to four carriers. The Japanese joined Hitler's criminal attack on civilization and had to bear the consequences, Yamamoto among them.—V.H.*

*   *   *

32

CAPTAIN Henry sat slouched over the detective novel in the sea cabin, his head on his hand, a cigarette burning down in his fingers.

"The aviators are breaking radio silence, Cap'n." Hines, the quartermaster, saluting in the doorway.

"Very well." He leaped up and hurried to the wheelhouse, where his attempt to settle at ease in his high chair deceived nobody. The ship's clowns had long been mimicking his stooped posture and quick cigarette gestures when he was tense. Knowing glances went among the men on watch as he crouched and smoked, staring out to sea. Through the bridge loudspeakers came scratchy talk from the weak faraway aircraft transmitters: "... *Earl, you take that one on the left ... Commencing our attack ... Hey! Zeroes at eleven o'clock ... Victor Sail Six, this is Tim Satterlee, I'm hit and ditching, wish me luck ... Wow, look at that big bastard burn! ...*"

"Sounds like they're doing pretty good, sir," ventured the exec, who was pacing and mopping sweat from his face.

Pug only nodded, straining his ears in vain for the timbre of his son's voice; the keyed-up youngsters out there all sounded alike. These garbled fragments peppered with hot obscenities brought laughter and noisy chatter on the bridge, which Pug for once overlooked in his own excitement.

When the transmissions petered out, Captain Henry glanced about him and the bridge talk died. Long silence, with crackling of static. Returning pilots began to give calm position reports, sometimes with a wry joke, as their fuel ran out and they prepared to ditch; from Warren, not a word. After a while radar reported "friendlies" approaching. The fleet swung ponderously into the wind. Pug's lookouts reported specks low in the western sky, which grew into airplanes roaring in over the screen to the carriers. The *Yorktown,* hull down far to the west, was landing its planes, too. As the aircraft came straggling into Pug's binoculars, he resolved *not* to worry if no SBD made a wing-waggling pass over him.

Warren would have a fuel problem like the rest, and might be ditching. Still, as the *Enterprise* dive-bombers landed, he counted them. Thirty-two had departed. Ten . . . eleven . . . twelve . . . A long interval went by; long for him, anyway. Plane after plane kept landing on the *Hornet;* a few on the *Enterprise,* but no more dive-bombers . . .

"*Dauntless off the starboard bow, Captain!*" A shout of the quartermaster from the other wing. Pug darted through the bridge house. Rocking its white-starred wings, the plane thrummed over the forecastle and veered off toward the *Enterprise,* the goggled pilot waving a long arm. Victor Henry kept his face seaward, watching the aircraft come in to land. He would not put a hand up to his wet eyes. Nobody on the bridge came near him. So several minutes passed.

From the bridge house, the exec called, "*Yorktown* reports many bogies on radar, Captain. Bearing two seventy-five, distance forty. Closing speed two hundred knots."

Pug managed to articulate, "Very well. Go to General Quarters."

On the *Enterprise,* the landing officer sliced a paddle past his throat in a grinning cut. Warren's wheels thumped on the deck. Joy swept him as the drag of the arresting gear strained him against his belt. *Home!* He gunned forward over the flattened barriers, killed the engine, and jumped out with his chart board, slapping Cornett on the back as the radioman leaped to the deck. Quickly the handlers shoved the plane toward the elevator.

"Well, we made it," Warren tried to yell over the engine noise of another bomber slanting in to land. The sudden wailing of the general alarm drowned him out. Sailors streamed over the flight deck to battle stations, avoiding the Dauntless that slammed down (*6-S-9, Pete Goff, God bless him!*). Bells clanged, and the loudspeaker bellowed, "*Stand by to launch fighters.*"

Cornett trotted off. Warren dropped into the nearest AA tub. The helmeted gun crew turned surprised eyes at this aviator fallen among them, and the telephone talker gestured toward the flat gray hump on the horizon to the west. "Fire control reports a mess of bogies going for the *Yorktown,* Lieutenant."

"Sure, they've come on her first. Better look sharp, all the same."

"Bet your ass," said the sailor whose steel helmet was stenciled *Gun Captain.* "Sir," he added, showing white teeth, and they all laughed.

In his exaltation Warren thought that these were wonderful-looking American kids, that the weather was amazingly fine, that there was nothing to beat combat in the world, and that this victorious return in a damaged plane, with the fuel needle jammed at zero, was like starting life over with a million dollars. The launching of fighters commenced. Fingers to their ears, Warren and the gun crew peered toward the *Yorktown,* while planes howled off the deck one by one. They were still taking off when a smoke column grew out of the distant gray shape. "Shit, they got her," said the gun captain sadly.

"Maybe their screen's just making smoke," said another sailor.

"That ain't no smoke screen, you idiot," said the gun captain. "That's a goddamn bomb hit, and—*Jesus Christ!*" He frenziedly trained the weapon at a cluster of specks in the sunny sky. "Here comes a gang of the bastards. Straight *at* us."

"*All gun crews, attention.*" The loudspeaker took on an urgent tone. "*Planes approaching on the port quarter are not, repeat not, BOGIES, they are FRIENDLIES. Hold your fire. They are returning* Yorktown *aircraft, low on fuel and requesting emergency landing. The* Yorktown *has been hit. Repeat HOLD YOUR FIRE. Stand by to take planes on board.*"

Plane handlers scampered out on deck with red, yellow, and green jerseys showing under their life jackets. Warren jumped from the gun tub, sprinted across the windy deck, and went below. A glance into the torpedo squadron room sobered him. The teletype was clicking away, and on the unwatched screen words crawled,

YORKTOWN REPORTS THREE BOMB HITS HEAVY DAMAGE BELOW DECKS

Acey-deucey sets, packs of cards, girlie and sports magazines lay about the vacant leather reclining chairs. Ashtrays heaped with cigar and cigarette butts gave off a heavy stale smell. Good God, Lindsey's squadron must have had a bad time! Still, maybe they were elsewhere, in the wardroom or in sick bay, the ones who had got back. . . .

His own squadron room, though far from full, was lively and noisy. Of the ten fliers here, two were reserves who had not gone out. Eight of the eighteen returned so far, then. Only eight! They were talking, laughing, holding coffee or a sandwich in one hand and gesturing airplane maneuvers with the other. Overhead the *Yorktown's* planes were thumping down with snarling engines, while the teletype clicked out a new damage report. She was on fire, dead in the water; damage control parties were beginning to master the blaze, but the *Enterprise* would have to land her search planes, too.

Warren gave the debriefing officer his combat account, chalking out his dive maneuver on the blackboard, while the jubilant pilot talk went on and on—who had gotten a hit, who had missed, who had been attacked by Zeroes, who had been seen on fire or going in the water, who might have ditched on the return leg. About Warren's hit there was no argument: solid, spectacular, confirmed. The rest of the attack was shrouded in dissent, even to the number of carriers observed—five, two, three, four, no consensus whatever; not about that, not about the hits, not even about the near-misses, and some disagreements verged on the acrimonious.

A telephone call from his squadron commander summoned Warren to Air Operations, and he hurried to the dark low crowded plotting room, clamorous with loudspeaker blare. Amid ozone-reeking, green-flashing radar scopes, and big Plexiglas compass roses still marked with orange grease-pencil tracks of the Jap attack, Gallaher was huddling with a refugee lieutenant from the *Yorktown*. McClusky had returned wounded, Gallaher said, so he would lead the group to attack the fourth carrier. Search planes were out to pinpoint its position now. His exec was missing, and Warren was next in line. Warren would have to scratch together a bomber squadron at once, with the surviving pilots of Bombing Six, Scouting Six, and the *Yorktown* aviators. Instant promotion to squadron command seemed quite normal to Warren on this radiant day. Gallaher went off at a call from Miles Browning. Warren sketched an attack plan with the *Yorktown* squadron leader, a hard-faced Southerner itching to strike back at the Jap flattop that had disabled his ship.

Back in Scouting Six room, Warren called together the *Enterprise*'s Dauntless fliers and the *Yorktown*'s refugees. Arms akimbo before the blackboard, he explained the new orders, and briskly warned against any further contention between Bombing Six and Scouting Six over hits in the morning strike. "Here's another shot for all hands," he said. "It's our asses if we don't operate together like old buddies, so save your pugnacity for the Japs."

The meeting went smooth as glass. From the first, the Bombing Six fliers and the *Yorktown* strangers accepted Warren's leadership. The aviators and their pro tem skipper quickly decided on new wing mates and section positions. He could sense them coalescing, as they talked, into a working make-do squadron. Warren forgot his fatigue. He almost forgot the missing pilots. The one thing he loved even above flying was leadership of any sort. He had not had a command since his Academy battalion.

Even the news that the *Yorktown*, after quelling the fires and resuming fleet speed, had been torpedoed in a second attack, was again ablaze and listing, and might be abandoned, could be taken in stride. The main thing was that the fourth carrier had been located, and the attack was on. Warren's last briefing to his hastily formed squadron went by like a dream, and he found himself in the cockpit of an SBD-2, with Cornett as usual in the rear seat. A dizzy, numbed but far from unpleasant sense filled Warren. He was riding a rocket of hours, staying alert on nervous energy, unafraid, and happy. Great events were swirling over his head, but he had to keep his part clear and simple: fly this plane, lead this squadron, find that carrier, and get a bomb hit.

On his launch the sense of heading out into the unknown was almost gone; Warren wryly thought that it was a little bit like the second time with a woman. There were no torpedo planes or fighters to wait for. The fighters had to stay behind to guard the *Enterprise* and the smoking *Yorktown;* and the torpedo aircraft were finished. A *Hornet* dive-bomber squadron was supposed to join the strike; but seeing no launch activity on the *Hornet,* Gallaher decided to get going, and he led his group westward. It was a straight quiet flight into the sun over a cloudless blue sea. After an hour the Jap flattop showed on the horizon, straight ahead on the predicted bearing, in a heavy protective ring of ships. Southward in the distance, in a blaze of afternoon sunshine, the three ruined smoldering hulks of the other carriers still floated in a line, listing crazily this way and that: slaughtered bulls, dumped outside the bullring. Gallaher hooked all the way around the fourth flattop, so as to attack out of the sinking sun. With plenty of fuel, with only one carrier to attack, he could indulge in drilled doctrine, Warren thought, instead of making the pell-mell dives of the morning strike.

The sea winked with antiaircraft guns like a lawn full of fireflies. Black bursts filled the air. Zeroes swarmed up to meet them. Different business this time! The carrier, boiling out a thick white curving wake, heeled far over in a confusing flank speed turn. Now the newness of the squadron showed in ragged dives. Warren saw bomb after bomb splash. He went into his own dive, trying to shut out the distractions—the salvos of Cornett's gun, the green-brown Zeroes zooming and swooping like chicken hawks and spitting red tracers, the wild rattle of shrapnel on his wings, and the damned curving course of the carrier. He managed to hold the ship in his scope as he plunged thousands of feet, popping his ears and sweating; but the unfamiliar plane wobbled and the carrier kept sliding away. He made his decision to drop. Instantly he regretted it. As his hand obeyed his will and released the bomb he knew it would miss. When with a sinking stomach and aching loins he pulled up and looked back, a column of white water was kicking up ahead of the ship. But even as the water splashed on the tilting bow a giant fire sprang out of the afterdeck like a terrible red and yellow flower, and a second smoky explosion forward sent the whole elevator flying out of the deck and slamming back against the island, streaming flames and debris. So someone else had done it, thank Christ. Scratch another carrier.

Antiaircraft shrapnel was churning up the foamy blue waves as Warren dodged along the surface through the dark puffs, gunned straight between two big yellow-blinking ships—a battleship and a cruiser, he thought—and blasted out at full throttle to the open sea. Amazingly, despite the AA storm and the alerted Zeroes, when the straggling planes joined up and formed on Gallaher, Warren counted only three missing. Behind them, the thick smoke rolling up above the carrier was reddened within by leaping fire, and without by the low sun. The triumphant radio talk indicated four sure bomb hits, perhaps five. This was more like battle as he had pictured it: danger, losses, but victory with discipline unbroken. It was not too unlike an island raid. The morning attack by comparison had been a bloody botched mess. But of course this fourth carrier had been such a pigeon only because the first strike had already incinerated most of the Jap air force. Only the sight of the tardy *Hornet* dive-bombers high overhead, heading the other way half an hour late in the red sunset light, recalled the morning foul-up.

Warren found the *Northampton* in the great spread of screening ships, and made his wing-wagging pass. When his wheels touched down in the last glow of sunset, exhaustion flooded him. Barely keeping his eyes open through a perfunctory debriefing, he stumbled off to his cabin. He thought he would drop off to sleep when he fell in his bunk. Instead he lay awake, though aching with fatigue, staring at the squadron exec's neat bunk. They had been roommates, but hardly close friends. There on the blanket was a half-empty pack of Camels. There on the bulkhead smiled the picture of his girl, Lois, a Navy junior. The short dark-haired sallow Ken Turner from Front Royal, Virginia, was gone. He would never manage that Hereford farm of his father's; or could he be alive somewhere out there on a raft? When Warren with an effort closed his eyes, yellow decks began coming up at him, and airplanes were exploding in rainbow spurts of flame.

"To hell with this," he said aloud and went to Gallaher's stateroom, where other wakeful pilots were discussing what was in store tomorrow;

mainly, how to split up the search and the attack assignments. Obviously, there would be a high-speed pursuit all night; search at dawn, launch for attack at sunrise. The Japs must be given no respite. Without air cover, their battleships and cruisers were as vulnerable as the *Prince of Wales* and the *Repulse* had been. Here was the big chance of the war to smash the Nip fleet, and there would be plenty of hunting tomorrow for dive-bombers. So the talk went, mixed with exultation about the gutting of the four carriers. They had not been seen to sink, so finishing them off might also be in the next day's work. But Gallaher thought that destroyer torpedoes would do that job.

Fliers came and went in the room, *Yorktown* aviators and Bombing Six pilots joining the remnant of Warren's squadron. After a while someone suggested a raid on the wardroom for cold meats and coffee, and they marched off in great good humor. Warren dropped out, returned to his bunk, and fell fast asleep. When he awoke he foggily thought it must be the next morning, for he felt refreshed and slept out; but the glowing watch dial read 10:45. He had dozed off for less than half an hour.

This was no good, he thought. He showered, put on a uniform and a windbreaker, and went topside. A bright moon was paling the stars. Warren remembered wondering twenty-four hours ago whether he would live to see stars again. Well, there they were, and here he was. As he strode the cool breezy flight deck long mental vistas opened. This battle marked a divide in his life—truly "midway" it was! He'd been a hellion and tailhound, but an outstanding student, an outstanding engineer, an outstanding deck officer; and he had graduated to gold wings. With some cheerful departures from Dad's prudish ideas and ways, he had really been aping his father. But he had gone past all that in the last twenty-four hours.

Flying was great, but a few more battles like this would give him a bellyful of glory and achievement. As a peacetime career the Navy was a sterile cramped long pull at bad odds. Dad had wasted his life and fine abilities, pretty much. In five combat minutes he, Warren, had done more for the country than Victor Henry had accomplished with his whole naval career. He didn't look down on his father—that could never be, he thought him a man superior to most—but Warren felt sorry for him. The model was out of date. His father-in-law was a better model. Ike Lacouture moved in the real world of money and politics. By comparison the Navy was a queer little planet whirling in an austere void. It served a purpose, but it was nothing but a tool for the real leaders.

The fresh wind, the rhythmic walking, relaxed Warren as these notions flickered in his tired mind. This battle wasn't over, and would still draw hard on his stamina and his luck. He knew that, but after the worst day the stars still shone on him. He stopped to stretch and yawn, and only then took notice that the Big Dipper and the North Star hung broad on the pórt beam, and that the yellow moon was sinking dead astern.

God Almighty, the task force was heading east. Admiral Spruance was withdrawing from a beaten enemy!

This discovery astounded Warren like nothing else in his life. It violated the first law of the Navy, gravely spelled out in *Rocks and Shoals:* never to withdraw from possible action; always to seek out a fight; a violation too of a basic maxim of war, to give no respite to a defeated foe. Was there some late word about gigantic Jap reinforcements—six fleet carriers or something—closing Midway?

He hurried down to the ready room, and found only Peter Goff, gloomily slouched on his back-tilted chair, puffing at his corncob and staring at the vacant teletype screen. "Where's everybody, Pete?"

"Oh, still in the wardroom chowing up, I guess."

"Is there any news?"

The ensign gave him a bleary sour look. "News? Just that we've got ourselves a chickenshit admiral. Do you know that we're retreating?"

"Yes. What's going on?"

"Who knows? All hell's breaking loose in flag country. You should hear the talk in the wardroom. They're saying Spruance can be court-martialled for this."

"What's his reason? He must have a reason."

"Look, this bird just has no stomach for fighting, Warren," said the ensign, his face pink with anger. "The staff could hardly get him to launch today. That's the word. He kept stalling and dillydallying. If not for Captain Browning we'd never have gotten off the deck for the first strike. The Japs would have creamed us, instead of the other way around. Jesus, if only Halsey hadn't come down with the crud!"

"Where are we going? Any word on that?"

"I'm not sure. I think we reverse course again in the morning, so as to give air cover to Midway at dawn. By then, naturally, those yellow monkeys will be halfway back to Japan."

Warren yawned, picked up a sandwich from a piled tray, and lounged in the chair beside Goff. He was disappointed, but obscurely relieved, too. "Well, we did get the carriers. Maybe he wants to quit while he's ahead. That's not bad poker."

"Warren, he's blowing our chance to destroy the Jap fleet."

Warren was too weary to waste words with the youngster. "Look, maybe they'll still try to take Midway tomorrow. Then it'll be another big day. Better catch some shut-eye."

"Warren, what did it really feel like, getting that bomb in there?" Rubbing his bushy beard, Pete Goff callowly, awkwardly grinned. "I missed twice, by a country mile."

"Oh, it was a great feeling. Absolutely great. Nothing like it." Warren yawned and stretched. "However, Pete, I'll tell you something. On that long flight back, I got to thinking about all those Japs burning up, and their bodies flying around, and those planes going up like firecrackers, and that magnificent ship all wrecked up and frying and drowning everybody. Then I thought we get paid for doing some strange work in this fucking Navy."

The day broke cloudy. There was no dawn search, and so no daylight attack. At sunrise the task force was plowing through iron-gray swells at a sedate fifteen knots. No air operations whatever had been ordered. On the hangar deck the clang and shriek of all-night airplane repair still echoed. In the ready rooms a slump was taking hold. The edgy aviators, having breakfasted at 3 A.M., were waiting and waiting and waiting for something to happen. By ten the sun was breaking through. Still no orders came. There were no alarms. Except for the turns into the wind to launch and recover the overhead combat patrol, it was like peacetime steaming. The mutterings mounted that the admiral had let the Japs escape.

Meantime, the teletype burbled conflicting news.

Midway search planes had found the fourth carrier, smoking but still afloat, and under way.

No, that had actually been a *fifth* carrier, which Army B-17s had hit.

No, the fourth carrier had disappeared.

No, the Japanese fleet was splitting up, one force heading west toward Japan, the other withdrawing northwest with a smoking carrier.

The positions jumped about on the chart and made no sense. A feeling spread among the pilots that, after a glorious first day, something was going very, very wrong "up there."

In fact, Rear Admiral Spruance and Halsey's staff were at loggerheads.

To the staff officers, Raymond Spruance was still the screen OTC who by a fluke had been thrust into command of a battle that Halsey should have fought. The Old Man had assured them of Spruance's rare brilliance, but the night retreat had badly shaken them. Put to the test, he seemed to be muffing a historic victory.

Spruance for his part was losing confidence in them. He had assumed that they would execute combat operations with seasoned skill, but in reality this was their first battle. Until now, Vice Admiral Halsey had led only hit-and-run raids on atolls. The laggard first launch, the wrong estimate of the enemy's movements, the miscalculating of Point Option, had been disheartening bungles. The heavy damaging of four enemy carriers (for Spruance still had no confirmed news of sinkings) was a great result; but fuel exhaustion had put down more American aircraft than the enemy had done. Three torpedo squadrons had gone unescorted to the slaughter. The *Hornet* aviators, except for the suicidal Torpedo Eight, had entirely missed the battle. This was wretched work. Then in the second strike, the staff had—unbelievably—failed to notify the unlucky *Hornet* of the attack order, hence their tardy, useless flight.

Now the staff, still surly over the retreat at night, wanted to steam after the enemy at full speed, and launch search-and-attack sweeps at once, clouds or no clouds. But Spruance would not leave Midway unguarded until he knew the Japanese were out of air strike range; and he was keeping back his surviving machines and aviators for direct attacks, based on hard knowledge of where the foe was. This was the impasse in flag country. The restless aviators in the ready room, because their necks were at stake, quite accurately surmised that something was rotten "up there."

It was past one o'clock when orders at last came down. The fleet was speeding up to twenty-five knots. The squadrons would chase the Jap formation reported retreating with a "smoking carrier." The Dauntlesses were to sally forth on the cold trail, make a wide search, and hit anything they found; returning before dark, because they had not drilled in night landings. Glances soon began to pass among the pilots, as they plotted the orders on their flight charts. A peculiar silence fell.

Warren Henry was called to Earl Gallaher's stateroom. Pallid and weary, Wade McClusky sat in Gallaher's armchair, his khaki blouse bulging over bandages. Gallaher, chewing on a cold cigar, closed the door. "Had a chance to plot out the new attack plan, Warren?"

"Yes, sir."

"What do you make of it?"

"It's a plan for a swimming meet."

Wade McClusky, his face scored with worry lines, put in, "You know Spruance, don't you?"

"My father does, sir."

"That'll do." McClusky pushed himself up. "Let's go talk to the CO."

The captain of the *Enterprise* was waiting for them at his desk, in a large office bright with sunshine through open portholes. McClusky briskly stated the problem, asking him to intervene with Browning, and if necessary with Spruance. The captain stared at him, slowly nodding, his fingers idly expanding and contracting a thick rubber band. He was in an unenviable spot, squeezed between his aviators and his admiral's staff. "Well, okay, Wade," he said with a sigh that came out a groan. "I'm assuming you can use dividers and add. Maybe somebody on the staff can't. Let's go up to the flag shelter."

Perched on Halsey's favorite stool, Captain Miles Browning was looking over a large chart of the attack plan. For the first time since Halsey had left the ship, the chief of staff was happy. The admiral had been stalling and stalling, waiting for word of a definite enemy sighting from the Midway search planes. At last, in exasperation, Browning had pointed out that sunsets do not wait; that if they did not launch soon, a whole day of battle would pass without aggressive action; and that might take explaining soon in Pearl Harbor, not to mention *Washington*.

Quite casually, as though permitting an extra liberty for all hands, Spruance had thrown in the towel. "Very well, Captain. Prepare and execute an attack plan."

This chart was the result. Rapidly whipped up by the staff, beautifully drafted in blue and orange ink, it called for a majestic sweep of the widening triangle of ocean where the fleeing Nips might still be found. The area had fanned out like all hell with the passing hours, of course. If only Spruance had listened sooner! Yet the boys might still catch the Japs. Rear Admiral Spruance stood on the platform outside, elbows on the bulwark, watching the spotting of planes for the launch. At least the man did not resent being overborne. In his quiet way Spruance was even more stubborn than Halsey, but once he gave in he bore no grudge. Browning had to grant him that.

Trampling feet mounted the ladder, and the three aviators entered the shelter, led by the ship's captain. McClusky flatly told Miles Browning that the attack plan would splash every dive-bomber left on the *Enterprise*. Even with five-hundred-pound bombs, the distance, time, and fuel factors did not add up, yet the plan called for thousand-pound bombs. Nor was there any margin for gas consumption in combat. Mildly the ship's captain suggested that the staff might recheck the plan.

Browning retorted that there was nothing to recheck. The plan was an order. Let the fliers watch fuel economy and not botch their navigation, and there would be no splashes. Sharpening his tone in return, McClusky declared that if it meant a court-martial he would not take his air group out on those orders. Both men began shouting.

Rear Admiral Spruance strolled in and asked what the matter was. First Browning, then McClusky angrily put their cases. With a glance at the chronometer Spruance sat down in the armchair, scratching at his hairy face. Not to shave in combat was a Halsey staff custom, and he was conforming, though with his starched spotless khakis and gleaming black shoes the brown and gray bristles looked decidedly odd.

"Lieutenant Henry, you've been given your orders!" Spruance surprised them all by bursting out at Warren in a harsh grating voice, with a furious look. "What the devil does this temerity mean? What's your problem? Do you suppose the staff hasn't worked out this plan with the greatest care?"

Under Spruance's icy ugly stare, Warren spoke up shakily. "Admiral, the staff doesn't fly."

"That's an insubordinate response! Wouldn't your father in your place just carry out his orders? Just get in his plane and do as he'd been told?"

"Yes, Admiral, he would. But if asked—as you're asking me, sir—he'd mention that you wouldn't see any of your aircraft again. Because you won't."

Pursing his broad well-cut lips, his large sober eyes glancing around at the others, Spruance rubbed his chin, then clasped his hands behind his head. "Well," he said, turning to Wade McClusky, "I'll do what you pilots want."

"What!" The word broke from Browning like the cry of a stabbed man. He dashed his cap to the deck, stamped scarlet-faced out of the flag shelter, and his rapid steps thumped down the ladder. The cap rolled to the feet of Spruance, who picked it up and put it on the chair arm, saying placidly, "Call the operations officer, Wade."

In thickening weather, the dive-bomber squadrons finally left the *Enterprise* and the *Hornet* at three in the afternoon, on a modified plan. They saw only white clouds and gray patches of water in their wide sweep. Returning in a scarlet-flaring sunset, they came upon a lone Japanese destroyer and pounced on it. The vessel dodged and twisted under the hail of bombs, vomiting red AA tracers, even shooting down one plane, until darkness forced the air group commander to let it go unscathed. As the Dauntlesses roared off through the fast-falling night, homing on the Y-E signal, Warren wondered how the hell they would get back aboard. He stewed too about his own gross miss on this destroyer, and on the failure of an entire squadron to get even one hit.

On the *Enterprise,* Browning had thought better of his tantrum, and had returned to the shelter in a calm professional mood. Spruance's manner to him was as pleasant as always. As night fell and McClusky reported the search group on the way back, Spruance took to pacing like Halsey, for the first time in the battle. Both men strode here and there in the gloom until Browning burst out, "Admiral, we've got to turn on the lights."

The dim form of Spruance halted. "What about submarines?"

"Sir, we have a screen out there. If a son-of-a-bitching sub has gotten through the screen, that's too bad. The boys have to land."

"Thank you, Captain Browning. I agree. Illuminate at once."

In after years, in one of his rare specific statements on his war conduct, Raymond Spruance declared that he was concerned only once in the war, and that was when the planes were returning in the dark off Midway.

So to Warren's amazed relief, a white blaze suddenly starred the dark sea far ahead. The carriers stood out like perfect little ship models. The operations officer came on the radio with emergency instructions. Warily, nervously, the pilots came in for the first carrier night landings of their lives. The brilliant searchlight illumination made it seem a sort of circus stunt. Warren was surprised at how simple it actually was. He slammed down and caught the number two cable in the glare as though it were noon sunshine; then he hurried to the landing officer's platform to watch the other planes come in. The instant the last bomber touched down—with only one dropped in the sea, and its men handily rescued by the plane guard destroyer—the lights went out.

Ships, planes disappeared. The night sky leaped into view.

"What do you know?" Warren said to the landing officer. "Stars."

On the *Northampton's* blacked-out bridge, Victor Henry happily told the exec to secure from General Quarters. The astonishing blaze-up, while forcing the cruiser on immediate submarine alert, had lifted a load from his heart. Pug didn't believe that the one unlucky plane had been Warren's. He sensed too that this spectacular night recovery was the real end of the battle. There might be mopping up of stragglers for a day or two, but the Japs were gone. Spruance would not follow them far. The screen destroyers were getting near their fuel limits, and in these waters he could not leave them behind. Pug had followed Spruance's maneuvers with intense if frustrated admiration. The withdrawal on the first night, and the cautious pursuit tactics, had secured a substantial victory against the Japanese powerhouse. He had socked them and rocked them, and not lost his shirt.

Now, standing out on the wing of his bridge under the stars, Pug Henry allowed himself to think about Warren again. This two-day vigil had aged him; he could feel it in his nerves, in his very breathing. On that fearful first morning a Bible verse had kept running through his mind, a verse over which he had once broken down, reading the Bible with his family long ago. Each morning a member of the family had taken a turn at a chapter, and the last battle of David and Absalom had fallen to him.

"O my son, Absalom, my son, my son, Absalom! Would God I had died for thee, O Absalom, my son, my son!"

Under the bright solemn eyes of the three children he had choked over the verse, slammed the book shut, and hurried from the room. Yesterday morning, as his agonized father-feeling had welled up, those words had repeated and repeated in his brain like a torturing old song; and like a smashed record, it had stopped at the sight of Warren's Dauntless flashing over the forecastle. Ever since, Pug had shut out thoughts of his endangered son, almost as he blocked away the hurtful remembrance of his faithless wife. He had even forced himself to stop watching the air operations on the *Enterprise*. Warren's second pass yesterday had been reassuring. Yet Pug knew he would not draw an easy breath until he saw his son again in Pearl Harbor. He was not absolutely sure that Warren was alive, and there was no seemly way of finding out. But the big risks were past, and now there was only the waiting.

Victor Henry thought he was not likely ever to endure a more harrowing time than these two days of futile steaming in command of a major warship with silent guns, while his son fought a battle at the highest hazard, as it were before his eyes.

In the flag shelter, the atmosphere had calmed. When Spruance set the pursuit speed for the night at a mere fifteen knots, there was no argument. He and the chief of staff now understood each other. Browning wanted hot pursuit at reckless fuel cost; oilers were bringing up the rear, in case fuel ran low. Spruance was conserving fuel for possible extended combat with no chance for refueling. The verdict between them now lay with their superiors and with history.

Early next morning an urgent Nimitz dispatch gave Miles Browning a sweet foretaste of that verdict, for Cincpac agreed with him. He hastened to deliver the message himself to Spruance, who was brewing coffee in his quarters before dawn. Nimitz said in the dispatch that the sole survivor of Torpedo Eight had been rescued, and had confirmed great damage to three Jap carriers. The time therefore was ripe to close the enemy and attack. Both men understood the veiled language of high command dispatches. This was a rough rebuke for excessive caution, and a warning of possible responsibility for letting a wounded enemy escape. The report of the rescued pilot was padding.

Calmly initialling the flimsy sheet, Spruance inquired, "What have you done about this?"

"Our dawn search is ready to launch, Admiral. The *Hornet*'s bombers are standing by, armed with thousand-pound bombs, ready to attack at contact."

"Excellent." It was a word Spruance had rarely used. "Have the cruiser float planes follow up any sighting, Captain, and keep the enemy in view."

Warren put himself on the dawn search. Weary though he was, flying was pleasanter than fretting in the ready room. The starlit launch, the long flight in the dawn and the sunrise, gave him a sort of second wind. He saw nothing, but he heard Peter Goff radio a long excited report from the southern sector. Two large vessels, cruisers or battleships, had apparently collided in the night. They were moving slowly in a gigantic oil slick, screened by destroyers, and the bow of one appeared to be crushed. Poor Pete, flying without a bomb over a couple of huge unmaneuverable cripples! This would be the great chance for the *Hornet* bombers to improve their sad score. Approaching the screen on his return, he dropped once more to fly over the *Northampton,* and saw his father on the bridge nonchalantly wave. The *Hornet* bombers were already taking off.

In the *Enterprise* ready room, the fliers listened avidly to the jocular, occasionally obscene radio exchanges pouring from the loudspeaker as the *Hornet* planes found the two cripples and plastered them with half-ton bomb hits. When the attack ended, the patrolling cruiser plane reported the ships appallingly battered and on fire, but still under way at dead slow. The teletype, turning playful in the sunshine of victory, spelled out:

LOOKS LIKE MORE TARGET PRACTICE FOR ENTERPRISE

At this, Ensign Goff let out a rebel yell that raised a wave of guffaws, and some headshakes among the slumping red-eyed pilots.

"Well, Pete, here's your moment," Warren tiredly grinned. "Just lay it in there this time, nice and easy."

His face set and pale, Pete Goff said, "I'll put it down the smoke-stack."

As they were leaving the ready room, Warren tapped Goff's shoulder. "Look, Pete, belay that down-the-smokestack stuff. It's just another bombing run. You'll get a hundred more chances in this war."

Pulling on his helmet, the ensign set his red-bearded jaw with a youthful obstinacy that reminded Warren strongly and sadly of Byron. "I'm just tired of not earning my pay."

"You earn it when you fly."

The wind had now shifted to the west. Smoothly, swiftly, McClusky—back in action despite his injuries—led the group off to the attack. Bone-weary as the aviators were, Warren could see they were getting better and better at join-ups. Combat was the school, no doubt of that.

Over the horizon, after half an hour's flight, smoke pointed down at the victims. McClusky had three surviving torpedo planes in his group, but orders were to use torpedoes only if no AA was still firing. Seen through binoculars from ten thousand feet, the two vessels were unbelievably smashed up—guns askew, bridges dangling, torpedo tubes and catapults hanging crazily, amid drifting smoke and jumping flames. The *Hornet* fliers had reported them as battleships, but to Warren they looked much like a pair of ruined *Northamptons*. Both ships were putting up meager little squirts of AA tracers and a few black explosions.

"Well, that lets out the TBDs." McClusky's voice came in clearly. He assigned the dive-bomber sections to the two cruisers, and the attack began.

The first section, led by Gallaher, did a businesslike job: at least three hits sent up smoke and flame in billows, and the AA fire died away. As Warren prepared to lead his section down to the fiery shambles far below, he looked back at Peter Goff, and held up a palm outward, in a last friendly admonition to take it easy; then he pushed over in the familiar maneuver, straightened into a dive, and there was the blazing cruiser squarely in his telescope sight.

When he had dived about a thousand feet through sporadic and feeble AA, Warren's plane was hit. At the alarming jolt, and the grinding, gruesome noise of tearing metal, and the queer sight of a ragged piece of his blue wing flying away, with cherry-colored fire licking out of the stump, his first feeling was stupefied surprise. He had never thought he would be shot down, though he had known the risks. With his death sentence before his eyes he still could not believe it. His future stretched before him for so many years—so well-planned, so real, so important! But he had only a few more seconds to pull off something miraculous and even as these vertiginous thoughts whirled through his shocked brain and he jerked futilely at the controls, the fire flared all along the broken wing, and in the earphones he heard Cornett screaming something frightened but incomprehensible. The plane fell sideways and began to spin downward, shaking fearfully, with fire shooting from the engine. The blue sea turned round and round before Warren's eyes, framed in flames. He could see white breaking wave tops not far below. He tried frantically to open his canopy, but could not. He called to Cornett to jump, with no response. The cockpit grew hotter, and in the intense heat his rigid body hanging there in his straps struggled and struggled and struggled. At last it involuntarily relaxed. There was nothing more to do, after all. He had done his best, and now it was time to die. It was going to be tough on old Dad, but Dad would be proud of him. His last coherent thought was this one, of his father.

The water was thrusting up toward him in tossing revolving foamy waves. *All over already?*

Horrible pain seared Warren as fire leaped across his face, blinding his last living moments. The crash into the water was a terrific blow in the dark. Warren's final sensation was a soothing cooling one: the sea, bathing his scorched face and hands. The plane exploded, but he never knew that, and his torn body began its long slow descent in peace to its resting place on the bottom of the trackless sea. For a few seconds, a thin black smoke plume marked the place where he fell. Then like his life the plume melted into the wind and was gone.

† † †

O my son, Absalom, my son, my son, Absalom! Would God I had died for thee, O Absalom, my son, my son!

PART THREE

Byron
and
Natalie

33

IN mid-July, still recovering from the terrible news, Rhoda left Washington by train for the West Coast. Madeline was in Hollywood and Byron was attending a submarine attack school in San Diego, so whenever he got leave, they could at least be together. Train journeys, even in wartime, were cheering, and just packing for this one relieved her agony. Her first dining-car meal woke a sluggish flow of life in her chilled veins. She knew that her black linen suit, dark hat, and dark stockings looked smart. After dinner men in the club car eyed her. A bemustached, beribboned Air Force colonel tried his luck at buying her a drink. What rotten taste! Couldn't the man see she was in mourning? She quenched him with one sad glance.

Bedding down between crisp heavy Pullman sheets, she was a long time dropping off. The clacking of the wheels, the rhythmic sway of the berth, the chugging and wailing of the locomotive, the old train smells in the upholstery and the green curtains, the vibrating roll through the night, bathed her in nostalgia. So she had lain as an engaged girl of nineteen, aquiver with love and with erotic visions, riding down to Charleston to visit Pug; so they had lain together in a lower berth, on their brief rapturous honeymoon; so she had lain as the mother of one infant, then two, then three, as the family dragged from one duty station to another. Now again she lay alone, on her way to the two grown-up children left to her.

Oh, Warren's wedding day, and the songs and the champagne in the car on the way to the Pensacola airport! Oh, that last glimpse of him, that last reunion of her little family to all eternity! He had looked so handsome driving the big Cadillac and singing along as the whole family, crowded in with his blonde bride and Byron's dark Jewish girl, were harmonizing.

Till we meet, till we meet,
Till we meet at Jesus' feet . . .

Rhoda accepted the death of her son as a personal punishment. An excruciating, cleansing catharsis of remorse had been racking her for weeks. She was determined to cut her misconduct out of her life like a cancer. This resolve was turning the death of her firstborn son into a redeeming experience; she was spending much time and pouring out many tears in church. Like most service wives and mothers, Rhoda had thought herself steeled against bad news, but the ringing doorbell at seven in the morning a few days after the Midway battle had frightened her, and the words on the yellow telegraph form had blasted her soul. Warren! The winner, the best, always carrying off prizes and top grades, going to the right schools, marrying the right girl, rising in the Navy faster than his father had—Warren, gone! *Dead!* Her firstborn son, lost to her, lying somewhere on the bottom of the Pacific, miles down, in the wreckage of an airplane! Would a funeral, and a last look at him in a coffin, have been easier or worse than this dry notification that her son, out of her sight for two years, was dead? She could not tell. The funerals of her mother, her father, and her older brother had not hit her like this. A funeral was a release of a sort, a vent for grief. Her only release had been one wild long flood of tears over Pug's letter.

She had meant to schedule an overnight stop in Chicago to break with Kirby, but he was away from his office, so she would have to do it on the way back. In the majestic shadow of her son's death, their middle-aged amour seemed not so much soiled and wicked as ridiculous. They had both needed it, or had thought they did, and so they had accommodated each other. That was the reality. The rest had been romantic illusion. Now it was finished. She was Pug's till death. He might be too good for her, his magnanimity might be crushing, but she hoped to become more worthy of him in the years that remained.

Buried under all this wholly sincere repentance was an intuition that the Kirby thing had peaked anyway. Forbidden fruit has its brown spots, but these are not seen in the dusky glow of appetite; one has to bite and taste the unpleasant mush. Her civilian lover had turned out not so very different from her military husband. He had less excuse for neglecting her, yet like Pug he had shut her out and absented himself for weeks at a time. Answering her fatal divorce letter, Pug had warned her that Fred Kirby was too much like himself for the thing to work. Wise old Pug! In fact, Palmer rather despised her. She knew this, though only with Warren's death had she squarely faced it. If she forced the issue he might marry her, but it would be a mere entrapment. When all was said and done, she had been a fortyish fool. It happened to lots of women, and it had happened to her. All she wanted now was to end the thing and save her marriage. Around and around this pivotal resolve her thoughts circled, chasing each other until she dozed off in the rocking berth, to the sad hoots of the whistle and the rhythmic clatter of the wheels.

Young men in white and khaki uniforms swarmed through the tumultuous mob in the sweltering Los Angeles terminal, three days later. Rhoda kept looking for a red beard as she wandered here and there, followed by a sweating porter with her bags.

"Here I am, Mom."

The shock when she turned and saw him so weakened her that she sagged into her smooth-shaven son's arms. He wore dress whites with a splash of campaign ribbons, his gold dolphins looked much like gold wings, his face had filled out, and a cigarette slanting from his mouth completed a frightening resemblance to Warren. They had never looked much alike to her, but this stern-faced tanned apparition was a shivery blend of the two. She buried her face against the starchy uniform and cried. When she could control herself she choked out, wiping her eyes, "I received the most beautiful letter from Dad. Have you heard from him?"

"No. Let's go. I've got Madeline's car."

At the wheel he slouched in a Byron-like way, and smiled with a mouth shape unchanged since infancy. "You've lost weight. You look very pretty, Mom."

"Oh, what does it matter how I look?" Her eyes overflowed again, and she put her hand on his. "It's so hot here, I'm perspiring like a NIGGER. I haven't had a proper bath in three days, Byron. I feel SLIMY."

His smile broadening, he leaned over and kissed her. "Old Mom." And he drove out into a brightly sunny avenue lined with palm trees and tall buildings; and into the thickest traffic jam she had ever seen.

"What news of Natalie?" Rhoda tried to sound naturally affectionate. Her Jewish daughter-in-law's name did not come easily to her tongue.

He took from an inside pocket and passed to her a long wrinkled airmail envelope half-covered with purple rubber stampings. "From that fellow Slote. I may have to go to Switzerland."

"Oh, Byron. SWITZERLAND? How can you? In wartime, and you under orders!"

"It's possible. Not easy, but possible. I can cross unoccupied France by train, or fly to Zurich from Lisbon. When this torpedo course finishes I've got thirty days' leave coming."

"But even so, dear. Once there, THEN what?"

Byron's face obstinately hardened. "Nobody cares about Natalie and that kid as I do. I can go there and see." When he looked like that, it was time to drop the subject, though his mother thought he was out of his mind. Slote's letter was a confused mess about exit visas and Brazil which she couldn't follow.

Rhoda had never before been to Hollywood. Walking through the lushly green hotel garden splashed with flowering hibiscus and bougainvillea she saw a real film star, Errol Flynn, sitting in swim trunks by the pool with a beautiful young girl, no doubt a starlet. She could not help being excited. "Before I do ANYTHING," she said as Byron carried her bags into the roomy villa Madeline had rented for them, "I must shower. I mean this SECOND."

"Where's Dad's letter?"

"You want to read it right now?"

"Yes."

The envelope was scuffed, the creases in the sheets of U.S.S. *Northampton* stationery were wearing through. Byron crouched in an armchair over the pages, written in his father's familiar firm clear Navy hand with heavily crossed *t*'s and plain capitals.

Dearest Rhoda:

By now you have the official word. I tried a couple of times to place a call to you, but it probably was for the best that I didn't get through. It might have been painful for both of us.

Our son made it through the worst of the battle. He would fly over my ship and rock his wings, coming back from sorties. Warren scored a direct bomb hit on a Jap carrier. He'll probably get a posthumous Navy Cross. Rear Admiral Spruance told me this. Spruance is a controlled person, but when he spoke of Warren there were tears in his eyes. He said that Warren turned in a "brilliant, heroic performance," and Raymond Spruance uses such words sparingly.

Warren was killed on the last day, on a routine mission of mopping up enemy cripples. An AA shell caught his plane. Three of his squadron mates saw him spin down in flames, so there's no hope that he ditched and is afloat on a raft, or cast up on some atoll. Warren is dead, we will never see him again. We have Byron, we have Madeline, but he's gone, and there will never be another Warren.

He came to see me just before the battle and gave me an envelope. When I found out he'd been killed (which wasn't until we got back to

port) I opened it. It contained a rundown of his finances. Not that
Janice had to worry, but he wasn't counting on his rich father-in-law.
He'd arranged to transfer your mother's trust fund to her, and there's
an insurance policy that guarantees Vic's education. How about that?
He exuded confidence and cheer before the battle. I know he expected
to make it through. Yet he did this. I can still see him standing in the
door of my cabin, with one hand on the overhead, one foot on the
coaming, saying with that easy grin of his, "If you're too busy for me,
say so." Too busy! God forgive me if I ever gave him that impression.
There was no greater joy in my life than talking to Warren, in fact just
resting my eyes on him.

It's been awhile since I've heard from you, and almost six months
since Madeline last wrote. So I feel sort of cut off, and don't know
what to advise you. If you can stay with her in New York for a while,
it might be a good idea. That girl needs somebody, and this is no time
for you to be alone on Foxhall Road. Janice is behaving well, but she's
kind of smashed up. Byron will probably mask his feelings as usual, but
I'm worried about him. He worshipped Warren.

I've just written my ship's battle report. It's one page long. We never
fired a gun. We never saw an enemy vessel. Warren must have flown a
dozen search and attack sorties in three days. He and a few hundred
young men like him carried the brunt of a great victorious battle. I did
nothing.

Somewhere a character in Shakespeare says, "We owe God a death."
Even if we could roll time back to that rainy evening in March 1939,
Rhoda, when he was on leave from the *Monaghan,* and he told us he
was putting in for flight training—in his typical fashion, just like that,
no fuss, confronting us with the *fait accompli*—and even if we knew
what the future held in store, what could we do differently? He was
born to a service father. Boys tend to follow their dads. He chose the
best branch of the Navy for effectiveness against the enemy; certainly
he proved that! Few men in any armed force, on any front, will strike a
harder blow for their country than he did. That was what he set out to
do. His life was successful, fulfilled, and complete. I want to believe
that, and in a way I truly do.

But ah, what Warren might have been! I'm a known quantity. There
are a thousand four-stripers like me, and one more or less doesn't matter that much. I've had my family; you might say I've had my life. How
can I compare to what Warren might have been?

Yes, Warren's gone. He won't have any fame. When the war's over,
nobody will remember the ones who bore the heat of combat. They'll
probably forget the names of the admirals, even of the battles that
saved our country. I now feel that despite all the present discouraging
news we'll eventually win the war. The Japs can't recover from the

shellacking they took at Midway, and Hitler can't lick the world by himself. Our son helped to turn the tide. He was there when it mattered and where it mattered. He took his life in his hands, went in there, and did his duty as a fighting man. I'm proud of him. I'll never lose that pride. He'll be in my last thoughts.

Other things will have to wait for a different letter. God keep you well.

Love,
Pug

Emerging from her room in a silk robe, Rhoda said, "Isn't it a beautiful letter?" Byron did not reply. He sat smoking a cigar, staring emptily, his face wan, the letter on his lap. Disturbed by his silence and his look, she chattered cheerily, combing her hair at a large mirror. "I'm saving it. I'm saving everything—the telegram, the letter from the Secretary of the Navy, all the other letters, even the invitation from the Gold Star Mothers, and the story in the *Washington Herald*. It's a nice write-up. Now what is this party again, Byron? Isn't she working for Hugh Cleveland any more? I'm all confused, and—oh, to HELL with this hair! There's no light, and no time, and I don't *care,* anyhow."

"She is working for him. This party's something else, a volunteer thing." Byron got up, took a red and yellow circular from a pile on the coffee table, and handed it to her. "It's a buffet before this wingding starts."

AMERICAN COMMITTEE
FOR
A SECOND FRONT NOW
Hollywood Division
MONSTER RALLY
AT
THE HOLLYWOOD BOWL

There followed a large alphabetical list of participants: film stars, producers, directors, writers.

"My goodness! What a star cast. And Alistair Tudsbury, too, HE's here! Why, this is a very distinguished group, isn't it, Byron? *'Madeline Henry, program coordinator!'* My heavens! If that little snip hasn't come up in the world."

At this moment Madeline burst in. "Oh, Mother!" The intensity of the exclamation, and the clutching embrace that went with it, bridged their shared grief. She wore a dark wide-shouldered dress, her dark hair was elegantly styled, and her talk was cyclonic. "I'm so GLAD you came!

Shoot, I hoped you'd be ready, but I'll just go, I guess, and then send Hugh's limousine back for you. Oh, God, there's so much to talk about, isn't there, Mom! This insane clambake will be all over tonight, thank Heaven, and then I can draw breath."

"Dear, we don't know these people, I'm tired, I have no clothes—"

"Mama, you're both *coming*. The Tudsburys will be sitting in your box. That's why they've stayed on, they want to see you. They won't be at the party, but you'll meet all the film stars. It's at Harry Tomlin's home on Lookout Mountain, a fabulous place, he's the biggest agent in the movie business. Wear anything! You must have a black suit."

"Well, I wore it to death on the train, but—" Rhoda went out.

Byron pointed to the pile of circulars. "Mad, isn't that a communist outfit?"

"Sweetie, not on your life. All Hollywood's in on it. It's a popular movement. With Soviet Russia doing all the real fighting and dying against Hitler, we *need* a second front now, and we've got to raise hell about it. Everybody knows Churchill hates the Bolsheviks, and wants to hold back and let the Soviet Union bleed itself white, fighting the Germans alone."

"Everybody knows that? I don't know it. How do you know it?"

"Oh, Lord, Byron, read your newspapers. Anyway, let's not argue, sweetie, it's not worth arguing about. I took this thing on because I thought it would be fun, and it *has* been fun in a bloodcurdling way. I've made some fantastic contacts. I don't want to be Hugh Cleveland's little sandwich-fetcher forever."

"I'm glad to hear that."

Madeline was making a long strident telephone call about the rally to a man she called "Lenny, darling," when Rhoda marched in, buttoning her jacket. "Let's go. Nobody will pay me the slightest attention. I'll pass as someone's poor aunt from Dubuque."

The home of Harry Tomlin was an opulent sprawl of redwood and glass angled around a flagstone terrace with a huge blue-tiled pool. Perched at the end of a scarily steep concrete road up into a canyon, it commanded a spectacular view of Los Angeles, which at the moment looked like a drowned city shimmering at the bottom of a brown lake. Madeline vanished in the babbling throng of guests, after introducing her mother and brother at the door to a man named Leonard Spreregen, the rally chairman, who—so she told them—had won two Academy Awards for screenplays. Rhoda saw that her concern over clothes was needless; Spreregen wore no tie, and his orange shirt collar flowed over his black and white houndstooth jacket. Madeline whirled into sight again and introduced her mother and brother to one star after another, all of whom were most cordial. To the astonished Rhoda they appeared peculiarly shrunken, seen as human beings rather than blown-up moving shadows.

"How on earth have you gotten to know them all, dear?" she exclaimed, catching her breath after a kind word and a smile from Ronald Colman.

"Oh, you do, Mom, when you mix into a thing like this. You just do. That's the fun of it. Ah, there we go."

White-coated butlers were sliding tall Chinese panels into wall slots, disclosing a long dining room and a heavily laden buffet table, where two chefs were sharpening knives over steaming hams and turkeys. As the guests drifted in toward the food, several men in sharply tailored Army uniforms fell into the line behind Madeline. She whispered to Byron that these were Hollywood types making training films. Hugh Cleveland was looking into this angle, she said. He had received a draft notice; if things got sticky he wanted an out. She blurted this artlessly, then caught the look on her brother's face. "Well, I realize how that must strike you, but—"

"How does it strike you, Madeline?"

"Briny, Hugh is totally unmechanical. He can't sharpen a pencil properly. He'd be an utter washout carrying a gun."

They brought their food to a little table on the terrace, where Leonard Spreregen joined them and talked with Madeline about the rally while she scratched notes on a pad. Spreregen's manner was bright and edgy, his speech pure New York. Madeline exclaimed, jumping up, "Omigawd, the trumpeters for the mass chant, of *course*. Sorry, Lenny. I *knew* there was something. Be right back."

"What a lovely party," Rhoda said to Spreregen, glancing around at French impressionist paintings crusting the walls, "and what a gorgeous home!"

He pleasantly smiled. He was a short lean man with thick curly blond hair and a hawklike face. His voice was deep, almost bass. "Well, Mrs. Henry, ten percent of my heart's blood is in it, but I don't mind, Harry's a terrific agent. Say, Lieutenant, how do you feel about the second front?"

"Well, I'm puzzled," Byron said, eating away at a heaped plate, "there are four or five fronts right now, aren't there?"

"Ah, the military precisionist speaks!" Spreregen nodded, with a keen glance at Byron that took in the ribbons and the dolphins. " 'The Committee for a Second Front against Germany in France Now' would be more exact, I guess. People know what we mean. You're for that, aren't you?"

"I don't know if it's feasible now."

"Why, any number of military authorities are clamoring for it."

"But the Allied chiefs of staff are the military authorities that matter."

"Exactly so," said Spreregen, as though to a clever pupil, "and the chiefs of staff can't buck their political bosses. Economic and political motives can cause stupid military decisions, Lieutenant. Then you fighting men have to pay the price. The reactionaries want to let Hitler destroy the Soviet Union, before they finish him off. The reactionaries have a strong voice, but the voice of the people is stronger. That's why rallies like this are vital."

Byron shook his head, saying mildly, "I doubt they can affect strategic policy. Why not put on a rally for the Jews in Europe? Such big propaganda shows might do them some real good."

Rhoda blinked at her son. At the word "Jews," Leonard Spreregen's eyes clouded, his mouth tightened, and he sat up straight, putting down the knife and fork on a slab of hot ham. "If you're serious—"

"I'm deadly serious."

Spreregen spoke fast, in a rattled way. "Well, I'm not sure what's happening over there, my friend, I don't think anybody here really knows, but the way to end all that misery is by smashing Hitler with a second front now."

"I see," Byron said.

"Excuse me. Nice meeting you," Spreregen said to Rhoda, and he departed, leaving his food behind.

Soon Madeline appeared, frowning at Byron. "Look, Briny, let's drop you off at the hotel on the way to the rally."

"What on earth!" Rhoda exclaimed. "Why suggest that?"

"He made an anti-Semitic remark to Lenny Spreregen."

Rhoda blinked in surprise. "What? Why, the man's a fool, all he said—"

"Forget it, Mom," Byron said. "I'll come along."

A gigantic yellow banner printed in red swayed above the main entrance to the Hollywood Bowl:

THE YANKS ARE NOT COMING TOO LATE.

Cars were streaming inside, and from nearby streets hordes of people on foot were converging toward the Bowl. But, although the entrance appeared mobbed, the audience in the big amphitheatre was sparsely clustering near the stage shell, below the tier of boxes. On the upper slope, slanting sunlight reddened rows upon rows of empty seats. Over the shell, which was draped with three large flags—the British ensign, the Stars and Stripes, and the red flag with its yellow hammer and sickle—huge cutout letters arched:

SECOND FRONT
NOW

Alistair Tudsbury, in a bulging seersucker suit and an eye patch, awkwardly got to his feet and kissed Rhoda when she came to the box. Pamela's smile was agreeable, but her eyes were puffy, her face was sagging and unpainted, and she was almost unkempt; she looked, Rhoda thought, as though she did not much care whether she lived or died. Madeline came dashing into the box. Grand panic backstage! Two stars had pulled out of the show, a third had laryngitis, and a frantic rearrangement of the program had placed Tudsbury in the closing spot, after the mass chant. Was that all right? Tudsbury agreed, remarking only that his talk would not be a high note.

"Oh, it will, it will. You have *authority*," Madeline said. "Sorry we didn't pull in more of an audience. Charging admission was a mistake." She scampered off.

It was a tedious patchy program, part singing and dancing to two pianos, part speech-making, with some labored comedy. The hit of the evening was a song, "The Reactionary Rag," in which actors dressed as paunchy nabobs in high hats and cutaways, with dollar signs on their white-waisted bellies, capered about expressing their sympathy with the Soviet Union, but finding funny reasons not to send military help. The mass chant was a business of many voices speaking up from all over the amphitheatre—a steel worker, a farm laborer, a schoolteacher, a nurse, a Negro, and so forth—each demanding a second front *now;* these solo declamations were punctuated with solemn unison readings from mimeographed sheets by the entire audience of quotes from Pericles, Shakespeare, Lincoln, Booker T. Washington, Tom Paine, Lenin, Stalin, and Carl Sandburg, while the orchestra softly played "The Battle Hymn of the Republic." The climax was a wildly syncopated audience shout, repeated in crescendo to the accompaniment of trumpets:

Open up that second FRONT
Open up that second FRONT
Open up that second FRONT
NOW! NOW! NOW!

It all ended in great applause and cheers.

Introduced by Leonard Spreregen, Tudsbury limped onstage to a standing ovation.

"On June 22nd, 1941, as you no doubt recall," his voice boomed on the loudspeaker over the great half-empty amphitheatre, now in twilight under a pale moon, "Nazi Germany invaded the Soviet Union.

"On June 23rd, 1941, my column in the *London Observer* bore the heading, *'Open Up a Second Front Now.'* "

This brought the crowd to its feet again. But the Bowl grew very quiet as he talked. Military realities, he began, were not easy to grasp or to face. He had had to spend several months in Moscow during the worst of the German onslaught, a month in falling Singapore, and a week in Hawaii before and after the battle for Midway atoll, before he had gotten a grip on this global war.

A major assault on the French coast in 1942 was, he now knew, utterly out of the question. Only a trickle of green American forces had as yet arrived in England. The U-boats remained a formidable and merciless barrier to a rapid buildup of these forces. Mastering that menace was a long-range struggle. A cross-Channel attack now would have to be all-British. Britain was already spread far too thin. Singapore had proved that! Any British action in France would so weaken the China-Burma-India theatre that the United States would have to take over there—at once, and massively—with whatever forces it could get past the Japanese fleet. For if India or Australia fell to Japan, the defeat of Nazi Germany would not win the war, nor assure the survival of the Soviet Union.

"Eastern Asia is the center of gravity of the war, my friends," Tudsbury declared in weary firm tones. "World War Two started there at the Marco Polo Bridge, not in Poland. China has been fighting the war longer than anybody. If Japan wins there, Russia faces catastrophe. Japan will mobilize the incredible resources of India, China, and the East Indies against the Soviet Union. A new Golden Horde will storm across the Siberian border, armed with tanks, with Zeroes, and with manpower and natural resources outweighing the West ten to one. The China-Burma-India theatre is the true, the forgotten second front. We must hold it if civilization is to survive."

Several catcalls rose from the audience at this point.

"The long-range prospects are *good*," Tudsbury defiantly boomed. "Our soldiers who died in Singapore, and yours in the Philippines, did not die in vain. They upset the Japanese timetable for seizing India and Australia. The crux of the war now is a fight for time. Your country's productive power is awesome, but slow to gear up. I'm surprised to find so little interest here in your victory at Midway. Had your Navy lost that battle, you might be fleeing California this evening. Your fliers and sailors who died there gave their lives for all mankind."

Coughing was spreading in the amphitheatre, and people were yawning and looking at their watches.

"A second front in France? Yes, I'm warmly for it, too. The plight of the Soviet Union grows worse and worse. But the Russians are strong. They will hold on. It's delightful to visualize millions of stalwart Anglo-American troops storming across the English Channel *now*. But it's a pipe dream. We will overwhelm the Axis in good time with a cataract of men and firepower. Till then, we fight for time, and for the turn of the tide on many fronts, including the home front. My final word to this home front is, *Believe in the honor of your leaders, and trust them. They are great men, and they are fighting a great war.*"

As he limped off the stage, feeble brief handclapping ensued, with more catcalls. The crowd began dispersing, in a muttering mood. A loud bald man in a loud jacket was saying to a pretty girl as they left the box beside Byron's, "Still trying to hang on to their Empire, aren't they? Just pathetic."

Returning to the box with Madeline, Tudsbury said cheerfully, "Well, wasn't that a resounding flop!"

"Well done," Byron said.

Rhoda jumped up, kissed him, and said tremulously, "I'll never forget your words about Midway. Never."

"You made good sense," Madeline fumed. "This crowd doesn't change, and never will. Maybe it penetrated a thick skull here and there. I must go and pick up the pieces."

Pamela stood up as Madeline scurried off. "Was it fun, Talky?"

"It was, actually, watching them gradually realize that I wasn't one of them, but just another Limey snake in the grass. I quite enjoyed it."

"So courageous," said Rhoda. "Pug would have talked like that—without your lovely command of language, of course."

"Pug would have stayed away, and so should I have done," said Tudsbury. "However, we wanted to see you, Mrs. Henry, so let's have a drink now at our hotel, shall we? Pamela and I fly on to New York tomorrow."

As they walked out, the press of the crowd thrust Rhoda alongside Pamela, who spoke low fast words. "Mrs. Henry, may I have breakfast with you tomorrow—just the two of us?"

They faced each other next morning on the lawn beside the pool over melons, toast, and coffee on a wheeled linen-covered table. It was a perfect California day: hot sun, pellucid blue sky, scents of grass and palms, a cool breeze stirring the gaudy red flowers of the hibiscus hedges. Two youths and three girls dove and swam and laughed in the pool, their brown skins gleaming, their jokes as merry and simple as the mating calls of birds. Pamela looked better today, her face carefully made up, her hair falling behind her ears in long glossy waves. The sleeveless gray dress showed the cleft in her pale bosom. Rhoda recalled that this odd young woman, who fluttered in her father's wake like a gull behind an ocean liner, had a way of shifting between mousiness and allure. Perhaps, Rhoda thought, she was on her way this morning to meet a man. She gave the impression of very taut nerves.

As they idly chatted, Rhoda said she wished she had a copy of Tudsbury's speech to send to Pug.

"Nothing easier. I'll see that you get one." Pamela quickly replied in her educated British accent that so impressed and charmed Rhoda. "I wrote it."

"Why, it was his style to the life."

"Oh, yes, I fake for him when he's indisposed or lazy."

"Why the eye patch, Pamela?"

"That eye is ulcerating. He needs an operation. We'd be in London by now, but Madeline did mention that you were coming west, so we stayed. I desperately wanted to talk to you."

"Really? What about?"

"About your husband. I love him."

Rhoda yanked off her sunglasses and stared at the English girl, who sat up straight, her head high, her eyes wide and combatively shiny. Rhoda's first coherent thought, through the fog of amazement, was that Pamela was a formidable rival if Pug really liked her. Let her have her say, she thought, reveal what she would reveal. Rhoda played with the glasses and drank coffee, just eyeing her.

"I know that you wanted a divorce," Pamela said, "and that he's asked you to reconsider."

"I have reconsidered!" Rhoda leaped at the opening. "Long since. That's all over with. He's confided in you, it seems."

"Oh, yes, Mrs. Henry," Pamela replied gloomily. "He's confided in me."

"Have you had an affair with my husband?"

"No." Their glances met in mutual search. "*No,* Mrs. Henry. He's remained faithful to you, worse luck."

Rhoda saw truth in Pamela's eyes. "Indeed? You're terribly PRETTY."

"He's been an ass." Pamela turned off the compliment with a hitch of her shoulder. "It would have been heaven. What's more, honors would now be even between you two."

The tone and the words stung. Rhoda said acidly, "But isn't my husband much too OLD for you?"

"Mrs. Henry, your husband's the most attractive man I've ever met in every way, including his loyalty to you, which has defeated me."

The passion in her voice alarmed Rhoda. She could see the difference between Pamela's young skin and hers, admire the sweet slim form of Pamela's upper arms—Rhoda now had to conceal her own because of a growing, revolting limp bagginess—and could envy that bosom. A small voice within her said that Pug had indeed been an ass, though she blessed him for it. "Did you see him after—after Midway?"

"Yes, I saw a lot of him. Through all his agony he kept worrying about you, about how you were taking it, about what he could do to console you. He even considered asking for emergency leave. He packed me off, though I tried to stay. He's a family man to the bone. If you can get to Hawaii, do it. He needs you. If there ever was a chance for me, the death of your son has ended it."

Touching a handkerchief to her eyes, Rhoda barely articulated, "Poor Pug."

"You were foolish to risk losing him. I can't understand you, I think it was terribly stupid of you, but don't do it again." Pamela gathered up her purse. "You say all that's over with."

"Yes, yes. Absolutely and forever."

"Good. You have a well-wisher who's written your husband several anonymous letters about you and this man. If you have no better reason to straighten up, there's one."

"Oh, God," Rhoda groaned. "What did the letters say?"

"Guess!" It was a scornful snap. In a softer tone Pamela said, "I'm sorry to hurt you in your bereavement, but I don't want you hurting him any more. That's why I've talked to you. I'll send the speech text to you by messenger. Our plane leaves in a couple of hours."

"Will you promise never to see my husband any more?"

Ugly lines strained Pamela's face. She contemplated Rhoda's proffered hand—lean, long, wrinkled, strong-fingered—then glared at her. "That's impossible! The future can't be controlled. But I'm out of your way now, rest assured of that." She looked around at the youngsters, drying themselves and giggling on the pool's edge, and her manner turned gentle. "This has been a bizarre conversation, hasn't it? A wartime conversation."

"I'm STUNNED," Rhoda said.

They both got up.

"One more thing," Pamela said. "I met your son Warren only once, in Hawaii just before the battle. There was a strange light about him, Mrs. Henry. It wasn't my imagination, my father sensed it too. He was almost godlike. You've had an appalling loss. But you have two other wonderful children. I hope you and your husband will console each other, and in time be happy again." With a quick feline movement Pamela kissed Rhoda's cheek and hastened out of the garden.

Rhoda walked to a lounge chair in the sun and fell into it, half out of her senses with surprise. When had Pug mentioned Pamela Tudsbury in his letters? From London in the summer of 1940; from Moscow late in 1941; and then just lately, from Hawaii. Of course, the father and daughter had been in and out of Washington, too. In a letter about the party at the Moana before the battle, Pug had remarked on "the Tudsbury girl's" sickly appearance, due to dysentery.

Poor Pug! Camouflage? An effort to stamp out romantic stirrings in his own inhibited heart?

As in a crystal ball, Rhoda saw pictures in the sparkling blue bowl of the now-deserted swimming pool: Pug and Pamela together in those far-off places, not making love, perhaps not even kissing, but just being together, day after day, evening after evening, thousands of miles from home. The bitter knowing smile on the face of this woman was a picture of Eve with something on Adam. Pamela Tudsbury had told a good story, she thought, but old Pug couldn't have been quite the holy

Joe she made him out. Rhoda knew better. The kind of passion that burned in Pamela Tudsbury did not kindle of itself. Pug had in some way, oblique or direct, wooed the girl. Perhaps indeed he had kept it platonic, so as to have his highminded cake and eat it; or perhaps they had slept together. It was hard to tell. As for the truthful look in Pamela's eyes, Rhoda knew all about truthful looks.

The anonymous letters were horrible to think about. What nasty biddy had done *that?* Nevertheless, the gap between her guilty self and her husband was narrower than she had dreamed, after all. She was jealous of Pamela, and scared of her; and Pug's desirability had shot up. She felt a warm unaccustomed stir of erotic longing for the taciturn old dog. The girl's renunciation meant little, of course. Pug had sent Pamela packing as she intended to do to Palmer Kirby. What had really gone on between them she might never know. It was a nice tactical problem, whether she should ever ask him.

With a start in her chair, Rhoda Henry realized she had forgotten for a little while that Warren was dead.

34

Louis stood fretting noisily in his crib, rattling the side bars. Siena in the summer was a bakeoven, and he took heat badly, his disposition becoming as rough and sore as the rashes that mottled him from head to toe. A diaper and a thin white shirt lay ready on the bureau top. He would probably howl when Natalie clothed him for the bus ride, so she was leaving that for last. As she tightened the suitcase straps, the sweat starting from this effort, Aaron looked in. "The car will be here in half an hour, my dear."

"I know. I'm ready."

In an old blue beret and a shabby gray suit he looked like any Italian bus passenger. Natalie had wondered whether to caution him about his usual flamboyant travelling clothes. He was showing good sense, happily, starting out. He glanced up at the mildewy ceiling with its peeling frescoed cherubs. "The whole place has certainly gone to seed. I hadn't really noticed until now." Gesturing at the open window and the distant cathedral, he added as he left, "But you won't soon have another view like this from your bedroom, will you?"

To Natalie the departure was not yet real. How often had she left this godforsaken Tuscan villa for good; how often had she seen once again, with sinking heart, the old gate with the wrought-iron peacock, the cracking yellow stucco garden wall, the red-tiled tower Byron had slept in! How lightly she had first set foot here in 1939, expecting to stay two or three months while she tried to recapture Leslie Slote; what a quicksand it had proved! Memories of her very first night in this room were haunting her—the musty smell of the satin-draped four-poster bed, the rat noisily gnawing in the wall, the crashing thunderstorm, lightning-lit Siena luridly framed in the open window like El Greco's Toledo.

Last-minute doubts were assailing her. Were they doing the right thing? They had just about settled down to a bearable house-arrest existence. Except for Werner Beck, nobody was bothering them. There was milk for the baby—goat's milk, but he thrived on it—and enough food. The Monte di Paschi bankers, aware of Aaron's wealth in New

York, would not let them lack for money. All true. But she had acted out of instinct after that last meeting with Beck, and now the die was cast. Aaron had been handling Beck quite suavely since then, sending him outlines for broadcasts, flattering him by accepting his suggestions, and at last wheedling official permission to get away from Siena's heat, in a week or two by the sea, as guests of the Sacerdotes in their Follonica beach house.

The straps on the two suitcases were secure. One was full of Louis's stuff, the other contained her barest necessities. Rabinovitz's instructions were stark: *"no baggage you can't handle yourself walking twenty miles with the baby."* Since getting his message Natalie had been walking six miles a day. Her feet had blistered, then healed in calluses, and she felt very fit. What a shock when Castelnuovo had offered her the rolled-up cigarette paper with a magnifying glass! "Just like the cinema, eh?" he had said. Now was the time to get rid of that paper. She took it from her purse, and unrolled it on her palm.

> dear natalie happy you are coming tell uncle travel very light you take no baggage you can't handle yourself walking twenty miles with the baby i care for your baby and i care for you it will be all right love

The tiny words, barely discernible to the naked eye, stirred her yet. No letter had come from Byron in months. She had read to tatters the few she possessed. Her memories of Byron were as unchanging and repetitious as old home movies. Her life and his had been unfolding apart for the last two years and she was not even sure he was alive. His last letters that the Red Cross had forwarded—written from Albany, a tiny town in southwest Australia, months ago—suggested that combat was changing him; he sounded nothing like the lighthearted young dandy who had bewitched her. The news that Castelnuovo was in touch with Rabinovitz, and the cigarette-paper message, had thrown her in a turmoil that persisted, though common sense told her there was nothing in the Palestinian's words but Jewish kindness.

It was hard to give up the paper, but rolling it in a tiny ball, she flooded it down the bathtub drain. She dressed the baby; then she took a last look around at the big frilly candy box of a room, and stared long at the big bed in which for years she had not known a man's arms around her, only empty teasing dreams and fantasies.

"Come on, Louis," she said. "Let's go home."

There were no farewells to the servants. Aaron was leaving closets full of clothes, a whole untouched library, and stacked folders of the

Luther book drafts on his desk. Natalie had given the maid and the gardeners orders for work to be finished when she returned in two weeks. But servants are wise, Italian servants especially. The cook, the maid, and the two gardeners were lined up at the iron gate. Their good-byes were cheery but their eyes were solemn and their manners fumbling. The cook gave the baby a stick of candy, and as they drove off she cried.

At the wheel of Sacerdote's car was the surly son who was remaining in Siena, and—so his family suspected—taking Catholic instruction because of his Christian girl. The anti-Jewish laws forbade conversions, but in Siena Fascist edicts were often ignored. In a light open shirt, his hair thick and unruly, a cigarette hanging from a corner of his down-turned mouth, the youth wordlessly drove them to the almost deserted Piazza del Campo, and left them there.

Siena had never been lively; now it scarcely seemed inhabited. The few vending stalls in the broad plaza stood empty and untended. Later, if a truckload of vegetables or fish came up from the coast there might be some buying and selling, but not much; rationing controlled everything down to garlic and onions. The long shadow of the Palazzo Pubblico tower oozed along the hot pavement, and mechanically the few gossipers moved with it, like toy figures on a huge sundial. Natalie and Aaron sat outside the one open café, drinking imitation orange soda with a metallic taste. She remembered the roaring mob of the Palio filling this amphitheatre of Renaissance palazzos, the rainbow parade of the *contrade,* the wild horse race: all stopped, all gone! Years of her life had melted away in this town bypassed by history. That Aaron had chosen to settle here was bizarre; that she had shared his exile was an aberration beyond fathoming.

The car came back, and the young man grumbled at them that the bus was about to leave. They had avoided waiting at the station because of the police. The permit to visit Follonica was an extraordinary document originating in Rome; the less they exposed it the better. At the station the bus driver impatiently waved them inside, and off they went under the eyes of a yawning policeman.

The bus chugged out through the high town wall and bumped down a narrow dirt road, heading west. The Sacerdotes, though dressed modestly, sat with the dignity of rich proprietors, their expressions abstracted and sad, and as in the faces of many old couples, very much alike. Louis fell asleep in Natalie's lap. Through the open windows of the bus sweet farmland odors swept in, mixed with the strangely pleasant gasogene fumes from the charcoal burner, like the scent of a wood fire. Miriam chattered happily to her mother, while her father stared out at the passing scenery. Grand panoramas of mountaintop villages, green hillside farms, and terraced vineyards opened up at every turn of the road. The bus ground down past Volterra in a steepening descent, and ended its run in Massa Marittima, a tiny old hilltop town quiet as Siena, its old gray stones shimmering in noon glare.

Here in the little square the futility of the Mussolini regime struck Natalie anew, in the contrast of the garish hollow victory posters and the old weathered façades of the church and town hall. Italy was too weary, too wise, too charming to play the armed bully. It had all been a showy fake and a waste. Unfortunately, the Germans had imitated the bloodthirsty charade with heavy Teutonic seriousness and run amuck with it; so Natalie tiredly thought, as she trudged to the railroad station holding the limp baby and one suitcase; Aaron was carrying the other, and one for himself.

A small narrow-gauge train tweeted into the station, and the conductor punched tickets with scarcely a glance at the passengers' faces. Nobody checked their papers either in the station or on the train. In all Massa Marittima they had seen only one policeman, dozing against his propped bicycle. Awake again, Louis looked out with mild interest at the farmers on the slopes, at the grazing sheep and cattle, and at the ugly gashes of mines in the hillsides, with their great brown rubbish heaps, tall conveyor belts, and rough wooden trestles and towers. The train wound around a rocky bend and there far below the Mediterranean glittered. Natalie caught her breath. Off on the hazy horizon she could see dots and humps of islands, their escape route to Lisbon.

The Sacerdotes' summer home in Follonica was a boxlike stucco house right on the beach, painted blue. Across the road a public park full of high old shade trees and wide-spreading palms gave exceptional privacy. Inside the boarded-up house all was stifling hot darkness and dank stale smells until Castelnuovo and his wife took down storm shutters and opened windows to a sea breeze. Natalie put Louis to bed in a crib that had once been Miriam's, and Sacerdote took her and Aaron to the small *carabinieri* station. The sleepy-eyed police chief, looking very impressed at the permit document from Rome, made the necessary stampings and notations, and stood up to shake hands with them. He had a brother in Newark, he said, a florist who made good money. Italy had no real quarrel with America. It was the Germans. What could you do with the damned Germans?

A week passed. No word came from Rabinovitz. Natalie sank into animal enjoyment of the beach as an anodyne for her mounting anxiety. As for Louis, playing in the sand with Miriam all day, and now and then getting dipped in the sea, he took on color and shed his rashes and his crankiness. On a Sabbath evening they were sitting down at the candle-lit table when the doorbell rang and a grimy man with a bluish three-day beard came in. His name was Frankenthal, he said, and he came from Avram Rabinovitz. His manner was matter-of-fact, tired, and abrupt until the Sacerdotes asked him to stay for dinner. Then he took off a ragged cap and looked pleasanter and slightly abashed. Pointing to the candles on the dining table he said, *"Sabato?* I have not seen that since my grandmother died."

He was a dock worker in Piombino, the iron-ore shipping port north of Follonica, he told them as he ate. His father too had worked on the docks. His grandfather had been a Hebrew scholar, but the family had dropped all that. He himself knew nothing but that he was a Jew. Once the children were put to bed he got down to business. The news was bad. The Turkish freighter that had been running refugees illegally from Corsica to Lisbon had lost its British navicert, and could not transit Gibraltar. That route was finished.

Still, they were to go on to Corsica via Elba as planned. Rabinovitz was arranging to bring them from Corsica to Marseilles, where most of the rescue agencies operated. Several routes existed for going on from Marseilles to Palestine or Lisbon. That was Rabinovitz's message. But Frankenthal told them of a more direct way to get to Marseilles. Vessels carrying iron ore from the mines of Elba and Massa Marittima for transshipment to the Ruhr made the run from Piombino every week or so. The British navy did not bother the ore boats. He knew a captain who would take them straight to Marseilles for five hundred dollars a passenger.

They were still at the table, drinking chicory by the light of the waning candles. Jastrow said drily, "I sailed from New York to Paris for five hundred dollars, first class."

"Professore, that was peacetime. The other way, God knows how long you'll be stuck in Elba or in Corsica. On the boat you'll sleep in beds, a direct trip, three days, the children safe."

He left to catch the last bus for Piombino, saying he would telephone in a day or two for their decision. "Take the ore boat," were his parting words.

Jastrow spoke first, with acid amusement, when he was gone. "If we do take the ore boat, this fellow will get a fat cut of our money."

"Do you trust him?" Natalie asked Castelnuovo.

"Well, I know he comes from Rabinovitz."

"How do you communicate with Avram?"

"Cables about innocuous matters. Otherwise, messengers like this fellow. Why?"

"I'm thinking of just going back to Siena."

Sacerdote said to his son-in-law, putting his arm around his frightened-looking wife, "She's right. You said we would go to Lisbon and never set foot in France."

"Yes, Papa, and now that has changed," Castelnuovo said with exaggerated forbearance, "and so, we're having a little chat."

Natalie turned to Jastrow. "When I went to meet Byron in Lisbon, the Vichy police pulled me off the train to check my papers. They were in order, luckily. My spine went icy when they asked whether I was a Jew." She turned to Castelnuovo. "What recourse would we have now in France, Jews travelling illegally? Suppose they jail us? I could become separated from Louis!"

"Avram will arrange transit visas for us," said Castelnuovo. "Papers can always be had."

"Fake papers, you mean," said Sacerdote.

"Papers that will pass."

Jastrow said, "Let's not be faint-hearted. We have set out. I confess I never liked the island-jumping plan. As long as we're going to Marseilles, I say let's take the ore boat. One big bribe, one comfortable trip, that's my notion."

Castelnuovo made an impatient gesture with both hands. "Now look, I already knew all about the ore boats. They dock in a maximum security area of Marseilles, behind a high fence with French military patrols, and German inspectors from the Armistice Commission. The captain cares nothing about you. It's just your money. If any danger arises to him—pauf!—his neck comes first. Going through the islands, we'll be in the hands of people Rabinovitz knows."

"I imagine my wife and I will go back," Sacerdote said very solemnly to Jastrow. "We must still talk it over, of course. But our son is there, you know." The old woman was sniffling into a handkerchief.

Jastrow quickly said, "It's natural. It's your home. For us it's safer to go on."

The old couple went upstairs. Jastrow and Castelnuovo debated some more about the ore boat. Castelnuovo hated to trust his family's lives, he said, to a bribed Italian. The price could jump in mid-passage;

the man could take the money and fail to perform; he could in fact sell them out. Resistance people stood for something more than an itching palm.

At last Jastrow said, "Look here, is our organizing principle democracy or authority? If it's authority, you decide."

Castelnuovo sourly laughed, waving off the suggestion.

"Well, then, I vote for the ore boat."

Anna Castelnuovo said, "Two votes."

"You're a mule," her husband said, but the tone was wryly affectionate. He turned to Natalie. "Well?"

"The ore boat."

Castelnuovo pursed his mouth, lightly struck the table, and stood up. "Settled."

On a gray cool afternoon, coming back from an eight-mile walk, Natalie noticed from a distance a parked car near the house. There were few private cars in Follonica. Her steps quickened, and something like a prayer flitted through her mind: "Let it not be trouble." As she drew nearer she recognized the Mercedes. In the house Jastrow and Werner Beck sat at the dining table over tea and a platter of cakes. Yellow typescripts of Jastrow's broadcasts lay scattered on the bare table.

Werner Beck got up, smiling and bowing. "Delighted. It's been so long!" She could barely choke out a civil response. He glanced down at his SS uniform with an apologetic little laugh. "Ah, yes. Never mind my formidable masquerade. I'm on a tour of the western ports, Mrs. Henry, in connection with an unaccountable shortage of fuel oil, which my country has to supply to Italy one hundred percent. We're sure the black market is draining it off. Italians are more forthcoming with the truth when they see this uniform. My SS commission is purely honorary, but they don't know that. Well, now, the sea air has done wonders for you. And the baby? How is he? I'd love to see him."

Natalie said in as normal a tone as she could muster, "Shall I fetch him? How long can you stay?"

"Regrettably, not long. I have business in Piombino. Follonica's only a short way off the main road, so I thought I'd drop by and pay my respects."

"Let me get him, then."

On the second floor the Castelnuovos, their faces pallid and strained, sat in their bedroom with the door wide open. The doctor beckoned to her and whispered, "Is that the man?"

"Yes."

"I heard him mention Piombino."

"He's on an inspection tour."

In the other room Miriam was amusing Louis with a ragged toy bear. She looked up like a worried grown woman when Natalie lifted him from his crib. "Where are you taking him?"

"Downstairs, just for a moment."

"But downstairs there is a German."

Natalie put a finger to her lips and bore off the yawning Louis. She halted on the staircase, hearing Beck raise his voice. "But Dr. Jastrow, all four broadcasts are fine as they stand. Why, they're gemlike essays. You can't change a word. Why not record them now? At least the first two?"

Jastrow's voice, quietly serene: "Werner, a publisher once urged the poet A. E. Housman to print some essays he was discarding. Housman cut him off with these words: *'I did not say they were not good. I said they were not good enough for me.'*"

"That's all very fine, but for us time is a key factor. If you could not polish these talks to your taste before the war was over, it would all be pretty pointless, hm?"

Jastrow's chuckle was appreciative and jolly. "Very neat, Werner."

"But I'm absolutely serious! I'm shielding you from painful harassment. You told me that a week or two by the sea was all you'd need. If this matter is ever taken out of my hands, Dr. Jastrow, you'll be extremely sorry."

Silence.

Natalie hurried down the stairs and into the dining room. Beck stood up, beaming at the child. "My goodness, but he has grown!" He slipped his glasses into a breast pocket and extended his arms. "May I take him? If you knew how I miss my Klaus, my youngest!"

Putting her son into the hands of this uniformed man gave Natalie a sick qualm, but Dr. Beck's manner of handling the baby was knowing and gentle. Louis smiled beautifully at him. Dr. Beck's eyes moistened, and he spoke in an artificial little voice. "Well, hello there! Hello, little happy boy! We're friends, aren't we? No politics between us, hm?— Well! Want my glasses, do you?" He pried the frames out of Louis's tiny clutch. "Let's hope you never need glasses. Here, your mother looks anxious, go back to her. Tell her I've never dropped a baby yet."

Natalie clasped Louis with relief and sat down. Resuming his seat,

Beck donned his glasses, and his face took on a severe cast. "Now then. I shall be returning from my tour in five days, and I propose to take you both with me to Rome. Dr. Jastrow, you must be ready to record the broadcasts. I've already made hotel arrangements, and I am going to be very firm about this."

With a resigned mock-humble gesture of bowed shoulders and out-stretched arms, Jastrow exclaimed, "Five days! Well, I can try to do something. But the second two scripts are out of the question, Werner. They're simply scattered notes. I can attempt to cobble up the first one or two, dear fellow, but if you insist on all four, I shall simply lie down in my traces like the overloaded horse."

Beck patted the old man's knee. "Just have the first two ready when I return. Then we'll see."

"Is it really necessary for me to come to Rome, too?" Natalie asked. "Yes."

"Will we return to Siena afterward?"

"As you wish," Beck said absently, glancing at his wristwatch and standing up. Aaron walked outside with him.

Down the stairs came the Castelnuovos, with Miriam tiptoeing behind her mother's skirts. She poked out her head at Natalie and stage-whispered, "Did the German go away?"

"Yes, he's gone."

"Did he hurt Louis?"

"No, no, Louis is fine." Natalie was clutching the baby as though picking him up after a fall. "Suppose I put you two out on the porch."

"Can he have a cake?"

"All right."

The four adults held a quick conclave in the dining room. That this was a crisis, that Jastrow had to move on, they took for granted. Castelnuovo had to consult Frankenthal, they decided, but not over the telephone. The afternoon bus was leaving in half an hour. The doctor clapped on his hat and departed. A grim evening followed. He returned early the next morning, to the immense relief of his wife, who had not slept. Frankenthal's advice was that they had better go on to the islands after all, for an ore boat had sailed only last week. The next ferry to Elba was day after tomorrow.

"It's off to Corsica, then," said Natalie, covering the thumping of her heart with dogged gaiety.

"Off to Elba," said the doctor. "There we'll have to wait. Nothing is organized for Corsica as yet."

"Well," said Jastrow. "Napoleon made it off Elba, and so shall we."

It rained and blew hard the morning they left. Waves were breaking high over the sea wall of the Piombino waterfront when the passengers began straggling aboard the small ferryboat pitching in its slip. Far off under a shed three waterfront customs guards, dry and snug, sat smoking pipes and drinking wine. Frankenthal had excursion permits ready, as well as tickets; the permits were required because of the prison on Elba. But there was no checking of papers. The fugitives boarded the ferry among other travellers under umbrellas; chains rattled, the diesel coughed stinking smoke, the ferry pulled unsteadily away from the slip, Frankenthal waved at them and shouted a casual good-bye, and they were *out!*

Looking back at the mainland veiled by the downpour and by smoke from the Piombino blast furnaces, Natalie recalled how, the night before, the red flaming mouths of the furnaces outside the train window had scared Louis into a screaming fit, attracting an inspector examining passengers' papers. Miriam had distracted both Louis and the official by chattering Italian baby talk in her bell-clear Tuscan accent, and he had laughed and walked off without giving them trouble. For all her nightmarish fears, that had been the only narrow moment in leaving Italy.

A slow nauseating trip over stormy waters, and Elba loomed through the drizzle, a broad mist-shrouded hump of green. They disembarked on a windy U-shaped waterfront lined with old houses under a long frowning old fortress. On Frankenthal's instructions, Anna wore a white shawl and Natalie a blue one, and Aaron had a pipe in his mouth. A mule-drawn carriage driven by a gnarled old man drew up. He gestured at them to climb in, and he closed the carriage with very dirty canvas rain curtains. A long, long uphill ride ensued, with much bumping and sliding. Seen through isinglass panels, the hilly vineyards and farms were green blurs in fog. The air inside the canvas curtains was mildewy and close, the mule smell chokingly strong. The driver never spoke. Louis slept all the way. At last the carriage halted, the driver pulled back the curtains, and Natalie stiffly stepped down into a puddle, gulping the sweet damp country air. They were in the stone square of a sloping mountain village. There was nobody else in sight; not so much as a dog. Twilight was falling, the rain had stopped, the wet stone front of the old church looked violet, and the stillness was almost shocking.

"Where are we?" Natalie asked the driver in Italian. Her ordinary voice sounded like a shout.

He uttered his first word, "Marciana."

35

STABLEHANDS were grooming many neighing, stamping horses in the Bel Air Canyon Riding Academy, but no other riders were about except Madeline and Byron. Madeline's habit was bandbox-new: fawn jodhpurs, softly gleaming brown boots, mannish feathered hat. Byron wore Warren's Annapolis blazer with faded dungarees and sneakers. A withered groom in very dirty clothes, appraising him at a glance, brought out a large coal-black steed called Jack Frost. Byron adjusted the stirrups and mounted; whereupon Jack Frost, flattening his ears and redly rolling his eyes, took off up the canyon like a lunatic. He was a powerful animal with a smooth gallop, and Byron let him run free. Passing a white rag lying on the trail, Jack Frost reared, bucked, neighed, and snorted in a Hollywood enactment of acute panic. With some effort Byron stayed in the saddle. The horse, apparently concluding that he could ride, calmed down and glanced around at him inquiringly. Byron saw Madeline trotting along, far back on the trail, through Jack Frost's settling dust. "Okay, this was your idea, horse," he said with a kick. "Keep going."

Jack Frost lit out again, darted into a steep narrow switchback trail, and thundered up the side of the canyon in a hair-raising run to the summit, where he stopped short, head down, blowing like a whale. Shaken up and exhilarated, Byron got off, tied him to a tree, and perched on a rock. After a while he heard hooves scrambling below, and Madeline came in sight coated with dust. "What's with your horse?" she called.

"I think he wanted some exercise."

She giggled as he helped her off her mount. "I thought maybe he had a breakfast date in San Francisco."

They sat side by side on a wide flat rock, looking out over the canyon at sunlit wild hills. Lizards rustled on the rocks, and in the air below them vultures wheeled screaming. The horses stamped and puffed, jingling their harness. These sounds only heightened the prevailing hush.

Byron waited for her to speak. She had begged him to come on this ride, giving no reason. After a while he said, "Everything okay, Maddy?"

"Oh, Briny, I'm in a peck of trouble. But no! No!" She burst out laughing. "Your face! It's like a *teletype,* sweetie. Christ, did I ever get off on the wrong foot *that* time! I'm not pregnant, Briny. Put down that shotgun."

He scratched his head and managed a grin.

She shook a roguish finger at him. "Such evil thoughts about your own sister! No, it's a question of changing jobs, and"—she quickly lit a cigarette with a gold lighter—"it's something I can't discuss when Mom's around."

"Can you smoke here? I saw a sign about fire hazard in this canyon."

She shrugged, heavily inhaling. "You remember Lenny Spreregen?"

"I sure do."

"Universal's making him a producer. He wants me as an assistant."

"What about Cleveland?"

"Furious! Having kittens." She smiled at Byron. Her face was flushed, her eyes zestfully sparkled. "But I've got to consider it, don't I? Two hundred a week is a *beeg* jump from one fifty, you know."

"Why, that's munificent, Mad. And getting away from Cleveland sounds great."

Her face remained sweetly amiable, but the hard Henry note began to ring. "Oh, you've always underestimated Hugh, haven't you? The public *loves* him. Of course, making films beats selling soap and laxatives, but I have a sure thing where I am. Hugh's even given me a little stock ownership in his company. It's a really tough choice."

"Madeline, grab the job at Universal."

"Tell me one thing. Did Hugh ever do something to offend you? If so, it had to be unintentional. He thinks you're terrific."

"He doesn't know me."

"You know what? I bet it's that kiss he gave me in Janice's house. Isn't it?" She archly grinned. "I bet that still rankles. My God, when you told me you'd seen us, you had murder in your eye."

It was a memory Byron still preferred to blot out: the soft plump married man clutching Madeline to him, her skirt riding up behind, uncovering pink thighs and white garters. "Look, you asked for my advice. I gave it."

"Briny"—her voice softened—"Hugh Cleveland wants to marry me." Byron's face showed no reaction. She hurried on, blushing, *"That's* the complication. That's why I've got to talk to somebody. Mom's so straitlaced, she'd just fall over dead at the idea. Anyway, she has enough problems and—my, that's a grim silence, darling! But you don't know Hughie. He's *our kind,* honey, he's really a very intelligent, vulnerable, and lonesome man."

"Wife and three kids aren't that much company, eh?"

Madeline bitterly laughed. "That had to come, I guess."

"He's proposed to you?"

"Oh, darling, people don't *propose* nowadays." She waved a scornful hand. "Did you propose to Natalie?"

"I did, in so many words."

"Well, you're a weird old-fashioned type. All us Henrys are. Hugh's already working on his divorce."

"He is?" Byron got up and paced on the pebbly dirt with loud crunches. "You should be talking to Dad."

"Dad? Perish the thought. He'd visit Hugh with a horsewhip."

"Is he divorcing his wife because of you?"

"Oh, Claire, that's the wife, is just a horror, a total paranoid, a stupid woman he married when he was twenty-one. She's insanely afraid of losing him, yet she treats him like dirt. She's always running to psychoanalysts. She spends money like a duchess. Why, a year ago she was throwing fits about me, threatening I don't know what. He had to placate her with a sable coat. She is one unholy mess, Briny, take my word for it. And of course, she's turned his kids against him."

"Listen to me. Call Universal today." He halted and stood over her. "Tell the fellow you'll go to work for him Monday."

"I figured you'd say that." She looked up at him solemnly and her voice faltered. "I'm just not sure I can do it."

Feeling a wave of sickened, poignant sympathy for his sister, Byron said, "It's serious."

"Yes."

He spoke low. "How serious?"

"I *told* you." Her voice turned testy. "It's not a matter for horsewhips and shotguns. But it's serious."

He scanned her face, and heavily sighed. The gentle open look of the girl was as opaque as a leather mask. "How old is he?"

"Thirty-four." She glanced at her watch. "Honey, you have to pick up Mom and meet us in the Warner Brothers commissary at noon. Let's finish our ride."

"Maybe I'll talk to him at the studio."

The pretty leather mask faintly suggested wistful relief. "You? What-ever about?"

"About this."

Her mouth curled. "Shotgun in hand, sweetie?"

"No. If he wants to marry you, he should be glad to talk to me."

"I can't stop you. Do as you please." She put her foot in the stirrup. "Give me a leg up, Briny, we're late."

In the large, crowded, sunny cafeteria on the Warner Brothers lot, Rhoda gawked about, round-eyed, scarcely eating, saying things like, "Why, Maddy dear, isn't that Humphrey BOGART?—My stars, and there's Bette Davis! She looks so YOUNG off the screen."

Hugh Cleveland explained that though the stars had their own posh dining rooms, they liked to drop into the commissary now and then for a sandwich and a glass of milk. Like the stars, Cleveland was lunching in a dressing gown, his face painted up for filming. Byron disliked him again at sight, but his whimsical rumblings and chucklings clearly amused Rhoda, and his sleek happy air of success impressed her. Two radio shows—the old *Amateur Hour* and the military *Happy Hour*—were going strong, and the film shorts promised still more revenue. Madeline's hundred fifty a week was about twice Byron's submarine pay; and if she took the Universal offer she would be out-earning her own father, the captain of a heavy cruiser.

And for what? Watching the filming of a *Happy Hour* short after lunch, Byron was disgusted. The soldiers and sailors were the merest butts for Cleveland's supposedly spontaneous jokes, which were held up off camera on large printed placards. There was no audience. Later, Madeline explained, the director would splice in shots of attentive, laughing, or applauding onlookers. Byron couldn't believe that the films would be entertaining even if the fraud came off. Nothing was there but a radio announcer with a calculated folksy manner, poking conde-scending fun at untalented kids in uniform. The sights and sounds of show business, however low-grade, obviously enchanted his mother, and he was glad she had this distraction from grief; but as for him, he yawned and yawned until his jaws hurt, in an agony of irritated tedium.

A break came in the filming, and Cleveland approached them, grin-ning, with two paper cups of coffee. "You seem to need this more than I do, Admiral."

Madeline bustled up. "Mom, Byron! Humphrey Bogart is shooting on the next sound stage now. Want to watch?"

"Is it all right?" Rhoda asked eagerly.

"Of course."

"I'm DAZZLED by all this," Rhoda said, following her.

Cleveland said to Byron, who didn't stir, "Not interested?"

"Mr. Cleveland, can I talk to you?"

"What's up?"

"Madeline's told me about the Universal offer."

"Oh ho. Come along." Byron went with him into a plywood dressing room, and they both sat down on chairs by a lamp-bordered mirror. "Byron, don't let her take that job."

"Why not? It's more money."

"Lenny Spreregen's a passable screenwriter, but he's no executive. He's fast-talked himself into this thing. He's a communist, what's more, a notorious one. He'll never last at Universal, and the day he goes—bye-bye Madeline, broke and alone in Hollywood."

"She says you want to marry her."

"Oh, wow!" With a warm beguiling grin, Cleveland rubbed fingers in his back hair. "By the way, call me Hugh, won't you?" He looked at a cheap alarm clock on the dresser, swallowed coffee, and humorously rumbled as he stood up, "But let's not open that can of peas during a coffee break, huh, Admiral? How long are you going to be here?"

"My leave is up tonight." Byron rose, blocking the narrow doorway. It was a casual act, but meanwhile Cleveland couldn't go out. "She says you're getting divorced."

Cleveland made a move toward the door, with a polite little gesture that Byron ignored. To leave he would have had to shove the submarine officer aside. His puffy face went sombre, then the charming grin with arched eyebrows reappeared. He rested a haunch on the dressing table, and rubbed his chin, looking quizzically at Byron's serious face. Rumpling his hair with both hands, he uttered a small groan. "Okay, Byron. Once over lightly, here goes. Claire, that's my wife, is a very unhappy and unfortunate woman. I'll say no more against her. We have three grand kids, but nothing else is left in common between us. Sexual interest is zero—not on my side. On hers. That's hell on earth, and I hope you never experience it. We've both been talking to lawyers, but these deals are messy and long. It's easy to get into marriage, but Christ on wheels, me lad, it's hard to get out."

"Do you love my sister?"

"You have a wonderful sister. She wasn't lying to you. I believe I can work this out, but it is one bitch of a bind. Now that's how it is,

Byron." With his warmest radio chuckle, Cleveland stood up and lightly slapped his shoulder. "Back to the salt mine. Maybe the three of us can have a drink together later. Tell her not to take that Spreregen job, Byron. It's a stinker."

Madeline was rushing about outside, carrying a script board and talking to people over one shoulder and the other. She came darting to Byron, who leaned against a wall near the exit amid a snarl of cables and lights.

"Well?" It was a tone of mock conspiracy.

"Well, what? Where's Mom?"

"Oh, she won't budge. The director invited her to stay and meet Bogart. You talked to Hugh?"

"Oh, yes."

"Come on. What happened?" Her look was worried, excited, searching. "Did he get mad?"

"No."

She smiled. "No shotgun, then. He'd have blown his stack at that."

"Madeline, tell him you're quitting. Do it today. Hang it on me. Tell him I've got an insane temper. Tell him any goddamn thing you want."

Her face fell. "Did he deny that he wants to marry me?"

"He fudged. Quit, I tell you. If he's what you want, maybe that'll get him moving."

"Why, Byron Henry." Her eyes slyly narrowed. "That's how a girl thinks. Or should."

"And if he's stringing you along, you'll find that out, too."

She tossed her head, and the lithe hips in a pleated yellow skirt swished away.

In the villa, hours later, Byron was napping when a gentle knock at the door woke him. "Briny!" Madeline's voice, soft and excited. "Are you decent?"

Slant sunlight made big patches on the drawn red curtains: cocktail time. He sat up, stretching, naked except for shorts. "Oh, reasonably."

She swept in, and stood with her back to the closed door. "By Christ, I did it!"

"Great. Where's Mom?"

"I don't know. Not here. Briny, I never *dreamed* I could. It's incredible. I feel as though I've broken out of Alcatraz and swum ashore." The red glow through the curtains exaggerated the wild animation of her face. "And the way he took it! In a hundred years, I couldn't have predicted that. Byron, he was nice as pie! Utterly sweet! Not a harsh word! I'm in a daze. Can I have a drink?"

Byron put on a robe, and they went into the living room. He lolled on the couch, smoking, while she paced around and talked, highball in hand, yellow pleats flapping. She had done it in the dressing room, only an hour or so ago, upon finishing a review of the next day's script. Cleveland had been gentle, understanding, and not in the least surprised. "Oh, what a clever dog he is! You know what he said first thing? 'Well, kid, when you consulted your brother, that was it. That meant you already wanted to leave.' But, Byron—and this may really floor you—he says you're *right*. It's much better for me to get out while he pushes the divorce. Otherwise Claire could make real trouble about me. Thank Christ you came here."

"It's all set? It's definite? You've quit?"

"Absolutely. Isn't that terrific?"

"When do you go to work for this Asparagus person, or whatever?"

Madeline tried to hold her offended look, but her lips tightened and then she exploded in laughter. *"Asparagus!* Honestly, Byron, you're a sketch. What's so hard about Spreregen?"

"Sorry. When do you start with him?"

Still giggling, she said, "Next month. I called Lenny, he's agreed, and—"

"Wait a minute. Next month?" Byron sat up and swung his hairy naked legs to the floor.

"Sweetie, of course. I had to give a month's notice. I can't walk out overnight, that's childish." Byron crashed a fist on the coffee table so that books and ashtrays jumped. Frightened, Madeline raised her voice. "Oh, I can't *stand* you! How can you be so unreasonable? Could you or Dad walk off your ship without a replacement?"

Byron leaped to his feet. "Goddamn you, Madeline, are you comparing the garbage Cleveland does to what I do? To what Dad does? To what *Warren* did? I'll go see this fellow again."

"No! I don't want you to!" Madeline began to cry. "Oh, how ugly and cruel you can be! Did I mention Warren?"

"Hell, no, you haven't since I got here."

"I can't bear to!" Madeline screamed, shaking her fists at him. A storm of tears burst from her eyes. "And neither can you! Oh, God, why did you say that? Why?"

Rocked back by the outburst, Byron muttered, "Sorry," and tried to put an arm around her.

She pulled away, drying her eyes with a shaky hand. Her voice was tremulous but hard. "My work's important to me, Byron, and to millions of people. Millions! It's honest work. You're just bullying me, and you have no right to do it. You're not Dad. And even he doesn't have the right anymore. I'm not sixteen."

The door opened and Rhoda walked in, juggling large parcels. "Hi, kids, I've BOUGHT OUT Beverly Hills! Swept down Wilshire Boulevard like a typhoon! They'll be clearing the wreckage for WEEKS! Byron, I'm roasting, make me a nice tall gin and tonic, will you, dear?" She went on into her bedroom.

"Oh, Lord," Madeline muttered, wiping her eyes. She had turned her back as her mother entered.

"Go wash your face, Maddy."

"Yes. Fix me another drink, too. Strong."

In a new gay print robe, Rhoda soon looked into the kitchenette where Byron was mixing highballs. "Dear, are you really going back to sub school tonight? That's so awful. It seems I've barely laid eyes on you."

"I'll stay with you tonight, and drive down early. And I'll be back next Sunday."

"Oh, lovely! You and Maddy have brought me back from the DEAD, you truly have. In Washington I felt ENTOMBED. I've bought a RAFT of these California clothes, they're so smart, and light, and *different*. Amazing the stuff they've got out here, war or no war. It's a whole wardrobe for Hawaii. I intend to knock Dad's eyes out."

"You think you can get there?"

"Oh, I do. I do. There are ways and means, darling, and I'm absolutely determined—oh, thank you, pet. I may just dunk myself in the pool before I drink this."

Madeline said in a placating tone, when they were alone again sipping drinks, "Byron, will you really go to Switzerland after sub school? Will the Navy allow it?"

"I don't know. It depends on what I can find out from the State Department, and the legation in Rome. I won't start up with the Navy unless I have to."

She walked to his armchair, sat on the arm, and caressed his face. "Look, don't be so hard on me."

"Can't you quit in two weeks?"

"Trust me, Byron. You've been a big help. It'll work out, I swear." Madeline's voice shifted to loud cheerfulness as her mother came out in a bathing suit, carrying a towel. "Hey, Mom, big news! Guess what? I'm going to work at Universal Pictures!"

36

Early in August, in the American legation in Bern, the Jastrow-Henry case came to a sudden boil.

Dr. Hesse, Slote's friend in the Swiss Foreign Ministry, returned from Rome with the shocking news that Jastrow and his niece, having been granted the extraordinary privilege of a seaside holiday, had violated parole and vanished. A Jewish doctor from Siena, a secret Zionist, was involved. The Italian authorities were wrathful, and Dr. Hesse had been called in to the German embassy and asked what he knew. The roly-poly pink little diplomat was recounting all this to Slote in a sidewalk café, and half a chocolate éclair trembled on his fork as he described how he had told the German first secretary, a hard nasty customer named Dr. Werner Beck, to go to hell. The situation of Jastrow and his niece, in Hesse's opinion, was now hopeless. If they were hiding, they would be found; if they tried to leave Italy, they would be caught. On recapture, they would go straight to an Italian concentration camp. The government had confiscated Jastrow's villa, his bank account, and the contents of his safe deposit box.

Oh, God, thought Slote as he heard this upsetting tale, the same old Natalie, plunging headlong into incalculable risk, this time baby and all! He decided not to report this grave development to Natalie's mother or to Byron—who was writing him letter after letter—until he could find out more; and to do this, he decided, he would have to go to Geneva. There the big Jewish organizations, including the Zionists, had their Swiss offices. The American consulate dealt all the time with them; it had contacts too with the Jewish underground. He might learn nothing about the escape. On the other hand, one heard surprising things from the Jews in Geneva, and the information tended to be accurate.

It was through these contacts that the ghastly accounts of the German extermination camps were trickling in. Slote had been shutting his mind to these reports. After his failure to authenticate the Wannsee Protocol, and the strange death of Father Martin, he felt helpless, even threatened. Preserving himself and his sanity came first. Anyway, who was he to change history? Beyond the postcard beauty of the snowy Alps, there was not only a great war going on, but—he was all but sure —a vast secret slaughter. Meantime, the sun rose each day, one ate and drank, and one's desk was laden with work. There were diplomatic cocktail parties and dinner parties. Wartime life wasn't bad in Bern, everything considered, and the town itself was so clean and quiet and charming! On the Zytglogge tower the little jester jingled the hours, the golden giant clanged the bell with his hammer, the puppets did their dance; in the bear pits the tame bears sadly stumbled through their waltzes for carrots. On days when the *Föhn* blew away the Alpine mists, the snowy Oberland ridge sprang into sight, white and pink and azure, looking like the approaches to Heaven. The only link to the terror beyond these pretty peaks was the permanent line of refugees with haunted eyes outside the door of the American legation.

Slote entrained for Geneva in a glum frame of mind. When he returned to Bern three days later, commercial work had piled up in his office. He ground through the heap with his secretary, grateful to be using his mind on rational matters. At the end of the day he declined a dinner with two other bachelors of the staff who had some visiting French ballet girls lined up. Telephoned at his flat by the married Swiss woman he now and then discreetly slept with, he stalled her off, too. After what he had learned in Geneva, petty sensualities seemed dirty to him. He ate some bread and cheese, then sank into an armchair with a bottle of Scotch.

What he had picked up about Jastrow and Natalie was only a vague third-hand report; still, it sounded plausible and cheering. Unfortunately, and unwillingly, he had also found out much more about the exterminations. The thought of resigning from the Foreign Service was circling in his mind, like a recurring slogan on an electric sign. Hard behind it there flashed the red reminder that he would at once be drafted into the Army.

Leslie Slote found himself reviewing his ambitions, his origins, his moral values, his hopes, in an agony of self-stripping, as before a decision to try a new career, or to give up a woman or marry her. He cared nothing for the Jews. He had grown up in a Connecticut suburban town where they could not easily buy homes. His father, a quiet philosophical Wall Street lawyer, had had no close Jewish friends. At Yale Slote had kept his distance from the Jewish students, and his secret society had tapped none. Natalie Jastrow's Jewishness had once seemed to Slote a flaw about half as bad as being a Negro.

Nor had he really changed. Now as always he was strictly out for himself, but by chance the Wannsee document had come his way. Because he knew German history and culture, what struck others as utter fantasy he believed to be true. Between the episode of the Minsk documents, and his stridency about the Wannsee Protocol, he was already suspect. If now he raised his voice about the new evidence, he would mark himself "Jew-lover" at the State Department for good. So Slote ruminated, sunk in his armchair, as the whiskey dwindled in the bottle.

Yet even the new Geneva evidence, though shocking and sickening, was not irrefutable. How could it be? *Where were the dead Jews?* Nothing surely proved murder except the *corpus delicti*—in this case great mounds of murdered people or mass graves full of them. How could one gain access to such proof? Photographs could be faked. There would never be irrefutable proof of this thing until the war ended; and then, only if the Allies won. The Geneva evidence, like the Wannsee Protocol, was only words: words spoken, words written, mixed with other words that were hysterical bosh, and still others, like the story of factories making corpses into soap, that were stale atrocity propaganda from the last war.

Slote could blame nobody for hesitating to believe in this weird gigantic massacre. Pogroms were an old story, but only a few people died in a pogrom. The Nazis did not bother to hide their persecution and looting of the Jews; still, they dismissed as Allied propaganda or Jewish ravings the ever-multiplying stories of secret murders in the hundreds of thousands. Yet these murders were happening, or at least Slote believed they were. The plan in the Wannsee Protocol was simply being carried out, in a grisly world of killers and victims as inaccessible as the unseen side of the moon.

Glass after glass of Scotch and water coursed down his throat, leaving a warm glowing trail, relaxing and comforting him, floating him above himself. Almost, he could look down like a released spirit at his skinny bespectacled self stretched on the chair and ottoman, and feel sorry for this clever chap whose future might be sacrificed for the goddamned Jews. How could he help it? He was a human being, and he was sane. If a sane man who knew about this insane thing didn't fight it, there was not much hope for the race of man, was there? And who could say what one man might not accomplish, if only he could find the right words to utter, to proclaim, to shout to the world? What about Karl Marx? What about Christ?

When a solitary boozing session got around to Marx and Christ,

Slote knew it was running down. It was time to reel off to bed. He did.

Next morning he was in his shirt-sleeves, typing a letter to Byron Henry about what he had learned of Natalie, when his secretary came in, a fleshily sexy blonde girl named Heidi. Heidi kept flirting with Slote, but to him she was like a cream pastry in a skirt. "Mr. Wayne Beall from the Geneva consulate says you expect him."

"Oh, yes. Tell him to come in." He locked the letter in a drawer and donned his jacket. As Wayne Beall entered, Heidi made cow eyes at the handsome young American vice consul, a short man going very bald in front, but so straight-backed, flat-stomached, and bright-eyed that the bald brow didn't matter. He had dropped out of West Point on developing a heart murmur, but at thirty he still strode like a cadet, and kept trying to get back into the Army. Beall regarded Heidi's hind parts thoughtfully as she twitched out.

"You didn't bring your papers?" Slote closed the door.

"Hell, no, my hair stands on end to think of losing such stuff on a train. If the minister decides to act, I'll send him everything I've got."

"Your appointment is for ten o'clock."

"Does he know what it's about?"

"Certainly."

Beall's bald brow became corrugated with worry lines. "I'm in way over my head on this, Les. You'll join us, won't you?"

"Not a chance. I'm considered bonkers on this subject."

"Hell, Leslie, who considers you bonkers? You've read the files. You know who these informants are. You have a reputation for brilliance. I've never been suspected of that. Damn it, come along, Les."

Resignedly, and with a sense of foreboding, Slote said, "You'll do the talking, though."

The minister wore a Palm Beach suit and well-chalked white shoes. He was going to a garden luncheon, he said, so this interview would have to be a brisk one. He dropped into his swivel chair and keenly regarded with his living eye the two men sitting side by side on the couch.

"Sir, I appreciate your giving me this time out of your busy schedule," Beall began, somewhat overdoing the briskness in tone and gesture.

The minister made a tired deprecatory hand wave. "What new information have you?"

Wayne Beall launched into his report. Two hard separate confirmations of the massacre had come into his office from very high-level persons. From a third source, he had eyewitness affidavits of the mass murder process in action. He said this at length, with much talk about disaster, American humanitarianism, and the minister's wisdom.

Leaning his face on one hand like a bored judge, the minister asked, "What high-level persons gave you confirmation?"

The vice consul said that one was a well-known German industrialist, the other a top Swiss official of the International Red Cross. If the minister needed the names, he would try to get the gentlemen's consent to be identified.

"You've talked to them yourself?"

"Oh, no, sir! Neither one would level with an American official. Not unless they knew him very, very intimately."

"How did you get their reports, then? And how do you know they're authentic?"

With a trace of embarrassment Beall said that Jewish sources had given him the reports: the World Jewish Congress and the Jewish Agency for Palestine. Slote perceived the fall in the minister's interest: a wandering of the live eye, a slump of the shoulders. "Indirect reports again," Tuttle said.

"Sir," Slote spoke up, "what other kind can there be about a secret plan of Hitler's?" He could not keep irritation out of his voice. "As to this German industrialist, I spoke to the chap at the WJC myself, and he—"

"What's the WJC?"

"World Jewish Congress. He all but named the man. I know who he means. This man is very high up in German industry. I also read the file of eyewitness affidavits. They're substantial and shattering."

"And that's not the whole story yet, sir," said Beall.

"Well, what else?" The minister took an ivory paper cutter and slapped it on his palm.

Beall described how he and the British consul in Geneva had sent home identical coded cables about the new evidence, for confidential transmittal to Jewish leaders. The British Foreign Office had forwarded it at once to the designated British Jews, but the American State Department had suppressed the telegram. Now the Jewish leaders in both countries, besides being in a turmoil over the disclosures, were up in arms over the State Department's action, which had been found out.

"*That* I will look into," the minister declared, throwing the paper cutter down on his desk. "You'll be hearing further from me, Wayne, and now I'd like a word with Leslie."

"Certainly, sir."

"See you in my office, Wayne," Slote said.

When the door closed behind Beall, the minister said to Slote, looking at his watch and rubbing his good eye, "I've got to go. Now listen, Les, I don't like this business of suppressing cables. The Division of European Affairs puzzles me. It's already ignored two letters of mine, about the visa regulations, and about your photostats."

"You did write about the photostats?" Slote burst out. "When?"

"When the Polish government-in-exile's stuff came out. That gave me second thoughts. How on earth could they fabricate all that? The statistics, the locations, the carbon monoxide vans, the midnight raids on the ghettos? That business of searching the dead women's rectums and vaginas, for God's sake, for jewelry? How could anybody just imagine such things?" Slote stared dumbfounded at the minister. "But okay, let's assume the Poles are unreliable. Let's say they're blackening the Germans to cover their own misdeeds. What about that business in Paris? The Vichy police separating thousands of foreign Jews from their kids and shipping off the parents, God knows where! In front of news cameras, this was. Nothing secret about it. I got a YMCA report on the details. Just heartrending. That was when I wrote the department about your photostats, but it was like throwing a stone down a well. And the visa thing, Les, is just too much."

"Good God, I hope you mean the good conduct certificate!" Slote exclaimed. "I've been battling that nonsense for months."

"Exactly. I can't look these Swiss officials in the eye anymore, Leslie. We're not fooling them, we're simply disgracing our country. How can an escaped Jew produce a good conduct certificate from his hometown police in *Germany?* It's an obvious gimmick to keep the Jews piling up here. We're going to have to waive it."

Staring pallidly at Tuttle, Slote cleared his throat. "You're making me feel human again, sir."

The minister got up, combed his hair at a closet mirror, and fitted on his broad-brimmed straw hat. "Besides, the railroad intelligence is getting damned strange. These huge jammed trains really are hauling civilians from all over Europe to Poland, and then turning around and rattling back empty, while the German army's hurting for cars and locomotives. I know that for a fact. Something funny is going on, Leslie. I'll tell you something *entre nous.* I wrote a personal letter to the President about this business, but then I tore it up. We're losing the goddamned war, and he just can't be burdened with anything else. If these Germans do win, the whole world will become one big execution yard, and not just for Jews."

"I believe that, sir, but still—"

"Okay. You tell Wayne Beall to pull his material together. Go to Geneva and help him. Get that Red Cross big shot to put what he knows in writing, if you possibly can."

"I can try, sir, but these people are all petrified of the Germans."

"Well, do your best. I'll send the stuff straight to Sumner Welles this time. In fact, you may be the courier." The good eye sparked appraisingly at Slote. "Hey? How does that strike you? A nice little Stateside leave?"

Slote instantly recognized in such a mission the final ruin of his Foreign Service career. "Isn't Wayne Beall your man for that, sir? He's collected the stuff."

"The specific gravity isn't there. And he hasn't mastered this subject as you have."

"Mr. Tuttle, the car is waiting," the desk loudspeaker grated.

Tuttle left. Returning to his office, Slote heard merry laughter as he opened the door. Wayne Beall and Heidi stood there looking sheepish, and Heidi hurried out. Slote relayed the minister's instructions to Beall. "The sooner we get at it, the better, Wayne. The minister's hot on this at last, so let's keep up the momentum. Shall we go down to Geneva on the two o'clock train?"

"I just made a lunch date with your secretary."

"Oh, I see."

"In fact, Les, I thought I'd stay overnight, and—" He gave Slote a man-to-man grin. "Do you mind?"

"Oh, be my guest. We'll go tomorrow."

Soon Slote heard more laughter from the next room. One pretty girl on hand counted more than a million vague people suffering far away; nothing would ever change that fact of nature.

On his desk in the morning mail lay a formal report from Dr. Hesse, summarizing the Henry-Jastrow situation. Slote dropped it into a file marked *Natalie,* then tore up the unfinished letter to Byron. Perhaps good news would come in soon from some Mediterranean consulate, or even from Lisbon. For bad news there was always time.

37

PALMER FREDERICK KIRBY sat in shirt-sleeves at an old rented desk in a grimy office building near the University of Chicago campus, trying to finish a report before Rhoda's arrival by train. He was in a low mood; partly from dread of this encounter, partly because Vannevar Bush demanded facts and detested gloom in reports, and all the facts about the availability of pure graphite for a uranium reactor were gloomy. So was the weather. On this sultry gray August afternoon, opening the window admitted a gale off Lake Michigan warm as a desert sandstorm, and—what with Chicago's airborne dust and detritus—perhaps half as gritty; and shutting it gave him a gasping sense of taking a steam bath with his clothes on.

The graphite problem typified the grotesque enterprise in which Dr. Kirby was now passing his days. The languid trickling effort on uranium had become since Pearl Harbor a rising river of ideas, money, people, and problems tumbling along in murky secrecy. Kirby worked for the S-1 Section of Vannevar Bush's Office of Scientific Research and Development. To the initiated "S-1" meant uranium, but—and this was the root of his trouble—to everybody else it meant nothing. In his quest for materials and building sites, he could not beat out the tough procurement men from giant corporations and the armed forces. The Chicago scientists were blaming the repeated fizzling of their uranium reactor on the graphite, demanding purer stuff; but it was not to be had, and the large chemical firms capable of producing it were swamped with war orders from stronger bidders. This was the nub of Kirby's report to Bush, with some half-hearted optimistic suggestions to sugar the pill.

A telephone call from Arthur Compton at the Physics Department interrupted him. The Compton brothers were two crushingly brilliant men; this one had a Nobel Prize, the other headed the Massachusetts Institute of Technology. Kirby knew them both. He knew most of these dazzling physicists and chemists who were trying, at alarmingly wasteful cross-purposes, to make an atomic bomb before the Germans did. With some he had gone to school. They had not seemed much superior to himself at bull sessions and dances, or even in the laboratory; ambitious hardworking youngsters, as fond as he of girls, beer, and raw jokes. But in achievement they had pulled away from him like racehorses from a milkwagon nag. Being on first-name terms with them gave him no illusion of equality. On the contrary, it was a chronic sore in his ego.

"Fred, there's a Colonel Peters here." Compton, dry and direct as usual. "He'd like to come over and talk to you."

"Colonel Harrison Peters? Army Corps of Engineers?"

"That's the man."

"I just sent a stack of reports to him in Washington."

"He got them."

Kirby looked at his desk clock; Rhoda was arriving in two hours. This was how everything happened in the uranium project. "Tell him to come along, Arthur."

Soon Peters appeared, windblown and perspiring. Kirby seldom met men taller than himself, but Colonel Harrison Peters was one. The colonel was lean and long-skulled, with heavy graying hair, broad-shouldered, very erect; his grip was hard and his blue eyes were hard, too. Kirby gestured to his oversize armchair and ottoman. With a grateful sigh, Peters sank down, stretched out his legs, dusted his khaki uniform and pulled it straight, and clasped long muscular hands behind his head. "Thanks. This feels good! I've been on the go here since dawn. I've seen a lot, but I'm so ignorant that not much penetrates. You're a physicist, aren't you?"

"Well, I got my Ph.D. at Cal Tech. I'm an electrical engineer. A manufacturer, now."

"At least that's close, electrical engineering. I'm a civil engineer, West Point and Iowa State." Peters yawned, a picture of relaxed chattiness. "Bridge-building is what I do best, but I've done a lot of general construction. Also some hydraulics, with all the harbors and rivers stuff the Corps handles. But this high-powered physics is out of my line. I don't know what the hell I'm doing on this assignment. We'll be invading Europe or Africa or the Azores in the next six months. I've been counting on a field command. However"—the long arms waved wide—"*Befehl ist Befehl,* the Krauts say."

Kirby gave a short nod. "If you know German, that can be of use."

"Why, is there much literature on uranium in German? I can hardly make out the stuff in English. I was very grateful for your material. Reading it was like wiping a foggy windshield. I began to see where I was at."

"Glad it helped."

"Well, I still think somebody's crazy, Kirby, trying to play guessing games with triple-A priority materials, in the middle of a war, on a scientific riddle that may have no answer. I foresee nothing for myself but a knobby skull from butting stone walls. How's your skull?"

"All knobs." They both laughed, and Kirby added, spreading his hands, "I'm at your service."

Shoving the ottoman forward, Colonel Peters sat up, long legs crossed, elbows on the arms of the chair, fingers interlaced. Kirby, with his stocking feet up on the desk, felt a trifle sloppy under the big man's scrutiny. "Okay, Kirby. You and I have things in common." The tone now was curt. "We're both outsiders to chemical engineering and nuclear physics. We were both dragged into this thing. We both seem to have the same essential job, I on the Army side, you for this S-1 outfit of Vannevar Bush's. You've been in it a long time. I'd like to get some guidance from you before I plunge in."

"Ask me anything."

"Okay, now I've been travelling around the country getting a quick look-see at this whole undertaking. To start with, all these scientists grind axes like mad, don't they? Compton and his crowd here in Chicago are sure that this new Element 94, produced in a reactor, is the shortcut to the bomb. Only their reactor doesn't work; gets warm, then dies out. Dr. Lawrence's people out in Berkeley push electromagnetic separation of U-235. But they produce no U-235, with all that mess of big contraptions. The Columbia University crowd—and I take it, the British—think that diffusion is the way—"

"Gaseous diffusion, not thermal diffusion," Kirby put in with a chop of a flat palm. "Get that straight. Vastly different."

"Right. There's the Westinghouse thing, too, the ionic centrifuge. That makes the most sense to me, as an ignoramus. You've got two substances intermingled—natural uranium U-238 and the rare explosive isotope U-235. Okay? One's heavier than the other, so you spin 'em and get out the heavier one by centrifugal force. Cream separator principle."

"That one's pretty iffy, Colonel. Very complicated when you try to go to the large-scale mechanics. Ionized gas molecules don't act like butter fat." The colonel slightly grinned, and nodded in understanding. "I'm betting on gaseous diffusion myself," Kirby went on. "Simply because it's an established principle. Working with a corrosive gas like uranium hexafluoride you get into some nasty design problems, but there's no new concept to be tested. If you build enough stages and build them right—acres and acres of barriered chambers, I grant you, thousands of miles of conduits, and very difficult tolerances—you've *got* to end up with U-235. That magnetic separator of Lawrence's is a brilliant short-cut concept. I'm a Lawrence man, in fact a Lawrence worshipper, and my firm supplies him with high-performance equipment, but his whole idea just may not work. Nobody knows. It's a new principle. You're in green fields. Same thing with Compton's reactor. It has never been done anywhere on God's earth, unless the damned Germans have already brought it off."

"I spent two hours today," Peters said, "in that reactor setup under the football field bleachers. Ugly, sullen damned thing, this black heap towering to the ceiling, just standing there. Sooty technicians hovering around it, like devils fussing with a fire in hell that won't burn."

"Well put!" Kirby said with a sour smile. "There again, great concept. You nudge uranium with a neutron source and get it to splattering more neutrons around and splitting itself up. In theory if you design it right, you should get a chain reaction and blow up Chicago—except that the controls seem foolproof, so you just boil up a lot of heat and radiation and produce this new element, plutonium, that will also blow up with a hell of a bang, like U-235. That's what the pencil-and-paper gentlemen predict. Yet the thing keeps fizzling and dying out. Why? Nobody's sure. In a way I hope we're up against some fact of nature, some physical impossibility that nobody has discerned yet. That blank wall would stop the Germans, too. But is it really a solid wall? Or are we muffing the way through, while they're finding it? That's the damnable question."

"You rate gaseous diffusion first." Harrison Peters struck a stiff finger on the chair arm, as though to pin down Kirby's view.

"Yes, but I'm an ignoramus myself. We've got to assume the Germans are on all of these tracks, so we can't afford to bypass any of them. That's the position of the Office of Scientific Research and Development, so it's mine. I grind an axe too."

"Kirby, you keep looking at the clock. Am I keeping you?"

"I have to meet somebody at the Union Station at six. She hates to stand around waiting."

"Ah. A gal," said Colonel Peters. His smile turned to a goatish grin; he ran a hand along his handsome gray hair; his demeanor became charged with mischievous appetite. The Army brigadier general who had authorized Kirby to send Peters the secret reports had volunteered that "Big Pete" was a wild bachelor, with a plus score on pretty girls quite impressive in a man his age.

"Well, a lady," Kirby said.

"Good friend?"

"She's the wife of an old good friend. They just lost a son at the Battle of Midway, a naval aviator."

This wiped away, like a damp sponge swept over blackboard writing, the lecherous look of the colonel. His face went stiff and stern, his eyes clouded, and he shook his head. "That's rough."

"It's an all-Navy family. The father's commanding a cruiser, and another son's in submarines. She's been out on the West Coast, visiting the submariner and a daughter."

"Look, I won't hold you up then."

"I don't have to go yet."

"Can I pick your brain on one more point?"

"Shoot."

"If I understand it, the Army has come into this picture for the big production jobs. S-1 will carry on the experimental work, the pilot plants, and so forth."

"That's the general idea," Kirby said. "The Army should have been in long ago. I've learned *that* lesson, trying to get priorities for S-1. No corporation will pay attention to a pack of mad scientists with a secret Buck Rogers weapon, when the President's ordered sixty thousand planes a year, eight million tons of shipping, forty-five thousand tanks and God knows how many AA guns and shells. Yet this project begins to look like such a stupendous strain on this country's total resources, Colonel, that only the Army can handle it."

The colonel's eyes glinted. "Possibly, but won't S-1 and the Army be bucking each other? We'll want the same triple-A stuff, won't we? Won't you and I end up in a back-stabbing contest that I'll win, thus strangling your effort, which may be the key to the crucial advances?"

"Good question," Kirby replied, "but Vannevar Bush's uranium section can't last long now. The Army will soon take over in toto. I'm talking like a traitor, because Compton and Lawrence and company are having a great time running the whole thing themselves. Scientists have never played with such big chips. But at this point the problem is twenty percent theoretical science, and eighty percent industrial effort, a forced performance, Colonel, on a giant scale at top speed in dead secrecy." Kirby stood up, excited by his own words, and rapped the desk with a sweaty hand. "The muscle to ass-kick that performance out of

American industry has got to come from the United States Army. In six months I'll be out of here, and glad of it. Maybe I'd better get down to Union Station now."

Peters got up too, stretching his great arms. "Are we going to make a bomb?"

Kirby put on a tie and a jacket as he replied, "Ask me some other time. Today I'm down. That black pile you saw, they just can't get it going. This has been happening for months. They try one thing and another, and now they're blaming the graphite. They say boron impurities absorb too many neutrons, so the thing fizzles out. You're going to be hearing a lot about neutrons, and—"

"My head's swimming with them now. Fast neutrons, slow neutrons —between two dunderheads, what the hell is a neutron?"

"If you're serious—"

"Sure I am. I'm ignorant as a horse about this stuff."

"It's a particle without a charge, in the nucleus of the atom. An Englishman named Chadwick discovered it in 1932. Neutrons are what radioactive substances give off. They can penetrate another nucleus and knock it apart into two other lighter substances. A couple of Germans did that first, back in '39. That's splitting the atom, with a loss of mass and therefore a tremendous energy release."

"Einstein's law," Peters said, and he recited solemnly, as in a classroom, "*E equals mc squared.* I know that much."

"Okay. Neutrons aren't your job, of course. You'll just be looking at things like that dirty black pile and Lawrence's big electromagnet, all covered with dials and valves. Various Ph.D.'s and a Nobel laureate or two will yell at you for purer graphite or some bigger magnets or some other unobtainable thing. Someday something made out of uranium or Element 94 will probably go off with the biggest noise ever heard on earth. The smartest men alive think so. Whether it'll happen in our lifetimes, and whether we'll make that thing first—those are the crucial questions. If the Germans do it first, Hitler will shut down our effort rather rudely. And if they don't, and we don't make a bomb in time to use in this war—which is a real possibility, I assure you—well, Colonel, picture peace coming, and Congress learning that the Army blew in a few billion dollars on huge plants that produced a crock of horseshit. And start preparing your testimony."

Rhoda had spent two difficult hours in a swaying train compartment, grooming for this last encounter with the one guilty love of her life. Her charcoal shantung suit, a Beverly Hills purchase, set off her pretty figure with subtle charm; the purple hat added a sweet melancholy touch of color; gloves and shoes, still black. Her costume was appropriate for bereavement; also for an attractive widow getting ready to look around again. Two weeks of California sun and swimming had given her a rosy tan and cleared her eyes; and a nose veil so softened her features that a stranger might have taken her for a woman of thirty or so.

When a woman is about to discard a man—or to be discarded by him, for that matter—she often wants to look her best; arraying herself (so to say) for the last glimpse into the coffin of dead love. More prosaically, she simply prefers that he feel regret, not relief, if she can arrange it. The look on Palmer Kirby's face, when he first espied her at the train gate, rewarded her pains. Their talk in the taxicab was all about her family. Overshadowing Madeline's movie job was the news of Byron's orders to Gibraltar. He had telephoned it to her in great excitement from San Diego. His new duty, she supposed, was something hush-hush connected with submarines in the Mediterranean. He still meant to fly to Switzerland and work on freeing his wife and child; from Lisbon it was perhaps feasible, though Rhoda thought it a quixotic notion, and hoped they would get out of Italy before he tried it. Anyway, Byron had sounded happy, she said, for the first time since Warren's death. Those words slipped out. Then she and Kirby looked sadly at each other, and Rhoda turned away, her eyes watering.

The only hint of wartime in the famous Pump Room was the number of men in uniform, mostly bald or gray-headed colonels and captains. Expert waiters bustled about, chafing dishes flamed, rich roasts wheeled here and there, handsome bejeweled women devoured big lobsters, and the wine steward, clanking his brass tokens, hurried from table to table with bottles projecting from ice-filled buckets.

"We'll have wine, I suppose," he said to her when the waiter asked for their drink orders. "Would you like a drink first?"

"No wine tonight, I think," Rhoda returned with cool good cheer. "A very dry martini, please."

A long silence ensued between them, but the restaurant buzz made it tolerable. The drinks came. They lifted their glasses. Kirby shook his head, and spoke haltingly. "Rho, I keep thinking of the Berlin airport, the time you drove me there. I don't know why. There's no resemblance in the surroundings, God knows."

She peered at him through the veil, sipping at the martini. Delicately she put down the oversize glass. "That was a farewell."

"Well, we thought it was."

"Certainly I did," Rhoda sighed.

"Is this a farewell?"

Rhoda gave a slow bare nod. Her glance wandered away over the restaurant, and she began to prattle. "I once ate here with Pug, d'you know? We were on our way from San Francisco to Annapolis. BuOrd had stationed him in Mare Island to work on battleship turret design, and we were going back east for Warren's graduation from the Severn School. Ten years ago, I guess. Or is it eleven? All that's getting blurry." She stirred the martini, round and round. "You never know when you're happy, Palmer, do you? Imagine, I thought I had problems then! Byron kept failing in school. Madeline was fat, and her teeth were crooked. Big tragedies like that. Our house in San Francisco was too small, and on a noisy street. Dear me, I gave Pug a bad time about all those things. But how proud we were of Warren! He won the school sword, and a track medal, and the history prize—oh, hell." Her voice failed. She finished off her drink. "Please order me another, and then no more."

He signalled to the waiter for a second round, and said, slowly and gruffly, "Rhoda, let me speak my piece and get it over with. I won't embarrass you with a messy spill of my feelings. I have to accept your decision, and I do. That's all."

Rhoda's smile was sad and gentle. "Aren't you glad to be out of it, Palmer?"

"In your presence, I can't be."

Her eyes flashed at his intense look and tone. "A pretty speech, sir." She held out her hand, and they shook hands as though sealing a bargain. "Well! Now I think we can enjoy our dinner," Rhoda tremulously laughed. "It would be a pity at that, wouldn't it, not to have a good time in the Pump Room?"

"Yes. Change your mind about the wine?"

"Oh, why don't you order us a half-bottle?"

"Hello, Kirby."

It was Colonel Peters, following the head waiter past their table with a tall girl in a green dress. Kirby knew her slightly by sight: a large colorless female who worked in Compton's office. Now her eyes were excited, her dark hair was piled up in a beauty-parlor do, and she was painted in a most nonacademic way. The green dress was a shade too tight on her lush figure. They sat down nearby, and Kirby and Rhoda could hear Peters jollying the girl. Their laughter rang across the noisy restaurant.

Over their dinner and the half-bottle of Chablis, Rhoda told Kirby of her plan to go to Hawaii, of the varying advice some admirals on the West Coast had given her, and of her intention to close up, and perhaps sell, the Foxhall Road house. Kirby made little comment, and the topic lapsed. They passed some of the time watching, with amusement and ironic remarks, the rapid progress of Colonel Peters with the green-clad girl. He clearly did these things by the book, using basic principles and tested materials: smoked salmon, champagne, shish kebab on flaming swords, crepes suzette, and brandy. The joking and the laughter of the couple seldom paused, and the girl was glowing with aroused delight. Peters had an eye for spotting the prey, thought Kirby, as well as skill at netting it. Kirby was not above a play for a secretary when he got lonesome, but he had never given this big Miss Chaney in Compton's outer office a second thought.

Rhoda's train did not leave until midnight. By ten they had finished the meal, and there seemed to be nothing else to do. In other days they might have gone to Kirby's apartment, but that was unthinkable. Their relationship had run out like a phonograph record; their chitchat was the last scratching of the needle. Rhoda was acting friendly, and she was even being lightly funny about Colonel Peters's amorous tactics; but woman to man, she had turned distant as a sister. There she sat, in an elusive way made more desirable than ever by time and by grief; an elegant quiet lady, so correct and serene that his irrepressible mental pictures of her naked in the throes of passion seemed indecent falsehoods, or contemptible peeks into a bedroom.

The Army man was leaning over Miss Chaney, whispering as he helped her out of her chair, and they were both laughing richly. They had no problem about what to do next, thought Kirby; but he was confronted with this problem of a remote woman for two more long hours.

"I'm going to suggest something strange, dear," Rhoda said, "and if you become cross, you'll distress me."

"Yes?"

"Did you see that little theatre in the Union Station that shows nothing but newsreels and cartoons? Let's go there. Or if you're terribly busy, I'll go, and you can get back to your work. Do you still sit up nights, writing reports about that horrible THING you're working on, whatever it is?"

"No, no, I have nothing to do." Rhoda's proposal would at least kill the time until midnight. "That sounds just right. I'm awfully full of duck and wild rice."

Colonel Peters stood alone in the restaurant lobby looking pleased with himself. He straightened when he saw Kirby and Rhoda, and his face turned self-conscious and solemn. Rhoda went off to the lounge.

"Kirby, is that the lady who lost a son?"

"Yes."

Peters made a grimace of incredulity. "You could have told me the naval aviator was her husband, I'd believe you."

"She's a handsome woman," Kirby said. "Your Miss Chaney's the surprise. I never imagined she could gussy herself up like that."

"Oh, Joan's not a bad sort. A lot of laughs. You know, Kirby, my nephew Bob went and joined the RAF in 1939. Army brat, twenty-one, couldn't wait to get into the scrap. Got himself killed in the Battle of Britain. My brother's only son. Wiped out the line, because I've never married. Bob was a fine boy, a splendid boy. It just about destroyed his mother, she's been in and out of sanatoriums ever since. Your friend seems to be handling it better."

"Well, she has other children. And in point of fact, she's a very strong woman."

Miss Chaney came out of the powder room, her hips swaying, her bust quaking under the shiny green silk. With a wolfish grin, Peters put out his hand to Kirby. "That was a good visit we had today."

"Any time, Colonel."

Miss Chaney wiggled her fingers at Kirby, and rolled her eyes. "Well, Dr. Kirby, so we meet in the Pump Room! Beats the Physics Department, doesn't it?"

"In every way I can think of," said Kirby. Miss Chaney accepted this as a salacious compliment, and went off on the colonel's arm in a flurry of giggles.

Soon Rhoda emerged. What a difference there was in women, Kirby thought; how it showed in the very way Rhoda stepped along and held her head. At a disadvantage of so many years, she was far more alluring than poor Miss Chaney. To Kirby the natural sway of her slim body was potent as ever, or more so. An intense notion struck him to fight this dismissal. He could look forward to only ten or fifteen more years. Without Rhoda they stretched ahead bleak as an Antarctic landscape.

But they went to the movie, and sat beside each other watching *Silly Symphonies*. Palmer Kirby, who had so often roughly taken this woman all naked in his arms to share raptures, now hesitated to take her hand. At last he did. Rhoda did not withdraw it, nor did she keep it unresponsively stiff or limp. But there was no sex in the clasp; Kirby was just holding a friendly hand. After a while, feeling foolish, he put it back in her lap. The three little pink pigs were gambolling on the screen singing, *"Who's afraid of the big bad wolf?"* and Palmer Kirby knew that he had lost Rhoda Henry for good.

She kissed him just once, standing on the steps of the Pullman car. It was a cool kiss, not quite empty of sex. She drew her head back, lifted her veil, and looked hard into his eyes. Her own were dry and rather glittery. He felt that she was savoring his regret, balancing off once for all the months when he had neglected her, the hesitation he had displayed over marrying her. The thing had oscillated back and forth but never had worked; it had always been wrong to cuckold another man, above all a fighting man in wartime. He was well served, thought Kirby, and he must face his Antarctic landscape.

"Good-bye, Palmer dear."

"Good-bye, Rhoda."

After Rhoda settled her things in her compartment, she walked up to the club car for a nightcap. There she came upon Colonel Harrison Peters.

38

Iɴ Hollywood, Pamela had told Rhoda of her love for Victor Henry
because burning her bridges had seemed the best thing she could
do, for both these bereaved people. Now, sitting at her old portable, trying to start a letter to Victor Henry, it came very hard.

> Dearest Victor,
>   What is she doing in Cairo, do I hear you cry? I shall tell all, if heat
> prostration and a bout of Gyppy tummy don't finish me off first.

Slumped at the machine in a short shapeless Hawaiian flower-print, under which she heavily perspired, Pamela paused over these jocose lines.
The heat and the damp seemed to be melting her bones. She had just
ghosted an article for her father, and she felt wrung out. After a long
stare at the yellow sheet, she ripped it from the typewriter, rolled in another, and began again, shutting her senses as best she could to the street
vendors' haunting wails, and the spicy-fetid smells coming through the
open french windows. Typing hesitantly at first, she worked up to a
rapid clatter.

> Dearest Victor,
>   We saw your son Byron almost a month ago in Gibraltar. I've been
> meaning to write you about it. In fact, he asked me to. Censorship is
> heavy on his ship, and he didn't want to entrust the news about his wife
> and son to some faceless snoop.
>   Perhaps by now he's gotten word to you, but if he depended on me,
> I'm sorry. We've been in an unrelieved rush since we got to Egypt. The
> climate is enervating, and as my poor plump father wilts—he's never at
> his best in the heat—I must take on more of the burden. In fact, he's
> shared a couple of recent by-lines with me.
>   I'll presume you haven't heard from Byron. He's on temporary duty
> with the Royal Navy, attached to *Maidstone,* a submarine depot ship
> (you call them "tenders"), servicing a flotilla which includes some old
> Lend-Lease S-boats of yours. He's there with other Americans to assist
> in maintaining the S-boats. Actually the *Maidstone* personnel are quite
> up to the job, he says, and he's fallen into sinfully soft and pleasant

duty, including social forays to the Spanish side of the Rock. Of course food and bunks on a depot ship are of the best. Also, since the American mission on Gibraltar is chronically shorthanded, he's made some enjoyable air trips as a courier into unoccupied southern France. He looks tanned and well, but he itches to get back to "the war," as he refers to Pacific operations, and he means to do so as soon as Natalie's situation clears up.

Now about that. Byron's information comes from Leslie Slote, who's now the political secretary at your legation in Switzerland. Some time ago, Natalie and her uncle disappeared from a seaside resort called Follonica, to the immense chagrin of the Italian authorities, who had extended very special privileges to them. Through contacts with Jewish organizations in Geneva, Leslie has ascertained that they may be making a run for Lisbon or Marseilles, aided by Resistance groups. All this has dissuaded Byron from attempting to go to Bern, where he could accomplish nothing, since the birds have certainly flown from Italy. Perhaps by now all has ended happily. At any rate, that was Byron's news a month ago.

It's always seemed passing strange to me, incidentally, that a son of yours married this girl, whom I knew long before I was aware you existed. Byron has much aged since I saw him in Hawaii. Removing the beard is part of it, for his mouth and chin are quite stern. The loss of his brother has hardened and thickened the texture of the young man. Less mercury than iron, now, one might say.

I should tell you, too, that we saw your family in Hollywood. Your wife said she would try to join you in Hawaii. I hope she has, and I must assume she's recounted a talk I had with her. Perhaps you're angry about that. It seemed to me that she'd better know there had been a risk of losing you. She asked me point-blank if we'd had an affair, so I told her. Whether she deserved your steadfastness is a closed question, but you should remember that for her the war when it broke out must have seemed the crash of everything.

That was how I felt in Singapore. Nothing mattered, *nothing*, with those snarling yellow men coming on. It was the worst moment of the war and of my life, until you returned from Midway; and I saw in your eyes what had happened, and felt that I was useless to you, and that it was over. That was worse.

Here in Cairo people are still rattled by the closeness of Rommel, but encouraged by your planes, tanks, and trucks pouring to our Eighth Army via the Cape of Good Hope, and on direct convoy past Malta. Talky has it straight from Churchill—Winnie flashed through here twice this month, raising a cloud of bloody nonsensical trouble—that all this is a drop in the bucket compared to the Niagara of equipment that you're flooding to the Russians. When or how your countrymen produce all this, I don't know. Your country baffles me: a luxurious unharmed lotus land in which great hordes of handsome dynamic people either wallow in deep gloom, or play like overexcited children, or fall to work like all the devils in hell, while the press steadily drones detestation of the government and despair of the system. I don't understand how America works, any more than Frances Trollope or Dickens did, but it's an ongoing miracle of sorts.

In London things are bad. The repair of the blitz devastation goes sluggishly. People drag themselves through the rubble in sticky weather on dwindling rations. Those in the know are frozen with fear of the U-boats. I'm not revealing secrets to you, I'm sure; Victor, they have sunk over *three million tons* just since you entered the war. In June alone they sank close to a million tons. At that rate you can't mount an attack against Europe, and we can't hold out much longer. The Atlantic's becoming impassable. It's a queer sort of menace, this invisible strangulation that shows up in thinner British bodies, fewer vehicles, sicklier faces, a general flavor of bad-smelling decay, and a creeping defeatism in Whitehall. There are mutters about coming to terms. When Tobruk fell, Churchill survived a no-confidence vote, but it was a red-light warning. Macaulayesque speeches won't keep him afloat much longer.

But bad as the surrender of Tobruk hit London, it was nothing to what went on here in Egypt. We missed the worst of it, but we hear it was like the fall of France. Rommel came roaring along the coast, all fueled up and rearmed with masses of stuff he captured at Tobruk. By the time he halted at El Alamein, two hours by car from Alexandria, government bureaus, military headquarters, and rich big shots were all fleeing eastward to Palestine and Syria in every available train and vehicle. Less-favored folk were clogging the roads on foot. In the cities there were strict curfews, empty hotels, abandoned streets and office buildings, looters, trigger-happy patrols, and all the rest. Little of this got past the tough censorship.

Things are less scary now. Some of the skedaddlers are sheepishly drifting back, but the more prudent ones are staying where they are. Obviously Rommel is retooling and gassing up for another try. There's little hope for a long respite, such as the Russians had once the Germans bogged down outside Moscow. It doesn't snow in Egypt.

Now, a little news about me, and I'll cease boring you. Duncan Burne-Wilke is in Cairo to take over the logistics of the air effort against Rommel. Unless I give him a discreet signal to desist, I suspect he's going to ask me to marry him. I saw quite a bit of him in London. Lady Caroline died of cancer a few months ago. I don't know whether you ever met her. She was a tremendous swell, most elegant, somewhat bossy and bristly, the daughter of an earl. Duncan married over his head, so to say, for he's "just" a viscount and his father, who made motor cars, bought the title.

The marriage hadn't worked well for a long time. In fact, Duncan once very sweetly proposed to me what we civilized Europeans call an arrangement. Well, I'm not very moral, but I've had my standards always. In all my misadventures (strike out Singapore) I've been passionately in love, or thought I've been. I was terribly in love with you at the time, you old iron man, and it would have been indecent to accept Duncan. The girls around the plotting table at Biggin Hill all sighed and languished after Duncan like a Gilbert and Sullivan female chorus, but the truth is I had no such feeling about him and I still don't.

Nevertheless, I suppose I must begin to think of what to do with my life. I can't go on and on with Talky; for I know he's failing. Duncan is a dear man, to be sure. I just don't see plunging into such a commitment now, though it would be ever so swanky a step up for me. Our family's respectable enough, in fact landed on my long-deceased mother's side, but I'm just a reasonably educated commoner, and my drawn face, alas, is my fortune. All that's fine, but Talky still needs me. We'll stay here for Rommel's onslaught, and I'm not looking past that. There's growing confidence here, based partly on Tommy Atkins's pluck, and partly on those heartwarming rows and rows and rows of olive-painted American trucks and tanks on the Alexandria wharfs.

Talky's slumbering noisily in the next room, having taken a sleeping cachet. Churchill's second whirl-through jangled and exhausted everybody. I must sleep, too. We leave before dawn tomorrow for Alexandria by train, and thence for a press-briefing by Montgomery out at his field headquarters. He's newly in command and opinions differ here about him. The buzz in the Shepheard's Hotel bar is about fifty-fifty pro and con; tactical genius, pompous eccentric showoff.

I really look forward to another trip out to the desert. Difficulties have been made about my gender, since the men strip naked out there to bathe in the sea, or wash, or just keep cool, and they perform natural functions casually. I was excluded from Talky's first trip, but he missed me and raised a great row, and now I go along. Presumably signals roll along the coast at my approach, "Female, take cover." I'm sure I'm a damned nuisance, but it's heartbreakingly beautiful out there—the glittering blue-green sea, the long white sand beach, blinding as snow, and then the slate-gray salt flats, the brackish lakes, the yellow and red sands of the desert dotted with brush—and oh, the sunsets and the clear starlit nights! The magnificent Australian troops stripped to trunks, bronzed as Indians! One of the rottenest aspects of this war, actually, is its beauty. Remember London on fire? And that tank battle in the snow we glimpsed in the distance outside Moscow, the flames from the burning tanks, reflected purple and orange on the mauve snow?

If not for the war what would I have been doing all these years? Something dull in some dull London office building, or something domesticated in some suburban house or, with luck, town flat. And I would never have met you—an experience, which, with all its chiaroscuro, I treasure as the chief thing in my history.

I shall give this letter to a U.P. man who is going back to New York. He'll mail it to your Fleet Post Office address, so you should get it soon. Victor, if it isn't unreasonable I should like just a word from you that I have your blessing if I go on with Duncan. I myself thought silence the best way to close out our beautiful but guillotined relationship, but then I did have to write you about Byron, and I feel most enormously happy and relieved. You too may feel better writing to me, however briefly. I think we understand each other, though we had to part before we could explore the depths.

My love,
Pamela

The U.P. man did bring this letter to New York, and it entered the complex Navy system for delivering mail to the far-flung ships at sea. Gray sacks for the *Northampton* followed the cruiser all over the Central and South Pacific; but the letter never caught up before the ship went down off Guadalcanal.

*   *   *

39

Global Waterloo
1: Guadalcanal

(from *World Holocaust* by Armin von Roon)

November 1942! No German should ever hear that month mentioned without shuddering.

In that one ill-omened month, four concurrent disasters befell our brief imperium: two in North Africa, one in Russia, one in the South Pacific. On November 2 the British offensive at El Alamein, begun in late October, sent Rommel's Afrika Korps reeling out of Egypt, never to return. On November 8 the Anglo-Americans landed in Morocco and Algeria. From November 13 to 16, the tide turned at Guadalcanal. And on November 19 the Soviet hordes broke through at Stalingrad and began cutting off our Sixth Army.

Historians tend to miss the awful simultaneity of the fourfold smashup. Our German authors harp on Stalingrad, with casual treatment of the Mediterranean and silence on the Pacific. The communist pseudo-historians write as though only Stalingrad was happening then. Winston Churchill dwells on El Alamein, a minor textbook battle, decided by the lopsided British advantage in Lend-Lease supplies. The U.S. writers stress their walkover in French North Africa, and strangely neglect Guadalcanal, one of America's finest campaigns.

The Global Waterloo was in fact a swift, roaring, flaming reverse all around the earth of our war effort, history's greatest—on the seas, in desert sands, on beaches, in jungles, in city streets, on tropical islands, in snowdrifts. In November 1942, the world-adventurer Hitler, to whom we Germans had given our souls, lost the initiative once for all. Thereafter the hangmen were closing in on him, and he was fighting not for world empire but for his neck.

Militarily speaking, the situation even then was retrievable by sound military tactics, and we had great tacticians. Manstein's classic fighting withdrawal from the Caucasus after Stalingrad, to cite but one instance, will find a place one day in history with Xenophon's march to the Black Sea. But Hitler as warlord could only go on compounding his own pigheaded mistakes. Since nobody could loosen his terror-grip on our armed forces, he dragged the German nation down with him.

The Far Reach of the Third Reich

To understand Hitler's swollen pride before his fall, one must picture Germany's situation before November 1942.

For the modern-day German reader, this is difficult. We are a cowed people, ashamed of our mighty though Faustian past. Our defeated and shrunken Fatherland is sundered. Bolshevism bestrides one half; the other half cringes to the dollar. Our economic vigor has revived, but our place in world affairs remains dubious. Twelve brief years of Nazi mistakes and crimes have eclipsed the proud record of centuries.

But in the summer of 1942, we were still riding high. On the eastern front, the Wehrmacht was rebounding to the attack. After storming Sevastopol and clearing the Kerch peninsula, we were thrusting two gigantic armed marches into the Soviet southern gut; one across the Don toward the Volga, the other southward to the Caucasus oil fields. Stalin's armies were everywhere fading back before us with big losses. Rommel's stunning capture of the Tobruk fortress had opened the way to the Suez Canal and had all but toppled Churchill.

Our comrade Japan had won Southeast Asia, and in Burma was advancing to the borders of India. Her grip on prostrate China's coastal provinces was solid. Her defeat at Midway was shrouded by the fog of war. Her armies were still triumphing wherever they marched. All Asia trembled at the shift of world forces. India was rent with riots. Its Congress voted for the immediate withdrawal of the British, and an Indian government-in-exile was forming to fight on the Japanese side.

In Arctic waters, with the famous rout of the PQ-17 convoy at the end of June, we severed the Lend-Lease supply route to Murmansk, a body-blow to the already staggering Red Army. This defeat epitomized the British decline at sea. The convoy screening force, warned that our heavy surface ships were approaching, ordered the merchant vessels to disperse and hightailed it home to England! The shades of Drake and Nelson must have wept in Valhalla. The slaughter that ensued was mere rabbit-shooting by our aircraft and submarines. The cold seas closed over twenty-three merchant vessels out of thirty-seven, and one hundred thousand tons of war matériel, with much loss of life. Churchill's shamed message to Stalin cancelling the

Murmansk run brought an angry Slav howl. The grotesque alliance of capitalism and Bolshevism was sorely strained.

On the visible evidence, then, we were triumphing in the summer and autumn of 1942 against all the odds, even with the United States thrown into the balance against us, even with all of Hitler's miscalculations.

———————

TRANSLATOR'S NOTE: *The Murmansk run was suspended during the summer months of long Arctic daylight, then resumed. In December, British destroyers escorting another convoy outfought a German task force, including a pocket battleship and a heavy cruiser. Hitler waxed so wroth at this fiasco that he ordered the fleet scrapped, and the guns put to use on land. Admiral Raeder resigned. Dönitz took over, but the German surface fleet never recovered from Hitler's tantrum.*

Roon's appreciation of Guadalcanal which follows is detached and reliable. No Germans were fighting there.—V.H.

———————

The Pacific Theatre

All of Europe from the Bay of Biscay to the Urals could be sunk without a trace between Honolulu and Manila, yet the Pacific campaigns were fought over far greater distances than that. Unheard-of military space, unprecedented forms of combined land, sea, and air combat: such is the fascination of the Pacific conflict. The period in history when such operations were feasible came and went quickly. A high point was the six-month melee which raged in the skies, on the water, under the water, and in the jungle, for the possession of a small airfield that accommodated sixty planes: Henderson Field on Guadalcanal.

Guadalcanal is a neglected campaign, a small Pacific Stalingrad swirling around that landing field. Had it been a British victory, Churchill would have written a volume about it. But Americans are apathetic toward their military history. They lack the European sense of the past, and writers of broad culture.

In my restricted research* I have yet to come upon an adequate relating of the Stalingrad and Guadalcanal campaigns, but one might say that the Second World War turned on those poles. We reached the Volga just north of Stalingrad in August. The Americans landed on Guadalcanal in August. General Paulus surrendered at Stalingrad on February 2, 1943; the Ameri-

———————

* General von Roon wrote in prison.—V.H.

cans secured Guadalcanal on February 9. Both battles were desperate and successful defenses of a waterfront perimeter: the Russians with their backs to the Volga, the Americans on a beachhead with their backs to the sea. Both battles were head-on clashes of national wills. With both outcomes the tide in a war theatre turned, for all the world to witness.

German readers must never forget that the war had a global dimension. We are obsessed with Europe, and that is how the Bolshevik historians also write. But under Adolf Hitler's flawed but kinetic leadership, our nation broke the ice of the entire world imperial system. For six years a world storm raged, and all was fluid. The land masses of the planet, fifty-eight million square miles of real estate, were at hazard. The Asian samurai surged forward to form an alliance with the Nordic soldier, seeking a just redistribution of the earth's habitable surface. That two martial showdowns should simultaneously explode on two sides of the globe therefore lay in the nature of this wrenching world convulsion. The stunning halt of the Japanese onrush at Midway resembled our halt before Moscow in December 1941. These were chilly warnings. But the fatal crunches came later and in parallel, at Stalingrad and Guadalcanal.

The differences of course are substantial. If we had defeated the Red Army at Stalingrad, history in its present form would not exist; whereas had the Americans been thrown off Guadalcanal, they would probably have returned later with new fleets, air groups, and tank divisions, and beaten the Japanese elsewhere. Stalingrad was a far vaster battle, and more truly a decisive one. Still, the parallels should be borne in mind.

Admiral King

It was a wheeze in the American navy that Admiral Ernest King "shaved with a blowtorch." A naval aviator with a long record of achievement, including the raising of a sunken submarine in the open sea, King had been put out to pasture on the General Board, an advisory panel for old admirals with no place to go. His cold driving personality had not made him loved. He had bruised egos and damaged careers. Shortly after Pearl Harbor, Roosevelt appointed him Commander-in-Chief of the United States Fleet. King is said to have observed, "When things get tough they send for the sons of bitches." In the Wehrmacht, alas, when "things got tough" the Führer sent for the sycophants.

Besides the problem of the rampaging Japanese, King had to contend with the fixed Roosevelt-Churchill policy, *Germany First.* The Combined Chiefs of Staff were neglecting "his" war in favor of the bigger conflict.

King's cold-blooded solution was the attack on Tulagi, which evolved into the Guadalcanal campaign.

Japanese War Aim

Despite some blustering rhetoric, the Japanese were not seeking to crush the United States of America in war. Their aim was limited. In their view, Southeast Asia was none of America's business. Thanks to our conquest of Europe the time had come to throw out the imperialist exploiters, and to found a peaceful Greater East Asia for the Asians, including a pacified China; a so-called Co-prosperity Sphere under Japanese leadership, friendly to the coming world master, Germany.

Their military aim was a quick conquest of the desired areas, then a tough perimeter defense on interior lines. The hope was that the far-off prosperous Americans would tire of a costly war in which they were not very interested, and would make a face-saving peace. This might well have worked, except for the attack on Pearl Harbor, which roused in the proud Yanks, and especially in their fine navy, an irrational cowboy thirst for frontier vengeance.

———————

TRANSLATOR'S NOTE *to the third edition, October 1973: The Viet Nam experience is making me wonder whether Roon is not absolutely right about this.—V.H.*

———————

American War Aim

On the other hand, for twenty years the United States Navy had been plotting to destroy Japan if American hegemony was ever challenged by "the yellow peril." Assuming the Japanese would be maneuvered into striking first, their war games had produced a cut-and-dried plan of counterattack. After the war, as has been said, Chester von Nimitz claimed the U.S.A. had won the war along the exact lines planned at the Naval War College. The plan was:

1. *Hold a line of communication to the main forward bases in Australia and New Zealand, with installations along a curve of islands outside Japanese aircraft range.*
2. *Batter northward through the archipelagoes of the southwest Pacific in flank attack.*

3. *Thrust the main assault westward across the Central Pacific atolls, in an island-hopping strike toward Luzon and Japan.*

But King had trouble getting enough force in his theatre to execute the plan. General George Marshall, the Chief of Staff of the United States Army, an able planner and organizer, was adamant on "Germany First," and a full-scale invasion of France in 1943. He wanted to concentrate on an immediate buildup in England of American manpower and matériel.

Happily for King, all the British leaders from Churchill down kept waffling on the invasion. They remembered the Somme and Dunkirk all too well. In July 1942, Marshall in great disgust therefore recommended to President Roosevelt that the Americans throw their weight into the Japanese conflict. King seized this favoring moment to push the execution of a quick modest aggressive move in the Pacific: the capture of a Japanese seaplane base in the Solomons, the small island of Tulagi. Though already authorized, the Tulagi operation had stalled in an army-navy argument over supreme command. Now it went forward, with a complicated deal on command, which temporarily dodged the impasse. Soon afterward the American and British war planners settled on the North African landings called "Torch," but King's operation meantime went ahead. It was called Operation Watchtower. His forces were so meager that in the field they dubbed it Shoestring.

TRANSLATOR'S NOTE: *I omit here a long Roon analysis of the conflict between the Army and the Navy over the Pacific command issue and the Tulagi idea. MacArthur wanted to try a more ambitious shot, the capture of the big Japanese air base of Rabaul. Roon comments, "Vanity of leaders can divert or wreck campaigns. The divided command problem between MacArthur and Nimitz haunted the Pacific war and resulted in the stupendous botch at Leyte Gulf." In a later chapter I include a controversial essay by Roon on the Battle of Leyte Gulf.—V.H.*

First Blood

Combat preparations for taking Tulagi were well along, when a coastwatcher intelligence report greatly raised the stakes of the operation. Only a few miles from Tulagi, the Japanese were building an airfield on the large island of Guadalcanal.

This was explosive news. Pacific combat turned on local air superiority, and air power meant either carriers or airfields in the battle zone. Flattops could move about, bringing power where needed; also, they could flee from strong threats. On the other hand, airfields were unsinkable, and land-based planes could fly farther than carrier aircraft, with heavier bombs. An operational airfield was the strongest piece in Pacific chess.

Seven hundred miles northwest of Guadalcanal, the Rabaul air base threatened the line to Australia and barred an advance toward Japan. Hence MacArthur's dashing plan, which King had vetoed, to strike there. But an airfield as far south as Guadalcanal was a menace King could not accept. Denying it to the foe, he would gain local air superiority in the Solomons, and American airpower could trade punches at long range with Rabaul. Shoestring forces already embarked received added orders: *Capture and hold the Guadalcanal airfield.*

And so America sidled, as it were, into its most arduous Pacific campaign. Guadalcanal itself, a potato-shaped island a hundred miles long and half as wide, was never the prize. For months the land fighting raged along a narrow plantation strip of the northern coast flanking the airfield. The rest of the mountainous island was left to the mosquitoes, the jungle wildlife, and the natives, who were probably both frightened and entertained by the noisy flaming fireworks along the north shore.

The small, ill-equipped Shoestring expedition had little trouble capturing Tulagi and the Guadalcanal airfield, but the severe counterstroke from nearby Japanese bases came fast. In a night action called the Battle of Savo Island, Japanese warships sank the entire U.S. fire support force, four heavy cruisers, and departed unscathed. They could have finished the job and extinguished Shoestring by sinking the helpless half-emptied transports, but they had to assume that American aircraft carriers were steaming close by in the darkness and would attack at dawn. So they left, giving the Americans the brief breathing spell that saved their campaign. In war, when a strong enemy is down, one is well-advised to cut his throat. In point of fact, Vice Admiral Fletcher was out of combat range with his carriers, preparing to fuel. Fearing air attack from Rabaul, he had left while the transports were still unloading.

Reprimanded by King earlier in the war for lack of aggressiveness, missing his chances in the Coral Sea, failing to launch all aircraft at once at Midway, Fletcher's career seems to have had one good moment: when he signalled Spruance at Midway, *I will conform to your movements.* By abandoning the transports at Guadalcanal he nearly lost the campaign at the outset. Whenever danger impended, this admiral seems to have been seized by an uncontrollable urge to steam away a couple of hundred miles and fuel. He fades from sight after Guadalcanal.

———————

TRANSLATOR'S NOTE: *Roon continues to make a goat of Frank Jack Fletcher here. My cruiser* Northampton *missed the Battle of Savo Island, but I know that the Japanese leadership, gunnery, and torpedo fire were good at Savo, and ours were miserable. That was why we lost four cruisers. It is true that Fletcher might have struck a counterblow, and that his retreat was conservative.—V.H.*

———————

Land Operations August 1942–February 1943

Like their navy, the Japanese army seems to have been plagued by over-confidence; probably they wrote off Midway as mere navy ineptness. After all, white men had yet to defeat the Japanese on land. Busy with plans to assault New Guinea and threaten Australia, the army committed troops only piecemeal to Guadalcanal, not enough and not adequately supported; and the United States forces formed a perimeter around the airfield, often dented but never broken by wild and bloody *banzai* charges.

Still, for a long time it was touch and go for the Americans. In effect they were stranded. Air bombardment, naval shelling, enemy night attack overland—and above all, malaria and other tropical illnesses—decimated them. Their weakened navy could sneak in only scanty supplies and rein-forcements. Hungry, thirsty, feeling forgotten and abandoned, they lived off captured Japanese rice, and burned Japanese gasoline. The few fresh aircraft and pilots that slipped in were quickly worn down or shot down. On one black day, Admiral Halsey's account avers, there was one *operating aircraft* on Henderson Field. President Roosevelt began publicly talking of Guadalcanal as a "minor" operation, a most ominous and pusillanimous signal. But the beleaguered marines and exhausted airmen clung to the perimeter until the tide turned.

In view of the poor record of American soldiers elsewhere, this epic defense of Henderson Field is striking. These defenders were marines, the navy's elite amphibious combat corps. The words of the American naval historian, Samuel Eliot Morison, perhaps explain all: *Lucky indeed for America that in this theater and at that juncture she depended not on boys drafted or cajoled into fighting but on "tough guys" who had volunteered* to fight and who asked for nothing better than to come to grips with the sneaking enemy who had aroused all their primitive instincts.

TRANSLATOR'S NOTE: Roon's slurs on our army are intolerable. The Germans never won a victory against us in two wars, if one ignores the brush at Kasserine Pass. We even won the Battle of the Bulge. We marched to the Elbe. We could have taken Berlin, had the Allies not already agreed that it would belong in the Russian occupation zone.

Considering our social and political background, and the traditional distaste of Americans for war, our soldiers became damned good. They were irreverent and ingenious, they had initiative, and they fought hard without hate. Roon's mentality cannot absorb American combat policy, which is quite simple and non-European: to lose as few lives as possible, yet win battles and wars.

Morison does get carried away by Guadalcanal, where the United States Marines in truth put up one hell of a show.—V.H.

Battle at Sea

At sea, the war took on a bizarre form. The sea mission of both sides was support of the troops fighting for Henderson Field. Holding the field, the Americans controlled the daylight hours, when their supply ships could move under the thin air umbrella. But the Japanese, with a much stronger surface force, traversed the Solomons in the darkness so regularly that the Americans called it the "Tokyo Express." Though missing each other in this alternation of night and day maneuvers, the two navies had numberless brushes, and the Japanese generally had the better of this fighting. But the Americans won the one all-out clash that counted, the Battle of Guadalcanal.

This was a diffuse four-day explosion of carnage at sea by day and by night. Both sides threw in almost everything they had; the Japanese, to land at last a massive troop reinforcement, the Americans, to prevent it. Eyewitness accounts tell of eerily picturesque nocturnal sea fights: red tracer showers in the darkness, blue-white searchlight beams stabbing for miles, detonating ship's magazines turning night into day, flaming ships drifting over wide areas of black waters. The losses on both sides were high. In the end only one thing mattered: American airplanes, carrier and land-based, sank seven out of the eleven Japanese troop transports, while the rest were driven up on the beaches and bombed to burned-out hulks. So ended the last Japanese try to retake the island.

Thereafter, as the American forces built up, the Mikado's troops became the stranded ones. In the end the Tokyo Express brought off this harried remnant in a tropical Dunkirk. But Japan had no rich and idle major power to come to her rescue, as England had had. She never recovered from Guadalcanal.

Admiral King had accomplished his purpose. The marines cursing and sweating under Japanese fire in the tropical night, the airmen spinning to their deaths, the naval officers and men whose bones litter the sea bottom off Guadalcanal, doubtless died damning the higher-ups who had sent them against such odds to such an out-of-the-way place. In the vulgar talk of American fighting men, Guadalcanal was and remains *"that fucking island."* But war theatres tend to be self-generating, and once King had committed Franklin Roosevelt to the Pacific with Guadalcanal, he was assured of enough men and ships to fight the Japanese while our beleaguered Third Reich was going down; not afterward, when the Japanese would have been entrenched and the Allies war-weary. King may have, in this way, deprived Japan of the negotiated settlement that was her war aim.

———————

TRANSLATOR'S NOTE: *Roon puts the above vulgarism in quotes in English. Considering the language prevalent in current literature I think the readers of this volume will not be too outraged. Incidentally, that remains my own exact opinion of Guadalcanal.*

In view of his biting criticism of Admiral Halsey later on in the Leyte Gulf chapter, I wish Roon had given him his due here. The turnabout in the Guadalcanal campaign occurred when Halsey relieved Vice Admiral Ghormley as ComSoPac. Fatigue had made Ghormley a defeatist, and MacArthur's spirit was down, too. Halsey's belligerent and inspiring leadership got everybody going again.—V.H.

*   *   *

40

NATALIE had pictured a flight via an "underground railroad" as something swift, organized, secretive, hairbreadth, and romantic. All they did in Marciana was wait for a very long time, not communicating with anybody, not even with the villagers. The little walled hamlet of old stone cottages, straggling along a spur halfway up Elba's highest peak, was picturesque and pleasant enough. The fugitives might have come for a rusticating vacation, except that they weren't paying.

This delay wore on and on. Castelnuovo seemed unconcerned. He had told Natalie and her uncle little about the plan of escape or the people helping them, and she could understand that. The less she knew, if they happened to be caught, the better. Once when they were alone—almost a month had then passed—he remarked, "Look here, Natalie, everything is all right. Just don't worry." She tried not to.

They were housed in a tumbledown cottage of stone and cracked plaster at the end of a steeply climbing alley, which beyond the house became a donkey path through terraced truck gardens and vineyards; where, from sunup to sundown, silent villagers harvested, loading little donkeys with produce and sometimes riding them about. The views were magnificent, though the villagers ignored them as they ignored the newcomers: off to the west the crags of Corsica poking above the water, eastward a hazy line of mainland ridges, north and south green islands of the archipelago, like Capraia and Montecristo, with their little wreaths of cloud; and down the mountainside the blue sea breaking on the wooded coast dotted with fishing villages. Natalie passed much time climbing around up here among the gardens and orchards, enjoying the panoramas, the birdsong, and the sight and fragrance of September fruits and flowers.

During the first week a fat very ugly girl, who had more warts than words, brought them net bags of vegetables and fruit, coarse bread, goat's milk and cheese, and sometimes fish wrapped in wet seaweed. After that Anna Castelnuovo foraged and shopped in the small marketplace. If rationing existed on Elba, there was no way of knowing it in

Marciana; if there were *carabinieri,* they were incurious about the mountain towns. Natalie's edginess faded. The cottage had only two dark moldy-smelling rooms—one for the Castelnuovos, one for herself and her uncle—with an outdoor privy, and a wood-burning stove layered with black grease. She had to fetch water in pails from a communal pump, sometimes standing in line with barefoot children, and she slept on straw. But she and her baby were free from the menace of Werner Beck in a quiet remote hideout. For the time being, that was enough.

Aaron Jastrow took to the halt with philosophic placidity. Old Sacerdote had given him as a parting gift a mildewed Bible in Hebrew and Italian from the Follonica beach house. All day he sat on a bench under an apple tree with this Bible and his dog-eared Montaigne. Toward evening, he would walk out on the donkey paths. He seemed to have shed, with his tight work routine, his irritating traits. He was calm, undemanding, cheerful. He was letting his beard grow out, and looking more and more like an aging peasant. When Natalie one sunny morning late in September fretted to him about the inaction he shrugged and said, "Would you mind waiting out the whole war on Elba? I wouldn't. Unlike Napoleon, I've no delusion that the world greatly misses or needs me."

The Bible was open on his lap. She peered at the pages of heavy Hebrew lettering and old-fashioned Italian print, all stained and mottled with time and sea damp. "Why are you reading that, exactly?"

"Aristotle said"—Aaron faintly grinned—"that in his old age he became more interested in myth. Care to join me?"

"I haven't studied Hebrew since I walked out of the temple's Sunday school when I was eleven."

He made room on the bench. She sat down, saying, "Oh, what the hell, why not?"

He turned the book to the first page. "Do you remember anything? Read."

"Let's see. That's a *B. Beh-ray-shis.* Right?"

"Summa cum laude! 'In the beginning.' Next?"

"Oh, Aaron, I'm a dolt at this, and I'm really not interested."

"Come now, Natalie. If you don't like to learn, I like to teach."

Heavy double knocks at the wooden door.

A young man smiled at Natalie in the doorway, stroking a droopy black mustache. The pudgy olive face was insolent and uncultured; the brown eyes took her in with a gleam of appetite; the baggy corduroy trousers and short red jacket were like stage clothes. *"Bonjour, de la part de Monsieur Rabinovitz. Prêts à partir?"* Strange harsh accent.

An open hay wagon blocked the alley, hitched to a bony mule twitching long ears.

"Eh? Partir? Tout de suite? Je crois que oui, mais—entrez?"

He shook his head, grinning. *"Vite, vite, je vous prie."*

Castelnuovo sat at the table with the others in the back room, eating the monotonous daily lunch of bread and vegetable soup. "Good!" He wiped his mouth and stood up. "I've been expecting him for a week. Let's pack up."

Aaron said, "Who is he?"

The doctor made a vague gesture. "He's a Corsican. Please hurry."

The fugitives bumped downhill for hours in the slow wagon, heading west. Miriam and Louis larked about in the hay. They stopped and got off at a fishing settlement, a few houses on a stony beach. Nobody was around, but rough clothes drying on lines and damp nets draped on beached rowboats showed it was inhabited. The Corsican led them aboard a sailing boat piled with fishing tackle, tied to a rickety wooden pier. Two unshaven men in ragged sweaters came out of the blue-painted deckhouse and hoisted a filthy gray sail. The boat heeled and went slipping out to sea, as the two men shouted hoarse gibberish at each other. The mule, left tied to a tree, stared after the boat like an abandoned child.

Natalie braced herself against the deckhouse, watching Miriam and the baby play on a pile of dry nets. The young Corsican, whose throaty patois sometimes lost her, said the worst was over. They had met no police, and the coast guard seldom patrolled here, so they were free of the Fascists now. Once in Corsica she and her friends would be safe, and they could remain as long as they chose. Corsica had rigid traditions about fugitives, *les gens qui prennent le maquis.* Corte, where he lived, was an old rebel citadel in the mountains. German and Italian armistice commissioners avoided Corte for their health. His own name was Pascal Gaffori. His older brother, Orlanduccio, who lived in Marseilles, had shipped often with Monsieur Rabinovitz on French freighters in peacetime. Now Orlanduccio had a job in the harbor master's office. The Marseilles waterfront was full of Corsicans, and the Resistance in the port was very strong.

The wind was plastering Natalie's old brown wool dress against her, and as he talked the Corsican was taking in with relish the curves of her breasts and thighs. Natalie was used to the eyes of men, but this blunt stare was unsettling. Still, there was no menace in his gaze, only strong Latin appreciation—so far.

Did he know, she asked, trying to distract him, what the further plans were? He did not. They would stay with his family until some message came from Monsieur Rabinovitz. Had he talked to Rabinovitz? No, he had never met Monsieur Rabinovitz, all this had been arranged by his brother. Were the two men in the deckhouse also his brothers? He snorted. They were Bastia fishermen, doing this for money. Times were bad, the armistice commission had beached the fishing boats. Hulls were drying up, seams were opening; these fellows had spent two days secretly caulking their bottom. They were tough guys, but she need have no fear of them.

Natalie was starting to wonder how much she had to fear Pascal. She was at sea with three ruffians in international waters, with no legal record of their departure. What of Aaron's well-stuffed money belt? What of the zipped-up compartment of dollars in her own suitcase? The boat was hissing along on the swells toward the sun sinking behind the Corsican mountaintops, the sail hummed and slapped, and all this was really happening, but how dreamlike it was, the sudden ride on the sea after the long stagnation in Marciana! This brigandlike stranger could easily rape her if he chose. Who could stop him? Poor Aaron? The genteel doctor? The two coarsely laughing horrors in the deckhouse, who were now passing a jug back and forth? They would only cheer him on and probably await their turns. Natalie's vivid anxious imagination ran through the scenario: this fellow knocking her down on the nets, shoving up her skirt, forcing apart her bared thighs with those big hands—

Spray from the roughening swells flying over the deck stung Louis's eyes and he wailed. She pounced on him and comforted him, and then Pascal let her alone.

The sun disappeared in a glow behind Corsica. The wind freshened. The boat canted steeply and ran fast. Swells broke over the gunwale. Anna became seasick, retching over the side while Castelnuovo patted her back and Miriam looked on in alarm. Aaron staggered to Natalie in the lee of the deckhouse, sat down beside her, and commenting on the pretty view of Elba astern, began to philosophize about Napoleon. Napoleon had left Corsica to rampage through Europe, he said, destroying the old regimes, spreading waste and death, turning the French Revolution into a reactionary comic opera of tinsel empire, only to come full circle and end up on Elba within sight of his native island. The same sort of thing would happen to Hitler; these upstart monsters inevitably generated the counterforces to crush them.

It was hard for Natalie to pay attention amid the noise of wind and water, but she had heard most of it before, in interludes of their Hebrew readings, and all she had to do was nod now and then. If only this scary passage would end! The coastline of Corsica was still below the horizon, and it was getting dark. Louis was whimpering in her arms. She was hugging him to keep off the cold, and feeling remorse at risking him in a tiny wallowing boat on the open sea; but these fishermen surely had been out here in worse weather a hundred times. Pascal came groping to them with a flask. She took a swig of raw brandy, and in the kindling warmth of it forgave him the presumably accidental grope at her breasts.

Made sleepy by the brandy, the rocking, and boredom, Natalie numbly endured the slow passage of time, the wetting of her feet and legs, the pitching of the boat, for she could not tell how long. At last the boat moved into calmer water. On the dark coast ahead, she could discern moonlit trees and boulders. Another half hour or so, and the boat closed the shore. One fisherman dropped the sail; the other jumped with a manila line to a big flat rock. Pascal helped the passengers off with their meager luggage. At once the boat hoisted sail and slipped off into the night.

"Well, now you are in Corsica, and so you are in France," he said to Natalie, taking her suitcases, "and we must walk about three kilometers."

With Louis in her arms, she easily kept pace with him along a footpath through swampy-smelling fields, but they had to slow down for the others. The ground rocked under her feet after the long sail. So they walked for almost an hour. At a dark farmhouse Pascal led them to a hut in back. "Here you will sleep. There is some supper at the house."

The food was soup and bread which Pascal served out. Nobody else appeared. In the candlelight at the plank table Natalie could see octopus tentacles in the tureen; loathsome, but she ate every scrap in her bowl. Pascal gave Louis bread dipped in goat's milk, which he devoured like a dog; and they all bedded down in the hut fully clothed, on straw.

Next morning they had only a glimpse of Bastia's narrow streets and old houses, very like a Tuscan town, as Pascal drove them through in an old truck. A train of three small cars carried them up a hair-raising mountain pass. The passengers, some dressed like Pascal and others in shabby city garb, were amused by Louis, who in his merry morning mood prattled nonsense on his mother's lap and clapped his hands, looking wisely about him. Pascal joked with the conductor, handing him the tickets, and the man ignored the fugitives. Natalie felt in nervous high spirits. She had slept like a rock, and breakfasted on bread, cheese, and wine. Grand mountain views were unfolding outside the open window and an exquisite, pungently flowery odor was drifting in. Pascal told her that she was smelling the *maquis,* the famous aroma which Napoleon in St. Helena had sadly yearned to breathe again.

"I understand him," she said. "It smells like Paradise."

Pascal gave her a heated look through half-closed eyes. She could hardly contain her laughter, he so much resembled Rudolph Valentino emoting in a silent movie. For all that, he rather scared her.

Pascal's father was the son, thirty years older; stouter, also dressed in corduroy, with white mustache and hair, with the same oval face and the same uncivilized brown eyes, set in aged leathery pouches. His manner was courtly, and his house on three levels of a steep street below the hilltop fortress of Corte had the look and the furnishings of prosperity. In a ceremonious lunch around a long polished oak table in a gloomy room, he welcomed the fugitives. His wife, a shapeless figure in black, and two silent-walking daughters, also in black, brought the food and drink: identified by Pascal with some provincial pride as blackbird pâté, goat stew, a cake of chestnut flour, and Corsican wine.

Over the first glass of wine Monsieur Gaffori made a little speech, sitting erect in his heavy carved armchair. *Le docteur Jastrow,* he understood, was a famous American author, in flight from the infamous Fascisti. America would one day rescue Corsica from its oppressors. The Corsican people would rise up and do their part by cutting many German and Italian throats; as in the past his ancestors in Corte had cut Genoese throats, Spanish throats, Turkish throats, Saracen throats, and Roman and Greek throats. The old gentleman's soft fierce repetition of gorges—*"des GORGES espagnoles, des GORGES romaines, des GORGES grecques"*—gave Natalie the chills. Meanwhile, to help the famous author and his friends, said old Gaffori, was a privilege. The Gaffori house was theirs.

Pascal conducted them up a postern stair to a separate apartment. "Mine is the room exactly below," he said to Natalie, repeating the Rudolph Valentino look, as he showed her into a room with a crib. But under his father's roof, his menace had vanished; he was just a plump youngster suffering from endemic Mediterranean oversexiness, and he was, after all, her rescuer. She was on French soil, that was what mattered. She felt a pulse of gratitude toward Pascal.

"*Vous êtes très aimable, monsieur.*" She shook his hand, holding Louis in one arm, and gave him a brief kiss on the cheek. "*Merci mille fois.*"

His eyes glowed like blown-on coals. "*Serviteur, madame.*"

Avram Rabinovitz rode the little three-car train up to Corte the other way, from the port of Ajaccio. The single-track road was reputed a scenic wonder, but he slumped with closed eyes at a window seat, chain-smoking vile Vichy French cigarettes as the splendid valleys and crags slid by. Shutting out the sunlight and the moving scenery somewhat relieved a migraine headache, which was clacking in his skull to the rhythm of the wheels. Some of the most beautiful views in the world had been wasted on Avram Rabinovitz: the Pyrenees, the Tyrol, the Dolomites, the Alps, the Danube valley, the Turkish coast, the Portuguese backcountry, and the Syrian mountains. In all these sublime settings his preoccupation had been finding enough food and water to keep fugitive Jews alive and on the move.

Not only was his taste for pretty scenery extinct; Rabinovitz's outlook on geography and nationality was altogether peculiar. Countries, borders, passports, visas, languages, laws, currencies, were to him unreal elements in a tawdry risky game played on the European land mass. His attitude was in that sense criminal. He recognized the law of rescue and no other. He had not always been such a freebooter; quite the contrary. His parents had come to Marseilles from Poland after the First World War. His father, a tailor, had taken to making naval and merchant marine uniforms. So Avram had grown up with French schooling and French friends, and had gone into the French merchant marine as a cabin boy, working his way up to a chief engineer's certificate. Well into his twenties he had remained a conforming Frenchman, only dimly aware of his Jewish origins.

With the coming of Hitler, and with anti-Semitism rising in Marseilles like the seep of sewer gas, Rabinovitz had wakened to reluctant Jewish consciousness. A wealthy Swiss Zionist had recruited him to run Jews illegally to Palestine. He had taken three hundred people down the Danube and across the Black Sea to Turkey in a hulk like the *Izmir,* and thence through the Turkish and Syrian backcountry to the Holy Land. The exploit had changed his life. Thereafter he had done nothing else.

Settling in Palestine, he learned some Hebrew and married a Haifa girl. He changed his Frenchified name, André, back to Avram. He tried joining the Zionist movement, but the party quarrelling bored him and put him off. He was at heart a French Jew still, baffled by the fast-spreading hatred for Jews in Europe, and determined to do something about it. He looked no further than the saving of lives. In those days he was hearing the complacent Jewish byword about Hitler's threats in many languages, *It's always hotter cooked than eaten,* but to him the Nazis meant business. He stopped arguing with the Zionists about doctrine and politics, and used their money and connections for rescuing Jews, as he had done with Herbert Rose and the Sacerdotes.

After the fall of France he had returned there and joined the Resistance in Marseilles, as the best base for continuing rescue work. In effect he had been a Resistance man for years. He was already a competent forger, smuggler, spy, liar, confidence man, and thief. Once, to save more than forty people, he had killed an informer in Rumania who was blackmailing him for hush money; striking him harder with a piece of iron than he intended and leaving the man in an alley gasping, his eyes glazing. The episode recurred to him in low moments—the feel of bone cracking under metal, the gush of blood from the bushy hair of the fallen extortionist—but he felt no conscious regrets.

Rabinovitz's migraines tended to come on him when he was over-tired, or frustrated, or doing something he knew was stupid. He had no business reason to be riding this Corsican train. He merely wanted to see Mrs. Henry. Though he had talked with her on the *Izmir* only a couple of times, she remained a radiant memory. For Rabinovitz, as for many European men, American women were glamorous. Natalie Henry fascinated him: a Jewess, an unmistakable darkly glowing Jewess, yet as American as Franklin D. Roosevelt, niece of a famous writer, married to a United States submarine officer! In Marseilles in peacetime, visiting American warships had brought with them an aura of distant power. The young officers in white and gold walking in twos and threes on the boulevard had seemed to Rabinovitz almost the kind of supermen the Germans fancied themselves to be. Byron Henry, an image on a snapshot, added much to Natalie's magic in Rabinovitz's eyes.

He had no designs on her; she seemed a very proper wife and mother. He was just greedy for the sight of her. He had done his best on the *Izmir* to suppress his pointless feelings, even though he thought she liked him. That Naples situation had been complicated enough, without the addling of his wits in a futile romance. Nevertheless her disembarking had been a blow.

The news from Siena in June—first, that Mrs. Henry and her uncle were still there, and then, that they were coming with the Castelnuovos —had deeply stirred him. For a week after learning that Mrs. Henry had reached Corsica, he had resisted the urge to go there. Then he had given in. The migraine had hit him on the overnight boat; and as the little train groaned up the hairpin turns and steep grades toward Corte, what with the turmoil in his heart and the throbbing agony in his head, he had to wonder at his folly. Yet he was happier than he had been since the death of his wife.

When he arrived at the Gaffori house, the object of his infatuation was in the small upstairs apartment in an old gray wool wrapper, bathing her baby in the kitchen sink. She had just washed her hair and put it up in pins. Splashed all over with soapy water by the frolicsome baby, she was not just then an erotic dream figure.

A knock. Aaron's voice through the door. "Natalie, we have a visitor."

"Who?"

"Avram Rabinovitz."

"Christ!"

She heard Jastrow laugh. "He makes no such claim, dear, though he is a savior of sorts."

"Well, I mean, how long will he be here? Louis is all soap from head to foot. So am I. I'm an absolute fright. What's the news? Are we leaving?"

"I gather not. He's staying for lunch."

"Well—oh, blast, I'll be down in a quarter of an hour."

She dressed hurriedly in the white wool dress with the scarlet brass-buckled belt that she had bought in Lisbon for her meeting with Byron. For a long time after Louis's birth she had been too plump to get into it. Packing up in Siena, she had on a last-minute impulse slammed it into a suitcase; *some* time in her wanderings she might want to look well! She put on Louis a little corduroy suit Madame Gaffori had given her, and she strode into the garden, carrying him in her arms. Rabinovitz rose from a bench in the grape arbor where he sat with the others. He looked rather different from her recollection of him: younger, not so stout, not so desperately drawn.

"Hello, Mrs. Henry."

Her dark hair, still damp despite furious towelling, was swept up over her head. He remembered this heavy beautiful hair, and the slant of the huge eyes, now twinkling at him in the friendliest way, and the shape of the generous mouth when she smiled, and the way her cheeks curved. The feel of her brief cool handshake was enchanting.

"I've got a surprise for you," she said, setting Louis down on the brown grass. "Stretch out your arms to him."

Rabinovitz obeyed. She let go, and Louis, with a keen excited look on his chubby face, took a few uncertain steps and fell into the Palestinian's arms, laughing and crowing. Rabinovitz swept him up.

"He's starting to talk, too," Natalie exclaimed. "Imagine, it's all happened in one week! Maybe it's the Corsican air. I feared I was raising an idiot."

"You never did." Jastrow sounded indignant.

"Say something," Rabinovitz told Louis, who was inspecting him with sharp eyes.

Louis pointed a finger at Rabinovitz's broad nose. "Daddy."

Natalie turned scarlet. Even the Castelnuovos, sitting in glum silence, burst out laughing. Natalie gasped, "Oh, God! I've been showing him a snapshot of his father."

Delighted with the sensation he had produced, Louis shouted, "Dadee! Da-dee!" pointing at Castelnuovo and at Jastrow.

"Horrors, that'll do, you little beast!"

The old man and Pascal ate in farming clothes. Pascal, grimy and tousle-haired in his old goatskin jacket, was giving Natalie his Valentino looks again. In his father's presence he had until now been more careful. The dress, she thought uneasily, was setting him off, and she kept glancing at Rabinovitz, who took no visible notice. The conversation around the table was about the war news. The latest rumor in Corsica, said old Gaffori, was that all the North Africa hints were a deception. The Allies would hit Norway, drive across Scandinavia and Finland, and link up with the Russians. This would relieve Leningrad, open up a good Lend-Lease supply route to the Red Army, and put Allied bombers close to Berlin. What did Monsieur Rabinovitz think?

"I don't believe the Norway story. Too late in the year. Your son and I once served in a freighter that made port in Trondheim in November. We got icebound for weeks."

"Orlanduccio told us about that," said Gaffori, reaching for a stone jug and filling Rabinovitz's glass and his own. "He told us about some other things, monsieur, such as the little affair in Istanbul." He raised his glass to Rabinovitz. "You are always welcome in this house, as long as you live. Thank you for sending us the great American author and his friends."

Jastrow said, "We feel we're a burden."

"No. You may stay, monsieur, until we are all freed together. And now Pascal and I must go back to work."

Natalie said quietly to Rabinovitz as they stood up from the table, "I must talk to you. Have you time?"

"Yes."

He walked with her up the steep cobbled steps of the street outside, which led to the open gateway of the ruined fortress. "Shall we climb up?" she said. "The view is marvelous from the top."

"Okay."

"What was the business in Istanbul?" she asked as they began to mount a narrow stone staircase along an inner wall.

"Nothing much."

"I'd like to know."

"Oh, well, this guy Orlanduccio used to drink a lot and raise hell when we made port. This was before he married and settled down. I was on deck working on a broken winch, and I saw him come staggering along the wharf about midnight. Some hoodlums jumped him. Those waterfront rats are all cowards, they pick on drunks, so I just ran down there with a crowbar and broke it up."

"Why, then, you saved his life."

"His money, maybe."

"And the Gafforis are being kind to us on your account."

"No, no. They're in the Resistance, the whole family."

On a level terrace choked with brown grass and weeds, goats were wandering in and out of the broken walls of a roofless stucco structure with bars in the windows.

"Guardhouse," said Rabinovitz. "Not much good now."

"Tell me about the *Izmir*," she said, leading him across the terrace to another staircase that went higher.

"The *Izmir*? That's long ago." He shook his head, looking sad and troubled. "It wasn't so bad when we started out, but the weather got pretty wild by the time we reached Haifa. We had to unload the people into boats at night in a storm. That damned Turkish captain was making trouble, threatening to leave. There were some drownings, a few, I don't know just how many. Once the people reached the shore they scattered. We never got an accurate count."

Natalie asked soberly, "Then I was right to get off, after all?"

"Who can say? Here you are in Corsica now."

"Yes, and what happens next?"

The higher staircase, its steps ground deep by climbers, was very steep. He spoke slowly, breathing hard, "The American consul general in Marseilles knows you're here. He's a good fellow, James Gaither. I've had dealings with him. He's all right. Some of the other people in that consulate are no damn good. He's handling your problem himself, on a strict confidential basis. When all your papers are in order you'll come to Marseilles and proceed by train the same day to Lisbon. That's Gaither's idea."

"When will that be?"

"Well, the tough thing is the exit visa. Up to a month or so ago you could have gone by train to Lisbon like any tourist. But now the French have stopped issuing exit visas. German pressure. Your embassy can get things done in Vichy, so you'll receive visas, but it'll take a while."

"You've already managed all that!"

"Don't give me credit." It was a sharp sour reply. "Gaither had a cable from the U.S. legation in Bern to be on the lookout for you. When I told Gaither you were in Corsica, he said, 'Hooray!' Just like that." They were at the top now. Over windswept battlements, they looked down on a valley floor of farms and vineyards, surrounded by wild forested mountains. "Well, I see what you mean. Fine view."

"What about the Castelnuovos?"

He cupped a cigarette in his palms to light it. "Much tougher proposition. The German armistice commission made a raid on Bastia in September, because refugees were escaping to Algeria through there. That broke up my arrangements, so you got stuck in Marciana. Still, it's good they left Siena. The OVRA started pulling in Italian Zionists in July. They'd be in a concentration camp by now. I'm working something out for them, so please try to keep the doctor from getting impatient. If the worst comes to the worst, the Gafforis will always look after them." He puffed the cigarette and glanced at his watch. "We'd better start back. You wanted to talk to me? The train leaves for Ajaccio in about an hour."

"Well, yes. That young fellow, Pascal—" she hesitated, gnawing a knuckle.

"Yes, what about him?"

"Oh, hell, I must confide in you. And I couldn't talk in the house. Night before last, I woke up and he was in my room, sitting on my bed.

With a hand on the covers. On my leg." She began rushing out the words as they went down the windy steps. "Just sitting there! My baby's crib wasn't two feet from us. I didn't know whether I was dreaming or what! I whispered, 'What is it? What are you doing here?' And he whispered, *'Je t'aime. Tu veux?'* " Rabinovitz stopped short on the steps. To her astonishment he was blushing. "Oh, don't worry, he didn't rape me or anything, in fact I got rid of him." She tugged at his elbow. Frowning, he resumed the descent. "It may have been my fault. Even in Elba he was making eyes at me, and on the boat he got sort of fresh. I did one damn fool thing when we got to the house. The trip was over, I'd made it safely, and I was grateful to him. I kissed him. Well, he looked at me as though I'd taken off my skirt. And since then, it's as though I've never put it back on. And now this thing the other night—"

"How did you get rid of him?"

"Well, it wasn't so easy. First thing I whispered was, 'It's impossible, you'll wake my baby.' " Natalie took a quick side glance at Rabinovitz. "Now, maybe I should have gotten on my high horse and just thrown him out, yelled for his father, whatnot. But I was sleepy and surprised, and I didn't want to wake Louis, and I felt more or less at these people's mercy. So then he whispered, 'Oh, no, we'll be as quiet as two little pigeons.' " Natalie nervously giggled. "I was scared as hell, but it was just too ludicrous, *'deux petites colombes'*—"

Rabinovitz was smiling, but not pleasantly. "So what broke it up?"

"Oh, we whispered like that, yes, no, back and forth. He wouldn't leave. I thought of appealing to his Corsican honor not to harm a fugitive under his roof. Or threatening to tell his father. All that seemed long and complicated. So I just said, 'Look, it mustn't be, I'm unwell.' He snatched his hand off my leg and jumped from the bed as though I'd pleaded leprosy."

For a seafaring man, she thought, Rabinovitz was oddly prudish. He looked very ill at ease at this.

"Then he stood over me and whispered, 'You're telling the truth?' 'Of course.' 'Madame, if you are simply refusing me, you are making a grave mistake. I can promise you ecstasy.' " She assumed a baritone voice. " *'Je peux te promettre l'extase.'* His very words. With that, thank God, he tiptoed out. I fear he's going to try again. What shall I do? Shall I talk to his father? The old man's so formidable."

Rabinovitz was rubbing a palm on a very worried face. "I'm thinking where I can put you in Marseilles. Unless you want to try that ecstasy."

She said nothing, and again the puffy face reddened. "Sorry, I shouldn't make fun of you, I'm sure it's distressing."

She replied a touch mischievously, "Oh, well, it's made me feel young and so forth. But no, I'll forgo Corsican ecstasy."

He gave her a curious smile, with much sadness in it. "Good. Not for nice Jewish girls."

"Oh, you don't know me," Natalie retorted, though not—to her surprise—annoyed by the description. On Rabinovitz's lips the words had a caressing sound. "I've always done exactly as I pleased, or God knows I wouldn't have married Byron Henry. Or put myself through other wringers that nice Jewish girls usually avoid. Anyway, you think you'll move us to Marseilles?"

"Yes. I don't want trouble with the Gafforis. They're very important to me, especially Orlanduccio. And at the moment they're my one sure place for the Castelnuovos. Orlanduccio's told me about this Pascal, he's no good. You might be better off in Marseilles anyway. When your papers come through, you can leave, one two three. That's an advantage."

"And the Castelnuovos?"

"They stay here."

"But I don't want to abandon them."

"*Abandon* them?" Rabinovitz's voice turned harsh as they walked across the terrace past the tumbledown guardhouse. "Don't use such a silly expression, please. The U.S. consul general will step in for you if anything goes wrong, but they'd have no protection, none whatever. Marseilles is full of police and informers. I can't possibly move them there. Please don't encourage the doctor with such ideas. I'm having enough trouble with him as it is."

"All right. Don't be angry with me. Louis and Miriam are like brother and sister now."

"I know. Listen, that Bastia raid was rotten luck. If the doctor will be sensible, he and his family will be all right."

"While we're in Marseilles, will we see you now and then?"

"Sure."

"Well, that will be good."

He hesitated, and spoke very gruffly. "I was disappointed when you left the *Izmir*."

Natalie suddenly kissed his cheek. It felt bristly and cold.

"Mrs. Henry, doing that is what got you into trouble."

"I don't think I'll wake to find you in my bedroom."

"To a Frenchman that's no compliment."

They smiled uncertainly at each other, and descended into the town.

That evening it was Natalie's turn to cook. As she served out a scrappy ratatouille in the little upstairs kitchen, a recipe from her Paris days, there was little talk. Even Miriam was grave. She went off to bed while the adults lingered in the kitchen over a coffee substitute made of roasted grains, mere sour brown water. Castelnuovo said, "Well, it'll be hard on the children, won't it?" This was the first open reference to their coming separation.

She had stopped noticing his appearance from day to day, but now she was struck by the alteration in him since Siena. Then he had been a self-assured, charming, handsome Italian doctor. His good looks were fading, his eyes were hollow, the lids were heavy.

"It'll be hard on me, I know that," she said.

Aaron Jastrow said, "Isn't it possible we'll still rejoin, and go out together?"

Castelnuovo's headshake was slow, emphatic, and weary.

"What are his plans for you?" Jastrow insisted. "Can't we be frank with each other?"

"In Marciana we still hoped to go by ship to Algiers," said the doctor, "and make our way east to Palestine. But that's closed off. It seems we can go out illegally either to Spain or Switzerland. People go in groups, with guides who sneak them through the woods. I guess Spain's better. At least it's on the way to Lisbon."

"The trouble is," Anna said, with a pointless smile, "that to get to Spain we have to cross the Pyrenees on foot. In November. There's no other way. Miles of walking in the wilds, with snow and ice, and the border patrols to watch out for."

"What about Switzerland?" Natalie asked.

"If they catch you, back to France you go," said Anna. "Into the hands of the French police."

"Not necessarily!" Her husband spoke angrily to her. "Don't exaggerate. Every group has a different experience. There are rescue agencies in Switzerland, too, who can help you. Rabinovitz prefers Spain, but Anna is worried about Miriam walking over the mountains."

"But the vessels that were going to South America," said Jastrow, "the fishing boats to Morocco—all those other possibilities we've talked about?"

Castelnuovo's hopeless shrug and dark empty look made Natalie herself feel trapped as never before. "You'll be all right," she said, very cheerfully. "I trust him."

"So do I," said the doctor. "He tells the truth. He knows what he's doing. It was I who decided to leave Italy, and I was right. We're not in a concentration camp. If Miriam has to walk over the Pyrenees in the snow, why, she'll walk over the Pyrenees. She's a strong healthy girl." He got up and hurried out.

Natalie said to Anna Castelnuovo, whose eyes were wet, "Anna, can I take Miriam into my bed tonight?"

Anna nodded. The drowsy little girl came to Natalie's bed herself later, without a word, and fell asleep in a moment. Natalie loved the feeling of the small warm body snuggled beside her. When the sun woke Natalie next morning Miriam was gone. The girl had crawled into the crib and was sleeping with Louis in her arms.

41

A GRAND armada was now on the high seas, converging upon North Africa. Not since the Japanese Imperial Fleet had set out for Midway, and before that never in all history, had the oceans of earth borne such a force. Aircraft carriers, battleships, cruisers, troop transports, and newfangled landing ships crammed full of small craft, tanks, trucks, and mobile guns; also destroyers, minesweepers, submarines, and assorted supply vessels; from several directions, in far-flung formations, these warships of frowning shapes and many sizes, painted gray or in gaudy camouflage colors, were crawling the watery curve of the planet. They came thronging south from the British Isles, and, in an ocean-borne assault new in size and reach, they came steaming east from North America. Axis intelligence knew nothing of all this. The speculations at a Corsican dining table were being echoed aboard Hitler's command train heading for a Party rally in Munich. Though mounted in chatterbox democracies, the great attack was being kept as secret as the Japanese assault on Pearl Harbor.

Winston Churchill had closed his defiant oration after Dunkirk with a pledge to carry on the struggle *"until, in God's good time, the New World, with all its power and might, steps forth to the rescue and the liberation of the Old."* Now it was happening, two and a half years later, the Churchillian dithyramb coming to majestic life: a swarm of fresh seapower with the ever-rising roar of American technology behind it, bearing veteran British divisions and the first wave of America's newly recruited soldiery. If romance could exist in industrialized war, this was a romantic hour, the approaching hour of Torch.

But the American invaders, despite a Patton here and there, would have been embarrassed by Churchillian dithyrambs about what they were doing. The career challenges and the technical risks interested the professional soldiers; otherwise, generals and privates alike regarded Torch and the whole war as a dirty job to get over with. George Marshall disapproved altogether of Torch as a diversion from the big landing in France, and the commander-in-chief of the expedition himself, a newcomer on the world scene named Dwight Eisenhower, feared that the decision for Torch "might go down as the blackest day in history." Still, given their orders, he and his staff had methodically set about the business.

Loading the odds in their favor was much to be desired, however unromantic; and if a fight could be avoided altogether, so much the better. So the notion had arisen to bring into the combined Anglo-American high command a famous French general in a window-dressing role, to induce the Vichy forces in North Africa not to fight, no matter what their German-ruled government might order. Thus began a comedy worthy—except for the magnitude of the stakes—of a Parisian boulevard farceur's pen.

In this scherzo interlude in the heavy march of the war, Byron Henry became caught up. The reader therefore needs a brief sketch of what the foolery was about.

For this role of high-brass catspaw Charles de Gaulle was available in London, where he was sounding forth as the voice of "Free France," exhorting his countrymen to resist their conquerors. The trouble with de Gaulle was that Vichy's generals and admirals loathed him to a man. Nor did the Resistance much love him. Sonorous defiance from a London hotel suite did not greatly charm French hearts just then. The personage the Allies hit on instead was one General Henri Giraud. Giraud had fought well against the Germans in 1940, had been captured, and had escaped from a German prison. He was now lying low in France, and the plan was to hunt him up, spirit him from his hideout to the Mediterranean coast, take him aboard an Allied submarine, and speed him to Gibraltar to join Eisenhower.

This was a complicated project, and when secretly approached, Giraud made it more complicated. On points of honor General Giraud turned out to be a fussy man. Earlier in the war British warships had bombarded a French fleet to prevent its falling into German hands. Henri Giraud therefore would not consent to be rescued by a British submarine. But the only suitable subs on hand at the moment flew British flags. A British submarine had to be put under nominal command of an American captain, with a couple of other American officers along for verisimilitude, to fetch the Frenchman. The British skipper and crew naturally operated the boat as before; the Americans rode along and tried to act busy. This "American" submarine duly picked up General Giraud off the coast near Toulon, and brought him to Gibraltar.

There—to round out the Giraud epic, before narrating Byron Henry's small part in it—on being ushered into the presence of Eisenhower in his command-post cave, Giraud calmly thanked the American generalissimo for his services to date, and informed him that he, Henri Giraud, would now relieve him as commander-in-chief, and would himself conduct the invasion of North Africa. This happened less than forty-eight hours before the start of the assault, with some four hundred fifty ships approaching the landing beaches. Details of this remarkable chat are lacking, but we know that Giraud was deaf to argument. Taking supreme command was, he insisted, a point of honor with him. But Eisenhower insensitively declined to be relieved. The Frenchman thereupon went into a profound sulk and played no part in the invasion.

As things turned out he was not missed. In the early hours of the landing a certain Admiral Darlan, the most influential Vichyite in Northwest Africa, noted chiefly for his extraordinary hatred of England, America, and Jews, fell into the invaders' hands. Knife to his throat, they pressed him into the Giraud role. He did a fine job of pacifying the French forces, terminating the sporadic resistance, and establishing order under the Allies. Willy-nilly, Darlan prevented the deaths of many American and British soldiers, far better than Giraud could have.

A loud long cry at once went up in the Allied press against this cynical use of such a bad man. Political trouble ensued. General Eisenhower contemplated resigning, and President Roosevelt underwent prolonged newspaper savaging, more strident than usual. Then by another lucky chance of war the matter was cleared up. An idealistic French student shot Darlan. Some time afterward, at the Casablanca Conference, General Giraud, yielding to a lot of coaxing, consented to pose sullenly for pictures with Churchill, Roosevelt, and de Gaulle. So it is that one knows today what the man of honor looked like. He was tall and thin, but not as tall and thin as de Gaulle. He had the larger mustache.

It was during the frantic spate of communications back and forth about Giraud's honor that Byron Henry got sucked into the affair. Oddly, his submarine experience had nothing whatever to do with it. He was swept like a cork in an eddying stream, from Gibraltar to Marseilles, around and around, with no inkling of what the propelling force was, simply because he had a high American security clearance. Gibraltar was chronically short of American couriers; with invasion imminent, even more so. Since his encounter with the Tudsburys, Byron had been sent on several of these errands, but never before to Marseilles, though he had been in touch with the consulate by mail and telephone, inquiring about Natalie.

Like everybody at the Rock he knew that a big operation was afoot. The power hum vibrating throughout the base, the gathering of warships and warplanes, the descent of high brass with their scurrying self-important staffs, all brought to his mind Pearl Harbor before Midway. But whether the objective was Africa, Sardinia, the south of France, or even Italy, Byron did not know. He had never heard of General Henri Giraud. Nor was the name mentioned to him now. At eight in the morning, black with grease, he was aboard a decrepit S-boat alongside the *Maidstone,* trying to get a defunct air compressor to work; and by noon, hastily cleaned up and in civilian clothes, with the courier's leather pouch once more chained to his wrist and the diplomatic passport in his pocket, he was on his way to Marseilles.

He had heard nothing from Lesile Slote in over two months. His repeated inquiries to the Marseilles consulate had proven fruitless. Still, since he was going there, he meant to check around. His instructions were to hand the locked pouch of documents to a certain vice consul, wait for a coded reply, and bring it back posthaste. He would have time, he figured, to press a few inquiries. And so it was that he did find Natalie, though the final linkup was fortuitous. Had she not left Italy, and had he not gotten himself to Gibraltar, it naturally could not have happened, but the gap was closed by luck.

Arriving in a pouring cold rain at the consulate, he unchained the pouch and delivered it to the vice consul, a man named Sam Jones, with a nondescript face and nondescript clothes to match; a good inconspicuous sort to be handling covert military intelligence. As Byron doffed his dripping raincoat he asked Jones, "Is Lucius Babbage still stationed here?"

"Luke Babbage? Sure. Why?"

"I want to talk to him. How much time have I got?"

An incongruous foxy look creased Jones's average face; the intelligence man, peeping through the drab vice consul. "You've got time. Luke's office is down the hall. Frosted glass panel door."

A pinch-faced woman with a tight net on her grizzled hair was typing away inside the frosted glass door, at a desk stacked with official forms. Refugees crowded the anteroom, most of them looking as though they had been sitting there for days. The secretary's cold glance dissolved in a charming smile as she took in his face, and the American sport jacket and slacks in which he ran his courier errands. He had no trouble getting past her to see Babbage.

Pale watery light from the wide windows of the inner office fell on life-sized framed photographs of President Roosevelt and Cordell Hull; also on a large bad reproduction of *George Washington Crossing the Delaware*. Behind the desk a plump bald pink man rose to shake hands with Byron, his blue eyes twinkling through gold-rimmed glasses. "Lieutenant Henry, eh? I recall your letter, Lieutenant. Your phone calls, too. Lousy connection to Gibraltar. Good old American name, Henry. No relation to Patrick? Ha ha! Submariner, isn't it? My son wanted to join the Navy but couldn't make it. Eyes. He's in the Air Corps, quartermasters. How's the war looking from Gibraltar? I guess these courier trips are interesting, but I'd think you'd be out in the Pacific. Well, sit down, sit down."

Lucius Babbage wanted to know when Byron had last been in the States and whether he had seen any major league baseball games. Rocking back and forth in a squeaky swivel chair, he said that agitation to draft stars like DiMaggio and Feller was fomented by people of dubious motives. If a few great ball players could keep millions of laborers diverted while turning out planes and tanks, where was the sense in marching them off to carry rifles in the mud, leaving the big leagues to Army rejects and misfits? During this aimless persiflage the prominent eyes stared through the gold rims, and Babbage kept rubbing the back of his hand on jowls as smooth-shaven as a priest's.

"Well!" Babbage said, changing his tone as though with a flip of a switch, "the problem is your wife, as I recall it. Suppose you tell me the story again, and save me pulling out your letter again? There's an uncle, too, isn't there?"

"Yes. His name's Aaron Jastrow. He's the author," Byron said. "Hers is Natalie. Mrs. Byron Henry. My son is Louis, an infant in arms. I've lost track of them, but I have reason to think they might be in or around Marseilles."

Babbage kept nodding through all this, his face blankly beaming. "They're Americans?"

"Of course."

"Passports in order?"

"Yes."

"What would they be doing in the free zone, then? We sent everybody home ages ago."

"Then I take it they've not turned up?"

Babbage pulled a yellow pad from a drawer, and picked up a pen in his left hand. He nodded at Byron with a warm smile, his eyes squeezed almost shut. "Why not give me all the facts, as long as you're here? When and where you last had news of their whereabouts, and so on and so forth? The more I know, the more thoroughly I can look into it."

Some instinct made Byron tread cautiously. "Dr. Jastrow was living in Siena, retired from teaching history at Yale, writing his books. Natalie worked as his secretary. They were caught there when we got into the war. So—"

"Let me interrupt you right there, Lieutenant. All the Americans who were interned in Italy were exchanged in May." Babbage was smiling and scrawling as he spoke, his left hand curled around the pen. "So they should be home by now, no problem."

"Well, I was out in the Pacific then. I don't know what happened, but they weren't exchanged."

"How odd."

"And last anybody heard, they were going to try to get to France."

"You mean illegally?"

"I really don't know any more details."

"What's her uncle's name again?"

"Jastrow."

"Spell it, please."

"J-A-S-T-R-O-W."

"Well-known author?"

"The Book-of-the-Month Club took one of his books."

"Good enough. Which book was that?"

"*A Jew's Jesus.*"

This did bring a reaction from Babbage. His smile flared out, his eyebrows went up, and his eyes shone. "Oh? He's a Jew?"

"Not a practicing one."

"Few of them are, it's a question of nationality, isn't it?" Slight pause, and a happy grin. "Your wife is one, too?"

"Yes, she is."

"You're not, obviously."

"No."

The left hand scrawled and stopped. With a genial nod and a wink, Babbage got up and walked into the anteroom, saying, "Half a sec." He was gone about five minutes, while Byron stared at George Washington, at Roosevelt, at Hull, and at the grimy rain-beaten buildings across the street. Babbage returned, sat behind his desk, and clasped his hands before him. "No, they're not in Marseilles. And there's no record of them anywhere in the unoccupied zone. Have you checked with the International Red Cross? What with their being Jewish, and the kind of books he writes, they may well have landed in an Italian concentration camp."

"Suppose they'd made it to Toulon, or Algiers? Would you know?"

"If they'd reported in to American authorities, I'd know. The roster of all Americans in the area is my responsibility. Now, if they attempted an *illegal* transit of France—well, let's just hope they didn't, Lieutenant. The French police are getting damned tough with Jews on the run." He cheerily smiled. "But I don't know why they should have done such a silly thing, if their papers were in order. Right?"

"Right." Byron abruptly stood up.

"Well, it's an unusual case." Babbage rubbed his jowl with the back of his hand. "You a submariner, your wife working for this relative who writes these leftist books, and—"

"What? There's nothing in the least leftist about *A Jew's Jesus.*" Byron allowed hard annoyance into his voice. "It's a historical work, and very brilliant."

"Oh? Well, I'll have to read it. I thought it might be one of those tripey things that make out Our Lord to be a revolutionary. That's the old leftist line, isn't it?"

"Much obliged." Byron stalked out, galled by this frustrating finale to the long trek from Australia: a bureaucratic stone wall, mildewy with snide anti-Semitism, in a Marseilles consulate. He had the addresses of a Quaker agency and a Jewish committee, and he decided to walk off his irritation, though it was still raining. He had last visited Marseilles in 1939, in his vagabonding after dropping out of graduate school in Florence, and he retained pleasant memories of the Canebière boulevard with its opulent window displays and seafood restaurants, and the noisy cheerful people, so unlike the glum French elsewhere. Rain or shine, Marseilles had been a delight.

It had much changed. The people appeared peaked, weary, and impoverished. The long, wide, quiet Canebière, all but empty of auto traffic, had a plague-stricken look. The rain-blurred shop windows offered scanty dusty things like badly made garments, cheap Vichy propaganda books, and cardboard luggage. The famous food markets were pitifully shrunken. The meat stalls that were not barred shut vended horrid scraps caked with black blood: tails, ears, guts, lungs. The few vegetables for sale were sparse, wilted, and wormy-looking. There was no fruit. Amazingly, there was no fish. All the famous stalls, which once had been piled with gleaming bright-eyed fish wet from the sea, and all manner of shellfish in beds of seaweed, were shuttered. The cancer of German conquest was visibly eating at Marseilles.

Outside the Quaker office Byron found a great jam of children on the streaming sidewalk, blocking the entrance; children by the dozens, from toddlers to adolescents, huddled under dripping umbrellas. Inside, type-writers were clattering amid much high-pitched French gabble. A fat American woman herding the children into a line said that she had no time for him; Congress had passed a special resolution, allowing five thousand Jewish children into the United States: no parents, only chil-dren, and the Quakers were rounding them up as fast as possible, be-fore Vichy changed its mind about releasing them, or the Germans grabbed them to ship them east, or the State Department threw in a new monkey wrench. Byron despaired of accomplishing anything here, and he left.

The Jewish office, called the "Joint," was in a different neigh-borhood. He had to ask directions. The first two Frenchmen he ap-proached skulked off without a reply. He persisted, and found his way to the place. In so doing he walked right past the building where Rabin-ovitz had ensconced his wife and child; just one more wet gray four-story Marseilles apartment house in blocks and blocks of them. He strode by, hunched against the rain, in a close blind chance miss, as two submarines running silent can pass each other in the undersea dark by inches and not know it.

In the small crowded anteroom of the agency office, a hollow-eyed young woman at one desk frantically banged at a typewriter, but Byron could not approach her; a long line waited at the desk, coiling all around the room and snaking through people sitting in chairs or lounging on their feet, some holding battered valises, all talking every known lan-guage (or so it seemed to Byron) but English. Sad fear pervaded this crowd, visible in faces and sounding in voices. Byron leaned against the wall, wondering how to proceed. A plump dark young man in a trench coat came out of a door behind the desk, looked busily about, and shouldered toward the street entrance. Passing Byron, he stopped and said, "Hi."

The American monosyllable was clear as a bell. Byron replied, "Hi."

"Got a problem?"

"Sort of."

"I'm Joe Schwartz."

"I'm Lieutenant Byron Henry."

The man arched a heavy black brow. "Had lunch?"

"No."

"Ever eat couscous?"

"No."

"It's pretty good, couscous."

"Okay."

Schwartz led him a block away to what looked like a tailor shop; at least there was a headless unclothed dummy in the narrow gloomy window, and a yawning cat. They passed through the shop to a back room where at small oilcloth-covered tables people were eating. The couscous, served by an unshaven man in a skullcap, was a sort of farina with vegetables and a hot spicy meat gravy. Acting again on instinct, Byron told this stranger his story, including everything he had withheld from the American consul. Schwartz kept nodding as he ate with appetite. "Leslie Slote. Bern. Thin blond fellow," he said. "I know him. Very smart. Nervous type, very nervous, but he's all right. That fellow Babbage is bad news. These fellows here in Marseilles vary. It's an individual thing, some are fine guys, and the man you want to talk to here is Jim Gaither. If anybody knows anything about your wife, it'll be Gaither."

"Who's Gaither?"

"The consul general. He's not here now, though. He had to go to Vichy."

"I must return to Gibraltar today."

"Well, maybe you can phone or write to him."

"What do you do?"

"Right now I'm organizing thirty typewriters. One thing the Germans have is typewriters, so they trade them with the French."

"What do you need thirty typewriters for?"

"The Joint office in Lisbon. That's where I work. The American consulate in Lisbon has a total of three typewriters. It's unbelievable. So we're going to have plenty of typewriters from now on, and volunteer typists to fill out papers. Jews aren't going to be stuck in Lisbon any more, when a ship becomes available, because of a lack of typewriters."

"If my wife passed through Lisbon, would you know?"

"I'd know about her uncle." Schwartz looked thoughtful. *"A Jew's Jesus.* Who hasn't read it? Now listen, Lieutenant. Some decent Italian or French people could well be hiding them. Be optimistic."

"How bad is the situation?"

"You mean, of the Jews?"

"Yes."

Joe Schwartz's voice went deep, the face stony. "Very bad. In the east Jews are being murdered, no question about it, and the French are letting the Germans take them away. However"—he returned to his good-natured manner, even smiling—"there are many decent Christians, willing to risk their lives to help. Things can be done. It's a complicated picture, and we do what we can. Did you enjoy the couscous? How about some tea?"

"Sure. Thanks. The couscous was good."

"What's he like, Aaron Jastrow?"

Byron hesitated. "Very regular in work habits. Quite a scholar."

"That shows in his work. Informative. But *A Jew's Jesus* is a best-seller for Christians. You know? It's bland. Vanilla-flavored. Nice. Christianity has been hard on the Jews. The Crusades, the Inquisition, and now this. The Germans are supposed to be Christians."

"I'm a Christian. Or rather, I try to be," Byron said.

"I didn't mean to offend you."

"You didn't, but nothing Jesus taught leads to Hitler."

"That's very true, yet if Jesus hadn't walked the earth, would such things have happened? Europe is a Christian continent, isn't it? Well, what's going on? Where's the Pope? Mind you, there's one Catholic priest right here in Marseilles who's a saint, a one-man underground. I only hope the Gestapo doesn't murder him." Looking at his watch, Joe Schwartz shook his head. "How did we get into this? Yes, *A Jew's Jesus*. Well, anyhow, it's a good book. It brings Jesus down from the stained glass, the big famous paintings, the huge crosses, where he's always dying or dead. It shows him walking around among Jews, a poor Talmud scholar, a boy prodigy, a real living Jew. That's important. Maybe it's enough. More tea?"

"I've got to get back to the consulate."

The rain was blowing in slant sheets outside. They paused in the doorway to turn up their collars. Schwartz said, "I know where you can hire a cab."

"I'll walk. Thanks for lunch. Tell me something," Byron said, looking hard at Schwartz. "What can somebody like me do?"

"You mean about us, about the Jews?"

"Yes."

The heavy lines reappeared in Schwartz's face. "Win the war."

Byron held out his hand, and Joe Schwartz shook it. They went their separate ways in the rain.

Back in Gibraltar, Byron boarded the *Maidstone* dog-tired, after turning in his pouch at Allied headquarters. He meant to collapse on his bunk in his clothes, but a dispatch lying on his desk jolted him alert.

FROM: BUPERS
TO: CO HMS MAIDSTONE
VIA: COMLANT
LIEUTENANT (JG) BYRON (NONE) HENRY USN DETACHED TEMPO-RARY LIAISON DUTY ROYAL NAVY X PROCEED SANFRAN REPORT CO USS MORAY PAREN SS 345 PAREN X CLASS TWO AIR PRIORITY AUTHORIZED

Aster!

In a recent U.S. Fleet letter, Byron had seen a roster of new-construction submarines and their skippers, including *USS MORAY (SS 345)—Carter W. Aster, Lt. Cdr. USN.* This was Aster's style, to ask BuPers for officers he wanted, instead of taking what he got. Byron dropped on his bunk, not to sleep but to ponder. A gladsome, an electrifying prospect, suddenly; putting one of these new fleet subs in commission, to sail again with Lady Aster against the Japs!

He could leave the *Maidstone,* he knew, when he pleased. The tender captain had not requested the American technicians, didn't really need them to maintain the S-boats, and faintly resented the whole arrangement. Had this dispatch come a few days earlier, Byron would have packed and left at sunrise. But another courier trip to Marseilles was scheduled, and he decided he would make that last trip, in the hopes of seeing Consul General Gaither. That fellow Joe Schwartz seemed to know what he was talking about.

42

A MASTER plumber named Itzhak Mendelson owned the flat and the building where Natalie was holed up with her baby and her uncle. A Polish Jew, Mendelson had come to Marseilles in the 1920s and had done very well. His firm serviced the municipal buildings; he spoke excellent French; he knew magistrates, police chiefs, bankers, and all the most important criminals. So Rabinovitz had told Natalie. Mendelson was no Resistance man, and the Jews who slept on his parlor furniture or randomly on the floor were not underground types wanted by the Gestapo or the French police. They were objects of compassion, innocuous drifters like Jastrow and Natalie, lacking the proper papers to reside in Marseilles or to get out of France legally.

The apartment was enormous, for Mendelson had knocked down walls and merged several flats to fashion this labyrinthine warren, where Louis kept disappearing down dim corridors with racketing children who yelled in Yiddish. Two other younger families, refugee relatives of Mendelson, lived in the place. Natalie had trouble sorting out the transients from the residents, but it didn't really matter. The common tongue in the flat was Polish-Yiddish; in fact, the master plumber prided himself on a Yiddish historical romance he had written in his Warsaw youth, about the false Messiah Shabbatai Zvi. He had evidently paid to have it translated into French, for yellow-bound copies of *Le Faux Messie* lined the walls of the small room where Jastrow, Natalie, and Louis now dwelled. Glancing at this version, Natalie found it very silly stuff, though not bad for a plumber. Aaron, of course, with his flawless Yiddish, was right at home in the Mendelson ménage; and as *der groiser shriftshteller* he received immediate deference. Louis had a boil of children to play with, Natalie could get along with her rusty Yiddish, and all in all it was a warm, noisy, homey milieu. She was grateful to Pascal Gaffori, when she thought about it, for having driven her to this little Jewish oasis in Marseilles to await her freedom.

At first she didn't feel that way. The third night they were there, the police made a sweep of the neighborhood to round up alien Jews.

Warned by his high-placed friends, Mendelson had notified as many Jews as he knew; and he assured Natalie and Aaron that his building would not be entered. When at midnight she heard excited talk in the front rooms, she jumped from her bed and went to watch. Peeking through the curtains with the others, she saw two police vans surrounded by a docile crowd, much like onlookers at an accident, except for the valises they carried, and the small children among them. Under the eyes of a few gendarmes, they all peaceably got into the vans. The only odd detail was the frills of nightgowns, the legs of pajamas, and even bare feet, showing below the overcoats of some. Mendelson was right, the police never entered his building. The vans drove off, leaving the blue-lit street empty, and Natalie frightened.

She cheered up next day when Rabinovitz came with the news that the American consul general was expected back from Vichy in a day or two. Jim Gaither was a man of his word, the Palestinian said, a decent guy, a bonded officer with money and authority to deal with the Resistance. Since he had taken over the consulate, hundreds of people had received visas whose departure would otherwise have been blocked. A great admirer of *A Jew's Jesus,* Gaither was handling the Jastrow-Henry file himself, taking no chances on a leak. Nobody else in the consulate knew anything about it. Once Gaither got back they could count on a prompt departure.

About the Castelnuovos Rabinovitz was less sanguine. The headstrong doctor was negotiating directly for passage to Algiers with the Bastia roughnecks who had brought them from Elba. Rabinovitz said these fellows were unreliable, even dangerous, except when dealing with old Gaffori. He wanted the Castelnuovos to stay where they were until some safer way to leave opened up. Corsica was a good refuge, with enough to eat and drink. But Castelnuovo was becoming obsessed with an itch to move on. "So far, luckily, those scoundrels are asking for more money than he's got," Rabinovitz said. "So maybe he'll stay put. I hope so."

When Byron returned to Marseilles with another pouch for Sam Jones, the vice consul told him that Gaither had returned; and that, on hearing the name and rank of the expected courier from Gibraltar, he had exclaimed, "Hooray!"

"He wants you to report to his office at once. Second floor. You'll see the sign," Jones said. "*Without fail* were his words. Is he an old friend of your family, or something?"

"Not that I know of," Byron replied, with the greatest false show of nonchalance in his life. "Tell him I'm coming." He leaped up the stairs to the second floor.

"Well!" exclaimed the consul general, standing up and extending a hand over his desk. "D'Artagnan!" In his yellow pullover and gray slacks he looked like an old tennis pro: tall, stringy, brown, with close-cut straight white hair.

Byron blurted, "Where are they?"

"What? Sit down." The consul general laughed at the impetuous question. "They're in Corsica. Or they were, last I heard. They're fine, the three of them. How the devil have you pulled this off?"

"Corsica!" Byron gasped. "Corsica! God Almighty, so close? How do I get there? Is there a boat? An airplane?"

Gaither laughed again, very agreeably. "Take it easy, young fellow."

"You say they're fine? You've seen them?"

"I've been in touch. They're quite okay. There's no airplane to Corsica. The boat runs three times a week, and it takes eleven hours. They'll be leaving for Lisbon in a few days, Lieutenant, and—"

"They will? Why, that's marvelous, sir. Are you sure? I have orders to return to the States. I'll get to work on priorities, and maybe take them with me."

"Could be." Gaither shook his head, smiling. "You're an energetic fellow. Aren't you in submarines? How do you come to be in Gibraltar?"

"Can I talk to them on the telephone? Is there phone service to Corsica?"

"I wouldn't recommend that." Gaither leaned back in his chair, pulling at his lower lip. "Now look, Sam Jones has got an urgent job for you. You'll have to return to Gibraltar tonight. Sam will bring you to my house for dinner about six. How's that? We'll have a long talk. I repeat, they're fine, just fine, and they'll be out of here in a few days. Incidentally, Sam Jones knows nothing about all this. Nobody does. Keep it that way."

Impulsively Byron grasped his hand. "Thanks."

"All right. Steady does it. Don't get impatient."

Jones gave Byron two sealed envelopes to deliver by hand to an unnamed place. A silent ghost-pale young man in a ragged sweater drove him out along the coast in an old taxicab, ceaselessly glancing at the rearview mirror. The ride took over an hour, ending in a bumpy ride down a dirt road to a small villa within sight of the blue calm sea, almost hidden by overgrown shrubs and vines. A wary woman half-opened the door to Byron's knock. He could see behind her a tall mustached man looking keenly toward the door, hands jammed in the pockets of a red dressing gown. So he caught a good look at General Henri Giraud; though only long afterward, coming on a picture story of the Casablanca Conference in an old *Life* magazine, did he realize what his courier errands had been about, and who the man had been. It was after five o'clock when he returned to the consulate. Sam Jones said, rubbing his eyes and yawning, "Ready to go to the boss's house? He's waiting to give you dinner."

Natalie put on the white dress for the Friday night meal, and arrayed Louis in his cleanest shirt and jumper. Rabinovitz was coming, and they were going afterward to his apartment in the Old Town. She had herself proposed this in all innocence, during their last chat in the clamorous living room. She wanted to be alone with him, to talk in unhurried peace. Yet the last time she had invited herself to a man's flat, her love affair with Slote had ensued; and, a bit laggardly, this thought was troubling her. On impulse she pinned to her dress the brooch of purple stones that Byron had given her in Warsaw.

On this night she did something she had not done before in her life; she lit Sabbath candles. It seemed more mannerly to do it than to decline, when Mrs. Mendelson, a stout, incessantly busy, incessantly cheerful red-faced woman, came to tell her the candles were ready. Scrubbed and dressed-up children crowded around their mothers by the long dining table, where eight candlesticks stood on a fresh white cloth. Covering her head with a kerchief, putting the match to two cheap sputtering candles, stammering the Hebrew blessing as Louis watched her with enormous eyes, Natalie felt decidedly peculiar. Mrs. Mendelson elbowed her and made a genial joke to the others: *"Zeh, zi vert by unz a ganzer rebbitzin."* ("Look, we're making her into a rabbi's wife.") Natalie sheepishly joined in the laughter.

While the children were being fed, Rabinovitz arrived. Above the piping tumult of the children, he said, "Jim Gaither's back. I missed him at the consulate, but I'll go and see him tomorrow morning. That's a pretty piece of jewelry."

When the children swarmed out of the dining room, the adults gathered at the reset table. Rabinovitz was just sitting down beside Natalie when the doorbell rang. Mendelson answered it. He came back to tap Rabinovitz on the shoulder, and without a word Rabinovitz got up and left. He tended to come and go like a wraith, and nobody commented. The seat was left vacant beside Natalie. Twelve people, including several famished new transients, fell to the meal. It was all black market fare, obviously: baked fish, fish soup, and boiled chickens, the bones of which the transients loudly gnawed to splinters. Brown bottles of fiery potato spirits went round, and Aaron Jastrow quaffed more than his share.

Ever since his arrival, Aaron had been holding forth at table, overawing even Mendelson. Tonight he was in good form. The sacrifice of Isaac came up, for it was in the Sabbath Torah reading. Mendelson had a brash atheist of a son-in-law named Velvel, his partner in the plumbing business, characterized by a lot of bushy red hair and strong opinions. Velvel said the story exposed the Jewish God as a fictive Asian despot, and the author as a Bronze Age savage. Coolly Aaron put Velvel down. "The story's about Abraham, not God, don't you understand, Velvel? Even a *goy* like Kierkegaard could see that. Read *Fear and Trembling* some time. The people of Father Abraham's time burned children to their gods. Archaeology confirms it. Yes, Abraham took up the knife. Why? To show for all time that he cared no less for God than the pagans did for their bloody idols. He trusted God to make him drop the knife before he hurt the boy. That's the whole point of the story."

"Beautiful," said Mendelson, adjusting a large black yarmulka on his white hair. "That's a beautiful interpretation. I must read Kierkegaard."

"And suppose," Velvel grumbled, "God hadn't told the old fanatic to drop the knife?"

"Why, the Bible would end at Genesis twenty-two," Aaron retorted, smiling. "There'd have been no Jewish people, no Christianity, no modern world. Holocausts of children might still be going on. But you see, He did tell him to drop it. Western civilization turns on that stark fact. God wants our love, not the ashes of our children."

"What a depressing conversation," said Mrs. Mendelson, jumping up to collect dishes. "Burning children, slaughtering a boy! *Feh!* Velvel, play something happy."

Velvel got his guitar and struck up a Sabbath hymn, *Yah Ribon,* which everyone sang. Even Natalie knew that this instrument playing violated orthodox rules. In the Mendelson ménage everything went eccentrically. The women cleared the table and brought on tea and coarse cakes, and the singers grew very jolly in a ditty about an Old King Cole sort of rabbi sending for fiddlers, drummers, fifers, and so on. Natalie joined the women in the kitchen to get the dishes and pots washed before the electricity went off. In the dining room Velvel began to play an old lullaby, *Rozhinkes mit Mandlen* (Raisins and Almonds). This song was now Aaron's solo; he was vain about knowing all the Yiddish verses. Softly accompanied by the guitar, Aaron began the haunting nonsense refrain that stirred Natalie's heart with powerful childhood echoes:

> *Under my darling's cradle*
> *Lies a little white goat.*
> *The little goat went into business,*
> *That will be your career.*
> *Raisins and almonds,*
> *Sleep, little boy, sleep, dear.*

She heard the outside door open and close. Avram Rabinovitz appeared in the kitchen doorway, his face pale and smiling. "Natalie?" She came to the doorway, drying her hands on her apron. In the hallway, redolent of Sabbath food aromas, dim light from a wall bracket fell slantwise on Byron in his gray raincoat, standing with a large valise in one hand, and a leather pouch in the other. Natalie's legs almost gave way at the shock. He looked much changed, but there was no mistaking him.

"Hi, darling," Byron said.

*   *   *

43

Global Waterloo

2: Torch

(from *World Holocaust* by Armin von Roon)

The Torch assault on North Africa was an Anglo-American gesture to placate Stalin. Since the day we invaded the Soviet Union, he had been nagging the British to open a "second front NOW in Europe." This demand was empty noise and Stalin knew it. The British were too weak for that.

But once Japan was goaded into the Pearl Harbor attack, enabling Roosevelt to make the gleeful plunge into world war, Stalin's demand became clamorous. The unscathed American Union, sitting prosperous and happy beyond bomber range, could field ten million men. Its capacity for making the tools of war was immense, and the Soviet Union was hard-pressed.

Yet the warmongering President had only a half-trained expanding army of green recruits, led by an unblooded officer cadre. Civilian morale was unstable. Mild rationing ordinances brought wails of protest; austerities that we Germans had been taking for granted for years seemed to the spoiled Americans the end of the world. What was worse——and this was fundamental, and Roosevelt knew it——like the Italians, *the American people were incapable of accepting substantial battle losses. This fact shaped all of Franklin Roosevelt's war decisions, including the North African landing.*

Roosevelt's solution of his problems can be starkly stated. The formula that won world empire for the U.S.A. was twofold:

1. Germany First.
2. Shed German blood by shedding the blood of others.

How Roosevelt did it will be an enduring study for political and military historians.

Roosevelt In Trouble

Roosevelt's people did not share his aim of "Germany First." They wanted to avenge Pearl Harbor. As Wake Island and the Philippines fell to yellow-skinned attackers, the racial outrage of the Americans grew intense. Thousands of Japanese Americans were thrown into concentration camps, precisely like Jews behind the German lines, and for precisely the same reason: they were wartime security risks. The weepy indignation with which Roosevelt protested our security measures concerning the Jews was not in evidence on this matter.

TRANSLATOR'S NOTE: *The Nisei were abominably treated because of war hysteria. They were not murdered en masse, they all survived the war, and they got their property back. It was an indefensible business, but the distinction seems to escape General von Roon.—V.H.*

Moreover, the President soon discovered that war was not all beer and skittles.* Along his Atlantic coast and in the Caribbean, our U-boats played havoc at night, when the glow from the brightly lit coastal cities set up the targets. Strident calls for arms and action poured in on Roosevelt from the retreating Philippine defenders, from the forces in Hawaii, from the hard-pressed Chinese, from England's home front, from the British in Africa, Burma, Australia, India, and—loudest and ugliest—from the Soviet Union. Yet American war production was not in gear, and Roosevelt had his own army and navy to equip. He was in trouble.

Still, the Anglo-American planners had to go to work on a second front. The American General Staff officers, who had yet to smell gunpowder, were thinking in textbook terms: force the Channel coast as soon as possible, and smash across the northern plains to Berlin. But the British hated that notion. They proposed operations in Norway, in North Africa, in the Middle East; anywhere, in fact, but where we stood in force. Let the Red Army grind up the Wehrmacht; and if that meant a weak postwar Russia, all the better!

The "transatlantic essay contest" between the two staffs, as it came to be known, swayed back and forth. Roosevelt allowed the letters, memoranda, visits, and conferences to run on and on. He never strongly backed General Marshall in the American proposal:

* German: *Krieg ist kein Honiglecken.*

1. A vast buildup of men and supplies in Britain;
2. A contingent scheme for an emergency landing in France in 1942, **if** Russia seemed about to collapse;
3. Otherwise, an all-out cross-Channel attack in 1943.

Roosevelt did not push for this because something very different was in his mind.

Roosevelt's Basic War Plan

The Battle of Midway set him free to destroy Germany in his own fashion. Before that, with an all-triumphant Japan menacing his rear, he could make no big move against us. Had Yamamoto won at Midway—as by all the odds he should have—public opinion would have forced Roosevelt to go all-out in the Pacific. But with the great Nimitz-Spruance victory in hand, he could devote his "forested mind" to winning world rule with other people's blood. In effect, this meant at all costs keeping the Soviet Union in the war.

Franklin Roosevelt's basic plan for winning the Second World War was to take Germany from the rear with a brute mass of Russian troops. Everything else was secondary. He saw his main chance cold and straight. Militarily, it was a clear and brilliant plan; and brilliantly, alas, did it work.

This explains his hardheaded distribution of American supplies. He starved his Pacific forces so that they barely made it through the fierce Guadalcanal campaign, while he lavished matériel on the ungrateful and ever-demanding Russians through the Persian Gulf and the northern route. And he amply supplied the British in Egypt via the Cape of Good Hope and the Red Sea, while Rommel's stalled army withered under Hitler's neglect. Thus Roosevelt made sure that when his raw troops went ashore in French North Africa against feeble Vichy opposition, our tough and dashing Afrika Korps would be embroiled at a disadvantage, two thousand miles away at El Alamein.

Rooseveltian Chicanery

Moreover, he skillfully put the blame on the British for reneging on the second front in France.

He allowed the "transatlantic essay contest" to drag on until Marshall reported to him from London that the two staffs were stalemated. Admiral Ernest King had long been pushing for a turn to the Pacific; and the frustrated and infuriated Marshall, a stiff autocrat in the George Washington image, advised the President that an all-out shift to the Pacific was the only answer to British obduracy.

This was the moment Roosevelt had been playing for. In his lordly fashion, he notified his Joint Chiefs through his gray eminence, Harry Hopkins, that it would be wrong to "pick up our dishes and leave." Roosevelt loved to use homely phrases to mask his subtle machinations. The western Allies had to fight the Germans somewhere in 1942, to keep faith with Russia. If the British were really all that cautious and battle-worn, why, he would graciously give in and accept one of their proposals: French North Africa was all right with him.

Marshall warned that opening the Mediterranean theatre meant cancelling the cross-Channel attack in 1943; but in soldierly fashion he did Roosevelt's bidding. So Torch took form as a concession by Roosevelt to the British, when in fact it was just what he wanted.

TRANSLATOR'S NOTE: *General von Roon here ventures into mind reading. Mr. Roosevelt as I observed him—sometimes from close at hand—was an astute improviser, solving problems day by day with common sense, and a good grasp of historical facts and logistical limits. For the long view he was smart enough to trust long heads like Marshall and King, which sufficed.— V.H.*

Churchill shouldered the responsibility to bring Stalin the bad news, for Roosevelt was ostensibly "giving in" to him, by sending the American army into an operation which could not fail. French North Africa was the softest of touches. Not one German soldier faced the invaders. It was out of Luftwaffe range. All Roosevelt had to worry about was French "honneur" (which his deal with the arch-collaborator Darlan neutralized), and some freak of weather or tides that might drown some of his G.I. Joes, or wet their feet and give them pneumonia as they plodded ashore. True, the logistical mounting of the armada was impressive. Mass production and organization were and still are the American forte.

In Moscow Stalin vented much rage on Churchill; but of course he was not really angry. It was all political show. Stalin always tended to defer genially to Roosevelt; possibly because, being the world's greatest mass murderer himself, he bowed to this master politician who could get others to do his slaughter for him.

In an engaging passage of his history, Churchill describes how Stalin, after treating him with barbarous rudeness at a long Kremlin conference, invited him to his private apartment, called for wine and vodka, invited in

Molotov as a butt for jokes, and had a jolly midnight snack of a whole roast suckling pig; of which Churchill, who had a splitting headache, declined to partake. The picture lingers—the relish of the arch-Bolshevik consuming a pig, and the weary nausea of the aged arch-imperialist.

The British were wise to balk at the landing in France at that time. The Dieppe raid in August, when we killed or captured most of the Canadian raiders, suggests the warm welcome that would have awaited the Anglo-Americans, especially the neophyte G.I. Joes, in a landing attempt in France in 1942 or even 1943. But in the North Africa landing they had exactly the tea party that Roosevelt planned; they did, that is, until Rommel crossed the vast deserts after El Alamein and gave them their first rude taste of real war.

TRANSLATOR'S NOTE: *Roon deliberately belittles the largest, most difficult, most successful long-distance sea-borne invasion in history. If it looked easy, that was because it was well planned and well executed. It could have been a gigantic Gallipoli.—V.H.*

*   *   *

44

S HE threw herself into his arms. The dangling pouch struck her hip. The blow, the hard embrace, the warm eager kiss on her mouth, all scarcely registered, she was so shattered and dazed.

"Where's the boy?" Byron asked.

Clutching his hand, unable to talk, trying to infuse all her astounded love in her grip, she pulled him past the dining room down the gloomy halls. A romp was going on in the back of the flat: laughing and shouting boys were chasing squealing girls around a big bedroom. On the bed one little girl sat holding a baby in a clean blue jumper.

"There. That's your son."

In the dining room, many voices were joining in the chorus:

> *The little goat went into business,*
> *That will be your career.*
> *Raisins and almonds,*
> *Sleep, little boy, sleep, dear.*

Byron stood staring at the infant. At the sight of him the children stopped running, and their hubbub subsided. Exerting all her willpower not to cry, Natalie said, "Well, what do you think?"

"I guess he looks like me."

"God, does he ever! He's a stamped-out miniature."

"Will he be afraid if I pick him up?"

"Try it!"

Byron walked to the baby through the silent children, and lifted him. "Hello, boy. I'm your dad."

The girl who released the baby wrinkled her face at the English words. Louis looked from his mother to his father, then put his tiny hands to Byron's cheeks.

"He's a heavy kid," Byron said. "What have you been feeding him?"

"You wouldn't believe me if I told you. Octopus. Blackbirds. Anything!" She was unaware of the tears springing from her eyes till he brushed her cheek with his knuckles, and she felt the sliding wetness. "He's a travelling man, you see. A hell of a lot of goat's milk and cheese. Byron, do you like him?"

"He's all right," Byron said.

The other children were watching and listening with scarcely a whisper or a smile, their faces set in solemn curiosity. And Natalie could see Byron as it were through their grave wide eyes: a tall tanned Gentile with a tough countenance, in alien clothes, with a leather bag chained to his wrist; in looks and language not of the tribe, yet handling one of themselves in a fatherly way.

"Come, you've got to see Aaron! Then we'll go to my room and talk, my God, we've got to talk! You've got to tell me how you did this, I'm still gasping." As she took the baby from him, the leather pouch swung between them. "Byron, what is this thing?"

"I'll tell you about that, too."

Byron's visit to the dining room was a protracted and tumultuous sensation. Aaron's drunken amazement, his excited explanation in Yiddish—*"Natalie's mann fun Amerika, fun Amerikaner flot!"*—the general babble, the handshaking all around, the setting of a new place beside Rabinovitz, the parade of food and drink for them, the rousing welcome song in Yiddish while Byron forced down a few bites he didn't want; all this took time, but one couldn't fight off Jewish hospitality.

Bemused, Natalie stood in the doorway, holding Louis. There he sat amid the Mendelson ménage, Byron Henry, at a table where eight Sabbath candles burned, two of which she had herself lit—the most amazing sight in her life. Out of place though he obviously was, he was making cordial responses to the Yiddish compliments from all sides as Jastrow translated, and these people were warmly accepting him. He was her husband. That was enough. He was also an American naval officer. If the American consulate had rebuffed the applications of some visas, it didn't matter. Like the French, like most of Europe, they were waiting for the American counterattack against Hitler as their believing ancestors had waited for the Messiah. Nor did they seem surprised at Byron's thunderbolt appearance. Americans were supermen. Anyway, startling events were an everyday thing for these people; life was in chaos, and no one occurrence was very much stranger than another.

The contrast between Rabinovitz and Byron bit deep into her as the two men sat there side by side in candlelight, for the electricity had now shut off. The white-faced stumpy Palestinian, his shoulders bowed, his expression in repose a mixture of weariness, sadness, and resolve, was of another breed than Byron. Her husband had the clear-eyed self-assured naïve air of an American. His face bore new marks of experience she had yet to hear about, but Byron Henry, if he lived to be ninety, and if all his years were hard, would never look like Avram Rabinovitz.

"Sorry, now I go." Byron stood up. They let him leave, with a clamor of good-nights. Carrying Louis, she led him to the little room lined with yellow books. There Mrs. Mendelson, by the light of a tall candle burning on a dresser, was gathering Aaron's pajamas and dressing gown from a closet. The double bed Aaron usually slept in had been freshly made up. Natalie's cot was folded away. "Your uncle will sleep somewhere else, good Shabbas, good-night," she rattled in Yiddish, and she walked out, giving Natalie no time to smile, or blush, or thank her.

"I didn't understand a word," Byron said, "but there's a fine woman. How does that door lock?"

"With two bolts," Natalie said uncertainly, putting the yawning Louis down in his crib.

"Okay, lock them." He undid the chain from his wrist with a key and dropped the pouch on a chair. "I'm a temporary diplomatic courier, Natalie. That's what this thing is, and that's how I got here. I'm stationed on a submarine tender in Gibraltar. I've been there since August."

"But how did you manage that? And how did you find me? And—oh, sweetie—"

"All in good time." He was sweeping her into his arms.

She yielded to his powerful embrace, to his kisses, trying to please him, stupefied as she was. She thought of the revolting underwear he might uncover if they made hasty love right now; gray heavy cotton things, fit for a sow, all one could find in Siena. She still had her treasured pretty lingerie from Lisbon, but how could she stop him to change? Natalie would have lain naked on the worn carpet for him then and there, she was flooded with marvelling admiration and gratitude, but what she could not do was feel aroused. He had smashed back into her life like a cannon shell.

Unexpectedly his kisses stopped, his embrace loosened. "Natalie, that kid's watching us."

Louis indeed was standing up, holding the crib rail, regarding them with a lively expression.

"Oh, it's all right, he's only a year old," she murmured. "He's just curious as a raccoon."

"Raccoon, hell. He looks as though he's taking notes."

Natalie couldn't contain a giggle. "Maybe he is, dear, at that. It'll be his turn one day, you know."

"I swear I'm embarrassed," Byron said, and he let her go. "It's ridiculous, but it's the truth. That kid has grown-up eyes."

"Actually, honey," Natalie said, trying to keep her deep relief out of her voice, "why don't I clean him up for bed? Would you mind that? We can talk, and I can get a little used to you."

"Sure, go ahead. That's better than my idea, which was to cover his crib like a parrot's cage."

"Look, love, you should feel reassured," she giggled. Byron's drolleries had always amused her, and her nerves were stretched fiddlestring-tight. "The procedure is obviously quite new to him."

"I guess so. Is it true that he walks and talks?"

She took him from the crib and set him down on his feet. Louis toddled a few steps, looking to Byron for applause; for which, it was clear, he had developed a great taste.

"Well done, sprout. Now say something."

"Oh, you wouldn't understand him." She caught Louis up, and at a sink in the corner stripped and began washing him. "He babbles a mishmash of Yiddish, Italian, and French."

"I'd like to hear it."

With a shy sidewise glance she said, "You look so trim."

"You've grown far more beautiful."

Sweet warmth washed through her. "And your father, and Warren? Have you heard from them? Are they all right?"

"Warren? What do you mean? Didn't the Red Cross forward my letters? I wrote to Slote too about Warren."

His harsh tone made her turn scared eyes at him. "I got your last letter in May."

"Warren's dead. He died in the Battle of Midway."

"Oh! Oh, *darling—*"

"He got a posthumous Navy Cross." Glancing at his watch, Byron began to pace the narrow room. "Look, the train for Barcelona leaves at midnight. That's four and a half hours from now. You'd better start thinking about packing, Natalie. You won't have to take a lot. The shopping in Lisbon is still good."

She said dizzily, "Packing?"

"Aaron will have to wait till the consul general clears him, but I'm taking you and the baby with me."

"What! My God, Byron, did the consul general *say* you could?"

"We're going to his apartment now."

Like the dwellers in the Mendelson flat, James Gaither was hard to surprise. Wartime Marseilles was such a bubbling stew of political double-dealing, financial corruption, racial and nationalist crisscrossings, refugee agonies and tragedies, and Mediterranean finagling dating back to Phoenician times, that compared to Gaither's daily grind, melodramas and spy yarns paled. And this was only his legitimate work. In his covert dealings with the Resistance groups his experiences were right out of cheap cinema; of a drab sort, since sexy eyefuls never got into the action. All in all, in his two Marseilles years he had seen—so he liked to say—just about everything.

Still, Byron Henry's story was something new, and he was writing an account of it in his diary, in pajamas and dressing gown, when a knock came at the door. There stood Lieutenant Henry, pouch under his arm.

"Sorry to disturb you, sir."

"You again?"

"Sir, my wife and baby are downstairs."

"What! Out at night, without papers?"

"Rabinovitz is with them." Glancing down at the consul general's pajama legs, Byron said, "I regret the intrusion, sir."

"Never mind that. Get them all up here, fast."

Mrs. Henry came in with the baby in her arms, giving him a sweet apprehensive smile. Though her clothes were shabby, her hair carelessly combed, her whole aspect flustered and disarrayed, one look at her made the submariner's romantic feat easier to grasp. Well might a man work his way around the world for this one! The fair infant she carried was a babyish replica of the lieutenant. Avram Rabinovitz slouched in behind Mrs. Henry, looking unusually depressed and anxious.

Byron was still explaining his plan when Gaither began to wonder how best to quash it. It was a terrible idea, rash and highly dangerous. Yet with Natalie Henry sitting there holding that baby, he quite understood the young husband's impetuosity. Gently does it, he thought. "Lieutenant, the chargé d'affaires in Vichy has the exit visas. The telex came in confirming that today. We'll be getting them any day now. Perhaps as soon as tomorrow."

"Yes, sir, so you told me at dinner. But I've been thinking, and I don't see why I shouldn't just take Natalie and Louis along now. The thing is, I believe I can get them on the plane to the United States with me."

The wife cleared her throat and said in a charming husky voice, "He's good at that sort of thing."

"No doubt, Mrs. Henry, but there's the problem of crossing the border."

Byron sat beside his wife on the sofa, tense, erect, but collected. "Sir, flashing my diplomatic passport will suffice. It cuts through immigration red tape like a hot knife through butter. You know that yourself."

"Not always. Suppose you run into a nasty French border inspector or a German agent? I have myself. There's a lot of both kinds on that railroad route. You've got your transit visa. Your wife and child have nothing."

"I'll have a story."

"What's the story?"

"The baby got sick as hell in Gibraltar. We rushed him to Marseilles at night. We didn't bother with visas. I'll talk in broken French. I'll yell. I'll be the dumb angry American official. I'll make it stick, that I can promise you."

"But their passports have no Gibraltar stamps, no French stamps, only Italian stamps months old."

"Sir, all that flummery won't matter, I promise you. I can handle it."

"And unfortunately for your story, I've never seen a healthier-looking baby, Lieutenant. He's in the absolute pink."

On Natalie's lap, Louis was yawning like a crocodile. He did have excellent color, and his blinking eyes were clear and bright.

"It could have been appendicitis, something like that, just a false alarm."

Gaither turned on Natalie. "Are you prepared to sustain this story?"

Byron quickly struck in as she hesitated, "By the time we get to Perpignan we'll have it all rehearsed and down cold. Please don't worry, sir."

Gaither went to a telephone and summoned the consulate car and driver. "How about something to drink, all around?" he asked. "Chilly night."

Byron said, "Thanks, but we'd better keep clear heads."

"I'll take something," Natalie said. "Thank you."

"So will I," said Rabinovitz.

Gaither mixed drinks, still thinking, *Gently does it.* Walking up and down the room, whiskey in hand, white hair in disorder, dressing gown flapping, he said, "Lieutenant, I want to talk plainly to your wife."

"By all means, sir."

"Mrs. Henry, as I said, there are Gestapo agents on the trains and at the border. When they're on the trains, they do exactly as they please. They ignore all regulations. Rabinovitz knows that. Your husband may indeed get you by. He's a resourceful man, that's clear. On the other hand, the Gestapo has a keen nose for Jews travelling illegally. Those agents are hard and cruel men. You may be pulled off the train."

"She won't be," Byron interrupted, "and if she is, I'll go along."

"In that case," Gaither went on to Natalie, as though Byron hadn't spoken, "when you're questioned, your baby may be taken away from you. That's how the Germans do things." At the look of horror that passed over her face Gaither added, "I'm not predicting this will happen. But it may. You can't rule it out. Can you sustain a fake story once they do that?" Her eyes were reddening as she sat silent. He went on, "And once you and your baby are taken into custody, I can't protect you. We have a file of such cases pending now—people halted with questionable American documents. Some are still in police custody. A few, unhappily, are already in Rivesaltes."

"Rivesaltes?" Natalie choked the word at Rabinovitz.

"French concentration camp," he said.

Byron stood up and faced Gaither. "You're trying to frighten her."

"I'm trying to be honest with her. Are you, young fellow? You're carrying classified documents. Once you're detected in this bluff, the Gestapo can take the position that you're an imposter, confiscate that pouch, and slash it open."

Byron's face was getting pale and drawn. "It's a negligible risk," he said after a pause. "I'm ready to take it."

"It's not up to you."

Byron adopted a quieter, almost pleading manner. "Mr. Gaither, you're raising bugaboos. It'll all go smooth as oil, I assure you. Once we're across and out, all this will be forgotten. You'll laugh at your fears. We're going to chance it."

"You are not. I'm the senior American officer in this area, and I have to order you not to do this. I'm very sorry."

"Byron," Natalie said, in a faltering tone, her eyes wide with alarm, "it'll be a few more days at most. Go. Wait for us in Lisbon."

He whirled on her. "Damn it, Natalie, all hell's about to break loose in the Med. There's hundreds of planes lined up wing to wing in Gibraltar. At the first sign of trouble they'll close the borders." She was looking desperately at him, as though hoping for a convincing word and not yet hearing it. "Good God, darling, we went from Cracow to Warsaw with the war blowing up all around us, and you never turned a hair."

"We've got Louis now."

Byron faced Avram Rabinovitz. "Don't you think we can make it?"

The Palestinian, crouched over a cigarette, turned his head sideways to look up at Byron. "You're asking me?"

"Sure."

"I'm afraid."

"*You're* afraid?"

"I've been taken off that train to Barcelona by the Germans."

Byron stared long at him. "I guess this is why you told me to come here first."

"Yes, it is."

Dropping into a chair, Byron said to Gaither, "I'll take that drink, sir."

"I have to go," Rabinovitz said, and with a last sombre glance in Natalie's eyes and a caress of Louis's cheek, he departed.

Pouring more whiskey and soda, Gaither thought of a leading article in *Le Cahier Jaune,* the French anti-Semitic journal that he had glanced through on the train coming back from Vichy. The photographs had been taken at a French government exhibit in Paris called "Jewish Traits and Physiognomies": huge plaster models of hook noses, blubber lips, and protruding ears. Louis Henry didn't fit the specifications; but if French immigration inspectors, or the Gestapo, laid hands on him, he would be just a Jew like his mother. Otherwise, of course, Mrs. Henry could bluff her way through any border point, even without the lieutenant; a beautiful woman, a mother, an American; ordinarily no problem! But the Germans had turned routine travel in Europe, for Jews, into a risk like jumping from a burning building. Trivial bits of paper could mean life or death; Gaither knew Jews with valid passports and exit visas who were staying on in France merely for fear of facing the Gestapo at the borders.

The silence in the room was leaden as Gaither passed the drinks. To ease the strain, he talked about how he had gotten British pilots out of France on this train to Barcelona, posing as firemen and engineers. But they were tough men, he explained, trained in the escape art, prepared to confront the Gestapo; and still there had been some bad incidents.

When the consulate car arrived, Gaither became all business again. It still lacked an hour of train time, he said. Byron could get to the terminal in twenty minutes. Would he like some time alone with his family? The driver would bring up Mrs. Henry's luggage; now that she was here, she had better remain until the exit visas came. In the morning he would send for Jastrow, too, and keep the three of them under his eye until they left for Lisbon. He would himself go with them to the border, or send someone trustworthy in his place.

He showed Byron and Natalie into a small bedroom, and closed the door. Not looking at Byron, Natalie laid the sleeping baby on the bed, and covered him with her coat.

Byron said, "You surprised me."

She faced him. He leaned against the doorway, hands in his pockets, one leg crossed over the other, in the exact pose in which she had first laid eyes on him, when she had called for him on a Siena street in Jastrow's car.

"You're terribly angry."

"Well, not really. He frightened you. But I think we could have made it. Cigarette?"

"I don't smoke any more."

"I recognize that pin."

"Warsaw seems a million years ago."

"I'll wait for you in Lisbon, Natalie. I've got thirty days' leave, and I'll just wait. I'll inquire every day at the consulate." His smile was gracious and distant. "I doubt I can book that honeymoon suite in Estoril."

"Try."

"All right, I will."

That started them on reminiscences. Carter Aster's name came up. Byron chatted about his orders to the *Moray,* and about how fine the new fleet submarines were. Natalie did her best to act interested, to respond, but it was lifeless talk. He made no move to take her in his arms. She was afraid to move first herself. She was afraid of him, ashamed of her cowardice. The wretched suspicion was growing on her that his spectacular feat in finding her was the worst thing that could have happened to them, given the time and the circumstances. Yet what could she have done about this miserable turn of events? To the Germans and the Vichy French agents, the baby was a Jew. That was a terror impossible for Byron Henry to grasp. On that rock their marriage might split, but there it was.

"I suppose I ought to think about moving along," he said at last, in a dry cold manner, getting up.

That triggered a reaction from Natalie. She ran to him, clutched him in her arms, and kissed him wildly on the mouth, again and again. "Byron, I'm sorry, I'm sorry, I can't help it. I can't defy Gaither. I think he's right. I'll be there in a week or less. Wait for me! Forgive me! Love me, for God's sake! I'll love you till I die. Do you doubt me?"

He returned her kisses gently; and he said with his strange melancholy smile, the smile that had intoxicated her from the first, "Why, Natalie, you and I will never die. Don't you know that?" Walking over to the bed, he looked down at the flushed slumbering infant. "Goodbye, sprout. I'm glad I got a look at you."

They went into the living room together, and after a handshake with Gaither, he was gone.

PART FOUR

Pug
and
Rhoda

45

I N helmet and life jacket, Victor Henry stood on the port wing, watching red tracer shells of his main battery salvo streak off into the sultry night. The shadowy line of enemy ships off Guadalcanal showed up under a drifting cluster of green-white star shells, partly obscured by smoke and splashes of straddles from the *Northampton*'s guns.

"Torpedoes! . . . Torpedoes one point on the port bow! . . . Torpedoes to port, Captain, target angle ten!"

The clamor broke from the lookouts, from the telephone talkers, from officers and sailors all over the bridge. Though Pug's ears were half-deafened by salvos and his eyes half-blinded by muzzle flame, he heard the cries and saw the approaching wakes. On the instant he barked, *"HARD LEFT RUDDER!"* (Turn toward the wakes, and hope to comb them; the only chance now.)

"Hard left rudder, Captain." The helmsman's voice was loud and firm. "Rudder is hard left, sir."

"Very well."

The two phosphorescent lines cut through the glassy black water almost dead ahead, at a slight angle to the ships' course. It would be a close thing! Three other heavy cruisers, already torpedoed, were burning astern in blotches of yellow under dense high smoke columns: the *Minneapolis,* the *Pensacola,* and the *New Orleans.* Torpedoes were shoaling like herrings around the task force. Where in God's name were they all coming from? A pack of submarines? In its first fifteen minutes this action was already a catastrophe, and now if his own ship went—! As the vessel rolled, the two green wakes disappeared, then came in sight sliding past far below, directly under the captain's gaze. Confused shouts rose all around him. Christ, this was going to be close! He gripped the bulwark. His breath stopped—

LIGHT!

The night exploded into sun glare.

• • •

The night action on November 30, 1942, in which the *Northampton* went down has faded from memory. The Japanese navy is extinct, and the United States Navy has no reason to celebrate the Battle of Tassafaronga, a foolish and futile disaster.

At the time, the United States already dominated Guadalcanal by sea, in the air, and on land. To supply their starved sick garrison, Japanese destroyers were skulking past the cove called Tassafaronga, tossing overboard drums of fuel and food for small craft to come out and retrieve. They were not looking for a fight. But on Halsey's orders an American cruiser flotilla came six hundred miles from the New Hebrides to Guadalcanal, to halt and sink a large new enemy landing force. In fact, there was no such force. It was a phantom of false intelligence.

The rear admiral commanding the flotilla had taken over only two days before. His force was formed of broken units, remnants of many Guadalcanal sea fights. He was new to the area, and his ships had not trained together. Still, with the advantages of radar, surprise, and superior firepower, his Task Force Sixty-seven should have wiped out the enemy. With four heavy cruisers, a light cruiser, and six destroyers, he faced only eight Japanese destroyers.

But his operation plan assumed that the Japanese destroyer torpedo, like the American weapon, had a range of twelve thousand yards. Actually, the Japanese torpedo could go about twenty thousand yards, and twice as far on slow setting; and its warhead was much more destructive. At the admiral's conference before the run north, Victor Henry had mentioned this; he had written an intelligence memorandum in 1939 on the Japanese torpedo, which had altered his whole career. But the new admiral had coolly repeated, "We will close to twelve thousand yards, and open fire." Pug could argue the point no further.

So the Japanese destroyer admiral, trapped against the coast without sea room on the night of November 30, heavily outgunned, with eight-inch cruiser shells raining around him, star shells glaring overhead, splashes and smoke enveloping his force, desperately launched all torpedoes toward the distant muzzle flashes. This shotgun blast of warheads caught all four American heavy cruisers. The Japanese fled victorious and all but unscathed.

• • •

The thundering concussion tore at Pug Henry's ears. He was thrown to his knees. He sprang up, staggering. The whole ship was shuddering like a train off its track, and worse than that, worse than the fire shooting up on the port side, was the sudden list. Ten degrees or more, he groggily estimated—in seconds. What holes those torpedoes must have blown!

Seared into his memory was the story of the *Juneau,* torpedoed and vanishing in a giant explosion. He darted into the bridge house and seized a microphone. *"This is the captain speaking."* He heard the grating bellow of his own voice over the deck loudspeakers. *"Flood magazines of number three turret and jettison five-inch ready ammo. Repeat, flood magazines of number three turret and jettison five-inch ready ammo! Acknowledge!"*

A telephone talker shouted that the orders had been heard and were being carried out. The deck was still quivering. Almost, the *Northampton* might be bumping over a reef, but Pug knew that he was out in six hundred fathoms of water. When he strode out on the port wing, microphone in hand, the heat hitting his face surprised him. It was like opening a furnace door. The fire was roaring all over the stern, casting an orange glow far out on the dark water.

"Now, all hands, this is the captain speaking. We've taken a torpedo hit, possibly two, on the port quarter. Expedite damage reports. Forward fire-fighting and damage control parties, lay aft to help control fires and set flooding boundaries. Exec, lay up to the bridge—"

The orders formed readily in Pug's mind after months of hard drilling. Drills were a hell of a nuisance to the crew, but they would pay off now. In the bridge house the telephone talkers were relaying damage reports in controlled tones. The OOD and the quartermaster were hunched at the chart table over the ship's diagram, hatching the lower deck compartments with red and black crayons; black for salt water penetration, red for fire. Bad first reports: three propeller shafts stopped, communication and power failing, water and oil flooding on C and D decks. As Pug kept issuing orders he was already thinking of a salvage strategy. Holding back fire and flood long enough to make port was the thing to try for. Tulagi was eighteen miles away. The three other cripples were already heading there.

"After fire room, secure ruptured fuel and steam lines. All stations that have power pump fuel port to starboard. Pump overboard all port side water ballast, and—"

Another *BLAST!* jerked the deck under his feet. Far aft behind the boat deck a thick geyser of black oil climbed like a Texas gusher and toppled in the firelight, drenching the mast, the gun director housings, the boat deck, and number three turret in a thick gummy rain. Flames began climbing the oil-soaked mast, making a tower of bright rising fire against the smoky sky. More sheets of oil sprang from below-deck explosions, feeding the flames.

The ship could not live long at this rate. Despite her formidable length and big guns, she was a vulnerable monster. Her stability and her damage control characteristics were poor. She had been built not to military requirements, but to the stupid limits of a politicians' treaty. Pug had known that all along, hence his zealotry for disaster drills. Alas, the torpedoes had lucked into the heavy cruiser's weakest spot, just aft of the skimpy armor belt, tearing open main fuel-oil bunkers and —almost certainly—the cavernous engine and fire rooms. It would be all uphill to Tulagi. The sea must be cascading in below.

But the pumping had yet to take hold. This long hull contained some two million cubic feet of air space. That was a lot of buoyancy. If his vessel wasn't about to blow up, if the enemy didn't put more torpedoes in her, if the fires didn't break out of control, he might make port. Even if he had to beach her, the *Northampton* was of immense salvage value. The fire-fighting parties, clumps of moving shadows in the glare, were dragging their handybillies and hoses here and there on the slippery deck, and sparkling streams were raising great clouds of orange-red vapor. Damage reports were pouring up to the bridge house, and the tones of officers and sailors were becoming businesslike. The forward engine room still had power; one propeller was enough to shove this cripple into Tulagi.

For all the heartsickness at the torpedoing of his ship, and the defeat in the making, for all the macabre light and sound of a warship stricken at night—the glare, the crackling tumult, the shouts, the alarms, the smell of burning, the eye-stinging smoke, the worsening list, the nightmare glow on the black sea, the cacophony on the bridge of TBS and sailors' voices—for all the acute peril, for all the drastic decisions he had to make fast, Victor Henry was not bewildered or beset; on the contrary, he felt himself coming fully alive for the first time since Midway. Back in the bridge house he spoke over the TBS, *"Griffin, Griffin, this is Hawkeye, over."*

In reply, a formal drawl: *"Hawkeye from Griffin, come in, over—"* An older voice broke through. "Hold on, son, that's Pug Henry over on the *Northampton*. I'll talk to him. . . . Say, Pug, is that you?" Admirals ignored communication procedure. "How are you doing, fella? You look pretty bad from over here."

"Over here" was the *Honolulu,* the one unscathed cruiser left in the task force, a lean long shadow to the northwest, racing with the destroyer screen out of the torpedo water.

"I've got one engine room and one propeller, Admiral. I'll head for Tulagi too. We're effecting repairs, or trying to, as we go."

"That's one hell of a fire there on your stern."

"We're fighting it."

"Do you require assistance?"

"Not now."

"Pug, radar shows these bandits retiring westward. I'll sweep around Savo Island to engage them beyond torpedo range. If you need help, holler, and I'll send you a couple of my small boys."

"Aye aye, sir. Good hunting. Out."

"Good luck, Pug."

During this talk the executive officer arrived on the bridge, his moon face under the helmet streaked with soot and sweat, and he took charge of damage control while the captain conned the ship. Through battles, bombardments, long voyages, and a Navy Yard overhaul, Pug had developed confidence in this quiet chubby man from Idaho, though their personal relationship remained by mutual choice a distant one. In Grigg's last fitness report, Pug had reported him qualified for command. The latest Alnav had promoted Grigg to four stripes, and they expected him to get the *Northampton* any day. Pug already had orders to fly back to Washington for reassignment "when relieved." With Grigg handling damage control, Pug had time to reflect. His evil luck was certainly holding! Grigg's orders were probably on the way, but the delay had pushed him into this ill-omened night battle as captain. If he lost his ship, he would have to answer to a court of inquiry, and he could not plead that an inept admiral with an ill-conceived op-plan had led him into torpedo water.

The fires were no longer spreading so rapidly, and the main bulkheads were holding out the sea; so the reports went. But Pug was watching two indicators: the clinometer, which kept creeping left, and a plumb line that he had rigged which showed the ship settling by the stern. He was trying to head around northeast to Tulagi. All the telephone systems had failed, even the sound-powered lines; grounded by salt water, burned out, jarred loose. Messengers were carrying each order down the foremast, along the main deck, through black smoky passageways awash in water or oil, down several more decks to the forward engine room. Conning his ship by this slow process was exasperating, yet she was coming around. Meantime, Grigg was sending rescue teams to release trapped men from flooding compartments. The wounded were being brought topside. The fire-control crews, caught in the oil-drenched gun directors on the burning mainmast, were being saved from roasting alive by asbestos-clad rescuers, slowly mounting the mast behind fog nozzles and helping them down.

Dead ahead on the horizon, Florida Island bulged, with Tulagi lost in its shadow. The list was now up to twenty degrees, about as far as the heavy cruiser rolled in a gale. The *Northampton* hung lifelessly to port in a sea smoothed by leaking oil. It would be a race between the flooding and the remains of the power plant. If Grigg could keep the ship afloat till dawn it might make Tulagi behind the three other cripples, far ahead and brightly smoking. So Pug was thinking when Grigg came to him, mopping his brow with a sleeve. "Sir, we'd better lie to."

"Lie to? I've just now got her on course."

"Shoring is giving way on C and D decks, sir."

"But what do we do, Grigg, sit here and drift, filling up? I'll take some turns off the engine."

"Also, Captain, Chief Stark says the lube oil supply to number four engine is failing. The pump can't overcome the list."

"I see. Well, in that case maybe I will ask the admiral for a couple of destroyers."

"I guess you should, sir."

Grigg's news about the lubricating oil was close to a death sentence. Both men knew it. They both knew, too, that the lube oil system was poorly designed. Long ago, to no avail, Pug had requested an alteration.

"Yes, but meantime let's close Tulagi, even if we burn out our bearings."

"Captain, with any way on, we won't hold out the sea."

"Then what's to be done?"

"I'll counterflood all I can. We're low on pumping capacity, is the trouble. If I can right her five degrees and double up the shoring we can try getting under way again."

"Very well, I'll lay below for a looksee. You ask Griffin for the destroyers. Tell him we're afire, dead in the water, listing twenty-two degrees, and down hard by the stern."

Pug descended to the steeply slanting main deck, and slipped and slid ankle-deep in malodorous black oil past the fire-fighters to the huge rip in the afterdeck through which the oil had spouted up. Leaning outboard, he could see ragged hull plates sticking straight out into the water, blown out by the torpedoes. That was a sight he would never forget: a black hole in his ship, rimmed in broken metal like a crudely opened can. The other hole below the water line was reported to be yet larger. Leaning over the lifelines, Pug dizzily felt that the ship might capsize then and there. The list was rapidly getting worse, no doubt of that. He passed horribly wounded and burned men lying in rows on the fantail deck, tended by the pharmacist's mates. Time was needed to get those men off. Sadly, he returned to the bridge, called the executive officer aside, and told him to prepare to abandon ship.

About an hour later, Victor Henry took his last look around the deserted bridge. The little steel structure was quiet and clean. The quartermaster and the officers of the deck had taken away all the logs and records. The secret publications had been thrown overboard in weighted bags. Below, the crew was mustering at abandon-ship stations. The sea was a black still lake, with four scattered vessels burning on it like fallen yellow stars. The rescue destroyers were on their way. Sharks would be a hazard, and some sixty officers and men, at last muster, would never leave the ship; missing, or killed by fire, water, or explosion. Still, the loss of life would be low if nothing else went wrong.

By now Pug was in a fever to get his crew off. Crippled heavy ships were a prime prey of submarines. The last thing he did was to take from his sea cabin a pair of gloves and the folding photograph frame, containing Warren's Academy graduation picture and an old photograph of the whole family, in which Warren and Byron were gangling boys, and Madeline a little girl in a paper crown. Tucked into the frame were two small snapshots: Pamela Tudsbury, huddled in gray fur in the snow outside the Kremlin, and Natalie holding her baby in the Siena garden. About to descend the ladder, he noticed the *Northampton*'s battle flag folded on a flagbag. He took that.

Grigg was waiting for him, firelight flickering on his face, on a main deck slanted like a ski slide. He gave an unhurried muster report.

"Okay, let's abandon ship, Grigg."

"You're coming, then, Captain?"

"No." He gave Grigg the battle flag. "I'll get off in due course. Take this. Fly it in your next command. And here, try to keep my family dry for me, will you?"

Grigg tried to argue that counterflooding was still possible, that a number of pumps were working, and that damage control was his specialty. If the captain wouldn't leave, then the first lieutenant could man the motor whaleboat and look after the men down in the sea. He wanted to remain.

"Grigg, abandon ship," Pug interrupted in sharp cold tones.

Grigg stood as straight as he could and saluted. Pug returned the salute, saying, in an informal tone, "Well, good luck, Jim. I guess that turn west was a mistake."

"No, *sir!* You couldn't do anything else. We had the range. We had the bastards straddled. How could you let them retire scot-free? Pete Kurtz claims we hit a cruiser with that last salvo. He saw the explosions, just after we took those fish."

"Yes, so he told me. Maybe we can get that verified. Still, we should have hauled ass like the *Honolulu*. But it's done."

The exec looked forlornly up and down the steep-slanting deck. "I'll miss the *Nora-Maru*."

Surprised, Pug smiled. This was the sailors' nickname for the ship, and neither he nor Grigg had used it before. "Go ahead, over the side with you."

Swung out on the davits, the motor whaleboat loaded with wounded was so close to the water that the sailors had only to cut the falls. Balsa rafts flew over the side. Hundreds of nearly naked sailors went swarming down nets, sliding down ropes, many crossing themselves before they went. Below, there was a great sound of splashing, and those in the water cried thinly to each other and to the men on deck.

Soon they all were down in the sea. Rafts, boats, and bobbing heads drifted away on the current. In the distance the two destroyers shadowily approached. The crew's voices carried up on the slight warm breeze—men shouting for help, blowing whistles, calling out to each other in the dark. Well, none would die by fire now, Pug thought, and few if any by water, though sharks might be a hazard. Fortunately the floating oil had not ignited.

Pug was remaining aboard with a small volunteer salvage party of sailors and one chief. Strange things happened to damaged ships. Fires could burn out. Vagaries of flooding could even right a listing hulk. At Midway the captain of the *Yorktown* had in some embarrassment climbed back aboard his ship long after abandoning it, and if not for a submarine attack next day he might have salvaged it. Pug and his volunteers might be caught in a capsizing or a torpedoing, but if the *Northampton* stayed afloat till dawn they could rig the line for a tow.

The silence, the unprecedented filth on the vast empty deck, were strange and dreamlike. Clutching at cleats, stanchions, lifelines—for to keep his footing was becoming harder all the time—he groped his way to the forecastle to see how the towing rig preparations were coming along. Looking back at his sinking ship, he observed that his guns, arrested in the elevation of the last portside salvo, paralleled the sea, so steep was the list. Here the *Northampton* looked like her old self, except for the crazy tilt and the yellow glow that silhouetted the masts and the guns. Good-bye, then, to the *Nora-Maru!*

Around abandoned hand pumps and over coiling hoses he staggered aft, amid heaps of detritus—clothes, food, cigarette wrappings, books, papers, shell cases, coffee mugs, half-eaten sandwiches, oil-soaked life jackets, shoes, boots, helmets, all in a rotten stink of garbage and excrement, for the men had been relieving themselves topside; but the prevailing smells were of burning and of oil—above all *oil, oil, oil!* The sour stench of disaster would forever, for Victor Henry, be the smell of crude petroleum.

For another hour he watched the salvage party stumble about their work, mainly pumping and fire-fighting. The sailors had to move monkey-fashion, using hands and feet on deck projections to keep from sliding on the oily plates. Firelit faces stern, mouths taut, they kept looking out to sea at the two destroyers picking up survivors. Pug at last decided, at a quarter to three, that the *Northampton* was a dead loss. Staying on any longer, he would only risk sailors' lives to make himself look good. She might or might not float for another hour; she might also capsize with little warning.

"Chief, let's abandon ship."

"Aye aye, *SIR.*"

At the word the sailors pitched the last large balsa raft overboard. It sailed down and struck with a loud splash. The chief, a gray-headed big-bellied man, the best machinist on the ship, urged the captain to go first. When Pug brusquely refused, the chief kicked off his shoes, stripped to oil-smeared jockey shorts, and tied his life jacket around his thick sweaty white rolls of fat. "Okay, you heard the boss man, let's go." He scrambled like a boy down the straight-hanging cargo net, the sailors after him.

In this last minute alone on deck, Pug tasted a bitter private savor of farewell. Going down with the ship was out of the question; in the United States Navy you saved yourself to fight another day. The other tradition was stupid, though romantic and honorable. He could not help the war effort by drowning. Pug murmured a prayer for the dead men he was leaving in the hulk. He stripped to shorts, and drew on the gloves he had fetched from the bridge. In abandon-ship drills, he had always gone hand over hand down a dangling hawser. Aside from gratifying his petty vanity—he was agile at it—this had set many of the crew to imitating him, a useful thing. In emergencies ladders and nets might not be available when ropes were.

Rough manila slithering through his bare legs, Pug lowered himself into the black tropical sea. As he let go and splashed, the water felt good; warm as a bath and very salty. He swam through sticky gobs of petroleum to the raft, which still rode to a long painter tied to a cleat on deck. Naked sailors jammed the raft and swimmers surrounded it clinging to loops of cord.

"Chief, are all the men here?"

"Yes, Captain."

Several sailors offered to make room for him on the raft.

"Stay where you are, the lot of you. Cast off!"

A knife flashed in the firelight. The painter fell away. The men paddled the raft from the foundering ship. Trying to wipe foul oil from his hair and face and to rinse the taste from his mouth, Victor Henry watched her sinking. Seen from below she was a grandiose spectacle, a vast black shape stretching across half the horizon in sluggish toppling agony, with one end burning like a torch. The men on the raft were chanting long wailing halloos and blowing on shrill whistles at the nearby destroyers and motorboats. A swell washed over Pug, and oil got in his eyes. He was bathing them when he heard yells of *"There she goes!"*

Rearing up on his wrist cord, he saw the *Northampton* roll over and lift her dripping bow high. The fire went out, and she slid downward. The men ceased hallooing and whistling. It was so quiet on the raft that, over the lapping of the water, as the bow sank from sight, Pug heard the mournful sighing rush and roar of the vortex that swallowed his ship.

46

A YELLOW blaze lights the night sky in a different part of the world. Berel Jastrow, ankle-deep in snow outside the hideously stinking latrine blockhouse, stops in his tracks and stares at the high flare. It is the test: scheduled, postponed, rescheduled, postponed again. All week long SS bigwigs have been stomping through the puddles in the ice-cold raw cement structure, down in the enormous underground chambers and up above at the untried furnaces, their impatient brusque comments echoing to the splash and thump of boots.

The Commandant himself has been there with his frozen-faced entourage, watching civilian technicians work their heads off on twenty-four-hour shifts side by side with the shaven-headed bone-skinny inmates in their striped pajamas. Very strange they have looked in Auschwitz, these well-fed healthy outsiders with full heads of hair, wearing the almost forgotten polite costume of overcoats, trousers, jackets, ties, or else workmen's overalls; cheerful businesslike Poles or Czechs, talking technical jargon with the German supervisors about retorts, generator gases, fire bricks, draft cross-sections, and so forth; normal fellows, doing a normal job, acting normally.

Normally, except for the way they look at the prisoners. It is as though the striped ticking gives a man the invisibility of a fairy-tale cloak. The technicians do not seem to see you. Of course they are not allowed to talk to inmates, and they fear the SS overseers. Still, not even to show, with a flicker of the eyes, that they see fellow human beings? To look through them as though they are air? To walk around them as though they are posts, or piles of bricks? A strange thing.

The high red-yellow flare at the chimney top flutters and almost dies as clouds of black smoke swirl in the fire; then it burns clear again. No mistaking what this sight is. The tall square chimney shows up plain in the smoky glow from the disposal pits out beyond. Successful test; and why not? The best German workmanship has been going into this installation, the finest machinery and equipment—generators, ovens, blowers, electric hoists, giant ventilators, novel cradles that roll on rails right into the oven mouths—all first-class. Berel has himself been working at cementing this factory-new apparatus into place. He knows quality when he sees it. German wartime shortages have not affected this job. Highest priority! Down in the lower level, those long cavernous chambers are rough work by comparison, except for the airtight doors; excellent workmanship in those heavy doors, in the stout frames, in the double rubber gaskets.

Swinging his club, a trusty slogs by Jastrow toward the latrine, giving him an ugly look. Jastrow has his armband pinned on; rank has its privileges, he can relieve himself after dark. But armband or no, a trusty can crack you on the ass if he pleases, or for that matter smash in your skull and leave you bleeding to death in the snow, and there will be no fuss. Hurrying back to his barrack, Jastrow looks into the block chief's room: clean comfortable digs, with German travel posters of the Rhine, the Berlin Opera, and the Oktoberfest on the plank walls.

The block chief, a tall thin horribly pimpled *Volksdeutscher* burglar from Prague, is smoking a pipe in an old wicker chair, muddy boots up on a stool. Plenty of tobacco around in the camp now; also soap, food, Swiss francs, dollars, medicine, jewelry, gold, clothes; all manner of precious things, available at great risk, at high price. The SS men and the trusties are skimming the cream, naturally, but the inmates trade also; some to eat better, some to grab profit, a daring few to implement resistance or escape. This tide of goods has been sweeping in with the Jewish transports from the west, which have been mounting in number and size month by month. During the summer typhus epidemic, all camp discipline sagged. The trickle of contraband from "Canada," the luggage disposal barracks, became a corrupting flood. The Auschwitz black market, though a mortally dangerous racket, is now unstoppable.

The block leader blows out a sweetly fragrant gray cloud, and with a wave of his pipe dismisses Jastrow, who makes his way down the long frigid crowded blockhouse, his wooden clogs sliding in the ropy mud of the floor. Not an unendurable trusty, he thinks, this old green-triangle type from Dachau and Sachsenhausen, ready as a whore to do anything for money or luxuries except risk his neck or his job. At roll call he puts on a tough show for the SS, clubbing inmates about, but in the block he is just a lazy good-for-nothing. Now and then he messes behind his closed door with one or another of the *peipls,* the perverted boy inmates who drift through the blocks. The prisoners do not even slyly grin at that any more. Old stuff.

Many inmates are already snoring in their bunks, lying three and four to a tier like sardines. Jastrow pushes past the men roosting on the long central brick pipe which doesn't warm the place, but slightly mitigates, together with all the body heat of the prisoners, the subzero night. All the Birkenau huts—he has worked on constructing more than a hundred of them—are built on one German army plan: the field shelter, *Pferdestall,* for horses. These drafty barns, knocked up on the bare marshy ground with wood and tarpaper, are designed to shelter fifty-two animals. But a man needs less room than a horse. Three shelves per stall gives a hundred fifty-six spaces. Put three prisoners on a tier, deduct space for the trusty's room, the block office, the food service area, the slop vat area; result, about four hundred men per *Pferdestall.*

That's the regulation number, more or less; but regulations in Auschwitz are elastic, and heavy overcrowding is the usual thing. Sammy Mutterperl rescued Jastrow from a block where over a thousand men, mostly newcomers sick in the bowels, turned and squirmed all night in every inch of space, in the tiers and on the mud floor, faces jammed to assholes in the dark; where every morning ten or twenty glassy-eyed open-mouthed corpses had to be dragged outside to the roll call, and piled up for the meat wagons. Skilled artisans and foremen like Mutterperl are in the less crowded blockhouses like this one. The mushrooming camp needs these surveyors, locksmiths, carpenters, tanners, cooks, bakers, doctors, draftsmen, linguist-clerks, and the like; so life in their huts may include fuel for the stoves, endurable food, and good water and latrine privileges. Some of those fellows may even survive the war, if the Germans will let anyone survive Auschwitz.

The block of the Klinger kommando is bad enough. The lukewarm morning ersatz coffee, watery evening soup, and single slice of sawdusty bread are the usual Auschwitz ration: in itself, a sentence to slow death. But the kitchen has special orders about hard workers and skilled men: distribution twice a week of extra slices of bread, salami, or cheese to the privileged list. This enriched dole is still less than the "regulation" ration, for the SS consumes, or steals and sells, half the food consigned by Berlin for prisoners. Everybody knows that. They steal all food parcels for Jews from the outside, too; other prisoners, especially British inmates, can end up with part of their parcels. Still, the Klinger gang does well on the added calories, though some of them do gradually dwindle to *Musselmen.* These are a familiar Auschwitz type, the Musselmen; men starved down to dreamy emaciated moving mummies, doomed to be clubbed or kicked to death for slow work, when they don't simply drop and die at random.

Men like Mutterperl and Jastrow are not going to fade to Mussel-men. A different fate awaits them. The sardonic word has long since leaked down from the Labor Section: when the work is done, the kom-mando will have the great honor of going up the chimney first. Au-schwitz humor! Also probably the truth; a variation of the Sonderkom-mandos' fate.

With a practiced movement Jastrow slides feet first into the middle bunk that he shares with Mutterperl, who lies asleep in the blankets which he "organized" from Canada; and which, despite the prevailing thievery, nobody steals from him. The tier shakes. Mutterperl opens his eyes.

Jastrow murmurs, "They just tested."

Mutterperl nods. They avoid words if they can. Above them are three old inmates, but below with two old-timers lies a recent arrival speaking a fine Galician Yiddish, who claims to be a lawyer from Lublin. His skin color is fresh, not the Auschwitz gray, and his shaved scalp is white and unweathered. He bears no scars of quarantine camp. There is an odd expression in his eyes. Chances are, an informer for the Political Section.

The SS keeps searching out the feeble undergrounds that are stirring in Auschwitz; tiny secret groups germinating like weeds in some com-mon ground—political, national, or religious. They endure and grow until the Political Section detects and squashes them. Some last awhile, make contact with the outside, and even smuggle out documents and photographs. Betrayal is their usual end. In this narrow world of dis-ease-ridden famished slaves jammed in horse stalls in the snow, bounded by electrified barbed wire and guarded by machine gun towers and killer dogs, where life hangs by a hair and torture is as common as parking fines elsewhere on earth, informers of course exist. What is sur-prising is the number of straight fellows.

Mutterperl murmurs, "Well, never mind. It's set."

"When?"

"Tell you later." The words are barely breathed in Jastrow's ear. Closing his eyes, the foreman turns over.

Jastrow knows nothing about the escape scheme except what Mutter-perl has so far told him. That is very little. The bakery is the goal, a structure outside the barbed wire, near the woods by the riverbank. Berel's skill in baking will be important. He knows no more than that. Mutterperl will have the films, so if caught and hauled off to the bar-racks of the Gestapo's Political Section, Berel will have almost nothing to betray; not when the cross-examiners threaten to cut off his penis and testicles; not as the hedge-clipper blades are pushed into his crotch and coldly closed on his scrotum, and they give him his last chance to talk.

That's the rumor: the instrument is a plain crude garden hedge-clipper, sharpened like razors. They threaten you with it, and then they really use it. Who can say if it's true? Nobody would survive such a wound to tell the tale. Mutilated corpses are rushed straight to the old crematorium; nobody sees them but the Gestapo men and the Sonderkommandos. What is beyond German interrogators? If this isn't true, something just as bad is true.

One thing is sure: the flame in the night means death very soon for the Klinger kommando. Berel is prepared to try the escape; nothing to lose! So far Mutterperl has been his good angel. A Jew has to hope. Hungry, freezing, exhausted, he prays and falls asleep.

The test has in fact not gone well.

Chief Engineer Pruefer—from J. A. Topf and Sons of Erfurt, a fine company with international furnace patents—is embarrassed. The blowback has belched black smoke and scraps of burning flesh all over the damn place! Only by luck were the Commandant and Colonel Blobel standing clear. The disgusting stuff has spattered SS officers, civilian technicians, even Pruefer himself. Everybody has inhaled the nauseous greasy smoke. A real mess!

Yet Pruefer's conscience is clear. He knows he was right to fire off a mix of lumber, waste oil, and cadavers for the first test. In the new superheated retorts, the corpses will become fuel to accelerate the process; that's the whole point of these big-volume installations. For a serious test he needed actual conditions. As to the blowback, whatever the defect that caused it, he'll put it to rights. Tests show up problems, why else make tests? That Colonel Blobel was on hand is too bad. Topf and Sons did not invite him.

The Commandant and Colonel Blobel leave, coughing rancid smoke from their lungs. The Commandant is beside himself with rage. Civilian swine! Two months behind in delivery; then three postponements of the test; and by the worst luck Colonel Blobel himself has to show up, just today, for this fiasco. Oh, that buggering Erfurt engineer! In his nice comfortable tweed overcoat, English shoes, and fedora, assuring the Commandant that the test would go off all right! What he needs is a few months in Auschwitz, to teach him what lackadaisical performance in wartime means. Straight to Block 11, the swine!

Colonel Blobel says nothing. His disapproving smirk is enough.

They drive in the Commandant's car to the vicinity of the pits, flaring red and smoky over a broad area. Together they walk out on the fields, upwind, and—oh, hell, another foul-up. The Sonderkommandos are using flame-throwers. The Commandant gave strict orders: no flame-throwers while Colonel Blobel is in the camp! These old rotten bodies, some of them from pits dug in 1940 and 1941, just won't burn away. That's the plain fact. When the fire dies you're left with big piles of charred slop and bones. Yet the order from Berlin is, *Eradicate*. What else is there to do but clean up the mess with flame-throwers? But it's a waste of fuel, a confession of poor work. Does Blobel have to know that Auschwitz Establishment can't solve a combustion problem? The Commandant has asked Berlin in vain, over and over, for some decent officer material. They just ignore him, they send him the dregs. He can't do everything himself.

In the crimson firelight, Blobel stares at the flame-throwers, a supercilious look on his face. Well, he is the expert. Now he knows, let him do his worst. Let him tell Müller. Let him tell Himmler! Better yet, let him make suggestions on how to improve things. The Commandant is only human. He has fifteen square miles of installations to worry about. Big munitions and rubber factories going full blast, and more under construction. Dairy farms, plant nurseries. New subcamps and factories springing up. More political prisoners dumped on him by the thousands all the time. Major shortages of lumber, cement, pipes, wiring, even nails. Serious health and discipline problems, all over the area. And to top it all, Jews keep arriving by the trainload, in bigger and bigger batches. The special treatment facilities get overloaded, naturally. More mess! That tough guy Eichmann is no real planner. He runs a jerky hit-or-miss operation, always either no action or too much. Dirtiest part of the whole assignment. Has to be done, but not productive, except for the stuff in Canada.

What a pyramid of responsibilities! How can a man do a decent job under these conditions?

Fortunately, Blobel is an architect, an intellectual. He's no Eichmann. As they drive back to the villa for dinner, he has the taste to avoid criticism. He senses the Commandant's feelings. Once they've bathed and dressed and are having drinks in the library, he turns cordial. Colonel Blobel likes his drop, as the Commandant knows, and before the Polish maid curtseys to announce dinner, he has downed almost half a bottle of Haig and Haig. Fine, let him get mellow. One thing Blobel can have here is liquor, all he can guzzle. Surprising what the Jews manage to bring along in their suitcases. Even wine. At dinner the Colonel tells the Commandant's wife that not since peacetime has he drunk such a succession of wines at table. She blushes with pleasure. Blobel praises the roast veal, the soup, the cream chocolate cake. Cook has done herself proud, in fact. Blobel makes little jokes with the boys about their studies, and about their appetite for cake. His forbidding manner is melting away. He's a good fellow, after all, once he's had a few! The Commandant is feeling more optimistic about the unpleasant business talk still to come, but then—

AOW! AOW! AOW! The damned escape siren!

Even here, way down by the river front, the wailing, screaming escape alarm of Auschwitz shakes the windows and the walls, and all but drowns out the distant spatters of machine gun fire. *Of all times!* Stiffening in his armchair, Colonel Blobel turns a hard face to the Commandant, who excuses himself and tramples upstairs to his private telephone, seething. The dinner ruined, too.

A plane flying low over Auschwitz now—though no such thing is possible, the air space over these fifteen square miles of Polish backcountry is strictly off limits, even to the Luftwaffe—would come on a striking sight: thousands upon thousands of men and women ranked on the long parade grounds of the Birkenau camps under glaring floodlights in gently falling snow; a quasi-military sight, except for the unmilitary costumes of vertical-striped thin cotton rags.

The scream of the sirens has really startled the inmates, who have come tumbling out under the clubbing and curses of the SS and the trusties. Escape roll calls have been discontinued for months. Why now, all of a sudden?

Roll call is daily torture. One day the books will play up more gruesome aspects of Auschwitz: the medical experiments on women and children, the collecting of tons of female hair and the skeletons of twins, the mutilating tortures of the Gestapo, the casual sadistic murders of slave workers, and of course the covert asphyxiation of millions of Jews. All these things happen, but most working prisoners do not encounter them. Roll call is as bad as anything they endure. They stand motionless in ranks morning and evening for a couple of hours in all weathers. The hardest work is preferable. At least you warm yourself when you're in the swing, and distract your mind. At roll call hunger gnaws, bowels and bladder agonize, cold eats into bones, and time stops. Roll call is when Musselmen tend to keel over. By the time roll call ends on a bitter winter morning, bodies litter the ground. The meat wagons collect the dead; the inmates carry the living into the block-houses, or drag them off to work if clubbing revives them.

But there are big rush jobs under way in Auschwitz, and killing off workers with roll calls is no help. The authorities therefore decided way back during the typhus epidemic to cut down on these extra roll calls at an escape alarm.

So what now?

What has happened is that the Commandant has telephoned his dep-uty and warned that if the swine who escaped isn't promptly caught, there will be summary death sentences for negligence in the SS. Some-one will pay! Heads will roll! As for the prisoners, call them out! Let them stand at attention until morning, the shitasses! Then let them march off to work.

It's ten below zero outside. The Commandant knows he's cutting off his nose to spite his face, for these orders will kill a lot of marginal working hands. Never mind! Paul Blobel of Kommando 1005 is his guest. Stern measures are in order. Auschwitz Establishment cannot be disgraced. The roll call shows he means business. When the SS gets scared, it produces. They'll catch the shitass.

• • •

Are escapes then possible from Auschwitz?

Yes. As concentration camps go, Auschwitz is a sieve.

One day Auschwitz will acquire an awesome name in the world as an impenetrable fortress of macabre horrors. In actuality it is a sloppy in-dustrial sprawl, always expanding, always anarchic. Something like seven hundred escapes will be recorded in its history. A third of those will succeed. The unrecorded ones may add up to twice as many. No-body will ever know.

There is no other German concentration camp like Auschwitz.

The German camps early in the Nazi era simply imitated the gulags of Lenin's Bolsheviks; they were isolation and terror dumps for political opponents. But in wartime these camps have swollen, proliferated into hundreds dotting all Europe, filled up with foreigners, and become slave pens for German-run factories; where, to be sure, prisoners die in droves from bad conditions. But in only six camps, all in Polish back-

country, does the SS murder Jews en masse upon arrival, with an elaborate hygienic hoax of disinfection.

The German names for these six places are Chelmno, Belzec, Sobibor, Treblinka, Maidanek—and Auschwitz.

Auschwitz is in a class by itself, and not only because of its reliance on a cyanide pest-killer gas, while the other five massacre centers use exhaust fumes from truck engines. That is a minor distinction. The main thing is that the other camps serve no purpose but slaughter, though there may be some slave use of overflow Jews for a while. So from the others escape is very tough.

Auschwitz stands alone: at once the biggest asphyxiation center, the biggest corpse-robbing center, and the biggest slave-factory center of German-ruled Europe. It is the colossus. Hence its laxness. It is too huge, too complex, too improvised, for proper control. The effect of the Jewish plunder is also very unsettling. There is too much of it. Most of the Jews are poor, and they bring only two suitcases apiece; but in such multitudes, the loot adds up. The gold from the teeth alone is mounting into the millions of reichsmarks. SS training and morale break down, more even than from the temptation of scared submissive Jewesses in the women's work camp. Despite the fiercest penalties, the little gold ingots keep disappearing from the smelting laboratory and floating through Auschwitz, a strange secret currency for perilous deals.

The fact is, the Commandant lacks the manpower to run his show. His complaints are just. The battle of Stalingrad is on, and the army is demanding more and more men. Himmler is forming SS battle divisions, too. Which Germans are left from the comb-out? The stupid, the feeble, the elderly, the disabled, the criminal—frankly, the scum. And even of those there's not enough. The trusty system has to expand and take in foreign prisoners.

There is the trouble. Certainly a lot of these bootlick the SS and brutalize other prisoners to save their own skins. Auschwitz is a machine for debasing human nature. Still, too many of these non-German trusties remain soft. Hence the Resistance. Hence the escapes. Poles, Czechs, Jews, Serbs, Ukrainians, they're all alike. Not really trustworthy. They even soften up some confused Germans.

Yes, there are plenty of escapes from Auschwitz.

The Commandant hears from Himmler about them, time after time. The problem threatens his career. So he wants to impress Colonel Blobel with a recapture, at least. The man who heads Kommando 1005 has Himmler's ear.

• • •

An hour passes.

An hour and a half.

Two hours.

In the library, the Commandant keeps glancing at his recently acquired antique clock, as Colonel Blobel talks on; or rather maunders on, for he is consuming an amazing quantity of brandy. At another time, the Commandant would be relaxed and happy, hearing such alcoholic confidences from such a high-placed insider. But he is on pins and needles. He really cannot enjoy the talk, nor the twenty-year-old Courvoisier. He has airily assured the colonel that his garrison will "catch the bugger straight off." Risky thing to say! Now his head is on the chopping block.

Out on the parade ground there are only crude ways to gauge the passage of time. Snow piling on shoulders, for instance; or the spread of frozen numbness in your limbs, your nose, your ears; or the count of prisoners falling to the ground. Otherwise how can you tell time? Motion measures time. There is no motion here but the tread of a passing trusty on guard, no sound but his boots squeaking in the snow. No stars move overhead. Light white snow falls randomly in white glare on striped-clad immobile shuddering ranks. By the feeling that he has no legs below the knees, Berel Jastrow guesses that about two hours must have passed. Klinger will be unhappy at morning roll call. Berel can see thirteen men down.

The new fellow from Lublin, between Jastrow and Mutterperl, suddenly takes his life and theirs in his hands, exclaiming, *"How long does this go on?"*

In the silence the strangled gasp is like a shout, like a pistol shot. And at this moment the block chief walks by! Berel can't see him, but he hears the boots behind him, he knows the footfall, he smells the pipe. He waits for the club to crash on the fool's thin cotton cap. But the trusty walks on, does nothing. German blockhead! He should have slammed him with the club. He didn't have to hurt him. One good result of the roll call: the SS plant identified.

But SS plant or not, the man isn't shamming agony. Not much later he plops down with a groan on his knees and tumbles over on his side, eyes rolling and glassy. Well fed, new to the camp, he should have done better than that. Camp weakens or toughens you. If the Resistance doesn't murder that one, he'll end as a Musselman.

Colonel Blobel is well into his cups now: slumped in the armchair, slurring his words, drooping his glass at an angle that slops brandy. His assertions and boasts are getting wild. The Commandant suspects that, drunk as he is, Blobel is cutely playing cat-and-mouse with him. He still has not mentioned the problem that has brought him to Auschwitz. The escape will give him some nasty leverage, if it isn't foiled—and soon.

Blobel is now claiming that the whole Jewish program is his idea. In the Ukraine, where he headed an *Einsatzgruppe* in 1941, he grasped how shoddy the original SS plan was. Back in Berlin on sick leave, he presented a top-secret memorandum to Himmler, Heydrich, and Eichmann, three copies only—so hot that he didn't dare keep a copy himself. Therefore he can't prove that he conceived the present system. But Himmler knows. That's why Blobel now heads Kommando 1005, the hardest of all SS tasks. Yes, the honor of Germany rests in Paul Blobel's hands. He realizes his responsibility. He wishes more people would.

What Blobel saw in the Ukraine, so he says, was terrible. He was then an underling following orders. They assigned him to Kiev. Just ordered him to go in there and do a job. His part went off smoothly. He found a ravine outside the town, collected the Jews in batches and got them out to the ravine, called Babi Yar or something, a few thousand at a time. It took days to get it done. There were more than sixty thousand Kiev Jews, the biggest job anybody had yet tried. But everything he didn't organize himself was bungled. Not only did the army fail to keep Ukrainian civilians away from Babi Yar; half of the crowds of onlookers were German soldiers. Disgraceful! People watching the executions as though they were at a soccer game! Laughing, eating ice cream, even taking pictures! Pictures of women and children kneeling to be shot in the back, tumbling into the ravine! This was damn hard on the morale of the rifle squads; they didn't appreciate getting into such snapshots. He had to call a halt, raise hell with the army, and get the place cordoned off.

Moreover, the Jews were shot with their clothes on, and with God knows what money and jewelry concealed on them, and sand was bulldozed over them. Idiotic! As to their empty homes in Kiev, why, the Ukrainians just walked in and helped themselves. The Reich got nothing of their property. Everybody knew what was happening to the Jews.

Blobel perceived then and there that Germany was going to lose billions in Jewish property, if the whole thing wasn't done with more system. His memorandum laid the plan out properly, and Himmler jumped at it. Auschwitz and the whole revised Jewish solution resulted.

The Commandant isn't about to argue with Blobel, but all this is eyewash. Maybe not about the Ukraine; but long before the Wehrmacht ever got near Kiev, he met with Himmler about the Jewish question, and afterward with Eichmann. It was Eichmann's setup in the Vienna Jewish Emigration Office, way back in 1938, that was the economic model for Auschwitz. The Commandant has heard all about that Vienna setup. The Jews went in one door of the building rich proud bourgeois, passed down a row of offices signing papers, and came out the other end with bare asses and passports. As for the *Aktion Reinhardt,* the official general collection of the property of the Jews after special treatment, Globocnik has always handled that. So when Blobel tries to claim—

R-R-R-RING!

The sweetest sound the Commandant has heard in his life! He jumps to his feet. The telephone doesn't ring in the villa at midnight to report failure.

The sound of the drum is muffled by the snow, so Berel doesn't hear it until it starts up in the next camp. So they've nabbed him, and are marching him through Birkenau already! Well, if he had to be caught— God pity him—better now than later. For the first time in months, Berel has been fearing his knees would give way. Hearing the drum gives him strength. Two SS men are carrying the flogging frame out on the parade ground now. It will soon be over.

And here the guy comes. Three officers lead him, three follow him, leaving him plenty of room for his solo performance. One prods him with a sharp stick, to keep him dancing as he beats the drum. The poor devil can scarcely stay on his feet, but on he comes, jigging and drumming.

The clown suit is getting bedraggled with use. The bright yellow cloth is stained in the seat and the legs with blood. Still, it is a terribly ludicrous sight. Around his neck the usual sign dangles—HURRAH, I'M BACK—in big black German lettering. Who is he? Hard to tell, through the crude paint on his face, the red mouth, the exaggerated eyebrows. As he dances by, feebly whacking the drum, Berel hears Mutterperl hiss.

The flogging is short. The fellow's behind, when they bare it, is raw bleeding meat. He gets only ten more blows. They don't want to weaken him too much. The Gestapo interrogation comes first. They want him to stay lively enough so that the torture will make him talk. They may even feed him for a while to build him up. In the end, of course, he'll be hanged at a roll call, but there won't be much of him left to hang. Ticklish business, escaping. But if the alternative is going up the chimney, a man has little to lose, seeking another way to leave Auschwitz.

The chilled ranks break. The SS men and the trusties curse, club, and whip the slow-moving inmates back to the barracks. Some stumble and fall. Their rigid legs held them up while they didn't move. Bend those frozen joints, and down you can go! Berel knows about this. He found it out on the march from Lamsdorf. He walks on his own numb ice-cold legs as though they are iron braces, swinging them clumsily along with his hip muscles.

The block, where the temperature must be about zero, but at least the snow isn't falling, seems a warm refuge: in fact, home. When the light is turned off, Mutterperl pokes Berel, who rolls close and puts his ear to the foreman's mouth.

Warm breath; faint words. "It's off."

Berel changes position, his mouth to Mutterperl's ear. "Who was the guy?"

"Never mind. All off."

The Commandant laughs uproariously with relief and with genuine amusement, as he hangs up. The dogs tracked the fellow down, he tells Blobel. The poor bugger tried to escape in one of the big cistern carts that carry off the crap from the mass latrines. He didn't get far, and he's so covered with shit that it's taken three men to hose him off. Well, that's that!

Blobel slaps his shoulder. An escape that fails, he says wisely, is not a bad thing for discipline. Make an example of the bastard. This is the psychological moment, the Commandant thinks, and he invites Blobel upstairs to his private office. He locks the door, unlocks the closet, and brings out the treasure. Lovingly he spreads it out on the desk. Colonel Blobel's bleary eyes widen in an envious admiring gleam.

The stuff is women's underwear: exquisite fairylike things, soft works of art, lacy pretty nothings that give a man a hard-on just to look at them. Panties, brassieres, shifts, slips, garters, in filmy pastel silks, perfectly laundered, ready for movie stars to put on! The best in the world! The Commandant explains that in the undressing room he has a man just to collect the sweetest stuff he sees. Some of these Jewesses are ravishing. And oh, Christ, what lovely stuff comes off their asses. Just look.

Colonel Paul Blobel scoops up a double handful of panties and girdles, crushing them against his crotch like a woman's rump, with a wide grin at the Commandant and a masculine growl—RRRRRR! The Commandant says that the stuff is a present for Colonel Blobel. There's plenty more, tons of it. But this is the best of the best. The SS will deliver a package to the colonel's airplane with a good selection, also some decent Scotch and brandy, a few boxes of cigars, and so forth.

Blobel shakes his hand, gives him a little hug, becomes a different man. They sit down and talk turkey.

First he lectures the Commandant on the merits of crematorium versus burning pit. He has definite and informed ideas. He gives some technical tips on how to improve the pit performance. Damn useful! Then he comes to the point. Auschwitz has been sending him garbage, not workers. Kommando 1005 duty is very hard work. These fellows he's been getting don't last three weeks, whereas it takes three weeks just to show them the techniques. He is tired of complaining to Berlin. He knows that the way to get things done right—as the Commandant has been saying—is to do them himself. So he has come to Auschwitz to settle this thing. It has to be straightened out.

The tone is friendly. The Commandant responds that he will do what he can. He is caught in a bind himself. Himmler can't make up his mind what the function of Auschwitz is. Is he trying to eliminate Jews? Or put them to work? One week the Commandant gets a bawling out from Eichmann for sending too many Jewish arrivals to the work camp, instead of to special treatment. The next week, or the next day, for that matter, Pohl from the Economic Section will be down on him for not putting enough Jews into the factories. A directive has just come in, four pages long, with orders to nurse sick Jews back to health on arrival, and put them to work, if there's six months of potential labor in them. To a person who knows Auschwitz, it's utter nonsense. Just bureaucratic bumpf! But there you are. He has a dozen factories to man, and a perpetual labor shortage.

Blobel waves all this aside. Kommando 1005 has the highest priority. Does the Commandant want to ask Himmler? Blobel is not leaving Auschwitz—and now the tone is not so friendly—without an assurance that he will get four or five hundred able-bodied Jews in the next shipment. *Able-bodied!* Fellows who can deliver three or four months of hard labor before you have to get rid of them.

The Commandant is resourceful under pressure. In this business he has to be. He has a brainstorm. Colonel Blobel has seen the kommando at work in Crematorium II, he says. There's a fine working gang, well-fed fellows with strong backs, no better stuff in the camp. They are due to be liquidated when their work is done. The crematorium fires off next week. How about it? Kommando 1005 can have the Crematorium II kommando. Will that do?

This is highly satisfactory to Blobel. The two officers shake hands on it, and open another bottle of brandy.

Before they stagger off to bed, at three o'clock in the morning, they have agreed at length that their work is dirty but honorable, that the SS is the soul of the nation, that front-line soldiers don't have it as tough, that obedience to the Führer is the only salvation for Germany, that the Jews are the Fatherland's eternal enemy, that this war is the historic chance of a thousand years to root them out for good; that it only seems cruel to kill women and children, that it's one hell of a rotten job, but the future of European civilization and culture is at stake. They are seldom this frank about the things that trouble them, but to a surprising extent they find themselves kindred spirits. Arms around each other's shoulders, they lurch to the bedrooms with almost loving good-nights.

A week later, trucks take the crematorium construction kommando to Cracow. Before the work gang leaves Auschwitz, word comes down from the Labor Section about Kommando 1005. It is just a postponed sentence of death. Still, escapes from 1005 are reputedly easier. In Cracow they board trains for the north. Mutterperl and Jastrow carry identical rolls of undeveloped film, slipped to them after they were searched, stripped, and issued different clothes for departure. Both men have memorized Resistance names and addresses in Poland and Czechoslovakia, and a destination for the films in Prague.

* * *

47

Global Waterloo
3: Rommel

(from *World Holocaust* by Armin von Roon)

The Hinge of Fate

In his history, Winston Churchill calls the Battle of El Alamein "The Hinge of Fate." Actually, it was an interesting textbook encounter, a revival of World War I tactics in a desert setting. The double political impact of El Alamein and Torch was certainly serious. Just as America was dipping a gingerly toe into the European war at one end of North Africa, the legendary Desert Fox was driven from Egypt at the other end. The world was amazed. Spirits rose among the Allies and fell in Germany; Italian morale collapsed.

Nevertheless, despite the great distances and colorful battles, North Africa was a secondary theatre. Once Hitler backed off from the Mediterranean strategy, his last chance to win the war, the front dwindled to a costly and tragic sideshow; and when he too late plunged into Tunis in force, it became a military hemorrhage. Typically, Churchill devotes some twenty pages to El Alamein, and about seven pages to Stalingrad and Guadalcanal combined. Historical myopia can go little further.

Churchill's Greatest Blunder

What Churchill fails to mention at all, of course, is that his own stupid interference with his army commanders created the North African situation in the first place.

Mussolini took Italy into the war in 1940 as France was falling, after the British had left their ally in the lurch at Dunkirk. The Italian dictator thought he could snatch spoils on the cheap from two defunct empires, so from his huge arid territory in Libya he launched an invasion of Egypt. It was a case of the hyena mistaking an ailing lion for a dead one, and biting prematurely.

The British air force and navy were still almost intact. So was their Middle Eastern army. They not only counterattacked by land and air and sent the Italians fleeing westward; they also marched light forces south and took Somaliland and Abyssinia. This cleared the Red Sea and the whole East African coastline for British shipping.

Meantime, along the Mediterranean coast the Italians were routed. Wherever the British armored columns appeared the Italians gave up in droves, though greatly outnumbering the enemy. It appeared that England had North Africa won, to the very border of neutral French Tunisia. This meant sea and air control of the Mediterranean, with the gravest consequences for us.

Absorbed though Hitler was at that time with his plan to invade Russia, these events roused him to dispatch an air wing to Sicily, and a small armored force to Tripoli to stiffen the collapsing Italians. And so it was that there came on the scene the immortal ROMMEL. In February 1941, when the then little-known junior panzer general landed in Tripoli, the Italians were on their last legs. His Afrika Korps of ten thousand men was quite inadequate to hold off the fast-approaching British forces. But Churchill, with his worst blunder of the entire war, gave Rommel his historic chance.

At that time, the feckless Mussolini was in trouble in Greece, and Hitler wanted to pacify the Balkans before our assault on Russia. That we might invade Greece to clean things up was apparent. Anticipating this, *Winston Churchill halted the march of his victorious African forces, yanked out four of their strongest divisions, and shipped them to Greece!* His old Balkan mania, which had led to his Gallipoli disgrace in World War I, was cropping out again.

In both wars Churchill was haunted by the absurd fantasy that the polyglot squabblers of the Balkan peninsula, that patchwork of small countries formed of the debris of the Ottoman Empire, could be induced to unite and "rise up against Germany." This time his folly cost England a disastrous defeat in Greece and Crete, the "little Dunkirk," and her chance to secure North Africa as well. By the time the defeated divisions returned to Libya, their equipment battered, their élan gone, Rommel was entrenched, and the Desert War was on. It would take two years of hard fighting and the whole gigantic Anglo-American invasion to retrieve Churchill's idiocy, and win for England what she had in hand before he threw it away.

TRANSLATOR'S NOTE: *No great man fails to make mistakes. Churchill's shift of forces from Africa to Greece was mistimed. Churchill doesn't admit this, in his unabashedly self-serving though fine six-volume history called* The Second World War. *One has to read a few other books, including works like Roon's, to get a clearer idea of what really went on.*—V.H.

———————

Desert Warfare

The North African desert war oscillated for a year and a half between two port bases fourteen hundred miles apart: Tripoli in Libya, Alexandria in Egypt. A game of hare and hounds went on turn and turn about. First the Afrika Korps, then the British, stretched their supply lines to attack, ran low, and withdrew to base. *Supply* so far governed this war that Rommel wrote, *"Any desert campaign was won or lost by the Quartermaster Corps before a shot was fired."*

In Erwin Rommel's masterly desert tactics, the ruling concept was the *open southern flank.* On the north lay the Mediterranean. To the south lay the sandy void. Conventional rules of land war melted before the oceanlike open flank. It was Rommel's flank moves that won victory after victory, as he kept varying his tricks to bedazzle his stolid foe.

But a desert army's range, like a fleet's, is dictated by the amount of fuel, food, and water it can carry along, with the reserve needed to double back to base. The dashing Rommel was somewhat neglectful of this limitation; fortunately his good staff kept it in mind. It was something Adolf Hitler could never understand. His mentality was that of a World War I foot soldier. In Europe adequate supply lines were taken for granted, and our troops could live off fruitful invaded lands like France and the Ukraine. The picture of armored columns proceeding through vast sterile flat voids was beyond Hitler. He saw the newsreels regularly at Headquarters, but they made no dent in his obtuseness.

I was present on two occasions when Rommel flew to the Führer's HQ in East Prussia to plead for more supplies. Göring was there once. The bored uncomprehending glaze in the eyes of the two politicians must have sickened Rommel. Hitler's response each time was the same: airy-fairy chaffing of this great field general as a "pessimist," voluble promises to improve supplies, warm assurances that Rommel would "pull it off no matter what," and a new medal.

Göring reacted only once, when Rommel was describing the power of the new American Tomahawk fighter-bomber that the British were using. At this pinch of his Luftwaffe toes he smirked, "Nonsense, the Americans are good at making only refrigerators and razor blades."

Rommel retorted, "Reichsmarschall, the Afrika Korps will appreciate a large issue of such razor blades."

But Rommel's fearless talk to the bigwigs came to nothing. To save Mussolini's face, the African theatre was maintained as an Italian command; and the Italians broke promises of more supplies as fast as Mussolini made them.

Tobruk: Poisoned Fruit

Rommel's great storming of Tobruk in June 1942 marked the high tide for us. Coming when Sevastopol was falling to Manstein and our U-boat sinkings were spiking upward, the fall of Tobruk shook the world. The British retreated all the way to the El Alamein line in Egypt, only eighty miles from Alexandria. The Tobruk booty was lavish—gasoline, food, tanks, guns, ammunition, in quantities known only to the enemy, never to us. The worn and spent Afrika Korps, like a starving lion that has caught and devoured a gazelle, came back to roaring life. Rommel demanded freedom to drive for decisive victory. Hitler gave him the green light. On to Suez; maybe to the Persian Gulf!

Those were heady days in the map room. In my mind's eye the pallid puffy-faced Führer still leans on the table map of North Africa with stiff arms, his favorite posture, wearing the very thick reading glasses the public never saw, lifting a pudgy white hand to sweep it with a slight tremor from Tobruk across Suez, Palestine, and Iraq to the mouth of the Euphrates. Unfortunately, the Führer tended to fight his wars with just such visionary arm sweeps. Logistics bored him. He either dismissed these gritty supply realities, or terrorized with screaming fits generals who pressed him too hard about such mundane details. Since his fearsome willpower did sometimes work wonders, he had become accustomed to demanding the impossible.

This time he really demanded the impossible of Rommel, for he used the fall of Tobruk as an excuse to cancel "Operation *Herkules*," the capture of Malta. The small but strong fortress island base lay athwart Rommel's supply line, a hundred miles off Sicily. Mussolini yearned to capture it. But Hitler, his mind on the eastern front, had hemmed and hawed for a year, and now he dropped the plan. This was a radical error. Malta's interdiction was ceaseless, and each tanker, each ammunition ship, that was sunk weakened Rommel. Hitler believed that Luftwaffe bombardment would neutralize Malta, but the British patched their airstrips, flew in more aircraft, slipped in more submarines, fought through in convoys, and kept the garrison supplied.

Tobruk convinced Hitler and Mussolini that the superman, Rommel, could manufacture victories out of thin air, and that his complaints about supply were prima donna tantrums. Pressure for supplying him relaxed. The Tobruk cache melted away as he drove up to El Alamein, and made an assault late in August which barely failed. And still supplies did not come. His own reputation was strangling him.

The British Buildup

On the British side, the fall of Tobruk had the opposite effect.

Churchill was in Washington at the time, and Roosevelt asked how he could help. Never bashful, Churchill at once demanded three hundred Sherman tanks, the U.S. Army's brand-new weapon. Over the army's grumbling, Roosevelt granted this request; added another hundred Grant tanks, and a lot of new antitank guns and other matériel. At highest priority a big convoy sailed off for Egypt via the Cape of Good Hope. When this convoy unloaded in September, the munitions and supplies it delivered *alone outweighed everything the Afrika Korps had on hand to fight the Battle of El Alamein.* Meanwhile, the British had been heavily rearming Montgomery too, via the Mediterranean. Moreover, Persia's refineries and the military reserves in Palestine were there to draw on.

In fact it was now no contest. Rommel has been much criticized for not declining battle and withdrawing from El Alamein, for the British buildup was becoming monstrous.

TRANSLATOR'S NOTE: *Roon here gives a table showing British advantages of five to one or better at El Alamein in tanks, planes, and troops. Dubious, but the figures in British accounts are lopsided enough.—V.H.*

But Rommel *could not* leave. So poor were his logistics, so badly had the Supreme Command failed him, so costly was the interdiction from Malta, that the Afrika Korps virtually lacked the gasoline to pull across Libya. Rommel had to stand and fight, using up in battle what fuel he had. Beyond El Alamein lay Alexandria, a richer supply dump than Tobruk; beyond that, Suez still beckoned. He had beaten the British often. He had their measure. One more fight, one more victory, and all might yet be well!

El Alamein was a long-prepared British fall-back position, well fortified and mined. The front stretched some forty miles from the coast to the Qattara Depression, where steep cliffs dropped to a vast bog of salt marsh and quicksand, two hundred feet below sea level. It was perfect for the World War I mentalities in charge of England's forces, and unsuited to Rommel's desert tactics.

He too sowed stupendous mine fields nine miles deep all along the front, mainly with captured British mines. He fortified the high ground, husbanded the fuel and ammunition, begged and pleaded and raged for more supplies, and waited for the enemy to attack. But his opponent, Bernard Montgomery, was in no hurry. Montgomery combined a flair for flamboyant and belligerent rhetoric with extreme caution in planning and fighting. Eisenhower once called him a good "set-piece commander." Montgomery wanted his set piece against Rommel to be a sure thing.

Erwin Rommel was not a well man, and his health gave way. He flew back to Germany on sick leave. When the battle began he was still in the hospital, and the Anglo-American armada was already on the high seas, bound for French North Africa.

El Alamein Erupts

Montgomery attacked on the October full moon. One thousand massed artillery pieces laid down a Verdun-like barrage; waves of infantry then crossed the mine fields to seize advanced positions; sappers cleared mines yard by yard in narrow corridors; and behind them came crawling the tanks. It was heavy, unimaginative, slogging warfare, orthodox as a Sandhurst field exercise. Montgomery had the weight of men, shells, and metal, and was not trying tricks. Our troops and some superior Italian divisions, well dug in all along the line, stoutly resisted. By daylight the attack was bogged down in the mine fields, facing rings of heavy antitank guns.

Hitler ordered the Desert Fox from his sickbed to fly to El Alamein and resume command. The unequal battle raged for a week. Throwing in men and machines with World War I abandon, Montgomery failed to break through. Rommel fought back brilliantly, switching his dwindling handful of tanks here and there, virtually counting his shells and gasoline jerrycans before each counterattack.

In London, Churchill was impatiently waiting for the breakthrough. He wanted to order the victory bells rung throughout England, for the first time in the war; just as Mussolini had flown over to Libya in July—entourage, white horse, and all—for his grand entry into Alexandria. But as the days dragged on, the bell-ringing had to be put off. In plain fact, the Afrika Korps had Montgomery stopped. Concern in Alexandria and in London grew that the engagement might have to be broken off, a desert stalemate very much like the Western Front in 1916.

But the attrition became too much for Rommel. His tank force was shrinking away. His shells were almost gone. He had no air support; and the RAF pounded him at will. Having no tanks left to consume gasoline, he could now use what fuel remained to truck his forces back to Libya. This he decided to do, but he made the terrible mistake of telegraphing Hitler for permission to withdraw. The answer of course shot back, *Hold fast at all costs, no retreat, the troops must write a glorious new page in German history,* and so forth and so on.

This delayed the loyal Rommel's escape by a full forty-eight hours, and forced him to abandon his Italian infantry division in order to save the Afrika Korps. Two days earlier he might have extricated the lot, but now he had to put first things first and preserve his striking arm. Montgomery was slow in pursuit, and the Desert Fox made good his retreat to Libya and to Tunis.

Such in truth was the vaunted "Hinge of Fate" Battle of El Alamein.

By October 1942, the Afrika Korps was already all but done for, due to the criminal failures of supply. After the most formidable preparations, Montgomery placed the pistol of the Eighth Army at the prostrate Rommel's temple, pulled the trigger—and missed. The Desert Fox sprang up and escaped. That is essentially what happened.

That the needed supplies could always have been sent in a flood—troops, tanks, fuel, aircraft, antitank guns—was amply proved, too late, once the Anglo-Americans landed. Stung in their sensitive political nerves, Hitler and Mussolini rushed whole armies to Tunis by air and sea, gradually building up to almost three hundred thousand men. Such reinforcements to Rommel in July would have carried German arms to the Persian oil fields and to India. Slipping away from his dawdling pursuers, Rommel crossed the continent in a great fighting retreat, took command of the Tunis pocket, and made a shambles of the Allies' Mediterranean timetable. But the dream of Suez and beyond was over.

Torch: Summary

The Anglo-American North African campaign was a poor show even before Rommel entered the picture. The key was the Bizerte-Tunis port area at the Sicilian Narrows, scarcely one hundred miles from Europe. The British wanted to land near there and dash for the objective. But the American army, facing its first battle test, feared venturing so far inside Gibraltar Strait. What about German air power, the inexperienced Yank generals asked; what about possible intervention by Spain, which could cut off the expedition's supply lines? They wanted a cautious landing in the rough Atlantic surf at Casablanca, on the outer bulge of Africa, connected to the key terrain only by a single rickety railroad line. The final compromise plan retained the Casablanca landing, with beachheads inside Gibraltar much too far from the main objective. Axis reinforcements crossed the Mediterranean by sea and air and seized Tunisia first.

Yet winning the race for Tunis was but a snare into which the two dictators blundered. With all of Fortress Europe to defend, we could not in the long run triumph in North Africa against the rich and untouched American industrial system. Our armies in Tunis were foredoomed to become as big a prisoner bag as the Sixth Army at Stalingrad. Even Rommel's generalship could not avert this, though he did wreck the Allies' plan for a quick win. North Africa was our most useless defeat, under our best general; another disaster of the *Führerprinzip* in war.

Triumph of Roosevelt

Roosevelt got out of the Torch landing just what he wanted: a "victory" to pep up his home front, a battleground where his raw recruits and bright-buttoned generals could make their first mistakes (they made many) at a light price, and a plausible second front to placate the Russians. Marshall was right in predicting that the sideshow would lengthen the war by at least a year, but meantime the politician Roosevelt reaped his profits. The easy Torch success froze Spain in her neutrality, kept Turkey quiet, and ensured the early fall of Mussolini.

All this Roosevelt accomplished in French North Africa at a cost of about twenty thousand Americans killed or captured, and less than half as many British casualties. When one adds that in four years of war that brought the U.S.A. de facto world hegemony, America lost in all theatres less than three hundred thousand men in battle deaths—*about equal to the force we lost at Stalingrad*—while the Russians sacrificed something like eleven million soldiers, and we lost perhaps four million, one must call Franklin Roosevelt's overall war strategy a work of malevolent genius.

Churchill never did ring his bells. Rommel had pummelled the Eighth Army too badly before retreating. Moreover, with Torch about to go with green American troops, Churchill may have feared a debacle there. In any case, he thought better of it, and even in defeat, Rommel silenced the church bells of England.

———

TRANSLATOR'S NOTE: *In view of Roon's exalted estimate of General Rommel, one sentence from Rommel's Memoirs may be in order here: "The battle which began at El Alamein on the 23rd October, 1942, turned the tide of war in Africa against us and, in fact, probably represented the turning point* of the whole vast struggle." In this matter Rommel evidently shared Churchill's "myopia."

Rommel is an important and controversial figure in any discussion of military ethics. He was implicated in the generals' plot on Hitler's life in 1944. Most of the generals remained slavishly loyal to Hitler, and the Führer sent two of these to finish off Rommel. They offered him the choice of a public trial for treason, or a quiet death by poison (with a cover story of a heart attack) and a "hero's funeral," with safety guaranteed to his family. He took the poison, and they delivered him dead to a hospital. Hitler duly proclaimed a day of national mourning for the great Desert Fox.

Rommel had fought for Hitler to the last. When he was murdered, he was already a broken man, done in by illness and a bad automobile accident. He knew about the extermination camps. He considered the Führer incompetent to command. He bemoaned the waste of life and property in continuing a lost war. He hated the whole Nazi gang that was sacrificing what was left of Germany to prolong their clutch on power. Yet he went on fighting until he was incapacitated; and then he took the poison that the Führer sent him by the hands of his fellow generals.

Rommel's career is some sort of object lesson for military men in the difficult borderline between steadfast loyalty and criminal stupidity.

As for Roon's assertion that "Americans cannot take battle losses," I have heard that a little too often from Europeans. A Russian general once told Eisenhower that his way of clearing a mine field was to march a couple of brigades through it. We Americans fight differently, when we can. Yet in the Civil War we fought some of the most sanguinary battles in history, and the South was living on grass and acorns when it quit. Nobody knows yet what the American people can do in the last extremity.

Our moral climate does seem to be going to hell in a handbasket—I am writing in 1970, the "counterculture" era—but my superiors were making that complaint in the 1920s, the "flaming youth" era, which then more or less included me.—V.H.

*   *   *

48

J ANICE answered a ring at the front door and blinked. Victor Henry stood there hunched, his eyes troubled and weary, his face as gray as his ill-fitting work uniform. He carried a wooden footlocker and a bulging leather portfolio.

"Hi." The voice too was troubled and weary.

Clutching at her open housecoat collar, she exclaimed, "Dad! Come in, come in! What a surprise! The place is a mess, and so am I, but—"

"I tried to telephone. I know the rule against surprising the female persuasion. The line was busy, and I'm crowded for time. I had a problem finding where you'd moved."

"I wrote to you."

"I never got it." He glanced around the small living room, his eyes jerkily avoiding Warren's photograph on the wall. "Furniture's sort of jammed in here."

"Does it seem a comedown? It's all Vic and I need now."

"Have you stored my stuff?"

"No, it's all there in Vic's room."

"Good. I'll need my dress blues and bridge coat."

"How long will you be in Honolulu?"

"A few hours."

"Wow! No more?"

He raised heavy eyebrows in which Janice saw new flecks of gray. "I've got orders back to Washington. Class One air priority." The quick tart grin, with a flick of a knuckle across his nose, was a Warren mannerism that gave her a turn. "In the Nouméa NATS terminal I bumped an Australian newspaper editor. He was madder'n hell."

"Why the rush?"

"Beats me."

"Well, there's a whole closet full of your Stateside things."

"Good. I can use whatever's here. That footlocker is empty. Even this outfit is borrowed."

It was her opening to say softly, "I'm sorry about the *Northampton*."

"Was it in the papers?"

"Grapevine." Embarrassed, she hurried on, "How about some breakfast?"

"Well, let me think now." He dropped in a chair, rubbing his eyes. "I could use a hot bath. I've spent three days and nights in NATS planes." His head down on a hand, he spoke in a remote exhausted tone. "The thing is, I'm wanted at Cincpac at two, and my plane takes off at five."

"My Lord, they're pushing you!"

"Where's the baby?"

"Out there." She pointed to french doors opening on a sunlit garden. "He's no baby, though. He's grown like King Kong."

"Jan, suppose I see him, then clean up and rest a bit before I pack? If you'll wake me and just give me some scrambled eggs about noon, we can talk and—what's the matter?"

"Why, nothing. That's just fine."

"Got something else on?"

"No, no, that's just what we'll do."

She picked up the telephone as he went out to the grassy yard. His grandson, in swimming trunks in the blazing sun, was making a coal-black Scottie jump for a red rubber ball. A young Hawaiian girl sat watching the tanned plump child.

"Hi, Vic. Remember me?"

The child turned his head to inspect him, said, "Yes, you're Grandpa," and threw the ball for the dog to chase. He had Warren's eyes and jaw, but his cool response struck Pug as pure Byron.

"You know who has a dog like that, Vic? The President of the United States. What's your doggie's name?"

"Toto."

The dog chased the ball under a clothesline, where Janice's pink two-piece swimsuit dangled beside a man's flower-print trunks. Janice came out in the sunshine, pushing up her thick blonde hair with both hands. "Well, what do you think of him?"

"Perfect physical specimen. Mental giant."

"How unprejudiced. This is Lana." The Hawaiian girl smiled and bobbed her head. "She follows him around, or tries to. Problem about lunch. You remember Lieutenant Commander Aster?"

"Sure."

"We were going on a picnic today. I was making the sandwiches when you arrived. So—"

"Well, just go ahead with it, Jan."

"No, no. I'll call it off. The thing is, his room at the Royal Hawaiian doesn't answer. He may get here while we're eating. That won't matter, will it?"

"Why scrub the picnic?"

"Oh, it couldn't be more casual. We're a five-minute walk from the hotel. You know, SubPac's taken it over. Carter was teaching Vic to swim there yesterday, so sort of to thank him I suggested a picnic, but we can do that any time."

"I see. Well," Victor Henry said, "me for that hot bath."

In the Tulagi hospital cot, and dozing in iron bucket seats on the planes, he had kept dreaming of the *Northampton*. His nap now was broken by such a nightmare. He and Chief Stark were aboard as the ship dizzily heeled up on its beam ends, and black warm water came rushing along the deck, engulfing them to their thighs. The feeling in his dream of being drenched was real and not unpleasant, like settling into a bath. The chief seized a sledgehammer and banged at the brackets that held a life raft, his eyes bulging with terror, and Pug Henry woke with a shudder. The hammering became a knocking at the door. Relieved to find himself dry and in bed, he could not at first recollect how he came to be in this yellow nursery room decorated with animal pictures.

"Dad? Dad? It's a quarter past twelve."

"Thanks, Jan." Memory flooded in. "What about Aster?"

"Come and gone."

He appeared in the yard in a white dress uniform. He was spruce and straight, and his color was better. The clothesline was empty. The Hawaiian girl sat by Vic on the grass as he fed himself yellow mush from a tray, smearing half the stuff on his nose and chin. "Got his appetite back, eh?"

"Oh, yes, long since. Do you mind eating in the kitchen?"

"I'd like it."

They talked haltingly over eggs and sausages. There were so many sore topics—the unknown whereabouts of Natalie, the sinking of the *Northampton,* the uncertainty of Pug's future, above all the death of Warren—that Janice had to force voluble chatter about her job. She was working for the Army. A colonel with the sonorous title of Director of Materials and Supplies Control had met her at a party and pirated her away from Cincpac. Martial law now ruled the territory, and under the jolly surface of Honolulu—the leis, the brass bands, the luaus, and the beautiful scenery—there was a cold tough dictatorship. Her colonel had the newspapers cowed. He and he alone decided how much paper to import, and who would get allotments, so the editors grovelled to him and to the Military Governor. There was no criticism in the editorials. Military tribunals, called "provost courts," had superseded the law, handing out strange verdicts like sentencing offenders to buy war bonds or donate blood.

"It's all more or less benign," she said. "The Army does keep order, and takes good care of us. There's nothing rationed but booze and gas. We eat like lords, and most everybody's happy as a clam, but it's disturbing, when you see its inner workings as I do. It's not America, you know? If we ever get a Stateside dictatorship, God forbid, it'll start as a military emergency measure."

"Mmph," said her father-in-law. His end of this conversation was nothing but such grunts. Perhaps, she thought, he disliked criticism of the military. She was just trying to keep the talk going. The change in him hurt her to see. There was about the quiet man an air of loss, a smell of ash. His accustomed silence now seemed a threadbare cloak against misfortune. Despite his impeccable air and the dogged toughness in the worn face, she pitied him. Once Warren's father had seemed so formidable—this brilliant senior naval officer, this intimate of President Roosevelt who had talked with Churchill, with Hitler, with Stalin . . . how he had dwindled! He looked all right. He was eating. His core of strong energy showed in this bounce back after a short nap. He was a hard nut to crack, but he was being squeezed hard. So his daughter-in-law thought, without knowing anything of the betrayal by his wife.

Over coffee, she showed him Rhoda's latest letter, hoping the warm sprightly run of chitchat would cheer him up. Rhoda had taken to church work; details of this, and some Navy gossip, filled three sheets. A postscript mentioned that Madeline's movie job had fizzled out, and that she had returned to New York to work for Hugh Cleveland.

Pug's face darkened over the letter. "Damned idiot of a girl."

"I thought you'd be pleased about Madeline. Hollywood's such a sinkhole."

He threw the letter on the table. "Incidentally, what's that canal out in front of your house?"

"The Ala Wai Canal. It runs down to the yacht harbor."

"Got trouble with mosquitoes?"

"You would think of that. I didn't. Monsters, by the millions."

"Rhoda and I have rented a lot of tropical houses. You learn."

"Well, I got it for a steal. A fighter pilot from the *Yorktown* had it. His wife went home after—" Janice's voice wavered. "Actually, Toto was their dog."

"You don't want to go home?"

"No, I feel I'm in the war here. When you and Byron come back, here I'll be. You'll both have a place near the beach. Vic will get to know you."

"Well, that'll be nice for Byron." Pug cleared his throat. "About me, I dunno. I'd guess I've had my shot at the blue water."

"But why? That's not fair."

Again the quick acid grin. "Why not? The parade moves fast in wartime. You lose step once, you drop to the sidelines. I can make myself useful in BuOrd or BuShips." He drank coffee, and spoke on thoughtfully. "My judgments under fire may be questioned at Cincpac today. I just don't know. Our loss of life was small. Still, my portfolio contains fifty-eight letters I've written to next of kin. That's how I passed the time, flying here. I regret every man we lost, but we took two torpedoes in a running gun battle, and that was it. I'll be moseying along. Thanks for lunch."

"Let me drive you to Cincpac."

"I cadged a Navy car." He went into the bedroom and brought out the footlocker and portfolio, carrying over his arm a heavy brass-buttoned blue coat that smelled of camphor. "You know, I started out for Moscow over a year ago in this coat, going the other way. It's circling the world." Halting before Warren's picture, he briefly looked at it, then at her. "Say, tell me about Lieutenant Commander Aster."

"Carter? Oh, he's becoming one of the famous submarine skippers. The *Devilfish* sank twenty thousand tons under his command. Now he's putting a new fleet sub in commission, the *Moray*. In fact, he's gotten orders for Byron to the *Moray*."

"Then what's Aster doing here? New construction's in the States."

"There's a flap with BuOrd about some radar he wants. He flew here to twist arms at SubPac. Carter doesn't fool around."

"What's the fellow like? I've never quite figured him out."

"Neither have I. But he's nice to Vic and to me."

"Do you like him? Not that it's my business."

"Yes, it is." Her jaw was set, her eyes faraway and clouded. Pug Henry had seen this sort of look on her face often after Midway.

"You're asking me if it's serious, aren't you? No. I'm not interested in becoming widowed twice in one war."

"He'll be rotated to the beach after a year or so."

"Oh, no!" She spoke with swift flat assurance. "ComSubPac sends the high-scoring skippers back out as often as they'll go. I'm sort of sorry Byron's been ordered to the *Moray*. No doubt he'll love it, but Carter's too adventurous for me. Vic and I swim with him, and every now and then he takes me dancing. I'm the widow lady, the backup date when there's no hotter action." Her crooked-tooth smile was wryly pretty. "Okay?"

"Okay. Does Aster have any word on when Byron's due back?"

"Not that I know of."

"Well, I'll take my leave of the senior officer present."

Vic slept on a spread-out blanket in the shade, still holding the red ball, with the dog curled at his feet. It was very hot. Lana drooped dozing over her magazine, and the child was perspiring. Victor Henry contemplated him for perhaps a minute. Glancing at Janice, he saw her eyes glittering with unshed tears. A look like a long conversation passed between them.

"I'll miss you," she said, walking out with him to a gray Navy sedan. "Give my love to my folks. Tell them that I'm all right, will you?"

"I'll do that." He got in and closed the car door, whereupon she tapped on the glass. He rolled down the window. "Yes?"

"And if you see Byron, tell him to write. I treasure his letters."

"I will."

He drove off, never having mentioned Warren. It didn't surprise her. Since the Battle of Midway, the name of his dead son had not once, in her presence, passed his lips.

Pug had no notion of what to expect at Cincpac. At three that morning, in mid-flight, the co-pilot had brought him a scrawled dispatch: PASSENGER VICTOR (NONE) HENRY CAPTAIN USN REPORT CINCPAC DUTY OFFICER 1400. In the red beam of the flashlight the words had looked ominous. A favorite saw of Pug's had once been, "I've had a lot of troubles in my life, and most of them never happened," but this incantation had lately lost its force.

The new gleaming white Cincpac building, high on Makalapa Hill above the submarine base, showed the way the war was going. It had been built fast, it was a work of power and wealth, and the lanais encircling the upper stories were sophisticated adaptations to the tropics.

Inside, the building still smelled of fresh plaster, paint, and linoleum. The thronging staff—officers sporting aiguillettes, enlisted men in whites, and many pretty Waves—had a sprightly look and walk. Midway and Guadalcanal, and the bristling array of new warships in the Yard, all showed in that bouncy new pace. It was not a change to triumph or even to optimism yet. Rather, the open confident look of Americans at work had come back. Gone were the stricken expressions of the days following Pearl Harbor, and the driven tension of the months before Midway.

Ensconced in the glass-partitioned cubicle of the duty officer, inside a bastion of junior officers and Waves, sat the youngest three-striper Victor Henry had ever laid eyes on, with lanky blond hair and a creamy face that appeared never to have been shaved. "A full commander," thought Pug, "and the Cincpac duty officer? I'm really out of step."

"My name is Victor Henry."

"Oh, Captain *Victor Henry!* Yes, sir." In the inquisitive eyes, at the utterance of that name, Pug could see the burning *Northampton* going down. "Please have a seat." The fellow gestured at a wooden chair and pressed an intercom button. "Stanton? Find out if the chief of staff is available. It's Captain Victor Henry."

So Spruance would be the interrogator. A tough man to face; old acquaintance would count for exactly zero. Soon the intercom gabbled, and the duty officer said, "Sir, Vice Admiral Spruance is in conference. Please wait."

While sailors and Waves scurried to and fro, and the duty officer answered the telephone, made calls, and scrawled in a log book, Victor Henry sat reviewing possible lines of questioning. If Spruance was taking time to see him, the battle had to be the topic. The duty officer's commiserating peeps at him were like wasp stings. So a very long half hour went by before Spruance summoned him. Pug remembered into old age the narrow girl-smooth face of the duty officer, the furtive pitying glances, and the tension of that wait.

Spruance was signing letters at a stand-up desk by a window. "Hello, Pug. Just a minute," he said. He had never used Henry's first name before; he addressed almost nobody that way. Spruance looked trim in starched khakis: face gaunt, color high, waist board-flat. Again Pug thought, as he had so many times, how ordinary this victor of Midway looked and acted, compared to Halsey with his battering-ram jaw, glaring eye, bushy brows, and imperious or rollicking humors.

"Well, now." Carefully inserting the pen in a holder, Spruance faced him, hands on hips. "What the Sam Hill happened out there off Tassafaronga?"

"I know what happened to me, Admiral. The rest is sort of a blur." The truthful words were scarcely out of his mouth when he regretted them. Wrong tone of levity.

"You're to be commended on the *Northampton*'s small loss of life."

"It's nothing I ever hoped to be commended for."

"We're going to be able to repair those other three CAs."

"Good. I wish I could have made port, too, Admiral. I tried."

"What went wrong in the battle, exactly?"

"Sir, we found ourselves in torpedo water after we'd opened fire at twelve thousand yards. That was supposed to be beyond torpedo range. Now, either we were ambushed by submarines—which seems unlikely in view of our sizable destroyer screen—or else the Japs have a destroyer torpedo that far outranges ours. We've had intelligence about such a weapon."

"I recall your memo to BuShips about that, and your recommendation on the battleship blisters."

Victor Henry allowed himself a short thankful smile. "Well, Admiral, now I've been on the business end of a couple of those things. They exist."

"Then combat doctrine should be modified accordingly." The large eyes scrutinized Pug. The stand-up desk served the purpose of keeping conversations short, Pug thought. He was making an effort not to shift from foot to foot, and he decided, if ever his time became valuable again, to have a stand-up desk, too. "A word with Admiral Nimitz might be in order," Spruance said. "Let's go."

Hurrying to keep up, Victor Henry followed Spruance down the corridor to tall royal-blue double doors with four affixed gold stars. Admiral Kimmel had received him in such an office in the old building, he remembered, all brave smiles and good humor, as his blasted fleet smoked in the sunshine beyond the windows. Pug had walked in to see Kimmel with calm confidence. He felt very shaky now. Why? He was now more or less in Kimmel's shoes, that was why. Another loser.

They went straight in. Nimitz stood alone, arms folded, at a window. To all appearances he was sunning himself. His handshake was cordial, his square tanned face pleasant; but the direct blue eyes under the thatch of sunlit white hair had a slaty look. That kindly, almost gentle face with those hard eyes, half in sunshine and half in shadow, made Victor Henry yet more nervous.

"Captain Henry says the Japs have a destroyer torpedo of very long range," Spruance said. "That's how he explains Tassafaronga."

"How long is very long?" Nimitz asked Pug.

"Possibly as much as twenty thousand yards, Admiral."

"What do we do about it?"

Forcing words through a tight throat, Pug replied, "In future engagements, Admiral, once our destroyers have made their torpedo attack, the battle line should open fire at much longer range, and make radical evasive turns during the action."

"Did you make radical evasive turns after you saw the other CAs get hit?" Nimitz spoke in an easy Texas-tinged drawl, but there was nothing easy in his look or manner.

"No, sir."

"Why didn't you?"

Victor Henry now had to answer, face to face with Cincpac, the question on which his career hung. He had already tried to handle this question in a fifteen-page action report.

"Admiral, it was a mistake made in the heat of battle. All my guns were bearing. I was straddling the enemy. I wanted vengeance for the three cruisers he had set afire."

"Did you get your vengeance?"

"I don't know. My gunnery officer claimed two hits on two cruisers."

"Confirmed?"

"No, sir. We'll have to await the task force report. Even then I'll have my doubts. Gunnery officers are troubled with creative eyesight."

Nimitz's eyes glinted at Spruance. "Any other observations?"

"I've listed a few in my report, sir."

"For example?"

"Admiral, flashless powder was a BuOrd project way back in '37 when I was there. We still don't have it. The enemy does. We discourage use of searchlights in night action, so as not to show where we are. Then we fire a few salvos and disclose our bearing, target angle, and speed of advance. Our battle line that night looked like four erupting volcanoes. It was a glorious sight, sir, very soul-satisfying. It also gave the Japs their torpedo solution."

Nimitz turned to Spruance. "Get off a dispatch to BuOrd today, and a personal follow-up letter to Spike Blandy on the flashless powder."

"Yes, sir."

Rubbing a stringy hand, which was missing a finger, across his square chin, Nimitz said, "Why the devil was our own destroyer attack a total failure? They achieved surprise with radar, didn't they? They had the drop on the other fellow."

Pug felt himself—so to say—back in torpedo water. This question might well become the crux of a court of inquiry on Tassafaronga. "Admiral, it was a reverse action, forces moving on opposed courses. Relative closing speed fifty knots or better. The torpedo problem developed very fast. When the destroyer commander requested permission to attack with torpedoes, Admiral Wright preferred to close first. The enemy was abaft the beam before he let him go. So it became an up-the-kilt shot at extreme range. That's how it looked in the *Northampton* plot."

"Yet the enemy had the identical problem, and he got an excellent solution."

"They won the torpedo duel hands down, Admiral."

After an excruciating pause Nimitz said, "Very well." He moved away from the window and offered Pug his hand. "I understand you lost an aviator son at Midway, who distinguished himself in combat. And that you've got another son serving in submarines." He bent his head toward the dolphins on his own khaki blouse.

"Yes, Admiral."

Holding Pug's hand in a lingering clasp, looking deep in his eyes, Chester Nimitz said, "Good luck, Henry," in a sad personal tone.

"Thank you, sir."

Spruance took him to the crowded smoky operations room. "There's your battle," he said, pointing to a heavily marked chart of Guadalcanal on the wall, "as we've reconstructed it." They passed into a small anteroom, where they sat down together on a sofa. "The *Northampton* was a beautiful ship," Spruance said. "But there were stability problems."

"I can't fault my damage control people, Admiral. We were unlucky. We took two torpedoes aft of the armor belt. I should have turned away. Gotten the hell out of there, the way the *Honolulu* did. Maybe I'd still have my ship."

"Well, the rage of battle is a factor. Your blood was up. You tried to reverse a rout."

Victor Henry made no comment, but it was as though Spruance had cut ropes holding a heavy burden on his back. He took a deep breath and audibly sighed.

Spruance went on, "Where to next?"

"I have orders back to BuPers for reassignment, Admiral."

"Last time around you were fighting shy of staff duty. I need a deputy chief of staff for planning and operations."

Unable to help it, Victor Henry blurted like a boy, "Me?"

"If you're interested."

"Good God." Pug involuntarily put a hand to his eyes. In the light of the huge growth of the Pacific Fleet, Spruance was offering him a golden prize; a long leap toward flag rank, toward responsibility on the scale of great men; precisely the second chance he had told Janice he could not expect. Victor Henry was not three weeks away from splashing naked through black oil toward a crowded raft, with his ship afire and sinking behind him. After a moment he said hoarsely, "You've achieved surprise, Admiral. I'm interested."

"Well, let's hope BuPers will go along. We've got some fine battle problems ahead, Pug. You should start thinking about them. Come."

Dazed, Victor Henry followed Spruance back into the operations room, to a large yellow and blue table chart of the Pacific. Spruance began to talk with a curious enthusiasm, half-pedantic and half-martial. "At the College, did you get in on the old problem, the recapture of the Philippines after Orange invades and occupies? That's more or less the war we've got."

"No, sir, in my tour we did the Wake Island problem."

"Oh, yes. Well, the thing boils down to two lines of attack. The geography dictates that. A drive across the Central Pacific, reducing the Jap island strong points, and consolidating in the Marianas for the jump to Luzon." Spruance's right hand moved over the chart as he talked, traversing thousands of ocean miles to pantomime a sweep through the Marshalls, the Marianas, and the Carolines to the Philippines.

"And a campaign northward from Australia—New Guinea, Morotai, Mindanao, Luzon." His left hand passed from Australia across New Guinea, with the fingers doing a slow crawl as though to suggest—as they vividly did to Pug—armies slogging over tropical mountains. "General MacArthur naturally is hot for that second strategy. Land fighter. But in the water route you've got a mobile flank attack on the enemy supply lines that keeps him guessing. He can't be sure where you'll hop next. Makes him scatter his strength. The other is a frontal assault overland through mountainous jungle. Jap fleet on *your* flank, alert Jap armies opposing you." Spruance shot Pug a puckish look. "To be sure, the general would strongly desire to lick some Jap armies."

Spruance's right index finger now stabbed at an island off New Guinea. "Still, even he concedes that the way is barred by Rabaul. That's what he saw in the Guadalcanal operation, a stepping-stone toward Rabaul. In any case, we're tooling up here for the Central Pacific. It'll be a big effort. Meantime MacArthur will pursue his drive, of course."

For Victor Henry, still shaken by this turn in his life, the unfolding horizons were magnificent. From command of a cruiser, a cramping task, he foresaw passing to the planning of gigantic sea campaigns. Ideas boiled up in his mind from War College problems and studies of Pacific war. Thin abstractions they had then seemed, algebraic toying with forces and situations that would never exist. Now they were materializing in thick and flaming realities. There surged in him a reviving sense of global combat as his own job to do, in an anonymous slot; all he could ask for.

Spruance tapped the chart at Guadalcanal. "You know, Tassafaronga was a pretty sour note for Admiral Halsey, after the magnificent way he turned that campaign around. Did you see him at all?"

"Yes, sir, when I passed through Nouméa he sent for me."

"How is he?"

"On top of the world. He's got everybody in SoPac on their toes, I'll say that. When I got to his office he was roaring mad about something or other. Everybody in sight was quailing. Next minute with me he was gentle as a parson. Very sympathetic about the *Northampton*." Pug hesitated and added, "Said at least I went after the bastards."

"How is Warren's wife?"

"I've just seen her." Pug's voice roughened. "She's all right. She's working for the Military Government."

"What about your submariner's wife? Did she ever get out of Europe?"

"I'm hoping there'll be news of her at home, sir."

"Warren was an outstanding fighting man." Spruance shook hands. "I'll never forget him."

Victor Henry said abruptly, "Thank you, Admiral," and he left. It was less than an hour to his plane time. He turned in the car at the pool office, and caught a cab to the NATS terminal. There, at a small newsstand inside the shed, he picked up a *Honolulu Advertiser*, not having read a newspaper in months. Banner headlines bawled of Allied breakthroughs in Morocco, the flight of Rommel, the encirclement of the Germans at Stalingrad. These things he had seen, put in less bubbling terms, on the Cincpac teletype board. Lower on the page a smaller headline hit him like a blow in the face.

ALISTAIR TUDSBURY
KILLED AT EL ALAMEIN

49

ALISTAIR TUDSBURY'S sixty-year-old secretary put her white head in through the doorway. "A Mr. Leslie Slote is here, Pamela."

In the tiny old office on Pall Mall, Pamela sat in her father's big swivel chair, crying. A cold wind was rattling the loose windows, purple with December gloom at midday. Even bundled in her gray lambskin coat, with a wool shawl tied over her head and ears, she was chilled. The ancient oil heater was having little effect in the room; the place smelled hot, so to say, but no more.

Dabbing her eyes with both hands, Pamela jumped up as Slote came in. He carried a Russian fur-lined greatcoat and a big brown fur hat. He had always been lean, but now his pinstripe suit hung in folds on him, and his eyes burned redly in black sockets.

"Hello, Leslie."

"I'm very sorry about your father, Pam."

"I wasn't weeping over his death. I'm used to that. What brings you to London? Are you finished in Bern so soon? Will some whiskey warm you up?"

"God, it'll save me."

She pointed at a typescript on the desk. "That's the last thing he wrote. He didn't quite finish it. The *Observer* wants it. I'm winding it up, and I'm afraid it brought on the tears."

"What is it? A news dispatch?"

"Oh, no, that would be dead as mutton. It's a battlefield sketch. He called it 'Sunset on Kidney Ridge.'" She handed him half a tumbler of neat whiskey, and gestured with another. "Cheers. He was dictating it, actually, when Monty's press chap rang to say that the interview was on."

Pamela's careworn countenance, the swollen eyes, the slipshod hair, the flat voice, could be ascribed to grief, Slote was thinking, but she seemed altogether quenched. At her lowest in other days—and Pamela had been very low—she had not lost a certain defiant sparkle, an enticing bravura beneath the quiet surface. Slote was looking now at a dull sad woman past thirty.

"Do you believe in presentiments?" Her voice was hoarse from the whiskey.

"I'm not sure. Why?"

"Talky had one. I know. I was supposed to go in that jeep. I'd even been cleared by Montgomery's press chap, quite a break for a female. Talky suddenly, mulishly, bumped me. He was downright nasty about it, and I got nasty too. We parted in anger, and that's why I'm alive, sitting here now, drinking with you." She raised her glass sadly, and drained it. "I'm an utter skeptic, Leslie, I believe only in things you can see and hear and measure, and all that. Still, he knew. Don't ask me how. Hitting a land mine is a random accident, I realize, yet he knew. That piece on Kidney Ridge is a deathbed sort of thing."

"You remember Byron Henry?" Slote asked.

"Why, of course."

"I met him in Lisbon last week. I fear there's more bad news. The *Northampton*'s gone down." Slote had been looking forward with sour relish, of which he was slightly ashamed, to making this disclosure. Not that he wished her ill, or Victor Henry either, but in their romance he had briefly figured as a feeble also-ran, and the bad taste lingered. She showed no emotion. "You're very well connected here, Pam, aren't you? Can you find out whether Captain Henry survived, and cable Byron? The only word he could get in Lisbon, from some Navy people there, was that the ship was sunk in battle."

"What about your naval attaché here?"

"He's off in Scotland."

"All right," she said briskly, almost gaily, "let's find out about Captain Henry." It was a peculiar reaction to grave news, Slote thought; mighty peculiar. Merely talking about the man animated her. She told the secretary to call Air Vice Marshal Burne-Wilke. "Well! And what news about Byron? And Natalie?"

"He found her. Found her, and the baby."

"I'll be damned. *Found* her! Where?"

"In Marseilles. Told me about it for two hours over dinner. It's a saga."

"Honestly, that family! How did he do it? Where's Natalie now?"

Slote had just started on Byron's tale when the telephone rang. It was Burne-Wilke. Pamela told him about Pug Henry and Byron in a quick affectionate way, calling him "darling." She hung up and said to Slote,

"They have a direct line through to Washington. He'll get on it as soon as he can. Have you ever met my fiancé?"

"Once. On a receiving line at your embassy in Washington. You were there, but he wasn't your fiancé then."

"Oh, of course. And Captain Henry was there, and Natalie, too. Now go on with what happened in Marseilles. More whiskey?"

"Absolutely, if you can spare it."

"People have been kind. I've bottles and bottles."

Slote told the story of the encounter at some length, and said Byron was still trying to learn his family's fate. On the day the Allies had invaded North Africa, the telephone lines to Marseilles had shut down. Intermittent contact had since been restored, with long delays, but none of his calls had gone through. He had thirty days' leave, and he was spending them hanging around the rescue agencies' offices in Lisbon.

"What on earth came over Natalie to balk like that? I don't blame Byron for being furious," Pamela said.

Slote stared at her. Blankly he repeated, "What came over her?"

"Leslie, that's the girl who climbed up to your second-story window on the rue Scribe, when you lost your latch key. Remember? Remember how she faced down the gendarmes in Les Halles, when I cracked Phil's head open with a soup bowl? The lioness, we called her."

"What's all that got to do with it? She'd have been insane to try to run the border with Byron."

"Why? He had his diplomatic pass. How could she be worse off than she is now?"

The eyes in the dark sockets luridly flared. Slote looked to Pamela as though he were running a high temperature. He replied with soft exaggerated calm, "Why, sweetheart, I'll try to tell you exactly how much worse off she could be. Can I have just a tot more of your firewater?"

He pulled a pen from his breast pocket, and while she poured, he sat down at her desk and began to sketch on a yellow sheet. "Look, this is prewar Poland. All right? Warsaw to the north, Cracow to the south, Vistula connecting them." It was a skilled rough map, drawn as quickly as the hand could move. "Hitler invades. He and Stalin partition the country. Zip! To the west of this line is German-held Poland. The Government General." The irregular stroke cut Poland in two. Slote drew three heavy ink circles on the western side. "Now, you've heard about concentration camps."

"Yes, I have, Leslie."

"You haven't heard of these. I've just spent four days talking to Polish government-in-exile people here. That's actually why I came to London. Pam, this is quite a news story. You're carrying on your father's work, aren't you?"

"Trying to."

"Well, this may prove the biggest story of the war. The reporter who breaks it will have a place in history. In these three places—there are more, but the Polish government-in-exile has eyewitness accounts on these right here in London—the Germans are exterminating human beings like rats, in multitudes. They ship them here from all over Europe in trains. It's a massacre by railroad. When the Jews arrive, the Germans kill them with carbon monoxide or rifle squads, and they burn up the bodies." The pen darted from circle to circle. "This place is called Treblinka. This one is Lublin. This is Oswiecim. As I say, there are more, but on these there is *proof*."

"Leslie, concentration camps aren't news. We've had these stories for years."

Slote gave her a ghastly smile. "You don't grasp what I'm saying." He achieved emphasis by dropping his voice to a grinding whisper. "I'm talking about the *systematic execution of eleven million people. It's well under way as you and I are talking.* A fantastic plan, a gargantuan secret operation with vast facilities built to carry it out! You don't call that a story? What is a news story then? This is the most enormous crime in the history of the human race. It dwarfs all wars that have ever been fought. It's a new aspect of life on this planet. And it's *happening*. It's about half-accomplished right now. Isn't that a news story, Pamela?"

Pamela had read stories of gassing chambers and of mass rifle slayings. There was nothing new about any of it. Of course, the Gestapo was a gang of monstrous thugs. The war was worth fighting, just to rid the world of them. The plan to wipe out all the Jews of Europe was naturally a morbid exaggeration, but she had read of this, too. Somebody obviously had sold the whole package to Slote; and, perhaps because his career was going badly, or because he had never gotten over Natalie, and was now having guilt feelings about having jilted a Jewess he adored, he had fastened on this thing. She murmured, "It's quite beyond me to handle, dear."

"Well, I don't think so, but we were discussing Natalie. Refusing Byron took amazing guts, a hell of a lot more than climbing to a second-story window. She didn't have her exit visas. The Gestapo swarms on those trains. If there'd been a snag, they'd have taken her and her baby off the train. Then they might have put her in a camp. Then they might have put her on another train going east. Then they might have murdered her and her baby, and burned them to ashes. Now that was a bad risk, Pam, and if she didn't know the details she sensed that in her bones. She knew that exit visas were coming. She knew the Germans have a lunatic respect for official paper, it's the one talisman that restrains them. She did the right thing. When I tried to tell Byron that, he turned white with rage, and—"

The telephone was ringing. She made an apologetic silencing gesture. "Hello? What, so *quickly?*" Her eyes opened enormously, and went brilliant as jewels. She nodded hard at Slote. "Well! Marvelous. Thank you, thank you, dearest. See you at eight." She hung up, and smiled radiantly at Slote. "Captain Henry's all right! You know, getting that information out of our Admiralty would have taken a week. Your War Department put Duncan through to Navy Personnel, and he had the answer almost at once. Captain Henry is on his way back to Washington. Shall I cable Byron, or will you?"

"Here's his address in Lisbon, Pam. You do it." Slote hastily scrawled in a notebook and tore out the sheet. "And look, the Poles here are amassing a book of their documents. I can get you the galley proofs. What's more, they've got a man who escaped from Treblinka, this camp up here"—a skinny finger jabbed at the sketch on the desk—"near Warsaw. He made his way clear across Nazi Europe on sheer nerve, just to bring photographs and tell the story. I've spoken to him through interpreters. It's impossible not to believe him. His story is an Odyssey. A terrific scoop, Pamela."

Pam was finding it hard to pay attention. *Pug Henry alive and safe! Returning to Washington!* This put a new light on her plans, on her life. As for Slote's "scoop," he seemed to her more than a bit obsessed. She could almost hear her father saying, *"No chance. None whatever. Old stuff."* The new stuff was victory—victory in North Africa, in Russia, in the Pacific; victory too against the U-boats, after four years of catastrophe, the true great turn of the war. That the Germans were terrorizing Europe and maltreating the Jews was as familiar as the tide tables.

"Leslie, I'll talk to my editor-in-chief tomorrow."

Slote thrust an emaciated hand straight at her. The palm was wet, the grip loose. "Splendid! I'll be here two more days. Call me either at the Dorchester or the American embassy, extension 739." As he put on his fur coat and cap, the old Paris smile lit the gaunt face and haunted eyes. "Thank you for the booze, old girl, and for listening to the Ancient Mariner."

He stumbled out.

The editor-in-chief listened to her next day in a bored slump, gnawing at his cold pipe, nodding and grunting. The Polish government-in-exile, he said, had long since offered him all this material. He had run some pieces. She could see these in the files, standard propaganda stuff. By any journalistic standards the stories could not be verified. The business about the plan to kill all the Jews was coming from Zionist sources, to pressure Whitehall into opening up Palestine for Jewish immigration. Still, he would be willing to see Mr. Slote next week. Oh, the man was leaving tomorrow? Too bad.

But when she offered to go to Washington and write some stories on the war effort there, he brightened. "Well, why not? Do try your hand, Pam. We know you were drafting Talky's copy toward the last. When will you let us have 'Sunset on Kidney Ridge'? We're frightfully anxious for it."

Slote knew of two Foreign Service officers who had disappeared on ferry command bomber flights between Scotland and Montreal. The North Atlantic sky was not the route of choice, certainly not in midwinter. Big comfortable airliners flew the southern route—down to Dakar, a hop across sunny seas to the bulge of Brazil, then north to Bermuda and so on to Baltimore. But that was for big shots. The choices offered him were a ten-day voyage in a convoy, or an RAF ferry command trip.

On the train to the Scottish airport, he fell in with an American ferry pilot going the same way: a wiry middle-sized Army Air Corps captain with a toothbrush mustache, a wild eye, three banks of ribbons on his khaki tunic, a richly obscene vocabulary, and a great store of flying stories. The two men had a compartment to themselves. The ferry pilot kept nipping brandy, explaining that he was getting plastered and intended to stay plastered until they were well off the Prestwick runway. Crashing on takeoff was a hazard at Prestwick. He had attended two mass funerals of pilots who had died on the runway. Dangerous overloads of gasoline had to be accepted, when you were flying westward into North Atlantic gales. The ferry command had to keep hauling pilots back, because shipping disassembled aircraft by sea was slow and cumbersome, and the U-boats got too many of them. It was the ferry pilots who were really building up the Allied air forces in the war zones.

Nobody gave a shit about them, but they were the key to the whole war.

As the old dusty train clanked its slow way through snowy fields, the pilot regaled Slote with his autobiography. His name was Bill Fenton. A barnstormer before the war, he had since 1937 been doing various flying jobs, civilian and military, for various governments. He had flown cargo carriers on the India-China run ("over the hump," he called it); taking off from a runway that had to be cleared of cows and water buffalo by a honking jeep, then climbing five miles and more to get over icy storms that whirled higher than Everest. He had joined the Royal Canadian Air Force to ferry planes to England. Now he was flying bombers for the Army Air Corps via South America to Africa, and on across to Persia and the Soviet Union. He had crash-landed in the desert. He had floated for two days in the Irish Sea on a rubber raft. He had parachuted into Japanese-held territory in Burma, and walked out to India on foot.

By the time they reached Prestwick in a snowstorm, Slote was not only tired, sleepy, and drunk from his share of Bill Fenton's brandy; he had a whole new vision of the war. In his fumed brain pictures reeled of aircraft crisscrossing the globe—bombers, fighters, transports, by the thousands—battling the weather and the enemy, bombing cities, railroads, and troop columns; crossing oceans, deserts, high mountain ranges; a war such as Thucydides had never imagined, filling the skies of the planet with hurtling machines manned by hordes of Bill Fentons. He had not until now given the war in the air a thought. For once, the everlasting Wannsee Protocol, the map of Poland with the three black circles, and the European trains carrying hundreds of thousands of Jews each month to their deaths faded from his mind. He was moreover so scared at the prospect of the flight that he could hardly walk off the train.

When they arrived at the airfield the plane was warming up. Waddling out of the check-in office in cumbersome flying suits, heavy gloves, and life vests, with parachutes dangling behind their knees, they could not at first see the aircraft through the falling snow. Fenton led him toward the motor sound. It was inconceivable to Leslie Slote that a machine could take off in this weather. Inside the four-engine bomber there were no seats. On the board floor about a dozen returning ferry pilots sprawled on pallets. Slote's armpits coldly dripped and his heart raced as the plane heavily took off. Fenton screamed into his ears, over the engine roar and the groan of retracting wheels, that the weather briefing predicted head winds of a hundred miles an hour. They might well have to put down in Greenland, the asshole of the Arctic.

Leslie Slote was a coward. He knew it. He had given up fighting it. Even riding in a car with a fast driver gave him bad nerves. Every airplane ride, just a one-hour hop in a DC-3, was an ordeal. This man now found himself in a stripped-down four-engine bomber, setting out to cross the Atlantic westward in December; a howling rattletrap that sucked in the cold through whining and whistling air leaks, climbed through hail that made a machine gun racket on the fuselage, and bucked, dipped, and swerved like a kite. Slote could see, in dim light from iced-up windows, the greenish faces of the sprawled pilots, the sweat-beaded foreheads, the shaking hands bringing cigarettes or bottles to tight mouths. The fliers looked fully as terrified as he felt.

Fenton had explained on the train that the North Atlantic head winds were strongest at low altitudes. Planes flew high to climb over the weather and conserve fuel in the thinner air; but up there they could accumulate ice too fast for the de-icers to work. Also, the carburetors could get chilled from pulling in subzero air, and they could ice up. Then the engines would quit. That no doubt was the way so many planes vanished. When ice began to build up you could keep trying to climb above the wet cold into the dry cold, where one needed an oxygen mask to survive. Otherwise you had to drop back down fast, maybe down to the wave tops, where warmer air would melt your ice. Against his better judgment, Slote had asked him, "Can't the icing conditions prevail right down to the water?"

"Hell, yes," Fenton had answered. "Let me tell you what happened to me." And he had launched into a long hideous anecdote about a near-spin into the water off Newfoundland under a heavy ice load.

The plane kept climbing and climbing; loose things persisted in sliding toward the rear. Some pilots huddled under ragged blankets and snored. Fenton too stretched out and closed his eyes. A sudden metallic crashing and banging along the fuselage stopped Slote's heart, or so he felt. Fenton blinked, grinned at Slote, and pantomimed ice forming along the wings, and rubber de-icers cracking it off.

Slote wondered how anybody could sleep in this howling torture chamber in the sky, hammered at by breaking ice. He could as soon sleep, he thought, nailed to a cross. His nose was freezing. There was no sensation in his hands or feet. Yet he did doze, for a nasty sensation woke him: a smell of rubber, a cold thing pressed to his face as in anesthesia. He opened his eyes in the dark. Fenton's voice yelled in his ear,

"Oxygen." Somebody lit a dim battery lamp. A shadowy figure was stumbling here and there with masks that trailed long rubber tubes. Slote thought he had never been so cold, so numb, so sick all over, so ready to die and get it over with.

All at once the plane dived, roaring. The pilots sat up and looked about with white-rimmed eyes. It was an obscure comfort in Slote's agony that these skilled men were so scared, too. After a horrendously steep long dive, ice crashed along the fuselage once more. The floor levelled off.

"Never make Newfoundland," Fenton yelled in Slote's ear. "Greenland it is."

*   *   *

Ven Der Fuehrer says,
"Ve iss der Master Race,"
Ve Heil (phfft!)
Heil (phfft!)
Right in Der Fuehrer's face.

In the wooden barracks beside the Greenland runway, this song was grinding out of the phonograph, hour after hour. It was the only record on hand. The airfield, a treeless spread of steel netting sunk into mud and drifted over with snow, was a drearier place than Slote had imagined could exist on earth. The runway was short and chancy, so the refueled aircraft had to wait for endurable takeoff conditions.

Not to luff Der Fuehrer
Iss a great disgrace
So ve Heil (phfft!)
Heil (phfft!)
Right in Der Fuehrer's face.

Here in this witless ditty, Slote thought, was the fatally soft American idea of Hitler and the Nazis—the ranting boob, the dumbbell followers, the *heils* and the razzes. The musical arrangement mixed various funny noises—cowbells, toy trumpets, tin cans—with the oom-pahs of a German band. The pilots were playing cards or lolling about, and when the record ended somebody simply moved the needle back to the start.

Fenton lay on the bunk underneath Slote's, leafing a girlie magazine. Slote leaned over and asked him what he thought of "Der Fuehrer's

Face." Fenton yawned that it was getting to be a pain in the ass. Climbing down, Slote sat beside the captain and unburdened himself about the massacre of the Jews, bitterly observing that when a song like that could amuse people, it was small wonder that nobody believed what was happening.

Turning the pages of naked females, Bill Fenton calmly remarked, "Shit, man, who doesn't believe it? *I* believe it. Those Germans have to be weird people, to follow a nut like Hitler. Some of them are fine aviators, but taken as a nation they're a menace."

> *Ven Herr Goebbels says,*
> *"Ve own de Vorld und Space,"*
> *Ve Heil (phfft!)*
> *Heil (phfft!)*
> *Right in Herr Goebbels' face.*

> *Ven Herr Goering says,*
> *"Dey'll neffer bomb dis place,"*
> *Ve Heil (phfft!)*
> *Heil (phfft!)*
> *Right in Herr Goering's face . . .*

"But what can anybody do about the Jews?" Fenton tossed the magazine aside, stretching and yawning. "Fifty million people will die before this war's over. The Japs have been fighting the Chinese since 1937. Do you know how many Chinese have starved to death? Nobody does. Maybe ten million. Maybe more. You ever been to India? There's a powder keg. The British can't keep the lid on much longer. When India blows, you're going to see Hindus and Sikhs and Moslems and Buddhists and Parsees cutting each other's throats till hell won't have it. The Germans have killed a lot more Russians than Jews. This world is a slaughterhouse, man, it always has been, and that's what all these fucking pacifists keep forgetting."

> *Iss ve not der Supermen?*
> *Aryan pure, Supermen?*
> *Yah! ve iss der Supermen*
> *Sooper DOOPER Supermen!*

Fenton enjoyed the sound of his own voice, and he was getting worked up. He sat erect and poked Slote on the shoulder. "Tell me this.

Is Stalin any better than Hitler? I say he's the same kind of murderer. Yet we're flying half of the bombers we're producing over to him—free, gratis, and for nothing, and some damn good pilots are getting killed at it, and I'm risking my own ass. And why? Because he's *our* murderer, that's why. We're not doing it for humanity, or for Russia, or for anything except to save our own asses. Christ, *I* feel sorry for the Jews, don't think I don't, but there just isn't a thing we can do about them but beat the shit out of the Germans."

> So ve Heil (*phfft!*)
> Heil (*phfft!*)
> Right . . . in . . . Der . . . Fuehrer's . . . face.

. . .

At the enormous Canadian Air Force Base outside Montreal, Slote telephoned the Division of European Affairs, and the division chief told him to hurry along to the Montreal airport and catch the first plane to New York or Washington. While this was going on, Fenton passed the telephone booth. A tall pretty girl in a red fox coat was clinging to his arm, hips rolling with each step, devouring the pilot with lustrous green eyes. A casual wave with his smoking cigar at the booth, a man-to-man grin, and the ferry pilot passed from view. A short life and a merry one, thought Slote, with a flicker of rueful envy.

To his pleased surprise, Slote found that he did not mind the takeoff of the DC-3, or the bumpy climb through heavy clouds. The airliner seemed so huge, the interior so luxurious, the seat so broad and soft, the stewardess so entrancing, that it was more like being on the *Queen Mary* than on something flying through the air. He could not tell whether the bomber ride had cauterized, as it were, his fear of flying, or whether he just had no nerves left, and was on the verge of a total crack-up. Anyway, not to be frightened was delightful.

He had snatched a *Montreal Gazette* from the newsstand. Now he unfolded it, and a picture of Alistair Tudsbury and Pamela on the first page made him sit up. They stood beside a jeep, Tudsbury grinning in balloonlike army fatigues, Pamela looking pinched and bored in slacks and a shirt.

SUNSET ON KIDNEY RIDGE

By Alistair Tudsbury

By wireless from London. This dispatch, dated November 4, 1942, the famous British correspondent's last, was dictated shortly before he was killed by a landmine at El Alamein. Edited by his daughter and collaborator, Pamela Tudsbury, from an unfinished draft, it is reprinted by special permission of the London Observer.

The sun hangs huge and red above the far dust-streaked horizon. The desert cold is already falling on Kidney Ridge. This gray sandy elevation is deserted, except by the dead, and by two intelligence officers and myself. Even the flies have left. Earlier they were here in clouds, blackening the corpses. They pester the living too, clustering at a man's eyes and the moisture in the corners of his mouth, drinking his sweat. But of course they prefer the dead. When the sun climbs over the opposite horizon tomorrow, the flies will return to their feast.

Here not only did these German and British soldiers die, who litter the ground as far as the eye can see in the fading red light. Here at El Alamein the Afrika Korps died. The Korps was a legend, a dashing clean-cut enemy, a menace and at the same time a sort of glory; in Churchillian rhetoric, a gallant foe worthy of our steel. It is not yet known whether Rommel has made good his escape, or whether his straggle of routed supermen will be bagged by the Eighth Army. But the Afrika Korps is dead, crushed by British arms. We have won here, in the great Western Desert of Africa, a victory to stand with Crécy, Agincourt, Blenheim, and Waterloo.

Lines from Southey's "Battle of Blenheim" are haunting me here on Kidney Ridge:

> *They say it was a shocking sight*
> *After the field was won,*
> *For many thousand bodies here*
> *Lay rotting in the sun;*
> *But things like that, you know, must be*
> *After a famous victory.*

The bodies, numerous as they are, strike the eye less than the blasted and burned-out tanks that dot this weirdly beautiful wasteland, these squat hulks with their long guns, casting elongated blue shadows on the pastel grays, browns, and pinks of the far-stretching sands. Here is the central incongruity of Kidney Ridge—the masses of smashed twentieth-century machinery tumbled about in these harsh flat sandy wilds, where one envisions warriors on camels, or horses, or perhaps the elephants of Hannibal.

How far they came to perish here, these soldiers and these machines! What bizarre train of events brought youngsters from the Rhineland and Prussia, from the Scottish Highlands and London, from Australia and New Zealand, to butt at each other to the death with flame-spitting machinery in faraway Africa, in a setting as dry and lonesome as the moon?

But that is the hallmark of this war. No other war has ever been like it. This war rings the world. Kidney Ridge is everywhere on our small globe. Men fight as far from home as they can be transported, with courage and endurance that makes one proud of the human race, in horrible contrivances that make one ashamed of the human race.

My jeep will take me back to Cairo shortly, and I will dictate a dispatch about what I see here. What I am looking at, right now as the sun touches the horizon, is this. Two intelligence officers, not fifty yards from me, are lifting the German driver out of a blasted tank, using meat hooks. He is black and charred. He has no head. He is a trunk with arms and legs. The smell is like gamy pork. The legs wear good boots, only a bit scorched.

I am very tired. A voice I don't want to listen to tells me that this is England's last land triumph; that our military history ends here with a victory to stand with the greatest, won largely with machines shipped ten thousand miles from American factories. Tommy Atkins will serve with pluck and valor wherever he fights hereafter, as always; but the conduct of the war is passing out of our hands.

We are outnumbered and outclassed. Modern war is a clangorous and dreary measuring of industrial plants. Germany's industrial capacity passed ours in 1905. We hung on through the First World War by sheer grit. Today the two industrial giants of the earth are the United States and the Soviet Union. They more than outmatch Germany and Japan, now that they have shaken off their surprise setbacks and sprung to arms. Tocqueville's vision is coming to pass in our time. They will divide the empire of the world.

The sun going down on Kidney Ridge is setting on the British Empire, on which—so we learned to say as schoolboys—the sun never set. Our Empire was born in the skill of our explorers, the martial prowess of our yeomanry, the innovative genius of our scientists and engineers. We stole a march on the world that lasted two hundred years. Lulled by the long peaceful protection of the great fleet we built, we thought it would last forever. We dozed.

Here on Kidney Ridge we have erased the disgrace of our somnolence. If history is but the clash of arms, we now begin to leave the stage in honor. But if it is the march of the human spirit toward world freedom, we will never leave the stage. British ideas, British institutions, British scientific method, will lead the way in other lands, in other guises. English will become the planetary tongue, that is now certain. We have been the Greece of the new age.

But, you object, the theme of the new age is socialism. I am not so sure of that. Even so, Karl Marx, the scruffy Mohammed of this spreading economic Islam, built his strident dogmas on the theories of British economists. He created his apocalyptic visions in the hospitality of the British Museum. He read British books, lived on British bounty, wrote in British freedom, collaborated with Englishmen, and lies in a London grave. People forget all that.

The sun has set. It will get dark and cold quickly now. The intelligence officers are beckoning me to their lorry. The first stars spring forth in the indigo sky. I take a last look around at the dead of El Alamein and mutter a prayer for all these poor devils, German and British, who turn and turn about sang "Lili Marlene" in the cafés of Tobruk, hugging the same sleazy girls. Now they lie here together, their young appetites cold, their homesick songs stilled.

> *"Why, 'twas a very wicked thing!"*
> *Said little Wilhelmine.*
> *"Nay, nay my little girl!" quoth he—*

Pamela Tudsbury writes: "The telephone rang just at that moment, as my father was declaiming the verse with his usual relish. It was the summons to the interview with General Montgomery. He left at once. A lorry brought back his body next morning. As a World War I reserve officer, he was buried with honors in the British Military Cemetery outside Alexandria.

The London Observer asked me to complete the article. I have tried. I have his handwritten notes for three more paragraphs. But I cannot do it. I can, however, complete Southey's verse for him. So ends my father's career of war reporting—"

"It was a famous victory."

• • •

The airplane was humming above the weather now, the sky was bright blue, the sunlight blinding on the white cloud cover. Slote slumped sadly in his chair. He had come a long way from Bern, he was thinking, not only in miles but in perception. In the hothouse of the Swiss capital, under the comfortable glass of neutrality, his obsession about the Jews had sprouted like some forced plant. Now he was coming back to realities.

How could one arouse American public opinion? How get past the horselaugh of "Der Fuehrer's Face," the acid cynicism of Fenton? Above all, how overcome the competition of Kidney Ridge? Tudsbury's piece was touching and evocative, describing a great slaughter; but there was no Kidney Ridge for the Jews of Europe. They were unarmed. It was no fight. Most of them did not even comprehend that a massacre was going on. Sheep going to the slaughter were uncomfortable to contemplate. One turned one's eyes elsewhere. One had an exciting world drama to watch, a contest for the highest stakes, in which the home team was at last pulling ahead. Treblinka had small chance against Kidney Ridge.